A SIMPLE MAN

BOBBY HALL

ISBN 978-1-64028-314-5 (Paperback)
ISBN 978-1-64028-315-2 (Digital)

Christian Faith Publishing, Inc.
296 Chestnut Street
Meadville, PA 16335
www.christianfaithpublishing.com

Printed in the United States of America

The best index of a person's character is how he treats
people that can't do him any good, and how
he treats people who can't fight back!

Preface

J ustin Hayes, a hardworking Christian man, is fortunate enough to retire early and build a beautiful new home in the Appalachian Mountains of North Carolina, but his near perfect life is flipped upside down when his rich neighbor, Jack Billings, decides that he absolutely must own the forty-three acres of land that Justin now lives on. But unbeknownst to Jack, he has much bigger problems than a stubborn neighbor who doesn't want to move. A guest at his house is being watched closely by the Central Intelligence Agency and the Department of Homeland Defense. Jack will stop at nothing to remove Justin Hayes from the land he wants, and Justin will need all the skills he acquired so many years ago in Vietnam plus the help of friends and the man upstairs to fight off his cunning and evil neighbor.

There is an old saying that I'm sure all of you have heard at least once in your life. It goes: "There is no shame in failing. The only shame is in not trying!" With that thought in mind, I decided several years ago to write a book. If someone had told me prior to that that someday I would write a book, I would have strongly encouraged that person's family to immediately enroll them into a drug intervention program. A lot of people were surprised that I wrote a book, but no one was more surprised than me! To this day I don't know why I wrote it, or how I ever got through it.

If you choose to read *A Simple Man*, I sincerely hope that you enjoy it. If you don't like my book...well, that's okay too.

May God bless you and yours.

Fly Fishing on the New River

The wooly-bugger touched down lightly near the opposite side of the river and began its slow descent downstream. Justin couldn't see the small black lure but had placed a bright green line-finder about three feet up the leader so he could tell exactly where his lure was by watching the luminous float. The fly line picked up speed and he slowly took in slack as the lure slammed into a large rock and swirled around it. Instantly the line snapped tight and Justin jerked the nine foot fly rod straight up.

The sudden rush a person gets from a fish strike is always the same, no matter how many fish you have caught, and this strike was no different.

Justin was standing about fifteen feet from the bank in water about two feet deep. He started downstream as soon as the trout did and was trying desperately to turn the fish around. The trout stalled and made a dash to the opposite side of the river, turned, and came straight back across, tail-walking and splashing the whole forty feet. Justin kept the pressure on as he slowly moved downstream and retrieved his line. The fish made one more run back toward the middle of the river, but Justin managed to turn him before he got into the rushing water, and eased him gracefully into his landing net.

Justin sloshed back to the bank and sat down on a picnic table-size rock. The adrenaline rush left him out of breath and exhausted.

The trout would probably weigh about four pounds but when it was swimming with the current it felt like it weighed much more.

He was beautiful, like all rainbow trout, and Justin dropped him in his creel with the other two trout he had caught since daylight.

It was Friday, April 6, 2006, opening day of trout season in North Carolina, and Justin Hayes had been fishing for three hours and had three fish—two rainbow trout that would weigh around three and a half pounds, and the last one which was maybe four pounds. It would be enough fish for lunch today and Justin was looking forward to lunch like a kid on Christmas Eve waiting for Santa Claus.

Justin's son Travis was on his way home from Norfolk, Virginia, with a friend of his named Dwight McMasters. Travis and Dwight were in the Navy and had just returned home from a six-month deployment on the nuclear aircraft carrier USS *Theodore Roosevelt*. It seemed like Travis had been gone for six years instead of six months and Justin couldn't wait to see him.

Justin and Travis were closer than most fathers were with there sons. It probably was because Justin raised Travis since he was ten years old by himself. It was a very hard time in Justin's life having to run his son to school, ballgames, karate practice, dances, and whatever else came up.

There were meals to prepare, lunches to be packed, laundry to do, doctor appointments, homework, science projects, grocery shopping, trips to the mall, and when you got time you had to work a forty- to fifty-hour work week as a lineman for the power company. But it was well worth all the time and hard work to watch his son grow into manhood. He was very proud of his son.

Justin was feeling rested now so he gathered up his creel and fly rod and slid off the rock into the river once more. It was probably a quarter of a mile walk back to his truck and then a two mile drive to his new house. He carefully waded across the New River and climbed the bank until he stepped onto River Road.

It was a perfect day. The sky was blue and the air was clean and crisp. Springtime in the Appalachian Mountains brought new life not only to the land, but also to everyone around it.

Travis would be arriving in two or three hours and Justin was planning on fixing a big meal to welcome him home. He wondered if Travis would reenlist in the Navy or stay home and maybe go to college or start a photography business. He had joined the Navy right after graduating from high school and signed up for five years so he could get the job he wanted, which was a Navy photographer. Travis had always liked photography and was very good at it. In every profession you find a few people who have a knack for it and Travis definitely had a knack for photography. He had won almost every photo contest he had ever entered, and his pictures were frequently selected to be posted on the Navy website. But Justin didn't want to get his hopes up that Travis would stay home because he knew that he was undecided about his future.

Justin started walking down the road toward his old Toyota truck when ten yards in front of him a groundhog burst out of the tall grass and ran across the road. In less than a second he dropped his fly rod and drew his Model 642 Airweight .357 magnum revolver.

The groundhog stopped at the entrance of his den and took one more look at Justin before diving to the safety of his home. Justin laughed and slid the little revolver back in the side pocket of his fishing vest. If it had been a rabid raccoon instead of a groundhog it would have been dead before it could have attacked. Years of handgun competition had honed his reflexes with a handgun that only a few men could match.

Justin picked up his fly rod and continued walking down River Road. River Road was an eleven-mile stretch of asphalt that ran all the way from Highway 117 to the confluence of the New River where the north fork and the south fork joined back together. The highway twists and turns as it follows the river and small farms with cattle and horses and sheep pop up every half mile or so. There are only two houses in the last three miles of River Road—Justin's house which was one mile from the end, and Jack Billing's house, or mansion, which sat at the dead-end of the road in between the north and south forks of the river. Justin could see Jack's house from his front porch on a clear day but it was a mile away, and he thought that was a good distance for neighbors-to-be.

The last two years had been a whirlwind for Justin. First his mother died at the age of eighty-eight. She died peacefully in her sleep one night and even though she was in her late eighties it surprised everyone because she was in such good health and so chipper. Her estate also surprised everyone because she had over four hundred thousand dollars in various investments. Justin and his only sister Rebecca were named co-executors of the will. After the sale of his mother's house and the funeral expenses were paid, he and his sister each received a check for $227,000.

Then his friend Roy Hepler was found dead from what the authorities say was a farming accident. Roy was found underneath his tractor at the bottom of a very steep mountain. Justin didn't believe for a minute that Roy's death was an accident, but there was no way for him to prove it otherwise.

Roy and Justin had been friends for about ten years. Four or five times a year Justin would drive up to the mountains on Friday after he got off work and spend the weekend with Roy. Sometimes Justin would bring Travis along and other times Travis would spend the weekend with one of his friends.

Roy loved to hunt. Every time Justin came to visit they got up early on Saturday and hunted all day. They hunted whitetail deer, turkeys, squirrels, and grouse. If nothing was in season they hunted groundhogs. After a full day of hunting they would go back to Roy's house and cook a meal fit for a king and then sit around and talk about guns or farming or politics or whatever came up until they fell asleep. On Sunday morning they got up and showered and dressed, then drove six miles to the New River Baptist Church to attend services there. After church they would say their good-byes and Justin would head toward home.

Justin knew that Roy was lonely. Roy's wife, Verda, had died of breast cancer in 1997 and they didn't have any children, so Roy was by himself. Their weekend visits were the highlight of Roy's life and Justin knew it, but he was shocked to learn that Roy had left him forty-three acres of land and his old house on River Road. Justin knew that Roy had a sister and just assumed that she would inherit the property after his death, but Roy's attorney said that Roy left his sister an envelope with a dollar bill in it and that was all.

Justin had been living in a small community named Silver Hill for thirty-four years. He married his high school sweetheart there and built his home there. He had made many friends in Silver Hill and was well respected, but Silver Hill, like a lot of small rural communities, was getting crowded. A new school was first and then a grocery store. Then a Chinese restaurant and a car wash. The small farms around Justin's house were being bought up by land developers and realtors, and housing developments were popping up like prairie dogs in Nebraska. Silver Hill was located in the Piedmont-Triad of North Carolina and was surrounded by the towns of Asbboro, Lexington, Thomasville, and Winston-Salem, and the towns were slowly but surely growing together and strangling the small farms and rural communities. It was time for Justin to leave.

Justin had thirty-four years of service as a lineman for Triad Power and Light. His retirement plus his 401K, plus the $227,000 from his mother's estate, and another $186,000 from the sale of his house made the decision a no-brainer, so Justin retired at the age of fifty-six and moved himself and his possessions 135 miles away into Roy's old house and began building his new house right beside it.

Justin had first traveled into Ashe County in 1973 after being invited along on a groundhog hunt by a friend of his. He instantly fell in love with the rising mountains and the beautiful streams and rivers. He was also impressed by the local people who lived in these back-woods communities.

They were for the most part uneducated but were brilliant when it came to living off the land. They not only survived in a very rugged environment but they thrived on it. They had very strong morals and taught their children to respect other people and the land they lived in. They worked long hard hours and everybody worked until the work was done. They drove old, beat-up cars and trucks and lived in small shacks and farmhouses and were very content with their lives. If you ever heard one of them complaining it was usually about the government or taxes.

It took Justin a little over a year to build his new house and workshop, but now that it was finished he had time to do whatever he wanted. Lately he had been working in his gunsmith shop and doing some shooting on his gun range. Now that trout season was in he was planning on learning how to catch big trout with a fly rod.

Justin knew that he was a fortunate man. He had always worked very hard and led a clean, respectable life. He had fought for his country in Vietnam, and like a lot of soldiers, had seen and done things that no man should have to do, but he didn't think he had ever done anything to deserve the many blessings that he had. When he stood on his front porch and looked out over his property and Gods creation he felt very humble. "Sometimes I think I went to heaven early," he would sometimes say out loud.

Justin had finally reached his truck and tossed his gear into the bed when he heard a roar that was gradually getting louder. A black Ford F350 super-cab with huge mud grip tires came flying around a curve and Justin immediately recognized the driver as Billy Billings, Jack Billing's son.

Billy was spoiled rotten from birth and had never worked a day in his entire life. His dad had bailed him out of trouble since he was eleven years old and now he was twenty-five years old and was nothing but trouble waiting to happen. Everybody in Ashe, Allegheny, and Wilkes County knew Billy Billings and tried to steer clear of him.

As the big truck came flying by, Billy leaned out the window and hollered, "YEE-HAW!" and threw an empty beer can out the window onto River Road.

As the truck went around the next curve and out of sight, Justin walked over to the beer can and picked it up. He walked back over to his truck and tossed the can in the truck bed with his fishing gear. "Well, maybe I'm not in heaven quite yet," he said to himself.

Welcome to Sparta

Travis shifted his Jeep Wrangler from fourth gear to third gear as he steered into another blind curve. His friend, Dwight McMasters, or as his friends called him, DeMac, was leaning left and then right as they wound their way up the mountain.

They had left Norfolk, Virginia, that morning at five o'clock and driven five hours to Greensboro, North Carolina, to visit with Travis's mother. Travis's mother Kathy had run off with another man when Travis was ten years old and had been out of touch until recently when she wrote Travis a letter and asked him if he would come see her. Travis agreed to visit her but it was extremely awkward. Seeing her again brought back lots of painful memories that Travis had forgotten until now.

When Travis rung the doorbell and his mother answered the door, Travis didn't recognize her at first. She looked old beyond her years and was somewhat feeble. Of course she was thirteen years older now than she was the last time he saw her, but she looked more like she was seventy than fifty-seven. Travis wondered if she was dying and wanted to see him one last time before she passed on. She had fixed a sandwich platter and some potato salad for them, so they ate and made polite conversation for about thirty minutes and then excused themselves so they could get back on the road. Travis wondered if he should tell his dad about the visit or just forget it.

"So how close are we now?" DeMac shouted over the wind noise in the Jeep.

"As soon as we top the mountain it's about twelve miles to Sparta and then another twenty miles to dad's house," Travis shouted back.

Dwight McMasters knew exactly where he was and so did every member of his seal team who were already in place and tracking them by the GPS unit built into his cell phone. Not only were they tracking them, they were also listening to every word they said.

"So tell me about your dad. If I'm going to teach him how to fly fish I need to know something about him," DeMac hollered.

Travis downshifted again as he slung the Jeep into another never ending curve. "He's an amazing man. I didn't realize how amazing he was until I joined the Navy and left home. The first thing you'll notice about him is his arms and chest. He looks like a bodybuilder but he's never been to a gym in his life. He worked as a lineman for the power company for over thirty years and has always helped his neighbors get up hay and build fences or barns or whatever needed doing around their farms. He is a very powerful man even at fifty-seven years old."

"What about karate? Did he study karate like you did when you were growing up?"

"No. He carries his karate in a holster. He's always armed with some type of pistol, usually a J-framed Smith and Wesson. He calls his pistol Jay, and dad and Jay are always together. He competed in handgun competitions for years and was very good at it. A lot of people encouraged him to turn professional but he said he had a son to raise and didn't have time to travel around the country on the handgun circuit. You have got to see him shoot before you go back to Norfolk. You won't believe your eyes. And believe it or not, he's just as good with a rifle. I've seen him shoot groundhogs at four hundred yards that only had their heads sticking up."

DeMac knew that Justin Hayes was a good shot with a rifle. When he read his file at the start of this mission he saw that Sergeant Hayes had forty-seven confirmed kills in Vietnam and God knows how many he had that were unconfirmed.

They finally came across the crest of the mountain and Travis turned in at a scenic overlook. "I need to stretch my legs and take a piss," Travis said.

Travis and DeMac climbed out of the Jeep and stretched. Travis stepped over to the woods and relieved himself while DeMac dug around in the ice chest for two Pepsi's. He handed one to Travis when he returned and they both stood and gazed out over a beautiful valley. Since they had both been at sea for the last six months, standing on solid ground and breathing in the clean mountain air was a special treat.

DeMac took a swig of his Pepsi and then asked, "Does your dad have any hobbies besides shooting? Does he do any fly tying or woodwork or anything?"

Travis turned his Pepsi up and then threw the empty can in a trash barrel. "Nope, at least not yet. He just started fly fishing but knowing dad like I do, I'd be real surprised if he didn't learn to tie his own flies. His only other hobby is gunsmithing. He went to school at night for almost four years at Montgomery Technical Institute in Troy. It was thirty-seven miles from our house and Dad wouldn't get back home until after midnight. I was in high school and was working at Food Lion to help pay for my car so dad didn't have to drive me around anymore. He poured his heart and soul into learning to be a gunsmith and graduated with honors. He has built a machine shop behind his new house so he can walk out his back door and go straight into his shop. I haven't seen his shop yet because he built it after I left on this last deployment. I'm so glad that dad was able to retire early. He has always put everybody else before himself, whether it was me or my mom or even a neighbor who needed help. If anybody ever deserved to enjoy their final years on this earth it's my dad, and I hope he has a lot of years left to enjoy."

DeMac knew the spooks would want to know exactly what Justin Hayes was building in his new machine shop and for whom. "Does your dad ever do any work for the public or contract jobs for anybody?"

"No, not really," Travis answered. "Dad has been so busy building his new house that he hasn't had time to do much of anything up until now. He has built a few rifles for close friends of his, and he did build a couple of tactical rifles for the Davidson County Sheriff's Department, but besides that he mostly just works on his own stuff. I know on a couple of occasions he has fixed guns for people who couldn't afford to have them fixed. He could make a lot of money at it if he wanted to, but dad doesn't care anything about money."

"I don't think I ever met anybody that didn't care about money."

"That's why Dad is so amazing. He cares more about people than he does about money or property or possessions. He'll give you the shirt off his back if you need it," Travis said.

DeMac threw his empty Pepsi can in the trash barrel and he and Travis jumped back in the Jeep and headed for Sparta. "What if I tried to take your dad's shirt off his back?"

"He would tear you apart. And besides, you couldn't wear my dad's shirt. His chest is twice the size of yours,." Travis said, laughing.

DeMac grinned at Travis and finally started laughing himself. This Justin Hayes must be some kind of man, he thought to himself.

The twelve-mile ride to Sparta was quiet as both men just relaxed and enjoyed the beautiful countryside. They both were slowly unwinding from their six-month deployment to Afghanistan. Travis had been with DeMac's Seal team on three separate missions while they were overseas. His dad didn't know it but Travis wasn't just a Navy photographer but was a combat photographer. He had been trained in basic combat operations, wilderness and desert survival, escape and evade procedures, how to survive a helicopter crash in the ocean, and how to travel with a seal team without blowing their cover. His main responsibility was to record the mission on film so they could use the film for a record of the mission and also as a training aid. But the main thing was not to get them killed while he was trying to take pictures. DeMac's Seal team hadn't been thrilled about taking him along, but after a huge bar fight in Spain where Travis got a chance to show them his special skills they accepted him as one of their own.

Travis had invited DeMac to come home with him for several reasons. One, DeMac no longer had a family to go home to. Two, DeMac was an expert fly fisherman and could help his dad learn the secrets to catching big trout. And three, Travis and DeMac had become really good friends over the last few months and as far as Travis was concerned DeMac was always welcome in his home.

They topped another hill and Travis slowed down as they passed a new sign that said "Welcome to Sparta." The town of Sparta consisted of five city blocks of old brick buildings and a few strip malls on either side of town. There was a high school and a small stadium on their right and a livestock arena and animal hospital directly across the street. Most of the vehicles along the street were at least ten years old and some were much older than that. They passed an old barber shop and a hardware store where several old men in bib overhauls sat on benches and stared at passing motorists. It was almost like going back in time when you traveled through Sparta.

"I need to fill up with gas before we leave town, and we probably should buy another bag of ice for the cooler," Travis said.

"You got it, partner, but I'm buying this time," DeMac replied.

Travis slowed down and turned into a Hess service station and convenience store. There were three sets of gas pumps. At the first pump there was a travel-home and two couples that had to be in their seventies watching the meter as they filled their tank. At the second pump was a black Ford F350 with huge mud grip tires, and the third pump was vacant so Travis pulled up to it and shut the engine off. A cardboard sign was taped to the pump that said, "Prepay Only," so Travis started walking toward the store. The double doors of the store were propped open letting the breeze fill the store with the clean mountain air.

A big tabby cat came flying out the door followed by a twenty-something-year-old man dragging a kicking and screaming teenage girl. The man was approximately six feet two inches tall and weighed about one hundred and ninety pounds. He had long black hair that was pulled back in a ponytail and he hadn't shaved in at least three days. He had dark eyes and looked very angry and Travis could smell beer on him from fifteen feet away. He was the redneck from hell, Travis thought.

"Just get in the damn truck, Sheila!" he growled as he dragged the frightened girl through the double doors.

The girl was maybe sixteen or seventeen years old and was very pretty. She had a black Harley-Davidson tee shirt on that was cut off just above her belly button and blue jean shorts that were cut off just below her butt cheeks. Daisy Dukes as all the southern boys called them, named after the actress "Daisy" on the Dukes of Hazard television show. She was pulling as hard as she could but was no match for the tall redneck.

"Let me go, Billy. Let me go, dammit!" she screamed.

Then she bit him. She leaned forward and bit the blood out of the hand he was dragging her with. He screamed and let her go but instantly back handed her so hard her feet left the ground before she fell to the concrete, semi-conscious and dazed.

"You freaking bitch!" Billy screamed at her as he looked at his bleeding hand. He started toward her again but Travis stepped in between him and the now groaning girl.

"Whoa, partner, I think she's had enough for now. Just calm down and go home and I'll make sure she's all right," Travis said as he held his hands up with his palms out.

Billy was pissed. He was going to give Sheila a ride home and the ungrateful little bitch not only refused his offer, but she bit the blood out of his hand. And now soldier boy was trying to be a hero so he could take her home and that just made Billy furious.

"Butt out, asshole, or you'll be lying beside her!" Billy snarled.

Travis held his hands up again. "Come on, man, don't do this. I don't want to fight. Just let me make sure she's all right and I'll be on my way," Travis pleaded.

Billy had two men riding with him who were up until now just watching the charade. They were employed by Jack Billings to work on the farm but today their main responsibility was to babysit Billy and keep him from getting hurt or killed. They weren't worried about the outcome of this altercation one bit. Billy had never taken anything seriously in his life, except for taekwondo. He had a private tutor who was flown in to Jack's once a month to train with him, and Jack had even had a dojo built on the property just for their sessions.

So as far as they were concerned the outcome of this fight was already decided.

DeMac wasn't worried either, at least about Travis. He had seen Travis in action when a huge bar fight broke out in Spain. DeMac's Seal team was jumped by a local gang when they accidentally went into the gang's bar. There were sixteen Seals including Travis and about forty gang members. DeMac figured the photographer would cut and run, but he stood shoulder to shoulder with the team until the last gang member fell. Then he took pictures of all the gang members in case they needed proof of what happened. It turned out that they did need proof and the pictures helped clear the Seals of any wrongdoing. From that time on Travis was considered part of the team.

DeMac was a little concerned about the two big men standing by the truck. He turned his head toward his cell phone that hung on his belt and said, "Eagle, this is Red fox. There's a problem at these coordinates. Bring up the hounds but park across the street. Stand down until further orders."

"I got fifty dollars that says my man will kick your man's ass!" DeMac said loudly as he stepped toward the two big men.

"You're on, dumb ass," the biggest one said. "Billy doesn't ever lose. He just wins some quicker than others."

DeMac couldn't see any weapons on the two men but that didn't mean they weren't armed. Both of the men were big with the largest one being about six-foot four and about 285 pounds and the smaller of the two being about six-foot two and 240 pounds. The two men both started laughing and DeMac turned to see what was so funny.

DeMac couldn't believe his eyes. Travis was hopping up and down in front of Billy with his fists held up like a boxer would back in the early 1900s. He would hop on one foot and then on the other.

Billy couldn't believe what he was seeing either. Kicking this sailor's ass was going to be easier than he thought. He laughed out loud. "Say good night, hero. I told you to back off and you didn't so now you can join her," Billy said as he went into his taekwondo fighting stance.

"I might not be as easy to hit as that girl was, grease ball," Travis said as he hopped back and forth.

When Travis said grease ball, Billy spun around with a spinning back kick aimed for Travis's head. Travis dropped down and swept Billy's other leg out from under him and Billy fell flat on his back hard. Billy had a look on his face that could only be described as pure shock, but as soon as he hit the concrete he bounced right back up just like his Sensei had taught him. As Billy was coming back up Travis threw a roundhouse kick that caught Billy right on the side of his jaw and he fell to the concrete in a heap. He was out cold and the only thing moving was his chest as he breathed in and out. The fight was over in seven seconds.

The two men who were leaning against the black Ford truck immediately started running toward Travis.

DeMac stepped between them and shouted, "I believe you owe me fifty dollars, dumb ass."

"Here's your fifty dollars, asshole!" And he swung a meaty fist at DeMac's head.

DeMac easily side stepped the big mans punch and hit him in the solar plexus like a mule kicking a barn door. The air rushed out of the big mans lungs with a whoosh and he gasped for air as he fell to the concrete. The other man stopped running, planted his feet, and threw a punch that could only be described as a haymaker. DeMac actually had to wait· for the man's punch to arrive before he could block it, but he did and then kicked him right in the balls. The man groaned and fell on top of his buddy.

Travis checked the unconscious redneck for weapons and then stepped over to the pretty blond teenager who was struggling to get up. Travis held her up until she regained her balance. She was crying as she wrapped her arms around Travis's neck and squeezed him so hard that he had trouble talking.

"It's all right, honey. Everything is going to be fine," Travis said over and over.

A siren could be heard in the distance and it was getting louder. The lady in the convenience store must have called the police, Travis thought. DeMac was watching the two men that were piled up beside the gas pump as they groaned and cursed.

A navy blue Ford Explorer came sliding in the store lot and screeched to a stop. It had a magnetic blue light stuck over the driver's window and the decal on the door said Ashe County Sheriff's Department.

Sheriff Bill Sisk had been taking his midday nap when his secretary came banging on his door hollering his name. She said there was a fight at the Hess station, and as usual Billy Billings was involved. Sheriff Sisk grabbed his hat and his Sam Brown duty belt and flew out the door faster than a greased minnow. Billy's going to kill somebody one of these days and it's going to be the devil to pay, the sheriff was thinking as he jumped in his Ford Explorer and fired it up. The sheriff reached in his glove box and grabbed a cheap unregistered .25 automatic pistol he carried around just in case he needed to throw it down at the scene of the fight. That way they could claim the man pulled a gun on Billy and he acted in self-defense.

Billy got into a fight just about once a month. He always won, usually sending the victim to the hospital with a broken nose, missing teeth, cracked ribs, and occasionally a fractured knee. The fights were always considered mutual combat and no charges were ever filed.

Nobody in Ashe County would testify against Jack Billing's son anyway.

Bill Sisk had been with the Ashe County Sheriff's Department for twenty-three years. He was a deputy for thirteen years and had been sheriff for the last ten. Jack Billings was responsible for his victory on Election Day and everybody knew it. It wouldn't be a very wise career move to charge Jack's son with assault. Sheriff Sisk knew who buttered his bread and would do whatever was necessary to keep it that way. He stepped out of the Explorer and looked at DeMac who was still standing watch over the two groaning men. He quickly scanned the parking lot and saw Billy, who was now starting to squirm and grunt. He immediately jerked his pistol out of his holster and pointed it at Travis's head.

"Get on the ground! Get on the ground! Do it now!" he roared.

Travis could see that the crazed officer had his finger on the trigger and looked like he was insane. He held his hands up and tried to go to the ground but the still sobbing girl was clinging to his neck.

"Okay, officer, I'm getting down. Let me go, honey, so I can get down," Travis said loudly.

Sheriff Sisk stepped over Billy, and with his right foot pushed the still sobbing girl off Travis and she fell to the ground and began wailing.

DeMac stepped away from the men he was watching. He could see that the officer was over reacting to what he rolled up on. He turned his head toward his cell phone and said, "Hound Dog, send backup. If this idiot shoots the Rabbit you have a green light, over."

The side door opened on the van across the street and two men stepped out. They looked like tourists with their denim shorts and Hawaiian shirts. The van had "High Country Tours" on the side and all the windows were tinted black. The two men walked casually across the street and blended in with the crowd that was gathering. News travels fast in small towns, and the news that somebody kicked Billy Billing's ass went through town like an Amtrak Train.

Travis lay down and stretched his arms straight out. The officer stepped around behind Travis and put his knee in between Travis's shoulder blades hard. He pushed the barrel of his pistol against the back of Travis's head and Travis could feel the barrel trembling. Two more sheriff cars came flying in the lot, and one of the deputies ran over and put handcuffs on Travis. The other deputy stepped over to DeMac and began asking him questions.

"Sorry, Sheriff, but we were all the way across the river when the call came in," he said.

"Call for paramedics while I deal with this other clown," he said as he turned and headed across the lot. DeMac was explaining what happened to the other deputy when the sheriff walked up and ordered him to the ground. He instructed the deputy to cuff him and place him in one of the cars.

The deputy who cuffed Travis stepped over to Billy and helped him to his feet, but his legs were like rubber and he fell back down.

"Let me go, Jerry, dammit!" Billy hollered. "Arrest that son of a bitch. He hit me from behind with a pipe or something. I want him charged with assault with intent to kill. Do you here me!" Billy screamed.

Two paramedics emerged through the crowd and ran up to Billy.

"Leave me the hell alone!" Billy hollered as they reached for him. This time Billy got to his feet by himself and was steady enough to stand.

"I want that bitch over there charged with assault too. She bit the blood out of my hand," Billy said pointing at the teenage girl who was now standing with two other girls who looked to be the same age.

Travis was still on his belly with his hands cuffed behind his back. He looked over at the two men who DeMac had apparently neutralized even though he didn't see it when it happened. The two paramedics were helping them to their feet as the sheriff looked on. When Travis looked back all he could see was a boot coming straight for his face.

Apparently the deputy had stepped over to talk to the teenage girl, and the drunk redneck who they all seemed to know and call by the name Billy decided it would be a good time to kick Travis's brains out.

Travis rolled hard and fast but it wasn't quite fast enough. The boot glanced off Travis's cheekbone just below the eye. Billy tried to kick him again but the deputy pushed him away.

"Back off, Billy, or I'll cuff you too!" the deputy commanded. He then reached down and pulled Travis to his feet. Sheriff Sisk had turned his head toward Billy when he tried to kick Travis and saw the whole thing.

"Put that piece of shit in the car with his buddy and then run this crowd off," the sheriff said pointing his finger at Travis. "Billy, get your men loaded up and go home! And let one of them drive since you're obviously drunk."

"I want that son of a bitch charged, Sheriff. I mean it. That bastard blindsided me and then that bitch over there bit me! I want her charged too!" Billy hollered.

"They're going to jail, Billy, don't you worry. You just go home and let me take care of it," the sheriff said.

Deputy Jerry Morris led Travis over to the patrol car and put him in the backseat next to DeMac. Billy and his limping companions loaded up in their truck and tore out of the parking lot. The crowd slowly started leaving and the two men in the Hawaiian shirts crossed the street and got back in the van.

"Well, like the sign says, welcome to Sparta," Travis said, and he and DeMac both cracked up.

As soon as they stopped laughing, DeMac said, "What's with that ridiculous looking boxing stance and all that hopping around you were doing before the fight?"

"Well, that redneck made three mistakes," Travis said. "Number one, he was drunk when he started the fight. Number two, he used a technique that you should never start a fight with. It takes longer to strike your opponent when you have to spin all the way around before you strike. And number three, the worst mistake you can ever make in any fight is to underestimate your opponent. When he saw me in that stupid looking stance he thought this was going to be the easiest fight of his life. You should have seen the look on his face when I swept his leg out from under him. He didn't know whether to scratch his watch or wind his ass," Travis said, and both men busted out laughing again.

"Well, let's review our situation," DeMac said grinning. "A really hot looking young lady was being abducted by a big, mean looking, drunk redneck. You intervened, and after trying to diffuse the situation, were attacked by same redneck, and in self-defense knocked his dumb ass out cold. I, on the other hand, in an effort to keep things fair, intercepted two really large but untrained accomplices, and although I didn't knock either one of them out, they will both be real sore tomorrow, especially the smaller of the two. Then an insane man with a gun, who apparently is the sheriff of this county, came and almost executed you and then me.

"Then, after the big mean redneck, who apparently runs this county and everybody in it, regains consciousness, he kicks you in the face while you are in handcuffs in front of two officers of the law, who immediately scold him and send him home while you and I are being arrested."

Travis was still laughing as DeMac continued, "Let me take a moment here to just thank you for inviting me along on this vacation. I can't wait to see what happens next!"

Seal teams, Special Forces, Recon Marines, and other elite soldiers often use humor to keep up morale and to help them get through tough times. That was exactly what was happening in the backseat of that deputy's car as DeMac and Travis laughed and joked. An assistant deputy director for the Central Intelligence Agency wasn't amused. He had listened to the whole affair through the special cell phone on DeMac's belt, and was getting video from the van across the street. It wouldn't do enough damage to force them to scrap the mission, but he would have been much happier if they would have avoided a confrontation with the son of the man they were investigating. Now everybody in the county would be talking about the two sailors who rode into town and whipped Billy Billings and his gang. It was a bad way to start a covert operation, but the damage was done and there was nothing they could do about it now.

He pushed a button on his phone and said, "Sherry, get me all the information we have on that sheriff and bring it to my office please."

"Right away, sir," a pleasant voice replied.

DeMac and Travis watched as the sheriff and his deputies discussed their situation. The sheriff appeared to be getting madder by the minute. Then the two older couples that were filling up the travel home came over and joined in the fray. Travis and DeMac couldn't hear the conversation but they could tell the volume was increasing and the sheriff was getting madder. The lady who was running the convenience store came through the double doors holding up a video cassette tape, and the crowd filed into the store to view it. After several long minutes the sheriff stormed out of the store and threw the video tape on his front seat, jumped in behind the wheel and spun his tires as he tore out of the lot.

The two deputies came out of the store and walked over to the car where Travis and DeMac were being held. One went to one side and the other went to the other side and they opened the back doors simultaneously.

"We need to see some ID to make sure neither one of you have any warrants. The two couples who witnessed the fight gave a detailed description of what happened and the store video backed up their story. They also said that they would drive back down here from Pennsylvania to testify if necessary," the deputy said. They removed the handcuffs and Travis and DeMac gave them their driver's licenses. The other deputy took the licenses and stepped over to the other car, but returned quickly and handed them back.

"You're free to go," he said. "Where you guys headed, anyway?" he asked.

Travis started to answer but was cut off by DeMac. "We're just passing through, officer. You won't be seeing us anymore." DeMac said.

"Well, you two are free to go. My name is Buddy Dixon and this officer is Jerry Morris," he said, pointing at the other deputy. "Sorry we had to detain you but we needed to sort this thing out. That guy you knocked out was Billy Billings, and his daddy is a powerful man in this county. That's why the sheriff was so freaked out when he got here."

"No shit! I thought he was going to shoot me," Travis said.

"I can't believe that maniac is the sheriff of this county," DeMac added.

"That's why he is the sheriff of this county. He looks out for Jack Billings. When Jack says jump, Sheriff Sisk jumps. Billy gets into a fight about once a month and there's never any charges filed against him. Sheriff Sisk would lock up his mama before he would lock up one of Jack Billings's family," Buddy Dixon said.

The other deputy, Jerry Morris, started grinning and said, "Only this time, old Billy Boy got his ass kicked, and I can't think of anything that could make me happier than pulling up to this scene and seeing Billy lying there unconscious. I thought you shot him since he wasn't moving and the sheriff had his pistol stuck in the back of your head. Are you guys Seals or something? It's obvious you're in the Navy and you both have some skill when it comes to fighting."

Travis and DeMac had to wear their uniforms to be discharged from the ship early that morning. No one leaves the ship unless they are in uniform and salute the flag. When they got to Travis's Jeep, they removed their dress shirts and pulled on tee shirts that said Navy in bold letters across their chest, so everyone knew at a glance that they were sailors.

"No, we're not Seals. We're just sailors who just got back from a six-month deployment and need some downtime," DeMac said.

"What about you?" Buddy Dixon asked, looking at Travis. "No one has ever even hit Billy Billings and you knocked him out!"

"No, I'm not a Seal," Travis said as he stepped over to his Jeep and pulled out his uniform top. "I'm a Navy photographer," Travis said pointing to the patch on his uniform with a camera on it. "That guy was drunk and anybody could have put him down."

"Now you're lying to an officer. I'd arrest you if I thought I could. We watched the tape when we went in the store and saw exactly what happened. When you got in that boxing stance I almost laughed out loud. Billy is always drinking and he always wins his fights, so there is no doubt that you got some serious karate skills. Everybody in town will be talking about this fight for years. I wish I had a copy of that tape but the sheriff took it with him and it will never be seen again, you can bet on that," Deputy Morris said.

"Well, we better be going," DeMac said. "You officers have a good day and be careful."

"This has been one of the best days of my life." Buddy Dixon said with a grin.

"Me too," Jerry Morris said, laughing while he headed for his patrol car.

Travis turned to get in his Jeep and noticed the two elderly couples were still standing by their travel home. He walked over to them and DeMac followed him.

"Thank you so much for your help," Travis said. "If you hadn't gone to bat for me, I believe that sheriff would have locked us up."

"I couldn't believe that damn fool sheriff was going to arrest you boys," the smallest of the elderly woman said.

"And even after he saw the tape he wasn't satisfied," the other lady spoke up.

"Well, I'm just glad there are still some people around with enough character to take a stand when they need to. You folks are my kind of people and I thank you from the bottom of my heart," Travis said.

"And we're just glad there's still some young folks around that will take a stand and do what's right," one of the men said. "It did my heart good to see you step in and help that young girl, and I'll be damned if I was going to stand here and watch that idiot arrest you and do nothing about it. Here's a piece of paper with our names and

addresses and phone numbers on it. You call us if you need somebody to testify for you. We're from Pennsylvania but we're retired and
have all the time in the world to drive down here if we need to."

"I don't think there's going to be any charges filed but I would
like to keep your information in case something does come up,"
Travis said as he took the paper.

"Why wasn't that guy arrested? He assaulted a young girl, he
attacked you, and then kicked you while you were handcuffed in
front of a deputy, and they just let him go," the other man asked.

"Well, evidently his daddy is some kind of big shot in this
county and he can do whatever he pleases," Travis said. "The sheriff
won't arrest him because he's afraid he would loose his job."

"Well, at least he got a good ass whipping. The sheriff couldn't
protect him from your left foot. Damn that was awesome. I'll never
forget this, and if you don't mind I would like to take your picture," one of the elderly men said and he stepped up into the RV
and emerged with a Nikon 35 millimeter camera. Travis was going
to pose with DeMac but when he turned around to find him he was
gone. Then Travis remembered that DeMac was a Seal, and Seals
don't like to get their picture taken.

So Travis posed while the man took three or four pictures of him
standing by the RV and then a couple pictures with the two women
hugging him, and finally he set the camera on the gas pump and took
a picture with all of them huddled around him. The women finally
hugged him one last time and the men shook his hand and they
loaded up in their motorized home and drove away.

DeMac came out of the store carrying a bag of ice and dumped
it in the cooler. "I already paid her for twenty-five dollars' worth of
gas," he said.

"I forgot about getting gas," Travis said. "I'm glad you reminded
me or I probably would have left without it."

Travis put in twenty-five dollars' worth and he and DeMac headed out of town. As they neared the edge of town another new sign appeared on the side of the road. "Leaving Sparta, NC, Beautiful Country and Friendly People."

Travis and DeMac looked at one another and then back at the road before busting out laughing.

Visit from Jack Billings

Justin turned into his driveway at 1050 River Road and cut the engine off. He hopped out of his truck and crossed the road to his mailbox and came back across sifting through junk mail and sale papers. A deep bark followed closely by a shrill whine let him know that his two buddies were watching him from the front porch. Justin threw the mail on the passenger seat and looked up the mountain. Standing on the front porch like two soldiers at attention were his two dogs, a Rottweiler named Shogun and a Jack Russell terrier named Scooter.

Justin paused and stared at his new home. It was beautiful and he was very proud of it. He had built most of it by himself and it turned out much prettier than he expected. It was two-hundred yards up the mountain and was facing River Road.

Justin usually woke up every morning about daylight. He would pour himself a cup of coffee and let the dogs out the front door. Then he would stand on the front porch and watch the river roll by while the dogs ran back and forth doing what dogs do when you let them out first thing in the morning.

The house was approximately two-thousand square feet of living space, with a double carport built onto the back of the house. A thirty foot covered walkway led from the carport to the machine shop so that even if it was raining or snowing a person could go back

BOBBY HALL

and forth without getting wet. The carport and machine shop were behind the house and couldn't be seen from River Road.

The front of the house had large panels of glass separated by equally large panels of polished stone. From anywhere in the house you could look out and see the river and the mountains rising up beyond it. The front porch was covered and ran the whole width of the house and down the left side to the carport. The sides and back of the house along with the machine shop were veneered in a rustic brick that blended in well with the polished stone on the front of the house.

Justin hopped back in his truck and started up the asphalt driveway. Roy's old driveway was dirt and ran straight up the mountain. It was impossible to travel in bad weather unless you had good tires and a four-wheel drive vehicle. Roy used to say, "A good driveway cuts down on the quality of your company." Justin understood what Roy was saying but he wanted to be able to go and come in bad weather if he pleased so he built a new driveway that angled about forty-five degrees from left to right going up the mountain. Near the top it leveled off and turned back to the left and crossed by the front of the house and finally around the house and into the double carport.

Justin crossed by the front of his house as Shogun and Scooter ran for the carport. He pulled his truck in the carport and got out while his dogs waited impatiently.

"Hey there, guys," Justin said as he patted each one on the head. "Look what I got."

Justin reached in the truck-bed and grabbed his creel. He opened it and held it down so the dogs could see and smell it. Shogun looked puzzled at the strange creatures. Scooter, in true Jack Russell form, growled and then snapped at the three fish. "Easy, Scooter, I've already killed them for you. Shogun, I believe we need to send Scooter to anger management classes. He thinks he has to kill everything he sees," Justin said to the 125-pound Rottweiler. "Come on, guys, and I'll get you a dog biscuit. Scooter, you can kill the dog biscuit and eat it," he said to the Jack Russell terrier as it jumped up and down.

Justin stepped over to the back door of the house and punched in the code to disarm the burglar alarm. He unlocked the door and stepped into the kitchen where he set the fish in the sink and grabbed two dog biscuits out of the cookie jar, a small one for Scooter and a large one for Shogun. Justin gave the dogs their treat and they both remained seated holding their reward in their mouth waiting for permission to eat it.

"Now get out of here while I clean these fish!" Justin ordered and both dogs flew out the door and into the carport.

Justin cleaned the three fish quickly and placed them in a Tupperware container with a little marinade over them, and set the container in the refrigerator. He was planning on dipping the fish in melted butter and then battering them in a flour and cornmeal mixture before frying them in a cast iron skillet. To accompany the fish he planned on fixing mashed potatoes, garden peas, and a tossed salad. For desert he had a homemade apple pie, thanks to Carol Crissman who came by yesterday and gave him the still hot pie. Carol was in her late forties and had never married. She had set her sights on Justin as soon as he started attending services at the New River Baptist Church and was determined to make Justin Hayes her man. She was a very attractive woman and a very nice lady, but there just wasn't any chemistry between them so Justin didn't want to date her. When she dropped by yesterday unexpectedly to give Justin the pie, she was wearing a tight sweater and a skirt that was too tight and too short, and she had on so much perfume the dogs started sneezing and finally went outside to escape. Justin knew that sooner or later he was going to have to tell Carol he wasn't interested, but he was hoping that she would take the hint when he didn't return her calls. So far that plan wasn't working.

Justin started back out to the truck to get his waders and fly rod when the phone rang and stopped him in his tracks. The wall phone in the kitchen didn't have caller ID and Justin figured it was Carol calling to see if he had tasted her pie yet. Justin finally answered it on the fourth ring thinking it might be Travis calling.

"Hello?" Justin said.

"Yes, I'm calling to speak to Mr. Justin Hayes. Is this he?" the voice said.

"Who is this?" Justin asked.

"Sir, my name is unimportant. I'm calling on behalf of Mr. Jack Billings," the voice replied.

"Well, tell Jack to get someone to call me whose name is important. I don't talk to people who won't give me their name," Justin said as he hung up the phone.

Justin didn't like Jack Billings one bit. He was a thief, a liar, and a con man, and he had made millions of dollars by cheating people out of their property. His bank, Billings Savings and Loan was notorious for making bad loans to people and then foreclosing on their property. He had acquired several thousand acres of land in Ashe, Allegany, and Wilkes counties by convincing some elderly farmer to sign legal documents that they either didn't read, or they didn't understand.

Jack had put his fortune to work by placing people in key positions in the local government. He owned a couple judges, two city councilmen, the county manager, the register of deeds, and of course the sheriff. He gave lots of money to the sheriffs department, the fire department, and the local school system. He also gave money to local charities to build up his good name. So to some people he was a hero and to others he was the devil.

Jack had been trying to buy Roy's land from him before Roy died. He tried to get Roy to borrow some money to "fix the place up." He drove a brand new four wheel drive John Deere tractor up to

Roy's and had the paper work ready for him to sign and buy it. He even drove a new four wheel drive Chevy truck up to Roy's, but Roy was to smart for that and sent them packing.

Then they starting threatening and harassing him to scare him into selling out, but Roy wasn't scared of anything on two legs or four. He started getting phone calls in the middle of the night but the caller wouldn't speak. His dog, a redbone hound named Red, suddenly disappeared. His mailbox got torn down at least once every two weeks. He was even forced off the road and wrecked his old truck, but Roy had no intention of selling his home.

Then the news came of Roy's tragic farming accident. Roy was found crushed to death under his tractor at the bottom of a steep mountain. Roy had been driving tractors up and down these hills for over fifty years and would have never tried to drive any tractor up the hill where he was supposedly killed.

Justin felt sure that Jack Billings was responsible for Roy's death but had no way to prove it. He had to remind himself of the Bible verse that says, "Vengeance is mine, saith the Lord!" because he wanted to deal with Jack and his bunch of thugs personally instead of waiting for divine intervention or the so-called authorities to handle it.

The phone rang again and this time Justin answered it on the first ring.

"Hello?" Justin said.

"Mr. Hayes, my name is Cecil Wood. I apologize for not identifying myself when I called a few moments ago," the voice said.

"Now we're getting somewhere, Cecil. How can I help you?" Justin asked.

"Mr. Hayes, I am Jack Billing's business manager and attorney. Mr. Billings would like to speak to you about a very lucrative business arrangement that he thinks you would be interested in. Do you think we could make some arrangement for you to meet with Mr. Billings?" Cecil Wood asked.

"Well, Cecil, I can't imagine being interested in a business deal with Jack, but I'll be here all evening if he wants to see me," Justin said.

"Mr. Hayes, with all due respect, Mr. Billings is a very busy man and was expecting you to come to his house for this meeting," the attorney said sternly.

"I'm a very busy man too, Cecil!" Justin said just as sternly. "I got people coming over for dinner and I got fish to fry. Now if Jack wants to see me I'll be here all evening. Have a good day," Justin said and then hung up the phone.

Jack Billings was sitting across the desk from Cecil Wood and heard the conversation on the speaker phone. He wasn't accustomed to being called Jack by anybody but close friends and he didn't like it when Justin did it. Cecil Wood wasn't accustomed to being called Cecil or being hung up on and he didn't like it either. Most of the time just the mention of Jack Billings's name was all that was necessary to put people at their best behavior.

"He's a cocky son of a bitch, isn't he?" Jack said.

"Yes, he certainly is," Cecil replied. "It looks like you and I are going to have to pay Mr. Hayes a visit."

"No, not you and I. Me and Johnny will ride up there in a little bit. We'll see if Justin Hayes is as cocky face to face as he is on the phone," Jack said.

"I don't think that's a good idea, Jack. Why don't you let me go see him and try to soften him up some first?" Cecil asked.

"No, I'm going with Johnny. He won't be as cocky with me and Johnny in his face. Besides, when I make him this offer he's going to jump all over it. He'd be a fool not to!" Jack said.

Justin wondered if Jack was going to try and buy his property. He sure was interested in buying it from Roy, or rather cheating him out of it. Justin knew that it was just a matter of time before Jack would approach him about purchasing his property.

Justin retrieved his fishing gear out of his truck and carried it to his shop. He wiped everything off and put it away. Justin always cleaned up his fishing or hunting gear when he got home no matter how tired or busy he was. It was a habit that he acquired in Vietnam. When he got back to base, even if he had been in the bush for a week, he always cleaned up his gear before he took a shower and hit the rack. As soon as he got his gear squared away he returned to the kitchen to fix his meal for Travis and Dwight. He called Travis's cell phone and Travis answered on the first ring.

"Where you at, Hoss?" Justin asked.

"Were about twenty-five minutes away. We just left Sparta," Travis answered.

"Are you hungry?" Justin asked.

"I'm starving to death," Travis said.

"I can't wait to see you. Sounds like I better get busy in this kitchen though for now. You guys drive on around and park in the carport when you get here and come on in the back door," Justin said.

"Right on, Dad. We'll see you soon."

Justin started putting his meal together. He cut up some potatoes and put them in a pot of water on the stove. He started another pot of water for the peas and melted some butter to dip the fish in before battering them. He put the apple pie in the double oven on a low heat to slowly warm it up and then started cutting up the lettuce for the tossed salad. Just as he placed the first piece of trout in the frying pan he heard the dogs barking and turned just in time to see Travis running through the back door.

He looked great, Justin thought. He was six-feet one and about 190 pounds. He had sandy-colored hair and blue eyes and looked like he just stepped out of a catalog for men. He crossed the room and they hugged each other as DeMac came through the door.

"Dad, this is my friend, Dwight McMasters, but we all call him DeMac. DeMac, this is my dad, Justin," Travis said.

Justin shook DeMac's hand and said, "Nice to finally meet you, DeMac. I've heard an awful lot about you. Make yourself at home. You guys pick out a bedroom and stow your gear while I finish up in the kitchen."

Justin finished frying the fish and mashing the potatoes and set them on the table along with the peas and tossed salad. He took the biscuits out of the oven and was just putting them on the table when Travis and DeMac came back in the kitchen. They sat down and Justin gave thanks for the good food and that these two soldiers had returned safely.

There wasn't much conversation at the table for awhile. It wasn't clear who the hungriest man was as all three men were apparently starving. Justin finally retrieved the apple pie from the oven and a half a gallon of vanilla ice cream from the freezer and all three men dove in again like they were possessed. When the last bite of pie was finally eaten Justin cleaned up the kitchen while Travis and DeMac walked around the yard looking at the property. They all finally ended up on the front porch sitting in rocking chairs and relaxing.

DeMac was impressed with Justin and his new house. The house was beautiful and had a spectacular view of the river and the surrounding mountains. Watching the river roll by reminded him of home and he had to fight back tears and remind himself that this was a mission, and he needed to act accordingly. Travis was right about his dad's physique, DeMac thought. He looked like a body builder, with wide shoulders and big arms and legs. His picture was included in the folder that DeMac was given to review before they left Norfolk, but he looked bigger in person.

The weather was perfect for sitting on the front porch and relaxing. It was about 65 degrees with a slight breeze, and all three men and both dogs were totally content.

"It's been a long time since I had fresh trout and it was absolutely delicious, Mr. Hayes," DeMac said.

"It was all delicious and now I'm about to pop," Travis said, rubbing his belly.

"Call me Justin instead of Mr. Hayes, if you will. That way I won't feel so old," Justin said. "As for the trout, they were tasty, weren't they? I fished for over three hours to catch those three little fish. I can manage to catch fish, I just can't seem to catch any big fish. I hope you can teach me some secrets for catching big fish. Travis says you're the man when it comes to fly fishing."

"Well, I don't know much about the New River, but I grew up in Montana and my family guided fisherman on the Musselshell River, so I grew up with a fly rod in one hand and a boat oar in the other. I haven't been fly fishing in several years and I'm looking forward to it," DeMac said.

Scooter jumped up and started growling followed closely by Shogun. They were staring down the driveway and both dogs jumped off the porch and charged down the hill.

Justin hollered, "Whoa! Get back here! Come on now, heel!"

Both dogs stopped their charge. Shogun spun around and started back immediately but Scooter stood there looking first down the hill and then back at Justin.

"Scooter, get back here! Heel!" Justin ordered. Scooter finally turned and trotted back up the hill.

"There's a groundhog down there and Scooter can't stand it. She's got a den right on the other side of that big flat rock and every time she sticks her head up Scooter takes off like a jet," Justin explained. "If Scooter catches her before she can get to her den, she will probably tear him up. Pound for pound a groundhog is tougher than a grizzly bear."

"Why don't you just shoot her?" Travis asked.

"Well, I probably would have, but she's got three pups and I can't stand the thought of those pups starving to death if I kill their mother."

"I can see her now just to the left of the rock," DeMac said, pointing down the hill.

The groundhog was eating the fresh green grass along Justin's driveway, pausing only long enough to stand up and look for danger. Scooter started growling again and when Justin told him to hush he whined and then snorted to show his disapproval. Justin laughed at Scooter's obvious pouting and called the little dog over and placed him on his lap.

"Are you mad at me 'cause I won't let you fight the groundhog?" Justin said in a baby voice while he scratched the dog's head. "That groundhog will tear you up, Scooter, especially since she's got babies to protect," Justin said in the same silly voice. Scooter snorted again and tried to act mad. All three men were laughing at the little dog.

·"Speaking of tearing something up, who or what hit you in the eye?" Justin said to Travis.

Travis had forgotten about his eye and instantly reached up and felt the swollen mouse under his right eye. "That was the Sparta Welcome Wagon. You know, 'Beautiful country and friendly people.'" Travis and DeMac both started laughing. When Travis composed himself he told his dad about the "redneck from hell" and their little confrontation.

"Well, I'll be damned," Justin said. "I thought Billy was stupid up until now."

"You know this Billy?" DeMac asked.

"Everybody knows Billy. He's Jack Billings's son," Justin said as he pointed his finger down River Road toward the Billing's mansion.

DeMac suddenly realized that the man Travis knocked out was the son of the man they were investigating. I'll bet the spooks are pulling their hair out about now, DeMac thought to himself.

"What makes you think he's not stupid?" Travis asked.

"Well, he tried to kick you the first time and you knocked him out. The second time he tried to kick you, you were handcuffed and lying on the ground. I think that shows a certain level of intelligence," Justin said, laughing. "Maybe that's why his daddy wants to see me so suddenly," Justin added.

"His daddy wants to see you?" Travis asked.

"Yeah, his attorney and business manager, a man named Cecil Wood, called about fifteen minutes before I called you and said Jack had a very lucrative business deal he thought I would be interested in. I told him I would be home all evening if he wanted to see me."

DeMac couldn't believe his luck. The spooks wanted to know if Justin and Jack were connected in some way. It looked like he was going to have a ringside seat for this business deal Jack had to offer.

Justin got up and went inside for a couple of minutes. When he stepped back outside he was wearing a Carhart vest with a fleece lining and carrying a .45 automatic. He checked the clip to make sure it was full and then chambered a round before sliding it in a special pocket that had been sewn inside his vest.

"I don't really expect any trouble, but it doesn't hurt to be prepared," Justin said.

"What kind of .45 you got there?" DeMac asked.

"Well, it's a Heinz 57, I guess. Its fifty-seven ingredients all put together. I built it when I was in gunsmithing school. It's a Kimber frame with a Wilson Combat barrel and trigger. It has a Caspian slide and a set of Novak sights. The ejection port has been lowered and the feedramp has been polished so it won't jam. It will function with practically any kind of ammo and with the right ammo it will shoot in a ragged hole at twenty-five yards. I got fancier pistols than Heinz

57, but I don't have any that shoot better. Will take it up to the range in a little bit and you can shoot it if you want to."

"Daddy, I sure hate I started all this trouble," Travis said.

"You didn't start this trouble. This trouble has been up here for years. You did the right thing and I'm proud of you. Hell, you're a hero and don't even know it. There are a lot of people around here who have been waiting for a long time to see Billy get his ass kicked. I just wish I could have seen it when it happened. Maybe you can do it again for my birthday or something," Justin said, grinning.

DeMac just shook his head. "You southern boys are absolutely crazy sometimes."

"Oh, you haven't seen anything yet," Travis said with a grin.

"All kidding aside, you better watch your six 'cause I'm sure Billy and his thugs will come after you if they catch you out. Maybe you should carry old Jay with you until things cool down a little." Justin said as he slid the little Smith and Wesson .357 Magnum out of his back pocket and tried to hand it to him.

"I better not," Travis said. "I got a feeling if that sheriff sees me again he's going to pull me over, and if he finds a pistol on me, he'll either arrest me or shoot me, I'm not sure which."

"You're probably right," Justin said. "He's Jack's right hand man."

DeMac smiled at Travis and said, "Have I thanked you lately for inviting me along on this vacation?"

"Yes, you've thanked me several times today and just so you will know, you're quite welcome," Travis answered.

"Well, it looks like were going to get that visit after all," Justin said as a black Hummer turned into his driveway and started up the mountain.

It topped the hill and made the turn and came to a stop right in front of the porch. The windows were tinted so dark you couldn't even see movement inside the vehicle. Finally the driver's door opened and out stepped what anybody would recognize as a professional bodyguard. He was six feet five inches and weighed probably 250 pounds. He had a square jaw and broad shoulders that tapered down to his waist and custom tailored blue jeans to fit his muscle bound legs. His hair was dyed blond and styled in a spiked hair do. He had on dark sunglasses and his teeth looked like they were cosmetically whitened.

He was wearing a black tee shirt with a black windbreaker over it, and it was very obvious that he had a shoulder holster on under it. He thought he was the meanest son of a bitch on earth and wanted everybody to know it.

He walked around the Hummer and opened the passenger side door. Out stepped Jack Billings. Justin had never met Jack but bad seen him on the news and passed him on the road a few times. Jack was average size, about six feet tall at the most with just a little bit of a belly on him. His hair was slightly thinning and was black with just a touch of gray around the edges. Jack reached in the door and retrieved his black cowboy hat and put it on his head. He was smoking a big expensive cigar and was every bit as cocky as his bodyguard.

Scooter and Shogun didn't like what they saw anymore than Justin and both of them started growling.

"Hush," Justin ordered and they both became quiet.

"Are your dogs friendly?" Jack asked.

"Not particularly, but they're well trained and won't give you any trouble." Justin answered. "Come on up on the porch and sit down if you like."

"That's all right, Mr. Hayes, this won't take long so if it's all the same to you will just lean against the vehicle here," Jack said.

"Suit yourself. This is my son Travis and a friend of his. They're staying a few days to do some trout fishing. Anything you got to say to me you can say in front of them," Justin said.

DeMac removed his cell phone from the right side of his belt and clipped it on the left side facing Justin and Jack.

"Is this Cecil with you here?" Justin asked. Justin knew that the man standing beside Jack wasn't the man he spoke with on the phone but he wanted to see the bodyguard's reaction when he called him Cecil. The bodyguard didn't say anything but his forehead wrinkled up slightly and Justin could tell he was staring at him even though he couldn't see his eyes for the dark sunglasses.

"No, no, this is my driver, Johnny Steele. Mr. Wood is tending to some other matters and couldn't come. Mr. Steele is my driver and personal assistant," Jack said with a slight grin.

Justin Hayes was nobody's fool. He knew that Jack had brought Johnny Steele along to try to intimidate him. Justin wasn't the least bit intimidated by Johnny Steele or Jack Billings.

"That car must steer real hard to need someone with all those muscles to drive it," Justin prodded.

"Johnny likes to spend his free time in the gym when he's not working. He does a lot more for me than just driving," Jack said with a smirk on his face.

Justin wasn't ready to quit yet. The fact that he brought this gorilla along to try to scare him angered Justin to no end. He wanted them to know that he wasn't scared of either one of them.

"Does he ever talk?" Justin asked.

Travis snickered but not loud enough for them to hear it. Travis knew his dad better than anyone and he knew it was a mistake to try to intimidate him. His dad wasn't afraid of Satan, much less Johnny Steele.

"Well, Mr. Hayes, Johnny here is kind of like you said your dogs were. He's not particularly friendly, but he's well trained," Jack said. There was an obvious tone in Jack's voice. He was accustomed to being in charge of conversations and being shone a certain level of respect. Jack was thinking maybe someday he could arrange for Johnny to teach Justin some manners.

Johnny Steele just stood beside Jack with his huge arms crossed and his snow white teeth shining. He would like to yank that smartass off the porch and break every bone in his body, but like Jack said he was well trained and would wait for the right opportunity or the order to do it.

DeMac sat calmly and listened. A couple of things were already apparent. One, Justin Hayes was his own man and not someone to trifle with. And two, Justin Hayes and Jack Billings weren't connected in any way, shape, or form. DeMac felt a great deal of relief from the latter. He really liked Travis and Justin and was hoping that they weren't involved with Jack in any illegal activities. He knew that the spooks would arrive at the same conclusion since they were watching and listening to this meeting also. Video was being sent to the CIA from two different sniper hides and the audio was coming from the cell phone on his side. It wouldn't mean that they could cancel their mission because the spooks still needed to know what Jack was doing with Suitcase B, but it would shift the attention away from Justin and Travis and focus it on Jack.

Justin was satisfied that he got his point across. He chuckled at Jack's comparison of Johnny and Justin's dogs. "That's a good answer, Jack," Justin said. "Don't take offense now 'cause I'm just having a little fun. Now what's this business deal you have for me all about?"

"Well, Justin, I'd like to buy this property of yours. It was my understanding that after Mr. Hepler passed away that you were building a house on the place just to help sell it, but it appears that you've moved in to stay," Jack said.

Justin was careful not to tell anyone that he was moving in once he finished building the house. The whole time he was working on the house he had people asking him what his intentions were, and some of those people were no doubt sent by Jack Billings. The county building inspector was constantly calling and pretending to know someone who was looking to purchase some property in the mountains, and Justin knew exactly who that person was.

"Well, Jack, I have moved in to stay. I'm not interested in selling the place, but if I change my mind I'll be sure and let you know," Justin said in a tone that suggested that the matter was settled.

"Mr. Hayes, I've discovered over years of doing business that everybody has a price, it's just a matter of finding out what that figure is. Now I'm prepared to make you a very generous offer for this property, and I think out of courtesy you should let me make my offer since I have taken the time to drive over here," Jack said.

"Jack, you can make your offer if you want. I'll show you the courtesy to listen to your pitch, but I don't have a price or a figure like most people. I would like to know what it is about this property that is so important to you. Why do you want my land?"

"Well, I'll tell you why. Your land joins mine for one reason. And even though I do own lots of land, your land is the only land that I can see from my house that I don't own. I guess it's selfish but I want to be able to stand in my front yard and look in any direction and know that I own everything that I can see," Jack explained.

Justin knew that Jack was right about that. Jack's land started at Justin's boundary and ran all the way to the confluence of the river and back up the other side of the river past Justin's house for almost a half a mile. The property lines ran across the tops of the mountains and all the land that surrounded Justin's and Jack's land was part of the New River State Park. Justin didn't really believe Jack's explanation, but then Justin didn't really believe anything that came out of Jack Billing's mouth.

"I've actually got two offers to present to you," Jack continued. "Forty-three acres of land that borders the river is worth between $500,000 and $750,000, depending on what part of the river you're on. I don't know how much you spent to build your house, but I'm guessing that your house and machine shop cost about $250,000 to build, not including your machinery or furniture. So I figure your property is worth one million dollars at the most."

Justin never thought of himself as a millionaire until now. He considered himself just an old country boy who was richly blessed. He guessed that both accounts were probably right.

Jack went on. "My first offer is $1.25 million with a $250,000 bonus if you sign the paperwork and move out within sixty days." Jack paused to see Justin's reaction. "That's $1.5 million if you move within sixty days."

"Not interested" was all Justin had to say.

"Okay, my other offer is this. I own a sixty-acre farm on the north fork of the New River. It's on Cranberry Creek Road and it borders the river just like your place here. It's a beautiful little farm and was once owned by the McCullock family. I'll take your house plans and build an identical house on that property complete with a paved driveway and a machine shop just like you have here, and swap you my place for yours. I'll even pay for a moving company to move your furniture and your machinery. You'll have almost twenty more acres of land and be sitting on what most people think is the prettiest stretch of the New River in the whole county."

Justin pulled out a can of Copenhagen and put a pinch between his cheek and gum. After he returned the can to his back pocket, he said, "Well, Jack, those are both generous offers, I'll give you that. But I'm still not interested in selling. If I change my mind though I'll let you know." Justin leaned forward to spit.

Jack couldn't believe his ears. He needed this land to help seal off his property. A person with a good quality spotting scope could watch Jack's house from Justin's and see things that Jack didn't want seen. Besides that, Jack could put a couple of men here to warn him about anybody coming down the road or the river. It was only forty-three lousy acres of land but it was the piece of the puzzle Jack needed to finish his operation. Jack had made arrangements to remove that stubborn Roy Hepler and damn if he didn't leave the place to somebody just as stubborn. Jack felt sweat popping out on his forehead and he knew his face was turning red.

"Well, Justin, you tell me what it would take to purchase this property from you," Jack said louder than he intended.

"You don't have enough money to buy this land, Jack," Justin said just as loud as Jack.

"What will it take? Two million! Three million! You tell me!" Jack snapped. It was obvious that Jack was losing his cool. He wasn't accustomed to not getting his way.

"Jack, let me explain something to you. I'm just a simple man. I am one of the very few people on this earth that is totally content. I have no needs or wants. If I want to go fishing I can walk across the road and be in some of the best water in the state. If I want to shoot one of my rifles or pistols, I can step up to my shooting range and shoot all I want. I can hunt deer, grouse, turkey, coyotes, bobcat, or groundhogs and never leave my property. I have enough money coming in every month from my retirement and investments to pay my bills and still have plenty left over. I don't want a bigger house or more money or more land. I'm a very simple man that is totally content and happy with what the good Lord has seen fit to give me."

Travis and DeMac sat in their rocking chairs and listened as the conversation continued. Part of DeMac's Seal team was monitoring the conversation on their headsets while they videoed the action from their sniper hides. The other members of DeMac's Seal team were watching the video in their base of operations in an old abandoned tobacco barn about seven miles away. The video from the snipers was being sent by satellite to the old tobacco barn and the audio from DeMac's cell phone was being sent to the tobacco barn and the sniper hides. All the information was being carefully monitored at the pentagon by the CIA and several senior military personnel.

Travis was looking at Johnny Steele when he happened to notice that the groundhog they were watching earlier had come back out for a bite to eat. Shogun and Scooter were lying beside Justin and hadn't seen him yet.

"Dammit, Justin Hayes, you're telling me there's no amount of money that could buy this land from you," Jack said as he tossed his cowboy hat on the hood of the Hummer.

Scooter and Shogun jumped to their feet and started growling. Johnny Steele started reaching for his pistol, but before he could grab it Justin had drawn his .45 automatic and pointed it straight at Johnny's head.

"You touch that pistol and I'll blow a hole right through those pretty white teeth!" Justin shouted.

Scooter and Shogun were still growling but were now looking at Johnny Steele instead of the groundhog. "Hush!" Justin ordered and both dogs became quiet.

"If those dogs leave that porch I'll kill them," Johnny snarled.

"You'll never get that pistol out of your holster before I blow your brains all over that pretty black Hummer." Justin replied.

Johnny lowered his hand and said, "You got the jump on me that time, old man."

In all the excitement Travis hadn't noticed that DeMac was also pointing a pistol at Johnny. He didn't even know that DeMac was carrying one until now. DeMac had drawn his Kimber Ultra Carry .45 automatic out of his ankle holster when Johnny reached for his gun. DeMac lowered his pistol when Johnny lowered his hand.

Justin slid his pistol back in his vest and said, "Don't let this gray hair fool you, son. You reach for that pistol again and they'll bury you day after tomorrow."

Jack had run around to the other side of the vehicle but now came back around the hood. "Now see here, Justin Hayes, I don't know who the hell you think you are to pull a pistol on me, but I'll have your ass arrested if I need to."

"Jack, your man reached for his pistol first. My dogs were growling at that groundhog down there beside the driveway, not at you. I told you that these dogs were well trained and wouldn't hurt you but muscles here thinks he's got to shoot one of them. It almost got him killed."

"Well, Johnny's job is to protect me!" Jack shouted.

"Well, you might want to get somebody a little quicker, Jack!" Justin shouted back.

Johnny Steele was standing motionless staring at Justin Hayes and he was madder than he could ever remember being. The old man had humiliated him in front of Jack and he wanted to yank his Desert Eagle pistol out and kill everybody on the porch, including the two dogs. But the old man was faster than anyone he had ever seen so he would have to wait for another time. Maybe they could arrange for Justin to have an accident, like they did his friend Roy.

"As for your question earlier, there is one way I would sell this property," Justin said.

Jack thought every man had a price and Justin Hayes was no different. "How much?"

"Oh, it's not an amount Jack. It's a condition," Justin replied.

"Well then, what's the condition?" Jack asked.

"That the person or persons responsible for the murder of my friend Roy Hepler are arrested and convicted. Then I would sell this property," Justin said as he stared at Jack.

"That's the craziest thing I ever heard. That old fool killed himself trying to drive a tractor up the side of a mountain," Jack said.

"The only fool present the night they killed Roy were the people that killed him. Roy had two tractors. The tractor they chose to roll over on him wasn't running at the time of his so-called accident. Also, the tractor they chose didn't have headlights. Roy never drove his tractors at night but on this particular night he decided to drive one of his tractors up a steep mountain and he took the tractor that didn't have headlights and wasn't running at the time. It was no accident. Somebody killed him and God have mercy on their souls if I find out who did it."

"Maybe Roy was working on the tractor and got it running. Maybe he was test driving it," Jack countered.

"The carburetor off that tractor was in the floorboard of my truck the night Roy was killed. I had taken it home and rebuilt it for Roy and was going to bring it back on my next visit. It's in my shop now and has serial numbers on it that match the tractor. If you drive over to Jefferson to the junkyard you can walk back there and see for yourself. Roy's old tractor doesn't have a carburetor on it."

"You should have reported this to the sheriff's department," Jack huffed.

"To Sheriff Bill Sisk? He was probably there when they killed him," Justin said loudly.

"Sheriff Sisk is a fine officer and I think you're confused about the facts surrounding this accident. At any rate it's obvious that we can't come to any agreement today so Johnny and I will leave. But one thing you should know, Justin, I didn't get where I am today by taking no for an answer. I plan on owning this land, some way or another," Jack said angrily.

Justin stood up and leaned out from the porch and looked up at the sky. "What are you doing?" Jack said as Johnny opened the door for him to get in.

"Just making sure a tractor isn't going to fall on me," Justin said.

Jack got in and slammed the door. Johnny Steele walked around to the driver's side and stopped to grin at Justin before he got in. Justin grinned back at Johnny but didn't say anything. The Hummer turned around and finally left. Just as they started to pull out of Justin's driveway Sheriff Sisk drove by headed for Jack's place.

"Well, I thought that went pretty good," Justin said, laughing.

"Yeah, but when he gets home and sees that video of me kicking his son's ass, he's going to be pissed," Travis said, grinning.

DeMac shook his head. "You guys are absolutely insane. Have I thanked you lately for inviting me along on this vacation?" DeMac said and all three men cracked up.

Groundhog Trouble

Justin, Travis, and DeMac sat on Justin's front porch relaxing and watching the river roll by. They would occasionally see a deer or a turkey on the mountain behind the river. An Osprey glided gracefully over the river for several minutes and then suddenly dove down and scooped up a nice fish. The Osprey struggled to gain altitude with the flopping fish but finally was able to fly away to feed its fledgling chicks.

"That Osprey fished for five minutes and caught a bigger trout than I did and I fished for four hours," Justin said, grinning.

"What were you fishing with when you caught those fish this morning?" DeMac asked.

"I fished with everything in my tackle box I think and all three fish hit different lures," Justin said.

"Do you ever cut a fish open to see what they have been eating that day?" DeMac asked.

"No, I haven't. I always figured they were eating what they hit when I caught them," Justin answered.

"Well, sometimes they hit a fly out of curiosity. I'll show you how to cut one open and see what there eating on that particular day. If you have something similar in your tackle box you can increase your odds quite a bit. If you don't have anything similar looking you can always go home and make something if you tie your own flies. Then the next time you'll be ready," DeMac instructed.

"That makes a lot of sense," Justin said. "I'm already learning to be a better fisherman and I haven't left the front porch yet."

"Dad, I want to see your machine shop," Travis said as he hopped up out of the rocking chair. "But first I want to change out of this uniform. I've been wearing a uniform everyday for six months and I'm tired of it. I'm going to put on a pair of blue jeans and a tee shirt and my tennis shoes.

"That sounds like a plan to me," DeMac said as he jumped up.

Travis and DeMac changed into civilian clothes and then returned to the front porch. "Well, let's do it," Justin said as he pushed himself up.

The three men walked around the house and through the carport to the walkway that led to the shop. Justin opened the door and cut on the lights.

"Wow, Dad, this is awesome!" Travis said as he stared in amazement.

"Holy mackerel," DeMac added.

Justin's shop was twenty-four feet wide and forty feet long. It had a three foot metal door leading in from the walkway and a matching one at the other end of the building. On the left side of the shop was an eight foot by ten foot roll up door so you could pull a vehicle in if you wanted to. Justin's Honda Farm Boss four-wheeler was backed in facing the door. There were large windows with steel bars over them spaced about eight feet apart all the way around the building and four sky-lights in the roof. There were workbenches and metal cabinets on three walls and various pieces of machinery bolted to the concrete floor. There was a South Bend metal lathe, an electric band saw, a vertical milling machine, a bead blaster, a surface grinder, a Tig welder, an acetylene torch, bluing tanks, and several bench grinders and belt sanders. On the far end there was a gun safe and a reloading bench. An eight foot by twelve-foot area in the back-right corner was partitioned off with Plexiglas and had a concrete shooting bench inside. There wasn't one square inch in the whole building that wasn't spotless.

Travis and DeMac wandered through the shop like two kids in a toy store until they reached the far end.

"This is the shooting room," Justin said as he opened the wooden door leading into the room that was partitioned off with Plexiglas. He stepped over to a set of wooden shutters across from the shooting bench and unlatched them, letting them swing open. Travis and DeMac looked out the opening and saw a firing range that stretched all the way across the mountain.

"How far is the farthest berm?" DeMac asked.

"It's six hundred yards to the end," Justin answered. "When they were grading my driveway I worked out a deal with the owner of the grading company. When they left in the evening I would use their bulldozer to work on my shooting range. He had leased the equipment so he didn't care if I used the equipment or not as long as I filled them back up with fuel before they came back the next morning. So I pushed out a lane all the way to the edge of my property and used the dirt to build my berms. I have a berm at 25, 50, 75, 100, 200,300,400,500, and 600 yards. The berms aren't real tall but if you overshoot one of them the bullet will hit the next one. There's a gradual rise from this point to the far end."

Travis and DeMac looked down the range and realized what Justin was trying to say. All the berms were in a straight line, and each one was just barely higher than the one before it, so a stray bullet would be stopped at some point if it went over its intended target.

"I can work on a gun or build a new gun and test fire it without ever leaving the building. That's a nice feature on cold rainy days or when there's a foot of snow on the ground. I use the four wheeler to go hang my targets and to retrieve them."

A strange noise from somewhere down the mountain came through the open shutters. No one recognized what the noise was except Shogun. He growled and took off through the shop and out the door.

"Where's Scooter?" Justin asked. "Oh no, Scooter's fighting that groundhog!" Justin hollered.

Everyone suddenly realized that the noise they were hearing was a dog and groundhog fight, and everybody knew which dog and which groundhog were involved.

All three men bolted through the shop door and ran wide open around the house and down the hill. Travis was in the lead with DeMac right behind him and Justin was bringing up the rear as fast as a fifty-seven-year-old man could possibly run. As they crested the hill they just got a glimpse of Scooter and the groundhog rolling around on the ground before Shogun ran them down and tore the groundhog off of Scooter. Bones could be heard cracking as the Rottweiler crushed the groundhog in his powerful jaws and then shook him like he was strapped to a paint shaker. He finally threw the groundhog up in the air and when it came down it hit the ground with a thud. The groundhog was dead.

Scooter was whining and trying to get up. His head and shoulders were covered with blood and there was a four-inch gash above his left shoulder that was pouring blood. Travis and DeMac ran over to the whining dog to see how bad he was hurt. Travis looked around for his dad and saw him lying up the hill about thirty yards holding his leg. He immediately ran back up the hill to his dad.

"Dad, are you all right!" Travis said.

"I turned my ankle over and messed it up big time." Justin groaned. "How bad is Scooter torn up?"

"I don't know but he's pretty bloody," Travis said.

"Go take care of him first. I'll be all right for now," Justin said.

Travis ran back down the hill to DeMac and Scooter. DeMac had taken his tee shirt off and made a bandage out of it for Scooter's shoulder.

"Hold pressure on this and let me go get my sea bag. I have a medical kit in it somewhere. He needs some serious stitches to close that wound up, but we've got to try and stop the bleeding or he definitely won't make it," DeMac said.

Travis pressed hard on the bandage while DeMac ran up the hill toward the house. Justin tossed his keys to DeMac when he ran by and said, "Bring my truck when you come back."

DeMac caught the keys on the run and never broke his stride. In less than a minute the truck rounded the house and came straight down the mountain.

DeMac slammed on the brakes when he got beside Travis and jumped out with a medical kit. Justin had slid on his back down the yard until he was beside Travis and Scooter.

Shogun circled the group whining, apparently worried about his canine friend. "Do I need to sew him up or is there a vet close enough to do it?" DeMac asked.

"The only vet around here is in Sparta at the animal clinic. Call information on your cell phone and get them to connect you to the Sparta Animal Clinic. If were lucky maybe we can catch them before they leave," Justin said.

DeMac did as he was instructed and finally got someone to answer on the sixth ring. "Animal Clinic," a woman's voice answered.

"Yes, ma'am, we have a Jack Russell Terrier with a deep four inch laceration to its upper left shoulder that needs to be sewn up quickly or he will bleed to death," DeMac said.

"How far away are you?" she asked.

"About twenty-five or thirty minutes." DeMac answered.

"I'll wait for you. Keep firm pressure directly on the wound until you get here," she said.

"We're on the way." DeMac said.

DeMac ripped open several rolls of gauze and began wrapping them tightly around the tee shirt he had placed on Scooter for a bandage. Blood had already seeped through the thick bandage and onto Travis's hands, but DeMac knew better than to remove it. He worked with the speed and precision that only comes from hours of practice. When he got to the end of a roll Travis held it while he ripped open another roll and started back where he left off. After the sixth roll of gauze he quickly tied it off and picked up the now lethargic dog and placed him on the passenger side of the truck. He made a loop in the seatbelt and placed it directly over the wound and then snapped the buckle. The tension of the seatbelt would keep pressure on the bandage while he was in transport. It was obvious to Justin and Travis why DeMac was the Seal team leader. He reacted to a critical situation with speed and precision with no unnecessary movements and no unnecessary talking. He was amazing to watch.

DeMac shut the door and grabbed the medical kit up off the ground. He pulled out a plastic bag and tossed it to Travis.

"Keep your eye on him on the way to town. Keep talking to him and scratching his head to keep him awake. If he closes his eyes and starts going into shock, pull over and tear this open. Inside is a syringe with blood expanders in it. Don't give him the whole thing, maybe a fourth of it to start with. I really don't know how much to give a small dog. I'll stay here and look after you dad," DeMac instructed.

"Do you know where the animal clinic is?" Justin asked.

"I saw it when we came through town today," Travis said.

"Okay then, take off. Don't wreck and kill yourself trying to save my dog, you hear me!" Justin said.

"Yes, sir!" Travis said as he jumped in the Toyota truck and took off down the hill."

Scooter's eyes were open but he had quit whining and looked very sleepy. Travis scratched his head and said, "You hang in there, Scooter. Don't you die on me now."

DeMac stepped over to Justin as soon as Travis went out of sight. "You think it's broken?"

"I don't think so. I've had trouble with it before. I fell off the back of a bucket truck about twelve years ago and broke it. Ever since then it's been real easy to turn over," Justin said.

"Let me take your boot off and take a look at it," DeMac said as he unlaced Justin's boot. "This might hurt a little."

"You think Scooter will make it?" Justin asked DeMac.

DeMac wasn't sure if Scooter would make it or not. If the vet was ten minutes away instead of twenty-five he believed the dog would have a good chance, but the wound was so deep it wasn't going to stop bleeding until a doctor sewed it up.

"Yeah, he'll make it. Scooters tougher than Chinese arithmetic," DeMac said.

Justin could tell that DeMac wasn't sure about Scooter's chances, but he appreciated his compassion in keeping up his spirit. "Well, regardless of what happens I want you to know how much I—Ahhh! Damn, that hurt!" Justin screamed as DeMac twisted his ankle.

"I don't think it's broken either, but we need to get you to the house and get an ice pack on it before it swells up any more."

"Go get my four-wheeler. The keys are in the ignition. I can drive it all the way to the back door and then hobble inside," Justin said. "Do you know how to drive a four-wheeler?"

"Oh yeah."

"I guess that was a dumb question," Justin said. "If you grew up in Montana and guided fisherman you probably rode one all the time."

"Well, actually we never had one when I was growing up, but we've been using them in Afghanistan. I'm glad too 'cause I can't stand camels," DeMac said, grinning as he trotted up the hill toward the house.

Travis was driving as fast as he could on roads he wasn't familiar with. Scooter was still conscious but the blood was starting to seep through the gauze that DeMac had layered over the bandage. As he came in sight of town he turned on the emergency flashers and the headlights and slowed down to about fifty miles an hour. There weren't but three stoplights in Sparta and they were all green when he went through the first one but they turned red as he approached the main intersection of town. Travis slowed down until he could see that it was clear and then gunned the engine and flew through the red light. The next light turned green before Travis got to it, but an elderly man in a Volkswagen Beetle was stopped at it and wasn't moving.

Travis looked at Scooter and saw that he had closed his eyes. "Just one more minute, Scooter! You hold on for one more minute!" Travis hollered. Travis slung the truck in the left lane and passed the Volkswagen in the middle of the intersection, then swerved back in his lane just in time to miss a lady driving an old Cadillac with huge fins on the back fenders. She blew her horn and it sounded like the fog horn on a tug boat, Travis thought. The animal clinic was in sight and the truck tires squalled as Travis turned in the lot almost on two wheels.

A woman wearing a lab coat was waiting outside and ran to the truck before Travis had a chance to get out. She opened the passenger side door and immediately felt for a pulse on the lifeless dog. Travis ran around the truck and stood behind her holding the plastic bag that DeMac had given him with the blood expanders in it.

"He has a pulse but its very faint," she said as she picked the little dog up and cradled it in her arms like a baby. "Hold the door open for me," she said as she ran for the building.

Travis ran over and opened the door to the animal clinic and she ran inside. He followed her through a waiting area and then down a hallway and into a room that was already prepared for surgery. A powerful overhead light was on and surgical trays were laid out in preparation for there arrival.

"You'll have to help me," the lady said. "I'm the only one here. I was just starting out the door when you called."

"Can we get the vet on the phone?" Travis asked.

"I am the vet," she said. "My name is Jesse."

"Oh, okay, I'm Travis. Just tell me what you need for me to do," Travis said.

Jesse quickly started an IV on Scooter. Then she took a hypodermic needle and injected something into Scooter's right hip. She placed a mask over his nose and mouth and turned on a valve that started making a hissing noise. Travis watched intently but didn't ask any questions for fear of distracting her. Scooter was lying lifeless on the operating table with his eyes closed and Travis couldn't tell if he was alive or not. He sure hoped he was alive because he knew how much the little dog meant to his dad. The vet had been working furiously up to this point, but now stopped to listen to Scooter's heart with her stethoscope. They stood there for what seemed like a very long time in silence except for the hissing of the machine hooked up to Scooter's mask while the doctor monitored his heart. After what seemed like an eternity to Travis, the vet looked up at Travis and smiled.

Travis was suddenly aware of how beautiful this woman was. When she looked up at Travis and smiled, he felt a strange sensation run through him that he had never felt before.

"His pulse is gradually getting stronger. When you first pulled up he was almost dead. If we can keep enough fluids in him until we get him sewn up he might just make it," she said. She put the stethoscope away and began cutting the bandage off with a pair of scissors.

"You did a great job of bandaging him up before you left," she said.

"Well, that was my friend DeMac who bandaged him up," Travis said, staring at her eyes.

"If he lives you might want to thank him because he wouldn't have made it otherwise," she said as she removed the bandage. "What caused this wound?"

"A groundhog, believe it or not. Scooter jumped her and my dad's Rottweiler jumped in and finished it."

"Oh, I remember Scooter now. And your dad's Rottweiler is named Shotgun, isn't he?"

"Shogun," Travis said. "You know my dad's dogs?"

"Yeah, I think he brought them in for shots and transferred their medical records," she said. "I remember them because they were so well behaved. Okay. Hold him just like this," she said, and she took Travis's hands and placed them on Scooter just like she wanted them.

Travis felt that same sensation that he had felt before shoot through him. It was kind of freaking him out a little bit. Maybe it was the adrenaline rush leaving him after the mad rush for town he thought.

"How can a groundhog cut a dog open like that?" Travis asked.

"I'm guessing that the groundhog bit the dog on the shoulder and held on until your dad's Rottweiler ripped him off, causing the long tear in his shoulder. You know a groundhog's top teeth are sometimes over an inch long." Jesse placed a strip of surgical tape over the gash and began shaving a half inch strip all the way around the wound. When she finished she took a vacuum hose and sucked up the loose hair.

"Now I want you to hold the wound open while I flush it out and take a look at it," she said as she removed the tape covering the gash.

Travis pulled gently on each side of the laceration until it gaped open. Jesse put the vacuum line inside the wound and started flushing it out with a bottle of saline solution. After several minutes of sucking the blood and dirt and grass from the opening she stopped and started threading a long curved needle. She changed the almost empty I.V. bag and immediately started placing sutures deep inside the wound. After placing a whole row of sutures inside the wound she started slowly pulling the gash closed on the outside. Travis was holding Scooter just as she had instructed him and was amazed at how nicely the terrible looking gash was coming together.

"I can handle this by myself now. Maybe you should call your dad and give him a progress report. He's probably going crazy worried about him. I'm surprised he didn't come with you," Jesse said.

"He twisted his ankle when we ran to help Scooter or he would be here. You're right. I should give him a call and let him know what's going on," Travis said as he reached for his cell phone.

Justin was resting in his recliner with his injured ankle elevated and a chemical cold pack wrapped around it. DeMac had driven Justin's four-wheeler down the yard to where Justin was laying and helped him to get on it, and then Justin had driven it up the hill and into the carport as close to the backdoor as possible. Using DeMac as a crutch, he then hobbled through the house until he got to his recliner. DeMac dug around in his medical bag until he found the chemical cold pack and then wrapped it around the swollen ankle. Then he drove the four-wheeler back to the machine shop and parked it before returning to the house and sitting down across from Justin on the sofa.

"DeMac, I appreciate all you've done. You haven't had much of a vacation yet, that's for sure," Justin said.

"You're quite welcome," DeMac said. "I'm glad I was able to help."

"Are you planning on visiting your family in Montana?" Justin asked.

A lump formed in DeMac's throat and he coughed before answering.

"Well, actually, I don't have any family anymore. They were killed about five months ago when their house burned down in the middle of the night," DeMac said.

"I'm sorry to hear that, DeMac. Travis hasn't said anything about it and I didn't know," Justin said.

"That's all right. I didn't tell anybody for a long time. I think every time you spoke to Travis lately I've been standing right beside him so he probably couldn't tell you. Travis and I have grown pretty close over the last few months. You have a fine son that you can be proud of," DeMac said.

"How did the fire start?"

"Well, you know, I told you my family guided fisherman on the Musselshell River, but we also guided hunters during the winter months who wanted to kill trophy mule deer, whitetail deer, and elk. There were two men from Mississippi staying at the ranch who were hunting trophy mule deer. The water heater in the hunting lodge went out so dad moved them in the house until he could get to town and buy one. During the night one of the men decided to bring a butane heater in the house that he had brought along because he just couldn't get warm. Sometime later one of them apparently kicked some clothes or a blanket over against the heater and started the fire. When the men woke up they ran outside, but mom and dad, and my sister were trapped upstairs and couldn't get out. They were probably overcome with smoke before they could jump out the window. When the fire department got there they said the two men who escaped were sitting in their truck with the engine running. Neither one of them tried to help get my family out of the burning house," DeMac said with a cracking voice.

"I sure am sorry, DeMac," Justin said as the phone rang. He reached over and picked up the receiver.

"Hello?" Justin answered.

"Dad, this is Travis. The vet is almost through sewing up Scooter. She's done a remarkable job and Scooter's doing as well as can be expected but isn't out of the woods yet, she said to tell you," Travis said.

"Well, good. You tell that pretty young thing that if Scooter lives I'll dance at her wedding," Justin said.

"Dad said that if Scooter lives, he'll dance at your wedding," Travis said to Jesse.

"I'll hold him to that," Jesse said as she tied off the last suture.

"How's your ankle?" Travis asked.

"The swelling is going down. Dr. McMasters has everything under control," Justin said.

"Good. I'll let you know more when I can. Oh, by the way, Jesse said DeMac's bandaging was the only thing that saved him so we owe him a big thank you," Travis said.

"Okay then. Call me when you know more," Justin said and then hung up the phone.

Jesse was listening to Scooter's heartbeat with her stethoscope. "He seems to be doing fine. I'm going to clean him up a little bit and then we'll wait for him to come out of the anesthesia."

"Would you like me to go get you something to eat or a cup of coffee while we wait?" Travis asked.

"Actually, a cup of coffee sounds good. The Allegany Inn is about three blocks down if you turn right at the square of town. Their coffee is the best."

"Okay then. I'll be right back," Travis said. Travis jumped in his dad's truck and drove to the Allegany Inn and returned with two large coffees and a bag with cream and sugar.

When he walked back into the operating room Jesse was just finishing giving Scooter a bath. He was still unconscious from the anesthesia but his eyes were fluttering occasionally. Jesse had attached a heart monitor to Scooter so she could watch his heartbeat on a screen.

"Go grab a couple chairs so we can drink our coffee in here."

Travis grabbed two folding chairs from an adjacent room and they finally sat down to rest and drink their coffee.

Travis couldn't keep his eyes off of Jesse. He thought she was absolutely gorgeous but his dad had mentioned dancing at her wedding so she must be engaged. She wasn't wearing an engagement ring, but then she wouldn't dare wear one while she was doing surgery. She was about five feet eight inches tall with shiny black hair that she had put in a ponytail Her skin was a very light brown like some light skinned oriental women and her eyes were the most beautiful blue that he had ever seen. She was slender like a runner but had a nice figure, as best he could tell with her wearing a lab coat. When she smiled it was obvious that her teeth were perfect and it almost gave Travis chill bumps.

Scooter made a grunting sound and Jesse got up to check on him. She returned to her chair and said, "He's doing fine. He'll be awake in about fifteen minutes and you can take him home. Thankfully the laceration was confined to muscle tissue and didn't sever any major arteries or veins. I'll send some antibiotics home with you to prevent an infection and some pain killers. He's going to be awfully sore for a couple days and you need to limit his activities if that's possible with a Jack Russell Terrier. At least he can't reach the stitches with his mouth and tear them out."

"That's great. I can't thank you enough for waiting for us to get here. This dog means an awful lot to my dad, even though he probably wouldn't admit it. I was amazed at how nicely it came back together."

"It was a clean cut, almost like a razor. When the hair grows back it won't be very noticeable," Jesse said. Jesse couldn't help but to notice Travis staring at her and was somewhat flattered by it. He seemed like a nice guy and he was awful easy on the eyes. He was obviously in good physical condition and she could tell he had six-pack abs even through his tee shirt. He didn't have any piercings or gaudy tattoos, and he was polite and respectful like a gentleman.

"Do you live with your dad?"

"No, I'm just staying with him for awhile until I figure out whether to reenlist in the Navy or not. I just finished a five-year enlistment and I have thirty days to decide whether to reenlist or get out."

"You're not the sailor who came through town today and knocked out Billy Billings, are you?" she asked.

"Well, yes, that was me. I tried to avoid it though!" Travis said in his defense. "Boy, news travels fast around here, doesn't it?"

"I'm glad you didn't avoid it. You got to tell me about it," she said with that beautiful smile of hers.

Travis told Jesse everything that happened at the Hess station and she laughed until she cried. Conversation came easy between Jesse and Travis and they talked and laughed until time slipped away. Travis glanced over at Scooter and he was sitting up with his eyes open. "Look," Travis said, and he and Jesse jumped up and stood on opposite sides of the operating table.

"Hey there, fellow," Travis said as he rubbed Scooter's head.

Jesse checked Scooter's heartbeat and respiration one more time and then covered the wound with a Beta dine solution to keep it clean. She gathered up the antibiotics and the pain killers and gave one of each to Scooter while Travis held him. Then she scooped him up softly and walked outside with him.

"I need to see him first thing Tuesday morning," she said as she leaned over to hand the little dog to Travis.

When Travis leaned over to take Scooter from Jesse her pony tail brushed across his cheek and he could smell her wonderful scent. That strange sensation he had felt earlier flashed through him again and he knew this time it wasn't adrenaline.

"Here's my card. If you need me over the weekend don't hesitate to call. Try to limit his activity as best you can and be sure to give him those antibiotics religiously. It was nice to meet you, Travis, and tell your dad I'm going to hold him to his promise," she said and disappeared back into the animal clinic.

Travis just stood there like an idiot and didn't say a word. He didn't want to leave but he guessed he would have to. It was dark outside and Travis called his dad and told him that they were on the way. Travis drove through the curvy mountain roads at a much more leisurely pace then when he went to town. He was rubbing Scooter's head as he drove and the little dog was asleep after the first mile. Travis couldn't get Jesse off his mind. She was beautiful, smart, talented, and a lot of fun to be around. Her smile could melt glaciers, he thought. Her fiancé was a very lucky man.

Travis finally saw his dad's driveway and turned in. He drove up the driveway and into the carport and was welcomed by DeMac and Shogun. Scooter woke up and started whining when he realized where he was. DeMac reached in and gently picked the little dog up.

Shogun was anxious to see his little buddy so DeMac held him down so they could smell and lick each other.

"Welcome home," DeMac said.

"It's good to be home. Damn, what a day it's been!" Travis said. Travis gathered up the medicine that Jesse had sent with him and followed DeMac and Shogun through the house and into the living room where Justin was sitting in his recliner.

"Well, Scooter, it's good to see you," Justin said as DeMac placed the dog on Justin's lap. "I wasn't sure if I would ever see you again or not, at least alive." Scooter was whining and licking Justin's hand as he rubbed him. "I guess I'm going to have to cancel entering you in the Westminster Dog Show now that you got that scar across your back."

"Jesse said to limit his activity if we could. Here are the antibiotics and the pain medicine she sent. She wants to see him first thing Tuesday morning," Travis said. "I need a cold beer after a day like today." Travis headed for the kitchen.

"Bring us all one!" Justin said.

Travis came back with three long necks and passed them out before flopping down on the sofa beside DeMac. "What a day! First it was seeing mom after all these"

"You went to see your mother?" Justin asked.

Travis had messed up. He had decided not to tell his dad about the visit with his mother but it was to late now. "Yeah, I stopped on the way up here this morning and stayed about half an hour. She wrote me a letter about two months ago and begged me to come see her when I got back and I agreed to it," Travis said as if he was ashamed of himself.

"Well, that's okay. How is she?" Justin asked.

"She looks bad. I didn't recognize her at first. I think she must have cancer or something. She looks like she's dying to me," Travis said.

"I'm sorry to hear that," Justin said.

"Really, Dad? 'Cause I didn't know how you felt about her," Travis asked.

"I don't wish her anything but happiness. She broke my heart and broke up our home, but I'll always have some feelings for her, I guess. We had twenty good years together and she is the mother of my only child. Besides, hate will eat you up quicker than cancer," Justin said.

"Well, anyway, after leaving Mom's house we got into the fight at the Hess station, then we almost had the fight at the OK Corral on the front porch, then Scooter got torn up and we had to medi-vac him. It's just been a rough day," Travis said as be took a swig of his beer.

"You're looking at it all wrong, Hoss," Justin said. "You finally got to see your mom after fifteen years, you won the fight at the Hess station and saved a damsel in distress, we won the quick draw contest on the front porch, and Scooter lived through what almost certainly was a fatal injury," Justin said with a smile.

"I guess you're right, Dad. There was one more wonderful thing that happened today," Travis announced.

"Well, I wasn't going to mention that fabulous fish dinner I prepared," Justin said.

"No, not that!" Travis shouted.

"What then?" Justin asked.

"I met the most beautiful woman I have ever seen," Travis said as he stared at his empty beer bottle.

"She was pretty hot, but I wouldn't say she was the most beau-tiful woman I'd ever seen. Besides, she's probably only sixteen years old," DeMac said.

"Not the girl at the Hess station! The veterinarian! Jesse!" Travis said.

"Oh," DeMac said with a strange look on his face.

"Her fiancé is one lucky man," Travis said with a sigh.

"She's engaged?" Justin asked.

"Well, I guess so. You promised her you would dance at her wedding if Scooter lived," Travis said.

"Well, I will dance at her wedding, whenever she has one. That doesn't mean that she's engaged," Justin said.

"You mean she's not engaged as far as you know?" Travis asked.

"I don't think so. I have never seen any other vehicles besides hers at her house. She lives in a two-story farm house on the right just before you get to town. When I was building this house I had to run to town at least three times a week and I never saw any vehicles there except her Chevy Suburban she uses to haul her veterinarian supplies around in, and her red Jeep Cherokee she drives when she's not working."

Travis felt like a hundred-pound weight had been lifted off his chest. He wondered if the pretty veterinarian would consider going on a date with him. As he pondered this in his mind he could visualize her sitting beside him in a fancy restaurant smiling at him with those beautiful teeth, her shiny black hair falling across her shoulders.

"Hey! Hey, Romeo!" Justin hollered.

"Oh, I'm sorry about that I…uh, I was just—"

"You're daydreaming about playing doctor with the doctor." DeMac chuckled.

"No, I was just. uh, I'm just tired I guess," Travis said, blushing.

"Take that quilt that's in the toolbox on my truck and spread it out in the laundry room for these two knuckleheads to sleep on tonight. Bring their food bowl and water bowl in from the carport and put it in there with them, and shut the door so they can't get out," Justin ordered.

"Yes, sir, Master Chief, sir!" Travis said, grinning. He did as instructed and returned to the living room with three more longnecks. Justin was reading the labels on the medicine bottles that Jesse sent for Scooter.

"She already gave him one each of those for tonight," Travis said.

"That's good. And by the way, I agree with you concerning her looks. She is quite beautiful," Justin said.

"She's gorgeous," Travis said.

"I believe your son is in love, Justin," DeMac said.

"Yeah, it sounds like the real thing," Justin teased.

"No way. Besides, a woman that pretty and smart probably has men lined up to date her," Travis said.

"There aren't many eligible men around here," Justin said. "You ate that apple pie today and you know I don't bake apple pies."

"Yeah, you said that lady was pretty and real nice, so why don't you take her out, Dad, whatever her name is?" Travis asked.

"Carol Crissman is her name and she is very pretty and a very nice lady, but she would drive me crazy in less than a week. She's the kind of woman that would turn your covers down every night and fluff your pillows, and pack special lunches for you when you were going out with little love notes hidden in them, and follow you around everywhere you went when you were at home, and call you ten times a day when you were gone. Some men like that but it would drive me insane. Besides, she wears way to much perfume. I had to open the windows and cut the ceiling fans on when she left the last time."

"All this talk about women is making me sleepy," DeMac said. "I think I'll turn in. Goodnight, Justin. Goodnight, Romeo."

"I guess we can forget about fishing tomorrow since I can't walk," Justin said.

"You'll be ready by Monday morning," DeMac said.

"Good night, lover boy," DeMac said to Travis.

"Kiss my ass, DeMac," Travis said, grinning.

"I think I'll turn in too," Travis said.

"When you were telling Jack today about being a simple man that was totally content with his life. Is that true?" Travis asked.

"Yeah, for the most part it is. I'm very happy and content with my life and I don't really want anything that I don't already have. The only thing I would change is I sometimes get a little lonely, especially since I've moved away from Silver Hill."

"Well, I'm glad you're happy, Daddy, 'cause you deserve it," Travis said.

"I haven't ever done anything to deserve all this," Justin said.

"Yeah, you have too!" Travis said as he got up to go to bed. "Do you need help to get to bed?"

"I am in bed," Justin said as he reached over and cut the lamp off beside his recliner.

Trouble in Paradise

Travis was pouring himself a cup of coffee when DeMac walked into the kitchen. He turned around and handed DeMac the steaming mug and then reached into the cabinet to get another mug for himself.

"Good morning," DeMac said as he took a sip.

"Morning. Did you sleep all right?" Travis asked.

"Like a rock. I don't think I even turned over. How about you?" DeMac asked.

"I slept good once I got to sleep," Travis said.

"Couldn't get the doctor off your mind, could you?" DeMac asked.

"To be honest with you, I couldn't," Travis said.

"How are your dad and Scooter this morning?" DeMac asked.

"I don't know. Let's go out on the front porch and see," Travis said.

Travis and DeMac walked through the house and out the front door onto the porch. Justin was standing in the front yard drinking a cup of coffee and Scooter was hobbling around at his feet. Shogun was taunting them by running back and forth across the front yard just out of their reach. When he would run by, Justin would pretend to try and grab him and he would dodge and weave like a pro running back carrying a football.

It was a beautiful crisp spring morning as Travis and DeMac stood and watched the game of catch with the New River in the background flowing by under a thin veil of mist. Justin turned and slowly hobbled toward the front porch before he noticed he had an audience.

"Good morning," he said, smiling.

"How's the ankle?" Travis asked.

"It's a little tender but it's a lot better than I expected. I think keeping it elevated and a cold pack wrapped around it did the trick. Scooter's doing okay but he's so sore he can hardly move. I gave him his antibiotics and pain medicine and then brought him out here so he could stretch and use the bathroom."

"Did you guys sleep okay?" Justin asked.

"I slept great," DeMac said. "Romeo had a little trouble falling to sleep."

Justin turned around and saw Scooter hobbling down the hill toward the groundhog hole. "Well, they could never accuse Scooter of being a quitter, now, could they? Scooter, get back up here!" Justin ordered.

"What about the groundhog pups, will they just starve to death?" DeMac asked.

"I've been thinking about that this morning. I believe if we set a live trap at the entrance of their hole we can catch them. They're big enough to live without their mama if nothing kills them. I've got a live trap in the shop and if you boys will help me we'll see if we can catch them. That's the best we can do. If they stay here these dogs will eventually catch them and kill them for sure."

"Let's do it," DeMac said.

Travis didn't say anything. He was wondering if Jesse was up yet.

The morning wasn't going very good a mile away at the Billings household. Jack had been up and down all night with acid reflux. He had only slept a couple hours and his head hurt and his chest and throat felt like they were on fire. He sat on the edge of his bed and stared in the direction of Justin's house. He wanted a stiff drink of bourbon but he knew it would be like throwing gasoline on a fire the way his stomach was this morning. He finally stood up and stepped over to the intercom. "Ashley, bring me my coffee," he barked.

"Right away, sir," a women's voice answered.

Jack stood there nude and waited for his housekeeper, Ashley Yates, to bring him his coffee. It was only a matter of seconds before she entered the room carrying a steaming cup of coffee for her boss. She wasn't surprised to see him standing there naked. He was narcissistic enough to believe that she enjoyed it. She handed him his coffee and without ever looking at him, turned and left the room.

Jack walked across his bedroom and into the bathroom. He set the coffee on the counter and stepped into his shower and cut the water on. He stood on the magnificent marble floor that came from a quarry somewhere in Italy and waited until the water was hot before he stepped under the steaming spray that came from seven different nozzles. He needed to clear his head before the meeting that he had scheduled for eight o'clock. They normally met at noon on Mondays to touch base and plan the week's activities, but Jack had informed everybody that they would meet at eight a.m. on Saturday morning and by God they better be there. He had also sent word to his son that he was expected to attend even though he normally wasn't at their meetings. Jack stood under the deluge of steaming water and waited for a magical cure of some kind to seep into his body and make him feel better.

It was no wonder he couldn't sleep. When he came home yesterday from Justin Hayes's house he was furious. He couldn't believe that anyone was stupid enough to refuse an offer like he had made Justin Hayes. On top of that, he all but accused him of murder and damn near shot his bodyguard. Then Sheriff Sisk shows him the tape of Billy being knocked unconscious by a sailor and it turns out to be, of all people, Justin's son, Travis. It's a wonder that he didn't have a heart attack or stroke. After watching the video three or four times he started getting Ashley to bring him bourbon and Cokes, and he drank until he finally staggered to bed. The combination of the alcohol and the stress caused his acid reflux to flare up, and no amount of Nexium or baking soda or Rolaids could stop the burning when he would lie down.

Jack finally cut the water off and stepped out of the shower. He sat on the stool in front of the mirror and drank his coffee as he air dried. He had fought and clawed and run over anybody that got in his way to build quite an empire, but he was faced with two big problems. The first problem was Justin Hayes. There was something about him that made Jack nervous but he wasn't sure what it was. It was probably his total lack of fear that bothered Jack the most. Very few men could stand in front of Jack Billings and Johnny Steele and not feel at least a little anxiety if not downright fear, but Justin Hayes did and even taunted them. Some men tried to pretend they weren't scared, but Jack was an expert at reading body language, and he could tell that Justin Hayes wasn't pretending.

There was also the matter of Roy Hepler's farming accident that troubled Jack. Justin obviously knew that Roy's death was no accident, and although he couldn't prove it, Jack didn't want anyone drawing attention to it. But Jack also knew that there were ways to deal with people like Justin Hayes and sooner or later he would win that battle and own that property.

The other problem was something Jack didn't have a clue how to deal with and that problem was his son Billy, and his nephew Johnny. Jack was fifty-eight years old and needed to groom someone to run his business, and he wanted to leave the business in the hands of someone who was family. The trouble with that was the only family Jack had to leave it to was his son Billy, or his nephew Johnny Billings.

His brother Zeb had drowned nineteen years ago in the New River when he drove off the low water bridge and couldn't get out of the car before it rolled over in between two large rocks and filled with water. Zeb and Jack and two other men had been spotlighting deer and drinking white liquor that evening and all four of them were falling down drunk when Zeb announced he was going home and jumped in his car that fatal night. Johnny was only five years old at the time and Jack took him in and promised his dead brother he would raise him. Johnny's mother had left Zeb when Johnny was three years old after being beaten repeatedly ever since Johnny was born. She wanted to take Johnny with her but knew Zeb would kill her if she did, so she had to leave without him to save herself. Johnny was only four months older than Billy, and when he came to live with Jack it was almost like having twin sons running around the house. They grew up together and played together and Jack considered both of them his sons.

The problem was neither one of them could be left to run the business because neither one of them stayed sober enough to run anything. Billy was an alcoholic and Johnny stayed high on marijuana and cocaine or whatever he could get. Jack had put both of them in rehab a year ago but when they returned they both started back where they left off. Jack couldn't remember the last time he had seen either one of them when they weren't high. He could send them back to rehab but it would probably be a waste of time and money.

Jack took the last sip of coffee from his cup and pushed the button on the intercom. "Ashley, will you bring me another cup of coffee?" he said, a little more civil than the first time.

"Yes, sir."

Jack walked back in his bedroom and opened the plantation blinds over the double windows. The fog had lifted off the river and he could just barely see Justin's house a mile away on the side of the mountain. Ashley came back in carrying another cup of coffee and handed it to Jack and then left with his empty cup. Jack sipped the coffee and stared at Justin's house. He belched and felt the acid rise up and burn his throat again. His eyesight wasn't what it used to be but he thought he saw something move in Justin's front yard so he picked up his 10 × 50 Zeiss binoculars off the nightstand and placed them to his eyes.

There was Justin standing in his front yard playing with his dogs. The Rottweiler was running back and forth and Justin was grabbing at him when he went by. He looked like he was laughing and having a good time and Jack almost felt jealous for just a moment. He remembered what Justin had said yesterday about being "a simple man" and being totally content and happy with his life. "Bullshit," Jack said out loud. "We'll see how happy you are when I get through with you." And he walked into his walk-in closet to get dressed.

Justin had retrieved his Have-a-Heart live trap from the machine shop and sent Travis and DeMac down the front yard with it to try and catch the orphaned groundhogs. They baited the trap with a thin slice of cantaloupe and then placed a bite-size piece at the entrance of the den. Justin was hoping that they would come out and look for their mother when they got hungry. He had seen them about three days ago standing on the mound of dirt beside the hole their mother had dug, so he knew they were big enough to crawl out of the den.

"Let's go eat some breakfast," Justin said to Travis and DeMac as he hobbled up the front steps.

"Sounds good, 'cause I'm starving. What are we having?" Travis asked.

"Oh, we can have bacon, sausage, or ham with eggs or pancakes or French toast, and grits or hash brown potatoes or any combination of those things you want," Justin said.

"I want French toast and sausage," Travis said immediately.

"That sounds good to me," DeMac said.

"Okay then, it's French toast and sausage," Justin stated. "Oh, by the way, you've got to cook it. I'm going to rest my ankle."

Jack put on a pair of blue jeans and a white dress shirt and then slipped on his shark skin cowboy boots. He combed his thinning hair and brushed his teeth and put a drop of cologne behind each ear before he headed for the kitchen. Jack's kitchen would be the envy of any restaurant in North Carolina. It was bigger than most people's houses and equipped with anything a chef would want.

There were two chefs under Jack's employ., The main chef's name was Michael Bloom. He normally worked Thursday through Sunday from eleven a.m. until eight p.m. unless directed otherwise. The other chef's name was Steven Sanders and he worked every day of the week except Sunday from six a.m. till noon unless otherwise directed.

Steven was standing at the grill frying something when Jack walked in. "Good morning, sir. Would you care for some breakfast this morning?" Steven asked.

"Not till later, Steven," Jack responded. Ashley was sitting on a bar stool eating a sandwich and drinking a cup of coffee.

"Ashley, we're having a meeting this morning and I don't want to be bothered until it's over. I want you to bring me a ginger-ale on ice as soon as you finish your breakfast," Jack said.

"Yes, sir" was all Ashley said.

Jack walked through the kitchen and down a hall that led to the conference room. He passed by Steve Helm's office, Donald Crafton's office, and Cecil Wood's office and they were all unoccupied. When he entered the conference room all three men were already seated and nursing their first cup of coffee. A carafe filled with coffee and a platter of pastries sat in the center of the table.

"I hope you gentlemen slept better than I did last night," Jack said.

All three men answered in some way or another but the truth was that none of them slept very well because they were wondering why they were having an emergency meeting on Saturday instead of their usual meeting at noon on Monday. Ashley knocked and then entered the room with the ginger ale Jack ordered and promptly left. Johnny Steele came strolling in and poured himself a cup of coffee before sitting down. It almost seemed like the room got smaller when Johnny came walking in and Jack was suddenly reminded of the way Justin Hayes's humiliated Johnny the day before.

Jack's success was no accident. He had surrounded himself with the best men money could buy. It cost him a small fortune to employ men of this type but in the long run it was money well spent. Jack looked at the clock and saw the time was 8:02. Everybody was present except for Billy, and Jack felt the acid in his stomach churning when he thought about how irresponsible his only son was. He took a swallow of his ginger-ale to cool his throat before reaching over and pressing the intercom button.

"Ashley, call Tommy Sides or Lee Hayworth and tell them I said to find Billy and bring him to the conference room and I don't care if they have to drag him here!" Jack said loudly.

The four men who were present at the table were the only four men that Jack trusted on earth. Cecil Wood was an attorney that specialized in real estate. He was also Jack's business manager and was in charge of communications and security. He had five men who worked under him: Danny Comer, who was a communications expert; Brett Tranthum, who was an electronics genius; and three men for security, Johnny Steele, Tommy Sides, and Lee Hayworth.

Steve Helms was sitting beside Cecil Wood. He was in charge of the farm and garage. He had seven men under his direction: C. J. Tysinger, a master mechanic who kept everything on the farm running; Walt Setzer, who was a machinist and welder; Brooks Walker, Steve Weavil, and Charles Moses, who were primarily farmers; and two Mexicans who did all the landscaping and lawn maintenance, Horatio Hernandez and Antonio Penta.

Directly across the table from Jack sat the most intelligent man in the room, Donald Crafton. Jack would be lost without Donald and everybody knew it. Donald was in charge of running the Hideaway Hilton, the airplanes, the landing strip, and the kitchen: He also had seven assistants" the two chefs, Michael Bloom and Steven Sanders; a head waiter, Anthony Tussey; two maids, Tracey Skeen and Jennifer Lopp; and two pilots, Jerry Simmons and Coy Beard. The only other employee that Jack had was Ashley Yates, his housekeeper and bartender. She answered only to Jack.

Donald had the ability to look through a person and know exactly what they were thinking and Jack never hired anybody that Donald didn't interview first. It was the main reason that Jack's business was so successful and ran so smoothly.

"Well, gentlemen, we got some problems that need to be dealt with, and I didn't want to wait till Monday to do it, so I called for a special meeting this morning. Before I get started though, do any of you have anything to discuss. What about you, Cecil?" Jack asked.

"The only thing I have to discuss is the 128 acres of land we repossessed in Wilkes County is finally free and clear. I have the deed to it on my desk," Cecil said.

"Okay, that's good news. I don't want to sell that property until I know exactly what the DOT. has planned for the new I-73 corridor that's coming through there. See if you can find out where they're planning on crossing Highway 421. We might be able to sit on that property for a couple years and then make a killing on it when we sell it," Jack said. "What about you, Steve?"

"The forestry service has agreed to supply us with white pine seedlings if we plant them on Whistling Mountain, the only thing is we can't cut them for eighteen years if they supply them."

"Those bastards aren't going to tell me when I can cut a tree on my own damn property. Tell them 'Hell, no.' I'll grow my own seedlings," Jack snapped.

"I'll tell them. That's all I got to discuss," Steve said.

"What about you, Donald?" Jack asked.

"I don't have anything at all. We still have five guests at the hotel and as far as I know they plan on staying awhile," Donald reported.

"How about the last guy, the Arab or whatever he is?" Jack asked.

"He's Egyptian, he says. His name is Maschiek Abdullah Ignacio, and he's doing fine. He orders food sometimes that we don't have on hand, like eel and goat meat. He has also ordered wine that I can't find either, but we're looking for a supplier in the United States. But we have had no problems with him whatsoever, at least not yet," Donald said.

Jack had never had a foreigner stay at the Hideaway Hilton and was a little reluctant to agree to it, but this guy came through the same channels as all their guests and agreed to pay $6,000 a week instead of the usual $3,000, so Jack agreed to it. He was a little strange though because he stayed in his room practically all the time and he carried around a suitcase that was empty.

The sequence of events that led up to the building of the Hideaway Hilton still amazed Jack. He had built his house at the foot of a small mountain that was mined years ago by the Cisco Mining Company but was abandoned years before Jack bought the property. Jack built his house against the mountain for reasons of privacy and security. When you repossess land from people they tend to get angry. If someone tried to kill Jack, and there were several who wanted to, the only way they could get to him was from River Road. The south fork of the river crossed in front of the house, and the north fork crossed on the other side of the mountain behind the house, so to get to Jack you had to come up River Road and cross the bridge that led up to Jack's wrought iron gates, and then explain who you were and why you were there before they would open the gates. The front gate was monitored by a video camera and intercom and nobody entered unless Jack approved it.

The abandoned mine was worthless until it was renovated and turned into a five star hotel about five years ago. It wasn't something that was planned, it was just circumstance that created it. Billy and Johnny went to Atlantic City to party and gamble and when they failed to return, Jack flew to Atlantic City to find them. What he found were two twenty-year-old boys with gambling debts of over $200,000.

What made it worse was that they had borrowed about half the money from loan sharks. Jack told the loan sharks that he would have the money wired to him the next day and would pay them their money plus interest if they would leave the boys alone. They agreed to it of course and Jack put Billy and Johnny on a plane for home. The next day when Jack and the man escorting him arrived with the money, Jack overheard one of the men talking about needing a place to lay low for a couple months until he could figure out what to do.

Jack offered the men a deal. He would hide the man from the law for a couple months in exchange for the gambling debt. As the old saying goes, the rest is history. Jack and the mystery fugitive flew out that night in a private plane and landed at a private landing strip in Wilkes County where one of Jack's men picked them up. Since that night Jack had been hiding from three to seven fugitives at a time for the mob. The old mine was turned into a five-star motel and the guests paid $3,000 a week plus their tab. It was the easiest money

Jack had ever made. Donald Crafton masterminded the whole operation. After the construction of the underground hotel was complete, he had a huge hangar built over the entrance of the hotel and a landing strip built across the perfectly flat river bottoms beside the river. Because most of their flying was done at night, and the fog off the river was sometimes real heavy, the landing strip was brightly lighted and even had a control tower.

When they were notified by Jimmy Milano about a new guest, they would arrange to pick up the guest at any number of private airports scattered across the East Coast. This was always done at night and the numbers on the plane were always covered up prior to the guest's arrival so the plane couldn't be traced back to Jack. Then the guest was frisked and his luggage searched. No guns, cell phones, cameras, or drugs were allowed on the flight.

The guest was then placed on the plane and blindfolded for the flight to the Hideaway Hilton. After they landed, the plane would taxi into the hangar and pull up to the entrance of the hotel while the hangar doors were being closed behind it. Only then could the person remove his or her blindfold. Once they entered the hotel they were greeted by Donald Crafton and instructed as to what they could do and what they couldn't do. Whatever they wanted was available, such as alcohol, drugs, or even women, but the cost was extra and had to be approved by whoever was paying for the stay. All the money was paid to an overseas account and had to be paid weekly. Any problems with a guest were handled by Johnny Steele and he was always standing beside Donald when a guest arrived. When a guest got ready to leave they were placed on the plane and blindfolded before the hangar doors were opened, and they were flown out at night just like they arrived.

DeMac and Travis fixed French toast and sausage while Justin looked on and offered advice. After breakfast they relaxed at the kitchen table and talked and laughed as each one told funny stories about each other until they heard a growl coming from the front of the house and went to investigate it. Standing at the glass storm door were both dogs and they were both staring down the front yard and growling.

"I'll bet those pups are out looking for their mom," Justin said.

As the men slowly approached the front door and looked down the hill they saw two of the small groundhogs trapped in the cage and the third one standing beside it.

"Well, we got two of them," DeMac said.

"What do we do now?" asked Travis. "Do we take the two trapped groundhogs out of the cage and reset it, or what?"

"We could do that or maybe one of us could slip up behind the one that's loose and grab him with a fishing net," Justin said.

"Good idea," DeMac said. "I'll do it."

"Okay, we need to be careful and not let the dogs out when we leave, so, Travis, you watch the dogs while we slip out the back. I'll get my landing net out of the shop for you, DeMac," Justin said.

"If he goes back down in the den before I get to him just leave the dogs penned up for a couple hours and I'll wait on him to come back up," DeMac said.

Justin and DeMac slipped out the back door, and Justin returned in a few minutes to watch the action with Travis and the dogs.

DeMac crawled with a slow continuous motion like a snake. One skill that every Navy Seal was well trained in was crawling. There had been times when DeMac's Seal team crawled all day and into the night without ever standing up. This crawling was easy because it was a gradual downhill approach and the ground was soft and quiet. Justin had given DeMac the landing net that he used for fishing and the camouflage that he used for turkey hunting. It was a brown and gray pattern and included a head net and gloves. Justin had sewn strips of burlap all over the suit to help break up his outline when hunting and DeMac knew that he had learned those skills in the jungles of Vietnam.

DeMac paused before he got in sight of Justin and Travis and grabbed his cell phone from its pouch. "Eagle, this is Red Fox. It's me crawling down the side of the mountain in case you're wondering. We're trying to catch a baby groundhog so don't jump me or shoot me. Smitty, put the safety back on that fifty of yours. Everything is going fine. I'll check back in later today. Out."

Directly across the river from Justin's house, at the top of the mountain, 743 yards away under a huge rotting log, Specialist David "Smitty" Smith reached up and put the safety back on his McMillan M88 .50-caliber sniper rifle.

Justin and Travis watched as DeMac finally appeared, crawling down the mountain in the brush beside Justin's yard. When he got within one hundred feet of the groundhog he went from crawling like a snake to crawling like a worm.

It was impossible to detect any movement but over a period of fifteen minutes the camouflaged mound had mysteriously drawn within four feet of the confused groundhog pup, who continued to stand there waiting for his litter mates to join him and return to their den.

DeMac struck like a cobra and trapped the baby groundhog under the landing net. It happened so fast that Justin and Travis both jumped and Shogun and Scooter started barking. Justin and Travis slipped out the back door so the dogs wouldn't get out and hurried down the hill to help DeMac. DeMac pulled off the hood he was wearing and he was smiling from ear to ear. It was obvious that he had enjoyed this game and was tickled that he was successful. Justin stood the cage on its end and opened the door while Travis took the net and dumped the frightened groundhog in with its litter mates.

"Good job," Justin said. "That was awesome."

"You're the man!" Travis said.

"Eagle, this is Crow's Nest. We have three Tangos captured and ready to transport, over!" Smitty's voice came over the Seal team communications network. Eight Seals were watching the capture on video in an abandoned tobacco barn seven miles away, and all eight were standing and cheering their leader. There was even a small group of people at CIA headquarters in Washington, DC, clapping and cheering.

"Okay, if that's all the business you people have to discuss, I'll tell you why I wanted to meet this morning. We got a real problem with this jack-ass that inherited Roy Hepler's place. I offered him one and a half million dollars for his property yesterday and he practically laughed at the offer. He said the only way he would sell the property would be if the people that murdered his friend Roy were caught and convicted, so he knows that Roy's accident was no accident. Even though he can't prove anything the last thing we need is someone drawing attention to Roy's death, so I think something has got to a done. There's something about this guy that makes me real nervous and I don't know exactly what it is. All of you know how much I want that property so if we can make this guy go away we could kill two birds with one stone."

"You mean arrange for him to have an accident like his friend Roy?" Steve Helms asked.

"No. I don't want another fatal accident at the same place, it looks to suspicious. We need to figure out another way to accomplish it if we can," Jack said.

"What about a car wreck? We can arrange that pretty easy," Cecil Wood said.

"Well, I guess that's a possibility if we could set it up just right. We tried that with Roy and it didn't work out the way we wanted it to though," Jack said.

"What if our neighbor was arrested for something and died one night trying to escape from jail under the watchful eye of our trusted law enforcement officers," Donald Crafton said. "The tragic death would be documented and there wouldn't be any reason to suspect anyone but him."

There was a long pause as everyone considered this suggestion. Finally the silence was broken by Jack. "I like it. It not only would get rid of him, but it would tarnish his character. People would wonder what kind of crazy man he was and be glad he was gone, and there's no way it could come back on us either."

"How are we going to get him arrested?" asked Steve Helms.

"I don't know, but it needs to be a serious offense, something that would make him look real bad in the eyes of the community and something that would lock him up for at least forty-eight hours before his son could bail him out," Jack said.

"What about having him charged with rape? We could get one of the girls from Atlanta to accuse him of raping her and that would get him locked up with a huge bail amount," Steve Helms suggested.

"That's not a good idea for a couple reasons. One, they would call in special rape investigators as soon as she reported it, and two, if those investigators got her tripped up on her story she could start naming all of us. It's best not to bring anybody from outside our little group in on something like this. It's too dangerous," Cecil said.

"I agree with Cecil on that," Jack said.

The door opened to the conference room and in walked Billy, or rather in stumbled Billy. Tommy Sides stepped in the door and looked at Jack briefly to see if there was anything else Jack wanted him to do.

"Thank you, Tommy," Jack said.

Tommy just nodded at Jack and shut the door as he left.

"Well, well, I'm glad you could find time in your busy schedule to make the meeting this morning, son," Jack said sarcastically.

"Why the hell are we having a damn meeting on Saturday morning and why the hell do I have to be here?" Billy grumbled.

Everyone at the table looked at Jack and saw his face start turning red and his hands start balling up into fists. Jack could feel the acid start rising up into his throat again.

"Well, I'll tell you why, son. Number one, all the money you piss away on staying drunk and partying has to come from somewhere, so these gentlemen and I have meetings so we can run a business and not let you or your drug addict cousin run us all into bankruptcy.

"Number two, I run this business and if I want to have a meeting at three o'clock in the morning, then by God we'll have a meeting at three o'clock in the damn morning. Number three, when I was fourteen, I got up before daylight and went to work and worked sixteen hours a day because my daddy was like you and didn't give a shit if his family starved to death as long as he had plenty of moonshine to drink. And number four, I wanted to see how you were doing after your little altercation at the Hess station yesterday," Jack said in a cracking voice.

Billy was wearing a hooded sweatshirt and sunglasses and raised his head to glare at his father when he mentioned the Hess station. "I'm just fine. I just slipped and fell down. I don't know why everybody is making a big deal about it," Billy snarled.

"Pull your hood down and take off your sunglasses," Jack ordered.

"Come on, Daddy, I'm fine," Billy pleaded.

"Pull your hood down and take off your sunglasses or I'll come over there and do it myself," Jack said in a strained voice.

Billy did as instructed and pulled down his hood and tore off his sunglasses as he stared at his daddy. His right eye was black and his jaw was bruised and swollen.

"Damn, you fell down hard, didn't you, son?" Jack said. "What did you fall on, a sailor's left foot?" Jack said loudly. Jack reached over and picked up a remote control off a shelf beside him and pressed a button on it. A large screen television came to life on the opposite end of the conference room and there for everyone to see was the video from the Hess station. Jack let it play all the way through before he pressed the button to cut it off.

"You fell down, all right," Jack said. "Of course, I'll give you this, you were probably drunk. As a matter of fact, the odds that you weren't drunk are probably about a thousand to one."

"I'm going to hunt that son of a bitch down and beat him to death!" Billy snarled.

"Oh, you don't have to hunt very hard. You probably could stop at the first house you come to and find him," Jack said.

"What are you talking about?" Billy asked.

"That sailor that kicked your ass yesterday is Justin Hayes's son, Travis. He's staying with his dad for the next several days along with his Navy buddy so they can do some fishing. So if you drive down River Road and stop at the first house you come to, I'm sure you could find him," Jack informed his son.

"You mean Bill didn't arrest that son of a bitch?" Billy asked his dad.

"He couldn't arrest him! There were several witnesses that were willing to testify about what happened and there was this video that backed their stories up," Jack said.

"Well, that's all right. Dammit, if he's not locked up that means he's out running around. We'll just see how bad this sailor really is the next time we meet!" Billy boasted.

"There's not going to be another meeting between you and that sailor. That's another reason I wanted you at this meeting. I'm trying to make arrangements to buy the Hayes's property and I want you to stay clear of him until I do. You could screw up everything if you start a feud with them now. So leave him alone. When I get through with Justin Hayes, you can hunt him down and do whatever you want, but not until I say so. Understand?" Jack said sternly.

"Yeah," Billy said as he turned toward the door to leave.

"Wait a minute, there's one more thing," Jack announced. "You have thirty days to stop drinking or you're going back to rehab, and this time you're going for longer than two months. That goes for your cousin too."

Billy looked at his father with an evil face. "I'm not going back to rehab," Billy snarled. "I can promise you that."

"Well, let me rephrase that statement then," Jack said. "In thirty days, you and your cousin Johnny are going to be tested, and if either one of you test positive for alcohol or drugs, you will be living somewhere besides here. You can move out and get a job or you can go to rehab, whichever you choose, but by God you won't be living here. Do you understand that?" Jack almost shouted as he came to his feet.

"Whatever!" Billy snapped as he walked out and slammed the door.

"I'm sorry about that, men," Jack said as he sat back down and rubbed his face with his hands. "Let's take a forty-five minute break and get Steven to fix us some breakfast before we continue. Maybe we can come up with some ideas then."

Justin and DeMac were bouncing up and down in Justin's truck as they drove up an old abandoned sawmill road through the woods. They had the live trap with the three orphaned groundhog pups in the bed of the truck as they clawed their way through the ruts and the mud holes. This was the third location that they had traveled to looking for a safe place to leave them. Justin wasn't satisfied with the first two locations so they continued their search. The only problem was now they were headed toward the old tobacco barn where DeMac's Seal team had set up their base of operations. DeMac knew they would be tracking them by the GPS unit on his cell phone, so he wasn't worried.

"There's a small meadow back here that is maybe four or five acres that they don't farm anymore. They used to grow burley tobacco in it but it hasn't been farmed in two or three years. It might be the perfect place for Moe, Larry, and Curly,"

Justin had named the little groundhogs after the three stooges on television. They finally bounced and spun their way up a small grade and came out of the woods into the meadow. The tobacco barn was to their right on the far end of the field and DeMac was somewhat relieved when Justin turned left and headed away from it. There was a huge pile of rocks at the edge of the field that had been put there when they cleared the field years ago. Justin pulled up to the rocks and cut the engine off as he got out of the truck.

As Justin looked around the rock pile, DeMac cut his eyes toward the tobacco barn. There was nothing in sight to draw attention to it, but DeMac knew that inside it there was over a million dollars' worth of equipment and at least eight Navy Seals looking through the cracks at him.

"Right here is perfect," Justin said. "Look at this, DeMac."

DeMac stepped over beside Justin and looked at the ground beside the rocks where he was pointing his finger.

"Here's an old groundhog hole that's been abandoned. There are no trails leading away from it and there's a spider web across the entrance so I know it's not being used. They're to far away from the road to be bothered by hunters and there should be plenty of grass for them to eat. They won't have to dig another hole, all they have to do is clean this old hole out a little bit. If they can't make it here, they can't make it anywhere," Justin said.

DeMac retrieved the trap from the back of the truck and set it down at Justin's feet. Justin set the trap beside the old groundhog hole and started piling brush over it until it was completely covered.

"We'll leave the trap here for a couple weeks until they get settled in their new home. I'll just wire the door open on it so it won't snap shut on them and come back later to get it," Justin said.

Justin stepped over to the tool box on the back of his truck and got a piece of fourteen gauge wire and a bag with lettuce and apples in it. He knelt down beside the trap and opened the door, and then wrapped the wire around the door so it couldn't close. Then he threw the lettuce and apples down the old groundhog hole before he backed up to look at his work.

"Well, I guess that's all we can do for now," Justin said and he and DeMac got in the truck and starting driving back across the field toward the sawmill road. Just before they reached the edge of the woods, Justin looked in the direction of the tobacco barn and stopped the truck. "Look at that."

"Look at what?" DeMac asked.

"Something doesn't look right down there. Let's go take a look," Justin said.

Justin turned and drove across the meadow toward the old tobacco barn.

"I don't see anything strange down there," DeMac said, straining his eyes.

"Look at the field down there," Justin said. "The grass and weeds are laying flat on the ground, it looks like." Justin drove down the field and stopped about forty yards from the tobacco barn before he got out. He stood there looking at the ground as DeMac got out and joined him.

"Well, you're right. Something flattened out these weeds," DeMac said and he cut his eyes toward the barn again. Eight men were in the barn but none of them were moving. They had cut off all the equipment and turned off the light as soon as Justin started heading their way. They could only hope that Justin wouldn't want to look inside.

"I don't know what could have done this, do you?" DeMac asked.

"I sure do," Justin said. "It's the prop wash from a helicopter. It's perfectly round and right in the middle you can see where the skids were sitting."

"You're right. It is from a helicopter, but why would they be landing here?" DeMac asked, looking toward the barn.

"I don't know unless they were looking at that barn for some reason. It probably was somebody from the Historical Society. They love these old tobacco barns because they can disassemble them so easily and move them wherever they want them, and then reassemble them just like they were originally. Whoever owns this barn might be negotiating a price with them. That would be my guess anyway. Let's go to the store and get a moon pie and a Pepsi. That French toast is already gone," Justin said as he got back in his truck. DeMac got in the truck and back up the field they drove as eight Seals finally took a deep breath.

Jack came back in the conference room and picked up one of the pastries off the platter in the center of the table before taking his seat. He was too angry to eat breakfast like the other men did, but he felt better now that he had calmed down. Cecil Wood, Donald Crafton, Steve Helms, and Johnny Steele all filed in and took their seat.

"Well, let's just start back where we left off. Does anybody have any idea how we can get Justin Hayes arrested on a serious offense without exposing ourselves in any way?" Jack asked as he took a bite of a cinnamon roll. No one said a word for several moments so Jack continued, "Okay then, lets just think about it for now and we'll discuss it at our usual Monday meeting. In the meantime I want a full background check done on Justin Hayes. I want to know everything there is to know about him and I want that information as soon as possible. Cecil, can you get that done before our Monday meeting?"

"No problem at all," Cecil said.

"Okay, good. Steve, I want you to take one of your men to town and rent a roll-back tow truck. I want somebody to drive over to the big junkyard in Jefferson and buy the tractor that rolled over on Roy Hepler," Jack said.

"Why don't we just use our own roll-back?" Steve asked.

"Because it's got our name on the side of it and our license tags on the back of it. I don't want anyone to know that we're the ones that bought it. Don't drive any of our vehicles to town when you rent it and be sure to pay cash for it when you do. Take a fake driver's license with you because they'll want a photocopy of it before they will rent it to you. Take enough tarps along to cover it up once you get it loaded, and don't bring it back here until after dark. Once you get back here with it I want you to drain all the fluids from it and drop it down the number 7 mineshaft. Don't drop it until you check with Donald so he can distract our guests while you're dropping it."

"All right, I'll get it first thing Tuesday morning," Steve said.

"I want it done today!" Jack said.

"Oh, well, uh, okay." Steve stuttered.

"That tractor doesn't even have a carburetor on it. The tractor wasn't even in running condition when you rolled it down the mountain and Justin Hayes knows it, so it needs to disappear before somebody starts asking questions. He has the matching carburetor in his shop and when the time is right I want it thrown down the mine shaft also. This is damage control, understand!" Jack said sternly.

"Yes, sir," Steve said, blushing.

"That's all I've got. Does anybody have anything else?" Jack asked.

There was a moment of silence as everybody in the room stared at their coffee cups. "Okay then, let's get out of here." Jack said.

Good and Bad Neighbors

"Are you going or not?" Justin shouted from the carport.

"Yeah, I'm coming. Let me find my camera bag," Travis shouted back.

Justin decided he could probably go fishing with DeMac if he wrapped his sore ankle in an ace bandage and was real careful how he stepped. After he and DeMac took the baby groundhogs to their new home they had driven to the New River General Store at the corner of Highway 117 and River Road to get a snack and a soft drink. Sitting on the porch of the store watching the river roll by was just to much temptation for Justin, so he and DeMac had driven back home and started packing their gear for an evening of fly fishing. Travis finally decided to go along with them, but carry a camera instead of a fly rod. He didn't care much for fishing and Justin figured it was probably a gene defect from his mother's side of the family.

"We're leaving!" Justin shouted.

Travis came running through the house and into the carport wearing a photographer's vest and carrying his camera bag. "I'm coming, I'm coming!" He said as he hopped up in the bed of his dad's pickup truck. Justin drove about five miles up River Road before he came to the stretch of river he wanted to fish.

"This stretch of river is real easy to walk in," Justin said to DeMac as he slowed the truck down. Justin locked his truck in four-wheel drive and eased across the ditch beside River Road and then drove down beside the river before parking the truck. They bailed out and started the fifteen-minute drill a fly fisherman goes through to get ready to fish. Justin had bought DeMac some fishing gear as soon as he learned that he was coming home with Travis, so DeMac and Justin were well equipped. They sat on the tailgate of the truck pulling and tugging their waders on as Travis loaded film into his camera and snapped a telephoto lens on it. Justin and DeMac finally got their waders and their fishing vests on and assembled their fly rods. Justin took his Smith and Wesson Model 642 Airweight revolver and slid it in the side pocket of his fishing vest and DeMac took his Kimber Ultracarry .45 automatic and did likewise.

"Well, I guess we're ready, DeMac. I've done a lot of fly fishing in lakes and ponds, but very little in a river, so you tell me whatever you think I need to know," Justin said.

"Okay. First let's see what's on the menu today," DeMac said. DeMac reached in his vest and pulled out a fine mesh nylon net similar to the ones they use in pet stores to catch fish, except this one was a little larger. DeMac had brought it with him from Norfolk because he doubted that Justin had one. He waded out into the center of the river and plunged the net down into the rushing water and held it there, letting the river flow through it. Justin didn't know what DeMac was doing but watched intently.

"The biggest difference in fishing a river as opposed to fishing in a lake or pond is that a river is like a giant conveyor belt that is loaded with food. A fish in a river doesn't have to travel around looking for food because the food is flowing by them constantly, so if we figure out what's flowing down the river today we can tie on a fly that resembles it and probably catch fish," DeMac said as he raised the net up out of the water. "Look here, Justin. There's an assortment of nymphs in the net. There are several dragonfly nymphs and one Mayfly nymph, and a couple I don't even recognize. Let's tie on a fly that looks like a dragonfly nymph since there are more of those in the water today."

Justin unsnapped the little water proof tackle box on his vest and opened it up. DeMac pointed to one of the fly's and said, "Use that one. It looks like a dragonfly nymph but is a little larger than normal. If you're going after big fish as opposed to just trying to catch fish, use a larger lure. If there are three nymphs floating by a large trout, he will normally take the largest one."

They heard a click and then a buzz and looked around as Travis took a picture of the two men standing in the river.

"You can't go anywhere these days without the paparazzi bothering you," DeMac said.

"I know what you mean, DeMac. I had to live with the paparazzi before he joined the Navy," Justin said with a grin.

DeMac continued his instructions. "You always want to walk upstream as you fish if you can because the fish are always facing the current and they won't see you coming. If you walk downstream you're going to spook some of them because they will see you. Let's ease our way upstream and see what we can do."

Justin and DeMac slowly eased their way up the river wading against the current until they had traveled about sixty feet. DeMac stopped and looked closely at the water in front of them. "Okay, Justin, if you were the dominant trout in this section of river where would you be hiding?"

"I never thought about a fish being dominant. You mean the biggest fish?" Justin asked.

"Yeah, the biggest fish is going to be the dominant fish. If the biggest trout in this stretch of water weighs seven pounds, and there's a five-pound trout in a spot that he wants, then he'll run him off. If you can figure out where the best spot is for a trout to hide and feed then you are more than likely going to catch the biggest trout in this particular area. The next biggest trout, say maybe a five pounder, will get the next best spot and so on and so on. If someone catches the dominant trout or it dies, the number two trout will move into its spot. That's why you can repeatedly catch big fish in some spots on the river, because the next biggest fish will move in as soon as you catch the dominant fish."

"I understand," Justin said as he thought about what DeMac just said. "It's like everything in nature. The dominant whitetail buck runs off the smaller bucks so he can eat his fill or breed the does. The biggest tom turkey runs off the jakes so he can keep the hens to himself. It makes perfect sense to me now that I think about it."

"I imagine that you have been spooking some of the bigger fish simply because you didn't know where to cast. If you want to catch big trout you need to learn how to spot the best location and cast into it, and forget about the other places that probably have fish but not the biggest fish."

"What about this section of river. Where should I cast?" Justin asked.

"I like the looks of that spot over there under those overhanging tree limbs," DeMac said, pointing his finger. "The river flows through there nice and strong and the overhanging branches provide shadows for a trout to hide in. There's also a small stream flowing into the river right above it and that's always a good place to fish since the stream is carrying food with it as it empties into the river. If I was the biggest trout in this section of the river I would be lying right under that log that's washed up against that big rock. Cast upstream about thirty feet above that log and let the current carry your lure right by it."

Justin cast the floating Super Dragon upstream and let it drift by the log just as DeMac had instructed. When nothing happened DeMac told him to try again. After the fourth cast Justin was ready to move on but DeMac said to try again. Justin cast upstream again and watched the tiny fly as it drifted toward the same place as before.

Justin saw what looked like a shadow rise up slowly as his fly neared the log, and just when he realized it was a fish his fly disappeared from the surface of the river. Justin jerked as hard as he dared to set the hook and the battle was on. DeMac was hollering instructions to Justin as he battled the fish.

"Keep your rod up! Don't let him go behind the log! Walk backward!"

Justin's heart raced as he fought the big rainbow trout. He felt somewhat helpless because he couldn't muscle the fish and make him go where he wanted him to go, so he just held on and tried to follow DeMac's instructions. After what seemed like an eternity Justin gained a little of his fishing line back and thought he felt the fish starting to tire. As he fought the ·fish to within twenty feet of him his confidence began to grow and he thought the battle was over, but as soon as DeMac stepped over to net him the fish exploded back into the rushing water. The next three minutes were a repeat of the last three minutes with Justin pulling and grunting, backing up and stepping forward, DeMac hollering instructions, and the trout fighting for his life. The beautiful and majestic eight-pound rainbow trout was finally exhausted and so was Justin as he guided him into DeMac's landing net. Justin was as tired and as happy as he had ever been. DeMac twisted the landing net so the trout couldn't escape and held him under the water so he could breathe while Justin caught his breath and got his composure back.

"Wow! That's what I'm talking about! Let me see him," Justin said.

Justin stepped over to look at his catch when he and DeMac heard something and looked up to see Travis running up the riverbank toward them.

"I heard you guys hollering all the way around the next bend," Travis said, huffing. "What you got?"

Justin held up the beautiful fish. Just then the sun reflected off the side of the trout and gave the three men a magnificent light show that would rival a Fourth of July fireworks celebration.

"How about taking a couple pictures of him before I turn him loose," Justin said as he reached in his vest and pulled out a set of fish scales. "I'm finally going to get to use this set of scales I've been carrying around. I'm a little disappointed in my guide though. It took five casts before I caught the biggest trout that I've ever caught on a fly rod," Justin said as he slapped DeMac on the back.

Travis went to work with his camera, taking pictures from several angles of the two smiling fisherman and the beautiful trout. He even waded out into the river to get a few shots wearing blue jeans and tennis shoes until he was satisfied that he had every conceivable shot. Justin held the trout under the water until it was fully revived and then watched it as it darted away.

"What did it weigh?" DeMac asked. "It looked like maybe eight or eight and a half pounds."

"Seven pounds and fourteen ounces," Justin answered. "Thank you, DeMac, for your expertise. You don't know how much I appreciate it."

"You're quite welcome," DeMac said.

"Now, I'm going to take a break and watch you fish for awhile," Justin said.

"Sounds good to me," DeMac said and he and Justin started easing their way up the river.

Steve Helms was sitting in his office pouting when Brett Tranthum knocked on his door. "Come in," Steve said.

Brett stepped in the office and tossed a fake driver's license on Steve's desk along with a picture of Steve that he had used when he made it.

"There you go. One fake driver's license just as you ordered," Brett said.

"Thank you, Brett. That looks good," Steve said as he examined the merchandise.

"No problem. You need anything else?" Brett asked.

"No, this should do it. I appreciate it," Steve said.

"When are we going to go fishing? The season came in yesterday!" Brett said.

"I was going to see if you wanted to go today until we had that meeting this morning. Now I've got something I just have to do today because it won't wait until Monday," Steve said sarcastically.

"I believe I'm going to give it a try. It's just to pretty outside not to."

"I don't blame you one bit. I would too if I could. Let me know tonight how you did," Steve said.

"Okay," Brett said as he turned and walked away.

"Good luck," Steve yelled. Steve had planned to spend Saturday evening fly fishing on the north fork of the New River until Jack had ordered him to go get Roy's tractor from the junkyard. Over the winter months Steve had purchased a new fly rod from G-Loomis and a new fly reel from Vom Hofe, and had been anxiously awaiting a chance to try them out. The rod and reel had cost almost $900, but it was worthless standing in the corner of his office. He was tempted to get one of his men to go get the tractor but was afraid if he did that something would go wrong. He could tell by Jack's voice in the meeting that Jack blamed him for the fact that the tractor didn't have a carburetor on it when they used it to simulate the farming accident. How was he supposed to know the tractor wasn't running?

It was dark when they winched it up on the roll-back and even darker when they lowered it over that cliff.

Steve picked up his phone and called his straw boss, Brooks Walker. "You ready to go?" Steve asked.

"Whenever you are, boss," Brooks said.

"Okay, pick me up in five minutes in front of the house," Steve said. "We're going to drive Horatio's pickup truck so the license tag won't be registered to this address. I already told him and gave him fifty dollars for letting us use it so the keys are supposed to be in the ignition. Don't forget the chains and the tarps."

"I got the chains and tarps right here in front of me ready to go. I'm on my way," Brooks said as he hung up the phone.

Steve unlocked his desk drawer and opened it up. He reached in a small cash box and pulled out a stack of hundred dollar bills and another stack of twenties and slid the money into his front pants pocket. He locked his desk drawer and started out of his office.

As Steve turned to lock his office door he happened to glance over and see his new fly rod leaning in the corner.

"Shit," he said out loud as he locked his office door.

Billy kicked the punching bag in his dojo with a front kick and then followed it with a side kick. That was the technique he should have used on that sailor instead of the spinning back kick. Every time Billy struck the bag he envisioned the day he could use these techniques on that sailor instead of the punching bag. Billy was accustomed to fighting just average guys that were untrained in self defense and had greatly underestimated the ability of the sailor, especially since he was in that ridiculous looking boxing stance. The next time we meet it will be much different, he thought to himself as he kicked the bag. Billy was furious with his dad for showing that video in front of everybody in that meeting. There was no reason for humiliating him like that in front of other people. Sometimes I'd like to kick daddy in his mouth, and then his pet gorilla, Johnny Steele. Billy ran through all his kicks one more time. Front kick, side kick, roundhouse kick, back kick, and spinning back kick. He was soaked with sweat and wanted a cold beer, so he took off his Gi and dried off with a towel before putting on his blue jeans and tee shirt. He pulled on his cowboy boots and walked out of the dojo and headed for the garage. There was a refrigerator in the garage for CJ and Walt to keep their lunches and soft drinks in, and Billy always kept a couple six-packs of beer stashed in it even though he could tell that Walt didn't like it.

The garage was over a hundred yards from the house and the dojo, and before Billy got halfway to it he heard an engine fire up that literally shook the ground. Billy couldn't tell from the sound which one of the muscle cars it was. It didn't really sound like any of them.

Jack's only hobby besides making money was buying and restoring muscle cars and he had bought and restored quite a few over the last ten years. Of course he didn't actually restore them himself, that's what Walt and CJ did when they weren't working on the farm equipment or company vehicles. Jack had a metal building erected behind the garage that was climate controlled to store his collection of muscle cars and it was almost full. Billy's favorite car was a 1970 Dodge Challenger two door hardtop with a 426-cubic inch Hemi with dual four-barrel carburetors and 425 horsepower. There was also a 1970 Z-28 Camaro with a 350-cubic inch engine and 245 horsepower, a 1970 Chevrolet Chevelle Super Sport with a 396-cubic inch engine and 325 horsepower, two Plymouth Road Runners, a 1971 and a 1972, both with 426 Hemi engines, a 1968 Plymouth GTX with a 440-cubic inch wedge-head V8 Magnum that had 375 horsepower, a 1968 Ford Mustang Fastback with a 390-cubic inch engine and 325 horsepower, two Pontiac GTOs, one with a 389-cubic inch engine and three two-barrel carburetors and the other with a 400-cubic inch engine, a 1965 Corvette Stingray with a 396-cubic inch Mark IV engine and 425 horsepower, and finally a 1969 Oldsmobile 442. The next addition to Jack's collection was not going to be a muscle car, it was going to be a monster truck. Walt and CJ had been working on it forever it seemed like but were getting close to completing it.

Jack's birthday was on July 22 and they always threw a huge party every year that lasted for three days to celebrate it. The usual call girls were flown in from Atlanta and there was all the food and drinks you could imagine being served all day and all night from Friday morning until Monday morning. On Saturday morning they would drive all the muscle cars through the tunnel to the airstrip and drag race them all evening on the runway. They would measure off a quarter of a mile and rig up starting lights and a finish line complete with electronic timers and a camera to judge the winners. It was a real blast and Billy always enjoyed the racing. At the end of the day they would have a feast and award a trophy to the driver that won the most races and of course that was always Jack. It was considered part of Jack's birthday present to award him the trophy.

Billy heard somebody run up behind him over the rumble of the engine in the garage and turned to see his cousin Johnny as he came along beside him.

"What's up, cuz?" Johnny shouted. "You going to check out 'Jumping Jack Flash.'"

"Is it ready?" Billy shouted.

"That guy from Texas that came up here to paint it left two days ago, so it should be ready to go."

"That's got to be what CJ's running 'cause it's louder than any of the muscle cars," Billy shouted to Johnny as they walked toward the garage. Just as they rounded the corner of the garage holding their hands over their ears the roaring engine stopped.

Billy and Johnny stopped in their tracks and stared with their mouths open at the most massive and the most beautiful truck they had ever seen. It had been an ongoing project for over a year now and the finished product stood before Billy and Johnny and gave both of them chill bumps.

It was Steve Helms who originally had the idea to build a monster truck and pitched the idea to Jack a little over a year ago. He told Jack that it would be the perfect way to advertise his many businesses and would be a tax write-off because it would be considered advertising. They could list all of Jack's businesses on the sides of the truck and on the tailgate and drive it in parades and take it to car and truck shows and fall festivals or even take it to the state fair in Raleigh. Since Jack loved muscle cars and anything that had a big engine in it, it wasn't too hard to get him to agree to it, so Steve was put in charge of the planning and building of "Jumping Jack Flash." CJ Tysinger, the mechanic, and Walt Setzer, the machinist and welder, were as excited about the project as Steve Helms and worked on it every spare minute they had and sometimes after quitting time.

CJ was standing beside the massive truck holding the ten foot stepladder that Walt was climbing down after getting out of the truck. Billy and Johnny walked around the truck in absolute awe as CJ and Walt watched them and grinned. They were very proud of their creation, as well they should be after spending thousands of hours working on it.

"Damn, CJ, how much does this thing weigh?" Johnny asked.

"Fourteen thousand pounds," CJ answered without hesitation. "It's twelve feet high and a little over twelve feet wide."

"It's awesome," Billy said. "How much horsepower?"

"Somewhere around nine hundred horsepower. It' got a 454-cubic inch engine with a 671 blower and dual Holley carburetors bolted to a turbo 400 transmission. The truck body is a 1972 Chevy Cheyenne Super 20 body with Rockwell five-ton military axles and four shock absorbers on each wheel. There's seven leaf springs under each axle that were custom built for us by the St. Louis Spring Company. It's got a sixty-ton hydraulic winch on the front bumper and two spun-aluminum ten gallon fuel tanks. The tires are 66 inch

Terra tires and they weigh 957 pounds apiece," CJ said, sounding like a tour guide.

"It didn't look too impressive until that boy from Texas got through painting it. He charged almost $10,000 to paint it, but you can see why he gets that kind of money when you look at it," Walt chimed in.

The sides of the monster truck were a mural of a series of mountains with Christmas trees growing on them and a river winding through it. A monster truck was airborne as it jumped from one mountain to another and above it in bold letters it said, "Jumping Jack Flash." The various names of Jack's businesses were listed on the rocker panels and behind the rear wheels and on the tailgate: Billings Saving and Loan; Billings Real Estate; Billings Christmas Tree Farms; Billings Farm Equipment, along with their telephone numbers and websites.

"Walt and me have been waiting over a year for this day to arrive, haven't we Walt?" CJ said as he glanced toward Walt.

"You damn right we have," Walt replied.

"Has Steve seen it since it's been painted?" Johnny asked.

"Yeah, he's seen it and he's tickled pink. He gave me and Walt two front row tickets to the monster truck show in Winston-Salem tonight at the Lawrence Joel Coliseum and reservations at the Hilton Hotel for tonight and Sunday so we don't have to come back until Monday morning. As soon as we take some pictures of it, me and Walt are getting out of here," CJ said with a grin.

Walt and CJ walked around their new toy taking picture after picture until they had each used up a whole roll of film. Billy and Johnny held their ears as CJ climbed up the ladder to get back in the truck. The ground shook as CJ fired up the 900-horsepower engine and slowly backed the giant truck back into the garage stall where they normally worked on farm machinery like hay balers, combines, front loaders, and log skidders.

Everything in the garage was rattling until CJ finally shut the engine down.

"Check this out," CJ said, smiling as he reached up on the dash and flipped a toggle switch. The garage was instantly filled with the sound of Mick Jagger and the Rolling Stones singing their famous song "Jumping Jack Flash." CJ flipped the toggle switch back off and the music stopped. "It's got a sound system built in so we can play the theme song during parades and when it's on display," CJ said as he climbed out and started down the ladder that Walt was holding for him.

"I'll shut up the garage for you, CJ. You and Walt go on and get out of here," Billy said as CJ stepped off the ladder onto the concrete floor.

"Well, okay, Billy, but be sure and lock it up before you leave," CJ said.

"You guys have a good time," Johnny said.

Billy walked across the garage to the refrigerator and got out two beers for him and Johnny as Walt and CJ walked across the gravel lot toward their cars. As soon as Walt and CJ drove out of sight Johnny reached in his sock and pulled out a ladies make-up compact. He opened it up and pulled out a perfectly rolled joint and lit it. Billy handed him one of the beers and they both sat down on a pair of bucket seats that had come out of a car so long ago that nobody could remember which one it was.

"Dad says that if you and me aren't on the wagon in thirty days that we both have to go back to rehab," Billy told Johnny.

"You think he's serious?" Johnny asked.

"He said it in front of everybody in that meeting this morning," Billy answered.

"Oh shit. I can't go back to that hell hole, Billy," Johnny said.

"I'm not going back there, you can believe that," Billy said.

"What are we going to do?" Johnny asked.

"I don't know yet," Billy said. "You got another one of those joints."

Steve Helms watched as the forklift lowered Roy's Ford 601 Workmaster tractor onto the bed of the roll-back truck that Steve had rented in Independence, Virginia. Steve was too well known around Sparta to rent a truck there, so he had Brooks Walker to drive him to Independence, Virginia, to rent the roll-back. The only roll-back truck they had was a piece of junk that didn't have any power and had a busted muffler, so between the exhaust fumes and the constant roar of the engine he had acquired a splitting headache.

After he finally drove the fifty miles to the junkyard in Jefferson the grease covered man charged him $700 for the wrecked tractor. Steve knew the tractor wasn't worth half that amount but wasn't in a position to argue with him, so he paid the man and told him to load it.

"Can you help me chain it down and cover it up with these tarps?" Steve asked the man after he parked the forklift.

"I reckon, but I don't know why you want to cover it up. It's been sitting in the weather for two years," the junk man said. "What are you going to do with this tractor anyway? The fenders and hood are mashed, it doesn't have a carburetor or headlights on it, the radiator is busted, and the tires ain't no good."

"Uh, I need the transmission and the rear axles," Steve stammered. "I'm working on another one just like it back home."

The junkyard man looked at Steve's hands as he reached over to take the end of a chain from him and knew that he was lying about working on another tractor. Those manicured fingernails have never turned a wrench, he thought to himself. They got the tractor chained down and the tarps pulled over it and tied down and Steve was finally ready to go. Of course he was going to have to wait about five hours before he drove back to Jack's house because Jack said not to bring it back until after dark. Steve was hoping he could find a nice restaurant and eat a good meal before he left Jefferson. It would help kill some time and maybe help him get rid of his headache. He might try to find a fly shop or fishing store and do some browsing to help kill some time also.

Jack was making too big a deal over this tractor Steve thought. Hell, it had been almost two years since Roy was killed and this tractor had been sitting here ever since the sheriff's department had released it from their impound lot. But Jack wanted it done today, the first Saturday of trout season.

"I'd bet you thought you would never sell this tractor," Steve said to the greasy man.

"Well, that's what is so strange about the junk business. This tractor is a perfect example. It sat here for two years and nobody even looked at it, and then two days in a row somebody wanted to see it," he said.

"Somebody wanted to see it yesterday?" Steve asked.

"Yep. Said he was going to come back and buy it but it's to late now," the junk man said. "He even wrote the serial numbers down off the side of the motor."

A jolt of fear shot through Steve as he processed this new information. It was probably just a coincidence but what if somebody was taking another look into Roy's farm accident. It was probably that damn Justin Hayes nosing around, but what if he alerted the SBI or hired a private investigator to look into it.

"Was this guy about six feet one and maybe 230 pounds? Kind of muscular and in his fifties with sandy-colored hair with a little gray mixed in it," Steve asked.

"No, he was probably in his thirties and he was skinny with black hair," the junk man answered.

"Did he by any chance leave his name and number?" Steve asked. "I might be able to swap some tractor parts with him if I knew where to find him."

"Yeah, he left a couple business cards in the office. Stop on your way out if you want one," the greasy man said as he climbed back on the forklift.

Steve stopped beside the office on his way out of the junkyard and rolled his window down as the man stepped over beside the truck.

"You know, if you two guys start swapping parts with each other it kinda hurts my business if you think about it," the man said with a slight grin on his face.

Steve knew what the man was up to and reached in his pocket and pulled out a twenty dollar bill and handed it out the window. The man took the twenty dollar bill and handed Steve the business card as he slid the bill in his greasy coveralls.

"Thanks, mister. Come back to see us," He said as he turned and walked away.

Steve looked at the card. "Tommy's Tractors. Owner Tommy Jones. 1313 Academy St., Randleman, NC. Telephone 336-478-0101."

The card helped Steve to believe it was just a coincidence but it wouldn't hurt to check this guy out anyway. He jerked the truck in gear with a clunk and drove out the gate of the junkyard as he slid the card in his pocket.

As he pulled out onto the street the telephone lineman across the street snapped two more pictures of him. He had taken pictures of him driving in the junkyard, buying the tractor, loading the tractor, stopping at the office for the business card, and finally leaving the junkyard. He grabbed the lever on the bucket truck and started lowering himself to the ground. As soon as he got back into the cab of the truck he would plug his camera into his laptop computer and send the pictures to Washington, DC.

Billy was sitting behind the steering wheel of Jumping Jack Flash and Johnny was in the passenger seat. They were passing a joint back and forth and drinking their fourth beer apiece as they searched for the switch that CJ had flipped on to start the music. Finally Johnny flipped a toggle switch on the dash and the garage boomed with the music of the Rolling Stones' famous "Jumping Jack Flash."

Johnny and Billy bobbed their heads to the beat of the music and passed the joint back and forth giggling like two little girls. Johnny finally tossed the roach out the window and Billy flipped the switch to stop the music.

"Cuz, I have got to drive this big-ass truck, man," Billy said in a slurred voice. "I mean it. I want to feel what nine hundred horsepower feels like, you know."

Johnny giggled and said, "Well, fire this bitch up, man. Let's go!" Johnny started laughing the more he thought about it.

"CJ and Walt would shit if they found out about it," Billy said, and then he started giggling at Johnny who had tears coming down his face from laughing so hard.

"Well, CJ and Walt are on their way to Winston-Salem. Jack and Cecil flew out after the meeting headed for Chattanooga on business they said but everybody knows there going to go get laid. Steve had to go and pick up a tractor and won't be back until after dark and Donald left after the meeting and took Johnny Steele with him, so were the only ones around except for some of the hired help. Everybody's out partying except for me and you, so fire this mother-fucker up Cuz!" Johnny said.

Billy reached up and turned the key and it felt like the whole earth was shaking when the engine fired up. Billy revved the engine one time and something in the garage fell and shattered on the floor bringing on another round of laughter from the drunken cousins.

Billy let the clutch out and the truck leaped out of the garage. Billy headed across the gravel lot toward the cast iron gates that protected Jack from intruders.

"How are we going to open the gates, man?" Billy hollered.

"I think I got my key-chain remote," Johnny said as he fished around in his pocket. "Are we going down the road in it?"

"Hell yeah!" Billy shouted.

Johnny found his remote control and opened the gates just in time as Billy drove through the entrance and across the bridge onto River Road. Billy wound the truck up in first gear and then hit second gear and floored it and the monster truck did a wheel-stand much to the delight of its passengers.

Carol Crissman was driving down River Road looking in her rearview mirror checking her make-up one last time before she got to Justin's house. She had made a huge pot of chicken and dumplings to carry to church tomorrow for their after service meal. It was Easter Sunday and the congregation always gathered in the fellowship hall after the service to eat a covered dish meal before going home. Carol had dipped a portion of her dumplings in a Tupperware container for Justin to make sure that he got some of them.

Carol was anxious for Justin to see her in her new dress. She had ordered it three weeks ago over the phone from a catalog that she got in the mail and it had finally arrived yesterday. It was a black dress with a plunging neck line and there was a split up the side almost to her butt. She had spent the morning getting ready by going to the beauty shop and then buying a new pair of high heel shoes before she went home and squeezed into her new dress. She thought that if Justin Hayes didn't notice her now that he must be gay or something.

Carol had tried to call Justin before she left home but couldn't get an answer so she just decided to surprise him. He was probably out working in his shop or shooting one of his guns she thought since he wasn't answering the phone. She had driven by Justin's truck about four miles ago but didn't see it because she was putting on mascara and his truck was parked fifty feet from the road down next to the river. Just as Carol took her foot off the gas pedal to slow down to turn in Justin's driveway she noticed a big piece of farm machinery coming up River Road toward her. No, it couldn't be a piece of farm machinery because it was traveling way too fast for that so she put on her turn signal and stopped to let it pass. Just as Carol got stopped something else became apparent to her. There wasn't enough room on the road for this thing to pass by her and it was bearing down on her with no indication that it was going to stop. At the last possible moment Carol stomped her gas pedal and crossed River Road with her tires spinning, just barely avoiding being crushed to death under the huge truck. She went sideways into Justin's driveway and then slammed on her brakes causing the Toyota Camry to spin violently all the way around until it finally stopped. The Tupperware container on the passenger seat slammed into the dash and flew open, slinging chicken and dumplings all over the inside of the car. Carol looked in the rearview mirror and saw pieces of chicken and pieces of dumplings scattered through her hair and there was broth running down in between her breasts and pooling up where her dress was tight against her belly. She reached for a box of Kleenex in her glove box but was shaking so bad she couldn't open it, so Carol just laid her head on her steering wheel and started crying.

"Eagle, this is Crow's Nest. A black monster truck, I repeat, monster truck, traveling south at a high rate of speed, has just forced a white Toyota Camry off the road at the Rabbit Den. Monster truck did not stop and is occupied by two. There are no apparent injuries but car is not moving," Petty Officer Harold Hartley said.

"Eagle, this is the Wizard. Monster truck pulled out of the garage at my ten o'clock," Petty Officer Ozzie Curry reported from his sniper hide across the river from Jack's house.

"Roger that, Crow's Nest and Wizard. Continue to monitor situation," Eagle responded.

Special Agent Jimmy Hardy sat at the control board in the tobacco barn and pondered this new information. He was the on-site coordinator for the CIA in charge of this mission they had code named Red Rover. He didn't know why a monster truck was flying up River Road but he did know that Justin, Travis, and DeMac were up ahead.

"Duke, you and Sammy saddle up and double time it down to the river in case DeMac needs some back-up. They're only about one and a half clicks from here according to DeMac's GPS unit," he said. "Call sign Birddog."

"We're on the way," Petty Officer Jonathan Wayman said as he grabbed his pack and his Springfield MIA SOCOM II rifle. Petty Officer Sammy "Snake" Hedrick was right on his heels as they exited the tobacco barn and hit the woods in a run.

DeMac and Justin were having a grand time fly fishing in the beautiful New River. Occasionally DeMac's mind would drift back to Montana and he would imagine he saw his Mom and Dad and his beautiful sister drifting down the Musselshell River and tears would well up in his eyes, but he would shake it off and continue fishing. It had been a long time since he had held a fly rod and deep down he knew it was probably the best therapy he could get to help him grieve over his loss. But in between the moments of pain he really was enjoying fishing this beautiful river on a perfect spring day. He had managed to catch two trout: a rainbow that weighed three pounds and ten ounces, and a native brown trout that weighed seven pounds and thirteen ounces, one ounce shy of Justin's first fish. Justin had caught a couple more fish but they were smaller.

"What is that noise, DeMac?" Justin asked. "Is it thunder?"

DeMac had heard the noise just before Justin did and thought it might be a helicopter, but he didn't want to mention it since if it was a helicopter it was probably the one his team was using. The noise got louder and DeMac could tell it wasn't a helicopter.

"I think it's a car or truck engine," he said to Justin.

They stopped fishing and stood in the river listening as it got louder and louder. Finally the monster truck rounded a curve and they could see it.

"Well, I'll be damned," DeMac said.

"Oh shit, DeMac! Guess who's driving that thing. It's your buddy from the Hess station, Billy Billings," Justin said as the massive truck roared by.

Billy and Johnny were having a grand time also. They didn't see Carol Crissman sitting in the road until she gunned her engine and flew across the road in front of them. They almost had to stop the truck because they were laughing so hard. As they continued up River Road, Billy suddenly quit laughing when he noticed Justin Hayes's truck parked beside the river. He backed off the gas and searched the river as they continued up River Road. Then he saw them—two fisherman standing in the river about two hundred yards upstream watching them as they went by. Hate started flooding his soul.

Billy couldn't tell if the two fishermen standing in the river were the sailors from the Hess station but they probably were since daddy said in the meeting that they were here for a few days to do some fishing. All the laughing and giggling from the alcohol and marijuana suddenly turned into hate and anger. Billy swerved the giant truck to the left and gunned the engine and the massive truck easily jumped the ditch beside River Road and headed toward the river.

"What the hell are you doing, Billy?" Johnny screamed.

"I'm going fishing, Johnny. What does it look like I'm doing?" Billy said in an angry voice.

Johnny knew Billy better than anyone and he knew from the look on Billy's face and the tone of his voice that there was nothing he could say to change Billy's mind, so he snapped the cross chest safety harness on and held on for all he was worth. The monster truck plunged into the river like a champion Labrador retriever and Billy turned it hard to the left and started downstream. This particular stretch of the river was only about three feet deep in the deepest spots and most of it was under two feet deep which is why Justin chose this stretch because it was easy to wade. It was no obstacle for the monster truck with its sixty-six inch tires and Billy drove straight down the center of the river toward the two fishermen slinging rooster-tails of water toward the river bank on both sides of the truck.

"That ignorant moron!" Justin shouted as he watched the truck coming their way. "He's destroying the river with that thing."

"Justin, lets get on opposite sides of the river so they'll be between us. If this thing turns into a gunfight will have them in a crossfire," DeMac said as he sloshed toward the far side of the river.

Justin climbed the riverbank and laid his fly rod down and then slid his hand in his fishing vest grasping his Smith and Wesson revolver. DeMac did the same thing on the opposite side of the river about forty-five feet away. DeMac turned away from Justin briefly and held his cell phone up to his mouth. "Eagle, this is Red Fox. We got trouble. Send me some help," DeMac said softly.

Duke and Snake were winded as they reached the top of the mountain above the river where Justin and DeMac were fishing. It wasn't a tall mountain, maybe nine hundred feet above the river but it was fairly steep. They couldn't see the river or the truck for the massive white pine trees and the thick mountain laurel bushes but they could here it, so over the edge they went feet first, sliding on their butts holding their rifles up to protect them with one hand and using their other hand to grab bushes and vines to slow their descent.

"Birddog, this is Eagle. Red Fox has called for backup. What is your status? Over," Jimmy Hardy's voice came over Duke and Snakes earpiece.

"ETA is three minutes, Eagle. Over," Duke said into his voice-activated mouthpiece as he slid another thirty feet before grabbing onto a laurel bush.

"Roger that, Birddog. Eagle out."

Snake knew that if they slid all the way down this mountain in three minutes that they both were going to have sore asses tonight. Oh well, he thought, pain is temporary. Pride is for forever. Hoo-ahh!

Billy saw Justin on the left side of the river, and the sailor who stopped Charles Moses and Steve Weavil on the right side of the river, but not Justin's son Travis. "Damn it! Where is that little son of a bitch?" he screamed.

Johnny sat frozen in his seat and didn't say a word. He was scared to death that Billy was going to destroy Jumping Jack Flash, and if he did he knew that Jack would definitely send them both straight to rehab or kick them out one. Billy cut off the engine and glided to a stop right beside Justin.

"How's the fishing, Justin?" Billy said with an evil grin.

Justin was furious at Billy for this stupid and irresponsible stunt. The river had turned a dark brown from all the mud and silt that the truck had stirred up and a dead fish was floating by as Justin fought the urge to shoot Billy and rid the world of this human waste.

"Billy, you idiot. Get that truck out of this river before you destroy it anymore than you already have," Justin said through clinched teeth.

"Watch your mouth, old man, or I'll get out of this truck and"

"And what? Kick my ass. Come on and jump on this chest. If I can't shake you off you can live there!" Justin shouted as he stared into Billy's soul.·

DeMac could see the fury on Justin's face as he stared at Billy. Billy could see it too and it rattled him for a brief moment.

"I'm looking for a sailor about six feet tall, a hundred and eighty or ninety pounds, sandy hair. Have you seen him around by any chance?" Billy asked Justin.

"You would think after taking an ass-whooping like he gave you yesterday that you would have enough sense to stay away from him, but since you asked I think he went to the library with a copy of that tape from the Hess station and posted it on the internet under www.jackass.com," Justin said loudly.

DeMac heard something behind him and glanced back just long enough to see a small rock come bouncing down the mountain. He knew then that his reinforcements had arrived and he was glad because this situation was going downhill fast.

Billy slung his door open and looked down at the river rushing around the left front tire. "I've heard about all the shit I'm going to listen to from you, old man," Billy shouted as he looked down at the river.

"Billy! Crank this thing up and let's go!" Johnny pleaded.

"Shut-up Johnny. If I can figure out a way to climb back in here after I kick his ass I'm going to do it," Billy hollered at his cousin.

"Oh, don't worry, Billy. When I get through with you I'll throw you back in the bed of the truck and your cousin can drive you to the hospital" Justin said loud enough for everybody to hear. Even Duke and Snake heard it from thirty yards away as they watched the action from underneath a laurel bush. "At least your eyes will match each other when you wake up!"

Billy rose up to jump out and Johnny hollered, "Rehab, Billy! If you do this you and me will be in rehab by Monday morning. Please, let's just go!" Johnny said almost sobbing.

That stopped Billy in his tracks. Johnny was right. Jack had said to stay away until he said it was okay and if he fouled this up Johnny and him would be sent somewhere immediately. He slammed the truck door and cranked the truck back up. "I'm not done with you or your son!" He shouted to Justin as he let out the clutch.

Justin didn't reply because the truck was so loud he couldn't have heard it anyway. As Billy roared off Justin saw Travis burst through the mountain laurel on the other side of the river and run up beside DeMac. He instantly raised his camera and started taking pictures of the monster truck as it bounced and splashed its way down the river. Travis sloshed his way out into the river and continued taking pictures as Billy threw two beer bottles out his window into the muddy water. Billy finally turned and did a wheel-stand as he drove up the riverbank and out of the water. The massive truck bounced across the ditch and disappeared around the curve heading back home.

Justin was so mad he had tears in his eyes. Travis couldn't ever remember seeing his dad this angry. Justin stepped back down the bank and into the river as a three pound channel catfish floated by belly up followed by a pound and a half smallmouth bass.

"Take a picture of these dead fish, Travis," Justin said.

Travis took a couple pictures of the dead fish and one picture of his diver's watch to verify the time and date.

"I want to take that film to town this evening and get it developed," Justin said to Travis.

"I'll take it to town for you. I was going to try and catch Jesse and ask her out on a date anyway. I want to take a quick shower before I go though," Travis said.

"Well, let's go then. We can't fish this stretch of river anyway since that moron destroyed it," Justin said as he picked up his fly rod.

Carol Crissman had herself a good cry and was finally able to open the glove box and get the box of Kleenex out. She wiped off her face and chest and then the steering wheel and windshield as best she could. The greasy chicken and dumplings weren't easy to wipe off the windshield and she used every tissue in the box before she was satisfied that she could see to drive home. She took a couple of deep breaths to try and relax her before finally grabbing the key and cranking her car. She pulled the shifter down in drive and eased the Toyota Camry back onto River Road to head home. She didn't want Justin to see her with her hair matted and greasy and her makeup smeared. She looked at herself in the rearview mirror and saw streaks of mascara running down her face and when she looked back at the road her heart stopped. She screamed and jerked the steering wheel to the right and plunged into the ditch, narrowly avoiding being crushed to death for the second time by the same truck in less than half an hour. As soon as Carol hit the ditch she jerked the steering wheel to the left and the car jumped out of the ditch and crossed the road into the other ditch before finally stopping. She cut the ignition off and then promptly fainted.

"Birddog, this is Eagle. What's your status?" Jimmy Hardy asked.

Duke eased his finger up to the voice-activated microphone and tapped it twice with his fingernail to let Eagle know that he had received the transmission but was unable to respond at this time.

"Roger that, Birddog. Eagle out," Jimmy responded.

"Eagle, this is Crow's Nest. White Toyota is pulling out of Rabbit's Den and heading south," Harold Hartley said.

"Roger that, Crow's Nest," Jimmy said from the control board at the tobacco barn. Jimmy rubbed his face with his hands. This was the hardest part of any mission, waiting and wondering. He had retired from the Special Forces two years ago and had been working for the CIA ever since. He would rather be lying beside Duke and Snake right now instead of being stuck in this old tobacco barn, but his forty-two-year-old body just couldn't do what was necessary to be a special operations soldier. Well, at least I'm not stuck in a factory with somebody looking over my shoulder he thought to himself.

"Eagle, this is Crow's Nest. You're not going to believe this. Monster truck has just forced white car off the road again and white female appears to be unconscious," Harold said.

"Continue to monitor, Crow's Nest. Do not intervene," Jimmy ordered.

"Roger that, Eagle," Harold Hartley said.

"Eagle, this is Wizard. Black monster truck is returning to the garage at my ten o'clock," Ozzie Curry said.

"Roger that, Wizard," Jimmy said.

"Eagle, this is Birddog," a voice came over the speaker talking in a whisper. "Red Fox and Rabbit are loading up and returning to the Rabbit's Den," Duke said.

"Roger that, Birddog. Return to base," Jimmy said.

Travis held on as Justin eased his truck back across the ditch onto River Road. Justin shifted the Toyota truck out of four-wheel drive and slowly increased his speed to about thirty-five miles an hour.

"I'm glad Billy didn't jump out of that truck," Justin said to DeMac as they cruised down the winding road beside the river. DeMac was a little confused by that statement until Justin continued the conversation. "I'm not so sure I could have stopped myself from killing him if I ever got my hands on him."

"If the right people found out that he drove a monster truck down a river that is protected by state and federal environmental laws he could end up in some serious trouble. I don't think his daddy's influence reaches out far enough to shield him from that kind of trouble," DeMac said.

"That's why I want those pictures developed. I might just mail a few of them to the right people. It's one thing to be a drunk and a troublemaker, but when you start destroying a beautiful natural resource like the New River then you've stepped over the line," Justin said.

Justin rounded the last curve on River Road before you came to his driveway and saw the white Toyota Camry in the ditch on the right side of the road.

"Looks like somebody ran off the road," DeMac said.

"That looks like Carol's car. I believe it is," Justin said as he stopped beside it. Justin jumped out and ran around to the driver's door. Carol was slumped over and not moving so Justin jerked the door open and leaned over her.

"Carol! Carol! Can you hear me, Carol?" Justin shouted.

"Huh? What? Oh, Justin, you won't..." Carol moaned as she started waking up.

Justin reached under her legs with his left arm and around her back with his right arm and picked Carol up and carried her around the front of her car. Justin stepped over the ditch and sat down on his tailgate still holding Carol in his lap. Carol started crying and mumbling about a giant truck and Justin held her tight to comfort her.

"Lets get her up to the house and then you two can come back and get her car. There's a chain in my toolbox if you need it to pull her car out of the ditch," Justin said as he carried the sobbing woman around to the passenger seat and set her down. Travis and DeMac hopped on the back as Justin drove up the driveway and into his carport. Justin carried Carol inside his house and laid her on the couch while Travis and DeMac went back to retrieve her car. When DeMac and Travis walked back into the house Justin met them in the kitchen.

"I can't see any injuries on her anywhere. I think she's just shaken up a little bit. I covered her up with a blanket and she's sleeping now. I believe she will be just fine once she gets a little rest," Justin said.

"I'm going to take a quick shower and take that film to town," Travis said.

"Okay but keep your eyes open. This feud we got going with the Billings clan is probably going to get worse before it gets better," Justin warned.

"I'm going to clean up her car for her. I don't think it's damaged, but it sure is a mess," DeMac said.

"That would be nice of you, DeMac. There's a wet dry vacuum cleaner in the machine shop and everything to clean up a car is in that cabinet in the carport," Justin said. "I'm going to keep an eye on her for awhile to make sure she's all right."

All three men turned and went in separate directions.

Travis took a quick shower and put on a pair of khaki slacks and a light blue dress shirt. He was nervous about asking Jesse for a date but was looking forward to seeing her again. He put his favorite cologne on and grabbed the film and was out the door. DeMac was bent over inside Carol's car with a soapy towel in his hand when Travis walked by.

"Be careful, Romeo," DeMac hollered. "Watch your six."

"I will. I'll be back in a couple hours," Travis said as he jumped in his Jeep. As Travis pulled out onto River Road his mind went immediately to thinking about Jesse. He hadn't thought about anything else since he met her. He was more nervous about asking her out than when he asked Jenny McClure to go with him to the junior high homecoming dance when he was fifteen years old. He didn't understand how meeting somebody for just a couple hours could take total control of all your thoughts and feelings.

What was really confusing to him was the fact that he had been around lots of beautiful women in five different countries and never once felt like this before now. Travis wound his way through a series of turns as the road followed the twisting river until he passed a gravel road on his right marked by a sign that said, "Antioch Church Road." Just beyond the road a driveway turned to the left and went up to a beautiful A-framed house on top of a hill overlooking the river. A black Cadillac Escalade was sitting in the driveway and an attractive red headed lady was standing beside it with her arms crossed. Travis thought she looked upset so he stopped his Jeep and ran his window down.

"You got car trouble?" he asked her as she turned toward him.

"No, I got tree trouble," she said. "A big pine tree has fallen across my driveway and I can't get up to my house. I'm from Kernersville and I just bought this property so I don't know who I can call to have it removed."

Travis pulled his Jeep over to the side of the road and parked it. He got out and as he walked toward the lady he saw the huge pine tree laying across the driveway about half way between the road and the house.

"Hi. My name is Travis Hayes. I don't live up here but my dad does and he might know someone who can help you," Travis said as he pulled out his cell phone.

"Thank you so much for stopping. My name is Teresa Owens," she said as she reached out to shake Travis's hand.

Justin was sitting in his recliner watching Carol as she slept. She really is a nice lady Justin thought, but I know she would probably drive me crazy if I ever took her out. The phone rang and Justin answered it on the first ring hoping it wouldn't wake up Carol.

"Hello," Justin said.

"Dad, this is Travis. There's a lady up here who can't get up her driveway because a big pine tree has fallen across it. It's a big A-framed house on the left after you pass Antioch Church Road."

"I know exactly which house you're talking about," Justin said.

"She wants to know if you know anybody she can call to remove it. She's from Kernersville and doesn't know anybody around here yet," Travis explained.

"It will be hard to find somebody on Saturday evening to do it but I can take care of it for her. Tell her that I'll be there in twenty minutes," Justin said.

"Okay, Dad, I'll tell her. I'll see you in a couple hours," Travis said as he hung up.

"Justin," Carol said as she looked up from the couch. "What happened?"

"It's okay, Carol. You ran off the road and passed out but everything is fine now," Justin said as he leaned forward to stand.

Carol threw the blanket off her and swung her legs around to put them on the floor. The black dress with the slit up the side that Carol had bought to impress Justin was definitely impressing him now because in her sleep it had ridden up over her waist and the only thing covering her from the waist down was a pair of black bikini panties. She was still a little groggy as Justin came over and sat down beside her. She pulled her dress down and adjusted her clothes as Justin explained what happened.

"I remember everything now," she said and told Justin all about the events that led up to her ditching her car.

"I don't think you have any injuries, you just passed out. Sometimes a person's body will shut down from too much stress," Justin told her. "You've been sleeping for about a half an hour."

"Oh no, my car is wrecked and—"

"No, your car is fine. We pulled it out of the ditch and drove it up here behind the house and my son's friend DeMac is out there cleaning it up for you right now. Travis just called me and said the people who bought the A-frame house up past Antioch Church Road can't get up their driveway because a tree has fallen across it, so I'm going to run up there and cut the tree up for them. Just make yourself at home until I get back. If you want to wash your clothes or take a shower or fix yourself something to drink just help yourself. I'll tell DeMac when I leave that you're awake and might be walking around.

"Thank you so much, Justin. I'm sorry to have caused you so much trouble this evening," Carol said and she leaned over and kissed Justin on the lips.

"Umm, tastes like chicken," Justin said.

"Oh, well, I guess I probably do," Carol said, blushing.

"That's okay. I like chicken," Justin said, grinning.

"Justin, before you leave, do you by any chance have any wine? I could use a glass of wine after a day like today," Carol said.

"I got one bottle and I don't know what kind it is or if it's any good. It was given to me by a friend of mine when I retired from Triad Power and Light and you're welcome to it if you want it. Let me go get it for you," Justin said as he stood and left the room. Justin returned in a minute with the bottle in one hand and a glass and corkscrew in the other.

"It says 'Gossamer Bay' and then under that it says 'Chardonnay.' I don't drink wine so I don't know anything about it," Justin said as he twisted the corkscrew into the bottle.

Justin popped the cork on the bottle of wine and poured Carol about a half a glass full and handed it to her. She took a sip and then took a gulp. "Umm, this is just what I need. It's delicious."

"Well, help yourself, Carol. If you need anything you can ask DeMac. He's a real nice guy," Justin said as he turned to leave.

Justin walked out to his machine shop and got his Stihl 360 chainsaw and his gas can and carried them to his truck. He went back to his shop and returned with an axe and a wedge and placed them in his truck before walking over to where DeMac was working on Carol's car. DeMac had already finished the inside of the car and was just starting on the outside when Justin walked up. Justin told DeMac that Carol was awake and doing fine and where he was going before he backed out of his carport and started down the driveway as Carol watched from the window and sipped her wine.

Travis was wondering where he could take Jesse if she agreed to go out with him when it suddenly dawned on him that he was in the city limits and the speed limit was thirty-five miles per hour. He backed off the gas and put his right turn signal on as he approached the first stoplight and turned right just like his dad had told him to do. Justin told Travis before he left that there was a photo shop about two blocks down that did one hour processing. Travis saw a cinder block building with a sign that said "Sparta Photo Center" and he turned in and parked. As he entered the store he noticed the store hours were ten a.m. till six p.m. on Saturday and the clock on the wall said it was 5:17 p.m. Travis hoped he wasn't too late to get the film developed since it was Easter and they were probably going to be closed on Monday. A white haired man in his late sixties came walking up from the back of the store.

"Yes, sir, how can I help you?" he said.

"I got two rolls of film I'd like to get developed if you got time," Travis said.

The old man looked at his watch and studied the question for a moment before answering. "Well, I guess so," he said. "It's not like I'm busy doing anything else."

"I really appreciate it," Travis said. "I know it's close to your quitting time."

"As you can see, there's nobody in here that I have to wait on so I can develop your film. The photo shop business has gone to hell since all these digital cameras and computer software has come out and people can develop their own film. I can't even pay the power bill anymore," the man grumbled.

"All this technology has made photography much simpler, but I think you can still get better quality with chemical photography," Travis said to the elderly gentleman.

The old man stopped and looked at Travis. "Finally somebody comes in here with some damn sense," he said as he took the film and started walking toward the back of the store.

"I'm going to run an errand and come back, if that's all right." Travis said, "Go ahead, but be back by 6:15. That's when I'm leaving."

Jesse was totally exhausted. She had been on her feet since six o'clock this morning and her whole body was sore and achy. Actually she had been on her feet all week starting with the rabies clinic on Monday sponsored by the Ashe County Health Department. She had volunteered her services and had spent the day vaccinating dogs and cats and explaining to people the importance of getting their pets spayed and neutered, so she had started the week a day behind and had actually never caught back up. At least tomorrow was Easter Sunday and they were closed on Easter Monday, so she had two days off to relax. She might run herself a bubble bath and light some candles and let her body rejuvenate itself. Then she might just sit around and read a good book.

Jesse walked to the back of the clinic and opened a cage with a fourteen-year-old golden retriever in it. "Come on, Precious. Time to go home," she said as she slid a leash over her neck. Jesse had operated on Precious on Wednesday to remove a fleshy tumor from her neck. The tumor itself wasn't a health risk to the dog but it had grown so large that it was affecting her ability to swallow so it needed to be removed.

Jesse led Precious into the waiting room where three small children and their mother were anxiously waiting. The children swarmed the dog as soon as they entered the room and the dog was wagging its tail and actually smiling as the children hugged it.

"Be careful with her neck, kids. We don't want to hurt her," Jesse warned.

The children instantly stopped and started looking for the incision on the dog's neck as their mother stepped around them and walked over to Jesse.

"I might have to pay you a little along if that's okay Jesse," she said as she opened her purse and pulled out a tattered wallet.

Jesse knew that Sandy's husband had run off about three months ago leaving her with three children to raise by herself. The gossip around town was that he was living with a woman in Hillsville, Virginia. All three of the children were wearing worn out shoes and their clothes were starting to get ragged.

"You don't owe me anything, Sandy. I know things are a little tough right now for you so just consider it paid."

Tears flooded the woman's eyes and she was unable to speak.

Jesse stepped over and opened the door that led to the parking lot.

"Okay, kids. Take Precious home and be careful with her neck, all right?" Jesse said.

"Yes, Miss Jesse, they said as they filed through the door behind their dog. "Thank you" was all Sandy could manage to say as she hugged Jesse and then walked out.

"Crystal, let's close this place up and go home," Jesse hollered as she headed toward the back of the building.

Crystal Gordon was a high school senior who worked part-time for Jesse after school and on Saturday. Jesse started checking all the rooms to make sure no one had left their sunglasses or their cell phones when Crystal suddenly appeared in the doorway.

"Sheila Morgan is in the waiting room with three kittens in a box," Crystal said.

"Put her in room number two and then lock the front door. After I see her I want to go home. You can go on home if you need to Crystal" Jesse said.

Jesse finished checking the other rooms before she went to room number two. Sheila was standing beside the stainless steel examining table and a cardboard box was sitting on it.

"What can I do for you, Sheila?" Jesse asked.

Sheila turned her head and Jesse could see that Sheila's right eye was black and her right cheek was swollen and puffy. She had tried to cover it up with make-up but you could still see it if you looked closely.

Sheila was almost hysterical as she started telling Jesse about her problem. "Oh, Jesse, my cat has been gone since yesterday and I know something's wrong because she wouldn't leave her kittens unless something happened to her and I don't know what to do!"

Jesse picked up one of the meowing kittens and looked it over. "Well, I hope your cat is all right, Sheila, but these kittens are already weaned so you can feed them yourself and they will be fine."

"I know but daddy won't let me keep them in the house and that old tomcat has already come back and killed one of them and if I keep them outside I know he will come back and kill the rest of them or something else will. I don't know what to do. Do you know somebody that could take them?" Sheila pleaded.

"Okay, just calm down. Here's what we will do. I'll take the kittens on one condition. If your cat comes back home I want you to promise me that you will have her spayed or if you get another cat I want you to have it spayed or neutered. Understand?" Jesse said.

"Okay," Sheila whimpered.

"You promise," Jesse said firmly.

"Yes, ma'am," she said.

"Okay, I'll try to find them a home," Jesse said.

"Thank you so much," Sheila said, grinning.

"What happened to your face, honey, if you don't mind me asking?" Jesse said.

"That bastard Billy Billings slapped me down yesterday at the Hess station. He wanted to give me a ride but I said no because I know what kind of ride he was wanting, and he just started dragging me to his truck until I bit the shit out of him. When I bit him he let me go but he backhanded me and knocked me down."

"I heard about that, but I didn't know it was you,"

"Oh, you should have been there, Jesse. This sailor stepped in between me and Billy and he was a hunk too. He knocked Billy out cold and then held me tight until Sheriff Sisk kicked me down again and then almost shot him. I hate that bastard too," Sheila said with a frown.

"Well, you did the right thing by fighting back. You were real lucky that someone was there who could rescue you, especially from Billy Billings."

"I know and I didn't even get a chance to thank him before my mom showed up and dragged me home. If I ever see him again I'm going to thank him like you wouldn't believe. He's my knight in shining armor," she said, staring off into space.

Crystal appeared in the doorway again. "Jesse, I hate to tell you this, but Jake Bodenhiemer is on the phone and he says his horse ran·into a fence and cut its leg. He wants you to look at it and see if you think it needs sewing up."

That was the last thing that Jesse wanted to hear on Saturday evening at quitting time, but she knew she would have to go check it out.

"Tell Jake that I'll be there in thirty minutes and lock the door behind Sheila when she leaves. I'm going to slip out the back door and let you finish closing up," Jesse instructed.

"Yes, ma'am. I'll close up for you and I'll see you Tuesday after school," Crystal said as she led Sheila to the front door.

When Travis got in sight of the animal clinic he could see Jesse's Chevrolet Suburban parked behind the clinic and two cars parked out front. He was afraid that she would be gone since the business card she gave him said their hours on Saturday were eight a.m. till five p.m. and it was already 5:30 p.m.

Travis parked out front and took a deep breath. "Well, here goes nothing," he said out loud as he opened the door and stepped out. He walked up the sidewalk and just as he started to reach for the door knob he heard the door lock click and the door swung open.

"Oh my God, it's you!" the blond girl screamed as she ran up and hugged Travis. "I didn't think I would ever see you again!"

Travis finally realized who was hugging him when he got over the initial shock. Actually what she was doing to him was more than just a hug since she had one leg wrapped around him and was kissing his neck and ear. The girl that had unlocked the door grinned at Travis and closed the door behind her and then locked it.

Travis heard gravel crunching under tires and turned just enough to see Jesse driving around the building in her Suburban. Jesse drove past them and waved as Travis tried to pry the teenager off him so he could stop her. It was no use. He would have a better chance getting away from an octopus than this hormone-fueled teenage girl.

"Well," Jesse said to the kittens in the box beside her, "That's my luck for you, she got the hero, and I got the litter box."

Justin parked his truck behind the black Cadillac Escalade and got out. The driver's door on the Escalade opened up and a red headed lady stepped out and came toward him. Justin noticed immediately how beautiful she was. She reminded him of the actress Nicole Kidman but her hair was a much darker red.

"Hi. My name is Teresa Owens," she said as she reached out to shake his hand. She was wearing an olive colored pin striped business suit with matching high heels and a string of pearls around her neck.

"Hi. My name is Justin Hayes. I live about seven miles down the road from here. I can see your problem lying across your driveway."

"Oh, yes, Mr. Hayes. Can you possibly clear it enough for me to drive up to my house?"

"Call me Justin if you will, and to answer your question, yes, ma'am, I can clear your driveway for you."

"That would be great. I thought I was going to have to drive back home," she said, relieved.

"I'll cut a section out of the middle so you can drive on up to the house and then I'll cut up the rest of it for you," Justin said as he walked back to his truck to get his saw.

"When you finish come up to the house and I'll pay you," she said as she got back in her Cadillac.

Justin carried his chainsaw up the hill and set it on top of the loblolly pine tree that was lying across the driveway. It was a big tree, probably thirty inches in diameter and at least eighty feet tall. He grabbed the pull rope on the saw and gave it a yank. The saw spit and growled a little bit but didn't crank. The next yank brought it to life and Justin sank it in the tree sending rooster tails of sawdust into the air behind him. There is something about running a chainsaw that just makes a man feel good he thought as he finished his first cut and started his second. When he had made five cuts three feet apart he cut his saw off and rolled the pieces one at a time off the drive-way and then waved the pretty redhead through the opening. Justin watched her drive up to the house before cranking his saw again. That is one fancy lady, he thought, as he sunk the saw back into the tree. Justin couldn't help but wonder what it would be like to make love to a woman as beautiful as Teresa.

Teresa went immediately to the master bedroom to change out of her business suit into something more comfortable. As she pulled on a pair of sweat pants and a sleeveless cotton top she watched Justin through the window sawing up the tree. She had always been very good at judging people's character and she thought Justin was prob-ably a very nice man. You could tell that he had worked outside for a living from his face and arms but he was still quite attractive she thought. He had what people often called "rugged good looks." She was sick and tired of men who were prissy and spoiled. Most of the men she knew couldn't even change a flat tire much less cut up a tree with a chainsaw. Justin certainly looked like he could change a tire she thought. Hell, with a chest and a set of arms like that, he could probably hold the car up while somebody else changed it. Teresa went to the kitchen and got herself a beer and returned to watch

Justin cut up the tree. She couldn't help wondering what it would be like to make love to a rugged man like Justin Hayes.

Justin finished sawing up the tree and started carrying the logs over to the edge of the woods and piling them up. When he finished with the logs, he dragged all the brush over to the wood line and piled it up and was finally finished. He placed his chainsaw back in his toolbox and got out an old towel to dry off with. He was soaked with sweat and covered with sawdust but felt great after such a work-out. Some guys go to the gym and some guys cut wood he thought to himself.

The sun was sinking close to the horizon and it was starting to cool off as Justin pulled his tee shirt off and gave it a pop to shake the sawdust off of it. Justin hung his shirt across the side view mirror and leaned against the hood as he dried himself off with the towel. It was a gorgeous spring day and Justin was enjoying it. Teresa sipped her beer and watched Justin as he toweled off. She felt kind of guilty spying on him but she was certainly enjoying it. He was a powerful man and good looking and when he ripped his shirt off she felt a slight tingle run through her.

Justin put his tee shirt back on and drove up to the house. There was a deck built on to the back of the house overlooking the river as it tumbled over and around some huge rocks and Justin walked up on the deck and leaned against the rail to look at it. When he turned around to go ring the doorbell Teresa was already coming through the door and he couldn't believe the change in her since he saw her less than an hour ago. Instead of a suit and pearls she was wearing a sleeveless cotton tee shirt and a pair of sweat pants and instead of high heels she was wearing flip flops. One thing that didn't change was her beauty. She is one of those women who are beautiful wearing anything Justin thought. Justin didn't know a pair of sweat pants and a tee shirt could look like that and he felt himself getting aroused.

"Thank you, Mr. Hayes. Uh, I mean Justin. You don't know how grateful I am that you could clean that up for me," she said. "Now please tell me how much I owe you."

Teresa was holding a beer bottle in one hand and a wallet in the other. Justin figured her for a glass of wine or champagne instead of a beer. "Do you happen to have another one of those beers?" he asked.

"Why certainly. I should have offered you something to drink. I don't know what I was thinking," Teresa said as she disappeared back into the house. She returned in a minute with one for Justin and a fresh one for her.

Justin took a big swallow of the beer and gazed at the river. "This is beautiful," Justin said. "My house is facing the river but it's about 250 yards up on the side of a mountain from it. You're close enough to hear it and feel it and taste it."

"If we have a flood I think I'd rather be at your house though."

"That's a good point," Justin said and he turned away from the river and smiled at her. Teresa smiled back at Justin and they shared a moment of silence.

Justin finally broke the silence. "My son said you're from Kernersville."

"Yes, I am. I'm a realtor and I work the Winston-Salem area but my home is in Kernersville. My friends wanted me to buy a place at the coast when I started looking for a vacation home but I wanted to get away from crowds of people and traffic and noise. I wanted a place I could go to relax," she explained.

"Well, Teresa, you and I think a whole lot alike. I lived in the Silver Hill community until two years ago and then I built a house up here for the very same reason."

"Your son seemed like a very nice man," Teresa said. "I'm so glad he stopped to help me."

"He's been a wonderful son. It's been a blessing to raise him," Justin said as he turned back to look at the river.

"Did your wife mind moving way up here away from her friends?" Teresa asked.

"She moved to Greensboro fifteen years ago to live with a rich man," Justin said.

"Oh, I'm sorry," Teresa said but she really wasn't.

Justin suddenly put his finger up to his lips to signal Teresa to be quiet. He took her hand and pulled her up to the railing and pointed across the river.

"There's a doe deer and her twins coming to the river," Justin whispered in her ear. He could smell her perfume and fought the urge to smell her neck.

Teresa couldn't see the deer at first but they suddenly materialized like magic as they made their way to the river. They were beautiful and she and Justin stood motionless as they stepped into the river to drink. When they finally turned and left the doe deer stepped back into the woods with the grace of a ballerina, while her knobby-kneed twins looked like a couple of drunks.

Teresa was thrilled as she watched the deer leave and was equally thrilled to be leaning against Justin. It was strange to her that she felt so at ease around a total stranger but there was something about this man that made her feel safe. She was hoping the deer would stay longer so she could stay cuddled ·up to Justin. He smelled like gasoline and oil and sweat but instead if offending her she wanted to bury her nose in his massive chest and inhale it.

When the deer were completely out of sight Teresa and Justin stepped apart. "They were beautiful," Teresa said. "Thank you for pointing them out."

"My pleasure," Justin said, and he meant it because it had totally aroused him.

"Well, Teresa, it's getting dark and I guess I better be getting home. If you get in a bind or need some help you can call me since were not strangers anymore. I could stand here and gaze at this river all night but I still have something I need to do at home. It was nice meeting you," Justin said as he stepped off the deck.

"Well, first, Justin, tell me what I owe you?" She asked.

"Consider it a welcome-to-the-neighborhood gift," He said as he walked away.

"Nonsense. I must pay you something for all that work," Teresa said.

"You can't pay a man who already has everything," Justin said, still walking away.

"But I don't have your number if I need to call you," she yelled.

"It's 704-789-4395. Good night," Justin yelled back.

Teresa wrote the number down quickly in her check book. She was left stunned by this man. He was big and strong like a gladiator, but purred like a kitten when they stood and watched the deer. He seemed totally at home in the outdoors and had almost a spiritual connection with nature. He was confident without being cocky or arrogant. She had never met anyone in her fifty-two years who had such a presence that you could feel it from ten feet away. She definitely wanted to learn more about this man. She pulled out her cell phone and dialed the number for SOS Security Company in Winston-Salem. A man answered on the fourth ring. "SOS," he said.

"Ryan, this is Teresa Owens," she said.

"Oh. Hi, Teresa. Long time no see."

"Listen, Ryan, I know it's Saturday evening but I want you to check a guy out for me."

"Do you want basic information or do you want a detailed workup?"

"I want everything and I want you to fax it to me at my new fax number in the mountains. 704-789-0022."

"Okay, Teresa, tell me what you know about him?"

"I don't know much. His name is Justin Hayes and he lives on River Road in Ashe County and his phone number is 704-789-4395. That's all I got."

"Okay, Teresa. I'll send it to you as soon as I can."

"Thank you, Ryan. I appreciate it," Teresa said as she hung up. She had used Ryan's services in the past to check up on prospective clients in her real estate business. She normally just wanted to know if they had a criminal record and if they were financially able to purchase the property that they were looking at. It kept her from wasting her time on people who were just curious and had no intention of buying any property, and it also let her know if she needed to have someone with her when she showed them· the property. Realtors were easy targets for rapists and thieves. She hoped that Justin was all that she thought he was, but it was almost too good to be true.

Ryan hung up the phone and smiled. This was going to be the easiest $250 he had ever made. He had just finished faxing a background check to an attorney in Ashe County named Cecil Wood. The background check was on a man named Justin Hayes. All he had to do now was wait a few hours and send the same package to Teresa and then send her the bill. Ryan leaned back in his chair and thought about Teresa. He had asked her out on a date once but she declined. He was sorry too because that was one good looking baby doll.

Justin cut his headlights on as he cruised down River Road. It wasn't dark outside yet but it was getting there fast. Justin rounded a curve and tapped his breaks as three whitetail does bounced across the road in front of him. Seeing the does reminded him of Teresa's perfume when she leaned against him to see the deer come to the river. One of the reasons he left so hastily was that between her leaning on him and the smell of her perfume he had got totally aroused and didn't want her to see the bulge in his pants. He felt sure that what she was smelling wasn't as good. Justin thought that a good name for the way he smelled right now would maybe be "Chainsaw and Locker Room Number 9."

Justin turned in his driveway and noticed the house was dimly lit. He wondered if Carol had left already since the house wasn't lit up more than that. He hoped Carol was all right after having such a near miss and landing in the ditch like she did. She was a very pretty and sweet lady, Justin thought, just not the right lady for him. Justin drove by the front of the house and around to the carport where Travis and DeMac were leaning on Travis's Jeep.

"Did you get the driveway cleared?" Travis asked Justin as he stepped out of the truck.

"Yes, I did. You didn't tell me that my new neighbor was a gorgeous redhead. That's information that I need to know," Justin said, grinning. "Did you get a date with Jesse?"

"No, I didn't even get to ask her. That girl from the Hess station just happened to be at the animal clinic and was practically molesting me as Jesse was driving out of the lot," Travis said dejectedly.

"Sorry about that. What about the pictures?" Justin asked.

"They're on the kitchen bar. They turned out real good."

Justin glanced over at Carol's car and couldn't believe how shiny it was. It was so clean it practically sparkled and the tires had been blacked and were shining too.

"DeMac, I bet the next time Carol's car gets dirty she's going to drive over here and run it in the ditch. That looks good."

"It cleaned up real nice," DeMac replied.

"Speaking of Carol, how's she doing?" Justin asked.

"She's doing fine. She took a shower and washed her clothes and now she's waiting for them to come out of the dryer," DeMac said.

"I know somebody else that needs to take a shower, me!" Justin said.

"Dad, me and DeMac are going to drive over to Jefferson and eat a pizza. Do you want us to bring you something back to eat?" Travis asked.

"No, I'll eat a sandwich or something. Thanks anyway."

"Okay, we'll see you later on," Travis said as he and DeMac climbed in his Jeep.

"Be careful," Justin said as he walked toward the back door. Justin took his boots off in the carport and filled the dog bowls up with food and water. When he rattled the dog food bag Shogun and Scooter came running around the house. Well, Shogun was running and Scooter was in a fast wobble.

"What's the matter, boy, are you sore? Where have you knuckle-heads been?" Justin said to the dogs as he rubbed them. Justin finally stood up and walked through the back door and went straight for the kitchen to see the pictures that Travis had taken. He opened the package and flipped through the pictures until he came to the ones of the truck in the river. These are perfect he thought as he thumbed through them. He finally put them back in the envelope and grabbed a longneck before heading for the living room.

"Carol!" Justin shouted.

"I'm in the living room, Justin," he heard her say.

Justin walked through the kitchen and into the living room. Carol had lit all the candles that Justin had in the living room and had cut on the gas logs in the fireplace. She was leaning against the far wall looking out the front of the house toward the river. She had a glass of wine in her hand and was wearing one of Justin's flannel shirts.

"Carol, how are you? Are you feeling better?" Justin asked as he crossed the room toward her.

"I'm fine," she said and smiled at Justin. "I took a shower in your wonderful master bathroom and then washed my clothes. They're in the dryer now."

Carol looked sexier standing beside that window than Justin would have ever dreamed possible. It was because she wasn't squeezed into a dress that was to tight and her hair was hanging naturally instead of being in some ridiculous arrangement Justin thought as he looked her over. Justin was suddenly aroused again and turned toward his bedroom door.

"I'm glad you're okay, Carol. DeMac's got your car spotless. He must have really worked hard on it because it looks great. Anyway, I've got to take a shower because I'm filthy. There's stuff in the refrigerator for sandwiches if you get hungry," Justin said as he stepped into his bedroom and shut the door.

Justin quickly undressed and put his clothes in the hamper. He couldn't wait to get in the shower and wash away the sweat and dirt from his body. He walked into his bathroom and into his walk-in shower and cut the water on. After it got warm he stepped under the water and just stood there for a while letting the water massage his sore body.

Justin had splurged when he built this bathroom and he was glad he did. He had installed a tub that was big enough for him to stretch out in and it was jetted so it doubled as a whirlpool. He also installed double sinks and a vanity and a big walk-in shower with a corner bench seat so he could sit and relax as he showered. The walls and floor of the bathroom were covered with ceramic tile so water could splash in any direction and not cause any concern.

Justin went to work scrubbing the grime off and shampooing his hair before sitting down and just letting the water rain down on him. He didn't know whether he should take a hot shower or a cold shower after what happened when he saw Teresa and then Carol. Justin leaned back against the corner and shut his eyes as he relaxed and thought about his day. They had caught and relocated the baby groundhogs. He had caught the biggest trout of his life. Billy drove down the river. Carol drove in the ditch. He met a new neighbor who was gorgeous. Except for that idiot driving down the river and Carol running in the ditch, it had been a good day he thought.

Justin's mind drifted back to Teresa. Justin thought he could feel some kind of special connection between Teresa and him. Call it chemistry or compatibility or call it what ever you want to, but he could feel it. Justin visualized Teresa standing there in sweat pants and a sleeveless top. He started to get aroused and felt himself starting to swell again and then felt something else as Carol straddled his legs and sat down on him.

"Carol. We probably shouldn't"

Carol covered his mouth with hers and explored it with her tongue. She pressed her breasts against him and squirmed back and forth until she could feel him getting hard and then reached down and guided him into her. Justin and Carol both shivered with delight and moaned as the water rained down on them. Justin knew it was probably a mistake as he sat there and Carol rocked back and forth on his lap, but just as the river called to him earlier today as he stood on the porch of the store, Carol was calling him now and he was answering.

Something Doesn't Feel Right

Justin was listening to the rain beating against the roof and the side of the house as he watched the clock radio change from 5:44 to 5:45 a.m. It was Easter Sunday morning and Justin was lying in bed enjoying the sound of the rain as he slowly woke up. He had slept hard and felt good and rested. For some reason having sex always makes you sleep better he thought to himself as he stretched his arms and legs.

Carol had surprised Justin in the shower and they had made love there first and then an hour later in the bedroom before Carol got dressed and left. Justin thought that what happened between him and Carol last night was just the result of the circumstances surrounding yesterday's events but was probably something that they both needed at the time. His main concern was not to lead Carol on, so he told her that he wasn't looking for a permanent relationship and he didn't want to hurt her and she seemed fine with that. She said that she understood and that they would just play it by ear with no strings attached and no expectations. Justin was relieved to hear Carol say that, and he hoped that she meant it.

Justin got out of bed and stretched again before pulling on a pair of sweat pants and a matching sweat shirt. He slipped his feet into a pair of moccasins and headed to the kitchen to get a cup of coffee. His coffee pot was set to come on every morning at 5:30 a.m. because he always woke up between 5:30 and 6:00. Justin poured his coffee and headed through the house toward the front porch. He had fallen asleep last night before Travis and DeMac got home and didn't remember them coming in so he glanced in their bedrooms when he went by. Both bedrooms were empty and the beds were made up. A jolt of fear ran through Justin. Maybe Travis and DeMac didn't make it home last night. Justin practically ran through the house and onto the front porch. Travis and DeMac were standing at the porch railing drinking coffee and watching the rain come down in sheets.

"Oh, there you are. When I saw your rooms were empty it scared me," Justin said. "Why are you guys up so early?"

"Well, when we got home last night it was just ten o'clock and you were already asleep so we just went to bed too. I think all of us were worn out last night," Travis said. "You looked scared to death when you came through that door."

"I was scared! This feud we got going with the 'evil empire' has me a little jumpy, I guess," Justin said, pointing his finger toward the Billing's house. The three men stood silently drinking their coffee until Justin spoke again. "You know, I think all of us need to be real careful until this thing we got going on with the Billing's clan works it way out. I don't know what their plans are or what's going to happen, but I do know that they are capable of committing murder. All of us need to look out for each other for now."

"I think you're right," DeMac said. "Rich people don't like to be told no."

"Rich kids don't like to have their asses kicked either," Travis said.

"Let's just be careful and keep our eyes open for trouble. Gabriel has been warning me since last Wednesday that something is going on. I don't know what it is, but it is definitely out there. I can feel it," Justin said.

Travis and DeMac turned toward Justin and stared at him with a funny look on both their faces. "Who is Gabriel?" they said simultaneously.

"He's my guardian angel," Justin said, staring at the rain.

"Are you serious?" Travis asked.

"I'm very serious," Justin said. "I've had a guardian angel practically all my life and I don't know what his name is but I call him Gabriel."

"You never told me about Gabriel," Travis said.

"You wouldn't have believed me if I did. As a matter of fact you don't believe me now but I'm telling you he's real and he's been warning me since Wednesday that something's going on," Justin said.

"But this feud didn't start until Friday," Travis argued.

"I know, and that's why it's so strange because somebody has been watching me since Wednesday," Justin said.

DeMac was standing there drinking his coffee and wondering if the spooks were thinking the same thing that he was. DeMac had never believed in guardian angels but his Seal team had been in place and watching Justin since Wednesday morning, so he either had extrasensory perception or was psychic or had a guardian angel one.

"Once when I was in high school a friend of mine wanted me to go with him to town and I didn't because Gabriel warned me not to, and my friend was killed in a head-on collision thirty minutes later. Twice in Vietnam I changed my position because Gabriel warned me, and both times I would have been killed if I hadn't moved. Once at work I refused to grab an electric line that was supposed to be dead because Gabriel warned me not to and when we checked it there was 7,400 volts on it," Justin said as be stared at the rain. "Do you remember right before your mother left when we went to the beach and she got so mad at me because I made her get up in the middle of the night and pack up?"

"Yes, I do because I was mad too!" Travis said. "I wanted to go down to the beach the next morning before we went home."

"That motel burned to the ground three hours after we left," Justin said as he looked at Travis. "I had a hard time explaining to the Myrtle Beach detectives why we suddenly left in the middle of the night."

"Well, I'll be damned," Travis said as he stared back at his dad. "I can't believe you never have said anything about it until now."

"Well, like I said, no one would believe me anyway. I wouldn't have told you now but I'm a little worried because something doesn't feel right. I think Gabriel is trying to warn me about something."

As Travis tried to digest this new information the rain suddenly stopped.

"I've got to give Scooter his antibiotic and let him and Shogun out of the carport so they can use the bathroom," Justin said as he turned to leave.

"I'll help you," Travis said and he turned and followed his dad through the house.

Justin walked into the kitchen and grabbed the bottle of antibiotics off the counter and walked out the back door into the carport. Shogun and Scooter greeted them at the door and Justin and Travis immediately noticed the blood smeared across Scooter's back.

"Oh, no, Scooter, how did you manage to tear your stitches?" Justin said. Scooter's incision was partially ripped open and even though it had bled quite a bit, it had stopped bleeding now.

"Here's how," Travis said as he walked around the carport. Justin walked around to where Travis was standing. "He stood under my left front axle and rubbed it on the steering arm. You can see the blood and hair on it and on the floor," Travis said, pointing his finger at the floor.

"It must have been itching and he was scratching it," Justin said. "Even though it's quit bleeding we need to get it sewn back up."

"I'll call Jesse and see if she can sew him back up this morning. Maybe I can finally get an opportunity to ask her out on a date," Travis said as he went to retrieve his cell phone.

Justin pressed the button on the carport wall to raise the door so Shogun and Scooter could go use the bathroom and then went back into the kitchen to refill his coffee cup. Travis came in the kitchen followed by DeMac.

"I can't get an answer on her work number or her cell phone," Travis said. "She might have gone out of town since its Easter and their closed on Monday."

"She's probably still in bed. It's only six o'clock," DeMac said.

"You're probably right, DeMac," Travis said. "I'll take a shower and get ready to go and then try to call her. If I can't get her on the phone I'll drive over there and if she's not there I'll just drive over to Jefferson. There's an emergency animal clinic over there right across the street from where we ate pizza last night."

"Okay. I got to fix something to take to church for the covered dish lunch after the service so I'm going to get busy in this kitchen," Justin said. "If you get back in time come by and eat."

"You can count on that," Travis said.

Jesse was lying in bed wishing the rain hadn't stopped as early as it did because she was enjoying listening to it as she cuddled up under the covers. When she finally got home last night from sewing up Jake Bodenhiemer's horse she was totally exhausted so she took a shower and practically fell in bed. She needed to get on up and go feed the horses and let them out of the barn and then start doing laundry. She had been to busy this week to do laundry and everything she owned was dirty. After her shower last night she didn't even have a pair of clean panties to put on so she dug around in her drawers until she finally found a red thong that she had bought in college and put it on along with a tee shirt to wear to bed.

Jesse finally threw the covers back and got out of bed. She slipped on a pair of fuzzy bedroom slippers and walked out of her bedroom and down the stairs to the first floor of her two-story house to fix herself some coffee.

Jesse and her older brother Joshua had been raised in this house by their half-Cherokee grandmother and had never lived anywhere else. When Jesse was three and her brother Joshua was five, their father had killed their mother in a drunken rage and then killed himself. Jesse's grandmother raised them in the big two-story house and even though they were poor, there was always a lot of love and joy in this house. Their grandmother passed away three years ago and left the house and land to Jesse and Joshua and soon after that Jesse remodeled it. It would have been cheaper to have torn it down and built a new house rather than to remodel it, but there were too many good memories here to even consider tearing it down.

Jesse's brother Joshua was serving in the Army Special Forces in Afghanistan on his second tour there. He had joined the Army right after graduating from high school and Jesse missed him terribly sometimes since he was the only family she had left.

Jesse fixed her coffee maker and cut it on and then opened the back door to let Maggie in the kitchen to eat. Maggie was Jesse's Australian Shepherd and she watched out for everything on the farm, including Jesse. "Hey, girl! Good morning," Jesse said as she rubbed her head and back.

Jesse poured Maggie's food bowl full of Purina Dog Chow and poured some fresh water in her other bowl before pouring herself a cup of coffee, and sitting back down at the kitchen table. As soon as she finished feeding the horses and chickens and doing her laundry she was going to just relax until Tuesday. Running an animal clinic and a house all by herself didn't leave much time to do the things she enjoyed like reading and horseback riding and she was looking forward to having the next two days off.

Jesse got up and set her coffee cup on the counter and stepped over to the back door where a pair of dirty gray coveralls were hanging and started pulling them on. She would drink her cup of coffee when she got back from feeding the horses and chickens, but for now she wanted to get her outside chores done. Jesse stepped outside and slipped on a pair of knee high rubber boots and headed to the barn with Maggie trotting ahead of her. Jesse's three horses were snorting and nickering in anticipation of their morning meal as Jesse opened the door to the barn. She poured a large scoop of mixed grain into the food trough in each stall and tore off a section of hay from a bail for each horse before opening the back door of the barn so the horses could go out in the pasture and graze. Then Jesse got a large scoop of chicken feed and headed for the chicken house. Jesse opened the door of the chicken house and scattered the feed for her thirty domineckers to fight over when Maggie suddenly growled and took off running. Jesse ran to the door and saw Maggie tearing across the pasture about forty feet behind a gray fox.

"Get him, girl! Get him, Maggie!" Jesse hollered as the fox and Maggie went over the hill and out of sight. She didn't have to worry about her chickens as long as Maggie was around. Jesse walked back to the house and stepped inside and shut the door. She pulled off her coveralls and tee shirt and threw them in the washing machine along with some other dirty clothes and started the water running before heading for the upstairs bathroom to retrieve the overflowing laundry hamper. Just as Jesse stepped on the first step she heard the three kittens meowing on the back porch.

"Oh, I forgot to feed the kittens," she said out loud and headed for the kitchen to get the cat food and a carton of milk. Jesse walked back to the back door before it dawned on her that she didn't have anything to slip on to go outside and feed the kittens. She wasn't wearing anything but a red thong but she wasn't going to be outside but just long enough to pour some cat food and milk in a bowl.

Jesse had a special crate on the back porch for kittens since people thought that the local veterinarian was responsible for raising all the unwanted kittens in the county. The crate's roof was hinged so that it could be raised to put kittens in or take them out and also for feeding them. In one corner of the crate was a litter box and in the opposite corner was a box with towels in it for them to sleep on. Jesse had also rigged up an electric heater underneath the box of towels to keep them warm on cold nights. When Jesse got home last night she placed the kittens in the box and fed them and also plugged up the heater before she went inside.

Jesse looked around for something handy to slip on but didn't see anything, so she stepped outside wearing just the red thong and slipped on the knee high rubber boots before stepping over to the crate to feed the kittens.

Travis took his shower and got ready to take Scooter to Jesse's to get him sewn up and most of all to ask her out on a date. Travis stepped in the kitchen to tell his dad he was leaving but the smell of food cooking made him suddenly hungry.

Justin had fixed a large bowl of green beans and corn and had baked two pans of yeast rolls plus he boiled two dozen eggs to make deviled eggs.

Travis couldn't resist. "Can I have a boiled egg?" He asked.

"Yeah, man. Grab a couple eggs and a couple hot yeast rolls. There's butter and jelly in the refrigerator and some sourwood honey in the cabinet if you want some," Justin said. Travis put a couple boiled eggs on a plate along with a yeast roll and then grabbed the butter and honey before he sat down to eat.

"Where's DeMac?" Travis asked.

"He went for a run," Justin answered as he poured Travis a glass of sweet tea and sat down beside him.

"Dad, this guardian angel thing is kind of freaking me out. I believe you because you wouldn't say it if it weren't true, but I don't understand it," Travis said. "Do you hear a voice or what?"

"No, I don't hear a voice or see visions or anything like that. I don't really understand it myself to tell you the truth. I just get a strange feeling and I know something is about to happen," Justin said.

"Maybe you're a psychic or something?" Travis said.

"I think if I was psychic I would know it. The bible says that there are angels among us and I believe that a guardian angel has been looking out after me most of my life. I'm no bible scholar but that's what I believe for whatever it's worth," Justin said as the phone started ringing. Justin got up and answered it. "Hello?"

"Justin, this is Teresa Owens. You cleared my driveway for me yesterday evening."

"Oh, yeah. Hi, Teresa. You got another tree down?"

"Oh no, it's nothing like that. I felt bad for not paying you something for all that hard work so I decided that if you wouldn't take money from me, maybe I could fix you a meal. Would you be interested in eating lunch with me today?" Teresa asked.

"Well, Teresa, I appreciate the offer but we're eating a covered dish dinner after church today in the fellowship hall."

"Oh, I see," Teresa said. "Well, would tomorrow be any better?"

"Tomorrow would be perfect," Justin answered. "Would dinner be as good for you as lunch, say maybe six or seven o'clock?"

"Yes, that would be fine with me. What would you like to eat?" Teresa asked. "What about spaghetti and a tossed salad?" Justin suggested.

"That's sounds good to me," Teresa said. "So I'll see you around six or seven o'clock."

"I'll be there, and thanks for inviting me," Justin said.

"You're welcome. Bye now," Teresa said and then hung up.

Justin grinned at Travis. He knew that there had been some chemistry between Teresa and him when they stood on her deck and watched the deer drinking water.

"What are you grinning at?" Travis asked.

"Well, I don't know if you'll get a date with Jesse or not, but your old man has a date with that hot little redhead tomorrow night at seven o'clock at her house," Justin announced as he walked across the kitchen holding his hands up like he was signaling a touchdown.

"You old dog you," Travis said. "I got to get out of here."

Travis got up and went outside and loaded Scooter in his Jeep before heading toward Jesse's house. When Travis got in sight of Jesse's house he could see both her vehicles parked in the carport so he figured she was at home. He stopped after he turned into her driveway and dialed her number again. There was no answer so he drove up beside the house and parked. It was obvious that no one ever went to the front door so Travis picked up Scooter carefully and headed around to the back. As soon as Travis turned the corner he found himself staring at Jesse from behind as she bent over a crate wearing nothing but a red thong and a pair of rubber boots. It was quite a sight to say the least.

"There you go, kitties," Jesse said as she straightened back up and shut the lid. Jesse turned around and started for the door when she saw Travis and screamed. "Ahhhhh!" she screamed as she ran through the back door. "What are you doing here?" she hollered through the door.

"Scooter tore his stitches loose!" Travis hollered back.

"Why didn't you call before you came nosing around here?" Jesse said furiously.

"I did! I tried to call your office and your cell phone three or four times and couldn't get an answer. I'm sorry I scared you, Jesse," Travis said.

Jesse stepped over to the kitchen counter and checked her cell phone. She was so tired when she got in last night that she forgot to plug it in and it was completely dead. Jesse's face was as red as the thong that she was wearing. Of all the outfits to be caught out in she would have to be wearing a red thong and knee-high rubber boots. Jesse glanced out the kitchen window and saw Maggie coming for the house as hard as she could run. She knew that Maggie probably heard her scream and would attack Travis when she got to him.

"Come on in! Come in quick, my dog is after you!" she hollered as she grabbed a towel and wrapped it around her.

Travis saw the dog just in time and he jerked open the back door and jumped inside. Maggie was growling and scratching the door trying to get to Travis so Jesse told him to turn around and face the other way while she let Maggie know that everything was all right. She then told Travis to stay there while she went upstairs and got dressed.

Travis had never felt more awkward than he felt right now. His intentions were to ask Jesse out but he didn't know what to do now. Jesse returned in a couple minutes wearing a pair of jeans and a sweat shirt and Travis could tell that she was angry about the intrusion. She threw a sheet over the kitchen table and told Travis to place Scooter on the sheet.

"How did he tear them open?" Jesse asked.

"He got under my Jeep and rubbed his back against the steering arm last night," Travis said.

"It was probably itching. I'll give you some cream to put on it when you leave to keep it from itching him so bad. Let me get my bag and I'll sew him up right here," Jesse said as she turned and left. She returned in a few minutes with a medical bag and a tray full of instruments.

"I'm going to give him a local anesthetic instead of putting him under so hold him tight. I don't want to get bit," she said sharply.

Travis held Scooter tight as Jesse injected the anesthetic and after the initial jerk he settled down and was fine. Jesse stood there waiting for the medicine to numb Scooter before she continued.

"Jesse, I'm sorry for surprising you like that. I wouldn't have done that intentionally for anything in the world," Travis said sincerely.

"You're having quite a weekend, aren't you? You got hooked up with Sheila last night and then got a peep show from me this morning. You're going to have some real stories to tell your buddies when you get back."

As enamored as Travis was with Jesse, her comment angered him. "Actually I'm having a real shitty weekend. I didn't want to get in that fight with Billy Billings but I felt like I should in order to rescue a girl that was in serious trouble, and now there's a feud between my dad and the Billings clan. Then Scooter got torn up and almost died before I could get him to you to be sewn up. And then I decided to go to town yesterday evening to ask you out on a date and was attacked at your clinic by Sheila who wrapped me up so tight I couldn't stop you when you drove off. And then I tried to call you several times this morning before I came over here, and even tried from your driveway and couldn't reach you, and when I walked around the house and surprised you it embarrassed me as much as you. And just for your peace of mind, you don't have to worry about me telling my buddies any stories about you because I'm not that kind of guy," Travis said firmly.

Jesse didn't know what to say so she just bent over Scooter and started stitching him back up. When she finished she washed him off and put some cream on the incision before handing the tube to Travis and removing her surgical gloves.

"This will keep the wound from itching as much but you might want to keep him away from your Jeep if you can since he knows he can scratch it there."

"Thank you," Travis said as he scooped up Scooter and headed for the back door.

"Travis, wait. I'm sorry for what I said. I shouldn't have assumed you were stopping to see Sheila and I shouldn't have assumed you would go brag to your buddies about what you saw. I was wrong and I apologize."

"That's okay, Jesse, just forget about it," Travis said. Travis started out the door again and Jesse stopped him again.

"I forgot to plug up my cell phone last night when I got home and it is completely dead. That's why you couldn't reach me on the phone."

"I swear to you that I tried to call you several times this morning," Travis said as he finally turned around to face her.

"I believe you."

"And I had no idea that Sheila was at the animal clinic last night when I stopped. She grabbed me as soon as your assistant opened the door and I thought I would never get away from her."

"You mean you didn't leave with her?"

"No, I didn't leave with her. She kept saying that we should go to a place called The Point, but I went back home and me and my buddy DeMac went to Jefferson and ate a pizza."

"The Point is where all the teenagers go to make out," Jesse said. "It's a ridge that overlooks the river."

"Oh, I thought it was a restaurant or a night club or something." Travis said. "Listen, Jesse, I didn't ask you out on Friday night because my dad said he would dance at your wedding and I thought you were engaged. I went to the clinic last night to ask you out and Sheila attacked me and I couldn't stop you when you left. I was going to ask you out this morning since I had to come over here anyway to get Scooter sewn back up and that has obviously blown up in my face. So for whatever reason it apparently wasn't meant to be. I haven't thought about anything but you since we met and I'm sorry that things have turned out the way they have, but I still think you're a beautiful and wonderful woman and I appreciate all you've done for Scooter," Travis said and then walked out the door carrying Scooter with both arms.

Jesse wanted to say something but couldn't think of anything before he went through the door. She knew that she had hurt his feelings and felt bad about it even though she did apologize to him. Nobody had ever told her that she was all they had been thinking about and that she was beautiful and wonderful, and now that somebody finally did she ran them off. Jesse put her head in her hands and wondered what was wrong with her.

Donald Crafton was standing inside the airplane hangar that covered the entrance of the Hideaway Hilton trying to catch his breath. He had just completed his thirtieth lap around the 100 × 140 foot metal building and was winded after the three mile run. Donald tried to run at least twice a week and then swim a few laps in the pool before the guests woke up.

Donald walked through the front doors of the underground hotel and headed for the pool. The foyer of the hotel was empty as he walked across the marble floor and under the magnificent chandelier that hung in the center. The only movement in the room was the ever turning ceiling fans as he made his way through the foyer and down the main hall. There were five guests presently staying at the hotel but they wouldn't be awake at this time of the morning.

Donald passed by room number one. It was occupied by Billy Hagee, or Wild Bill, whichever you preferred. Billy was a top ranked member of the California Hells Angels and supplied the mob with Crystal Meth and any kind of gun they wanted. There was a warrant in California for his arrest for drug trafficking and murder and the Hells Angels were hiding him until they could find the witness that was scheduled to testify against him in court. Donald figured that if they were unable to find and eliminate the witness, then they would make arrangements to pick Billy up and then execute him. There was no way they were going to let the US Marshals or the FBI get their hands on him. Billy knew way too much about the illegal dealings of the motorcycle gang. Since the Hells Angels were footing the bill for his stay, Billy couldn't leave until they made the arrangements for him to be picked up. He was a prisoner in a five-star hotel and was too dumb to even know it.

Donald walked by room number two. It was actually occupied by two guests, but since one of them was the son of Jimmy Milano, and they were staying in the same room, they were only paying for one guest. Sonny Milano, and his personal bodyguard Quai Son Bien, were occupying room number two together. Sonny was wanted for aggravated assault, kidnapping, and rape. His bodyguard was wanted as an accessory since he was present and did nothing to stop it. Sonny's girlfriend had decided to break up with him after catching him with another woman and told him so in front of a crowd of people at a restaurant one night. Sonny dragged her out to his car by her hair and then drove her to an isolated spot where he repeatedly beat her and raped her as Quai Son Bien looked on. Sonny and Quai would have to stay at the hotel until Jimmy could convince Sonny's girlfriend and her family to drop the charges. Donald didn't think it would take very long for that to happen.

Room three was empty but room four was occupied by Ricky Stone. Tricky Ricky was the mobs main man in Atlanta and was wanted for drug trafficking and money laundering. Ricky had got careless and was busted by an undercover agent wearing a hidden microphone. As soon as he posted bond he fled to Chicago and they sent him straight to the Hideaway Hilton. The mob wasn't sure what to do with Ricky, but like the Hells Angels, they weren't going to let him be arrested. The only difference was that he knew it and Wild Bill Hagee didn't.

Donald traveled down the hallway until he passed room number six. It was occupied by Mike Savalous. Mike was from Miami, Florida, and transported huge amounts of drugs from Jamaica and the Caribbean Islands and also dumped hazardous waste into the ocean. The warrants for his arrest were for illegal dumping and tax evasion. Donald refused to send a plane to pick him up at first because there was so much heat on him. Then Jimmy Milano agreed to fly him to a secluded airstrip in Tennessee, so Donald finally agreed to send a plane for him. Mike was a multimillionaire and was just waiting for the heat to die down before he flew down to his mansion somewhere in the Caribbean Islands.

And finally, all the way at the other end of the hall in room number nine, was their Egyptian guest, Maschiek Abdullah Inacio. Donald agreed to let Maschiek stay there only because the arrangements were made through Jimmy Milano. Jimmy said that there were no warrants out for Maschiek and that he was not a criminal, but there were certain religious extremists trying to find Maschiek to kill him and he needed a safe place to stay for a couple months until his people could make arrangements to hide him somewhere else. Jimmy also said that Maschiek would pay double the going rate if they would take him so Donald agreed to let him come.

Donald turned at the end of the hall and walked toward the pool It was a magnificent pool just like everything else in the hotel. It was perfectly round and was one hundred feet in diameter. It was surrounded by the same kind of marble that was in the foyer and it was beautifully lighted and heated to the perfect temperature. There was a five-meter diving platform on the deep end that could be flooded to create a waterfall, and the shallow end had an adjoining hot tub and a marble table for the guests to set their food and drinks without ever leaving the pool.

Donald was wearing a pair of swim trunks underneath his sweatpants so he shucked off his pants and walked down the marble steps into the luxurious water and started swimming laps at a leisurely pace. After three laps around the pool Donald was tired and leaned back against the marble steps with just his head out of the water. He was thinking about the Egyptian guest, Maschiek Abdullah Inacio. Something was very strange about this man. He hardly ever left his room and when he did he always carried that empty suitcase with him wherever he went. They had inspected the suitcase before they let him on the plane and it was completely empty, but ·yet he insisted that the suitcase remain with him at all times. Donald wanted to know what was so special about that suitcase and why this man needed to stay hidden. He didn't completely buy their story about hiding from radical religious groups. Donald knew why all the other guests were hiding, especially Mike Savalous. Everybody was looking for him, the FBI, the IRS, the EPA, the Coast Guard, the US Marshals, the Florida Fish and Wildlife, and God only knows who else. He was featured on Americas Most Wanted last week on television so everybody knows what he looks like. All that trouble over dumping some chemicals in the ocean. Donald suddenly sat straight up on the marble steps. He had a great idea.

When Justin and DeMac drove up to the New River Baptist Church the first thing that caught their eye was Carol's shiny Toyota Camry. It was the only vehicle in the church parking lot that was clean and it stood out like a peacock in a room full of ducks. Carol met them at the door and hugged both of them. She thanked DeMac for cleaning up her car and thanked Justin for his "gracious hospitality." All the people in the church were decked out in their finest clothes and the church was full of smiling faces and noisy conversations as friends and neighbors caught up on the latest gossip. It always lifted Justin's spirits to see this tight knit group of hardworking people gather to worship. The pastor, Reverend Mark McDowell, preached on the resurrection as everyone expected him to, and after the service was over everyone headed to the fellowship hall to eat. Travis was waiting outside when Justin and DeMac went to the truck to get rid of their coats and ties.

"You're just in time to eat," Justin said. "Did you get Scooter fixed up?"

"Yeah," Travis said. "Jesse was at home but her cell phone was dead. She sewed him back up and gave us some cream to help keep it from itching."

"Well, good," Justin said. "Did you ask her out while you were there?"

"No, not really. I was going to but when I walked up to her house I caught her standing outside practically naked and she got mad and then I got mad, so it's just something that's not going to happen."

"I'm sorry to hear that, Hoss," Justin said. "Well, let's go eat and maybe you'll feel better."

"I think I'll just go home dad. I'm not really hungry."

Justin knew that Travis was heartbroken but there wasn't anything he could do about it. Like any dad he wished he could make him feel better but sometimes the best thing to do is to do nothing.

"Okay, Hoss. I'll fix you a plate before I leave and bring it home for you to eat later."

"Thanks, Dad. I'll see you at the house."

Donald Crafton walked in the kitchen in Jack's house and poured himself a cup of coffee. He had showered and dressed after his three mile run and three laps around the pool and he felt good as he headed for Jack's office. When Donald approached Jack's office he could here someone talking so he stopped and knocked before looking in. Cecil Wood was looking over some papers with Jack and Jack told Donald to come on in.

"Cecil and I were just looking over this background check on Justin Hayes," Jack said as he slid the paperwork across the desk for Donald to inspect.

Donald picked the papers up and began reading. Justin Hayes, born 9-23-1949, Father William E. Hayes (Lutheran minister), Mother-Mary Louise Harper (school teacher), both deceased, Sister-Rebecca Ann. Graduated High School-1968. Joined the Army-1968. Went to Vietnam November of 1968. 3rd Infantry Battalion. Decorated Sniper (47 confirmed kills). Came home December 1969. Married Kathy Sue Lambeth (May 1972). Son Travis Lee (2-12-81). Divorced March 1992. Employed with Triad Power and Light as a lineman for thirty-four years. Retired March 2004. CRIMINAL RECORD none. FINANCIAL INFORMATION: Income $2,286 retirement monthly, 401K $218,000 invested, Received $227,000 inheritance in 2004, Received $186,000 for sale of property in Davidson county in 2004. Diploma in Gunsmithing from Montgomery Technical Institute in Troy, NC (2002), Additional Information-Ranked as a Grand Master Class Shooter by the International Defensive Handgun Association.

"Looks like our boy Justin is clean as a pin," Donald said. "I don't think I want him shooting at me since he was a sniper in Vietnam and is ranked as a Grand Master Class Shooter by the IDHA."

"That's why he got the jump on Johnny when we were up there talking to him," Jack said. "Hell, he's a professional. He had his pistol pointed at Johnny before Johnny's hand even touched his pistol."

"Were going to have to be real careful with this guy," Cecil said. "I don't see any weakness in him."

"I have an idea about how we can get him arrested," Donald said.

Jack perked up. Donald's ideas were usually well thought out and sometimes brilliant. "How?"

"We can pour chemicals in the river right in front of his house and cause an environmental disaster. There would be an immediate

fish kill and the North Carolina Wildlife Department would investigate it and call the EPA as soon as they realized that there were
chemicals involved. The chemicals would be traced back upstream
to the exact spot where they were poured in. The chemicals we use
need to be the kind of chemicals that only a gunsmith would have
like copper remover, powder solvent, zinc phosphate, oxnate no.7, or
super stripper. With Justin being a gunsmith and the chemicals being
poured in the river right in front of his house, they would definitely
issue a warrant and arrest him," Donald said.

"That's brilliant," Jack said. "The clean up would cost at least a
million dollars and if they set a bond it would be more than he could
probably raise. People wouldn't be surprised he was found hung to
death in his jail cell."

"It is brilliant," Cecil said. "If the locals thought he poisoned
the river they would be glad that he hung himself."

"There's a supplier in Tennessee that has all those chemicals in
stock according to the computer. I could get Coy or Jerry to fly up
there tomorrow and pick them up if you want me to," Donald said.

"Go ahead and send them to get it. Will dump them tomorrow
night. I want that son of a bitch out of there as quick as possible,"
Jack said. "I'll tell the sheriff to expect a new prisoner."

Justin and DeMac sat in the fellowship hall of the New River
Baptist Church and ate like they were possessed. Justin's plate was
mounded up with fried chicken, succotash, potato salad, deviled
eggs, ham, cranberry sauce, candied yams, and of course Carol's
chicken and dumplings. It was a feast to behold and neither man was
going to waste it. After fifteen minutes of speed eating, Justin and
DeMac went to the dessert table. DeMac got a piece of pecan pie
and a scoop of homemade pineapple ice cream and Justin got a slice
of sweet potato pie and a double scoop of banana pudding. When
they returned to their seats Wade Shavers was standing there waiting

for them. Wade was fourteen years old and lived with his family all the way at the other end of River Road. The Shaver farm was the first farm on the left after you turned off of Highway 117 onto River Road and they mainly raised sheep.

"Hey, Wade. How are you?" Justin asked.

"Mr. Hayes, I got a rifle that needs some work done on it and I heard you were a gunsmith. Do you think you could look at it for me sometime?" Wade said, looking at the floor. "I got some money."

"What kind of rifle is it, Wade?" Justin asked.

"It's a Remington .308 and it's not accurate anymore. I can't hit a five-gallon bucket with it."

"I like to work on Remingtons. Why don't you bring it by the house tomorrow and we'll look at it," Justin said.

"Okay, Mr. Hayes. I appreciate it," Wade said and then turned and walked away.

"That boy looks like he just lost his best friend." DeMac said.

"He sure did. He's got something on his mind besides a rifle that's gone sour," Justin said. "Maybe I can find out what's bothering him tomorrow when he comes over."

Travis went through his closet until he found his favorite karate Gi. He had worn this Gi when he won the Battle of the USA in Washington, DC, in 2002 while he was stationed at Fort Mead, Maryland. He had entered the tournament on a whim and fought his way through all the competitors until he won first place. He remembered the championship match like it was yesterday. The guy he fought was awesome but he was also very predictable. One of Travis's friends from the ship's photo lab had videoed the guy fighting on Saturday so Travis could study the film that night in his hotel room. When the championship match started on Sunday, Travis knew what this guy was going to do before he even did it. When Travis got back to the base late Sunday night carrying the six foot tall first place trophy his shipmates had a surprise party waiting for him and they stayed up all night celebrating.

Travis changed into his Gi and started outside when the phone rang.

"Hello?" Travis answered.

"Hey, Hoss. You all right?" Justin asked.

"Yeah, I'm fine. I'm a little disappointed but I'll be all right," Travis said.

"Me and DeMac are going to ride up and down the river and look for some good places to fish. We can come by and pick you up if you want to ride along," Justin said.

"That's okay, Dad. I appreciate the offer but I think I'll just hang out here for awhile."

"Okay then. That heavy punching bag is in the storage closet in the machine shop if you want to work out. We're going to ride around some before we come home."

"Okay, Dad. I'll see you guys when you get here," Travis said.

Justin hung up DeMac's cell phone and handed it back to him. "He's going to stay at home and beat the shit out of that punching bag. He always does when he's pissed off."

Travis hung up the phone and started toward the machine shop. He grinned and shook his head when he thought about his dad reminding him where the punching bag was.

"I guess I'm pretty predictable too," he said to Shogun and Scooter as he walked through the carport.

Jesse unlocked the front door of the animal hospital and stepped inside. She walked to the back of the building to check on the patients but that wasn't the real reason that she had driven back to town. All the patients appeared to be doing fine so she went to the front desk and booted up the computer. A note was taped on the computer screen from Stephen White, the man that Jesse hired to look after the animals on the weekends. It said that Zach, the Schnauzer in kennel number 3, had thrown up after he fed him this morning. Jesse wasn't surprised since Zach was still recovering from being poisoned two days ago. Jesse figured that Stephen probably tried to call her, but like Travis, was unable to reach her because her cell phone was dead.

Jesse walked back to the kennel and checked on Zach again. He seemed to be doing fine but just to be on the safe side she gave him a medicine dropper full of penicillin. When she finished she walked back to the front and sat down at the computer. Jesse pulled up the patient list and scrolled down until she saw the name Justin Hayes. She clicked on it and took a pen and wrote the phone number on a post-it note.

After a fifteen-minute stretching regimen Travis attacked the bag with a fury. He had hung the punching bag in the center of the carport on a hook that he guessed his dad had put there just for that purpose. Shogun and Scooter sat and watched and occasionally whined as Travis struck the bag with palm heel and knife hand strikes. Travis was soon totally consumed with his attack. He led with a front kick and then a jumping side kick and then finished with a back fist. The combinations of hand strikes and kicks soon took on a rhythm as Travis quit trying to choreograph his moves and let it happen naturally. He could hear his sensei in the background saying, "Empty your mind. Quit planning your next move. Relax and breathe. Let your moves come naturally like dancing." It took five years of training before that ever happened, but when it did it was the greatest feeling on earth. Instead of tensing up for a fight you just relaxed and let your training dictate your blocks and strikes.

Travis finally collapsed onto the concrete floor and just laid there soaking wet and totally exhausted. The cool concrete floor felt good to him as he caught his breath and relaxed. Shogun and Scooter walked over to him and made sure he was all right before they laid down beside him.

Travis's mind soon went back to thinking about Jesse. He thought about Friday night when Jesse first sewed up Scooter's incision and how she looked up at him and smiled with those perfect teeth and how beautiful she was at that moment. He remembered how when she touched him a jolt ran through his body like he was being shocked with a cattle prod. He thought he understood for the first time why people sometimes said they fell in love with somebody as soon as they saw them. Travis had never felt the way he felt now about anybody and he wondered how he could love somebody that he didn't even know.

The phone in the kitchen started ringing and snapped Travis out of his trance. Lying on the cool concrete felt so good he started not to answer it but he was afraid not to since his dad and DeMac were out cruising around. He hopped up and ran into the kitchen and answered it on the fourth ring.

"Hello?" Travis said, panting.

"Travis, is that you?" the voice said.

"Yes, this is Travis. Who is this?"

"It's Jesse. You sound like you're out of breath."

"I am out of breath. I've been working out," Travis said as he tried to picture Jesse on the other end.

"I called to apologize to you for the way I acted this morning," Jesse said sincerely.

"You have already apologized Jesse and I totally understand why you were angry and why you said what you did and I don't blame you one bit."

"I know but I feel terrible about it."

"Don't beat yourself up about it Jesse. Really, everything is just fine. I accept your apology," Travis said.

"So everything is okay between you and me?" Jesse asked.

"Yes, everything is fine between us."

"Then what time are you going to pick me up?"

"Excuse me. What did you say?"

"I said, what time are you going to pick me up for our date?"

"Uh, I, are you asking me for a date?" Travis stammered.

"No, I'm accepting your offer. You said you wanted to take me out on a date and I need to know when you're coming," Jesse said.

"Well, uh—"

"Tomorrow evening around seven o'clock would be good," Jesse suggested.

"Well, yes, certainly, I'll be there at seven o'clock," Travis said.

"Just dress casual if you want to. We'll go eat a pizza or something if that's okay with you."

"That sounds great to me."

"I'll see you at seven o'clock. That's p.m., not a.m.," Jesse said, grinning.

"I'll be there. Thank you for asking, I mean, accepting my offer," Travis said.

"You're welcome. Bye."

"Whoopee!" Travis screamed as he ran out the kitchen door almost knocking Justin and DeMac down in the carport. Travis ran around the house hollering as Justin and DeMac looked on.

"Well, he either got a date with Jesse or he found my white liquor," Justin said.

"If your white liquor makes you feel like that, I want a glassful!" DeMac said as Travis made another lap by the carport.

Spring Is in the Air

Gyurman Yahamen Tahare-Azar sat in his room and watched the news on CNN. The war in Afghanistan and in Iraq was the only part of the news that interested him, but he watched all the news and another program called "Pimp My Ride" where they took automobiles and did ridiculous things to them. He was afraid that if he watched only the news about the war that it could lead to suspicion if they were watching him. He had been assured that there were no cameras or listening devices in his room, but he did not believe the filthy Americans. His brothers in Afghanistan and Iraq were counting on him to help them with their next attack on American soil. The next attack would make the first one look like a child's game thanks to the magnificent suitcase. He turned and looked at the suitcase standing against the wall. Such a simple looking thing but he knew that there was nothing simple about it. It was very sophisticated and way beyond his understanding even though he had a degree in engineering from Florida State University.

He had taken his phony passport that showed his name as Maschiek Abdullah Ignacio and flown from Egypt to New York and stood at the baggage claim waiting for the police to come and arrest him, but the suitcase soon came in sight so he picked it up and walked through the airport. The suitcase was loaded with trace amounts of all the ingredients necessary to create a "dirty bomb." A bomb that would kill one hundred thousand of the American dogs instead of the measly three thousand that were killed at the World Trade Center.

Gyurman thought that they were probably following him to see where he went with the suitcase and would arrest him later, so he walked out the front door of the airport and hailed a cab. He took the cab to the Red Roof Inn and sat in his room for two days waiting for the FBI to knock down the door and arrest him, but they never came. So he took a cab back to the airport and bought another ticket from a different airline and flew to Atlanta International Airport. There again he waited to be arrested but it didn't happen. After spending five days in Atlanta, Gyurman flew to Denver and then back to Chicago with still no arrest and no one following him. It was amazing that the x-rays and the bomb sniffing dogs and even the "sniffing machine" at the Chicago airport couldn't detect the chemicals that had been placed in the suitcase.

After waiting a week in Chicago he called the number that he was given by his contact and was flown to a remote landing strip where he was loaded on another small plane and blindfolded before he was flown here to wait for instructions from the Al Qaida leadership. He had removed the contents of the suitcase and flushed them down the public toilet in the Chicago hotel before he left so the suitcase was completely empty now.

Gyurman knew that no one really expected the suitcase to actually work and they were caught off guard when it did. They expected him to be immediately arrested and the suitcase confiscated. The man waiter, Mr. Tussey, had delivered a message to him that said he would receive a call today regarding his departure. The time of reckoning was near.

Travis was lying in bed watching the ceiling fan turn and thinking about his date with Jesse tonight. The anticipation had kept him from sleeping for most of the night but he didn't care. There was something very special about her and he couldn't wait to spend some time with her without having to hold a bleeding dog while they were talking. Meeting her last Friday night had completely consumed him and he couldn't quit thinking about her regardless of where he was or what he was doing.

DeMac cracked the door open and peeped in.

"Come in. I'm awake, man," Travis said.

"Let's go get a cup of coffee. Come on," DeMac said.

When DeMac and Travis walked in the kitchen they saw Justin sitting at the dining room table writing a letter and he had the pictures that Travis had taken of the monster truck scattered across the table. They got a cup of coffee and joined him.

"Well, we can't fish today, DeMac," Justin said. "It poured rain last night and the river is up and roaring like a runaway locomotive. It's also so muddy a trout couldn't see your fly unless you bounced it off his nose. It'll be two days before it calms down and clears up."

"I heard it raining last night when I got up to piss. It was really coming down around three o'clock," DeMac said.

"Yeah, I heard it too. At one o'clock, at two o'clock, at three o'clock, at four o'clock, et cetera, et cetera," Travis said, grinning. "What are you writing, Dad?"

"I'm enclosing a note with these pictures. It says,

Dear News People.

Recently when I was trout fishing on the New River, a monster truck came driving right down the middle of the river, turning over rocks and stirring up mud and trash and killing fish. If I would have had my pistol I would have shot that

ignorant son of a bitch in the head but I didn't.
I did have my camera on me and was able to get
these here pictures. I can't take these to the sheriff's department 'cause they got a warrant for my
arrest on account of I ain't paid my child support
in three months, so I thought I would just give
'em to you. I hope they arrest those dumb asses
and throw them in jail. They better hope I ain't
in there with them when they do.

A concerned citizen.

Travis and DeMac both laughed out loud.

"Who are you going to send them to?" Travis asked.

"I'm sending one envelope to the CNN building in Charlotte,
and another envelope to the Fox 8 building in Jefferson."

"But the mail isn't running today since its Easter Monday,"
DeMac said.

"I know. I'm not sending them in the mail," Justin said.
"Lawrence Cody is a courier for On Time Delivery. They deliver legal
papers, medical supplies, DNA and urine specimens, and whatever
else someone wants hand delivered. I talked to Lawrence at church
yesterday and he said the CNN building in Charlotte was two blocks
from their office and he's driving down there this evening, so he's
going to deliver it for me. He said to just leave it in my mailbox
and he would swing by and pick it up when he left. I told him that
I didn't want to be identified as the sender and he assured me he
wouldn't tell a soul. Now I need to figure out a way to deliver the
other envelope to Fox 8 in Jefferson late this evening. They probably
got surveillance cameras in the parking lot and in the lobby, so I don't
want to deliver it myself. Besides, I got a hot date at seven o'clock,"
Justin said and winked at Travis.

"I'll take it for you," DeMac said. "I can put on a disguise and walk in and drop it on the front desk and then turn around and leave. No problem."

"If me and Dad are both out on dates you won't have anything to drive," Travis said.

"I can drop your dad off at Teresa's and then come back and leave the truck at Teresa's and jog back here to the house. It's only seven miles."

"Or we could take my canoe and you could canoe back to the house after you dropped off the truck," Justin said.

"That sounds good to me. I'll drop the package, bring the truck back to Teresa's house, and then canoe back down the river until I get back here," DeMac said. "There should be just enough daylight to pull that off."

"Which pictures are you going to send?" Travis asked.

"This picture with Billy throwing the beer bottles out the truck window and this picture with all the phone numbers on the tailgate," Justin said. "I'm also going to send this picture. Do you see the road sign in the background?"

"Yeah, I see it but I can't read it," DeMac said.

Travis studied the picture and finally saw the road sign in between some trees in the distance. "Now I see it." It was the picture that Travis took when Billy was doing a wheelie when he left the river. A sign on River Road was just barely visible in the background.

"If they magnify that picture they should be able to read it. It says, 'No outlet. Road ends 5.6 miles.' That should give them all the information they need to locate the scene of the crime," Justin said with a grin.

"I think the fecal material is about to hit the rotating blades," DeMac said.

"Yeah, and the shit's about to hit the fan too!" Travis said.

"Go back to bed, Romeo!" Justin said.

Ozzie Curry sat on the edge of his cot in the old tobacco barn that the Seals were calling home these days and ate a pear as Jimmy Hardy did a radio check with all the sniper hides. They had five sniper hides with a two man team in each one. There was one sniper hide directly across from Justin's house and another one to the right of Justin's up near the top of the mountain. The other three sniper hides were surrounding Jack's house. One was directly in front of Jack's across the south fork of the river, one was to the right of Jack's on top of the mountain, and one was behind Jack's house on the other side of the mountain and across the north fork of the river overlooking the airplane hangar and the landing strip.

Ozzie, or as the team called him, Wizard, stood up and stretched before walking over to the spotting scope that they had trained on the groundhog hole where Moe, Larry, and Curly were living now. The Seals were taking twenty-four-hour shifts in the sniper hides and changing teams every night at 2400 hours, so he had seventeen hours to kill before he went back to work. Wizard looked through the spotting scope to see if the baby groundhogs were out feeding yet. The Seals had grown attached to the little fellows over the last two days. There wasn't anything to do when you were off duty except to clean your gear and watch the baby groundhogs as they cleaned out their den and grazed on the new grass that was popping up in the meadow. The Seals had been supplementing the baby groundhog's diet with apples and pears by throwing the fruit down in their hole when they left at night to hike to their sniper hides. Wizard didn't see the baby groundhogs so he stepped over to their makeshift kitchen to fix himself a cup of coffee.

"Eagle, this is Chief," a voice came over the communications network speaker.

"Go ahead, Chief," Jimmy Hardy said.

"Tell the guys to keep an eye on the babies. When I walked by there last night there were bobcat tracks everywhere. Over."

"Roger that, Chief," Jimmy said.

Billy Roe was the newest member of DeMac's Seal team but had already proved to all the team that he could be trusted to do his part. They called him Chief because he was a full blooded Cherokee Indian from Oklahoma. Chief always saw booby-traps and tracks before anyone else so they kept him on point when they were traveling through enemy territory. If he said there were bobcat tracks around the hole then you could bet on it.

Wizard took a swallow of his coffee and stepped back to the spotting scope. Now there was a baby groundhog standing at the entrance of their den, looking for any sign of danger before stepping out in the open. Wizard slowly pivoted the spotting scope from left to right on the tripod to see if there was any sign of the bobcat that Chief warned them about. He then pivoted the scope back across from right to left and was satisfied that all was clear until he twitched his ear. If a fly hadn't been flying around the big cat's ear he would have remained motionless, as only a cat can, and Wizard would have never seen him. He was hunched down on top of the rock pile, and blended in so perfectly, that when you blinked your eyes you momentarily lost sight of him.

"He's up there!" Wizard shouted. "He's on top of the rock pile waiting for them to come out!" he said as he stepped across the room and grabbed his McMillan 50-caliber sniper rifle.

"You can't shoot that damn thing in here," Jimmy said. "The building would probably fall in and none of us would ever be able to hear again."

"Well, I'm not going to let that pussycat eat those baby groundhogs," Wizard shouted.

"Let me take care of it. I got just the thing for this operation," Jimmy said as he stepped over to the CIA footlocker and unlocked it. Jimmy quickly removed an aluminum gun case from the footlocker and unsnapped the latches. He started pulling out pieces of a rifle and snapping them together. He twisted the barrel onto the action and then snapped a skeletonized plastic stock onto the back of it. Then he pulled out a scope and snapped it into place before grabbing a magazine full of cartridges and slamming it into the bottom of the rifle. Jimmy jerked the bolt back and then rammed it forward, shoving a round into the chamber before tossing the rifle across the room to Wizard.

Wizard caught the rifle and quickly shoved it through the large crack that they were using to watch their adopted babies and looked through the rifle scope. When he finally found the groundhog den in the scope's field of view he could see that one of the groundhogs had walked out into the meadow and another one was standing at the entrance to their den. He shifted the crosshairs over to the rock pile and desperately searched for the bobcat that blended in perfectly with the gray and tan colored stones.

"Hold about five inches high at that distance," Jimmy said. "It's about two hundred yards to the tree line."

All the Seals were up now, looking through any crack that they could find with binoculars and rifle scopes.

"He's still on the rock pile but he's fixing to jump," Duke said.

Finally the outline of the big cat materialized in the scope and Wizard started to squeeze the trigger when the bobcat gathered his legs underneath him and leapt off the rock pile toward the unsuspecting groundhogs. Wizard jerked the trigger but the rifle didn't fire. It just went "phssst" and didn't even jump from the recoil.

"You hit him but you need to finish him off," Snake said. "He's wounded."

Wizard was confused but he jerked the bolt back on the strange rifle and watched as a smoking brass case came flying out of the chamber, so he slammed the bolt back shut and peered back through the scope. The bobcat was cutting flips in the edge of the meadow so

Wizard timed his next shot so that it would arrive just when the cat would hit the ground.

"Phsst" was the only sound and the bobcat lay motionless where it hit the ground.

"Good shot, Wizard," Snake said. "And just in time too!"

"I thought the rifle misfired! I didn't know I even fired a shot, much less that I hit him," Wizard said as he examined the strange looking rifle. "What is this thing, Jimmy?"

"It's a custom-built take-down rifle chambered in 6.5 mm Whisper. The cartridge was designed by J. D. Jones about twenty years ago to be used in sound-suppressed rifles. It's based on a .221 Remington case necked up to hold a 6.5 millimeter bullet, and since the bullet is subsonic and never breaks the sound barrier, there is no crack when you fire it. It shoots 155-grain bullets at close to one thousand feet a second."

Smitty had been watching the show with binoculars and suddenly started laughing. "Did you see those groundhogs when that bobcat landed in the grass and started cutting flips? They started running around in circles trying to figure out what to do. I think the three stooges is a good name for them."

"Eagle, this is Chief. I got a young white male on a four-wheeler approaching the Rabbit Den. Occupant is armed with a bolt action rifle with a scope."

"Roger that, Chief, we're expecting him. He's a friend of the Rabbit," Jimmy said. "Oh, by the way, Bobcat has been eliminated by the Wizard. Thanks for the heads up."

"Right on, Wizard, I mean Eagle! I didn't hear the shot," Chief said.

"Neither did we!" Jimmy said smiling.

DeMac squeezed off another shot from the .45-caliber pistol that Justin called "Heinz 57." It was the fourth shot that he had fired and there was still only one ragged hole in the target that was hanging at twenty-five yards. This pistol may have been put together with scrap parts, but it was put together right, DeMac thought to himself. He fired shot number 5 and 6 in the same ragged hole but shot number 7 went to the right about a half an inch.

"Good shooting, DeMac," Justin said. Justin and DeMac were both wearing electronic ear muffs that blocked out the blast of the gunshot but allowed you to hear normal conversations.

"That pistol is sweet," DeMac said.

"I'm going to shoot the OK Corral," Justin said. "You have to double-tap each silhouette and then do a speed reload and double-tap each silhouette again, and then do another speed reload and shoot the nine inch gong at fifty yards. Justin had hung four silhouette targets at twenty-five yards. The first three targets were just standard silhouette targets that were an outline of a man's body, but the fourth target was a hostage target that displayed a mean looking fugitive holding a woman hostage in front of him with a knife to her throat. The only target area on the hostage target was the fugitive's face, which looked awful small at twenty-five yards. A stray bullet could easily hit the hostage and that would automatically disqualify you if you were shooting in a match.

Justin stepped up to the open shutters in the shooting room and faced the silhouettes. He was wearing a well worn Safariland Speed Rig with four spare clips hanging from his left front hip. The pistol was tilted slightly forward and it was the .45-caliber pistol that Justin used when he was competing. It was equipped with a muzzle brake to help control recoil and a beveled magazine well to help you change clips quickly.

Justin handed DeMac his PACT electronic timer. "When I get ready push this button," Justin said, pointing to the start button on the timer. "When you hear my last round hit the gong at fifty yards hit the stop button."

"Got it," DeMac said.

Justin stood facing the targets and DeMac could tell that he was "getting in the bubble," as shooters often referred to when they were shutting out everything around them so they could concentrate on the task at hand. Justin raised his hands up to shoulder level and said, "Whenever you're ready."

DeMac pressed the start button on the timer and after a slight pause it let out an electronic beep. Justin drew his .45 automatic and instantly had a rainbow of empty brass arching through the air as he shot each silhouette twice. Justin released the empty magazine and slammed another one in the pistol and again filled the air with empty brass as he repeated the process and then reloaded a second time before shooting the gong at fifty yards.

DeMac pressed the stop button on the timer and checked it. 13.42 seconds.

"13.4 seconds, Justin. Travis wasn't exaggerating when he said you could really shoot. That was awesome. Wow!" DeMac shouted.

"13.4 seconds would probably put you in about tenth place if you were shooting in a big match," Justin said. "And that's assuming that there aren't any penalties."

DeMac stepped up to the open shutters and looked at the targets. The three standard silhouettes had four holes in the center of their chest in the ten ring and the hostage target had four neatly clustered holes in between the eyes of the fugitive.

"The next time somebody pulls a gun on you, I'm not going to bother with pulling mine," DeMac said with a grin.

"Hey, Wade. How long have you been standing there?" Justin asked.

Wade was standing on the other side of the Plexiglas that petitioned off Justin's shooting room.

"I got here right before you started shooting, Mr. Hayes," Wade said. "That was awesome."

"Have you ever shot a pistol?" Justin asked.

"Just a .22 that my Uncle Steve had one time," Wade answered.

"DeMac, step out there and hang a couple fresh targets for Wade and stand these empty snuff cans up on the dirt pile," Justin said. "Wade, come on in here and let me show you a few things about shooting a pistol."

"I don't think I can hit anything with a pistol, Mr. Hayes," Wade said.

"I can have you hitting snuff cans at twenty-five yards in less than thirty minutes. Since you have never shot a big bore pistol before you don't have any bad habits to break, so I can teach you the right way to shoot a pistol in no time at all. Come on in here."

DeMac stepped out to the twenty-five-yard berm and stapled two new targets to the plywood and then stood the empty snuff cans in the dirt beneath them. Justin spent about ten minutes explaining to Wade how the model 1911 Colt .45 automatic worked and the way to handle it safely. He then taught Wade how to hold it, how to stand, how to sight it, and how to fire it.

Justin stepped over to a wooden cabinet and retrieved another set of electronic shooting muffs and a pair of shooting glasses for Wade. With Justin standing behind Wade coaching him, Wade slowly began to fire the pistol. In less than ten minutes Wade was placing most of his shots near the center of the target and was beginning to smile a little bit.

"Now shoot those snuff cans," Justin said.

"I don't think I can, Mr. Hayes."

"Sure, you can. Don't think about it, just do it. Relax, breathe, concentrate, aim and squeeze," Justin said.

Wade raised the pistol up to eye level and took a deep breath. After what seemed like an eternity the pistol fired and the snuff can flew straight up.

"You hit right under it. You're trying too hard. Relax. Once you get your sight picture go ahead and squeeze it off a little quicker," Justin coached.

Wade raised the pistol back up and aimed like he did before but this time fired quicker and blew the snuff can straight back into the dirt pile with a hole right in the middle of it.

"I did it! It's right through the center of it!" Wade shouted.

"Now shoot that gong at fifty yards," Justin said. "Aim for the top of it."

"But I—"

"Do it before I count to five. One, two, three—"

Wade took aim and fired. "Clang!"

"I hit it. I can't believe I hit it on the first try!" Wade shouted with a grin.

"I told you that you could do it," Justin said. "It's fun, isn't it?"

"Yeah, it's a lot of fun," Wade said.

"Good shooting, Wade," DeMac said as he patted him on the back.

"Did you bring your rifle?" Justin asked.

"Yes, sir. It's strapped down on my four-wheeler," Wade said. "I probably couldn't hit that gong with that rifle."

"Go get it and bring it in here and we'll look at it," Justin said.

Wade took off the shooting glasses and the ear muffs and walked through the shop looking at all the machinery. As soon as he was out of earshot, DeMac looked at Justin and said, "It tickled that boy to death to shoot that pistol."

"I knew it would," Justin said to DeMac. "I wanted to build a little trust between me and him and build up his confidence a little bit."

DeMac was starting to understand what Travis was talking about when he said that his dad cared more about people than about money. It was no wonder that his chest was so huge. It had to be to go around that big heart of his.

Wade came back in the shop carrying his rifle in one hand and petting Shogun and Scooter with the other. "I like your dogs, Mr. Hayes. What are their names?"

"The Rottweiler is Shogun and the Jack Russell is Scooter. Scooters healing up right now from a fight with a groundhog."

"He's lucky to be alive if he fought a groundhog," Wade said.

"He wouldn't be alive if it weren't for Shogun and this man standing right here," Justin said, pointing to DeMac.

"Attention!" Justin shouted and both dogs sat down and stared straight ahead.

"Present arms!" Justin shouted and both dogs started snarling, exposing all their teeth.

"At ease, soldiers." Justin commanded and both dogs laid down.

"Now would you soldiers rather be dead or be a Democrat?" Justin said like a drill sergeant and both dogs immediately rolled over on their backs and stuck their legs straight up and shut their eyes. DeMac and Wade were cracking up as Justin stepped over to a bench and retrieved a couple dog biscuits. Justin gave the two dogs their reward and ordered them outside before picking up Wade's rifle and examining it. It had seen a lot of use over the years. Practically all the bluing was gone from the barrel and the action and the walnut stock had been cracked and glued back together at some time. Justin removed the bolt and looked through the barrel The rifling was badly worn and was gone right in front of the chamber. It was no wonder that the rifle was inaccurate.

"Can you fix it, Mr. Hayes?" Wade asked. "Our sheep are having their lambs this time of year and the coyotes are killing them as soon as they hit the ground. I got a little money saved up if it doesn't cost too much."

"Yeah, I can fix it for you Wade, but you can't stand guard over your sheep all the time since you got to go to school and church and football practice and other things. I think you need a dog as bad as you need a rifle," Justin said.

Tears jumped out of Wade's eyes and ran down his cheeks. "I had a dog and the coyote's killed him. He chased them out of the pasture and when he didn't come back I went looking for him. They tore him to pieces.

Wade couldn't go on. He turned around so Justin and DeMac couldn't see him cry.

"That's okay, Wade. It's okay to cry. I had a yellow lab for sixteen years and when she died I cried for two weeks," Justin said.

"I'm going to kill those coyotes that killed my dog," Wade said, trembling.

"And I'm going to help you," Justin said. "Step over to that sink and wash your face and then we'll talk about a plan."

Wade walked over to the sink and washed his face before coming back over and sitting down with Justin and DeMac. He was obviously embarrassed for crying in front of them.

"Now here's what we'll do. I'll fix your rifle for you but I want you to come help me after you finish your chores. If your dad needs you to work on the farm then I don't want you over here. Understand?"

"Yes, sir."

"After I fix your rifle and you practice with it a little bit, we'll set a trap and try to ambush them. I've read a couple articles about it in my hunting magazines but I've never tried it, so it will be a learning experience for both of us," Justin said. "DeMac, did you ever hunt coyotes when you were growing up?"

"No, but I shot several of them. I can tell you this. They're smart and they're tough. You have to hit one solid to put him down."

"As far as the cost of fixing your rifle, I don't want you worrying about it. You and me will work something out between us. Maybe you can help me out around here some to help pay for it," Justin said.

"Well, that sounds good to me, Mr. Hayes. I really appreciate it and I'll pay you back as soon as I can," Wade said.

"When you get home I want you to tell your dad about our plan and make sure that it's okay with him. If he has any questions just tell him to call me."

"Yes, sir. I'm going to have to go for now 'cause Dad needs me to help him fix a fence, but I'll be back tomorrow if I can," Wade said.

"Okay, Wade. We'll see you sometime tomorrow," Justin said as Wade turned to leave. As soon as Wade left Justin walked over to the wall phone and punched in a number.

"Hayworth Kennels," the voice on the other end of the line said.

"Jimmy, this is Justin Hayes. How are you my friend?"

It was still ten minutes until noon but everybody was already seated in the conference room so Jack decided to start the proceedings. "Men, I want to skip over our usual weekly business and move right to our biggest problem, Justin Hayes. If any of you need to discuss anything else with me then just see me sometime tomorrow. As soon as we finish our meeting today Johnny is going to drive me and Cecil over to the Bass Pro Shop in Concord to do some shopping for four-wheelers and spotting scopes and other things we need around here, and then were going to spend the night in Charlotte and check out a couple of new ladies that want to work for us on a part-time basis. We should be back by midmorning tomorrow, so if you need something approved just wait until then."

"Just so everybody's on the same page, since our meeting on Saturday Steve picked up the tractor at the junkyard and dumped it down the number seven mine shaft, so that's been taken care of. Cecil got a background check done on Justin Hayes and there are several copies on the table if you want to see it. It doesn't help us much except it let's us know that we can't get in a shootout with this guy because we would definitely lose. He was a sniper in Vietnam and had forty-seven confirmed kills and is ranked as a Grand Master in the International Defensive Pistol Association. This guy can shoot!"

Johnny Steele picked up a copy of the background check and started reading it. No wonder he got the jump on me, he thought to himself.

"Anyway," Jack went on, "Donald has come up with a plan that is fool-proof and nobody's got to fire a shot. Tonight, between three o'clock and four o'clock, were going to send somebody up the road with several containers of toxic chemicals that only gunsmiths use, and were going to pour them in the river right in front of Justin's house. There will be an immediate fish kill, and of course we will report it to the State Wildlife Department as soon as we see fish floating by the front of the house. When the Wildlife Department tests the water and discovers chemicals in it, they will contact the Environmental Protection Agency and they will trace the chemicals to the front of Justin's house. As soon as they search Justin's house and discover those same chemicals, they will arrest him and we will let Sheriff Sisk handle it from there. Is there any questions?" Jack said.

"I wish we could figure out a way to do this without ruining the river," Steve said.

"Hell, Steve, the government will clean up the river and restock it if necessary. You'll finally get to see your tax dollars at work!" Jack snapped.

Steve didn't like it one bit, but he knew better than to argue with Jack. It was obvious that Jack had already decided to do this and nothing he could say would change his mind.

"Coy flew to Tennessee this morning and picked up the chemicals and is on his way back as we speak," Jack said. "The only question is who are we going to get to pour the chemicals in the river?"

"Tommy Sides or Lee Hayworth would be my choice," Cecil said. "They both were involved with Roy's accident and are in this thing just as deep as we are. And both of them are totally dependable when you need something done right."

"Let's get Tommy to do it then," Jack said. "He can drive the four-wheeler almost all the way to Justin's and then walk the rest of the way. Tell him to be sure and spill some of the chemicals on the river bank so it is obvious that they were poured in the river from that spot."

"I'll take care of it," Cecil said.

"I'm going to wave bye to that son of a bitch when we drive by there on our way to Concord, because he'll be in jail by Wednesday and in the graveyard by Friday or Saturday. I'll own that property sooner or later or by God die trying. Now let's get the hell out of here."

DeMac unloaded the Coleman canoe and carried it over his head down to the river beside Teresa's house and hid it in some brush. It reminded him of when he signed up to become a seal and was sent to BUD/S training in Florida. They divided everybody up into eight man teams and made them carry an inflatable boat everywhere they went. They carried that boat to the mess hall, up and down sand dunes, on ten mile hikes down the beach, and everywhere else they went for three weeks. Sometimes it felt like it weighed a ton and your arms would tremble and your arm muscles would burn. If you dropped your boat the drill instructors would make you do push-ups in the surf and then roll in the sand until you were covered in it. Then you had to pick your boat back up and run down the beach. The sand would chafe your crotch and legs until they bled and burned. That's why Seals never wear underwear. Eighty men started the BUD/S training but only twenty-seven graduated.

DeMac walked back to the truck where Justin was waiting for him. Justin was wearing a pair of khaki slacks and a blue long sleeved button down dress shirt and he looked good.

"When you get down to the house this evening just pull the canoe up near the mailbox and I'll stop and load it up when I come home," Justin said.

"What if you don't come home tonight?" DeMac asked and then winked at Justin.

"Then the canoe can just lay there until I do come home," Justin said with a grin. "If this lady lets me spend the night, I can assure you that I won't be worried about my canoe.

"She's gorgeous! Come on up to the house and I'll introduce you before you go."

Justin and DeMac walked up to the front door and Justin rang the doorbell. When Teresa opened the door Justin and DeMac could immediately smell the spaghetti sauce and it smelled wonderful. Teresa was stunning. She was wearing an almond colored sun dress with a pearl necklace and pearl earrings and she was absolutely beautiful.

"Teresa, this is a friend of mine, Dwight McMasters," Justin said. "Dwight, this is Teresa Owens."

"Nice to meet you, Dwight," Teresa said.

"It's nice to meet you, Teresa," DeMac said.

"Dwight's going to take my truck and run an errand for me and then bring the truck back here and leave it," Justin explained. "He's got a canoe down at the river and he's going to take it back to my house when he leaves."

"Dwight, would you like to eat before you leave?" Teresa asked.

"No, I'm going to have to get going, but thank you for offering," DeMac said. "It was good to meet you, Teresa. I'll see you later on, Justin. Bye now," DeMac said as he turned to leave.

"Well, you clean up pretty nice, Justin Hayes," Teresa said as she looked at Justin.

"Thank you, and you look stunning this evening," Justin said.

"Well, thank you. Come in and make yourself at home. Can I get you a glass of wine or a beer before we eat?"

"A beer sounds good to me. Your house is amazing! I love the white stucco walls and the mirrors. Did you hire a designer?" Justin asked as he walked around the living room.

"No, that's just something I came up with on my own. I'm surprised that you noticed. Most men aren't interested in decorating unless they're interior designers, and most of them are gay," Teresa said as she walked to the kitchen to get Justin a beer.

"I guess I noticed because I just got through building my house and decorating it," Justin said as Teresa came back in the room and handed him a beer.

"Did you hire a designer for your house?" Teresa asked.

"No, I just did it myself. I actually enjoyed it except for all the shopping for accessories."

"I would like to see your house sometime," Teresa said.

"Well, you're welcome anytime. We can go see it after we eat if you like."

"I would like that," Teresa said. "Speaking of eating, dinner is ready whenever we are."

"I really appreciate you inviting me over, Teresa," Justin said. "I'm looking forward to eating dinner with someone besides my two dogs."

"Well, I hope I can entertain you as well as your dogs do," Teresa said with a grin. "Come on in the dining room and I'll serve dinner."

"If it tastes half as good as it smells it will be delicious," Justin said.

Justin followed Teresa through the house until they entered the kitchen and adjoining dining room. Justin was impressed with the house and the hostess. They both had class. Justin figured that Teresa was probably about forty-four years old judging from her hands and just a tiny bit of wrinkling on her neck, but she was a gorgeous forty-four-year-old. He was a little concerned about their age difference though. He was fifty-seven, and if she was forty-four that would be a thirteen-year difference in their ages. He felt a little awkward being with someone that young.

Teresa brought Justin a generous helping of spaghetti on a beautiful white stone plate along with a wonderful salad. The salad was composed of leafy green lettuce and regular head lettuce with a small amount of chopped purple cabbage, and was covered with diced tomatoes and slivers of onions, cheese, and almonds. A basket of garlic bread sat in the center of the table, and as soon as Teresa served herself and sat down, Justin blessed the food. It was wonderful, better than any spaghetti that he had ever eaten and he fought the urge to gobble it down. Instead, he ate like a gentleman and tried not to stare too hard at the beautiful redhead on the other side of the table.

"This is incredible, Teresa. I've never eaten a better meal than this," Justin said.

"Well, I'm flattered. I'm glad you like it," she said, smiling. Teresa was trying to figure out why she was so attracted to this man. She started not to ask him over after reading the background check that Ryan had faxed her. The part about "forty-seven confirmed kills" bothered her. Justin was obviously a gun man and Teresa didn't like guns. She thought the world would be a better place if there weren't any guns. Teresa wondered if Justin's house had guns and animals hanging on every wall. That is why she wanted to see his house so badly. Having been a realtor for thirty years, she could tell a lot about a person from looking at their house.

"So Justin, tell me about yourself. You said that you can't pay a man who already has everything, so tell me about this man that has everything," Teresa said.

"There's really not much to tell," Justin said. "I hope I didn't sound boastful when I said that."

"No, you sounded sincere, I thought."

"Well, I was sincere. I'm just a very simple man. I'm fifty-seven years old and I'm retired, and I am very blessed. I have a very wonderful life and I'm very happy," Justin said.

"Well, that sounds good," Teresa said.

"When I get up in the morning, I do what I want to do. How much better can life be than that?"

"Not much," Teresa said. "What is it you like to do?"

"I've got a machine shop behind my house and a shooting range. Sometimes I work in my shop, sometimes I like to shoot my guns, sometimes I like to go fishing, sometimes I go for walks, sometimes I just read a book."

"So there's nothing that you would change about your life?"

"Well, I get a little lonely sometimes, especially during the winter months. From April to November I'll have friends coming from time to time to fish or hunt or to do some canoeing or kayaking, so it's not too bad. But from November until March, I get a little lonely. Aside from that, I wouldn't change anything about my life."

"You look like you're in great shape to be fifty-seven years old," Teresa said.

"Thank you. I've been real fortunate to be big and strong and have exceptionally good health since the day I was born. I guess that's the biggest blessing of all, especially when you look around and see all the people that are sick and crippled," Justin said. "Okay, it's your turn. Tell me about you."

"Well, like you said, there's really not much to tell. I'm fifty-two years old."

"Whoa, you're kidding me, right!" Justin said. "There's no way you're fifty-two years old."

"Born in 1954," Teresa said.

"I can't believe you're that old. I felt a little awkward coming over here because I thought you were in your early forties. There are at least a million women on this earth that aren't even thirty that would kill to look as good as you," Justin said.

Teresa blushed. "Well, you were born big and strong and I was born with incredible skin." Justin held his beer up and said, "A toast, to strong men and women with good skin."

Teresa held her wine glass up and giggled as they clinked their beverages together. She liked being around this man. There was something special about him that she had never sensed in any other man, but she didn't know what it was.

Justin stared across the table at Teresa. He knew what he wanted for dessert.

DeMac pulled Justin's truck around to the back of the Wal-Mart Superstore and parked beside the white van as he had been instructed. The manila envelope was opened and its contents were photographed before returning it to the envelope and resealing it. The man in the van handed the envelope back to DeMac along with a plastic bag that had a disguise and a map showing him where the Fox 8 studio was and where to park when he got there. DeMac put the fake beard and mustache on and the dentures in his mouth and then looked in the rearview mirror of Justin's truck. He didn't recognize the man that was staring back at him. He looked like he was in his early fifties. A greasy Carolina Panthers ball cap completed the disguise, so DeMac cranked up Justin's truck and headed for the news studio. The ball cap was wired for sound so DeMac decided to do a radio check.

"Eagle, this is Red Fox. Do you read?"

"Affirmative, Red Fox. After you park, wait for a signal. Over."

"Ten-four, Eagle."

In less than ten minutes DeMac arrived at the Fox 8 studio and parked the truck where the CIA told him to. After waiting about five minutes he was given the go ahead and he walked in the building and dropped the envelope on the vacant receptionist's desk and then returned to the truck and drove away. The whole operation took less than a minute.

Travis pulled in Jesse's driveway and dialed her cell phone. "Hello?" Jesse answered.

"Jesse, this is Travis. I just pulled in your driveway. Will your dog let me get to the door?"

"No. She won't bite you in the yard, but she won't let you touch the porch," Jesse answered. "Pull up to the back of the house and I'll let you in."

Travis drove up the driveway and pulled around to the back of the house. He was wearing dress blue jeans and brushed suede cowboy boots with a white Izod pullover shirt. Jesse was waiting at the back door to let him in. Maggie was growling as Travis walked up and Jesse ordered her to be quiet.

Jesse was beautiful. She was wearing blue jeans and open toed sandals with a button up white blouse that had an embroidered design across the upper chest and shoulders. Her beautiful black hair was pulled back in a pony tail and it was full and shiny. She smiled when Travis stepped up on the porch and Travis knew he had never seen a more beautiful face.

"Come in. I'm almost ready," Jesse said as she held the door open for Travis.

"Thank you. You look very pretty."

Jesse kissed him. She couldn't help it. She had never kissed a boy before when they walked up on their first date, but when Travis stepped in the door she leaned over and kissed him.

You could have knocked Travis over with a feather. His heart fluttered and his face turned red. "Wow!" he said.

"Just make yourself at home. I'll be ready in five minutes," Jesse said as she turned and went up the stairs two at a time.

Travis regained his composure and stepped into the living room. A small table and a Queen Ann chair sat in one corner, with a pewter lamp sitting on top of a beautiful lace doily.

There were several pictures arranged under the lamp so Travis stepped over to look at them.

The largest picture was of an elderly Indian woman wearing an apron and holding a headless chicken upside down by its feet. Her hair was white as snow and her face was heavily wrinkled by old age and hard living. There was another picture of a boy and a girl sitting bareback on a spotted horse. The boy was probably twelve years old and the girl, who Travis recognized as Jesse, was probably ten years old. She was sitting behind the boy with her arms around his waist holding on tight. There was also a picture of a soldier, and Travis thought it might be the same person as the boy on the horse, but he wasn't sure. He wore the uniform of the Army Special Forces and he had dark features and was handsome.

"That's my brother Joshua," Jesse said.

Travis turned around to see Jesse standing across the room. She was holding a sweater in one hand and a purse in the other.

"He's in Afghanistan right now on his second tour and I'm worried about him."

"I just got back from Afghanistan," Travis said.

"But you were on a ship, weren't you?" Jesse asked.

"No, not all the time. I traveled with a Seal team in country on three different occasions," Travis said. "You don't need to worry. The Special Forces are like the Navy Seals—they are the best soldiers in the world. Most of the time the enemy doesn't even know that there anywhere around until all hell breaks loose, and by that time their already gone. He'll be just fine."

"Well, that makes me feel better. That's exactly what he told me," Jesse said.

"He's telling you the truth. Who is this elderly woman in this picture?"

"That's my grandmother Leah. She passed away three years ago right before I graduated from college," Jesse said.

"How old is she in this picture?" Travis asked.

"I think she was seventy-eight or seventy-nine. I'm not real sure."

"If you look closely at her face you can see strength and determination. You also see wisdom and just a hint of happiness. Even though her life was hard, I think she was a cheerful person," Travis said as he stared at the picture.

Jesse stepped over beside Travis and picked the picture up and looked at it like she had never seen it before. "You just described my grandmother perfectly and you never knew her. All that from just a picture?" Jesse said and she stared at Travis with a look of bewilderment.

"I'm a photographer. I'm always looking for what's not obvious in pictures, like strength, weakness, happiness, sadness, pain, wisdom, or whatever is there," Travis explained.

"I think you have a gift!" Jesse said.

"Oh, speaking of gifts, I brought you something," Travis walked out to his Jeep and returned with a manila envelope. "Your dog let me back in the house without growling this time."

"Her name is Maggie. She knows you're supposed to be here now."

Travis handed the envelope to Jesse. "I didn't have a frame to put it in, but when I looked at this picture I thought about you so I decided to just give it to you."

Jesse opened the manila envelope and pulled out an eight by ten color photograph. It was a picture of a butterfly sitting on a rock in the middle of the river. The rock was protruding up through a section of rapids in the river, and the water surrounding the rock was spraying and splashing as it crashed around it. The colors were vibrant and beautiful and you could almost hear the water roaring when you stared at it.

"It's beautiful, Travis! Thank you so much," Jesse said as she wiped a tear from her eye. "Tell me what you see in this picture."

"Okay, but I hope you won't think I'm a fruitcake or something when I do."

"No, I won't. Go ahead. Please tell me. Please, please, please," Jesse begged.

"I'm a little embarrassed to tell you," Travis said, looking at the floor.

"Don't be. Please tell me."

"The contrast in this picture is what makes it special. You see the violence in the water as it crashes into the rock and then pushes and shoves its way around it, but only inches away there is this sanctuary where everything is peaceful and calm. And in the very center of this sanctuary, sits one of nature's most beautiful creatures. The butterfly reminded me of you so I decided you should have it," Travis said, blushing.

Tears came to Jesse's eyes as she stared first at the picture and then at Travis. "That's the sweetest thing that anyone has ever said to me Travis," and she put her arms around him and hugged him and then kissed him again, this time pausing slightly before she pulled away. She wiped a tear from her cheek and blushed slightly as she stepped over and grabbed a Kleenex from across the room.

Travis's stomach growled and he hoped that Jesse didn't hear it, but when she glanced back at him he knew that she had.

"Excuse me. I haven't eaten all day and my stomach is filing a formal complaint," Travis said.

"Why haven't you eaten today?" Jesse asked.

"I've been too excited about finally getting to take you out."

"Well, come on and let's get you something to eat before you pass out on me," Jesse said and she took Travis's hand and led him to the back door.

Teresa stopped her Cadillac Escalade after she turned in Justin's driveway and got out to look up the mountain at Justin's house. Justin got out and walked around the vehicle to join her.

"Well, what do you think? Tell the truth," Justin said.

"I think it's beautiful. It looks like it belongs there. The polished stone and large panels of glass are perfect," Teresa said. "I could sell this house from down here and not even show the inside of it."

"Well, as I told my next door neighbor day before yesterday, it's not for sale. "Come on and I'll show you the inside," Justin said as he got back in the Cadillac.

Teresa drove up the asphalt driveway and by the front of the house slowly, taking in everything just as if she were buying this property. It was much more than she expected but the real test was yet to come. She parked at the double carport and Justin got out and punched in a code on a digital keypad and the carport doors opened. Shogun and Scooter came prancing out and Justin introduced them to Teresa as he was opening the back door.

Teresa stepped in the kitchen and was pleasantly surprised. The kitchen was larger than most kitchens were these days and was furnished with commercial grade stainless steel appliances. There was an island bar in the center and the floor was a beautiful ceramic tile.

Teresa wandered through Justin's house with her mouth open, totally blown away by what she was seeing. The whole house was floored in hardwood except for the kitchen and bathrooms, and they were done in ceramic tile. The ceilings were vaulted with elaborate crown molding surrounding them, and the spacious living room had twelve foot ceilings and three columns that gave it an exotic look. The large glass panels on the front of the house provided you with a breath taking view of the river and the surrounding mountains, and the accessories that Justin had picked out were perfect. There was quite a lot of wrought iron and pewter arranged throughout the house in candle holders and lamps and light fixtures and it was all done very tastefully. It was the very best example of a rustic contemporary home that she had ever seen.

Teresa entered the master bedroom that was located on the front of the house beside the living room. It had ten foot ceilings and a double window facing the river with plantation blinds and vases with ferns on either side. There was a large ceiling fan with blades shaped like the branches of a palm tree in the center of the room and all the lighting was recessed. The king size master bed was covered in a comforter that was black with white stripes like a zebra, and of all the things that she thought she would never see in Justin Hayes's house, an abstract painting hung over the bed and it was beautiful.

Justin had followed Teresa through the house but hadn't said a word. She finally turned and faced him.

"Justin Hayes, you missed your calling! This house is truly spectacular. You should have been an interior designer."

"No, I didn't either. I hated all the shopping, and like you said, most interior designers are gay and I can tell I'm not gay every time I look at you," Justin said, grinning.

"Well, I guess I should apologize to you because I figured you lived in a log house with a dirt driveway and had guns and dead animals hanging on every wall. You fooled me and not too many people do."

"Speaking of guns, follow me out back and I'll show you my shop."

DeMac pushed the canoe out from the bank and into the current and soon was gliding swiftly down the beautiful New River. The river banks were full of overhanging trees with new blooms, and wildflowers were scattered here and there as spring slowly transformed a frozen wasteland into a beautiful greenhouse. The river was still flowing hard from the heavy rains so DeMac didn't have to paddle, all he had to do was steer the canoe around rocks and log jams.

DeMac soon found himself drifting back to his childhood, rowing down the Musselshell River in Montana. He could see his mother in the backyard hanging up clothes and his little sister swinging across the river on the rope their dad had hung high in a sycamore tree. He saw his dad unloading the lumber for their new barn and plowing their garden with his old worn out tractor. Suddenly DeMac couldn't see anything for the tears in his eyes so he glided over to the bank and sat there feeling foolish. Men aren't supposed to cry, especially Navy Seals. What is wrong with me he wondered? He thought about Wade and how the tears jumped out of his eyes when Justin told him he needed to get a dog. He remembered Justin saying he cried for two weeks when his yellow lab died. DeMac tried to visualize Justin crying but couldn't do it. What would the team think if they saw him sitting in this canoe crying like a baby? Maybe if he let himself go ahead and cry it would be over and done with. DeMac took the cell phone off his side and turned it off and wept.

Teresa let Justin drive them back to her house after she finished looking at his home. She watched him as he drove slowly up River Road looking for DeMac as they went. She thought she knew why she was so attracted to this man. It was his inner joy. Justin was a man that was totally satisfied with his life and was happy inside and out and that joy was reflected in everything he did. It made you want to be around him.

Justin slowed down and blew the horn. "There he is," he said and he stuck his arm out the window and waved. DeMac held his paddle up and waved it back and forth as he floated by.

"DeMac is a Navy Seal and he's a good friend of my son. His entire family died in a fire several months ago and he's still grieving but he doesn't want anybody to know it," Justin said. "He's a hell of a nice guy."

"I'm sorry to hear that. He seemed like a very nice man."

"I think if he spends a couple of weeks up here with me I can help him to get over the hump," Justin said.

Teresa thought that what Justin just said was sweet. The reservations that she had about Justin had completely dissolved. He was handsome and strong and had a lot of class. Even though he owned a lot of guns and did a lot of shooting, he wasn't the least bit ignorant or backward. Teresa thought that men who owned a lot of guns were backwoods rednecks with bad teeth until she met Justin. She could tell that he was an honest man with a big heart and had truckloads of confidence, and men with confidence were sexy.

Justin pulled the Cadillac up to Teresa's house and stepped around to open her door. Teresa intentionally slid off the seat in a way that would pull her dress up slightly and she could tell that it wasn't missed by Justin.

"Thank you, Justin. You're quite a gentleman."

"You're welcome, Madam," Justin said like a doorman at a fancy hotel and he offered her his arm to escort her to the door. "I think I'll get myself a beer and go out on the deck if that's okay with you."

"That sounds good. Excuse me for a few minutes and I'll join you," Teresa said. Teresa stepped into her bedroom and out of the sundress she was wearing. She hung the sundress up in her closet and pulled out a pair of black satin pants with a matching strapless top and slipped the outfit on. She looked in the mirror and was satisfied.

The top showed off her breasts and the satin pants clung to her hips and upper legs and didn't leave anything to the imagination.

Teresa stepped back into the kitchen to pour herself a glass of wine and saw Justin leaning against the porch railing, watching the river crash down through the large rocks behind her house. He looked like a modem day gladiator Teresa thought and she was suddenly aroused just watching him stand there. She poured a glass of wine and then stepped out onto the deck. Justin turned around and his mouth fell open when he saw her.

"I slipped into something more comfortable," she said as she walked over to Justin and leaned ever so slightly against him as she gazed out at the river.

"Teresa Owens, answer me one question."

"Okay, but just one," Teresa said, smiling.

"How is it possible for a woman as successful and beautiful as you obviously are, to still be single?"

"Well, all the men I have known in my life have fallen into one of two categories," she said. "The first category is the whiners, who spend all their time complaining about their lousy life and how they deserve so much more than they have. And the second category is the successful businessmen like doctors and bankers and lawyers and so forth that spend all their time bragging about all their accomplishments and all their possessions like big houses and fancy cars and expensive jewelry. I've dated both types and I'd rather be in hell with a broken back than to be married to either one."

"Which category am I in?" Justin asked.

"I said only one question," Teresa said as she turned toward Justin and set her wine glass down on the deck railing. Teresa put her arms around Justin and pulled him against her tightly and kissed him.

"Now that I've met you, Justin Hayes, I have to start a whole new category," she said, and she kissed him again. "Now answer a question for me."

"Okay, but just one," Justin said with a grin.

Teresa walked across the deck and slid the cover back on her Jacuzzi and then :flipped a couple switches on the control panel. The Jacuzzi came to life like a monster that had been suddenly awakened from a deep sleep.

"How long has it been since you have been in a Jacuzzi?" Teresa asked.

"I don't really know. It's been several years, I guess," Justin said. "But I didn't bring any trunks."

Teresa pulled her strapless top over her head in one smooth motion and her breasts bounced up and down and her pink nipples were hard and pointed. She then took her thumbs and pushed her black satin pants and her panties down to her ankles and then stepped out of them before stepping into the bubbling water.

"You won't need any," Teresa said.

Jesse and Travis drove to Jefferson and ate pizza and drank beer and both of them felt like they were the luckiest person in the world. They talked and laughed and giggled like two junior high kids on their first date until the waiters started giving them dirty looks for staying too long. Travis left a generous tip and Jesse took his hand as they walked back to Travis's Jeep.

"I want to stop at Wal-Mart before we go home," Jesse told Travis.

"There's nothing more romantic than a stroll through Wal-Mart," Travis said, looking into her beautiful eyes.

"I want to buy a frame for the picture you gave me and I want you to help pick it out."

"We can do that. I don't care where we go as long as were together," Travis said.

Jesse leaned over and kissed Travis on the cheek without breaking her stride as they walked across the parking lot. That was the third time that she had kissed him tonight and the evening wasn't over yet.

Jesse had almost forgotten how to have fun. When she was at N.C. State studying to be a veterinarian she didn't have time to party and date. Between her studies and her part-time job there wasn't any time or money to go out and just have fun.

After graduating and moving back home she went to work at the animal clinic for Dr. David Stetson, who had helped her get into college and was planning on selling the clinic to her in five years when he retired, but Dr. Stetson had a massive heart attack and died only a month after Jesse came home. So Jesse was forced to borrow the money so she could buy the clinic from Dr. Stetson's widow and had to work ridiculous hours to keep the business running and pay back the loan.

Travis drove them to WalMart and they picked out a frame for the butterfly picture and then drove slowly through the winding mountain roads toward Sparta. Jesse couldn't keep from glancing over at Travis as they wound their way home. If she could change anything about him she didn't know what it would be. He was handsome and strong and thoughtful and romantic. What little time that they had spent together had been wonderful so far. They had talked and laughed and shared stories about their childhood, and it just felt right to be with him. She was glad that she had swallowed her pride and finally called him, and that he had swallowed his pride and agreed to go out with her.

Travis finally turned in Jesse's driveway and pulled up behind the house with Maggie running around the Jeep barking. Travis rubbed Maggie's head as they walked up to the house.

"I want to put the picture in the frame as soon as I excuse myself," Jesse said. "I haven't drunk a beer in months and I forgot how they run through you."

"I know what you mean," Travis said. "I'm about to bust."

"There's a bathroom down the hall in between the living room and my office," Jesse said as she headed up the stairs. Jesse used the restroom and then changed out of her blue jeans and white blouse into a pair of khaki shorts and a bare midriff cotton top. When she went back downstairs Travis was just finishing putting the butterfly picture into the frame that they bought at Wal-Mart. Travis looked over at Jesse and almost dropped the picture when he saw her long shapely legs.

"I got into something more comfortable."

"Those shorts might be comfortable on you, but they're killing me!" Travis said, staring at her legs.

"Let me see it," Jesse said, excited.

"What do you think?" Travis said and he held the picture up so she could see it.

It was absolutely beautiful and the frame was perfect and made it look even more beautiful. As Jesse stared at the picture she thought about what Travis had said, "When I looked at this picture, I thought about you." That was the sweetest thing that anyone had ever said to her and it touched her heart as she stared at the picture. No one had ever given Jesse a gift except for her grandmother Leah and her brother Joshua, so this picture was very special to her already.

"It's beautiful," Jesse said as she wiped a tear from her eye. She crossed the room and kissed Travis again. "Thank you so much, it's beautiful and I love it. That's the sweetest thing that anyone has ever done for me."

"You're welcome, Jesse. I'm glad that you like it."

Travis reached around Jesse and held her and she laid her head on his shoulder and put her arms around him.

"Dr. Jessica Ann Longbow, I can't even begin to tell you how much I've enjoyed being with you this evening," Travis said in Jesse's ear. "I knew you were special the first time I met you and I haven't been able to think about anything else since that night."

Jesse was hugging him tight and he softly kissed her ear and felt her tremble.

"I also know that it's getting late and you have a business to run tomorrow, so as much as I don't want to, I'm going to leave so you can get some sleep."

Jesse raised her head and looked into Travis's eyes and then kissed him. "I don't want you to go."

"I can promise you that the last thing that I want to do is to go, but I probably should."

"No, don't go yet," Jesse pleaded, and she squeezed him like she could stop him from leaving.

"Can I come see you tomorrow?" Travis asked.

"You better come see me tomorrow."

"Oh, I almost forgot! I've got to bring Scooter in so you can check his incision," Travis said. "We can talk some more then."

"Will you help me hang my picture before you go tonight?" Jesse asked. "Sure I will. Where do you want to hang it?"

"Over my bed," Jesse said as she unsnapped Travis's jeans.

Gabriel Finally Gets Through

Justin was lying in bed slowly waking up. His eyes were open but he hadn't moved yet. He had slept hard and he felt good and rested. He finally rolled over and looked at the clock radio on his nightstand. Good grief, it was 7:16. Justin hadn't slept past six o'clock in years. It must have something to do with dating a redhead Justin thought. Justin rolled over on his back and thought about Teresa. Wow, what a woman!

Justin sat up and tried to shake the cobwebs out of his head but wasn't succeeding. It was going to take lots of coffee and a hot shower to bring him back to life this morning. First things first, slip on your sweatpants and moccasins and go to the kitchen and get a mug of coffee.

When Justin stepped out of the master bedroom and headed for the kitchen he could smell the unmistakable smell of sausage cooking. When he stepped into the kitchen he saw DeMac standing in front of the stove flipping sausage patties and whistling.

"Good morning," he said as he headed for the coffee pot.

"Well, well, well, it's the Love Doctor!" DeMac said, smiling. "That pretty redhead must have put you through the ringer last night."

"She did," Justin said. "I haven't slept this late in years."

Justin poured his coffee and no more sat down when Travis staggered into the kitchen. "Well, well, well, it's the Love Doctor that's in love with the doctor," DeMac said.

"I think you're right!" Travis said as he poured himself a cup of coffee and joined his father at the table.·

DeMac took the sausage out of the frying pan and slid it to the side of the stove before grabbing his glass of sweet tea and joining them.

"Okay, who's going to go first?" DeMac said. "I want to know about your dates and I want details."

"My date was awesome," Travis said as he stared at his coffee cup. "We talked and laughed and held hands and had a great time. We went to Jefferson and ate pizza and drank beer and then went to Wal-Mart. She's so sweet and so beautiful. I swear it makes you proud to be with her."

"How did she like the butterfly picture?" Justin asked.

"She cried when she saw it and then kissed me!" Travis said. "She said no one had ever given her anything before. Can you believe that?"

"Well, I'm glad you finally got a date with her and you kids had a good time," Justin said. "You were about to drive me and DeMac crazy!"

"I know I've been a pain in the ass lately," Travis said. "What about your date, Dad?"

"Well, you know us old folks are a little more conservative than the younger generation," Justin said. "We tend to be a little more laidback. I guess because we're going on sixty years old."

"Well, what did you old folks do?" Travis asked. "Sit around in rocking chairs and watch the TV?"

"No, we ate supper first, spaghetti, and a salad and I swear to you it was the best I've ever eaten. It was all I could do to keep myself from just gobbling it down. Then we drove back here because Teresa wanted to see my house."

"Did she like it?" DeMac asked.

"Yeah, she loved it. She said I missed my calling, that I should have been an interior designer," Justin said with a grin.

"Somehow I just can't see you as an interior designer," DeMac said.

"I can't either. Then what did you do?" Travis asked as he took a big swig of coffee.

"We went back to her house and got in the Jacuzzi and then I carried her up to her bedroom and banged her eyes out."

Travis sprayed coffee all over the table and all over DeMac and Justin. He had just taken a big swig of coffee and it came out his mouth and nose and went everywhere. Justin and DeMac were ducking for cover and laughing and soon Travis joined them until all three men were crying from laughing so hard. Travis was lying on the floor laughing and holding his stomach.

"Well, I was going to take a shower this morning anyway," Justin finally said wiping tears from his eyes.

"Dad, I can't believe you said that," Travis said as he dried his eyes.

"The truth will set you free, son," Justin said. "Besides, DeMac said he wanted details."

"That's right, Travis," DeMac said. "What base did you get to last night?"

"Home plate, but I wasn't going to brag about it!"

"You Hayes men are virile, if you're nothing else," DeMac said, stepping back to the stove. "I'm fixing hotcakes and sausage for breakfast this morning. Are you guys ready to eat?"

"Yeah, I'm starving," Justin said.

"Me too!" Travis said.

"I met Teresa last night and she is gorgeous just like you said, Justin, but when am I going to meet Jesse?" DeMac asked.

"Why don't you go with me this morning?" Travis said. "I've got to take Scooter back for his checkup."

"Okay, I will," DeMac said. "I've got to meet this woman that has cast this spell on you. Now do you want one big hotcake or three little ones?"

Justin tore Wade's rifle apart. He took the barrel and action out of the stock and then removed the scope and the trigger. He then clamped the barrel in a vise and unscrewed the action from the barrel. The action was the only thing that Justin was going to be able to reuse. The old stock, barrel, scope, and trigger were either worn out or no good.

Justin heard Shogun bark and stepped over to a window and looked toward the house. A black Cadillac Escalade was rolling to a stop in front of his carport. Justin walked out of his shop and down the walkway to the carport.

Teresa got out of the car and walked straight to Justin and kissed him hard, letting her tongue explore his mouth. She was wearing blue jeans and sandals with a cotton top and she was pretty as always.

"Good morning, beautiful," Justin said.

"Good morning, tiger," Teresa said. "I wish you would have been in my bed when I woke up this morning."

"I knew if I spent the night that I would never get back here this morning. I've got to fix a rifle for a fourteen-year-old boy and I need to finish it quickly before the coyotes kill all their baby lambs," Justin said.

"I can't imagine a fourteen-year-old boy owning a rifle," Teresa said.

"Well, he's about six feet tall and weighs about 180 pounds, so he's a big boy," Justin said.

"But he's only fourteen," Teresa said.

"Have you seen all the sheep grazing on the left side of the road when you first start down River Road?" Justin asked. "It's the first farm you come to."

"Yes, they're beautiful standing on the side of the mountain."

"Well, that's where he lives," Justin said. "He might be just fourteen years old, but he already knows how to drive a truck and a tractor and he can operate a chainsaw and fix a fence. He can also shoot a rifle when it's necessary. A rifle is just another tool on a farm."

"Did you say the coyotes were killing their baby lambs?" Teresa asked.

"They're killing them as fast as there born and they killed his dog too."

"Oh, that's terrible!" Teresa said.

"We're going to put a stop to it as soon as I get his rifle ready," Justin said.

"Well, I came by here because I wanted to see you again before I go back home," Teresa said and she kissed Justin again.

"Well, I'm sure glad you did," Justin said. "When are you coming back?"

"I got a house closing at two o'clock today and another one tomorrow morning at ten o'clock. I don't have to be present at house closings but I always attend as a courtesy to the buyer," Teresa said. "I wasn't going to come back until next weekend, but after what you did to me last night, I'll probably come back tomorrow evening— that is, if you promise me you'll come and see me," Teresa said, staring into Justin's eyes.

"A platoon of Recon Marines couldn't stop me from coming to see you. I might even cook supper for you if you act nice."

"If Travis and Dwight weren't here I'd drag you in the house and show you how naughty I can be," Teresa said as she ground her hips against Justin's leg.

"Dwight and Travis took Scooter to the vet's for a checkup. I'm the only one here."

"Then what are we waiting for?" Teresa said and she took Justin's hand and dragged him toward the back door.

Jesse walked into the examination room where DeMac and Travis were waiting with Scooter.

"Hey, Jesse. This is my friend DeMac. DeMac, this is Jesse."

Jesse turned and smiled at DeMac. "Hey, DeMac, it's nice to finally meet you."

"Same here," DeMac said.

"You did a great job of bandaging this little fellow up," Jesse said as she rubbed Scooter's head. "He would have never made it if you hadn't wrapped him like you did."

"Thank you. I just had to come today and meet this magnificent woman that has cast a spell on my friend here." DeMac said grinning. "Now I see why Travis. She's as beautiful as you said she was."

Jesse blushed. "Thank you."

"Now I'm going to excuse myself so you two can examine Scooter. It was nice to meet you, Jesse," DeMac said and grinned at Travis as he shut the door behind him.

The door wasn't even shut good before Travis and Jesse were in each others arms kissing passionately.

"I get off work at five o'clock. I should be home by 5:20," Jesse said in between kissing Travis.

"Don't you usually end up leaving about an hour late?" Travis said in between kisses. "Not today! Will you be there when I get home?"

"Damn, Skippy! I'll be there with bells on."

"Just be there with nothing on," Jesse said.

Lee Hayworth was standing on the bridge that crossed the south fork of the New River and led straight to the wrought iron gates in front of Jack's house. He was told to stand on the bridge until he saw dead fish floating by and then to call Steve Helms so that Steve could call the State Wildlife Department and report it, but he had been standing on the bridge for over an hour and hadn't seen one dead fish so far. He was tempted to go wake up Tommy and make sure that everything went okay but he hated to since Tommy had to be up half the night. It was a mile upstream where Tommy had to pour the chemicals in the river but you would think that there would be dead fish floating by here by now. Maybe he should just be patient and keep watching, but he hoped it wouldn't be too much longer. He was getting tired of standing here watching the river roll by under him.

Justin leaned in the Cadillac and kissed Teresa softly one more time before she left. "I'll see you tomorrow night."

"Why don't you just go with me?" Teresa asked as she leaned over and kissed Justin back.

"Any other time and I could have, but I need to get this rifle ready like I promised."

"Okay, I'll let you off the hook since you're trying to save baby lambs," Teresa said. "I'll probably call you tonight and talk dirty to you."

"I can hardly wait. Bye now."

Teresa backed out and waved as she drove away and Justin watched her as she went down the driveway:. He couldn't believe he was dating a woman as beautiful and sweet as Teresa. She seemed to be as taken with him as he was with her, and he was falling hard and fast for her.

After Teresa went out of sight Justin walked back to his shop and retrieved a new Shilen match barrel in .30 caliber out of one of the wooden cabinets and carried it over to the bench with the pieces of Wade's rifle. He had bought the new barrel to use himself when he built his next rifle, but he could order one for himself later. He was trying to decide where to start this project. He could go ahead and put the barrel in the lathe and cut the threads that screwed into the action and then cut the chamber, or he could true up the action and lap the locking lugs and reface the bolt. He decided to just lay all the parts out on a white towel before he started doing anything. He laid the barrel on the towel first and then went to a cabinet and retrieved a long cardboard box. He tore open the end of the box and pulled out a brand new McMillan A5 tactical stock with an adjustable cheek piece and adjustable recoil pad and laid it down beside the barrel. He went to the cabinet again and returned with a Jewell Trigger and a Leupold 4.5-14 × 50 variable scope with a mill-dot reticle. One more trip produced a set of scope rings and bases, a set of Butler Creek flip up lens covers, a new firing pin spring, a titanium firing pin, and a Harris bi-pod.

Justin was staring at all the parts when he suddenly realized ·something. He walked over to his gun safe and dialed the combination and then opened it up. After studying his rifle collection for a moment he reached in the back of the safe and carefully pulled out a matte black tactical rifle and carried it over to the workbench. It was almost identical to the rifle he was going to build Wade. It was a Remington short action and a Shilen barrel sitting in a McMillan A5 tactical stock. It had a Jewell trigger and it was chambered in .308 Winchester. The only difference was it had a Weaver 36× Target scope with a dot reticle and it didn't have a bi-pod on it, but Justin could switch the scopes and mount the bi-pod in about half an hour. The Weaver scope was a great scope but it was designed for target shooting at long distances and wasn't any good for a hunting scope.

Justin knew what he would do. He would give Wade his rifle to use until he had time to complete the other one, and then Wade could choose which rifle he wanted. That way they could go ahead and ambush the coyotes before Wade's family lost any more sheep.

It also meant that he could take his time building the rifle and wouldn't have to rush. Gunsmithing is a profession that requires lots of patience and when you try to rush you usually end up with a second rate job. Justin decided to switch the scopes on the rifles and mount the bi-pod. He would have Wade ready to go in thirty minutes.·

Gail Davis checked her makeup for the tenth time since she and the camera man had left Winston-Salem. In between putting on eye liner and lipstick and brushing her hair she had read all the information in the folder and studied the pictures of the huge truck going down the middle of the river. This was her big chance to make an impression on the powers to be at Fox 8 News and she wasn't going to blow the opportunity. She knew that if Brenda Edwards hadn't called in sick today that she would be the reporter sitting here instead of her.

Gail was scheduled to do a human interest story on Berry Farming in North Carolina until this came up. They decided at the last minute to send a reporter and a camera crew to the house of Jack Billings to get a statement before any of the other news channels got wind of the story. Gail's cell phone rang and she quickly answered it.

"Gail Davis," she said.

"Gail, this is Stephen in research. Since monster trucks aren't legal to drive on public roads they don't issue them license plates, so the truck is not licensed to Jack Billings; however, all the phone numbers and web-sites and businesses listed on the tailgate are owned by Jack Billings, so it's safe to say that he owns the truck. Also, if you look closely at the picture where the truck is leaving the river, you can see a road sign in the background. We enlarged the picture until we could read it and it says, 'No outlet, road ends 5.6 miles.' If you see a sign like that on River Road it might be the scene of the crime, and the truck is traveling down stream prior to exiting the river.

"Got it!" Gail said as she wrote furiously on her legal pad.

"Also, Jack Billings doesn't have a criminal record, but he's a controversial figure at best. His bank, Billings Savings and Loan, has repossessed more property than any other lending institution in the state of North Carolina. They have a well deserved reputation for making bad loans.

"That's interesting. Have they ever been sued?" Gail asked.

"Constantly, but they almost always win their cases," Stephen said. "Their damn good at what they do."

"What else do you know about Jack Billings?" Gail asked.

"He's a county commissioner, a member of the school board, a major stock holder and member of the board of directors at Ashe County Telephone, and a member of the local power company co-op. He owns the previously mentioned Savings and Loan, a Real-Estate office, a farm equipment dealership, a Christmas tree Farm, and has part interest in a number of companies in Ashe, Allegany, and Wilkes County. He owns two planes and has his own private landing strip behind his house on the other side of the mountain."

"It sounds like Mr. Billings is quite the entrepreneur," Gail said.

"Nobody really knows how many businesses Jack has his fingers in but it apparently is quite a few," Stephen said.

"What do you have on his personal life?" Gail asked.

"He was divorced in 1985 and has remained single. He has a son from that marriage, William Stanley Billings, who is twenty-four years old. He also adopted his nephew, Johnny Zebulon Billings, in 1987 when Johnny's father drove off a bridge into the New River and drowned. He is twenty-four years old also. Both his son and his nephew have been in rehab for drug and alcohol addiction. We are trying to determine if the two men in the monster truck are his son and nephew, but since we don't have a picture of their faces we can't be sure. One of the reporters from our Jefferson office where the pictures were dropped off says that he knows Billy and Johnny Billings and they are definitely the two men in the truck," Stephen said.

"But we can't prove it?" Gail said.

"No, we can't prove it," Stephen said. "That's all the information I have right now but if I find anything else I'll give you a call."

"Thank you, Stephen." Gail said.

"Go get him, tiger!" Stephen said and then he hung up.

"According to On-Star, the next road on the right will be River Road," Jerry said to Gail as they wound their way down Highway 117.

Gail thought that if she could impress the executives at FOX 8 as much as she had impressed Jerry that she would definitely be promoted to an anchor position. He had almost wrecked them twice because he was looking at her legs instead of at the road. They rounded another curve and could see the bridge that crossed the south fork of the New River. On the other side of the bridge was an old white two-story country store with a porch all the way across the front and down one side so that customers could sit and watch the river. The black Suburban bounced across the bridge and Gail could see the sign that said River Road.

"Here we go," Jerry said as they turned onto River Road.

"How long is River Road?" Gail asked.

"It's eleven miles to the dead-end. That's where Jack Billings lives," Jerry said as he studied the screen on the dash.

"Let me know when we've gone about five miles," Gail said. "I want to look for that road sign that says No Outlet."

Jerry set the trip odometer and then looked at Gail's legs. He loved his job.

"Lee Hayworth was pacing back and forth across the one-hundred-dred foot bridge that spanned the south fork of the New River when his cell phone rang. "Hello?" he said.

"Damn, Lee, why haven't you called me? I just woke up and it's almost ten o'clock," Steve Helms said drowsily.

"I haven't seen any dead fish yet!" Lee answered. "Did everything go all right last night" Steve asked.

"I guess so. After Tommy loaded up and took off on the four-wheeler I went back to bed."

"Well, you just stay put and keep watching the river. As soon as I get dressed I'm going to go wake Tommy and make sure he poured the chemicals in the river like we planned.

Maybe something happened and he couldn't do it. You should have seen some dead fish by now."

"Okay, Gail, we've traveled exactly five miles," Jerry said as he glanced at Gail's legs.

"If you see a road sign slow down," Gail said.

She had no more got the words out of her mouth when they rounded a curve and could see a road sign up ahead. "Here's one. Let's see what it says. 'No Outlet, Road Ends 5.6 Miles Ahead.' That's it. Stop! Stop!"

Jerry pulled the suburban onto the shoulder of the road and stopped. Gail took her folder and pulled out the picture with the road sign on it and hopped out. Jerry walked around the vehicle and leaned against Gail as he studied the picture.

"This is it. There are the two trees that you see in the picture. The man that took this picture was standing in the river right there through those two trees," Gail said, pointing with her finger.

"You're right," Jerry said. "You can tell this is the spot."

Gail turned when she heard a vehicle come around the curve and her heart sank when she saw who it was. A white suburban with a satellite dish mounted on the roof and CNN written all over it in large black letters came by them and the driver blew the horn and waved.

"Shit! Those bastards know about it too!" Gail shouted. "Hurry up, let's get down there before they get an exclusive."

219

Jerry ran around the suburban and jumped in just in time to see all the way up Gail's dress when she jumped in the passenger seat.

"If you would concentrate on your driving as much as you concentrate on trying to see my panties we would probably already be there!" Gail snapped.

Jerry cranked up the suburban and spun the tires as he swerved back onto River Road. Hell, what could he say? He was a man.

"Eagle, this is Snake. Over."

"Go ahead, Snake."

"I've got a white suburban with CNN written on it headed for Satan's palace, and a black suburban with FOX 8 News written on it right behind them."

"Ten-four, Snake. Did you copy that, Smitty?"

"Ten-four, I copied that," Smitty said.

"We need video from your location."

"Video's rolling, Eagle."

When the two vehicles came in sight of Lee Hayworth he sprinted back to the wrought iron gates and punched in the code to close them with him on the inside. Lee jerked out his cell phone and punched the speed dial for Steve Helms. Steve answered on the first ring.

"Lee, I can't find Tommy!" Steve said when he answered his phone. "He's not in his room and nobody has seen him."

"Steve, I got CNN and FOX 8 News pulling up to the gate as we speak," Lee said.

"Just stall them until I find Tommy," Steve said. "There must be a fish kill if they sent reporters down here. It might not have reached us for some reason. Maybe someone reported it and they got it contained before it got here."

"Do you think we should call Jack?" Lee asked.

"No, not yet. Let me find out what's going on first," Steve said.

"Okay, but hurry up and find Tommy if you can," Lee said.

The two Suburbans slid to a stop at the iron gates and both news crews jumped out and rushed to the gate. Gail recognized the woman reporter from CNN as Suzy Chung. She was Asian and like a lot of Asian women she was petite and had beautiful black hair and light brown skin and turned heads wherever she went. She beat Gail to the gate and started in on the guard immediately.

"I'm from CNN and would like to speak to Mr. Jack Billings."

"Mr. Billings is not here right now," Lee said.

"Do you know when he will be back?" Gail said as she stepped up beside Suzy. "No, I don't know when Mr. Billings will be back."

"What is your name, sir?" Suzy asked.

"I'm not at liberty to tell you," Lee said.

"You can't even tell us your name?" Gail asked.

"I'm afraid not," Lee answered.

"What do you know about the incident that occurred in the river?" Suzy asked. "I don't know about any incident that occurred in the river."

"Do you have a number that we could reach Mr. Billings at?" Gail asked.

"No, I don't have a number that you could reach Mr. Billings at," Lee said. "Listen, ladies, I can't answer any of your questions."

"Why were you standing on the bridge when we drove up? Are you guarding the gate? Are you in charge of security?" Suzy was bombarding Lee with questions when Jerry tapped Gail on the shoulder and motioned for her to step back to talk to him.

Gail stepped away from the gate and leaned over to whisper in Jerry's ear. "What is it?"

"The monster truck is in that garage! You can see the front end of it all the way at the end," Jerry said.

"Let's get the camera rolling and I'll point the truck out to the viewers and explain that the security guard won't let us enter and that he claims Mr. Billings is not on the premises," Gail said.

"Okay, but it will take us a few minutes to set up," Jerry said.

Gail rushed back to the FOX 8 suburban to check her make-up and her hair and in her baste she tripped on a black cord and went down on her knees. The only thing she hurt was her pride as one of the crew members from CNN helped her up.

"Are you all right?"

"Yes, thank you so much."

"You're quite welcome."

Gail stepped back to the suburban and looked at her knees. They weren't bleeding but she had ruined her hose. Fortunately she had learned early on to always carry extra clothing when she went to do a story and she had a bag in the back of the suburban with extra pantyhose. Gail stepped to the back of the suburban and pulled out her travel bag and grabbed the package of pantyhose. She looked all around to make sure there was no one looking and that there were no homes in sight and then she hollered at Jerry. "Don't come back here until I say so!"

"Okay," Jerry hollered back while be checked the camera.

Gail pulled her dress up over her waist and took her thumbs and pushed her pantyhose down. Her legs were her best asset and she would be damned if she was going to stand in front of a camera with runs in her hose.

"Hart! Hart!" Smitty said as he punched Harold Hartley. Smitty was running the video camera from the sniper hide directly across from Jack's house and Hart was lying behind the rifle watching the garage. Hart swung the rifle around until he could see what Smitty was so excited about.

"Oh my God!" Hart said as he watched the long-legged blond step out of her pantyhose and start pulling on the new ones. Hart knew that the rest of the team at the tobacco barn was probably gathered around the monitor whooping and hollering.

Justin set his rifle down on a set of sandbags on top of his shooting bench. He had switched the Weaver 36 × 42 for the Leupold 4.5 × 14 × 50 and had used a boresight to line it up. It would still need to be sighted in but at least it would be close. He retrieved a set of ear muffs and a pair of shooting glasses and a box of ammunition that had been loaded specifically for this rifle. Justin opened the shutters in his shooting room and then took a seat behind the rifle. He felt it as soon as he looked through the scope. It was like someone was pointing a ray gun of some sort at him and he was being pounded by an invisible force. It was Gabriel warning him of danger and there had been only one time in his life that he felt it this strong. It was in Vietnam when he and his spotter, Wayne Satterfield, had been in a hide on top of a hill overlooking a rice patty. He suddenly felt a strong force similar to what he was feeling now and motioned for Wayne to start backing out. Wayne didn't understand why but he slowly started backing out until they were in some trees and then they stood up and ran down their prearranged escape route. He asked Justin why they were leaving as they ran and Justin's only answer was "I don't know." About that time a barrage of mortars and machine gun fire erupted, covering the top of the hill they just left. Wayne never questioned Justin after that. The feeling Justin was getting now was the same but he couldn't run this time because this was where he lived.

"Where is he, Gabriel?" Justin said as he swung the scope back and forth across the mountain. "I know you're out there somewhere."

Smitty and Hart weren't the only snipers getting a firsthand view of the show that Gail was putting on unintentionally. Duke and Snake were in the hide to the right of Justin's near the top of the mountain. They were over 1,200 yards from the gate at Jack's but with the high quality optics that they were looking through they could see freckles at that distance. Duke was on the spotting scope and saw the long legged blond when she first stepped to the rear of the suburban and hiked her dress up over her waist.

"Snake," he said as he punched his partner.

Snake turned his head and Duke pointed with his finger toward Jack's house. Snake had the .50-caliber sniper rifle pointed at Justin's house and had to swing it almost ninety degrees to look at Jack's house. It was worth it. The long legged blond was pulling on a pair of pantyhose as she leaned against the tailgate of the suburban and it was as sexy as anything Snake had ever seen.

There, near the top of the mountain. Something moved. Justin knew that he wasn't imagining that. He definitely saw something move. Where was it? Justin reached up with his left hand and turned the magnification on the scope from 4.5 up to 14 power and then scanned the mountain again. There it is. A rifle barrel slowly swinging toward Jack's house. Jack has hired a sniper to kill me.

Justin pinpointed the sniper's location and then stepped out of the shooting room and over to the window where he had his Bausch and Lomb spotting scope sitting on a tri-pod. He located the gun barrel and then cranked the spotting scope up to sixty power. Justin saw the barrel of the rifle and suddenly got chills as he realized that from the size of the barrel and the huge muzzle brake on the end of it that the rifle had to be a .50-caliber sniper rifle. Jack must have hired a mercenary to kill me Justin thought to himself.

Justin ran across his shop and started pulling things out of a cabinet and piling them on a table. He then made a trip to his gun safe and placed those items on the table also. Justin looked closely at all the items to make sure he had everything he could possibly need. There was a ghillie suit, a pair of camouflaged hiking boots, a pair of pocket size binoculars, a Blackhawk neck knife on a chain necklace, a tactical vest with a built in shoulder holster and a built in knife sheath with a Ka-bar fighting knife hanging in it upside down, a compass, a fifty-foot roll of parachute cord, a .45 automatic pistol, and a pump 12-gauge shotgun with an extended magazine tube.

Justin started shoving 12-gauge double-ought buck shells into the shotgun until he shoved the seventh one in and then he jacked one into the chamber before inserting the eighth one. It was time to hunt the greatest predator that ever lived—man!

Gail couldn't believe her luck because just as soon as they went on the air someone cranked up the monster truck and pulled it out of the garage as if they wanted to show it off. It was definitely the same truck as the one in the pictures and it was so loud that Gail had to shout into her microphone so that the Channel 8 viewers could hear her.

Walt happened to look out and see the reporters and the television cameras and thought it would be a great way to introduce "Jumping Jack Flash" to the world, so he cranked it up and pulled it outside and even turned on the music. He couldn't wait for Jack to see his monster truck on the five o'clock news. He knew it would tickle him.

"As you can see in the background, the truck "Jumping Jack Flash" is the same truck that drove down the middle of the beautiful New River," Gail shouted into the microphone. "The security guard stationed at Jack Billing's gate claims that Mr. Billings is not here and that he doesn't know when he will return. This is Gail Davis, reporting live from the entrance of Jack Billing's house, in Ashe County. Wait, there's a black Hummer driving up to our location. Let's see if by chance this is Mr. Billings returning home."

Johnny Steele, Cecil Wood, and Jack Billings stepped out of the Hummer and were immediately surrounded by both news crews.

Jack was smiling like a possum eating persimmons as he stepped forward to speak.

Gail beat Suzy to the punch this time. "Mr. Billings, would you care to comment on the incident in the New River!"

"Yes, I would," Jack said. "I think the person responsible for pouring chemicals in the New River should be hunted down and prosecuted to the fullest extent of the law. To think that anyone could be irresponsible enough to poison a beautiful river like the New River is incomprehensible and I will do everything in my power to assist the authorities in apprehending them."

Gail Davis and Suzy Chung stood there with their mouths open looking at Jack wondering what in the world he was talking about.

"What chemicals are you talking about Mr. Billings?" Suzy finally asked.

"The chemicals that were poured in the river last night!" Jack said and he glanced down at the river with a confused look on his face. "That is why you're here, isn't it?"

"We don't know anything about any chemicals being poured in the river," Gail said. "We are here to see if you would give us a statement regarding this picture of your monster truck being driven down the middle of the river."

Gail showed Jack the picture of the truck in the river with Billy throwing the beer bottles out the window. "Can you tell us who these two men are that are driving your truck?"

Jack's eyes almost popped out of his head when he saw the picture and his face turned red.

"Mr. Billings you do realize that it is a felony to drive a vehicle down a river that is protected by state and federal environmental laws," Gail said.

Jack was in a total state of shock as he stared at the picture. He stood there looking at the picture and not responding to anything else. If a meteor hit the river and sprayed water over the crowd that was gathered on that bridge, he probably wouldn't have noticed because he was totally embarrassed and humiliated, and he was angrier than he had ever been.·

"Why did you mention chemicals in the river earlier, Mr. Billings?" Suzy asked. "We have not received any report of a chemical spill on the New River."

Jack stood there like a statue and finally Cecil stepped around to rescue him. "Excuse me, but Mr. Billings has just returned from a grueling business trip and is exhausted. My name is Cecil Wood and I am Mr. Billing's attorney. Neither Mr. Billings nor I have any knowledge of a truck being driven down the river but will immediately investigate the matter and issue a statement to the press. I, along with Mr. Billings, am in a state of shock after seeing this picture and would never allow such recklessness as this obviously portrays. Mr. Billings and all his employees are very conscientious of the environment and have always strived to protect it."

"Why did Mr. Billings mention chemicals being poured in the river, Mr. Wood?" Gail asked.

"Mr. Billings was asleep when we drove up and was not fully awake when you began questioning him. My only guess is that he was dreaming just prior to our stopping and just thought someone poured chemicals in the river. Now, if you will excuse us, we need to get Mr. Billings to the house," Cecil said.

"He's smoking a cigar, Mr. Wood! Does he usually smoke when he's sleeping?" Suzy Chung hollered as all three men jumped back in the Hummer.

Johnny Steele didn't have enough room on the bridge to drive around the news crews so he decided to just back out and leave. They needed to escape this nightmare even if they had to get Coy or Jerry to come pick them up in one of the planes at an airstrip. Johnny cranked up the Hummer and started to back up, but when he looked behind him all he could see was the front end of another suburban and there was another one pulling up behind that one. Channel 2 and Channel 12 had scrambled when they saw the first live shot from Fox 8, and put their crews on the road immediately. Like the old saying goes, better late than never.

The three-ring circus that was taking place on the bridge in front of Jack's house was being watched intently by Smitty and Hart who were videoing it from their hide four hundred yards away. It was also being watched by Duke and Snake from their hide on top of the mountain beside Justin's house and several people were watching it on monitors, including Jimmy Hardy in the old tobacco barn and several people in a room at the Pentagon. Chief and Wizard were in the sniper hide directly across the river from Justin's and couldn't see the action from their location so they just listened to the chatter in their earpieces. Chief looked through the spotting scope at Justin's house and then swung it over to look at Duke and Snake's sniper hide near the top of the mountain. That's strange, he thought to himself, he didn't remember a bush being right behind that sniper hide.

"Hey, Wizard! Look at Duke and Snake's hide. Do you remember a bush being behind them?" Chief asked.

Wizard swung the .50 over and looked through the scope. "That's not a bush! It's a man in a ghillie suit!" he shouted. "Give me a yardage."

Chief shot the range with a laser range finder. "It's 1,082 yards!"

"Tell Duke and Snake to keep their heads down and to be ready for my shot," Wizard said.

"Duke, this is Chief. Don't talk and don't move! You have a man ten yards behind you in a ghillie suit. Wizard is dialed in and ready to intercept!"

"Wizard, this is Eagle. You will not fire until person is identified or fires on our positions. Do you copy?"

"Copy, Eagle. Waiting for green light."

Duke slowly turned his head and looked right into the barrel of Justin's 12-gauge shotgun. "If either one of you even blink, I'll blow you in half! Now, one at a time, start undressing."

"Don't shoot, Wizard! It's Daddy Rabbit. We've been busted," Snake said.

"That includes moving your lips!" Justin said. "Now get undressed."

Time to Come Clean

DeMac was holding Scooter in his lap and scratching his neck as Travis drove them home from the Sparta Animal Clinic. "Did you two lovebirds let go of one another long enough to check Scooter's wound out, or did you just swap slobber for fifteen minutes?" DeMac asked.

"No, she checked Scooter out and said he was doing fine. She said to keep giving him the antibiotics and keep it coated with that cream."

"Well, I can see why you're walking around in a daze. She is truly a gorgeous woman," DeMac said. "I think the Navy is going to lose a good combat photographer."

"Man, I haven't even thought about the Navy since I got here," Travis said. There's been too much going on!"

"It has been kind of crazy," DeMac said. "It's not every weekend that you get in a fight with the son of a local dignitary, rescue a dog from a groundhog fight, meet a beautiful doctor, rescue a woman from a car wreck, and have to get out of the river so that you don't get run over by a monster truck."

"Speaking of monster trucks, look who's coming up River Road," Travis said.

A white van with a big 9 on the hood and Channel 9 News on the side passed by Travis and DeMac as they started down River

Road. They hadn't gone very far before they met the Channel 12 and Channel 2 news crews as they headed back toward Highway 117.

"I bet I know somebody who is really pissed off right now," Travis said.

"Oh, he's way beyond pissed off," DeMac said. "Jack will have to calm down for several hours just to get back to being pissed off."

"There's no way I could reenlist in the Navy and leave Dad up here by himself with this feud going on even if I hadn't met Jesse," Travis said. "Like Dad said, this thing is going to get worse before it ever gets better."

"Well, at least he's got a guardian angel," DeMac said as Travis turned into his dad's driveway. DeMac was thinking that Justin actually has about thirty guardian angels if you counted his Seal team plus the spooks.

When Travis topped the hill and started to turn to go by the front of his dad's house, he and DeMac could see a couple news teams parked on Jack's bridge with their satellite dishes run up in the air about forty feet. Travis drove around the house and hit his remote control garage door opener and waited for the door to raise up enough to drive inside.

As soon as the door came up Travis just reached up and cut the ignition off. Justin was sitting in a fold out lawn chair with a shotgun lying across his lap and his face and hands were painted green and black with camouflage cream. There were two naked men lying on the concrete floor with their hands and feet tied together with parachute cord, and Shogun was sitting at their heads watching them and he didn't look happy.

"You got here just in time, men," Justin said. "I was just getting ready to feed Shogun. I can't decide which one to feed to him first. If somebody doesn't start answering my questions I'm going to turn Scooter loose on them now that he's home. He's like a land dwelling Piranha."

"Hey, Duke. Hey, Snake," Travis said as he walked over beside his dad.

"You know these men, Travis?" Justin asked.

"Yeah, I know both of them. They're members of DeMac's Seal team," Travis said. "What the hell's going on?"

"They were up on top of the mountain above the shooting range watching me. Gabriel warned me that something was wrong so I kept looking until I spotted them and then I slipped around behind them and captured them. What do you know about all this DeMac?"

DeMac stood there and remained silent and Justin swung the shotgun barrel around until it was pointed at him. "Start undressing! You can join your friends here until I figure out what's going on."

A vehicle could be heard driving by the front of the house in a hurry, so Justin jumped up and took cover behind his truck and ordered DeMac to lie down. When the vehicle came in sight Justin followed it with the fiber optic front sight on his shotgun until it stopped behind Travis's Jeep. A man climbed out of the white van with his hands held high and Shogun and Scooter growled as he approached the carport.

"State your name and business and keep your hands up while you're doing it!" Justin shouted.

"My name is Jimmy Hardy and I'm with the CIA's department of Homeland Security. I have come here to explain why we have sniper's positioned around your house and to ask you for your help."

"I am not a threat to this country nor have I ever been. I fought and bled for this country in Vietnam and take exception to anyone spying on me on the grounds that they are protecting this country!" Justin said sharply.

"We know that now Justin, but we weren't sure at the start of this mission," Jimmy said. "Please just give me the chance to explain why we're here and why we need your help."

Channel 9, Channel 2, and Channel 12 sent their news teams to the Ashe County's Sheriff Department to find out if an investigation was underway, and if so, did they know the names of the two men in the truck and had warrants been issued for their arrest. CNN and Fox 8 left their crews in front of Jack's to await the statement that Cecil Wood had promised them they would get. They did finally move so that Jack could enter his property and Johnny Steele shut the gates behind them as soon as they drove through them.

As soon as Johnny stopped the hummer in front of the house, Jack stormed up to the front door and slung it open so hard that everyone expected the glass to break, but for some unknown reason it didn't. He needed to calm down so he could figure out a way to get out of this quagmire but right now he couldn't control himself. He had made a complete fool of himself on local and national television and somebody was going to pay for it.

Jack walked briskly over to his liquor cabinet and put three cubes of ice in a glass and started pouring Jack Daniels Whiskey over them. The whiskey bottle ran dry before it covered the ice and Jack slung the empty bottle across the room into the rock fireplace, sending pieces of shattered glass into the room in every direction. Jack drained the whiskey with one gulp and then turned to face the people in the room.

"Johnny, go find my son and my nephew and bring them to me immediately," Jack said through clinched teeth.

"Yes, sir," Johnny Steele said and he turned to leave.

"Somebody go tell Walt to pull that damn truck back in the garage and to shut the door!"

"I'll do it," Lee Hayworth said, happy to have an excuse to leave the room.

"Cecil, get us a copy of those pictures that the reporters were holding on the bridge."

"Right away, Jack!" Cecil Wood said.

"I want to have a meeting in thirty minutes with everybody except the hotel staff. Does everybody understand that?" Jack shouted sarcastically.

Everyone present said, "Yes, sir," and then quickly left the room. Jack opened up a bottle of Jim Beam and poured his glass full.

Jimmy Hardy cut his eyes over at DeMac, Duke, and Snake, who were sitting on Justin's living room floor with their backs against the wall. He was pissed off that these highly trained special operation soldiers were busted not by enemy snipers using thermal spotting scopes, but by a fifty-seven-year-old civilian using a hunting scope. You can train a man for years on techniques and procedures, but as soon as a long legged blond pulls her dress up, all the training goes straight out the window.

Travis had given Duke and Snake some old sweatpants to put on and had cut the parachute cord off their hands and feet. Travis was sitting beside his dad on the couch and the shotgun was still lying across Justin's lap. Jimmy Hardy was sitting in a chair directly in front of them and was holding a laptop computer.

"First of all, thank you, Justin, for not shooting our snipers when you spotted them."

"I wanted information from them!" Justin said angrily.

"I understand and I'm going to give you that information right now. Of course everything I'm about to tell you is classified and can't be repeated outside of this room. Justin, since you were a sniper in Vietnam, my superiors have granted my request to reinstate your classification at level 12. The fact that you actually worked for us on two separate occasions in Vietnam helped in getting you reclassified."

"I didn't know you were a sniper in Vietnam!" Travis said. "When were you going to tell me?"

"It's not something that I'm particularly proud of," Justin said.

"And like your father Travis, your clearance is also at level 12 since you're a combat photographer and have taken pictures of highly classified operations," Jimmy said.

"I didn't know you were a combat photographer!" Justin said. "When were you going to tell me about that?"

"I need to back up a couple years in order for you to understand what's going on," Jimmy continued. Two years ago, a Frenchman named Jacques de Sales, approached a research and manufacturing facility in Canada called Specialty Products about building a special suitcase for him to transport his wine in when he was traveling from one country to another. Now Jacques de Sales doesn't sell ordinary wine, he specializes in very old and very rare wines and spirits. His wine cellar has been passed down from one generation to the next since the thirteenth century and remained hidden during the war so it is filled with priceless wine. The market value of his wine cellar is unknown but is thought to be well over a billion dollars. When Blackbeard's ship was recently discovered there were several bottles of Ale in the wreckage and if you remember they were auctioned off. Jacques de Sales was the high bidder.

"Keep talking," Justin said.

Jacques de Sales lived in the Alsace Plain in France, east of Paris along the Rhine River where it forms the boundary between France and Germany. He was not a terrorist as far as we know, but he traveled back and forth between France and the Middle East, including Syria, Afghanistan, Egypt, Pakistan, Israel, Iran, and Iraq, selling his rare wines.

"He also traveled occasionally to Africa, South America, and the United States, but his best customers were the filthy rich Kings and Princes in the Arab world. That's why he was on our radar and we kept our eye on him," Jimmy said.

"You said he ordered a suitcase from Specialty Products in Canada," Justin said. "How does that involve me?"

"Jacques didn't just order a regular suitcase, he ordered a special one that would prevent x-rays from penetrating his precious wine bottles and would also prevent them from breaking in case the suitcase was dropped or was in an accident. Specialty Products has a research and design department that is second to no one in the world. They hire their engineers from MIT and Harvard and Yale and only the brightest and best are hired.

"They have designed and manufactured a lot of products for NASA and the United States military, but they will work for anybody if they have deep enough pockets. Jacques de Sales had deep enough pockets."

"Go on," Justin said.

"It took a team of engineers over six months to design and build the suitcase, and the finished product is truly spectacular. The suitcase is built out of a unique mixture of light weight metals like Scandium and Titanium in very thin overlapping layers and is coated with a composite material that Specialty Products calls Scales. They have applied for a patent on this material as well as several other patents pertaining to this suitcase. The materials in this suitcase completely block x-rays from penetrating the surface and as an added bonus the x-rays appear to be fuzzy pictures of folded clothes. The suitcase also has a special interlocking metal band that goes around it that is lapped together with a cutting compound under high speed vibration so that it goes together perfectly and forms an airtight seal. They have also applied for a patent on the metal band. The inside of the suitcase is a continuous series of small airbags that when inflated totally seals off the suitcase and protects its contents from breaking. The engineers at Specialty Products placed five wine bottles in the suitcase, and after pressurizing it, they dropped it on a concrete floor from as high as sixty feet without breaking any of the bottles. When the air-bags are inflated it's almost impossible to damage anything inside it, and since the metal band around the suitcase is interlocking, the pressure inside the suitcase just helps seal it off that much more."

"It seems to me that if you were flying at high altitudes that the pressure inside the suitcase would increase until the suitcase exploded!" Justin said.

"There's more," Jimmy said. "The suitcase is equipped with a miniature compressor that inflates the air-bags and also controls the temperature inside the suitcase, like a heat pump controls the temperature inside a house. It is also equipped with a drying tower and a purge system. All the systems that are built into the suitcase are programmed and controlled by a special laptop computer. When Jacques travels to Egypt with two bottles of wine that are worth $70,000 apiece, he can program the suitcase to maintain a constant 45 PSI and to keep his wine chilled at 60 degrees Fahrenheit."

"He can also set the humidity at whatever he pleases," Jimmy continued. "To answer your question about the pressure rising, if the pressure starts to rise, the purge system will bleed off the excess pressure and keep it at a constant 45 PSI. All the systems in the suitcase are almost totally silent, so a baggage handler or a customs inspector can't hear them running. A drug or explosives K-9 can hear the compressor running but they aren't trained to mark luggage by sound. They only mark luggage by smell, and so far they have failed to detect anything when it's been tested."

"Where's this story going Jimmy?" Justin said impatiently.

"Jacques de Sales was kidnapped on February 19 while traveling in Syria and was murdered a few days later. The people that kidnapped and murdered him are known Al Qaida terrorists and we think that they were after the suitcase. We also believe that they are planning to use the suitcase to deliver a dirty bomb into the United States and the suitcase is the absolute perfect vehicle to deliver it. We can't detect a bomb in the suitcase by x-rays or by sniffing it with a sniffing machine or by drug and explosives dogs. They could place a small nuclear device or possibly a biological device in the suitcase and fly it into this country with no problem. They have already tested it and it passed with flying colors," Jimmy said, staring at Justin.

"Jimmy, this is a very interesting story you're telling me but I want to know why the hell you have snipers positioned at my house!" Justin said angrily.

"The suitcase is at Jack's house," Jimmy said. "It was flown there over two weeks ago and it's still there as we speak."

"Now you got my attention," Justin said. "How do you know it's there?"

"The United States Government is by far the biggest customer of Specialty Products in Canada. Our space program and our military comprise over 60 percent of their sales, and were talking about billions of dollars annually, so they are very friendly with us to say the least. When we recognized the potential of this project we asked Specialty Products to build another one just like the original, but to equip it with a special GPS transponder that only we could detect so we could keep track of it wherever it went. They sold us the original suitcase for us to test, and then sold Jacques de Sales the second one, or Suitcase B, as we call it, to carry his precious wine in. We have been tracking Suitcase B by satellite since the day that Jacques walked out the door of Specialty Products with it in his hand.

After his kidnapping and murder, the suitcase remained in Syria until a little over a month ago when it was flown to Egypt and then to New York. The man traveling with Suitcase B is Gyurman Yahamen Tahare-Azar, a known Al Qaida member who was educated in the United States and goes by the name Maschiek Abdullah Ignacio. As soon as the plane landed in New York we seized the suitcase, and with the help of a couple of engineers from Specialty Products, we depressurized it and used a robot to open it up. It contained small trace amounts of different substances that can be used in a dirty bomb. We closed it back up and repressurized it and sent it down the conveyor for Gyurman to collect."

"And then this Gyurman flew to Jack's house?" Travis asked.

"No, not at first. He left New York and flew to Atlanta, and then to Denver, and then to Chicago, and then to a private airstrip in Pennsylvania, and then to Jack's house. They were testing the suitcase in different airports to make sure they could trust it to deliver a dirty bomb without being detected," Jimmy said.

"I can't understand why they would fly it to Jack's house?" Justin said.

"We didn't understand it either at first, but we do now," Jimmy said. "We've been watching Jack's house since the moment the suitcase landed there. We immediately tapped his phone lines and placed our own snipers in position to watch everything that went on there. We noticed immediately that something was wrong because nothing made any sense."

"What do you mean?" Justin asked.

"Well, first of all, Jack owns two airplanes. The one airplane he owns is a Cessna T210. It has been updated with all new electronics and displays and is probably a $300,000 airplane. That's a lot of money for most people but not for Jack, so we weren't shocked by that. But Jack's other plane is a King Air, with all the latest flat screen displays and digital electronics like XM Satellite Weather, Jepperson charts, the airplanes own weather radar, terrain and traffic warning systems, and top of the line communications including text messaging. This plane got our attention since it probably cost over three million dollars.

That's a lot of money and a lot of airplane for someone like Jack."

"Was that all that seemed out of place?" Justin asked.

"No, everything was out of place. Jack has twenty-three full time employees. That's too many people to run just his household and his farm. And they fly in too much food for that many people and a lot of the food is exotic and very expensive. The swimming pool behind Jack's house is 28 feet × 44 feet, but they fly in enough pool chemicals to treat a pool six times that size. They also fly in enough liquor to keep the whole staff drunk everyday of the week. And the most confusing thing of all was his phone lines. He had only three phone lines going into his house and they weren't being used nearly enough for that amount of people and that much business, and that was ultimately his downfall because we started looking for hidden phone lines and we found them. Jack has a secret duct system that runs from the back side of the mountain all the way to Highway 117. It follows the North Fork of the river until it reaches the highway and then goes into a manhole where it splices into the main fiber optic cable that runs from Sparta to Jefferson. Jack has two fiber optic lines dedicated entirely to him that run all the way to the Sparta Telephone Office. Once we discovered his secret phone lines we tapped them of course and things started to make sense. Jack is harboring fugitives. The mountain behind Jack's house has been converted into an underground luxury hotel for rich fugitives. He deals exclusively through Jimmy Milano, who is the head of the Chicago mafia."

"The mafia!" Justin shouted. "Jack is flying in fugitives and hiding them in the mountain behind his house?"

"When Jimmy Milano calls Donald Crafton, who is in charge of running the hotel, they take the King Air at night and fly to a private air strip to pick the fugitive up and then fly him back to Jack's. We have intercepted phone conversations and identified three fugitives and one of them is on the FBI's ten most wanted list. We know now why he orders so much food and liquor and pool chemicals. We think that Gyurman is staying at Jack's just to have a secure place to keep the suitcase until the leaders of Al Qaida can plan their next move."

"And you thought that I was involved in this somehow?" Justin asked.

"Justin, we don't assume anything in the CIA," Jimmy said. "We can't afford to under estimate anybody or anything. If we make a mistake it could cost the lives of tens of thousands of people, so we check everybody out, even if their flag flying Americans. Our biggest fear since the mission first started was that someone could use the suitcase as a blueprint and build another one just like it. You have the skills and the machinery in your shop to build almost anything if you really wanted to, so we had to set up on you and make sure you weren't involved," Jimmy said.

"Are you satisfied now?" Justin asked.

"We were satisfied as soon as we saw and heard this," Jimmy said as he turned the laptop computer screen so that Justin and Travis could see it. Jimmy punched in a code and the screen came alive with the video of Jack and Johnny Steele when they met with Justin to try and buy his property. You could hear Justin as he asked Jack if Johnny ever spoke.

"Well, I'll be damned," Justin said.

"How did you get the audio?" Travis asked.

"From DeMac's cell phone. We've been listening to everything that's been said since you two left Norfolk last Friday," Jimmy said. "We have your phone tapped also."

"What about Teresa? Is she one of your spies?" Justin asked.

"No, Teresa is not with the CIA, but we did check her out since she wandered into the circle. She's clean as a pin."

Justin felt a slight sense of relief when he heard that. He still thought she was too good to be true. "If you knew I was not connected to Jack after watching this video, why did you continue to watch me?" Justin asked.

"To protect DeMac. DeMac refused to participate in this mission when we first approached him about it, but we needed him so he was ordered to do it."

"Why did he refuse?" Justin asked.

"Because he didn't want to jeopardize his friendship with your son. Since he was friends with your son it was the perfect way for us to get someone on the inside, so he was ordered to do it, or face a dishonorable discharge. He finally agreed to it if we would let him use his team instead of our people and we agreed to it since they are highly trained and our people are stretched kind of thin since 9/11. DeMac's team will protect him at all costs and he knows that, but they will also protect you and Travis, that is if there not watching a long-legged blonde change her pantyhose," Jimmy said and he cut his eyes over to Duke and Snake.

"Sheriff, your wife's on line one," Sheriff Sisk's secretary shouted.

"Judy, how many times have I asked you not to call me at work?"

"Shut up, Bill, and turn on Channel 8. There are news people all over Jack Billing's place. They showed this film about an hour ago but they're going to show it again," Judy Sisk said and then hung up.

Bill Sisk hung the phone up and grabbed the remote control and turned on the television. When the picture appeared there stood Jack on the bridge in front of his house telling the reporters that he would assist the authorities until the person that poured chemicals into the river was apprehended. Bill wasn't surprised to see news coverage of the chemical spill but he was surprised that the Wildlife Department hadn't notified him yet.

Then the reporter held up a picture and Jack looked like a deer caught in the headlights until Cecil stepped around to rescue him. Channel 8 gave their viewers a close-up of the picture and you clearly see the backs of Billy and Johnny's heads as they drove the monster truck down the middle of the river.

Bill jumped up and grabbed his duty belt and ran to the back door of the Sheriffs Department. When he jerked the door open he was met by the Channel 2 reporter and camera man, and the

Channel 9 and Channel 12 crews were right behind them and they quickly surrounded him.

"Sheriff Sisk, what can you tell us pertaining to the pictures of Jack Billing's monster truck being driven down the New River?"

"I can't tell you anything until we complete the investigation," the sheriff said.

"So there is an active investigation into this matter?" another reporter asked.

"Yes. Yes, there is," Bill said.

"Is it possible that charges will be brought against Mr. Billings since it was his truck that was used in this attack on the river?" a reporter shouted over the crowd noise.

"I can't comment at this time about an ongoing investigation. As soon as we complete our investigation I will issue a statement and answer any of your questions. Now if you'll excuse me, I really must go," Bill said as he pushed his way through the crowd.

"Sheriff Sisk, are you aware of anyone pouring chemicals into the New River?"

"No, there has been no report of anyone pouring chemicals into the river that I'm aware of," Bill said as he climbed into his Ford Explorer and cranked it up.

Justin put his shotgun and tactical vest back in his shop and returned to his living room. Everyone was sitting in chairs now and Travis had poured everyone a glass of tea.

"Let me make sure that I've got all this straight," Justin said as he sat back down. "A known Al Qaida terrorist, who is carrying a suitcase that is capable of delivering a nuclear or biological bomb into the United States without being detected, is staying in the mountain behind Jack's house that has been converted into an underground hotel for fugitives."

"That's correct," Jimmy said.

"You said you needed my help. What is it you need me to do?" Justin asked. "Nothing. We want you and Travis to go about your daily routines just like nothing is going on and let us continue to monitor this situation. We think that Gyurman is going to fly out sometime Friday night. He received a message that suggested that but it hasn't been confirmed yet. When he flies out we're going to follow him until he meets his contact and then take them both down."

"What about Jack?" Justin asked.

"The CIA will give the FBI all the information that we have gathered over the last few weeks and they will use their Special Response Teams to take Jack and all his people into custody. We will assist them from the shadows but we cannot be connected to the actual takedown or investigations in any way, shape, or form. As soon as the suitcase flies out of Ashe County then the CIA and DeMac's Seal team will pack up and leave.

"What will Jack be charged with?" Justin asked.

"That will ultimately be up to the FBI, but there are numerous crimes besides harboring fugitives. There are two counts of accessory to first-degree murder, plotting to pour toxic chemicals into a federally protected river, tax evasion, money laundering, prostitution, drug trafficking, and the list goes on and on," Jimmy said.

"Would one of those murders happen to be my friend Roy?" Justin asked.

"Yes, it would. After your confrontation with Jack on Friday when you told him that Roy's tractor didn't have a carburetor on it, he sent one of his men to the junkyard in Jefferson to purchase the tractor and return it to his house. Jimmy turned the laptop screen around so Justin and Travis could see the picture of Steve Helms driving out of the junkyard. "They dumped it down the number 7 mine shaft."

"I knew that son of a bitch was responsible for Roy's death," Justin growled.

"How do you know that they dumped it down the number 7 mine shaft?" Travis asked. "Do you have somebody on the inside at Jack's?"

"No, but we have a prisoner and he is singing the blues. Last night between three a.m. and four a.m., a man traveling on a Kawasaki Mule pulled out of Jack's garage and eased up River Road slowly with his headlights out. We immediately sent the sniper team that is set up directly across from your house down the mountain to intercept him if it became necessary. He stopped about two hundred yards from your mailbox and proceeded on foot carrying two five gallon containers. When he reached your mailbox he turned toward the river and as he stepped across the ditch, the two Seals took him down. He had been sent by Jack to pour gunsmithing chemicals into the river at your mailbox to create a fish kill that would lead back to you and ultimately lead to your arrest. Once in custody, Sheriff Sisk was planning on drugging you and then he was going to hang you by a torn bed sheet making it appear that you committed suicide," Jimmy said.

"I'll kill that son of a bitch!" Travis said as he jumped up.

"Whoa! Whoa! This is where your assistance is needed. Instead of launching World War III, we need you to stay calm and let us handle everything," Jimmy said. "The man we have in custody has already told us about Roy's murder and Bill Sisk was there when they did it. As soon as the FBI steps in and takes over, Sheriff Sisk will be charged with murder and probably spend the rest of his life in prison. That's a worse fate than death, especially for a cop."

"What are you going to do with your prisoner?" Justin asked.

"We'll turn him over to the FBI when they step in and take over," Jimmy said. We've been wearing FBI clothing and flashing fake badges at him so he thinks were FBI agents anyway. He has no idea that we're CIA and that the two men that captured him are actually

Seals. We also seized the Kawasaki Mule and have it stored at the Federal Building in North Wilkesboro."

"I'll bet Jack's wondering where his man and his mule are," Justin said.

"I would almost bet you that they're having a meeting right now as we speak," Jimmy said.

"Well, Jimmy, I don't really see that I have any other alternative than to just sit back and let you and DeMac's team protect me," Justin said.

"I think we have you protected real well. There are two sniper teams watching your house and three watching Jack's house twenty-four hours a day. I have a cell phone for each of you to carry that will allow us to monitor conversations and give us a GPS signal so we will know where you are at all times. Travis, your cell phone is already programmed with your present cell phone number so that you don't have to carry both of them, and Justin your cell phone is programmed to ring on your home phone number. Of course both of you need to be real careful until this thing is over. Jack and his hoodlums are capable of trying anything and in some ways they are very sophisticated. We left a business card at the junkyard in Jefferson in hopes that if Jack sent someone to pick the tractor up that they would take the card back to Jack's and call the number from Jack's phones. The number on the card activates a special computer software tracing program at CIA headquarters at the Pentagon. The man that picked up the tractor took the card and called the number the next day. The computers at the Pentagon traced the call from Jack's house to Sparta Telephone, and then to a router in Texas, and then to another router in St. Louis, and then back to Randleman, NC. Jack's phone lines are hooked up to a series of routers in several different states so that no one can trace his calls. That's pretty impressive for a small time crook like Jack, so we want to be careful not to underestimate him or what he may try. But with five sniper teams watching twenty-four hours a day, you should be safe."

"Don't forget about my guardian angel," Justin said.

"I haven't convinced myself that you actually have a guardian angel yet," Jimmy said.

"I caught your snipers, didn't I?" Justin said.

"That you did," Jimmy said. "Point taken. So, will you guys work with us until this thing is over?"

"Under one condition," Justin said.

"I'm afraid to ask. What's the condition?"

"Do you have the video of that long-legged blond changing her pantyhose on that laptop?" Justin asked.

"You bet I do!" Jimmy said as he punched in the code on the computer.

Everyone at Jack's had gathered around the living room for the meeting. Cecil Wood, Steve Helms, Donald Crafton, Danny Comer, Brett Tranthum, Johnny Steele, Billy and Johnny Billings, Lee Hayworth, CJ, Walt, Brooks Walker, Steve Weavil, Charles Moses, and Ashley Yates all stood around the room waiting for Jack to start the meeting.

Jack was sitting in a swivel rocking chair facing the rock fireplace with his back to the crowd, drinking Jim Beam on ice. Bill Sisk came through the side door and joined the crowd as they stood there in silence. Finally Jack spun the chair around to face the crowd and start the proceedings.

Jack's cheeks were flushed and red and it was obvious that he was half drunk. He was surprisingly soft spoken and calm when he spoke. "Walt, I want you and CJ to rig Jumping Jack Flash up so that it looks like somebody straight wired it when they stole it. I also want you to take a big pry bar and pry the garage door open until you bust the lock, just like someone would if they broke into the garage. Don't let those reporters see you when you do it though," Jack said.

"Okay, Jack. If that's what you want, we'll sure do it," Walt said.

"Also, I don't want you to move the truck out of the garage without my permission."

"Yes, sir, Mr. Billings," Walt said.

"Okay, you and CJ can go then," Jack said and they both left the room. "Can someone please tell me why the chemicals weren't poured in the river like I ordered?"

"We don't know, Jack," Steve Helms said. "Tommy left here on the Kawasaki Mule with the containers and hasn't been seen since. He's missing and so is the Mule!"

"After I adjourn this meeting I want all operations to stop so that everyone can search for Tommy. I want Steve to coordinate the search. I want somebody to go to Sparta and look around and I want somebody to go to Jefferson and do the same. Cecil, I want you to call around to his family and friends and find out if anybody has seen or heard from him. Brett, I want you to grab your waders and fly rod and wade upstream past Justin's house to see if you can find any clues to his disappearance. Johnny, I want you to put together a pair of men on alternating shifts to watch Justin Hayes's house. I want them to take a spotting scope and hide somewhere on the mountain where they can watch his house at all times.

We have night vision goggles in the hangar and if you need to hire some of your old bodyguard buddies to make it work then go ahead and do it. I think there's something strange going on at Justin's and I want to know what it is."

"No problem, Jack, consider it done," Johnny Steele said.

"Danny, I want you to tap Justin's phone line and place a recorder on it. I want you to monitor it 24–7 and let me know about anything unusual. Brett can help you as soon as he finishes searching the river."

"Yes, sir, Mr. Billings," Danny Comer said.

"Cecil, do you have those pictures of the monster truck?" Jack asked.

"Yes, I do. I had Fox 8 to fax me these," Cecil said and he handed Jack a manila envelope.

Jack reached in and pulled out several pictures and studied them while everyone stood around and silently waited for whatever would come next. "This is some excellent photography. Not only can you read my name in about six places, but if you're from around here you can tell exactly who's in the truck," Jack said. "Who took these pictures, Billy?"

"I didn't see anybody take them!" Billy said quickly.

"What about you Johnny. Do you know who took these pictures?"

"It must have been Justin Hayes or his son's Navy friend. They were standing on the bank," Johnny said softly.

"Well, I guess they had to stand on the banks since you two were driving down the middle of the fucking river!" Jack said and his voice was getting louder the longer he spoke. "Hell, a man could get run over out there fishing if he wasn't paying attention!"

You could hear a pin drop as Jack stared at his son and nephew. Jack took another sip of whiskey and continued, "This is the damnedest mess that you two have ever gotten me into, but the good news is that it won't ever happen again. Actually the way to get out of this mess is pretty straight forward because we don't have a choice in the matter. We have got to claim that the truck was stolen from our garage and that someone took it for a joyride. I will offer to pay for any damages to the river since it was ultimately my responsibility to keep my truck from being stolen and will apologize to the people of North Carolina for my carelessness," Jack said and he stood to face Billy and Johnny. Jack was a little wobbly from the whiskey and his eyes looked like peach cobs.

"I've been pretty successful at everything I ever attempted except for raising you two boys. At that I have failed miserably," Jack said and then paused for a moment. There seemed to be tears in Jack's eyes when he continued. "I can't send the two of you back to rehab now because of the press. They would jump all over it if I did, especially since they have the pictures of you two in the truck. Luckily, there are no pictures of your faces in any of the photographs, but both of you can be identified by your long hair, so here's what we have to do. Both of you will have to get your hair cut short and dyed to another color. Ashley can cut and dye your hair before you leave the house."

"I'm not going to cut my damn hair!" Billy shouted.

"If you don't get your hair cut and dyed then I don't have any choice but to ask Bill to arrest you right now and carry you both to jail. It's your choice!" Jack said firmly.

"Damn it, Daddy, why can't we just stay here and lay low for a while?" Billy asked.

"Because neither one of you live here anymore, that's why," Jack said and he turned to face Cecil Wood. "Cecil, I want you to take the deed to that property we just repossessed on Mamie May Road and sign it over to Billy and Johnny. You two have just become the proud owners of a 1988 model 52 feet × 12 feet mobile home on 0.67 of an acre."

"You mean we have to live in that rusty old trailer?" Billy shouted.

"No, you can live any damn where you want to, except here!" Jack shouted back. "Cecil, I want you to cancel their bank accounts and credit cards immediately after this meeting and give each one of them a check for $2,000. That should get them by until they can find a job."

"I can't believe you're throwing us out like we're garbage!" Billy shouted.

"Moving day is tomorrow. I want both of you gone by dark tomorrow. You can get Horatio and Antoine to help you move if you need them."

"You're serious, aren't you?" Billy screamed.

"I'll tell you how serious I am!" Jack answered back. A tear ran down Jack's cheek as he continued. "Brett, after dark tomorrow I want you to reprogram the front gate and all the remote control openers with a new code that I will give you. If anybody let's either one of these worthless bastards onto this property without my knowledge or permission, their employment will be terminated immediately. Does everybody understand that?"

Everybody in the room said, "Yes, sir."

"This meeting is over!" Jack said and he sat back down and swiveled around to face the fireplace.

A Line Drawn in the Sand

I t had been a long time since Justin had heard an officer dress down a couple soldiers, but there was no mistaking what was taking place in his carport between DeMac and his two errant team members. Justin couldn't understand what DeMac was saying, but he understood why he was saying it. Carelessness will get you and your buddies killed quickly if you're a soldier, and even though in this particular case there was no real damage, the matter still needed to be addressed. Judging from the volume of the conversation, it was apparent that DeMac was sufficiently addressing the problem.

Jimmy Hardy stepped outside to put in his two cents worth but returned quickly to the living room carrying two cell phones. He gave Justin and Travis a brief demonstration on how to use their new cell phones and then asked them if they had any questions before he left. DeMac stepped back inside and went to his bedroom and then stepped into the living room carrying his sea bag.

"Where do you think you're going with that sea bag, sailor?" Justin said to DeMac.

"Well, I just assumed that I would move back to the tobacco barn since you found out that I was spying on you," DeMac said.

"Oh hell no!" Justin said. "You're staying right here. Put that sea bag back in that bedroom before I go back and get my shotgun. You and me haven't got to go fishing but one time since you got here and you're not going anywhere!"

"No fishing!" Jimmy said. "We can't protect you when you're fishing so I would prefer that you wait until this thing is over before you go back fishing."

"You're starting to piss me off, Jimmy," Justin said with a slight grin. "Okay, we won't go fishing, but I'm definitely going coyote hunting."

"Well, at least all of you will be armed with rifles if you go coyote hunting," Jimmy said as he answered his cell phone. Jimmy spoke briefly to someone and then hung up. "Wade Shavers is coming down River Road on his four-wheeler so I'm going to leave. It would be better for us to leave DeMac here with you, so I'm glad you want him to stay. Is there anything else before I go?"

"Yeah, there is," Justin said. "I want you to send another one of DeMac's men to stay here."

"I don't see a problem with that," Jimmy said. "Any particular reason why?"

"Yeah, I want you to send the one that knows the most about killing coyotes."

"Okay, I'll send you another man. It wouldn't be a bad idea to have someone else here for security reasons. I'll see if any of DeMac's team members know how to hunt coyotes, but officially he will be placed here for security reasons, not coyote hunting," Jimmy said.

"I understand," Justin said and he winked at Jimmy.

"You southern boys never cease to amaze me," Jimmy said and he shook his head as he turned to leave. Jimmy suddenly stopped and turned around to face Justin. "One more thing," he added.

"What's that?" Justin asked.

"No matter what happens, don't let Sheriff Bill Sisk arrest you! He'll kill you if he gets the chance," Jimmy said and then turned and left.

Danny Comer pulled his van over to the side of Highway 117, right beside the New River Telephone Access Node. All the telephone lines beyond this point were fed from here through a switch that was connected to the Sparta Telephone Company by a fiber optic cable. Justin Hayes's phone line was fed from this point to his house on a 200 pair copper cable that was numbered 101 to 300. The 200 pair copper cable traveled down Highway 117 on telephone poles until it reached the south fork of the New River, and then it dipped underground and went down River Road all the way to the dead-end at Jack's house.

Justin was connected to pair 237, which was the orange-black pair in the blue-red binder. Danny could have found the line and tapped onto it in the telephone pedestal in front of Justin's house, but would probably be seen doing it unless he waited till it was night. Since Tommy went missing at night in front of Justin's house, Danny thought it was a bad idea to try and tap his phone there. He could intercept Justin's phone line here and then send it to Jack's house on a vacant pair and it would be just as good and safer too. Having access to the Sparta Telephone Company's records made the job simple. Since Jack was a major stock holder and sat on the board of directors, Danny knew the code to access the phone company's computer files, and all the information that he needed was just a click away on his laptop computer.

Jack's house had a 12 pair cable run into it from the main cable that was numbered 221 to 232. The first three lines, 221, 222, 223, were in use, so Danny was going to use pair 224. Danny unlocked the large telephone cabinet and opened it up. He quickly ran a jumper wire from pair 237 to pair 224 using a wire wrap tool and then closed the cabinet and drove off. As soon as he got back to Jack's house he could tap onto pair 224 in Jack's telephone room, and be able to listen to any conversation that was taking place on pair 237, which was Justin Hayes's phone line.

Wade Shavers couldn't believe his eyes when Justin handed him the rifle and said he could use it until he could find the time to finish his rifle. It didn't have a fancy English walnut stock or any gold inlays or even any engraving, but it was the most beautiful rifle that Wade had ever seen.

Justin carried the rifle to the shooting bench and opened the shutters overlooking the shooting range. "Come over here, Wade, so that we can adjust the rifle to fit you."

Wade walked over to the bench and waited for instructions. "Sit down at the bench and do exactly as I say," Justin said.

"Okay, Mr. Hayes, but I didn't know you could adjust a rifle to fit you."

"You can this one. The length of pull and the cheek rest height are adjustable on this stock," Justin said. "Now lean down on the rifle just like you were going to shoot it."

Wade did as he was instructed and Justin made a few adjustments to the rifle stock. "Now sit back up and close your eyes," Justin said.

"You want me to shut my eyes?" Wade asked.

"Yeah, shut your eyes," Justin said. "Trust me."

"Okay," Wade said and he shut his eyes even though he didn't know why.

"Now without opening your eyes, I want you to lean back down and hold the rifle just like you did before. Pull it back into your shoulder just snug, not real tight. Rest your cheek on the stock firmly. Again, not too tight, just snug. Make sure it feels comfortable to you. It's important that you feel comfortable. Don't open your eyes until I say so."

Wade leaned down on the rifle and pulled it back into his shoulder and rested his cheek on the stock just like Justin had told him to. "Okay, Mr. Hayes, I'm comfortable."

"Now when I tell you to, I want you to open your eyes and look through the scope, but I don't want you to move your head or your arms or shift the rifle in any direction. Just open your eyes and sit perfectly still. Understand?"

"Yes, sir," Wade said.

"Okay, open your eyes."

Wade opened his eyes and sat perfectly still like Justin had instructed him. "Do you have a full field of view through the scope?" Justin asked.

"Yes, sir."

"Does the scope appear to be clear?" Justin asked.

"It looks perfect to me," Wade said.

"Do you see any shadows around the edges of the field of view?"

"No, sir. It's perfectly clear. It looks great!" Wade said.

"That's good, Wade," Justin said as he stepped over to the cabinet and retrieved two sets of shooting glasses and two sets of electronic ear muffs. "Let's burn some powder."

Johnny Steele dialed the number and waited for someone to answer it. "Security Concepts, how may I place your call?" A female voice said.

"I need to speak to Dave Setzer," Johnny said. "I'm an old friend."

"Who shall I say is calling, sir?"

"Tell him it's Johnny Steele."

"One minute, please."

Johnny didn't know if Dave would take his call or not, but after a moment he heard a click and then a deep voice say, "I hope you're calling to ask for your old job back so I can have the pleasure of telling you to kiss my ass."

"Dave, it's good to talk to you too!" Johnny said.

"What the hell do you want, Steele? You got a lot of nerve to even call me, much less to tell my secretary that we're old friends."

"We are old friends, Dave," Johnny said.

"I spent two years training you to be a professional bodyguard and you jumped ship on me after only four months, and you think we're old friends? If you got something to say you better say it quick before I hang up," Dave said.

"Okay, Dave, don't hang up," Johnny said. "This is a business call. I need two men to do some surveillance work for my boss."

"Why did you call me and what makes you think I would be interested in a surveillance job in North Carolina?" Dave asked.

"I called you because your men are the best, and you'll be interested because it's an easy job that pays big bucks," Johnny said. "I need two men to alternate on twelve hour shifts and just observe what goes on at a house that's located next door to my boss's house. The job may last a few days or it may last a few weeks."

"When do you need them?" Dave asked.

"Yesterday!" Johnny said.

"It'll cost you $2,000 a day with a $10,000 deposit paid up front before they ever board a plane to leave," Dave said.

"I'll wire you the money within the next hour. Fly them to Greensboro or to Charlotte and I'll send a private plane to pick them up. Tell your secretary to call me and give me their flight times," Johnny said.

"I'll put them on a plane as soon as I see the money, and not before," Dave said.

"Nice doing business with you, Dave."

"Fuck you Johnny!" Dave said and then hung up.

There was a trail of clothes from Jesse's back door, up the staircase and all the way to her bed. She had arrived home at 5:17 and Travis was in the backyard throwing a Frisbee for Maggie while he waited for Jesse to arrive. They couldn't wait until they got upstairs to start undressing each other so they started at the back door. There was a tennis shoe and a lab coat at the foot of the stairs and various other articles of clothing on practically every step until you reached the landing.

They were both madly in love, and as they lay on top of Jesse's bed holding each other and resting, they both knew that there was no other place that they would rather be than right here in each other's arms.

"Travis," Jesse said as she kissed his neck. "Have you decided whether you're going to re enlist in the Navy or not?"

"I can't reenlist in the Navy," Travis said. "I'm madly in love with you!" Travis could feel tears on his neck falling from Jesse's cheeks as he held her. She kissed his ear and squeezed him tight.

"I'm madly in love with you too, but I don't want to ruin your career."

"Listen Jesse, I joined the Navy because I didn't know what I wanted to do with my life, but now I know. I want to be with you. I have never felt like this before, and even though we've only known each other for a few days, I know that you and I are supposed to be together. I'm so happy right now that I could scream. I didn't know a person could feel this happy, so don't worry about ruining my career," Travis said and he kissed Jesse on her eyebrow.

"What will you do?" Jesse asked.

"I don't know exactly what I'll do. I could go to college on the GI Bill or I could maybe start a photography business, but one thing is for sure, I'm going to be with you!"

Jesse rolled over on top of Travis and kissed him. She had tears in her eyes but they were tears of joy. She was so in love with Travis that she felt like she might explode, and finding out that he felt the same way filled her with joy.

"I got a call today from Terry Shive. He's a student at N.C. State and he lives in North Wilkesboro. He wanted to know if he could work for me this summer as an intern. He's studying to be a veterinarian but he has one more semester before he graduates."

"What did you tell him?" Travis asked.

"I told him to call me back tomorrow," Jesse said. "I think I will tell him yes so that I can take some time off and be with you. I've worked a sixty to seventy hour work week for two years and I think I deserve a break!"

"That would be great if you think you can," Travis said. "I didn't think five o'clock would ever get here today. I wanted to see you so bad!"

Jesse kissed Travis's neck, and then his chest, and then his stomach, as she worked her way down his body. Travis moaned with pleasure.

"I couldn't wait to see you too," Jesse said. "Especially this part!"

Ashley Yates walked in the kitchen at Jack's and put her purse and the bag with the hair dyes down on the counter. Jack said that he wanted her to cut Billy and Johnny's hair and to dye their hair a different color so she had to drive to Sparta to Sally's Hair Supply and pick up some dye. She had attended Beauty College briefly after graduating from high school and was actually a pretty good beautician, but having to stand all day on your feet and listen to everybody's problems, plus having to work all day on Saturdays was too much for her and she quit and started dancing at a strip club in Nashville. The money she earned dancing was good and she only had to work twenty-four hours a week. Jack Billings took a special liking to her and soon was flying to Nashville every week to watch her dance. He always paid for a private room and was more than generous with his tips.

Life seemed to be good then but before long things got complicated. She started dating a biker named Jimmy and using drugs. Before she realized it she was strung out and her life started unraveling like a ball of twine on a steep hill. A drug deal went sour one night and Jimmy shot and killed a Hispanic man and before she knew what was going on, she was sitting in the Nashville jail charged with felony possession and accessory to second-degree murder. Her life seemed to be over until Jack contacted her through one of her girlfriends from the strip club and offered her a deal. Jack gave her the money to pay her bail and she skipped town and had been at Jacks ever since. She refused to have sex with Jack but he did ask her to dance for him about once a month when he was half drunk and lonely. She hated it but didn't have much choice since there was a felony warrant out for her arrest.

She was still basically a prisoner, but at least she was living in luscious surroundings and eating gourmet food instead of living in an 8 × 10 foot cell and sleeping on a cot and eating prison food. It just made her feel like a slave sometimes and when Jack asked her to dance, she felt dirty. It was different dancing at a club to make a living as opposed to dancing for your perverted boss so he could get his cookies off.

Ashley spread a sheet out on the floor to catch the hair and then she set a chair in the center of it. She was ready if she could just find Billy and Johnny.

Wade was watching the Copenhagen snuff can that was sitting on the three hundred-yard berm through Justin's 60 × 80 spotting scope. The empty snuff can was only two and a half inches across and looked awful small when you were looking at it through the 4.5-14 × 50 rifle scope, but it looked huge in the spotting scope. He had been shooting at one hundred and two hundred yards while Justin coached him and he was amazed at how well he had done. He knew that the rifle that he was shooting was the most accurate rifle that he had ever fired, and combined with the coaching that Mr. Hayes was giving him, he felt like he could kill a coyote on the far end of the county. His confidence was growing with each and every shot and he couldn't wait to get a coyote in his crosshairs.

Justin settled in behind the rifle and adjusted the sandbags so that he could shoot at three hundred yards. He gripped the rifle with a firm handshake style grip and pulled the stock snuggly back into his shoulder. Justin found the snuff can and placed the first mil-dot below the crosshairs directly on the can and then took a deep breath. Justin slowly blew all his breath out and then took a small breath and waited. Justin never consciously pulled the trigger on a rifle when he was shooting. He had fired so many thousands of rounds through a rifle in his lifetime that the art of squeezing the trigger had become a subconscious maneuver for him. But his sub-conscious wouldn't fire the rifle until he reached his natural respiratory pause, that fraction of a second when your heart actually pauses, making the rifle perfectly steady. Justin could see his heartbeat in the scope and it was gradually slowing down until it finally stopped, and the rifle fired.

"You nailed it, Mr. Hayes!" Wade shouted. "I don't even see it now."

"Now it's your turn," Justin said. "There's another snuff can to the left of where that one was."

Wade opened the door to the shooting room and took a seat behind the rifle. As he looked through the scope Justin started coaching him. "Wade, do you see those dots that are spaced evenly going down from the crosshairs?"

"Yes, sir."

"Those are called mil-dots. You need to place the first dot beneath the crosshair directly on the snuff can. That bullet is going to drop about eight inches between two and three hundred yards and you have to allow for it. Do you understand?"

"Yes, sir."

"I want you to take your time and make a perfect shot. If it takes you ten minutes to get ready to take the shot then that's fine.

When you start shooting at longer distances than normal you have to do everything exactly right because the distance magnifies your mistakes, so just relax and take your time, make sure that everything is just right and make the shot. I'm going to leave you with just one round of ammunition so you need to make it count. I'm not going to watch you or coach you. I'll be in the house until you fire. Okay?"

"Yes, sir," Wade said.

"Okay, you're on your own," Justin said and he walked through the shop and down to the house.

When Justin walked into the kitchen, DeMac stepped into the kitchen from the living room carrying a set of binoculars. "They got a man wading up the river pretending to be fly fishing, but if you watch him you can tell that he's looking for clues to what happened to their man and their Kawasaki Mule."

"I bet he would shit in his waders if he knew a Navy Seal was watching him through a scope that's attached to a .50-caliber sniper rifle!" Justin said.

"They also have tapped your phone line," DeMac said, staring at Justin to see his reaction.

"Well, that ain't nice!" Justin said. "I guess we're officially at war with each other now.

How do you know that they tapped my phone line?"

"We have a meter on your line that measures ohms," DeMac said. "About forty-five minutes ago the ohms meter went crazy and then gave us a reading that shows your phone line is twelve miles longer than it was before, so we did some checking and found the tap at the junction box on Highway 117."

"Did you remove it?" Justin asked.

"No, not yet. Jimmy wants you to go ahead and take a couple calls and let them listen so that they will think that their tap is good. Just be real careful what you say until we remove it. When we do remove it, we're going to rig it up so that it will read the same amount of ohms after we remove the tap, as it did before we removed the tap. They probably have a meter hooked up to their equipment also, but it will still read the same when we remove their tap."

"So they won't be able to tell that we've removed it by their ohm meter?" Justin said.

"Exactly." DeMac said.

The sound of a rifle shot rumbled across the mountain.

"Is that Wade?" DeMac asked with a concerned look on his face.

"Yeah, I left him alone with a three hundred-yard shot at a snuff can," Justin said. "I wanted him to think about the shot and make it without me looking over his shoulder. Lets go see if he hit it."

Justin and DeMac walked back to the shop and started toward the shooting room. As soon as they got in sight of Wade it was obvious that he had hit his target. Justin didn't think he had ever seen a boy grin that big in all his life. "There's no stopping him now," Justin said to DeMac as they crossed the room. "He has all he needs to be a crack rifle shot—an accurate rifle, good ammunition, knowledge, patience, and the most important ingredient of all, confidence."

"We need you to train our snipers," DeMac said.

"Let's mess with him a little bit," Justin said softly as they approached the shooting room.

"Hang on Wade and I'll get you another cartridge and you can try again!" Justin shouted as he headed for a cabinet across the room.

"No, Mr. Hayes! I hit it! I hit it with one shot! Look through the scope! It's gone!" Wade shouted.

"It's okay to miss, Wade. Everybody misses once in a while. Even that David Tubb fellow who has won the National High Power Championship about a dozen times misses every now and then!"

"But I didn't miss! Really, I'm not lying, Mr. Hayes! I really did hit it!" Wade said.

Justin walked over and looked through the spotting scope and then over at DeMac. "Well, I'll be a monkey's uncle! He did hit it, DeMac. He hit a snuff can at three hundred yards on his first shot!"

"DeMac held up his hands and gave Wade a double high five. "Good shooting, Wade."

"Well, don't just stand there, Wade, go get that snuff can and bring it to me!" Justin said.

"Yes, sir, Mr. Hayes," Wade said and he flew out the door and jumped on his four-wheeler. Wade tore out across the shooting range and returned in less than a minute carrying the snuff can like it was made of glass.

Justin took the snuff can from Wade and wrote on it with a Sharpie, "Wade Shavers, 300 Yards, One Shot, April 11, 2006, Witnesses: Justin Hayes and Dwight McMasters."

"I think we're ready to say hello to Mr. Coyote," Justin said. "I'm going to come over to your place tomorrow and we'll do some looking around and try to figure out where we need to set up our ambush."

"Mr. Hayes, there won't be anybody around there tomorrow," Wade said. "My mama's Aunt Hedrick passed away up in Galax, Virginia, and me and daddy are leaving real early tomorrow morning to go to the funeral. Mama left last night and she's going to stay up there for a few days, but me and daddy have got to come home tomorrow night to look after the farm. That's why I wanted to come over here today, because tomorrow we'll be gone."

"Well, I'm sorry your mom's aunt passed away. I might drive over there and do some looking around anyway if you don't think your daddy will mind," Justin said.

"No, he won't mind. I'll tell him you're going to come over and do some looking around."

"If I can figure out where a good place is to shoot from, we just might try to bust one on Friday," Justin said.

"I can't wait to get a coyote in my crosshairs!" Wade said.

"There's one more very important thing you need to learn about a rifle," Justin said.

"What's that?" Wade said.

"The proper way to clean it," Justin said. "Come on!"

Ashley had cut Billy's hair and styled it into a spike and then dyed it a light brown. Billy couldn't remember the last time he had a haircut, but his hair was hanging down past his shoulders before Ashley cut it. Ashley thought Billy looked good with his hair cut and styled and she was kind of proud of her work, but she kept her thoughts to herself. Billy was literally seething with anger as he sat there and watched his hair fall to the floor. Bill Sisk kept walking through the house to make sure that Billy and Johnny got their hair cut before they left the house, and that just made Billy that much madder.

Ashley finally finished with Billy and he got up out of the chair. "I'll go get Johnny for you," was all he said when he walked out of the room. Billy returned in about five minutes guiding Johnny to the chair. Johnny was so high that he could just barely function. He looked like he was looking through you instead of at you, and he would grin and then suddenly act scared. It was like a movie was playing in his head and he was the only one that could see it. He was pitiful.

Ashley tried to put a sheet around him before she cut his hair but he acted frightened by it so she just decided to cut his hair and let it fall all over him. In his condition he wouldn't even notice. When she picked up the comb and scissors and started toward Johnny he held up his hands to stop her and yelled, "No!"

"It's all right, Johnny," Ashley said. "I'm not going to hurt you. I'm just going to cut your hair."

"No!" Johnny yelled again.

Ashley felt sorry for him. She was strung out on drugs herself and was only able to get clean because she was locked up in a jail cell in Nashville. She remembered it like it was yesterday and it wasn't a pleasant memory.

"Let her cut your hair, Johnny," Billy said. "She won't hurt you. I'll stay here and make sure you're all right."

When Billy said that, Johnny seemed to calm down. Ashley started cutting his hair and he let her but he occasionally would turn his head from side to side.

"Just cut it like you think it would look the best," Billy said. "There's no need to ask him how he wants it when he's like this."

"You know, Billy, once your dad has a chance to cool down some I think he'll let you and Johnny move back in," Ashley said.

"Shit, he'll never let us move back in!" Billy said.

"Just try to get by for awhile and give him some time," Ashley said. "You'll see."

"What makes you think so?" Billy asked.

"That's the first time I've ever seen him cry," she said. "And I know him better than anyone here."

Johnny was staring at Ashley's chest and finally reached up and grabbed her left breast. Ashley took Johnny's hand and removed it but he just grabbed it again. Billy stood up and started across the room. "That's okay, Billy, he's not the first guy that's ever done that, and if it keeps him pacified then just let him hold it. He doesn't know what he's doing."

Billy sat back down. "I think I can find a job and get by okay for awhile, but what about Johnny? He can't work in his condition and I can't leave him alone in that trailer while I go to work. He would probably burn the place down or either I'll come home and find him dead from an overdose!"

"Billy, you have got to get Johnny dried out somehow. He can't go on much longer like this regardless of where he's living," Ashley said.

"How am I going to do that?" Billy asked.

"Call his mother if you can find out what her number is," Ashley said. "She use to call and try to talk to Johnny, but Jack wouldn't let her. She may be willing to help you."

"That's a good idea!" Billy said.

"Thank you."

"You're welcome," Ashley said.

"Why do you care what happens to Johnny?" Billy asked.

Ashley stopped cutting Johnny's hair and looked at Billy. She pointed the scissors at Johnny and said, "Been there, done that, got the tee-shirt."

Cecil Wood and Bill Sisk tried unsuccessfully to wake Jack up before they went outside to give a statement to the press. Jack was passed out in his recliner with a half empty bottle of Jim Bean whiskey sitting on the end table beside him and he was snoring like only a drunk can.

"We need to go ahead and give the press a statement." Cecil said. "We'll never wake Jack up in time and I don't think it would be a good idea to let him talk to them anyway."

"From the looks of that whiskey bottle, he won't wake up until tomorrow!" Bill said. "Billy and Johnny did get their hair cut didn't they?" Cecil asked.

"Yeah, and Walt and CJ have the garage ready too," Bill answered.

"Well, let's just go ahead and get this over with then," Cecil said, and he and Bill Sisk headed out the door and started walking toward the front gate.

Justin locked up his machine shop and walked down to the carport to feed and water his dogs. Scooter was back to normal, running and jumping, and the incision on his shoulder was healing nicely. After spending a few minutes rubbing them and playing with them, Justin filled their bowls and went inside the house.

Justin washed his hands at the kitchen sink and grabbed a beer out of the refrigerator. It had been a tough day and he was ready to kick back and relax for awhile. He couldn't wait for Teresa to call him. Even though he had been busy all day, he had still thought about her constantly. She was so beautiful and so much fun to be around that he had missed her and couldn't wait for her to call. He had only known her for a few days but he was already crazy about her. Justin knew that he and Travis both were falling in love. I don't guess I should be so surprised, he thought to himself. I've been praying that Travis would stay home and that I could meet someone to share my remaining years. It looks like I might get both my prayers answered.

Justin grabbed the remote control and turned the television on. When the picture appeared, there stood Cecil Wood and Sheriff Bill Sisk standing shoulder to shoulder. The caption said it was a live broadcast, so Justin got up and walked over to the nearest picture window and looked toward Jack's house. Justin grinned as he looked at the throng of vehicles gathered on Jack's bridge.

DeMac walked in and Justin sat back down and turned the volume up so he could hear.

"First of all, let me say that Mr. Billings and everyone that is employed by Mr. Billings are in a state of shock after learning about this terrible incident. Mr. Billings is so upset that he was unable to come out here and speak to you personally and has asked me to give you this statement. My name is Cecil Wood and I am Mr. Billing's attorney and business manager."

"I bet he is upset," Justin said. "And drunk too!"

"After seeing the pictures of the monster truck driving down the middle of the river, we immediately began to investigate the matter to determine how this could have happened. With the help of Sheriff Sisk, we have completed our investigation and have determined that two unknown men broke into the garage and straight wired the truck for the sole purpose of taking a joyride. The truck was returned to the garage after the joyride and no one knew that the truck had been gone until these pictures surfaced. After this press conference Sheriff Sisk will take you over to the garage and let you see where the perpetrators pried open the door to the garage and straight wired the ignition."

"Mr. Billings instructed me to announce to you that he will accept full responsibility for this atrocious act of vandalism, and he wishes to apologize to the people of Ashe County and also to everyone in the state of North Carolina for allowing someone to break in and steal the monster truck and then use it to damage one of this nation's most beautiful and undisturbed rivers. Mr. Billings has graciously agreed to pay for a team of Wildlife Biologists to study the river and determine what damages have occurred, and will pay whatever the amount is to restore the river to its original state. Are there any questions?"

"Sheriff Sisk, do you know who the two men are that are driving the truck?" Gail asked.

"At this time we do not know who the two men are that are driving the truck, but we will continue to investigate this matter in hopes of bringing them to justice," Sheriff Sisk said.

"According to some of the locals that we have spoken to, the two men in the truck are Jack Billing's son Billy Billings, and his nephew Johnny Billings," Suzy Chung said to Sheriff Sisk.

"None of the photographs give us a view of either man's face, so at best it will be difficult to positively identify who the men are in the truck. Our crime scene technicians will go over the truck and look for any evidence they can find, but since no one knew that the truck had been missing, several people have been in the truck and have even driven it, so we're not very optimistic that we will be able to gather any useful information. As for Billy and Johnny Billings, they were interviewed along with all of Mr. Billing's employees and they both had solid alibis for the time the crime was committed. Their alibis checked out so they are not suspects in this investigation."

"That lying sack of shit!" DeMac said.

"You can always tell when Bill Sisk is lying," Justin said.

"How?" DeMac asked.

"His lips are moving," Justin answered.

"Sheriff, we heard that truck running earlier today and had to shout into our microphones so the viewers could here us. It would be impossible to drive that vehicle out of this lot without someone hearing it!" Gail Davis said.

"Several people heard the truck running but assumed the mechanics were test driving it," Sheriff Sisk said. "The two mechanics that are normally in the garage during the day were on their way to Winston-Salem to see the monster truck show at the Lawrence Joel Coliseum and were absent at the time of the break-in."

"Sheriff Sisk, doesn't it seem strange to you that these men just happened to break in when no one was around, and that after they took this massive truck for a joyride that they would risk being caught by bringing the truck back to the garage where they stole it!" Suzy Chung said.

"It is unusual for car thieves, or truck thieves as in this case, to return the vehicle back to the place where they stole it, but it's not unheard of. From what we have learned from our investigation, it appears that the men did in fact return the truck back to the garage where they stole it. Now if you will follow me, I'll show you the garage door and the monster truck. Please don't touch anything since our crime scene technicians haven't arrived yet."

The throng of people started walking across the gravel lot toward the garage as Cecil Wood and Sheriff Sisk led the way. Gail Davis was walking beside of Suzy Chung.

"Hi. My name is Gail Davis."

"Hi. I'm Suzy Chung."

"Oh, I know who you are," Gail said. "Do you believe that story?"

"There lying through their teeth," Suzy said. "Someone stole a monster truck in broad daylight and took it for a joyride, and then returned it to the place where they stole it. Bullshit!"

"Yeah, I know," Gail said. "I don't buy it either."

"Everyone who sees the picture immediately identifies the two men as Billy and Johnny Billings. I'd like to know what their alibis are," Suzy said.

"Maybe we can track them down and ask them," Gail said.

"I doubt seriously that they would talk to us," Suzy said. "This whole thing is a dog and pony show, honey! They can't wait to show us this busted garage door and the straight wired monster truck. They're covering this thing up like a cat in a litter box."

"They do seem anxious to show us the evidence," Gail said.

"Cops don't ever show you the crime scene, especially before the crime scene technicians have seen it. The first thing they do is tape it off to keep the reporters out," Suzy said.

"You're right," Gail said. "And we're getting a tour!"

"There's politics written all over this," Suzy said. "And this tour we're getting has been carefully staged. I'll bet when we see the truck that they'll have it fixed so that we can see the straight-wired ignition."

"Like you said, a dog and pony show!"

"Justin, I appreciate you letting me stay here after learning that I was put here to spy on you," DeMac said. "I wouldn't blame you if you threw me out."

"You can stay here as long as you like, DeMac," Justin said. "You were following orders and didn't have a choice. Do you remember when Jimmy first started talking and he mentioned that I worked with the CIA on several occasions?"

"Yeah, I remember him saying it, but I already knew it because I read your folder before I left Norfolk."

"Well, technically it's true. I did work for them on two different missions, but I didn't like it. They didn't ask me if I would work with them, my C.O. called me to his quarters and told me when to be at the landing pad to catch my chopper ride. They picked me up and flew me around for hours and then dropped me off in the boonies. All I had was a picture of the person that I was supposed to kill, and a map with no names on it that showed me where to take the shot from and where to be to get picked back up," Justin said. "I didn't like it, but I did it because I was ordered to!"

"What made you decide to be a sniper in the first place?" DeMac asked.

"I didn't!" Justin said. "I was supposed to be a military policeman, but my rifle scores were so high that after I got to Vietnam they told me that I had been selected to take a three week course that they called Advanced Infantry Tactics. I didn't know it was sniper school until I got there."

"They threatened to court martial me if I didn't willingly participate!" DeMac said. "Of course this mission does have national security implications."

"I know that Travis feels the same way I do," Justin said. "You are a friend of his, and I consider you a friend, and there are no hard feelings in regard to this mission."

"Thank you," DeMac said. "I'm honored to call you my friend."

The phone rang and Justin reached to answer it. "I'll bet that's my redhead calling to talk dirty to me!"

"Don't forget that Jack's listening to your call," DeMac said.

"Hey, sweetie," Justin answered.

"Well, hey, darling!" Carol Crissman answered back.

"Oh, Carol, how are you?" Justin stammered.

"Who did you think it was?" Carol asked.

"I knew it was you the phone woke me up and I'm still sleepy headed," Justin lied.

"Have you been watching the news, Justin?" Carol asked.

"Yes, I have."

"Now I know who almost ran over me and killed me in that big truck. It was that damn Billy Billings and his no-good cousin Johnny!" she blurted out.

"Well, wait a minute, Carol," Justin said and he gave DeMac a weird look. "They said that Billy and Johnny had alibis for the time it took place."

"That lying Bill Sisk!" Carol practically shouted. "The only time he tells the truth is when he misunderstands the question! I've known those two boys since they were in first grade. I don't have to see their faces to know that it's them sitting in that truck. I've got a good mind to call Fox 8 and tell them!"

Justin had put the call on the speaker phone so that DeMac could listen to it, and DeMac was shaking his head back and forth as he listened.

"Well, Carol, I wouldn't jump to any conclusions. Why don't you just watch and see what happens over the next week or so?"

"I can't believe that you of all people are taking up for them!" Carol said.

"I'm not taking up for them, Carol. I, uh, was just thinking that in a way they did us a favor," Justin said.

"How do you figure that?" Carol snapped.

"Well, if they hadn't run you in that ditch then I wouldn't have carried you up to the house. And if I hadn't carried you up to the house, then you wouldn't have been here when I came home and took my shower. Understand?"

"Oh my God, I know what you mean now. That night when we were in the shower and the hot water was coming down on us as I sat on your lap and rocked back and forth—"

DeMac looked at Justin with his eyes wide open and Justin just put his face in his hands and closed his eyes.

"And then later on when you carried me to your bed, you were just amazing, Justin!"

"Well, you see where I'm coming from with this. Your car wasn't damaged and you got it washed and everything just worked out fine," Justin said and he blushed for the first time in years.

"Oh, I saw where you were coming from all right," Carol said in a sexy voice. "And I'd like to see it again! Why don't I come over there and we can take another shower?"

"Well, Carol, Travis and DeMac are over here and I just wouldn't feel comfortable, you know."

"I got a shower over here if you want to come over," Carol suggested.

"I'm just too tired, honey. It's been a hectic day and I'm just worn out," Justin said.

"Well, okay then," Carol said dejectedly.

"Carol, I wouldn't say much about the incident with the truck until I saw where the investigation went. If what you think is true, then it will come out sooner or later."

"I guess you're right," Carol said. "Well, I've enjoyed talking to you, Justin."

"It was nice talking to you too, Carol."

"I guess I'll see you Sunday, if not before. Bye now."

"Bye. Bye," Justin said and then punched the button to end the call.

DeMac was on his cell phone as soon as Justin hung up the phone. Jimmy answered on the first ring. "Did you hear that call?" DeMac asked him.

"Yes, and I've already got a team on their way over there. We'll have to protect her now that Jack knows she might call Fox 8. I sure didn't see this one coming! We're going to have our hands full just trying to keep this mission from coming unraveled."

"I think you're right about that," DeMac said.

"We can't let Jack get suspicious or this whole mission could blow up in our faces!"

"I know!" DeMac said.

"Well, tell Justin that he did good considering the circumstances and that we'll protect her until this thing is over," Jimmy said.

"Ten-four," DeMac said and then hung up.

"Call Travis and tell him this phone has been tapped before he calls over here and says something that we don't want said," Justin said to DeMac.

DeMac called Travis's cell phone and he finally answered it on the sixth ring. "Hey, Travis, be careful what you say if you call your dad because his phone has been tapped."

"They're getting serious, aren't they?" Travis said.

"Yeah, they're serious," DeMac said. "Better watch your six until this thing is over."

"Tell dad that I might spend the night over here unless he thinks I should be over there with him since we got a feud going on."

"There going to remove the tap before long and when they do I'll have your dad call you," DeMac said.

"Hey, DeMac!" Jesse could be heard saying in the background.

"Is she naked?" DeMac asked.

"Well, yes," Travis said.

"You lucky dog!" DeMac said.

"I know! Believe me, I know!"

DeMac hung up and looked at Justin with a grin. "So while Travis and me were gone to Jefferson to eat pizza, you and Carol were playing ride the wild horsy!"

"She surprised me in the shower I didn't plan on it," Justin said.

"Couldn't fight her off, I guess," DeMac said, smiling. "You old-dog you!"

DeMac's cell phone rang and he answered it. He spoke briefly with someone and then hung up. "You're going to get a call in a minute from a CIA operative pretending to be a salesman. Just go along with it, and when you hang up their going to remove the tap. They want to get that thing removed before anything else goes haywire."

"Okay," Justin said. "I'm glad they're removing it before Teresa calls, now that I think about it."

The phone rang and Justin answered it. "Hello."

"Mr. Hayes, this is Alan Loflin from Ashboro Toyota. How are you tonight, sir?"

"I'm fine, Alan. What can I do for you?"

"Well, Mr. Hayes, according to the DMV records you're still driving the same Toyota truck that I sold you several years ago."

"That's right, and it still runs like a Singer sewing machine," Justin said.

"Well, Mr. Hayes, I'm calling to just let you know that we're having a big sale this week end at Ashboro Toyota and I would love to put you in a new 2006 Toyota Tundra. This is a huge sale and I could make you a deal you wouldn't believe."

"I'm not interested in trading right now Alan, but I appreciate you calling," Justin said.

"Okay, Mr. Hayes, I won't take anymore of your time, but if you would happen to change your mind, just come on down Saturday and ask for me by name, Alan Loflin.

"Okay, Alan, if I change my mind I'll see you Saturday," Justin said and then hung up.

After a few minutes someone called DeMac and spoke with him briefly. DeMac hung up and turned to speak to Justin. "The tap has been removed so you can talk freely."

"Well, good," Justin said.

"Sometime tomorrow morning they will put the tap back on and stage another call just like this one, and then remove it again, just to reassure them that their tap is still working. There is a team protecting Carol already in place and Travis wants you to call him."

Justin called Travis and they talked for a few minutes before they hung up. Justin went to the kitchen and got himself another beer before returning to the living room. As soon as he sat down his phone rang again. "Hello?"

"I told you I was going to call you and talk dirty to you," Teresa said.

"I've been sitting beside this phone all day waiting for you to call!" Justin said.

"Justin Hayes, you're such a liar," Teresa said.

"Okay, but I have been looking forward to you calling."

"Do you miss me?" Teresa said.

"I wish you were here. How did your house closing go?" Justin asked.

"Oh it was terrible! It was a new attorney and he screwed it all up," Teresa said. "We were there for three hours!"

"I'm sorry," Justin said.

"Thankfully, the attorney that we have tomorrow knows his stuff, so we should be out of there quickly and I can get back on the road to Sparta," Teresa said. "I want to see you again Justin Hayes."

"And I can't wait to see you again, Teresa Owens," Justin said. "If you keep running up here to see me, you're not going to be able to sell any houses."

"I don't need to sell anymore houses, Justin," Teresa said. "It's the weirdest thing to me, that even though I have only known you since Saturday, I know I can tell you anything. I totally trust you and I just met you!"

"I'm flattered! I feel like I've known you longer than three days."

"I have several people working for me showing property and running the business, so I can stay in Sparta as long as I like," Teresa said.

"That's great," Justin said. "You must have won the lottery?"

"Well, sort of," Teresa said. "About nine years ago I bought a 250-acre farm outside the city limits of Kernersville and everyone told me I was crazy. I was hoping one day that I could afford to develop it. I paid $2,000 an acre, which amounted to $500,000. That was dirt cheap but it was still a lot of money to invest in something that might not happen."

"Yeah, a half a million is a chunk of change to gamble with!" Justin said.

"Have you ever driven by the Dell Computer Manufacturing Facility near Kernersville?"

"Yes, I have. I have a friend who lives near there. He was worried about the traffic after they built it," Justin said.

"That was my farm before Dell purchased it," Teresa said. "Wow! You were able to sell your farm to Dell Computers?"

"Yes, I did, for $40,000 an acre. It amounted to $10,000,000. I cleared over nine million dollars on that sale. It's the kind of deal that realtors dream of."

"I guess you don't have to sell any more property," Justin said.

"I plan on keeping the business and letting my employees run it. They need to keep working and they're my friends as well as my employees," Teresa said. "I'll get a small commission on everything they sell and it will be enough money to keep the business running."

"Well, it couldn't have happened to a nicer or more deserving lady," Justin said. "I know you grew up at the Baptist Children's Home in Thomasville, and have worked hard to be where you are today."

"Yeah, that's true. All I've ever done is work, work, and work. When I graduated from high school I went to work for a realtor in Winston-Salem cleaning up rental property and doing office work or whatever needed doing until I was finally able to become a realtor myself," Teresa said. "I had a baby to raise by myself so I had to get tough quick."

"I saw her picture in your bedroom and you could tell she is your daughter. She's beautiful just like you."

"Well, thank you, Justin. I got pregnant by a boy that I thought loved me when I was twenty years old. As soon as he found out that I was pregnant he hit the door running."

"I'll bet you could call him now and tell him you're worth ten million dollars and he would come back to you," Justin said.

"I'm sure he would and I'm also sure that I would take an aluminum baseball bat to his knees!" Teresa said.

"I've always heard that redheads had a bad temper!" Justin said laughing. "What about that picture of twins beside your daughter's picture, who are they?"

"I'm not going to tell you."

"Why not?"

"Because you might not want to date a grandma!" Teresa said.

"Those are your granddaughters?" Justin asked.

"Yes, they're nine years old and their names are Megan and Mindy and they are precious."

"They are absolutely adorable! I picked up that picture and looked at it and wondered if they were your grandchildren."

"I was a grandma in 1997 at the age of forty-three," Teresa groaned.

"That's wonderful Teresa! You're still young enough to enjoy spending time with them and can enjoy watching them grow up," Justin said.

"But I'm a grandma," Teresa said.

"I'll tell you one thing Teresa Owens, if they ever have a Miss USA contest for grandmothers then North Carolina will win it hands down."

"Justin Hayes, you're just a flirt!" Teresa said.

"You sure didn't act like a grandma this morning when you dragged me in the house and attacked me!" Justin said. "Boy; that was wonderful!"

"It was wonderful, wasn't it?" Teresa sighed. "To hell with a Special K breakfast; that's the way to start your mornings!"

"Where does your daughter live?" Justin asked.

"In Tampa, Florida. She was going to college at Wake Forest University studying to be a laboratory technologist when she met her future husband. He's a very successful transplant surgeon now and they live in a beautiful home on the outskirts of Tampa."

"That's great!" Justin said.

"I'm going to fly down there in a couple weeks and spend a couple days with them and then fly back with the twins and keep them for a week or so. Then my daughter is going to fly up here and spend a week with me before she flies home with the twins," Teresa said.

"I know you're looking forward to it," Justin said. "I was so thrilled to see my son when he finally got home last Friday."

"Will you go with me?" Teresa asked.

"You want me to go with you?" Justin said.

"Yes, I want you to go with me," Teresa said. "Besides, my daughter wants to meet you."

"You've already told your daughter about me?"

"Of course I have!" Teresa said. "Justin I know we just met. And I know that were moving real fast and I don't want to scare you off but I think I'm in love with you."

"Teresa, with your looks and sweet personality, and with a bank account like you have, you could have any man you wanted," Justin said.

"I know, you're exactly right. And the only man I would even consider is you."

"I don't know what to say Teresa. I'm flattered that you would want me to go with you. Since we have met, I can't go five minutes without thinking about you. I'm not sure but I think I'm in love with you too!

"Then say yes," Teresa said.

"Okay. Yes, I would love to go with you to Tampa," Justin said.

"Great!" Teresa said. "I can't wait for you to meet them and for them to meet you. We'll have a ball, I know we will!"

There was a brief silence and then Teresa started talking in a very serious tone of voice.

"When I met you the other night and saw how happy you were inside and how you were at total peace with your life, it made me stop and think about my life. After I sold the farm to Dell Computers and got a check for ten million dollars, I couldn't figure out why I wasn't happy. I actually got very depressed. Can you imagine that, get a check for ten million dollars and then get depressed! So I bought the house on River Road so I could get away from everybody and try to figure out what was wrong with me. I prayed that God would show me why I was so unhappy, and then you drove up."

"You were so happy and peaceful and so full of confidence that I knew you were sent from heaven," Teresa said.

"Well, I don't know about that?" Justin said.

"After being with you just one night, I knew why I wasn't happy. Over the years of struggling to pay my bills and raise my daughter and build up my business, I got my priorities all out of whack. There is no happiness in money! Happiness comes from being with your family, or helping a fourteen-year-old boy that has just lost his dog, or comforting a friend who is grieving over the loss of his family. Justin you showed me in one night where happiness comes from. I think you were the answer to my prayers and I'm in love with you!" Teresa said and it sounded to Justin like she was crying.

"Well, sweetheart, let me share something with you," Justin said. "I am at peace in my soul, and I know that I'm richly blessed, but I have been very lonely since I moved up here to Sparta. I love this country and these mountain people, but if it weren't for my dogs I believe I would have gone crazy. I've been praying that God would send me someone to share my life, so maybe God is answering both our prayers. I know this much, if God puts us together, then nothing can tear us apart!"

"I love you, Justin. I can tell that we are meant to be together and I can't wait to see you tomorrow."

"This has happened so fast that it's kind of scary, but I love you too Teresa and I can't wait to see you tomorrow," Justin said. "Do you want me to cook supper for us?"

"Why don't I just stop and buy a pizza on the way up," Teresa said. "Are you afraid to eat my cooking?" Justin joked.

"No, I'm sure you're a wonderful cook."

"Then why don't you want me to fix supper?" Justin asked.

"Because I want you in the Jacuzzi tomorrow evening, not in the kitchen!" Teresa said. "What have you got to say about that?"

"Hallelujah!"

The Right Thing to Do

I t took Johnny Billings several long minutes to figure out where he was when he woke up. He finally realized he was sitting in the back seat of the Cessna T210 and his buddy Chris Reid was sitting beside him fast asleep. The Cessna was parked inside the hangar and Johnny had no idea how he or Chris had managed to get in here.

Johnny remembered calling Chris to come pick him up at the front gate after Cecil gave him the check for $2,000. They got to the bank just in time to cash the check before the bank closed, and then they drove to North Wilkesboro to buy drugs. Johnny knew all the drug dealers in Wilkes County and he bought exactly $2,000 worth of cocaine, marijuana, amphetamines, and a couple blue tablets of window-pane acid. He could remember riding around with Chris and smoking a few joints, but he couldn't remember anything after that.

He looked around the hangar to make sure that no one was around. He wasn't allowed in the hangar or the hotel and they would throw him and Chris out if they caught them there. Then it dawned on Johnny that Jack was throwing him out today anyway, so it really didn't matter if they caught them or not. Jack might as well just shoot me, he thought to himself. He knows I won't be able to make it if I'm not living here. Deep down inside Johnny knew that he was in serious trouble, and he was scared to death of what tomorrow might bring. He pulled out his nasal spray bottle that he had filled last night with powdered cocaine and stared at it. Why not, he thought.

"KSJ 135 to Tower. Over."

"This is Tower, 135, go ahead," Jerry Simmons said.

"Run the deer off the landing strip Tower. My ETA is about three minutes. Over."

"Roger that, 135. Welcome home," Jerry said as he dialed Johnny Steele's cell phone.

"Hello," Johnny answered.

"Your boys are here, Johnny," Jerry said.

"I'll be there in a couple minutes," Johnny said.

Jerry climbed down the metal steps from the control tower and jumped in his pick-up truck and pulled out on the runway. He looked both ways and didn't see any deer standing on the runway so he punched the gas and headed for the hangar. Jerry ran the speedometer up to ninety miles an hour before backing off and he coasted to a stop right beside the tow motor. When Jerry stepped out of his truck he glanced down the runway and saw the King Air drop out of the clouds and line up for its landing. Coy set the plane down so soft the passengers couldn't tell they were on the ground until he started braking. He taxied up to the hangar and shut the engines down.

Jerry pulled the tow motor in front of the plane and attached the metal tow arm to the front wheel and then trotted up to the hangar and punched in a code on a digital keypad. The massive doors started to open and Jerry ran back to the tow motor and started slowly towing the plane inside.

Johnny Billings had finally got Chris to wake up and they were just starting to climb out of the Cessna when the hangar doors began to open, so they quickly climbed back inside the plane and hid. Jerry pulled the King Air inside the hangar and shut the hangar doors as Coy lowered the steps so the passengers could disembark.

Johnny Steele came through the tunnel that led from the back of Jack's house and walked up just as the two passengers stepped down. He recognized one of the men but not the other.

"Scott, glad you men are finally here," Johnny said. "Who's your friend?"

"Hey, Steele," Scott McMillan said. "This is Randy Rhodes. Randy, this is Johnny Steele."

"Nice to meet you, Randy," Johnny said. "Come on and we'll eat some breakfast. I know you've been in the air all night and you're bound to be hungry."

"We're starving, but we better secure our gear first," Scott said.

Jerry and Coy were straining as they slid a black footlocker off the plane and lowered it to the floor. There was another one just like it still on the plane waiting to be unloaded.

"I hope we brought all the equipment that we'll need. Dave just told us to grab our gear and catch a flight to Charlotte," Scott said.

"I could have saved you a lot of time packing because you're not going to need much gear, but Dave is still pissed at me and didn't want to talk," Johnny said. "Let's just set your gear over here beside the Cessna for now."

Jerry and Coy unloaded the second footlocker and carried it over beside the Cessna and Scott and Randy carried the other one over and set it on top of that one.

"What kind of toys did you bring?" Johnny asked.

"The bottom footlocker has video equipment, communications equipment, spotting scopes equipped with camera attachments, and night vision equipment," Scott said. "The top footlocker has four pistols, three Uzi sub-machine guns with thirty clips that are full of ammo, two M-16s with twenty 30-round clips, two tactical police 12-gauge shotguns with two hundred rounds of double-ought buckshot, and two sets of second chance body armor."

"Well, you won't be needing all that firepower," Johnny said. "This is strictly a surveillance job."

"You mean we aren't going to be protecting anybody or even doing security work?" Scott asked.

"Nope, just surveillance," Johnny said.

"Dammit, we could have left half this stuff in California," Scott said. "Well, it's too late now!"

"Your gear will be safe right here for now. Come on, let's go eat," Johnny led Scott and Randy through a door and down the tunnel to Jack's house and Coy and Jerry followed close behind.

"Well, you heard the man, didn't you?" Johnny Billings said to Chris Reid.

"What do you mean Johnny?"

Johnny pulled out his pill bottle and took out three amphetamines and chewed them up. He passed the bottle to Chris and he swallowed two tablets.

"He said they weren't going to need all that firepower."

Johnny could feel the drugs slamming into his bloodstream and he suddenly felt like Popeye on the cartoons when he took his spinach. The speed jacked up his central nervous system and his heart started racing.

"Help me carry that footlocker," Johnny said.

"Where are we taking it?" Chris asked.

"I hadn't figured that out yet."

Justin got just a glimpse of the King Air as it dropped under the clouds and disappeared behind the mountain. Jimmy had called DeMac and told him that they had intercepted a call from Johnny Steele to Security Concepts in California, and that Jack had hired two men to do surveillance work for him. Jimmy said they weren't sure how they wanted to handle this situation yet, but not to worry about it. Justin wasn't worried about anything. He was sitting on his front porch drinking coffee and watching Scooter and Shogun chase each other around the yard. Scooter had gone into the edge of the woods and found a pine cone and was teasing Shogun with it. He would set the pine cone down in front of Shogun and wait for him to try and grab it, and then scoop it up and run.

Justin cherished this time every morning when he sat on his front porch and drank his coffee. Sitting here looking out over the mountains and watching the river flow by put things in perspective for him. It made him realize how small and insignificant his problems were and it reminded him of how blessed he was. It was a good place to get your mind right before you started your day.

A Jeep turned in the driveway and started up the hill and Justin smiled when he realized it was Travis. Travis drove around to the carport and then joined his dad on the porch with a steaming mug of coffee.

"Good morning, Hoss," Justin said as Travis walked out on the porch. Justin had called Travis by the nickname Hoss since he was a baby.

"Good morning, Pop," Travis said as he took a seat in the rocking chair beside his dad.

"Jesse have to go to work?" Justin asked.

"Yeah, and I didn't feel right staying there by myself so I decided to come back here," Travis said. "She might get off early today if that intern comes on in to work."

Justin sat there quietly for a few minutes to let Travis drink his coffee and gather his thoughts.

"So what's on the agenda today?" Travis finally asked.

"I'm going to work on Wade's rifle for a couple hours this morning and then I'm going over to Wade's farm to look around and see if I can find a good place to ambush those coyotes," Justin said. "Then later on I'm going over to Teresa's house to spend the evening, and I can hardly wait to see her."

"You two have really hit it off, haven't you?" Travis said.

"Oh, we're beyond just hitting it off," Justin said. "We're both in love with each other."

"Isn't it weird that you and I both met total strangers, and had our first dates on the same night, and both of us have fallen in love with them. That's quite a coincidence."

"It's not a coincidence at all. It's the answer to my prayers," Justin said. "I've been praying that you wouldn't reenlist in the Navy, and also that I could meet someone to share my life with. I think that both my prayers have been answered."

"That's awesome, Dad," Travis said.

"God is awesome, son. Just look at his creation," Justin said, pointing at the mountains and the river in front of them.

"I see what you mean!" Travis said.

Justin and Travis sat in silence for the next five minutes and just enjoyed the view and sipped their coffee.

"Dad, since last Friday after stopping to see mama, I've been kinda torn up inside," Travis said. "I felt sorry for her when I saw how sick and feeble she was, and I also felt angry at her for leaving you and me."

"What you're feeling is perfectly normal. You have mixed emotions about her, and it's no wonder that you would. She abandoned you and me and it hurt both of us," Justin said. "On the other hand, she is your mother and she brought you into this world and loved you for ten years."

"It's been bothering me," Travis said. "I feel like I should go see her again, but I really don't want to."

"If it's bothering you, just imagine what it's doing to her!" Justin said.

"So you think I should go see her again?"

"You don't really have a choice."

"What do you mean I don't have a choice?" Travis asked harshly.

"You need to go see her again and tell her that you still love her and that you forgive her for leaving you," Justin said. "It's the only way you'll ever get rid of that burden you're carrying around inside."

"Shouldn't she be the one apologizing to me?"

"She wrote you a letter and asked you to come see her, didn't she?"

"Yeah, but she didn't apologize!" Travis stated.

"She wanted to but she was too scared. She feels so much guilt and pain that she probably can't bring herself to do it."

"Have you ever told her that you forgave her for leaving you?" Travis asked.

"Yeah, I did," Justin said. "I called her one night about six months after she left and told her that I was sorry she left but that I didn't wish her anything but happiness and I forgave her for leaving me."

"What did she say?" Travis asked.

"She laughed at me and then hung up," Justin said. "But I felt better after I made the call."

"I don't know if I can do that," Travis said.

"Just go see her again and when you get there just follow your heart," Justin said.

"How do you always know what to do?" Travis asked.

"I got a book with all the answers in it," Justin said. Justin's cell phone rang and the phones in the house rang at the same time. "Hello." He said.

"Good morning, sweetheart," Teresa said.

"Good morning, Sugar Monster," Justin replied.

"I just woke up and I wanted to hear your voice," Teresa said. "I'm not bothering you by calling, am I?"

"It would bother me if you didn't call," Justin said. "I can't wait to see you this evening."

"I can't wait either," Teresa sighed. "I love you."

"I love you too," Justin said. "I was just sitting here on the porch talking to Travis for a few minutes before I go to the shop and work on Wade's rifle."

"Well, I'll let you go so you can talk to Travis. I need to hurry up and get ready to leave anyway," Teresa said. "I just wanted to say good morning and I love you."

"I love you too and I'll see you this evening. Drive safely and call me when you get here. Bye-bye."

"Bye, darling."

When Johnny Steele walked into the kitchen with Scott, Randy, Coy, and Jerry following him, Jack was sitting at the kitchen table nursing a cup of coffee. He had finally woke up at five o'clock this morning still sitting in the recliner in front of the rock fireplace in the living room, and he had a killer hangover. He had pissed all over himself sometime during the night, so he made sure no one was around before he got up to leave the room. Jack took a handful of aspirins and sat in his shower for thirty minutes before he finally shaved and got dressed. His head still hurt and he had a mild case of the shakes, but he would be all right after he drank some coffee and stirred around some. He was drinking his third cup of coffee when the group of people entered the kitchen.

"Jack, this is Scott McMillan and Randy Rhodes. They work for Security Concepts. Scott and Randy, this is Jack Billings," Johnny said.

"Nice to meet you, men," Jack said as he reached out to shake their hands. Jack's hand was trembling as first Scott and then Randy shook it. "There will be a chef in this kitchen from six a.m. till eight p.m. for as long as you two are here, so feel free to utilize them. Johnny will be in charge of you, so if you need anything just see him."

"Thank you, sir," Scott said.

"This chef's name is Steven Sanders. You men just tell him what you want for breakfast," Jack said. "I'll be in my office if you need me, Johnny."

"Yes, sir. I'll touch base with you later on this morning."

Jack got up and walked out of the kitchen slowly. He looked like he had suddenly got very old, Johnny thought.

Justin was sitting in his machine shop and was lapping the locking lugs on Wade's rifle bolt. When he finished the two lugs would have even pressure on them, so that when the rifle fired the action wouldn't flex as bad and it would be more accurate. He had already recut the threads on the action so they were perfectly square and he had resurfaced the bolt face. Justin pulled the bolt out of the action and checked the locking lugs and they were both cutting perfectly even, so he stepped over to his parts cleaning sink and flushed the action and the bolt out with a warm solvent and then blew them dry with an air hose. All that was left to do to the action was to reblue it and he would wait until he blued the barrel to do that.

Justin glanced out the window at the outdoor thermometer. It was 63 degrees already and it wasn't even ten o'clock yet. It was going to be a hot day judging from that.

Johnny Billings and Chris Reid carried the footlocker from the hangar to the metal building behind the garage where Jack kept his muscle cars stored. Johnny slipped into the garage and when Walt wasn't looking he grabbed a five foot pry bar and carried it back where Chris was waiting beside the footlocker and he jammed it under the lock. With one fierce jerk he ripped the lock and the latch off and opened the lid. The speed in Johnny's body had his skin crawling and he rocked from side to side as he looked into the trunk.

"Check this shit out Johnny!" Chris said. "We can trade this stuff for a boatload of drugs man!"

Johnny took the pry bar and walked over to the metal building and jammed the end of the bar into the door jam. He jerked the bar toward him and popped the door open effortlessly. "Come on, man. Help me carry it inside!"

Johnny and Chris lugged the black trunk into the building and set it down behind the first car they came to. It was the 1968 Plymouth GTX with the 440 Wedge Head Magnum. It was silver with a black vinyl top and it had 375 horsepower. Johnny checked the ashtray and found the keys and stepped back to the car's trunk and opened it.

Johnny was feeling great. He was in charge, making decisions and taking action. He felt strong and powerful for a change. He had always been the weak one, the shy and inferior one, the follower instead of the leader. But it was time to change all that he thought. It was time to show Jack that he could take charge. Jack could throw him out, but he could no longer tell him what to do. No one can tell me what to do, Johnny thought.

Johnny pulled out his pill bottle and emptied the contents into his hand. He fished around until he found one of the blue tablets and then put the rest of the pills back in the bottle. Johnny slid the box cutter out of his back pocket and cut just a sliver off one side of the tablet and placed it under his tongue. He put the remainder of the tablet back in the pill bottle and put the bottle back inside his front jeans pocket. The window-pane acid coursed through Johnny's bloodstream like a runaway locomotive and slammed into his brain like a train wreck. Johnny felt like he staggered but he wasn't sure. He leaned over and reached into the footlocker and pulled out a shoulder holster that" had a Springfield Armory Tactical Response Pistol and a pouch with two clips full of 45 ACP hollow points. Johnny slid the shoulder holster on and rammed one of the clips into the pistol and racked the slide.

Chris was piling the guns and ammunition into the trunk of the GTX as fast as he could when suddenly the fluorescent lights came on inside the building.

"Just what in the hell do you boys think you're doing!" Walt yelled as he stepped inside the building.

Johnny raised the pistol up and shot Walt right through the heart. Walt slammed back against the door and collapsed on the floor. He was dead before he hit the concrete.

"Holy Shit Johnny, what are you doing man?" Chris hollered. "Oh man, were in deep shit now man! We gotta get out of here!"

Johnny picked up one of the Uzi submachine guns and several clips full of ammunition and threw them on the front seat of the GTX before stepping over and pushing the button that raised the roll up door in front of the car.

"Pull the car outside and I'll shut the door behind you," Johnny said calmly.

Chris jumped in the car and fired up the engine and pulled it outside the building. He thought about making a run for it without Johnny but he didn't have a remote control to open the front gate. He had already done a six month stretch in prison for possession with intent to sell and still had eighteen months of probation to complete. He didn't want to go back to prison, especially for murder!

Johnny pushed the button to lower the door and then dragged Walt's body all the way across the building until he came to the Dodge Challenger. Johnny found the keys in the ashtray and opened the trunk and then heaved the body into the trunk before slamming it shut. Johnny was soaring! He didn't know what he was going to do next, but he knew that he wasn't going to let anybody stop him. Then it suddenly dawned on him what was happening. He was playing his favorite video game, *Grand Theft Auto: San Andreas*, except he was acting it out instead of playing it on a TV screen. Instead of holding a controller he was holding a real gun, and the blood was sticky and it had a coppery smell to it. Johnny laughed like a child when he thought about it. He reached in his pants pocket and pulled out his nasal spray bottle that was still over half full of powdered cocaine. He removed the cap and sprayed cocaine up one nostril and then the other. It was time to go to the next level!

"It's like he vanished into thin air!" Steve Helms said to Jack. "There is no sign of him or the Kawasaki Mule anywhere. Brett waded all the way past Justin's mailbox and didn't see any sign of a struggle or any trace of Tommy or the Mule. No one has seen or heard from him, and his wallet and jewelry and other personal things are still in his room!"

"The answer is in that house on the side of that mountain," Jack said, pointing in the direction of Justin's house. "Justin Hayes either kidnapped him or killed him. It's the only logical explanation."

"I agree," Donald Crafton said. "People like Tommy don't just vanish. If he was planning on taking off he would have taken his wallet and jewelry with him. The only logical explanation is that he was kidnapped or murdered or both."

"I bet one of his dogs heard the Kawasaki coming up the road and alerted him and he slipped down the mountain and jumped Tommy before he knew what was happening."

"He probably tortured Tommy to find out what happened to Roy. He's damned determined to find out what happened to him," Jack said.

"Tommy's sister that lives in Boone has filed a missing persons report, so it's no secret now that he's missing," Sheriff Sisk said. "I could stop at Justin's and inquire about it since there's a report out."

"I think we need to back off for now," Donald Crafton said. "There's something real strange going on and until we can figure out what it is we need to sit back and just watch."

"We can't back off now!" Jack barked.

"Why not?" Donald said. "The tractor is in the bottom of the mine and even if he did grab Tommy and found out about Roy's accident he can't prove anything!"

"I want that son of a bitch dead!" Jack snapped.

"Jack, I'm telling you, there's something we're missing here," Donald said. "We intercepted that call from Carol Crissman and you can tell that Justin is trying to talk her out of calling Fox 8 and identifying Billy and Johnny. Why would he do that? And why doesn't he come forward and tell the media that he witnessed the truck being driven down the river since we know that he was there? And now Tommy has mysteriously gone missing. This whole situation stinks and we need to sit back and just watch him for awhile."

Johnny Steele knocked once on the door and then entered. "I took Scott and Randy to their rooms and there going to sleep for a couple hours and then we'll set up on Justin's house later this afternoon."

"Okay, Johnny, do they have everything that they need?" Jack asked.

"Yeah, they're pros," Johnny answered.

"Bill, since there is a missing persons report out on Tommy, it wouldn't hurt to stop at Justin's and ask a few questions. While you're there look around and see if there's anything unusual about the place. For right now we'll just keep looking for Tommy and monitoring Justin's phone calls until we get our surveillance set up," Jack said. "I'll be in this office all day as far as I know, so if anything happens, let me know immediately."

Everybody filed out of Jack's office and left Jack staring at the walls. Something Johnny said stuck in Jack's mind. "They're pros" Johnny had said about the men from Security Concepts. Maybe I need to hire a pro to get rid of Justin Hayes, Jack thought. If that's what it's going to take to get rid of him, then so be it. One man is not going to stop me from reaching my goal.

Justin had covered himself with bug repellant before he laced up his hiking boots and put on his tactical vest. It was a hot day and there was no question that there would be a lot of flies and other bugs on a sheep farm. He opened his gun safe to select a rifle to carry just in case he saw a coyote while he was walking around. The decision was an easy one. Justin pulled out a Ruger No. 1 single shot rifle chambered in the king of varmint cartridges, the 220 Swift. It was Justin's favorite cartridge and even after thirty years of shooting a Swift it still sometimes amazed him.

The 220 Swift shoots a 50- or 55-grain bullet at almost four thousand feet per second, and when a light weight bullet like that hits an object at extremely high velocity some truly amazing things usually happen. The Swift will shoot through a piece of 3/8-inch steel, but when shot into a groundhog it normally won't exit the body. The bullet spins on its axis at over 220,000 revolutions a minute, and when it is upset in something like muscle or soft tissue, the bullet's velocity plus its centrifugal force cause the bullet to fly apart almost like an explosion. Justin knew that a coyote that was shot with a Swift wouldn't suffer. Everything that he had ever shot with a Swift died instantly.

Justin slid ten shells in his vest pocket and carried the rifle to the carport and put it in his truck. Justin then went into the kitchen to fill his canteen with ice water when he heard Shogun and Scooter barking. He walked to the front of the house to see what they were barking at and saw Sheriff Bill Sisk driving up his driveway. Justin pulled his .45 automatic out of his tactical vest and made sure it was loaded before he returned it to the holster. He stepped out on the front porch and ordered Shogun and Scooter inside the house before he took a seat in one of the rockers. Sheriff Sisk stopped his Ford Explorer in front of the house and got out.

"Eagle, this is Crow's Nest. Sheriff is pulling into the Rabbit Den," Duke said into his voice-activated microphone.

"Give me video from Crow's Nest and from the Wizard. I got audio from daddy Rabbit's phone," Jimmy said.

"Roger that, Eagle. Video's rolling."

Justin detested Bill Sisk as much as he did Jack Billings if not more. Justin knew that the sheriff was going down with Jack in a matter of days and that he should just remain calm and not stir anything up, but when he saw him climb out of the Explorer he knew he couldn't do it. The fact that he participated in Roy's murder and was also planning to murder him was too much for him to ignore. If he started something, Justin planned on finishing it.

"Mr. Hayes, I'd like to ask you a few questions, if you don't mind," Bill Sisk said.

"Fire away, Bill," Justin said. He intentionally omitted using the title "Sheriff" to see if it irritated him. From the look in his eyes Justin knew that it did.

Bill let the remark pass and continued on. "There's been a missing persons report filed by a lady in Boone for a man named Tommy Sides who is her brother," Sheriff Sisk said as he walked up the porch steps and handed a copy of the report to Justin. "He was last seen riding a four-wheeler near here. Have you seen this man?"

"No, I haven't," Justin said as he stared at the picture of the man who was going to poison the river. "Why was he riding a four-wheeler near here?"

"He is employed by Jack Billings and was last seen driving out Jack's front gate heading this way," Bill said.

"When did he go missing?" Justin asked.

"Early yesterday morning."

"That's strange. I sit on this porch every morning drinking my coffee and I didn't see anybody on a four-wheeler yesterday morning."

"Well, it was real early, before daylight," the sheriff said.

"Why would anybody be riding a four-wheeler before daylight?" Justin asked.

"Mr. Hayes, why he was riding a four-wheeler before daylight is none of your business," Bill said sarcastically. "I just need to know if you've seen him."

"I've already told you that I haven't seen him!" Justin said.

"Well, if you don't mind, I think I'll look around some," Bill said as he reached for the storm door handle.

"I do mind. You're not looking around my house without a warrant," Justin said.

Bill pulled his hand back and turned to face Justin. "Sounds to me like you're hiding something!"

Justin stared straight into Bill Sisk's eyes. "I got nothing to hide. You said it was none of my business why he was riding a four-wheeler before daylight. Well, what's in that house is none of your business. So if you want to see it, go get a warrant!"

"Would you be willing to take a lie detector test?" Sheriff Sisk asked.

"I will if you will," Justin answered.

"What's that supposed to mean?" Bill Sisk asked.

"Don't you understand the English language?" Justin asked. "I'll take a lie detector test if you'll take one. I'll make a list of twenty-five questions for you to answer and you can make a list of twenty-five questions for me to answer."

"Just what kind of questions do you want to ask me?"

"Well, for one, I'd like to know how a sheriff who makes $75,000 dollars a year in salary can afford to buy a 180-acre horse farm with a three thousand-square foot brick home on it," Justin said.

"You need to keep your nose out of my personal business," Bill snarled.

"I'd also like to know where you were the night Roy Hepler was murdered," Justin said. "So when do you want to take our lie detector tests?"

"I got no intention of taking a lie detector test," Bill said.

"Sounds like to me that you're the one who's hiding something!" Justin said firmly.

"You listen to me Justin Hayes, and you listen good. This is my damn county and I'll look wherever I damn well please, with or without a warrant!" Bill reached over and opened the storm door and started to step inside but slammed the door shut as Shogun lunged for him. Shogun and Scooter slammed into the door and were both growling now as they stared at Bill through the glass door.

"You might want to watch those dogs, Bill. They have an even lower opinion of our local law enforcement officers than I do," Justin said calmly.

"I'll shoot those damn dogs if I have too!" Bill hollered.

Justin stood up and faced Bill Sisk. There was a difference in his look and in his voice. "You know, that's exactly what Johnny Steele said but I changed his mind."

The look that Justin was giving Bill Sisk unnerved him. As the top law enforcement officer in Ashe County he had been forced to prove his grit on several occasions and he had always responded, but this was different somehow. Bill could tell that this man that was standing in front of him was for real, and he felt something that he hadn't felt in a long time—fear! Justin stood there staring into his eyes and not blinking.

"If I didn't know better I'd think you were threatening me!" Bill said trying to retain his composure.

"I haven't threatened anybody, but I'm a citizen of the United States of America and you can't legally search my house without a warrant, so either go get a warrant or try to shoot my dogs. Frankly I don't care which one you choose as long as you hurry up and choose one or the other because I got things to do!" Justin said.

Bill was rattled. He stood facing Justin and tried to bluff him, but you can't bluff Justin Hayes. Justin could see the fear and indecision in Bill's eyes and was enjoying his discomfort.

"I'll be back!" Bill said as he turned and walked down the porch steps. Justin watched him get in his Explorer and drive away.

Chris Reid backed off the gas in the 1968 GTX as he and Johnny topped a hill and came in sight of the town of Independence, Virginia. He was totally freaked out when Johnny shot and killed Walt, but after they got up the road a few miles, Johnny gave him his nasal spray bottle and now everything was just fine. After taking a snort of cocaine up each nostril the fear of being caught and going back to prison was completely gone. Chris knew that no one could catch them as long as he was driving this silver rocket ship, and even if they did, Johnny and him could take care of business.

When they first took off from Jack's house they were just driving but now they had a plan. As soon as they filled the car up with gas they were going to head back to Jefferson, N.C. to sell the guns to a guy that Chris was in prison with that was a member of the Arian Nation. They would pay top dollar for the Uzi sub-machine guns, the M-16s, and the police shotguns, and then they could go back to North Wilkesboro and buy more drugs. Chris slowed down and pulled into the first gas station in Independence and pulled up to the pump.

Johnny hopped out and stuck the nozzle in the gas tank and punched the button for high test gas. Chris hopped out and stepped over beside Johnny and they stood there and watched the pump as the numbers spun by.

"You know something man, I don't have any money!" Johnny said. "Oh shit Johnny, I don't either!" Chris said.

Johnny started giggling and soon Chris joined him. "We're driving a car that's probably worth $200,000 and we have $20,000 worth of guns in the trunk, but we don't have any money to buy gas with!" Johnny said and then leaned across the trunk and burst out laughing. Chris soon was laughing too and had tears in his eyes when the tank finally filled up and the nozzle cut off. Johnny put the Nozzle back on the pump and the gas cap back on the car before wiping the tears out of his eyes.

"I'm going to grab a six-pack of beer while I'm here," Johnny said as he headed for the store. "Go ahead and crank up and pick me up at the front door."

"Walt? Where you at, Walt?" CJ hollered as he walked through the garage. CJ had been sitting in the bathroom for the last thirty minutes looking through the April edition of Penthouse Magazine and didn't have a clue where Walt had gone. CJ walked around behind the garage and noticed the door was slightly open going into the muscle car building so he walked up to the door and pushed it open.

The first thing he noticed was that the GTX was gone and he wondered why Walt was driving it. Then he glanced down and saw a huge pool of blood on the floor and he immediately turned and ran straight for Jack's house. CJ ran up to the side door and straight into the kitchen. Lee Hayworth and Johnny Steele were sitting at the kitchen table with Ashley Yates trying to impress her with tales of their adventures when CJ burst into the room.

"Johnny something's wrong!"CJ said, gasping for breath. "Walt's missing, and so is the GTX and there's blood all over the floor in the muscle car building!"

Johnny and Lee jumped up and ran out of the house and across the gravel lot to the garage. They ran through the garage and then back to the muscle car building and drew their guns before entering. Johnny walked slowly down one side of the building and Lee walked down the other side until they were sure that no one was in the building. The pool of blood was now four feet across and there were drag marks all the way across the floor of the building straight to the back of the Dodge Challenger. The key was still in the trunk lock so

Johnny pointed his Desert Eagle pistol at the trunk as Lee unlocked it and raised the lid. Lee turned Walt's body over and felt for a pulse and looked over at Johnny and shook his head. Johnny walked back across the building and looked in the empty footlocker as he dialed Jack's private number.

"What is it, Johnny?" Jack said when he answered the call.

"We got a major problem Jack!"

Johnny Billings walked into the Tank and Tummy No. 7 and headed straight for the beer cooler. Sylvia Culler normally wouldn't have noticed him but he was wearing a shoulder holster with a pistol in it and he certainly didn't look like a cop. She watched him grab a six-pack out of the cooler and then take his place in line behind a grossly overweight woman who was fumbling with her pocketbook as she paid for her gas. Since he was waiting his turn it made her feel a little better about him. The overweight woman finally waddled out the door and Johnny stepped up to the cashier and jerked the pistol out and pointed it at her head.

"Please don't kill me, I've got three kids!" she begged. "I'll give you whatever you want."

"Hand me the phone," Johnny said.

Sylvia reached behind her and picked up the desk phone and set it on the counter in front of Johnny. Johnny yanked the phone out of the wall and threw it across the store.

"Now hand me all the money," he shouted.

Sylvia opened the cash register and set the cash drawer on the counter in front of the wild eyed maniac.

"Put it in a bag!"

Sylvia's hands were shaking as she shoved the stacks of money into the plastic bag and then handed it to Johnny. Johnny took the bag and then just stood there staring at the trembling woman. He didn't know if he should kill her or just leave.

"I never had a mom!" He shouted at her.

"I'm sorry" was all Sylvia could manage to get out.

Johnny turned and walked out the door. Chris had pulled up to the door like Johnny had told him and when Johnny got in they took off squealing the tires. Sylvia fumbled with her purse until she found her cell phone and then dialed 911.

Corporal Don Gaines of the Virginia State Highway Patrol turned his cruiser out of the parking lot of the Independence Courthouse and headed south on Highway 21. He had just spent the last two hours sitting in a courtroom waiting to testify in a drunk driving case.

They finally called him to the stand and he gave his testimony and then returned to his seat. The man was found guilty of driving while impaired and ordered to surrender his driver's license and attend a class on substance abuse. Corporal Gaines was glad to be out of the courtroom and back on the road.

"All·units, report of a 10-17 at the Tank and Tummy on South Main Street. Two white males in silver-colored car headed south on Highway 21. Suspects are believed to be armed and dangerous."

Corporal Gaines was already headed south on 21 so he punched the gas and turned on his blue lights. When he came in sight of the store he could see two Independence City Police cars turning into the lot so he flew by the gas station headed out of town at about ninety miles an hour. Maybe he could get lucky and catch up to them before they reached the state line which was only twelve miles away. There wouldn't be much traffic on this road at this time of day, and while this road was only a two-lane road, it was a straight road that ran all the way to North Carolina up and down gently rolling hills. As he topped the first hill he got a glimpse of a car going across the top of the next hill almost a mile away. It looked like it was silver. There wasn't another car in sight so Corporal Gaines ran his cruiser up to 120 miles an hour and radioed his position.

"Be advised, suspect's car is a late sixties Plymouth GTX with no visible license plate. Vehicle is silver with a black top and is occupied with two white males in their twenties. Passenger is armed with a semiautomatic pistol."

Corporal Gaines knew that the policemen on the scene were looking at the store's video and sending out all the information that they could. He was glad to get it because if he caught up to them he could positively identify the car now. There just aren't many silver Plymouth GTXs on the road.

Chris was cruising at seventy miles an hour as he and Johnny drank their first beer. Johnny leaned out and threw his empty bottle at a speed limit sign and Chris just tossed his out the window and let it burst on the road. Johnny opened two more beers and handed one to Chris. Chris was thirsty and the beer hit the spot. As Chris raised the second beer up to take a swig he glanced into the rear-view mirror and what he saw snapped him out of his trance. "Oh shit, Johnny! Look behind us!"

Johnny turned around and saw the Virginia State Highway Patrol car as it overtook them and he just grinned. He snapped a clip into the bottom of the Uzi and jacked open the chamber. "Just hold her real steady," he said as he spun around in the seat and leaned out the window. Johnny pulled the trigger and held it back until the gun ran dry. The patrol car instantly backed off and pulled over in the grass beside the highway before it finally came to a stop.

"You got him, Johnny! He's outta here, man!" Chris squealed.

"Find a place somewhere up the road to pull over and let's put on that body armor before we go to the next level," Johnny said.

Chris didn't know what Johnny was talking about but he started looking for a good place to pull over.

Corporal Gaines pounded the dash with his fists. He had seen the passenger swing out the window and knew that he was probably going to shoot at him, so he swung his patrol car to the left to try to avoid being hit. He wasn't expecting what happened next. It sounded like a hundred rocks slammed into the front of his car and the windshield shattered and the right front tire blew out and the dash lit up when the engine died. He tried to restart the engine but it wouldn't even turn over, so he pulled off the highway and grabbed his microphone.

"Shots fired, shots fired. Suspects are armed with machine guns! I repeat, suspects are armed with fully automatic weapons and are traveling south on Highway 21 about four miles from the North Carolina border. Radio, I'm 10-50. I don't think I'm hit but my car is out of commission."

"Roger. Hang tight, 123, we got people coming for you."

Sheriff Sisk parked outside the Ashe County Courthouse and practically ran to the building. He felt like Judge Floyd might agree to a search warrant for Justin's house based on the fact that Tommy went missing near there and that Justin refused to let him enter his house and look around. If he had to he would get Jack to call him and then he knew the Judge would comply. As soon as he got the warrant he would have his deputies meet him there and then he would tear the place apart. I'll show Justin Hayes who runs this county Bill thought to himself as he stepped into Judge Floyd's office. Judge Floyd's secretary, Dena, was sitting at her desk going through a stack of legal papers.

"Dena, I need to speak to Judge Floyd if I can," Bill said. "It's kind of an emergency."

"He's in court, Sheriff, but they should be taking a recess for lunch anytime now," Dena said. "I can get a bailiff to take him a note if it's an emergency."

The sheriff's cell phone rang and he stepped away from Dena's desk when he saw who was calling. "Hello."

"I need you to call me from a secure phone somewhere and I need you to do it now!" Jack said. "We got a situation and it's critical!"

"I'll call you from my office in two minutes," Bill said and then he hung up. "I'll check by later, Dena, something's come up."

Bill turned and hustled out to his vehicle and could here them calling for him on his police radio even before he got to the Explorer. "Radio, this is the sheriff."

"Sheriff, we have received a call from the Virginia State Highway Patrol that said that two men armed with fully automatic weapons are headed our way on Highway 21 after robbing a gas station in Independence. Buddy and Jerry have been notified and have responded."

"Ten-four, Radio. I'm on my way to the office and I'll be there in thirty seconds."

Bill took off in his Explorer and squealed the tires as he turned onto Main Street. Why does everything have to happen at the same time he wondered? Jack has a critical situation of some kind and two armed fugitives are headed toward Ashe County, all at the same time! I really need to go back up Jerry and Buddy, especially since these fugitives have fully automatic weapons, but I need to call Jack first. He sounded like he was in a panic and was scared. Well, it won't take but a minute to stop and call Jack before I join Jerry and Buddy, Bill thought as he swung his SUV onto Church Street. Bill flew down the street by the First Baptist Church and slid to a stop in front of the Ashe County Sheriffs Department.

He ran into the building and down the hall until he came to his office and he shut the door. Bill called Jack's private number and he answered on the first ring.

"Bill, listen to me and listen good! Johnny and a friend of his named Chris Reid have stolen my 1968 Plymouth GTX and they murdered Walt in the process."

"Walt has been murdered?" Bill asked.

"Shot through the chest," Jack answered.

"Do you know where they went?"

"No, I don't have any idea where they went. They're probably high on drugs and they also stole some guns," Jack said.

"What kind of guns?" Bill asked.

"Hell, I don't know, Bill, just some guns!"

"Oh man Jack we can't sweep this under the rug. Not a murder!"

"Here's what I want you to do, Bill. I want you to find them and when you do I want you to kill Chris Reid. I don't know which one of them shot Walt but we'll claim that Chris did and then we'll charge Johnny with auto theft and drug possession and maybe DWI. He won't get too much time for that and it will give him a chance to dry out," Jack said in a strained voice.

"Billy's not involved with this, is he?" Bill asked.

"No, he was in his room packing boxes when it happened."

"Jack, I'll do what I can, but the district attorney will probably want to charge Johnny as an accessory to second-degree murder," Bill said.

"I'll take care of that, Bill, just find them before someone else does!" Jack shouted. "There in a silver 1968 GTX with a black top!"

"Okay, okay, Jack, I'll do my best," Bill said and he heard the line go dead as Jack hung up. He ran out of his office and back to the front of the building, stopping to talk with the dispatcher. "I'm on my way to back-up Jerry and Buddy," Bill said. "Where are they?"

"Jerry's at the intersection of Highway 117 where 21 joins it. He's going to block 117 so that they can't come to Sparta. Buddy's waiting with spike strips at the bridge over the south fork of the river."

"What are the suspects driving?" Bill asked.

"A late sixties model Plymouth GTX that's silver with a black top."

"Oh shit!" Bill said as he ran out the door.

Justin finally reached the top of the mountain behind Wade's house and sat down on a car sized boulder to rest. The view was great from up here he thought as he struggled to catch his breath in the thin mountain air. There must have been two hundred sheep standing on the side of the mountain that Justin just climbed and the big ram with the full curl of horns that Wade had warned Justin about was trotting back and forth letting Justin know that all those sheep were his. Justin kept his distance and kept walking to avoid a confrontation with him. Getting hit by that ram would be like getting hit by a Volkswagen at forty miles an hour Justin thought, and that ram kept looking at him like he owed him money.

Jesse had called Travis and told him that the intern had come to work and that she was leaving at noon so Travis took off for Jesse's house. DeMac had some legal papers pertaining to the estate of his parents and sister that he had to sign and get notarized and then mail them back to Montana by certified mail so he had gone to town. So Justin was by himself again, at least until Teresa got back from Kernersville, and he could hardly wait.

Justin had finally caught his breath and began to glance around and he wondered if this spot would be a good place to shoot from. He didn't know anything about calling coyotes but he knew a lot about picking out spots to shoot from. Justin reached in his vest pocket and pulled out his compass. He could see River Road and the New River from up here and they were due west from this spot, so if they were shooting across the pasture behind him they would be shooting due east. That wouldn't be any good in the morning because the sun would be in their eyes, but it would be perfect in the late evening. Justin turned around and looked across the pasture as he got out his laser rangefinder. He picked out a tree on the far side of the pasture and shot the distance. It was 514 yards. That's a long way to shoot at something as small as a coyote, especially if it's running. At the bottom of the valley in between Justin and the tree were some more large rocks similar to the one that Justin was sitting on. He focused his rangefinder on them and hit the button and the digital display showed 233 yards. That's a little more like it, Justin thought. If they could call them to the bottom of the valley then their chances of killing them would be much better.

Now Justin had to consider the biggest demon any shooter has to face—the wind. Justin figured the wind could be a problem on top of this hill even though it was still this evening. He turned his scope magnification up to 25 power and looked across the pasture to see the mirage. Mirage is simply the heat waves you can see rising up from the ground and it's always the best tool a shooter has to judge the wind. The mirage was angling slightly to Justin's right but not much. Justin was processing all this information when suddenly a coyote howled and another one joined in. Justin thought that coyotes howled only at night and was shocked to hear one howling at midday. He raised his binoculars and scanned the pasture and almost immediately saw him. He was standing right on top of the hill about fifty yards to the right of the tree that Justin had used to range the distance, right in front of a bushy locust tree and he had his head pointed straight up and was howling for all he was worth.

Justin eased to the ground and folded the legs of the bipod down before setting the Ruger No. 1 down on the ground. He settled in behind the rifle and quickly found the coyote in his scope. "Come on, Hayes, one shot, one kill. This one's for Wade's dog!" Justin said.

Justin clicked in five clicks of left windage to allow for the mirage he had seen earlier. It was slightly over five hundred yards and Justin knew from years of shooting a 220 Swift that in order to hold dead on at five hundred yards that he needed to be seven inches high at one hundred yards. Each click of Justin's scope equaled one-eighth of an inch at one hundred yards, so Justin needed to adjust his elevation 8×7 or fifty-six clicks to be able to hold dead on at five hundred yards. Justin watched his elevation knob as he spun it around to the proper setting. He looked back through the scope and found the coyote and placed the tiny dot in his scope right on the coyote's neck. If he shot a little high then he would still hit the coyote in the head, and if his shot was a little low it would hit him in the chest.

Justin's body went into automatic as he prepared to do what he had done at least ten thousand times over the course of his lifetime. He adjusted his body alignment and turned his toes outward as he lay on his stomach. He took a firm grip on the rifle and pulled it back into his shoulder and found his cheek-weld on the rifle's stock. He took a deep breath and blew it out and then took a very small breath and held it. The dot in the scope slowly began to settle down until it finally stopped and the rifle magically fired. Justin lost the sight picture because of the rifle's recoil but was busy jerking the lever down behind the trigger guard that dropped the falling block action and ejected the empty case. Justin shoved another round into the chamber and shut the action before he looked back through the scope for the coyote. At first he thought he might have missed him, but Justin saw something unusual and after careful examination he realized that it was one of the coyote's feet sticking up out of the grass and weeds. Justin watched the coyote to make sure it wasn't moving even though he had never seen anything move after being shot with a 220 Swift.

Justin thought it was strange that his ears were ringing so loud and then suddenly realized that his ears weren't ringing at all. It was a siren getting louder by the second. Now Justin knew why the coyote was howling. He could hear the siren long before Justin did.

Deputy Jerry Morris had his patrol car pulled across Highway 117 at the intersection· where Highway 21 joined it. If the fugitives coming from Virginia didn't turn on a side road before they got here then Jerry was going to force them to turn right on Highway 117 instead of letting them head toward Sparta. He was hoping he could shoot out one of their tires when they made the turn. He was standing behind his car and he was holding his Remington 870 shotgun and it was loaded with double-ought buckshot. Deputy Buddy Dixon had driven down the road to the bridge that crossed the south fork of the river and was waiting there with spike strips. If they could manage to flatten at least one of their tires it would keep them from ever reaching Jefferson or Wilkesboro. The main objective now was to keep these maniacs from ever reaching a populated area, especially since they had automatic weapons. If they shot at a Virginia state trooper then they probably wouldn't hesitate to shoot at anybody, and if there was going to be a shootout it needed to be in the country, not in the middle of town.

Deputy Morris was standing behind his car so he could use it for cover in case they shot at him when they went by, but he couldn't see up Highway 21 from this location. He knew that whatever happened would happen very quickly.

And it did. An elderly man and woman in an old rusty pickup truck came to a stop at the intersection. They had two small children, probably their grandchildren, standing on the seat in between them and the man was wanting to turn and head into Sparta but couldn't because Jerry's patrol car was blocking the road. He sat there staring at Jerry not knowing what to do. Jerry would normally write the man a citation for not having the children in child seats but now was not the time for that.

Jerry stepped around the front of his car to motion the man around when suddenly he heard a car gearing down hard as it approached the intersection. The silver GTX swung to the left to drive around the rusty pickup truck and was going to turn left until they saw the Deputy's car blocking the road, so they turned hard right and gunned the engine. The back end of the GTX spun around toward Deputy Morris and the driver with the blond hair stuck an Uzi out the window and fired twenty or thirty rounds. Jerry dove back around his car and heard the bullets as they ripped through the trees twenty feet away. He instantly jumped up and leaned across his hood with his shotgun to return fire but as he did the rusty pickup truck with the elderly couple and the two small children lurched into the middle of the road. The elderly man was trying to get his family out of danger and gunned his engine to back up but he was so scared that he forgot to put the truck in reverse. The truck literally leapt into the middle of the intersection completely blocking Jerry's line of fire so he swung his shotgun away from the truck and jumped in his car.

Jerry backed his patrol car up and then drove around the stunned people in the truck and punched the gas pedal to the floor.

"Shots fired! Shots fired! Suspects heading north on 117 between Highway 21 and the south fork of the New River. Get ready, buddy, they're headed your way. Radio, this is 154, in pursuit!"

"Roger, 154. Backup is on the way."

Deputy Buddy Dixon had pulled his patrol car over to the right side of Highway 117 just on the other side of the bridge that crossed the south fork of the New River. He retrieved his spike strips from the trunk of his car and crossed over to the left side of the bridge and stood behind the concrete pillar that the guard rail was attached to. It was the perfect spot to deploy the spike strips from because the suspects couldn't see him and would probably be concentrating on the patrol car on the other side of the road. Also the only one who could shoot at him would be the driver, and it would be hard to shoot and drive at the same time.

Deputy Dixon heard Jerry tell him to get ready. He reached up and pressed the button on his radio. "Radio, this is 169. Call Nancy at the New River General Store and tell her to get everybody off the porch and inside the store and to lock the doors."

"Roger, 169. I'm calling now."

Buddy could see the store from here and after a moment he saw Nancy step out on the porch and run everybody inside. He didn't want this to turn into a hostage situation or for someone to get hit by a stray bullet. Nancy kept a double barreled shotgun behind the cash register and if anybody tried to bust through the door she would probably ruin their day.

"169, this is the sheriff. I'm about ten minutes away. I want you to immobilize them and keep them contained until I arrive on scene. Suspects are believed to be Johnny Billings and Chris Reid. I want to talk to them if possible."

"Ten-four, Sheriff," Buddy responded. Buddy thought that the suspects probably wouldn't be in a very talkative mood since they already shot at a Virginia State Trooper and at Jerry. So far they had done all their talking with machine guns.

"154 to 169! We're approaching the bridge, 169! Get ready to deploy the sticks. I'm backing off. Over!"

"Ten-four. I'm ready and waiting!"

Buddy could hear the siren and saw the Silver car when it came in sight. They were probably running about eighty miles an hour when they started across the bridge and the passenger leaned out and opened up with automatic gunfire as soon as he saw the deputy's car parked on the right side of the road. Bullets were slamming into the rear of Buddy's patrol car. The rear windshield and then the light bar shattered as they drew closer and Buddy slid the spike strips across the road in front of them.

Johnny saw the spike strips slide across the road and tried to swerve but it was too late. He had changed places with Chris when they stopped to put on the second chance body armor because he wanted to drive the GTX for awhile and now they had cheated and used spike strips. Johnny was furious at them and decided to go back to Jack's and steal another car since his left side tires were punctured. He wasn't sure exactly what to do because when they stopped and put on the body armor he had taken another hit of acid and had snorted the rest of his cocaine and now his mind was flashing from one thing to another like an out of control movie projector. No, they would steal "Jumping Jack Flash" and then they could drive over the cop cars and drive across fences and through pastures or even down the river if they wanted to. Johnny threw the car into a hard slide in front of the New River General Store and headed down River Road spinning the tires. Johnny ran the car up to about eighty miles an hour. The road veered slightly to the left and then hard back to the right in front of the Shaver's farm, and even though Johnny was high on acid and cocaine, he knew that he was going to fast to make the turn on the rapidly deflating tires. The back end of the GTX lost traction and the car spun around one and a half turns before slamming into a guardrail and then sliding to a stop in the center of the road with the front end pointed back in the direction they were coming from.

Johnny got out and stumbled back to the trunk and opened it and started shoving clips of ammunition into the M-16s and stacking up the remaining clips. Chris had banged his head when they hit the guardrail and finally staggered back to where Johnny was.

"What are you doing man?" He asked.

"They cheated and now their going to pay!" Johnny said.

Jerry Morris wasn't real surprised to see the GTX turn down River Road. If it was Johnny Billings like the sheriff said then he was probably headed home. Jerry slammed on his brakes and slid to a stop beside Buddy's patrol car. Practically all the glass on the car was gone and the right rear tire was flat and gasoline was pouring out onto the pavement. Buddy jumped in the front seat beside of Jerry with his shotgun.

"Are you all right?" Jerry asked.

"Yeah, I'm fine, what about you?" Buddy said.

"I'm fine."

"Let's go get those chumps!" Buddy said.

Jerry and Buddy had been friends all their lives. They were raised on neighboring farms and grew up helping each other with their chores and hunting and fishing together. They rode the school bus together and played football for the Spartans together, and double dated together, and after high school they joined the Army together and served for three years before returning home and joining the Sheriff's Department together. They were closer than most brothers and they were both glad that the other one was all right.

Jerry took off and turned onto River Road. Nancy was standing on the front porch of the store and waved at the two officers when they went by like nothing had happened. Jerry accelerated to about fifty miles an hour. Jerry knew that the suspects wouldn't be going around these curves very fast with both their left side tires flat. They probably would just try and limp their way back to Jack's house.

As Jerry rounded the curve in front of the Shaver's farm, he and Buddy were caught completely off guard. The GTX was sitting in the center of the road pointed back at them and the two men were standing behind it, each holding an Uzi submachine gun. Jerry slammed on the brakes and went into a skid and even before the car got stopped they could hear bullets tearing through the sheet metal. Buddy opened his door and bailed out with Jerry right on top of him. They both immediately took a position behind the tires with Jerry crouched down behind the front tire and Buddy behind the rear tire as the gunmen sprayed the car with bullets.

The hail of gunfire was unbelievable and it was literally tearing the car apart. Glass was shattering and tires were blowing out and pieces of the car were flying off in every direction. A ricochet from underneath the car blew a bole through Jerry's left foot and a piece of shrapnel clipped his right ear. There was nowhere completely safe to hide under the relentless shower of bullets. Jerry rose up to engage the shooters with his pistol and his right hand was instantly shattered by a bullet sending the pistol flying behind him. He looked over at Buddy and what he saw shocked him. Buddy was sitting with his back against the rear tire and he looked pale. His right knee had been hit and was bleeding badly and he was trying to tie a bandage around it. Half of Buddy's little finger was missing on his right hand and a trickle of blood was running down his face from somewhere on top of his head. They looked at each other and were both thinking the same thing—we're going to die here today!

In between the relentless hail of gunfire Jerry could hear someone screaming "Cheaters" and wondered what that meant. Buddy was finally able to tie off his knee bandage and turned around so he could return fire. When he rose up with his shotgun the barrage started again and a bullet ripped through his upper left shoulder and spun him around until he was sitting right where he was before. Jerry pulled his backup pistol from his ankle holster and stuck just his left arm above the hood and started firing until a bullet grazed his arm and split it open like a knife. Jerry sat with his back against the tire just like Buddy as the bullets continued to fly.

They were finished and they both knew it. Buddy was slumped against the wheel of the car covered in blood and Jerry wasn't much better off with his right hand shattered, a bullet hole through his left foot, and his left arm ripped open from his wrist to his elbow. He reached up with his left hand and pressed the button on his microphone. "Shots fired! Shots fired! Two officers down. We need backup now. River Road. Hurry!"

Jerry looked back again at Buddy and saw that he was unconscious. Tears came to his eyes as he watched his best friend bleeding to death. "I'll see you on the other side, partner."

The gunfire had suddenly stopped and it was eerily quiet. Jerry slid down and looked under the car and what he saw scared him to death. There were two sets of feet walking toward him and he could hear the gravel crunching under their shoes.

"You shouldn't have cheated and used those spike strips Buddy and Jerry!" Johnny yelled. "Johnny, the sheriff will be here in a minute and he wants to talk to you," Jerry said.

"Good, I'm glad he decided to join the game. I want to kill him too!" Johnny said and he started laughing like a demon.

"Don't do this Johnny! Nobody's died yet so we can end this without anybody going to jail for murder!" Jerry pleaded.

"Oh, haven't you heard, Jerry? Walt's dead. I shot him through the heart so I don't have anything to lose."

A distant voice could be heard shouting from the top of the mountain. "Lay your weapons down now or I'll shoot!"

Johnny and Chris turned and looked toward the top of the mountain.

The voice repeated the command. "Lay your weapons down now or I'll shoot!"

Johnny pointed at the rocks on top of the mountain. "He's on top of the biggest rock, Chris. Shoot him."

Chris and Johnny raised their M-16s but before they could fire there was a sound similar to a person slapping the top of the water with a canoe paddle. "Ke-smack!" Chris hit the pavement like a giant fly-swatter had hit him. The sound of a distant rifle shot echoed through the valley as Johnny pointed his rifle at the mountain and emptied a thirty round clip. "Ke-smack" could be heard again as Johnny hit the pavement beside his buddy Chris. Jerry couldn't believe his eyes. The two assassins were both dead.

The Aftermath

Several members of the Shatley Springs Volunteer Fire Department were standing beside the bullet-riddled car holding fire extinguishers while several other firemen helped carry the stretchers and IV bags with the two wounded deputies to the waiting ambulance. A helicopter was standing by in the parking lot of the Grace Lutheran Church on Highway 117 waiting to transport the wounded officers to the Trauma Center at the Wake Forest Baptist Medical Center in Winston-Salem. Justin was sitting on the hot asphalt road with his hands cuffed behind his back watching the drama unfold.

Sheriff Sisk and the paramedics had arrived moments after Justin finally ended the murderous shooting spree, so Justin walked down the mountain and surrendered himself to Sheriff Bill Sisk. That was exactly what CIA operative Jimmy Hardy had warned him not to do. "Whatever happens, don't let Sheriff Sisk arrest you. He'll kill you if he gets the chance," Jimmy had said. But Justin's only choice was to kill the two men or sit and watch them execute the two deputies, and Justin couldn't do that. It wasn't an easy thing to do, but it was the right thing to do.

A North Carolina State Trooper came walking over to where Justin was sitting and squatted down in front of him. "I guess since you're the only one around here in handcuffs, that you're the one that finally shot those two maniacs," he said to Justin.

"Yes, sir, unfortunately I am," Justin answered. "How bad off are those deputies, trooper? Are they going to make it?"

"Yeah, I think they're going to make it. Jerry's right hand is shattered and his left arm is split open from his wrist to his elbow and he has a bullet hole through his left foot. And Buddy has been shot in the right knee and left shoulder and is missing a finger, but both of them are in stable condition and with a little luck they're going to make it."

"Well, I'm glad they're going to make it," Justin said. "It's a miracle that they're both not dead."

"That's why I walked over here, Mr. Hayes," the trooper said. "I want to thank you for what you did. Jerry told me what happened before he was loaded in the ambulance and he wanted me to thank you in person for saving their lives. I'm sorry that you have to sit here in handcuffs but that's standard procedure after a shooting and I can't do anything about that, but I can thank you for Jerry and Buddy and from myself for saving their lives."

"I appreciate that, officer," Justin said. "I'm just glad that they're both alive!"

"Not many men would have done what you did today. Nobody wants to get involved anymore. It's nice to know that there are still some real men out there that aren't afraid to step up and do the right thing. Thank you again," the trooper said and then walked away.

When Justin climbed on board that Freedom Bird in Vietnam in 1969 for that glorious flight back to the United States, he thought he would never have to look at another human being through a rifle scope again, but today had proven him wrong. Sitting on the hot asphalt in handcuffs even reminded Justin of how he was sometimes treated in Vietnam by some of the soldiers and even some of the officers. They called the snipers "Murder Inc." and sometimes treated them like they were morally deficient or sub-human, or like they were criminals of some kind or another. If a regular platoon of soldiers stumbled across a few enemy soldiers in the jungle they would sometimes fire over a thousand rounds of ammo at them and launch mortars and throw grenades and even call in artillery or air strikes to try and kill them, and they thought what they did was brave and honorable. But if a sniper team hid in the jungle and killed a couple enemy soldiers from a hidden position, then they were cowards and murderers. It never made any sense to Justin back then, and it didn't make any sense to him now. Justin didn't need anyone to justify what he did in Vietnam and he didn't need anyone to justify what he did here today. Every time he killed an enemy soldier in Vietnam, he knew that he was saving the lives of American soldiers, and today when he shot those two blood-thirsty fugitives he saved the lives of two deputies, and that was all the justification that he needed. He didn't want a medal or some kind of award for what he had done. All he really wanted was to be treated with respect, instead of having to sit on a hot asphalt road with his hands cuffed behind his back.

The crime scene was surrounded by yellow crime tape and was crowded with deputies, firemen, state troopers, and paramedics. There were even a few Virginia State Troopers standing on the fringes watching the action. The two dead men had finally been covered by sheets and Justin was glad that he didn't have to look at them anymore. A black Ford Crown Victoria came driving up River Road and parked as close as it could and a black van pulled up behind it and parked. The van had SBI Crime Lab painted on the side in bold letters. Four men got out of the car and three men and one woman got out of the van and they all were wearing tee-shirts and ball caps that said SBI on them except for one man who was wearing a suit. They immediately started clearing everyone out of the crime scene and the man in the suit approached Justin holding a badge out in front of him.

"Mr. Hayes, my name is Jerry Teddar and I'm with the State Bureau of Investigation," he said. "Has anyone read you your rights?".

"No, sir," Justin said and the man immediately started quoting the Miranda Act. When he finished he asked Justin if he understood his rights. "Yes, sir," Justin replied.

"Mr. Hayes, we are going to wait until we transport you to the Ashe County Sheriffs Department before we interview you regarding your actions here today, however there is one thing that I need to ask you now and that is where is the rifle that you allegedly used to shoot the fugitives?"

Justin turned his head and nodded toward the mountain behind him. "It's lying on top of a huge rock on top of this mountain and the empty brass is lying beside it."

"You mean these rocks on the far side of this river bottom?"

"No," Justin said. "I mean those huge rocks that are at the very top of the mountain. The tall rock on the far left is where you'll find the rifle."

Agent Teddar raised his head and peered at the top of the mountain. "That's a mighty long shot, Mr. Hayes. I'd guess it at almost seven hundred yards."

Justin could tell that Agent Teddar didn't believe that he shot the men from that far away and like most people he wasn't very good at judging distance either. "It looks longer than it is, Agent Teddar. It's only 472 yards," Justin replied.

Agent Teddar turned around and gave instructions to two of his men and they took off toward the mountain in a fast walk.

"I appreciate your cooperation, Mr. Hayes, and I see no need for you to sit on this hot asphalt any longer so I'm going to get someone to escort you to a car," Agent Teddar said.

"Thank you," Justin said.

Special Agent Jerry Teddar had been with the SBI for over twenty-five years and had seen hundreds of crime scenes, but he had never seen a car as shot up as the deputy's car he was looking at now. There wasn't one square inch of the car that wasn't perforated and how anyone could live through that was a mystery to him. There had to be at least three hundred bullet holes in the car and it was a miracle that the two officers were still alive he thought to himself as he stepped over to speak to Sheriff Sisk. He had worked with Sheriff Sisk a couple years ago on a bear poaching investigation and he remembered the sheriff as being cocky and uncooperative and he hoped that he had changed since then.

"Sheriff, I'm going to transport Mr. Hayes back to your jail and begin interrogating him while the rest of my team finishes gathering the evidence," Agent Teddar said.

"The hell you will!" Sheriff Sisk bellowed. "He's my prisoner and I intend to transport him and interrogate him myself!"

Jerry could tell that nothing had changed. The sheriff was still cocky and arrogant and uncooperative. "Sheriff, I understand why local departments are offended when we come in and launch an investigation, but you know as well as I do that anytime there is a shooting involving a police officer in the state of North Carolina that we're the ones in charge of the investigation."

"That's the damn problem!" Bill shouted. "There's things about that man that you don't know because you're not from around here. He's already a suspect in an investigation of a missing person and I think there's more to this killing than meets the eye! I plan on charging him with murder as soon as I get him back to town."

Agent Teddar thought it was a little strange that the sheriff was planning on charging this man with murder before he was even interrogated or the evidence was analyzed.

"Sheriff, from what I've seen and heard so far, if it weren't for Mr. Hayes, you would have two deputies to bury."

"Those deputies screwed up and damn near got themselves killed," Bill snorted. "I told them to isolate and contain the suspects until I arrived but they decided to shoot it out with them, so I don't feel the least bit sorry for them."

That comment shocked and angered Agent Teddar. Even if the officers made a mistake, they were doing everything they could to protect this community and almost lost their lives in the process. He stepped closer to Sheriff Sisk and looked him in the eye before he continued the conversation. "Sheriff, I didn't come over here to ask you for permission. I came over here to inform you of what my intentions are. Now out of courtesy I will wait until you are present before I interrogate Mr. Hayes, but I'm going to transport him myself and I'm going to do it right now!"

Agent Teddar could see the veins in Sheriff Sisk's neck bulging and his face was turning red and he wondered if the sheriff was going to take a swing at him, but he just let out a long string of curse words and walked away. Agent Teddar informed the rest of his team that he was heading to the Ashe County Sheriffs Department with the prisoner and then walked back over to where Justin was sitting.

"Okay, Mr. Hayes, I'm going to help you up and then transport you to town," Jerry said.

"Before you do, there's something you need to know," Justin said. "I have a .38 revolver in the small of my back."

"The sheriff didn't search you for weapons?"

"He took a .45 automatic off me and just figured it was the only handgun I had," Justin said.

"Why didn't you tell him you had it?"

"Because I thought he would be transporting me to town and I was going to use it to save my life if he tried to kill me," Justin said staring at Agent Teddar.

"So you think the sheriff would try to kill you?"

"There's not a doubt in my mind. If he gets the chance to kill me he will!"

Agent Teddar and another agent grabbed Justin by his huge upper arms and helped him stand up. After they got him up the other agent removed the .38 revolver and placed it in an evidence bag after he removed the cartridges. He then patted Justin down to make sure that he wasn't carrying any more weapons and then they started walking up River Road toward the black Crown Victoria. Justin didn't walk with his head down like most people do when they are being led to a police car. He held his head up and kept his back straight.

A crowd of people stood just beyond the crime tape trying to get a glimpse of the carnage. The local news stations were all represented and Justin happened to notice the tall blond reporter that had pulled up her dress to change her pantyhose on Jack's bridge yesterday. Justin wondered if he would have had the discipline to not swing his rifle around to look at her if he would have been in the same situation as the sniper that he caught.

The two SBI agents held the crime scene tape up so that Justin could walk under it and Justin saw Travis and Jesse standing in the crowd as soon as he stepped under the tape. DeMac was standing behind them and they all three waved and hollered when they saw Justin being led to the car. Justin winked at Travis to let him know that he was all right and then stepped over to get in the car. As soon as the agent opened the door for Justin to get in, Justin glanced up the road and saw her. A black Cadillac Escalade was pulled over on the shoulder of the road along with several other vehicles and Teresa was staring at Justin with her hands partially covering her face.

A fireman had told Teresa that there had been a terrible shootout between a couple guys and the sheriffs department, and that since there were several people dead, the road would probably be closed for several more hours. He also told her that she could drive around the roadblock by turning around and going back to 117 and turning right, and then go about two miles and turn right on Lucy Bell Road, and then take the second dirt road to the left and follow that until she came to Cranberry Creek Road, and then turn right and go until she came to a stop sign, and then turn right again and follow that until she came to Antioch Church Road and turn right again and it would eventually dead end at River Road. Teresa didn't know any of the back roads in Ashe County and was certain that she would get lost so she called Justin on her cell phone but was unable to reach him. She knew why now. He was being led to a police car in handcuffs. He was obviously involved in the shootout and her heart shattered when she saw him. Tears streamed down her cheeks and she put her hands over her face as she cried. All her hopes and dreams seemed to vanish as she watched them put Justin in the backseat of that police car. She had been absolutely sure that this man was her soul mate sent to her from God to spend the rest of her life with. She had fallen hopelessly in love with him after only one evening and now it appeared to be over as fast as it started.

She had been concerned at first when she read the background check on Justin because he had been a sniper in Vietnam and had killed so many men, but he had erased her fears with his warm personality and tender heart. Now it appeared that her suspicions had been right all along and she felt like a fool for being so gullible.

Teresa reached up to her ignition with a trembling hand and cranked the engine on her Escalade. She executed a hard three point road turn, slinging the pizza onto the floor of the Cadillac that she had bought for her and Justin to eat while they cuddled in the Jacuzzi.

She left squealing the tires on her way back to Kernersville.

Justin turned around in the backseat of the police car and watched as Teresa drove away. She looked like she was crying and he wished he could talk to her, but there was no way that he could pull that off. Maybe she was going to the jail to wait for him.

Agent Teddar and the other agent climbed in the front seat and they drove up River Road to the stop sign at 117 and turned left to go to Sparta. A white van with "High Country Tours" painted on the side pulled out of the parking lot of the New River General Store and followed them as they wound their way back to town. It was a quiet ride with everyone trying to gather their thoughts before they arrived at the jail.

When they finally arrived Justin was led to an interrogation room and Agent Teddar removed the handcuffs from his wrists.

"Mr. Hayes, you are not under arrest but are being held for questioning," Agent Teddar said. "Do you understand?"

"Yes, sir, I do," Justin replied.

"Can I get you a drink or something to eat?"

"I could drink a Pepsi or a bottle of water if it's available."

Agent Teddar nodded at his assistant and he turned and left the room.

"I promised the sheriff that I wouldn't interrogate you until he was present, but there are a few questions that I would like to ask you before he arrives. You do realize that you are entitled to have an attorney present and that everything you say in this room is being recorded and can be used against you in a court of law."

"Yes, sir, I'm aware of all that." Justin replied.

"Okay then, you and the sheriff are obviously enemies. He wants to charge you with murder even though you apparently saved the lives of two of his deputies, and you hid a handgun for protection in case the sheriff tried to kill you when he transported you to jail, but willingly gave it up when you realized that we were going to transport you. So what's going on between you two?"

"All I can tell you Agent Teddar is that I know some things about the sheriff that he doesn't want anyone to know. I can't prove anything yet, but I will eventually unless I have to spend the night in this jail," Justin said.

"Why would spending one night in jail make a difference?"

"Because I would be found dead tomorrow morning from an apparent suicide," Justin said. "Make no mistake about it, Agent Teddar, if Bill Sisk gets the opportunity to kill me, then I will be dead!"

"Then why didn't you run after you shot the two fugitives?"

"Because it would have made me look suspicious, like I had done something wrong. Besides, my truck is parked in the Shaver's yard and it wouldn't have taken you long to figure out that I did it."

The other SBI agent walked back into the room and set a can of Pepsi down in front of Justin.

"Thank you," Justin said and then took a long drink.

The sounds of doors slamming and heavy footsteps preceded Sheriff Sisk as he stormed into the room. His face was red and he was practically growling as he stepped over to the table that Justin was sitting behind.

"Why isn't this man in handcuffs Agent Teddar?" Bill almost shouted. "Because he hasn't been charged with a crime, that's why!"

"You don't think murder is a crime?"

"How do you figure that Mr. Hayes committed murder, Sheriff!"

"I'll tell you how, it's pretty clear to me what happened out there on River Road today. I believe that Justin Hayes was listening to a police scanner and knew the suspects were heading his way, so he grabbed a rifle and positioned himself on top of that mountain and shot out one of their tires when they came around that curve causing them to hit the guard rail and spin around in the road. That explains why there were three empty cartridge cases found beside his rifle. Then after the shootout, the two suspects decided to surrender and when they approached my deputies he shot them both dead. That's how I figure it was murder!" Bill shouted.

"What were you doing on top of that mountain with a rifle, Mr. Hayes?" Agent Teddar asked.

"I was coyote hunting," Justin answered.

"Coyote hunting!" screamed Sheriff Sisk. "That's a damn lie if I ever heard one. Nobody around here hunts coyotes and if they did it wouldn't be in the middle of the day!"

"Sheriff, if you don't calm down and quit acting like a raving lunatic, I will have you escorted out of this room and conduct this interview by myself! Do you understand?"

"I'm not in the habit of coddling murderers Agent Teddar!" Bill said angrily. "Why don't you ask him where the third bullet went?"

"Okay, I will, but you better calm down if you want to remain in this room during this interview. Do you understand?"

"Yeah, I understand," Bill said reluctantly.

"Mr. Hayes, the bodies of the two deceased men had what appeared to be one bullet hole each in their upper chest or lower neck region, but apparently they found three empty cartridges beside your rifle. Can you tell us where you fired the third shot?"

"I can tell you exactly where the third round went," Justin said. "I shot a coyote just moments before the shootout occurred."

"Bullshit!" Bill hollered. "Let me guess, the coyote wasn't dead and he ran away with your bullet inside him."

"No, sir, he's graveyard dead and he's lying on top of the next mountain over in front of a bushy locust tree with one of his paws sticking straight up above the grass," Justin said.

"All of us know that it's nothing short of a miracle that both those deputies aren't dead," Agent Teddar said. "Mr. Hayes, you have admitted to killing the two fugitives, but what I'm wondering is why you waited so long to intervene?"

"I didn't have a shot from where I was originally. The rock I was sitting on was small and it was about forty yards to the right of where I was when I shot the fugitives. I had to move to a higher location to have a clear shot of River Road. The natural curve of the hillside was blocking me," Justin said.

Agent Teddar pulled out his cell phone and called the agent in charge of the crime scene and began giving him the information on where to find the dead coyote.

"Before you hang up, Agent Teddar, tell him to look about forty or fifty feet in front of where I fired from for bullet drag marks," Justin said. "I was being fired on when I shot the two suspects. And tell them not to get close to that ram unless they want to get their asses knocked down."

Agent Teddar relayed this new information to his Forensics Team and then hung up.

"I guess those two boys you murdered just happened to look up on top of that mountain and saw you laying there with your rifle?" Bill said sarcastically.

"How is it, Mr. Hayes, that they were able to see you so far away?" Agent Teddar asked.

"Because I hollered for them to lay down their weapons or I would shoot. I actually hollered it twice before they fired on me."

"Okay, Mr. Hayes, I want you to start from the time you arrived at the Shaver's farm and tell me step by step what happened," Agent Teddar said as he reached for his ringing cell phone. Agent Teddar listened intently to the person on the other end of the call and then closed his phone and placed it back in his pocket.

"This interview is over. We are no longer in charge of this investigation."

"It may be over for you, but I'm not going anywhere until I find out the truth," Sheriff Sisk huffed.

The door to the interrogation room opened up and in stepped three men and one woman. They were all holding out badges that had FBI in gold letters across them and the man in front stepped over in front of Sheriff Sisk. "Sheriff, I'm Special Agent Dan Loggins, and this is Agent Robert Ritchie, Agent Fred Turner, and Agent Roseanna Lankford. I'm going to have to ask you and Agent Teddar to leave the room."

"What gives you jurisdiction in this matter?" Bill shouted. "You have no grounds to take over this investigation!"

"Oh, but we do, Sheriff Sisk," Agent Loggins said. "The two fugitives stole a car and then crossed over into Virginia, where they robbed a store and then shot at a Virginia State Trooper before crossing back over the state line again. That's what gives us jurisdiction in this matter!"

"Well, I guess the citizens of Ashe County don't need a sheriff if every time there's a crime the SBI and the FBI come charging in here and take over the damn investigation!" Bill Sisk shouted.

"There kinda used to it by now," Justin said calmly. "There hasn't been a real sheriff up here in years."

Bill Sisk dove across the table at Justin but was dragged back by SBI Agent Teddar and FBI Special Agent Loggins. Agent Loggins slammed Bill Sisk against the wall and held him there. "If you so much as touch that man I will arrest you for tampering with a federal investigation! Do you understand, Sheriff?"

Sheriff Sisk just stared at Agent Loggins and didn't say a word. Agent Loggins finally released him and ordered him out of the room.

Agent Teddar handed Agent Loggins his business card and said, "If you have any questions for me you can reach me here."

"Thank you for your cooperation, Agent Teddar. If you will brief one of my colleagues concerning what you know so far about this incident I will be grateful."

"No problem," Agent Teddar said and he left the room with Agent Ritchie and Agent Turner following him.

The remaining agents, Dan Loggins and Roseanna Lankford, took a seat across the table from Justin. Agent Loggins opened up a satchel and began writing something on a piece of paper. After a few minutes he stopped writing and looked at Justin.

"Mr. Hayes, you are aware that everything you say in this room is recorded and can be used against you in a court of law."

"Yes, sir, I'm aware of that," Justin answered.

"This is Special Agent Dan Loggins assisted by Agent Roseanna Lankford in the interrogation of Justin Hayes in regard to the shooting incident on River Road in Ashe County, North Carolina, on this the tenth day of April 2006 at 4:15 p.m. Mr. Hayes, if you will, look at these two photos and tell me if you recognize either one of these men," Agent Loggins said as he slid a folder across the table to Justin.

Justin opened up the folder and saw a hand written note. It said, "Everything we say in this room is being recorded and we are being watched, so be careful what you say and do. We have been sent by the CIA to rescue you, but we have to pretend to interrogate you first before we escort you out, so play along with us even if we get rough."

"No, sir, I don't recognize either one of them," Justin said and he closed the folder and slid it back across the table.

Agent Loggins asked Justin to tell him everything that happened from the moment he woke up that morning until now, and Justin did. Several times during the interview Agent Loggins and Agent Lankford tried to trip him up on his story, and they shouted and paced around the room. It was an act that would have won them an Oscar if it were in a movie and Justin played along just like the note said. Finally after about two hours they shut it down.

Justin was only caught off guard one time during the whole interrogation and that was when Agent Loggins told him the names of the two men he shot. Justin had no idea that one of the men was Johnny Billings. The last time he saw Johnny was when Billy drove the monster truck down the river and Johnny and Billy both had long black hair then. The two men that Justin shot both had short hair and neither one of them had black hair. It certainly explained why Sheriff Sisk was so upset. Justin also knew that Jack Billings would be insane with hate, and that until he was arrested Justin would have to be extremely careful.

The four FBI agents surrounded Justin and with Agent Loggins leading the way they stepped into the hallway and headed for the back door. Sheriff Sisk met them halfway down the hall and stood in the center to block their exit.

"Where in the hell do you think you're taking my prisoner?" He said. "He's not your prisoner and we're taking him home," Dan said.

"I can hold him for twenty-four hours and I intend to do just that!" Bill Sisk declared.

"You just don't get it, do you, Sheriff?" Dan said and he stepped forward until his face was inches from the Sheriff's. "You have nothing to do with this investigation or this person.

We have found no basis to charge this man with any crime and we are releasing him on the condition that he remains on his property until all the evidence is examined."

"I can charge him with murder without your permission Agent Loggins even though you're in charge of the investigation!"

"I think you would be surprised at what you can't do as long as I'm in charge of this investigation. Besides Sheriff, there isn't a district attorney on the East Coast that would look at this evidence and charge him with murder. The forensics technicians have already called me and given me the preliminary results. The skid marks and the damage to the guardrail indicate that the suspects were traveling in excess of seventy-five miles an hour when they entered that curve and both left side tires had been punctured by your deputies spike strips. That's why they slammed into the guardrail and spun around in the road. They also picked up over four hundred pieces of brass that the suspects fired at your deputies and confiscated five fully automatic weapons. The coyote that Mr. Hayes claimed he shot has been recovered and is being sent to Raleigh for a necropsy, and there are at least twenty bullet drag marks indicating that Mr. Hayes was being fired on when he shot the two fugitives.

"Now I don't personally know the district attorney for this area, but I can assure you that he's not stupid enough to charge Mr. Hayes with murder. Now I will ask you one time and one time only to step aside or I will have Roseanna arrest you and lead you outside for all the citizens of Ashe County to see on the ten o'clock news tonight!"

Bill Sisk paused but finally stepped aside and the group exited the back door of the jail and were met by reporters and cameramen from all the local stations. One of the agents had thrown his coat over Justin's head and they put him in the backseat of the Crown Victoria. Agent Loggins gave the press a brief statement and they were finally back on the road headed for Justin's house.

"I want to thank all of you for getting me out of there," Justin said as they wound their way down 117. "You probably don't even realize it, but you just saved my life."

"You need to thank Jimmy Hardy and the CIA for saving your life," Dan Loggins said. "We don't have a clue what's going on but it must be pretty big for the CIA to call us in to rescue you. Jimmy is waiting at your house to fill us in on what's going on."

"Is my truck still at the Shaver's farm?" Justin asked.

"No, we sent a roll-back to pick it up and haul it to our office in North Wilkesboro. We have to at least pretend to search it for evidence before we release it. We'll probably return it to you by tomorrow evening."

"That's okay. I got a feeling that I won't need it anyway," Justin said.

"We want you to stay on your property until we finish analyzing all the evidence. That way we can submit our reports to the Sheriffs Department and the SBI without arousing any suspicion," Agent Loggins said.

Justin hardly even heard Agent Loggins. He was wondering if Teresa had been trying to call him.

"Bill, it ends tonight! I don't care how you do it, but do it as soon as possible. Do you understand?" Jack Billings shouted as soon as Bill Sisk answered the phone.

"He's not here, Jack," Bill said.

"What the hell do you mean 'he's not there'?"

"The FBI took over the investigation and they are taking him back to his house where he is to remain until all the evidence is analyzed."

"That son of a bitch has pointed a handgun at me and Johnny Steele, kidnapped Tommy, and now has murdered my nephew and you're telling me you can't hold him in your jail!" Jack screamed.

"Jack I tried, but the FBI took over and they escorted him out to their car. I couldn't stop them!" Bill said frantically.

"I think we might need some fresh blood in the sheriff's office as soon as the next election rolls around. Seems to me that you lost your nerve Bill. Dammit, I need somebody that can get things done when I need it done!" Jack screamed.

"Jack, I almost got myself arrested for—".Bill realized that Jack had hung up and he threw the phone off his desk and onto the floor.

"Agent Loggins, can you slow down and look to your right and tell me if there are any lights on in that big A-framed house on the hill?" Justin said when they came in sight of Teresa's driveway.

"Sure" he said and almost came to a complete stop. "It looks dark to me. I don't see any lights."

"Thank you," Justin said dejectedly.

"Friend of yours?" Agent Loggins asked.

"I'm not sure after today," Justin said.

They finally got to Justin's house and pulled up to the carport. Shogun and Scooter somehow knew that Justin was in that car and they were both excited when he finally got out. Justin led the way as he and the four FBI agents walked into the kitchen.

Justin went straight for the refrigerator to get a cold beer but was practically tackled by Travis when he came running from the living room. There were tears in his eyes when he hugged his dad.

When Travis and Jesse first drove up to the roadblock on River Road he saw his dad's truck parked in the Shaver's yard and then heard someone say there had been a shooting, and he thought his dad had been shot. When DeMac and Chief arrived they told Travis what had happened and it felt like a thousand pound weight had been lifted off his chest. It was the first time that Travis had thought he lost his dad and it scared him to death. He now realized how much pain that DeMac had been carrying around.

"I love you, Dad!" Travis said. "I thought I lost you today and it scared me to death!"

"I love you too, son!" Justin said. "Is Jesse around here?"

"I took her home so she could feed her animals. I figured it was a bad idea to bring her over here with the CIA and the FBI all gathering here to talk."

"Well, if you leave right now you might get there in time to see her feed the kittens again."

"I'm afraid to leave you until this thing is over!" Travis said.

"I got more protection right now than the President of the United States," Justin said. "Hell, you can't walk through the house without tripping over a CIA operative or a FBI agent or a Navy Seal. On top of that there are snipers surrounding the house and if the truth was known they are probably watching the house from a satellite! Go back to Jesse's and stay there for now, but be extra careful until this thing is over."

"Okay, but call me if anything happens," Travis said.

"I will. Get out of here. Go! Scram!" Justin said, smiling.

Travis took off through the kitchen door and Justin turned around and was looking straight into Jimmy Hardy's eyes.

"Well, let me turn around and bend over so you can kick me in the ass!" Justin said.

"Don't think that I wouldn't if I got the chance!" Jimmy said. "Of course you would probably shoot me if I did!"

"I'm sorry Jimmy, I really am. I know I've made your life hell today," Justin said.

"You have no idea the hell I've been through today, and it's not over with yet!"

"I was in a bad situation, Jimmy! I had to do something and I didn't know that one of them was Johnny Billings!"

"I know that it wasn't entirely your fault. It was just a freak coincidence but it almost destroyed this mission," Jimmy said. "By the way, that was some damn fine shooting you did. I'm assuming that it was no accident that you shot those two punks an inch and a half above their body armor."

"Just a lucky shot, Jimmy," Justin said. "A blind hog will find an acorn every now and then."

"Bullshit, Justin! People don't make lucky shots on a forty-degree angle at almost five hundred yards! And a blind hog will find just as many acorns as the rest of the hogs because they find them with their nose, not their eyes. Anyway, go drink your beer and relax. I got to fill in Agent Loggins on what's going on."

"Oh, Jimmy, before I forget it, I hid that cell phone on top of the mountain before I surrendered," Justin said.

Jimmy walked over to a briefcase and pulled out Justin's cell phone and handed it to him. "We found it," he said and then walked off.

Justin hurried into his living room and checked the caller ID beside his phone. His heart sank when he read the dial: "No calls."

Perspective

Justin was tired. He sat in a recliner in his living room looking out the big picture windows toward the river and the mountains beyond it. It was dark outside and it had started raining, so Justin couldn't really see anything but it didn't matter. He really wasn't looking as much as he was thinking.

DeMac came walking into the room followed closely by another man who was obviously a soldier. He had features of an American Indian and his hair was cut high and tight, as they called it in the military. Other than that he looked like a pit bulldog. He was probably about five feet eight inches tall with a square jaw and piercing black eyes. His shoulders were wide and he was very muscular everywhere. He looked like he could tear a normal man apart.

"Justin, this is Billy Roe," DeMac said. "Billy, this is Justin Hayes, Travis's dad."

"Nice to meet you, Billy," Justin said.

"A pleasure to meet you, sir," Billy responded.

"Like everyone on my team, Billy's got a nickname," DeMac continued. "We call him Chief for obvious reasons."

"I'll call him Chief if he calls me Justin instead of sir," Justin said.

"That's a deal, sir. I mean Justin," Chief said.

"Chief here is a bona fide coyote expert. He was raised on the Cherokee Indian Reservation in Oklahoma and trapped and hunted coyotes for extra spending money when he was growing up, so he knows all about killing coyotes. Jimmy sent him to help' us with Wade's problem."

"That's great!" Justin said. "Glad to have you on board, Chief."

"Thank you, sir, I mean Justin."

"He can bunk in Travis's room since Travis is staying over at Jesse's," Justin said.

"That's okay, Justin. Me and Chief have bunked together in swamps, and in the desert, and on top of snow covered mountains, and even on a submarine, so bunking in your spare bedroom is not a problem," DeMac said.

"Suit yourself, but it's there if you want it," Justin said. "Chief, I want you to just take charge of this coyote hunt. None of us have ever tried to call in a coyote so we don't know shit from shinola. Just tell everybody what they need to do and where they need to be and maybe we'll get lucky. I would like for Wade to get a shot if possible. He needs to kill a coyote to even the score since they killed his dog. It will be up to him to make the shot if he gets one, but I would like to set it up so that he gets the chance."

"I've already done some scouting on the Shaver farm and I have a plan in my head for whenever you're ready, sir," Chief said.

"Let's go ahead and plan on doing it tomorrow before they lose any more sheep!" Justin said. "I won't be able to be there because I'm confined to my property until they finish their investigation, but Wade is familiar with DeMac and he will be comfortable as long as he's there."

"Very well, sir. I'll work out the details and we'll plan on trying it tomorrow evening," Chief said.

"And one more thing, Chief," Justin said.

"What's that, sir?"

"Just call me sir instead of Justin. I believe it will be easier for you," Justin said with a smile.

"Yes, sir," Chief said. DeMac and Chief went into DeMac's bedroom to stow Chief's gear and Justin grabbed another beer before heading to his machine shop to get some privacy.

Justin needed a quiet place to go so he could sort out his feelings and do some thinking. After all, it had only been a few hours since he had shot and killed two men. The killings were justified and he knew it, but you still had to carry it around with you for awhile.

Justin had known men that enjoyed killing but he had never learned to like killing another human being, even when he knew the person he killed would have gladly returned the· favor.

When Justin finally returned home from Vietnam in 1969 he was able to bury his feelings because in his mind everything that happened was in another world. It was almost like he had been abducted by aliens and taken to another planet where he had to fight to win his freedom back to the world. Now those feelings and bad memories were flooding back to him and he felt guilty. But what was he guilty of'! Doing his duty! Obeying orders! Should he be ashamed of himself because he was the best rifle shot on that firing range thirty-eight years ago? It wasn't his fault that he had killed so many men. The pilots of the helicopter gunships and the men who fired the big artillery pieces had killed hundreds of more men than him. But there was a big difference in the way they killed men and the way a sniper plied his trade. They never had to look at their eyes seconds before they died. They never had to watch them crumble to the ground and twitch until their nerves quit pulsing!

The shop door opened up and Justin turned to see who was invading his privacy. Reverend Mark McDowell shut the door behind him and took off his raincoat.

"Mind if I join you?" He asked.

"Come in preacher!" Justin said. "Kind of a nasty night to be visiting!"

"I had to go by the church anyway so I thought I would stop in since I was this close," Pastor McDowell said. "I rang the front doorbell and some man told me you were back here."

"Some of my son's Navy buddies are staying here and trying out some of the local trout streams," Justin said.

"I hope their luck is better than mine!" Reverend McDowell said. "Sometimes it's enough to make a man cuss!"

"Well, that's one thing that sailors are good at!" Justin said.

"You have an amazing shop here, Justin!"

"Thank you, preacher," Justin said. "I'm kind of proud of it."

"Justin, I heard what happened out there today, and I just wanted to come by and make sure you were all right," Reverend McDowell said.

"Well, I appreciate you stopping by preacher. I'm fine, I guess. I was just at the wrong place at the wrong time!"

"I think you were at the right place at the right time!" Reverend McDowell said. "As a matter of fact, I know you were!"

"Just for the record preacher, I don't like killing people, but I sure have done my share of it."

"Well, Justin, the Bible is full of stories about people being killed. People have been killing each other since the beginning of time and they will continue to the end of time."

"But if I remember correctly, Reverend, the seventh commandment says 'Thou shalt not kill.'"

"I think it's the sixth, but it doesn't really matter," Reverend McDowell said. "The bible says in Judges 15, verses 14 and 15, that when Samson was brought to Lehi that the Lord came mightily unto him and that he found the new jawbone of an ass and slew a thousand men. He was just an instrument of the Lord that day Justin, and I believe that you were just an instrument of the Lord today when you shot those two men."

"I would like to think that that was the case preacher," Justin said.

"Do you think that it was just a coincidence that the best rifle shot in Ashe County was sitting on top of that mountain today overlooking a shootout that almost surely would have been fatal for those two deputies?" Reverend McDowell asked.

"I don't know what to think anymore, preacher," Justin replied.

"Well, don't beat yourself up Justin! What you did was the Christian thing to do even though you had to kill two men. Sometimes killing somebody is the right thing."

"Well, that makes me feel a little better anyway," Justin said.

"Now Justin, even though I try to stay close to the Lord, I can't read minds. If you need me for anything or you want to talk about this some more, just call me. I can't stay long tonight because I got to get home and help my wife with the kids."

"I didn't think you and your wife had any kids?" Justin asked.

"We don't!" The preacher said as he turned to leave. "We're keeping Buddy and Judy Dixon's two children for a couple days so that Judy can stay at the hospital with her husband while he recuperates. They have a little girl that is five and a little boy that is two. You saved their daddy's life today, Justin."

Pastor McDowell walked through Justin's shop but paused before he opened the door. "Those kids are too young to understand what happened today, but they would be hugging your neck tonight instead of mine if they did. Goodnight!" The preacher said as he opened the door and stepped out into the rain.

Justin wiped a tear from his eye and then smiled. Pastor McDowell had certainly put things in a different perspective. Now that Justin stopped to think about it, a big portion of a preacher's job was to put things in perspective for people. He was glad now that the preacher had come by and put an end to the pity party he was giving himself. Now it was time to deal with the other thing that was bothering him. Justin pulled out his cell phone and dialed Teresa's phone number.

"Hello?" she answered.

"Hi, sweetheart," Justin said.

"Oh. Hi, Justin," Teresa said solemnly. "Is this your one phone call from jail?"

"I'm not in jail, Teresa, I'm at home," Justin said. "Where are you?"

"I'm at home too in Kernersville," she said. "How did you manage to get out of jail? I saw them arrest you!"

"They didn't arrest me, Teresa. They just took me in for questioning and then released me," Justin said.

"The fireman that I talked to said that there was a shootout and that there were several people dead," Teresa said.

"There was a shootout and there were two deputies wounded and two other men that were killed."

"Were you involved in the shootout?"

"Yes, I was, unfortunately."

"Did you kill anybody?"

"Well, yeah, I killed two men."

"Well, I guess that puts you up to forty-nine, doesn't it? One more and you'll have an even fifty!"

"What are you talking about, Teresa?"

"You killed forty-seven men in Vietnam, so the two men you killed today make it forty-nine and if you can get one more you'll have killed an even fifty!"

"Who told you I killed forty-seven men in Vietnam?" Justin asked.

"I had a background check done on you when we first met Justin. I guess that it will make you mad but at this point I don't guess it matters. Your military records show that you have forty-seven confirmed kills in Vietnam."

"Teresa, listen to me. First of all, I'm not mad that you did a background check on me. There's nothing in my background that I'm ashamed of. And secondly, a confirmed kill is when an officer witnesses the shot and reports it, or the body of the victim is recovered.

Ninety-five percent of the time there wasn't an officer around when you were shooting and in Vietnam you very rarely recovered the bodies."

"So that means that you killed a lot more than forty-seven, I guess?"

"Yes, I did, but the numbers don't mean anything, Teresa. I was just doing my job! We were at war, and every time I shot an enemy soldier, I was saving the lives of American soldiers!"

"I'm sorry, Justin, but killing people just comes too easy to you."

Justin felt like somebody had run a sword through him. His chest was hurting and he was having trouble breathing. He had fallen in love with this woman in just a few short days, but it was as strong a love as he had ever felt, and now it appeared to be over. Justin remembered when his ex-wife Kathy ran away with another man and how hurt he was for days and weeks before he finally was able to move on.

"Are you still there, Justin?"

"Yeah, I'm still here."

"Justin, as much as it hurts me to say this, I just don't think that I can be with somebody that can kill another human being."

"That's okay. If that's the way you feel then I understand. I don't guess that God intended for us to be together after all, but I want to explain something to you before you hang up.

When I was fifteen years old my family moved to a community near Lexington and we had a neighbor named Homer who was a gunsmith. Homer took a liking to me and he taught me how to shoot. We used to shoot at plastic jugs in his pasture on Saturdays. Sometimes we shot for hours and we had a great time doing it. By the time I graduated from high school I had become a crack rifle shot. I could bust a two liter Pepsi jug at five hundred yards even on a windy day. When I graduated from high-school I joined the Army, and when we went to the rifle range I shot the second highest score that had ever been recorded on that range, so the Army decided to make me a sniper. They didn't care what I wanted to do, they put me to doing what I did best, and that was shooting a rifle."

Justin paused to take a deep breath. There was nothing but silence on the phone line.

"It has never been easy for me to kill another human being. I've known men that enjoyed it, but I never did and never will. I didn't want to kill those two men today but they were firing machine guns at two deputies and I knew that if I didn't kill them that those two deputies would surely be killed. So please don't ever think that killing comes easy to me, it doesn't. And please understand that there are some people on this earth that need to be killed."

"I never have had to kill anybody!" Teresa said crying.

"Then you are very fortunate and I hope that you never have to. Please don't cry Teresa. It hurts me to hear you cry."

"Dammit, Justin Hayes, I was in love with you! Don't you tell me not to cry!"

"Teresa, I'm still in love with you! I think that you are the most wonderful woman that I have ever met, but I didn't have a choice in Vietnam and I didn't have a choice today!"

"That's just it, Justin! You did have a choice and you chose to shoot those two men today," Teresa said, still crying.

"Teresa, if you were keeping your twin granddaughters at your house and some man kicked in your door and started to grab one of them, would you shoot him if you had a gun? Now before you answer, just remember that you have a choice. You don't have to shoot him. You can let him rape and murder her, or you can shoot him."

The line went dead. She hung up. Justin just sat there and stared at the wall for awhile. He finally got up and went over to the bench where all the pieces of Wade's rifle were spread out. Justin picked up the Shilen match barrel and carried it over to the lathe and began chucking it into the lathe. He might as well go ahead and thread the barrel and chamber it and then cut the crown on the other end of the barrel. He wasn't going to be sleeping anyway.

Tears and Cheers

"Anthony speaking."

"Anthony, you can let our guests out of their rooms and cut the lights back on," Donald Crafton said. "The FBI just drove out the gate."

"Right away, Mr. Crafton!" Anthony replied.

Donald stood in the glass-enclosed sun room that had been built onto the end of Jack's house and watched as the three FBI agents drove through the wrought iron gate and headed up River Road.

The agents had pulled up this morning at 6:45 a.m. and began looking over the garage and muscle car building. They took a few pictures of the blood on the floor and in the trunk of the car and seized the footlocker that the machine guns had been stolen from. They interviewed Johnny Steele and CJ and then arrested Scott McMillan and Randy Rhodes from Security Concepts. Walt's body had been picked up yesterday by the Ashe County Medical Examiner and transported to Winston-Salem for an autopsy.

Donald had gone to each guest individually and explained to them that someone had stolen one of Jack's cars and crossed the state line and then robbed a gas station, and because of that, the FBI was sending a couple agents to look at the garage and take a few pictures but that they would be perfectly safe. However, just as a precaution, they wanted each of their guests to remain in their rooms with the lights out until the agents were gone.

Needless to say the last thing that these guests wanted to hear was that the FBI was going to be snooping around, so Donald further assured them that if the agents appeared to be the least bit suspicious that they would be loaded onto the King Air and flown out immediately to a secluded airstrip until it was safe to return. All of the guests were jumpy after learning this new information and all of them gave Donald a piece of their mind. By the time he had spoken to the last guest he had a splitting headache. Donald found it interesting that the guest who was the most upset was Mr. Inacio. He was the only guest who supposedly wasn't a criminal so he had no reason to be afraid of the FBI.

Donald also had the two maids, Tracy and Jennifer, to clean out Johnny's bedroom. They were ordered to remove any weapons, pornography, or drug paraphernalia and to change the sheets and pillow cases before the agents inspected it.

As it turned out, it was a waste of time. The agents didn't inspect the airplane hangar or ask to see Johnny's bedroom. Everyone was breathing a big sigh of relief when they finally loaded up and left—that is, except for Donald. He was glad that they were gone, but he found it very strange that they were so lax. His bullshit alarm was going off like a tornado siren in Kansas!

Justin fired his fifth round and checked the target at the one hundred-yard berm. All five shots were clustered in a circle that was under three quarters of an inch wide. Not bad for a new rifle and factory ammunition. After he got the barrel broken in and had time to experiment with some handloads, he knew the rifle would shoot groups under a half an inch.

He had been up all night working on it. After Teresa broke up with him he knew he wouldn't be able to sleep, so he decided to stay busy to help take his mind off of her. He had put the new rifle barrel in his lathe and cut the threads so he could fit it to the action. Then he took a set of reamers and slowly and carefully cut the chamber and set the headspace. Then he spun the barrel around and cut an eleven-degree target crown on the muzzle and bolted the whole works into the McMillan A5 tactical stock. He installed a Jewel trigger and set it at two pounds and twelve ounces and then fitted a titanium firing pin and a new firing pin spring into the bolt body. Next Justin took the scope bases and rings and attached the 4.5 × 14 × 50 Leupold scope to the rifle. He added a set of Butler creek flip up lens covers to the scope and attached a Harris bi-pod to the end of the stock. He boresighted the scope to get it close and then fired three rounds to get it zeroed in and five more to see how it grouped, cleaning the bore after every shot. He was totally exhausted but he was pleased with the rifle.

The shop door opened up and Travis and DeMac came walking in. Travis was carrying two cups of coffee and handed one of them to his dad.

"Thank you, Hoss," Justin said. "Check that group out at one hundred yards. Not bad for a new rifle and factory ammunition."

Travis looked at the group through the spotting scope and then took a seat across from his dad. "The rifle and the target look great, but you look like hell! Your eyes are red and they have bags under them, so what's going on?"

"Well, I couldn't sleep last night after shooting those two boys, so I just stayed up all night working on Wade's rifle."

"Did Teresa ever call you?" Travis asked.

"No, but I called her. We're going to give each other some space for right now."

Travis stared at his dad. He was a terrible liar and always had been. When Travis was twelve, his Labrador retriever was hit and killed by a car and Justin told him that he had run off and was probably living happily with another family. Travis knew his dad was lying then and he also knew that he was lying now.

"So you and Teresa broke up!"

"Okay, yeah, we broke up." Justin sighed. "She said that she just couldn't be with someone that could kill another human being."

"Does she not know what happened out there yesterday?" Travis asked.

"I don't know Hoss, but it really doesn't matter. She's not a gun person, and you're not going to change that. Life goes on though. The sun came up this morning and the birds sang anyway!"

"Well, I'm sorry you two broke up dad," Travis said.

"Is Jesse working today?" Justin said trying to change the subject.

"She went in real early to do a couple surgeries but she should be back home by now. As soon as she showers we're going to Greensboro to see my mom."

"Well, I'm glad you decided to go see her," Justin said. "Hey, since you're going to be in Greensboro, do you think you could run by Jimmy Hayworth's for me?"

"I don't see why not. Are you going to go to bed and get some sleep?" Travis asked.

"Yeah, as soon as I clean up this shop. There's cutting oil and metal shavings all over my lathe and I can't go to sleep until that's squared away."

"You go take a shower and get into bed. Me and DeMac will clean up this shop!"

"Okay, I will. Thank you!"

"You're welcome, Dad," Travis said. "I love you!"

Donald went searching for Jack and found him and everyone else in the conference room. Cecil Woods, Steve Helms, and Johnny Steele were seated around the marble table talking when Donald walked up.

"Come in, Donald," Jack said. "I was just going to send some-one to find you."

Jack looked dirty and disheveled. His hair was greasy and needed combing and he had bags under his bloodshot eyes. He hadn't shaved and the shirt he was wearing was heavily wrinkled. Jack had always been very particular about his appearance and Donald was surprised to see him like this.

"Well, I've finally had enough," Jack said loudly. "Everything we've tried has blown up in our damn face! We don't have anybody to do surveillance on him since the FBI arrested those two guys from Security Concepts, and the trace on his phone hasn't provided us with anything so we're right back where we started from."

Donald felt a sense of relief. Maybe Jack would forget about Justin Hayes and get back to business as usual. The only thing that concerned Donald right now though was the fact that Jack was drink-ing a bourbon and coke and it wasn't even ten in the morning yet.

"I've decided to hire a professional to deal with Justin Hayes," Jack continued. "I should have done that in the first place."

"You mean a hit man?" Cecil asked.

"That's exactly what I mean!" Jack said as he took another swal-low from his glass. "Don't you think it would look awful suspicious if he turned up dead now?" Steve asked.

"I don't give a damn how it looks!" Jack barked. "The son of a bitch killed my nephew and I mean to see him dead!"

"I could give it a try if you want," Johnny Steele said. "It's just one man and I owe him one anyway."

"Have all of you lost your minds!" Donald said. "In one week's time we have two men dead and one man that is missing and prob-ably dead, and you still want to go after this man because he owns forty-three acres of land that you want!"

"I'm not going to let one man stand in the way of what I want, and besides that he killed my nephew!" Jack hollered.

"Jack, we got all the news channels watching us since Billy drove the monster truck down the river and now the FBI is involved. We have got to let things cool down and return to normal around here before we try anything else."

"The news channels don't have shit on us and neither does the FBI," Jack said as he mixed himself another drink. "I'm not afraid of any of them!"

"Neither was Al Capone or John Gotti and they both went to prison."

"Donald, I don't like your tone," Jack said.

Donald started to tell Jack that he didn't give a shit if he liked his tone or not and that he needed to get his head out of his ass before he got them all arrested and sent to prison, but there was a knock on the door and Danny Comer stepped into the conference room.

"You wanted to see me, sir?" Danny asked.

"Yes, I did, Danny," Jack said. "Has there been any activity on Justin's phone line?"

"Not much. He doesn't use his phone much," Danny said. "About once a day he'll get a call, but it's usually a salesman or a telemarketer."

"Okay then, just let me know if you here anything besides that."

"Yes, sir, I will!" Danny said and then left.

"Now Donald, what is your problem?" Jack asked.

"Jack, I'm just trying to warn you! Something stinks about this whole mess. Tommy was a good man and he's missing and there isn't a trace of him or the Kawasaki Mule. The FBI took over the investigation of the shooting for some reason and I don't understand why they didn't just let the SBI handle it like they normally do. And on top of that, they didn't come over here yesterday after the shooting, they waited until this morning to show up and they didn't want to see the hangar or Johnny's bedroom. Now think about it, Jack, a drug-crazed man stole five machineguns and tried to kill a Virginia state trooper and two Ashe County deputies, and they don't want to see his bedroom! That's bullshit, Jack, and you know it! They normally would have shown up immediately after the shooting and they would have torn this place apart, especially Johnny's bedroom!" Donald explained.

"They got what they wanted!" Jack said. "They arrested those two men from Security Concepts because the machineguns were in their 'care and custody' when they were stolen. All they wanted was to arrest someone for letting the machine guns get stolen. They don't give a shit about Johnny!" Jack suddenly had tears in his eyes and took a big drink of his bourbon and coke to try and hide it. Tears ran down his cheeks and dripped onto the table. Johnny was like a son to him and he was hurting inside like he had never hurt before.

Johnny would probably still be alive if he hadn't thrown him and Billy out and the guilt he was feeling was like a water-soaked quilt draped over him.

Donald knew that there was no need to talk to Jack anymore so he stood up and left. One by one everyone in the room excused themselves and left Jack by himself to grieve. After a while Jack finally composed himself and he picked up the phone and dialed the man that he knew could help him hire a hit man, Jimmy Milano, the head of the Chicago mafia.

"Jimmy, this is Jack Billings," Jack said once he got through.

"We don't ever call names over the phone!" Jimmy said. "It's not the way we do business."

"I'm sorry. I know better than that but I'm not thinking clear right now."

"Maybe you should call back when your head clears up."

"No, no. Please, I'm in a bind and I need help! These phone lines are secure. You know that because you helped me set them up! If they weren't, me and you would already be in prison."

"Okay, okay, just calm down and don't use any more names. Now what's the problem?" Jimmy asked. "Is my son all right?"

"Yeah, yeah, he's fine. It doesn't have anything to do with him."

"Okay then, how can I help you?"

"I need to hire a hit man."

"Holy Jesus and Mother Mary, we don't talk about that over the phone either!"

"Please help me, he killed my nephew. He shot him yesterday with a high powered rifle!"

"Who? Who shot your nephew?"

"My neighbor did. He's after me and he's picking my people off one at a time! I need help and I need it quickly. Do you think you can help me?"

"Hey, you know me! You know I look out for my friends. Sure I can help you."

"Thank you. Thank you so much," Jack said. "How does this work? Will you have him call me?"

"I don't need to have him call you. You can talk to him in person."

"What do you mean?"

"He's already a guest of yours."

"You mean your son?"

"No, his bodyguard."

"You mean Quai Son Bien?"

"Jeez, you're using names again!"

"I'm sorry, I'm sorry!"

"Yes, Quai Son Bien. He's probably the best man on the East Coast."

"That's great because I need somebody right now."

"You deal directly with him. I got nothing to do with this. You tell him that it's okay with me if he wants the job. Okay?"

"Yeah, sure. So you think he's the best man on the East Coast?"

"That's why I hired him to be my son's bodyguard. I was afraid if I didn't that someone would hire him to kill me and I think he could do it! Keep your family and friends close, but keep your enemies closer."

"Thank you," Jack said.

Justin had taken a shower and fell into bed and had slept for about three hours when DeMac came into his room.

"Justin! Justin!" DeMac said.

"What time is it?" Justin asked as he rose up.

"It's noon. I hate to wake you up but we're having a pow-wow to discuss the coyote hunt and I thought you might want to attend," DeMac said.

"Yeah, sure, I want to attend," Justin said and then yawned. "Give me a couple minutes."

"Okay. We're meeting in your machine shop so just come on back when you get ready."

Justin got up and walked into his bathroom and took a quick shower to help him wake up. He pulled on a pair of bib overhauls without a shirt and slid his feet into his moccasins before heading back to his shop. DeMac, Chief, Wizard, Snake, and Wade were sitting on work benches and trashcans and an empty chair was waiting in the middle for Justin's arrival.

"Are you okay, Mr. Hayes?" Wade asked. Wade hadn't seen or talked to Justin since he heard about the shootout.

"Yeah, I'm fine, Wade," Justin answered. "Thanks for asking. Have you been introduced to all these men?"

"Yeah, and they're all Navy Seals! I can't believe that a Seal team is helping me hunt coyotes!"

"Well, you need to keep that a secret for now."

"Yes, sir, they already told me that."

"What do you think of your rifle?" Justin said pointing to it sitting on the workbench. "Where is it?" Wade asked looking around.

"Right here," Justin said pointing to the rifle.

"This is my rifle?" Wade said with his eyes wide open.

"That's it," Justin said.

"Wow, Mr. Hayes! I can't believe that that's my rifle."

"Well, it is."

Wade was speechless as he studied the new rifle.

"Chief, I'm sorry I held you up. Tell us what we need to know," Justin said.

Chief stood up and walked over to a workbench and leaned against it as he turned and faced the group of hunters. "My understanding is that none of you have actually done any coyote hunting. I know that a few of you have shot a coyote, but it was a random kill and not a coyote hunt, so I'm going to start by telling you a few facts about a coyote."

"First of all, do not take him lightly. He is a very worthy opponent. If you under estimate him, he will make a fool of you. His hearing, sense of smell, and eyesight are incredible. If you blow a dying rabbit call just one time and then remain quiet, a coyote as far away as a mile can place your position within nine feet. If there is any breeze at all and he circles downwind of you then you will never see him. He will smell you and head for safety. If you are totally camouflaged and remain completely still, you can fool his eyes, but there is no better animal at spotting motion than a coyote. If you move the slightest bit when he is even remotely looking in your direction, then he will turn tail and run. And while we're talking about running, a coyote can run very fast. Very few dogs can catch a coyote in a foot race."

"Coyotes are also very smart. They have evolved over hundreds of years into very smart and very tough predators. In all the places that the coyote has migrated to over this whole country, no one has ever been able to run him out. He has been poisoned, trapped, shot, and hunted with hounds, but he still thrives in practically every state in this nation. They have a tremendous tenacity for life. I have seen a coyote that was shot in the spine and couldn't use its back legs crawl to a fifty-foot river crossing and swim across the river using only its front feet, even after losing a large amount of blood. So it takes a solid hit to put one down. Any questions so far?"

No one said a word, so Chief continued. "As smart and tough as they are, they are not invincible. We do have a couple big advantages today. Number one, these coyotes have never been hunted and there's a good chance that they will come in running. And number two, mutton is their favorite food. They absolutely love to eat sheep, so we will use that to our advantage today."

Chief turned around and spread an aerial photograph of the Shaver's farm out on the workbench.

"Wow Chief, where did you get that?" Wade said.

"That's one of the advantages of being a Navy Seal," Chief said. "We have access to lots of resources. After the meeting you can have it to put up in your room."

"Gee thanks!" Wade said.

"Your welcome. Now if everyone will gather around I'll show you my plan. I am going to take a week old lamb and tape his mouth shut and stake him out in this pasture right beside these rocks," Chief said, pointing to the spot on the photo. "I will hide in the rocks and when everyone is in place, I will untape his mouth and let him cry. A coyote can tell from the cry that it's a baby lamb and if they see him standing alone in the pasture then they will probably come in fast. DeMac, I want you and Wade to set up here on top of this hill overlooking the pasture. It's 225 yards from where you will be laying to where the lamb is staked out, so set your rifle for a two hundred-yard shot. Snake, I want you to set up here on the far end of the pasture. When the shooting starts a coyote might run your way since its straight downhill from the lamb. Wizard, I want you to crawl all the

356

way over to here so you can watch the next pasture over. If one of the coyotes gets away from us and goes back across the mountain then you should be able to engage him. I'm going to un-tape the lamb's mouth at 1800 hours, so everybody needs to be in place at least thirty minutes before so that things can settle down before we start calling. Any questions?"

"When's 1800 hours?" Wade asked.

"It's six o'clock," Chief said smiling.

"Okay, there's one more thing. No one can predict if any coyotes will come or not, and if they do come, we don't know if there will be one coyote or seven coyotes, so we'll just have to wait and see what happens. But if we do manage to call in a coyote and it comes toward the lamb, I'm going to bark like a dog when it's about forty yards away. When I bark the coyote should stop running and try to find out where the dog is that he just heard. When it stops, the first shot is Wade's. Wade, you will have about three or four seconds to shoot before it either turns and runs away or comes on in after the lamb. I'll be armed with a 12-gauge shotgun, and if you miss him then I'm going to kill him, understand?"

"Yes, sir," Wade said.

"Okay. I'll see you guys at 1800 hours."

Coy Beard was vacuuming the carpet inside the King Air when the vacuum cleaner suddenly cut off. "Dammit, who unplugged my cord?" He shouted and then turned to see Donald Crafton step up into the plane.

"I need to talk to you in private," Donald said.

"Have I screwed something up?" Coy asked with a concerned look.

"No, no, this isn't an ass chewing," Donald assured him.

"Whew! I'm glad of that," Coy said.

"We have two guests that are flying out on Saturday night, the Egyptian, Mr. Inacio, and the guy from Atlanta, Ricky Stone. We are going to drop them off in Ohio at a private airstrip near Dayton. The reason I say 'we' is because I'm going with you," Donald said.

"I think everyone is ready to get out of here after all that's happened this week!" Coy said. "Probably so Coy, but I'm not coming back."

"What do you mean you're not coming back?" Coy asked.

"I mean I'm leaving for good. I don't intend to spend the rest of my life in prison and I think that Jack Billings and everybody associated with Billings Enterprises are right before going to prison for a long, long time.

Donald had Coy's attention now. "What makes you think that?"

"Well, Tommy disappearing into thin air for one thing, but the biggest clue is the way the FBI handled this shooting investigation. They didn't show up until the next day, and when they did they didn't look in the hangar or in Johnny's bedroom. And on top of that, they never even talked to Jack and it was his nephew that was the shooter! They gave us plenty of time to clean up our act and when they finally came they barely even looked around. That's not the way the FBI operates, Coy."

"I see what you mean, Donald," Coy said.

"And now Jack is trying to hire a hit man to kill Justin Hayes! Once that happens I think the FBI will be all over us. As soon as everybody is arrested then someone will want to cut a deal and we'll all end up being charged with murder and harboring fugitives and tax evasion and God knows what else."

Coy put his head in his hands and then rubbed his face. He was obviously scared now. "I don't want to go to prison, Donald."

"You won't have to if you go with me. I need a pilot so I'm going to make you an offer. I own a cabin in Oquossoc, Maine. It sits on the shore of a large lake and nobody, including Jack, knows that I own it. I bought it just in case something like this ever came up and I needed a place to hide," Donald explained.

"Won't they be able to trace it to you?" Coy asked.

"I bought it under a fake name so they won't be able to connect me to it. There's a logging road about a mile from the cabin but the only practical way to get to it is with a float plane. That's why I need a pilot and that's where I'm heading if you want to go along.

"But how will we survive? What will we do for money?" Coy asked.

"Money's not ever going to be a problem for us," Donald said with a grin. "I handle all of Jack's overseas accounts. When I set up his account, I went ahead and set one up for me. We couldn't keep all the money from the hotel in an account in the United States because it would look to suspicious and we would have to pay taxes on it, so most of Jack's money is in an account in Switzerland. Right before we take off on Saturday night, I'm going to transfer all of Jack's money into my account. Jack won't have enough money to pay the light bill, but he won't need it anyway if he's in prison."

"How much money are we talking about?" Coy asked.

"Almost nine million dollars," Donald said. "Of course, we're going to have to buy a float plane and some other things, but we should be able to live the rest of our lives with that kind of money."

"What will we do with the King Air?"

"Abandon it. Just leave it sitting."

"But it's probably worth three and a half or four million dollars!" Coy said.

"You can't spend money in prison!" Donald said. "Once the FBI arrests Jack then every law enforcement agency in the United States will be looking for that plane, and they will find it very quickly, so we need to just walk away from it."

"Well, count me in, Donald. I'd rather be shivering in Maine than sitting in prison," Coy said.

"Oh, we won't be in Maine during the winter months. We'll be in the Caribbean or in Cancun, Mexico, or maybe even Spain or France."

"Now I know I want to go!" Coy said.

"Here's what we'll do. I'll transfer the money on Saturday night before we take off with Inacio and Stone. We'll drop them off in Ohio and then fly to Dallas International Airport in Texas."

"Texas! Why Texas?" Coy asked.

"A couple reasons. The first reason is that's where I want to dump the King Air. If they find the plane in Dallas, then they will assume that we fled to Mexico or Central America and they will concentrate their search there. And secondly, my half-brother lives in Corpus Christi and he can drive up to Dallas and pick us up. We can stay with him until we can get new identities and new passports and he can help us find a good float plane to buy."

"Sounds like you have everything figured out to me," Coy said. "I've never been to Maine, but it's got to be better than Leavenworth, Kansas."

"It's beautiful up there from late spring to early fall. The fishing and the hunting are great, and if we get bored we can always fly to the coast to get away and party for a few weeks.

And if for some reason they ever do get on to us, we can fly into Canada in less than an hour."

"I'm ready to go," Coy said. "Just you and me or will there be anybody else?"

"Just the two of us," Donald answered. "Don't say a word to anybody and don't pack a suitcase. We'll have plenty of money to buy whatever we need."

"I guess I'll see you Saturday night!"

"Keep this plane ready to go in case we have to leave before Saturday night. If anybody knocks down the front gate, meet me here at the plane as fast as you can!"

"I'll be here waiting when you get here!"

Travis was a nervous wreck as he reached up and rang the door-bell at his mom's house. He stood there with Jesse waiting for some-one to come to the door and he could feel his knees shaking. He had seen some combat and had fought in some major karate tournaments and had never been as scared as he was now. A very pretty Hispanic woman opened the door.

"Hi, my name is Travis Hayes. My mother is Mrs. Kathy Maxwell. I would like to see her if I may," Travis said.

"Please come in," the maid replied.

Jesse and Travis stepped into the foyer and waited as the maid closed the door.

"Please wait right here and I will see if Mrs. Maxwell can see you," the maid said and she turned and left the room. After several long minutes she returned. "Please follow me," she said and Jesse and Travis followed the maid through the magnificent house and down a beautiful hallway that was adorned in expensive looking paintings until they came to a huge bedroom. The maid gestured with her hand for Jesse and Travis to enter.

The bedroom was the most luxurious room that Jesse or Travis had ever seen. The ceilings were at least fourteen feet high and there were several huge columns in various places through-out the room. The crown molding that surrounded the room was very ornate and quite intricate and was obviously very expensive. The bedroom walls were stucco and they were painted a soft blue and the room was lighted by several huge chandeliers and also some recessed lighting. A set of glass French doors led to a sitting room that overlooked a garden and a beautiful oval swimming pool and matching hot tub. One wall was covered in photographs and instantly drew Travis's attention. There was a picture of his mom in Acapulco wearing a bikini and one of her skiing in Aspen. There was another one of her standing in front of the Eiffel Tower and another one of her standing on the Rock of Gibraltar in Spain.

She was smiling in all the pictures but for some reason Travis didn't think she was happy in them.

Kathy came walking into the bedroom from the master bathroom. She was wearing a nightgown with a bathrobe on over it. "Excuse me for making you wait. I was trying to fix my hair and touch up my makeup but I didn't do a very good job," she said as she patted her hair with the palm of her hand. "I am tickled to death that you're here Travis and who is this that you brought with you?"

"Mama, this is Jessica Longbow. She is the veterinarian in Sparta and my girlfriend," Travis said and he wondered if that sounded right when he said it.

"It's nice to meet you, Jessica," Kathy said.

"It's nice to meet you also, Mrs. Maxwell," Jesse said.

"Well, Travis, if she's a veterinarian then you know she's smart, and she is obviously very beautiful, so she has looks and brains too!"

"Thank you," Jesse said.

"Let's go sit in here," Kathy said and she hobbled toward the French doors. "Would either of you like something to drink?"

"No, thank you," Travis answered.

"I can't tell you how thrilled I am to see you again!" Kathy said.

"We had to come down this way today so I thought we would stop and say hey."

"Well, I'm glad you did."

They all took a seat in the sitting room and sat there waiting for someone to speak. It was obviously very awkward for Kathy and also for Travis and Jesse was caught in the middle. Kathy was pale looking and had a slight tremble like a person with palsy, and even though she was trying to hide it, it was apparent that she was very sick.

"Mama, I don't know how to say this and it might not be any of my business, but you look like you're sick," Travis said, and he instantly wished that he hadn't said it.

Kathy smiled. "I am sick," she said. "You can tell that you're Justin Hayes's son because you say what's on your mind."

"I didn't mean to hurt your feelings. I'm sorry if I did," Travis said.

"No, you didn't hurt my feelings. This is very awkward for me and I'm sure it's very awkward for you also. I have breast cancer and cirrhosis of the liver, so I am a very sick woman."

"After stopping to see you last Friday, I couldn't help but wonder if you wanted me to stop so you could see me one last time before you died. I told daddy about it and he said I needed to go see you again, and now that I'm here, I don't know what to say."

Tears came to Kathy's eyes and she grabbed a tissue from a box on the coffee table that separated her from Travis and Jesse. "You don't have to say anything Travis. I abandoned you when you were ten years old and I don't deserve or expect you to have a relationship with me now. I really didn't expect you to stop last Friday and I can't get over the fact that you came back to see me today. You were right about why I wanted to see you. I am dying and I wanted to see you one last time before I passed on."

"What are the doctors saying?" Travis asked. "What's the prognosis?"

"They're not sure, but they think it will be less than a year."

Now Travis was suddenly teary eyed and he grabbed a tissue also. "Well, from the looks of the pictures on your bedroom wall you've had a wonderful and exciting life," Travis said.

"The only part of my life that has been wonderful and exciting was the years that I spent with your father. He was a wonderful husband and a wonderful father and I was a fool to ever leave him. But I grew up poor and when I met Paul he had beautiful homes and fancy cars and expensive jewelry and he traveled all over the world. He told me that I would never have to work again and that I could have anything I wanted if I would just go with him, so like a fool I did. The pictures on that wall are his fond memories, not mine."

Travis and Jesse saw the pretty maid that had let them in, walk out to the pool and start unbuttoning her uniform. She let her uniform fall to the concrete revealing a small white bikini under it, and she dove in the pool just like she owned it. When she surfaced she slung her long beautiful black hair behind her and then floated on her back.

"You really know how to treat your help around here," Travis said as he watched the beautiful woman floating effortlessly.

Kathy turned around and saw the woman :floating in the pool and then turned back around to face Travis and Jesse. "That's Maria," Kathy said. "She's not really a maid. She's sleeping with my husband but she doesn't know that I know it. Paul has always kept two or three mistresses, but since I've been so sick he decided to move one of them in the house."

"Oh, I see," Travis said.

"A business man like Paul needs a wife to sometimes travel with him to seminars and formal dinners. It looks better on him to have a faithful wife by his side when he attends some of the functions that he is invited to."

"I'm sorry, Mama," Travis said.

"I am too," Kathy said. "I'm sorry that I left you and your father. Justin is a remarkable man and he has such a big heart and I know that I hurt him and you and I am so sorry that I did. Do you know that he called me one time and told me that he wished me the best and that he forgave me for leaving him?"

"He told me about that and said that I needed to do the same thing," Travis said.

Tears started pouring out of Kathy's eyes and she covered her face with her hands. "I just don't want you to hate me, Travis!" She cried and then broke down and started sobbing.

Travis and Jesse were both crying now and Travis moved over beside his mother and took her in his arms. "Mama, I don't hate you and I never have. I still can remember you playing with me in the yard and packing my lunches for school and fussing at me for tracking dirt in the house. Those are the things that I remember! I didn't understand why you left me and dad, but I do now and I forgive you. Mama, I still love you."

"You have no idea what that means to me Travis. I love you too!"

Travis and his mother held each other for a long time. Travis told his mother about his junior-senior Prom and his karate tournaments and his adventures in the Navy and how he met Jesse, and after awhile the tears turned into laughter. Finally Travis told his mother that he and Jesse had to leave.

"Mama, Jesse and I have to leave to tend to some other business, but I promise to stay in touch," Travis said.

"Thank you so much for coming, Travis. I'm so proud of you and I think that you and Jesse are both wonderful."

"I'll call you tomorrow," Travis said.

"Travis, do you think it would be wrong for me to call your father?" Kathy asked. "I would like to apologize to him before I…I mean, while I can."

"He would love to hear from you. Give him a call. Here's his number and my cell number and you can call me everyday if you like."

"Thank you so much!" Kathy said. "I love you."

"I love you too! We'll see ourselves out. I'll call you," Travis said and he and Jesse exited the room.

Johnny Steele turned the black Hummer onto Mamie May Road and drove about two miles before he turned into the muddy driveway that led up to the 52 × 12 foot mobile home where Billy was living since yesterday.

"Just stay in the car, Johnny," Jack said as he stepped out into the mud. Jack started walking toward the trailer but stopped when he heard the front door swing open and slam against the side of the trailer. Billy stepped out onto the porch holding a Remington 1100 12-gauge shotgun. Jack had bought it for him for his fifteenth birthday but had forgotten about it until now.

"I'm going to have to ask you to leave this property!" Billy shouted. "I'm not welcome on your property and you're not welcome on mine!"

"Billy, I want to talk to you!" Jack said.

Johnny Steele started to step out of the Hummer but stopped when Billy leveled the shotgun on him. "If you step out of that car then I'm going to show you how to cut Steele in half with lead!" Billy shouted. "Understand?"

"Get back in the car, Johnny," Jack said. "Billy, let me talk to you!"

"I don't allow anybody except me to drink on this property, kind of like your place, Dad. You look like you're three sheets in the wind and it's not even two o'clock yet!" Billy hollered. "What's the matter, your conscience bothering you since you killed your nephew!"

"I loved him, Billy, and you know it."

"Yeah, you loved him so much that you threw him off your property. You threw a drug addict off the only place on earth that he had ever known. You might as well have shot him yourself!"

"What was I supposed to do, Billy?" Jack said, crying.

"Well, I'll be damned. The great Jack Billings is asking me what he was supposed to do. I have never heard you say those words until now. You always thought you knew the answer to everything."

"Billy, please."

"Shut up and listen for a change. You were supposed to spend time with him and talk to him! You were supposed to talk to experts in the field and find out about treatment plans! You were supposed to quit worrying about making a dollar and start worrying about your nephew's well being for a change!"

"Billy, please, I came over here to ask you to move back home!" Jack pleaded.

"This is home! I'd rather live in hell than to live under your roof again. Now get off my property!"

"Billy, I need you son!"

"Well, how does it feel? Johnny needed someone too!" Billy shouted and then slammed the door shut behind him.

Travis found himself once again reaching to ring a doorbell, but this time it was at Teresa's house in Kernersville instead of at his mom's house in Greensboro. They had left his mom's house and driven to the Olive Garden Restaurant to grab a bite to eat and hopefully rejuvenate themselves after a very emotional morning. Travis couldn't stop staring at Jesse when they were eating and it made him realize just how hurt his father must be after breaking up with Teresa.

When they finished eating they drove over to Jimmy Hayworth's place like he promised his dad, and while they were there he looked up Teresa in an old phone book and got her address. Jimmy told Travis how to get there from his place and Travis had driven straight to it. Teresa's black Escalade was parked in the carport so Travis figured that she was at home. He didn't have a clue what to say to her, he just knew that he had to say something. Travis rang the doorbell and then stepped back beside of Jesse.

"Who is it?" A voice could be heard from inside.

"It's Travis Hayes Teresa, Justin's son," Travis shouted.

The door cracked open and Teresa peeked out. Her eyes were red from crying and Travis took that as a good sign. "Come in, Travis," Teresa said solemnly.

"Teresa, this is Jessica Longbow. Jessica, this is Teresa Owens."

"It's nice to meet you, Jessica. Aren't you the veterinarian in Sparta?" Teresa asked.

"Yes, I am," Jesse answered.

"I remember Justin mentioning your name. Come in and have a seat."

Travis and Jesse sat down in the living room on a love seat and Teresa sat across from them in a matching white leather arm chair.

"Can I get you something to drink?" Teresa asked.

"No, thank you, Teresa. We just left the Olive Garden in Greensboro not long ago."

"They have wonderful food," Teresa said.

Travis was looking at Teresa and for the first time he realized just how pretty she really was. He had seen her only one time before and that was when he stopped to help her when the tree was across her driveway, and he hadn't really noticed how beautiful she was then.

"Teresa, I'm sure you probably know why I'm here. I am hoping that I can convince"

"Convince me to forgive your father and go back to him?" Teresa said.

"No, not exactly," Travis said. "I don't really see anything there to forgive."

"Travis, he killed two human beings! They might not have been very nice people, but nonetheless they were human beings."

"And in the process he saved the lives of two Ashe County deputies!"

"I know that, but I don't think you can justify killing people by adding up the people you might have saved," Teresa said.

Travis didn't know what else to say. Maybe his father was right when he said that Teresa wasn't a gun person and you wouldn't ever be able to change that. Why couldn't Teresa understand that his dad didn't have any options in the shooting? If he had sat and watched those two deputies being executed and not done anything he would have never forgiven himself.

"When I sat in the Olive Garden today eating my lunch, I was staring at Jesse and trying to imagine the pain I would be in if we broke up, and the thought of that was overwhelming to me," Travis said. "I know my dad is in love with you, and he must be really hurting inside, so I had to come by here today and at least try to talk to you about it."

"I was in love with him too Travis and I still am," Teresa said, teary eyed. "But the guns and the killing people bother me."

"As close as me and my dad are Teresa, he never told me that he was a sniper in Vietnam. He was never proud of it, and besides, he didn't have a choice! In 1968 the Vietnam War was in full swing and the Army didn't give him a choice of duty. He had to be a sniper because of his amazing ability with a rifle!"

"I can understand that, but didn't he have a choice yesterday?" Teresa said.

"Not a very good one!" Travis said.

"Can I use your phone, Teresa?" Jesse asked.

"Yes, you can. Just help yourself. Travis, I care deeply about your father but right now I'm confused. I've never been around guns and shooting and hunting!"

Jesse looked in her pocketbook and pulled out a piece of paper with a phone number on it and dialed it. When it started ringing she pushed the button on the phone to place the conversation on the speaker.

"Wake Forest Baptist Medical Center," the voice filled the room. "How may I direct your call?"

"I would like to speak to Buddy Dixon or to Jerry Morris but I don't know their room numbers," Jesse said.

"They are both in room number 327. One moment and I will connect you."

"What are you doing?" Travis asked Jesse.

"Hello."

"Is this Buddy and Jerry's room?" Jesse asked. "This is Jesse from the animal clinic."

"Oh, hi, Jesse. This is Pastor McDowell. Yes, this is their room and everybody is here. Buddy's wife Judy and both the kids and Jerry's wife Mary Lou."

Travis and Teresa had both quit talking and were now listening to the conversation. "How are they doing Pastor McDowell?"

"They are both doing remarkably well considering the circumstances," the pastor answered. "Buddy is a little groggy right now and can't talk to you. He's on a morphine drip and he's as drunk as a nine-eyed billy goat, but Jerry can talk to you."

"Hey, Jesse, this is Mary Lou. Thanks for calling. I've got to hold the phone up to Jerry's ear for him because one of his arms is in a cast and the other one is bandaged from his wrist up past his elbow, so hold on a minute."

"Hello?"

"Is that you, Jerry?" Jesse asked.

"Yes, it is, thanks for calling."

"How are you?"

"I'm doing real well. They operated on my right hand and my left foot and they sewed my left arm up and everything went real well according to the doctor."

"That's great, Jerry. I saw the car when they hauled it away and I don't see how you or Buddy ever lived through that," Jesse said.

"If it weren't for the grace of God and Justin Hayes we would both be dead!" Jerry said.

"So you think that if Justin hadn't killed those two maniacs that you and Buddy would have both been killed?"

"Oh there's no doubt about it! They were walking up to the car to finish us off when Justin hollered for them to lay down their weapons."

"So he ordered them to lay down their weapons before he shot them?"

"Oh yeah, twice!" Jerry said.

"Well, Jerry, I hope you and Buddy get well real soon. We'll be praying for you," Jesse said. "Is that sweet little girl of yours standing there?"

"Yes, she is. Hold on a minute Jesse. Honey, give the phone to Cindy."

"Hey, Miss Jesse," a little girl's sweet voice came on the phone.

"Hey, Cindy. How are you?"

"Miss Jesse, our cat went to heaven to be with Papaw Dixon."

"Oh, I'm sorry, Cindy. I got some real pretty kittens at my house if you want one."

"Really? I want a kitten, Miss Jesse."

"When daddy gets home you come over to my house and pick one out."

"Okay. Thank you, Miss Jesse."

"You're welcome, honey. How is your daddy?"

"Some bad men shot him with a gun."

"I know, honey, but daddy's going to be all right," Jesse said. "Is Colby there?"

"Hey."

"Hey, Colby. How are you?"

"I want a kitten too Miss Jesse."

"You can have one too, Colby, okay?"

"Okay."

"Hey, Jesse, this is Judy. You are so sneaky calling the hospital to get rid of kittens."

"When opportunity knocks, you have to open the door," Jesse said. "Seriously, is there anything that I can do for you or Mary Lou?"

"No, but thanks for asking. Pastor McDowell and his wife are keeping the kids so that I can stay at the hospital with Buddy, so were in pretty good shape right now."

"I forgot to ask Mary Lou when her due date was."

"It's July the Fourth, Independence Day," Judy said and then laughed.

"Well, if any of you need anything, please let me know."

"I heard you got a new man and he's quite a hunk. Is he the one that knocked out Billy Billings?"

"Uh. Judy, I got an emergency and I got to go, but call me if you need me. Bye now!" Jesse said and then pushed the button to end the call.

Travis was sitting there staring at Jesse with a look of astonishment. "What?" Jesse said to him.

"You're amazing. Absolutely amazing! I love you!"

Wade and DeMac were lying motionless on top of the hill that overlooked the pasture where Chief had staked the baby lamb out. He was wearing a ghillie suit that DeMac had given him and his face and hands were painted with olive green and black stripes. They had been here for twenty-five minutes but it seemed like two hours to Wade. Wade cut his eyes over to the grassy mound lying beside him. He couldn't see DeMac even though he was lying three feet away from him.

"What's the matter?" DeMac whispered.

"I'm scared. What if I miss?" Wade whispered back.

"Every man out here has missed shots before," DeMac whispered back. "I shot thirty rounds at a guy in Afghanistan and never touched him, and he was twenty feet away! The only thing I accomplished that day was messing up his underwear!" DeMac chuckled.

Wade giggled at DeMac's confession. "What does Justin always use for targets?"

"Snuff cans."

"Right, and there's a reason for that," DeMac whispered. "He was forcing you to shoot at a small dot instead of at a large paper target. If you get a shot at a coyote, imagine a snuff can sitting right on his shoulder and concentrate on hitting the snuff can instead of shooting at the whole animal. And if you miss don't worry about it. Just relax and enjoy the hunt. This is fun, isn't it?"

"Yeah, it's fun," Wade whispered.

The calm spring day was suddenly shattered by the wailing of the baby lamb. The week old lamb had never been separated from its mother and it cried for all it was worth. It was painful to sit and listen to the lamb and everyone, including the tough Navy Seals, felt sorry for it. The wailing went on and on for several long minutes and everyone was tense as they lay there waiting. Everyone was wearing a headset and suddenly there was chatter on it.

"This is the Wizard. We have four coyotes, no there's five coyotes at eight hundred yards and closing."

"Roger, Wizard," Chief said. "Get ready, Wade."

DeMac leaned over and whispered "Snuff can" to Wade to remind him to concentrate on a spot on the coyote's shoulder.

Five coyotes topped the hill in a tight pack, but two of them slowed to a fast walk to survey the situation before rushing in, and a third coyote slowed to a trot to check things out.

The other two coyotes never broke their stride and came down the hill like a yellow lightning bolt. When the two young coyotes were about forty yards from the lamb, Chief let out a deep bark that sounded like it came from a very large dog. Instantly all five coyotes slammed on the brakes and stopped to search for the large dog.

Like a lot of hunting situations, they had laid there for what seemed like an eternity and then in a matter of seconds you find yourself struggling to get ready. Wade found the closest coyote in his scope and placed the crosshairs right on the brass colored snuff can that he imagined was sitting on the coyotes shoulder. He squeezed the trigger and felt the rifle stock as it recoiled into his shoulder. The lead coyote crumbled and fell and the one standing behind him spun around to run but was cut down by a load of buckshot from Chiefs shotgun. The coyote that was halfway across the pasture turned and ran straight down the hill toward Snake, just like Chief predicted he might, and the two older coyotes that were still at the top of the hill ran back the way that they had come. Snake fired several three-shot bursts and then a lone shot to claim the third song dog. A loud crack, almost like a huge tree snapping in the wind, echoed in the next pasture over and after a five second delay it repeated itself and then all was silent. It was over in less than fifteen seconds.

DeMac grabbed Wade and started rolling over and over with him laughing and hollering. Snake came walking across the pasture dragging his coyote by its hind foot and Wizard appeared at the top of the hill with a coyote in each hand. They had killed all five of them. Wade was still in shock and had tears in his eyes as he and DeMac rolled around in the grass like two drunks at the county fair.

Quai Son Bien sat in Jack's office and studied the background check on Justin Hayes. Jack was sitting across from him babbling about all that had happened in the last week but Quai wasn't paying much attention to him. Several things bothered Quai about this Justin Hayes. For starters, he was an expert with a rifle and a pistol. You definitely couldn't get into a gunfight with this man. Another thing that bothered Quai was the man that Jack said went missing. The only explanation was that Justin killed him and got rid of the body. This meant that Justin Hayes had no qualms about killing another human being and wouldn't hesitate if the situation called for it. He also had two dogs that were apparently well trained. It was almost impossible to slip up on a house that had dogs. Their hearing was so much better than humans and even when they slept the slightest sound would wake them up. On top of all that, Jack said that he had wide shoulders and big arms and that he was in good shape, so you better make sure that you didn't have to wrestle him. Obviously this man was very dangerous and would need to be handled carefully.

"So what do you think?" Jack asked. "Do you think you can kill him?"

"I can kill anybody, Mr. Billings," Quai answered. "The only question is how."

"I can get you whatever you need—guns, poison, explosives. You name it and I can get it," Jack said.

"This man is too dangerous to try and kill at his house. He has access to too many weapons at his house and he has dogs that will alert him over the slightest noise. He must be killed somewhere else to do it safely."

"He's not supposed to leave his property until the FBI finishes their investigation, so I don't know how we could ever get him to leave his house," Jack said.

"Does he have a girlfriend?" Quai asked.

"Yes, her name is Carol. Carol Crissman."

"Does his girlfriend live alone?"

"Yes, she does. She lives by herself in a little white farmhouse."

"Are there lots of neighbors around his girlfriend's house?"

"No, there's not a house in sight from her house."

"How long would it take Justin Hayes to drive over to his girlfriend's house from his house?"

"Probably about fifteen minutes."

"Then that is your answer. You enter his girlfriend's house and tie her up. Then you call him and tell him that if he isn't over there in fifteen minutes that you will cut her throat. You also tell him that you have his phone tapped and if he calls the police or anybody, that you will kill her instantly. When he pulls up to the house, you use her as a shield and throw him a pair of handcuffs. After he puts the handcuffs on, you order him inside and then kill him. The only thing about doing it this way is you have to kill the girlfriend too. If you don't want to mess with the bodies you can make it look like a lover's quarrel, a murder-suicide."

Jack thought about the plan for just a moment before saying anything. "I like it. I want you to make it look like a murder-suicide. After shooting two men yesterday, if he was found dead from a murder-suicide, I think people would think that maybe he was distraught, or that he was just a violent man, a man with anger issues maybe."

"I need someone to drive me around tomorrow. I want to look at his house and his girlfriend's house. I need to make sure that the FBI isn't watching him and that he isn't wearing a monitoring device like a bracelet or an anklet. I also need to either see him in person or to see a picture of him."

"I can arrange all that," Jack said.

"We need to tap his phone line."

"It's already tapped. We did it several days ago."

"We also need to make sure that his phone line isn't also tapped by the FBI so that when we call him they won't be alerted."

"I'll get my communications man to check on that." Jack said.

"How many people know about this?"

"Just you and me," Jack lied.

"Let's keep it that way. I want you to drive me around tomorrow."

"Okay, Quai, whatever you want," Jack said. "There is just one more thing."

"What's that?" Quai asked.

"When you get Justin inside the house, can you call me and let me come over there and kill him myself?"

Quai stared into Jack's eyes. Not many men have the stomach to commit a one on one murder. Calling Jack over there would create a delay and someone could see him when he drove over there. "I will have to think about that Mr. Billings and let you know tomorrow," Quai said. "But if I agree to let you participate, I still get to kill the woman!"

Jack felt a chill run down his spine. "Okay, Quai. Okay."

Wade, DeMac, Wizard, Snake, and Chief all walked around the barn and into the backyard of the Shaver's house, each dragging a coyote. There were smiles all around as the men joked and laughed.

"When you barked like a dog Chief, those two closest coyotes went into a four-legged skid. I never saw an animal try to stop that fast!" Snake said laughing.

"I was waiting for Wade to shoot and when he did I saw dust fly off that coyote," Chief said. "Now I know why they say they 'dusted' somebody."

The four Navy Seals and the smiling fourteen-year-old boy walked past the white van that they had driven over there in and were shocked to see Justin sitting there on his tailgate.

"Good Grief!" Justin said. "I didn't know you were going to kill every coyote in the county. Did you leave any for breeding stock?"

"Mr. Hayes, I hit him. I imagined a snuff can was sitting on his shoulder and I knocked the dust off him!" Wade said holding up the thirty-five pound coyote.

"Good for you Wade. I'm proud of you!"

"I didn't think you were supposed to leave your place?" Wade asked.

"I'm not, but I did anyway. I had to see how you guys did," Justin said.

A Jeep turned in and drove up to the gathering and parked. Travis and Jesse jumped out and went to the back of the Jeep and raised the hatchback. Travis reached in and lifted an ice chest out and carried it around to the group of hunters while Jesse carried six extra large pizza boxes.

"I don't guess you guys are thirsty or hungry, are you?" Travis asked.

"You have a remarkable sense of timing," DeMac said. "We're starving!"

The crowd of hunters tore into the pizzas like a pack of, well, coyotes. There was beer for the men and some Pepsi for Wade. Wade's dad came out of the house and hugged his son and joined in on the celebration. It was a tailgate party for hunters instead of football fans, and everyone was laughing and giving Justin a play by play of the hunt.

Justin finally stepped over behind Travis and tapped him on the shoulder. "Did you go to Jimmy Hayworth's for me?"

"Yeah, and they're on the way. They should be here any minute."

"Is Jimmy bringing them himself?"

"No, he sent someone else," Travis said and then walked off.

Justin reached in the ice chest and grabbed a beer and then stepped away from the crowd for a minute. The pizza reminded him that Teresa was bringing them a pizza yesterday when she saw him being led to the police car in handcuffs. He suddenly found it hard to breathe and he took a deep breath. There were tears in his eyes and he wiped them with his sleeve. A vehicle slowed down and turned in but Justin didn't look to see who it was. He needed a moment to compose himself before he rejoined the party. Justin took another deep breath and then turned around. A black Cadillac Escalade backed up to the crowd and parked. Teresa got out and she stopped when she saw Justin. Justin's heart almost stopped when he saw her and he wondered if he was hallucinating.

"Could I have your attention please?" Travis hollered over the crowd. "Could everyone please give me their attention for just a moment?"

The crowd got quiet.

"We have a special presentation prepared for you tonight. If you will please welcome my father, Justin Hayes, he will take over from here."

Everyone was cheering and whistling as Justin reluctantly stepped back over to the crowd. His eyes were watering as he stared at Teresa and she had tears running down her face.

Justin started to speak and his voice cracked and he cleared his throat.

"First of all I would like to congratulate Wade on making a tough shot today under lots of pressure," Justin said and everyone clapped and slapped Wade on the back. "And I would also like to thank these men who helped make this hunt a tremendous success. Killing five coyotes on one stand is practically unheard of."

There was more clapping and cheering as Justin searched for the words he needed to say. "On a more serious note I don't think that there is any greater joy on this earth than to be able to help someone in their time of need. All of us need help once in a while, and it's a blessing to be in a position to help that person out. It's also a blessing for people to get together like this and laugh and joke and have a good time and I will never forget this special evening that we've shared here tonight."

The crowd was silent and standing motionless as Justin cleared his throat again.

"Wade, you lost a good friend a few weeks ago when your dog was killed, and none of us here tonight can bring him back, but we can help you to keep the coyotes away from here in the future with this gift from all of us to you."

Travis opened the back of Teresa's Escalade and two nine month old Australian Shepherds jumped out onto the ground.

"Oh my God!" Wade said as he went to his knees and started rubbing the two wagging dogs. "Thank you, Mr. Hayes, thank you!" Wade said as he looked back at Justin with tears running down his cheeks.

The crowd started cheering and Justin stepped away. The look that Wade had on his face was too much for Justin and he started to cry. When he turned back around Teresa was standing there looking at him with tears running down her face also.

"That was quite a presentation you made back there," Teresa said.

"I'm not much of a public speaker.' Justin stammered. "I wish Travis would have done it for me."

"He came to see me today," Teresa said.

"I didn't send him to bother you," Justin said.

"I know you didn't He came to see me because he loves you and doesn't want to see you hurt."

"Teresa I understand how you feel and you have every right to feel that way. Maybe you're right about me. I don't even know myself anymore."

"I made some new friends this evening," Teresa said as she stepped closer to Justin. "Buddy and Judy, and their two children, Cindy and Colby, and also Jerry and his wife Mary Lou."

"Who are they?" Justin asked with a confused look on his face.

"They're the two officers you saved and their families."

"Oh," Justin said.

"They hugged me like I was Mother Teresa instead of just Teresa Owens when Travis told them that I was your girlfriend. You're their hero, Justin."

"I'm no hero, Teresa. I'm just a simple man."

"Yes, you are whether you like it or not. What you said back there about it being a blessing to be in a position to help someone is very true. I wrote a check this evening for $5,000 and gave it to Buddy and Judy, and I wrote another one just like it for Jerry and Mary Lou. Their going to need some help to pay their bills over the next couple of months, and just like you said a few minutes ago, it's a blessing to be able to help people."

"Well, that was awful sweet of you, Teresa," Justin said. "I'm sure they were grateful."

"It was a wonderful feeling to be able to help them. I had forgotten how to give until I met you, Justin."

"Teresa."

"Justin, I was wrong! I jumped to conclusions before I took the time to find out what really happened. Instead of being there for you when you needed me, I ran back home to feel sorry for myself. It's just that you are such a wonderful man, and I love you so much, that I keep expecting something to happen to us, and I'm so sorry that I hurt you. I don't deserve you, but I would like to try it again if you'll have me back."

Justin was speechless. He didn't know what to say so he just reached out and took Teresa in his arms and kissed her.

As soon as Justin and Teresa went into each others arms it sounded like the home team scored a touchdown with two seconds left on the clock. Justin and Teresa turned around and saw Travis and Jesse and all the rest of the crowd cheering and whistling and jumping up and down.

"Let's go eat some pizza!" Teresa said.

"Are you kidding?" Justin said. "That pack of animals ate all the pizza and the boxes that they came in!"

"Yeah, I know," Teresa said. "But I got another one in the car for just you and me. I thought maybe we could fire up the Jacuzzi and"

"Let's go!" Justin said, and they ran for the Cadillac.

Battle Stations

J ustin leaned against the railing that surrounded the rear deck of
Teresa's house and sipped his coffee as he watched and listened
to the New River as it pushed and tumbled and fought its way
around the large rocks in its path. It was almost like listening to an
orchestra performing or watching a play.

He was leaning against this same railing just a few short days ago
when he first touched Teresa and he remembered how the moment
seemed special and how her perfume had aroused him. He never
dreamed that he would be waking up with this woman snuggled up
against him like she was this morning.

Last night could only be described as incredible. Teresa and
Justin had rushed away from Wade's house after the coyote hunt
like a newlywed couple running down the sidewalk of a church with
people cheering and throwing rice, except that particular crowd was
throwing pizza crust instead. Teresa had brought along an extra pizza
for them to eat, but neither one of them were hungry for food. They
started out with some heavy petting in the Jacuzzi but eventually
ended up in the living room in front of the fireplace, with the gas logs
providing the only light in the room, but definitely not the only heat.
Justin went to levels of passion and pleasure that he didn't even know
existed. At fifty-seven years of age you don't expect to experience
anything new in the bedroom, but what happened last night was way

beyond anything that Justin had ever experienced. They finally went to bed but neither one of them could sleep, so they just cuddled up together and talked for almost two hours until they couldn't stand it anymore and they made love again, this time very slow and deliberate, taking time to fully enjoy each other.

When Justin woke up this morning he held Teresa and watched her sleep for a long time before he finally slipped out of bed and pulled his blue jeans on. He went to the kitchen and made a pot of coffee, and as was his usual custom, he stepped outside to drink it.

Justin heard the door creak and turned to see Teresa stepping out onto the deck, cradling a cup of coffee in both her hands. She was wearing a pink bathrobe and white bedroom slippers and her hair was sticking up on one side of her head, but Justin was instantly aroused by the sight of this sensuous woman.

Teresa walked over to Justin and set her coffee cup on the railing and Justin did likewise and they took each other in their arms and kissed each other deeply.

"Good morning, sweetheart," Teresa sighed. "I love you."

"I love you more," Justin replied.

"Last night was incredible," Teresa said softly. "I'm still tingling all over."

"It was unbelievable, wasn't it?" Justin said smiling. "I can't imagine it being any better."

"It's definitely going to be hard to improve upon, but we can always try," Teresa said and then kissed Justin's neck.

Justin was holding Teresa tight and his mind was racing as he tried to figure out how to tell Teresa that she had to go back to Kernersville this morning. Jimmy Hardy had called Justin last night and told him that he could spend the night at Teresa's but that the CIA wanted her to return to Kernersville in the morning and stay there until Jack Billings and all his associates were arrested. It was for his and her safety and of course he was absolutely right. He also told Justin that he was posting two snipers at Teresa's to guard them until she left, and that whatever they did outside would probably be videoed. Justin knew that there was a sniper hiding somewhere and watching them at this very moment.

"Are you cold?" Justin asked.

"Not wrapped up in your arms I'm not," Teresa answered. "But it is chilly out here this morning."

"Let's step back inside and drink our coffee," Justin suggested.

Justin and Teresa stepped back inside and sat down at the dining room table to drink their coffee. Teresa stared across the table at Justin as she sipped her coffee and finally reached across the table and took his hand in hers.

"I just can't get over last night," she said. "I have never felt like that before: it wasn't just physical pleasure, it was somehow deeper than that. Somehow it was different than just great sex."

"I know exactly what you mean," Justin said. "I felt the very same way."

"And to think that just yesterday morning I was sitting around the house crying and feeling sorry for myself," Teresa said. "I'm so thankful that Travis and Jesse stopped to talk some sense into me."

"Love bears all things, believes all things, hopes all things, and endures all things!" Justin said.

"How beautiful!" Teresa said. "You constantly amaze me Justin Hayes. You look like a lumberjack, but you talk like a poet."

"I read that somewhere but I can't remember where," Justin replied. "I think that you and I are together for a reason Teresa. I think that there are powers at work that neither one of us are even aware of."

"You may be right, darling," Teresa said. "What we did last night didn't just feel right on the outside, it felt right all the way through. I have never felt anything that wonderful before!"

Justin's cell phone rang and he pulled it out of his jeans pocket and answered it. "Hello?"

"Justin, this is Jimmy. We're having a meeting this morning at your house at ten hundred. There are some new developments so it's important that you be there. Have you told her yet?"

"Not yet, but I will right now."

"All right, but be careful how much information you give her. We're listening to every word you know!"

"Yeah, I know. I'll see you at ten o'clock."

"Ten-four, Daddy Rabbit," Jimmy said and then hung up.

"Do you have to be somewhere at ten o'clock?" Teresa asked.

Justin didn't answer her. He just got up from the table and walked into the kitchen. He turned on the Bose radio and the sweet voice of Luther Van Dross filled the room. Justin placed his cell phone in front of the radio and then returned to the dining room table. He sat down across from Teresa and reached across the table and took her hands in his.

"Teresa, I have to ask you to do something but I can't tell you why, at least not yet. You've got to trust me, and like you said earlier, not jump to any conclusions."

"What's wrong?" Teresa asked with a look of confusion.

"Nothings wrong except for the timing of this whole mess. I've been sworn to secrecy so I can't tell you much about what's going on, but basically there's a bunch of criminals that live near here that are trying to kill me," Justin said.

"Is that what the shooting the other day was about?" Teresa asked.

"No, the shooting the other day was a weird coincidence, but some of the people involved were part of this group of criminals."

"Does the sheriff's department know about these criminals?"

"Just the sheriff," Justin said with a smirk. "The FBI knows about them though and there going to arrest them sometime in the next few days."

"The FBI!" Teresa shrieked.

"Yeah, the FBI," Justin answered. "These are some really bad dudes."

"Why do they want to kill you?" Teresa asked as she squeezed Justin's hands. "I can't tell you now, but I will later."

"Why don't you just leave until they can arrest them?"

"Because they might get suspicious. The FBI wants me to go about my business just like normal until they can gather all the evidence and spring their trap."

"I wouldn't care what the FBI wanted if my life was in danger!"

"I'm not really in much danger Teresa. There are snipers somewhere outside of this house guarding me right now and there have been snipers set up around my house for over a week now. That cell phone is the FBI's and they can hear my conversations and track my movements through the GPS system that is built into the phone."

"I was wondering why you turned the radio on and set your phone in front of it," Teresa said. "You said you had to ask me to do something."

"Yeah, I do," Justin said. "The FBI wants you to go back to Kernersville and stay there until they can arrest these guys. It's for your safety and for mine. They also want me to stay around my house so they can protect me better. They made an exception for us last night, but told me to ask you to go back to Kernersville this morning. It's only for a few days and then it will all be over with, but you can't breathe a word of this to anybody."

"Can I call you?"

"Yes, you can call me but they have my phone line tapped."

Teresa stood up and walked around the table and sat on Justin's lap with her arms around his neck. "Are you sure that you're safe?"

"I've got more protection than the president does. Yeah, I would say that I'm about as safe as a person can get," Justin said. "We just have to stay apart for a few days that's the only bad part."

"Life's not fair." Teresa sighed. "We finally get back together and now we have to stay apart."

"I know, sweetie. At least it's just for a few days."

"What time do you have to leave this morning?" Teresa asked.

Justin glanced at the clock on the wall before answering. "In about an hour and a half."

Teresa stood up and drank the last of her coffee and then untied her bathrobe and let it fall to the floor. She was wearing a pair of satin gold colored bikini panties and nothing else as she straddled Justin's lap and kissed him passionately. "Do you have any idea what we could do for an hour and a half?"

"Actually, one just popped up."

Bill Sisk parked his Ford Explorer next to the rear entrance of the Ashe County Sheriffs Department and slowly climbed out. He had just finished directing traffic at the High School and already felt tired. With two of his deputies in the hospital there weren't enough officers to go around and he had to help with some of their routine assignments, and on top of that he hadn't been sleeping very well lately. He had sent a request to the County Commissioners to hire someone part-time until Buddy and Jerry returned, but so far he hadn't heard anything back. Under normal circumstances he could have asked Jack to push the request through since he was a county commissioner, but this wasn't a good time for him to ask Jack for anything.

Bill shifted his stainless steel coffee mug into his left hand so he could fish out his keys and unlock the door. He finally found the right key and opened the door and walked down the hall until he came to his office door. He fumbled with the key ring some more until he found his office key and he opened the door and went inside. Bill tossed the key ring onto his desk and headed back up the hall to refill his coffee mug.

"Good morning, Sheriff," a voice came from the reception-ist's desk.

"Good morning, Jennifer," Bill answered. "Anything happening this morning that I need to know about?"

"Everything is quiet so far except for Jed Stuart. He called a while ago and I finally just patched him through to your answering machine."

"Was he drunk?"

"I can't tell the difference when he is and when he isn't," Jennifer responded.

"I'll see what his problem is and take care of it. I'll be in my office if you need me," Bill said as he filled his coffee mug up and headed back down the hall. Bill sat down behind his desk and hit the play button on his answering machine. "Thursday: April the twelfth, at 8:17 a.m. Sheriff, if that son of a bitch Thad Bodenhiemer don't put some mufflers on his damn truck I'm going to shoot the tires off of it. He rode up and down the road all last night and I didn't get a wink of sleep. I'm tired of it and either you can deal with it, or I'll deal with it, and I want something done today too!"

"Message Over. Next Message. Thursday, April the twelfth, at 8:26 a.m. Sheriff Sisk, this is Agent Dan Loggins of the FBI. We have completed our initial investigation of the shooting on River Road, and after analyzing all the evidence we have cleared Justin Hayes of any wrong doing and have no plans to charge him with any crime. A full report of our findings is being sent to you and the Ashe County District Attorney, and also the State Bureau of Investigation. If you would like to speak to me regarding the investigation please call the Wilkesboro Office and I will contact you promptly. Good day."

Bill pushed the stop button on his recorder and took a swig of his coffee. He wasn't surprised that Justin hadn't been found guilty of any wrong doing. He knew that when they led him out of the jail and took him home that they were planning on releasing him. Justin Hayes seemed to be armor plated because everything that was thrown at him just bounced off.

Bill knew that if he wanted to remain the sheriff of Ashe County then he needed to figure out a way to eliminate Justin Hayes. No one had ever challenged him on Election Day because they knew it would be futile. But if Jack Billings backed somebody else they would no doubt run and would probably win, and Jack was mad enough at him right now to do it! If he could only figure out a way to kill Justin it would put him back in Jack's good graces, but he didn't have a clue how to go about it. Justin showed no sign of fear when Bill had confronted him about Tommy's disappearance and Bill had a strong feeling that day that Justin was prepared to kill him if he had drawn his weapon. Maybe Justin could be ambushed at a traffic stop or forced off the road, but a fair fight was definitely out of the question Bill thought. Bill's phone rang and broke his train of thought.

"Sheriff Sisk," he answered.

"Bill, I need some information if you can get it for me," Jack Billings said.

"Certainly Jack, what do you need to know?"

"I need to know if the FBI has a tracking device on Justin Hayes, like one of those bracelets or anklets, and I also need to know if there watching him."

"They have officially cleared him of any wrongdoing so they can't legally put a tracking device on him and there would be no need to watch him now."

"Okay then, that's all I need to know."

"Wait, Jack! Why do you want to know that?"

"You don't need to know, Bill."

"Jack, I'm going to deal with this problem real soon," Bill said. "You can bet on it!"

"Bill you don't have the balls to deal with Justin Hayes. Besides, I've already made arrangements to eliminate the murdering bastard! Click!

The line went dead and Bill laid the receiver back down on the cradle and rubbed his face with his hands. He knew now beyond a shadow of a doubt that if he wanted to remain in office he better do something to impress Jack, and he better do it quickly too!

"Call me when you get home so I'll know you got there," Justin said as he leaned inside Teresa's car window and kissed her bye.

"I will," Teresa said. "I love you."

"I love you more!" Justin said as she drove off.

Justin jumped in his truck and followed Teresa down her driveway until she stopped at River Road. She turned left and he turned right and he missed her already. He pulled out his cell phone and dialed Teresa's cell phone.

"Well, hello, darling!" Teresa answered. "Did you forget something?"

"No. I miss you already," Justin answered.

"Oh, that's sweet. I miss you too, honey. What was it you said earlier? Love believes all things, hopes all things

"Love bears all things, believes all things, hopes all things, and endures all things."

"Well, I guess we'll have to endure a few days apart, but just imagine what it will be like when it's over." Teresa sighed.

"I just wanted to tell you one more time before you go back home how much I love you," Justin said.

"I love you too Justin Hayes. Please be careful," Teresa pleaded.

"I will. I'll see you in a few days. Bye now."

"Bye, darling. I love you more!"

Justin smiled and closed his cell phone as he cruised down River Road. When he got to his driveway he stopped and ran across the road to retrieve his mail and heard Shogun and Scooter howling for all they were worth. When he started up his driveway he could see Shogun and Scooter spinning around in circles until they bolted for the carport.

Justin pulled into his carport and was met by DeMac and Chief and two very happy dogs.

"Well, hey there, boys!" Justin said as he rubbed his dogs.

"If you would have been gone one more night we would have had to give those dogs a sedative. They paced all night waiting for you to come home," DeMac said.

"Well, now that I think about it, that's the first time I've been gone overnight since I got those dogs," Justin said as he shook DeMac's hand and then Chiefs. "Thank you both for what you did for Wade. That was an incredible coyote hunt."

"He took those dogs inside and let them sleep with him last night!" Chief said. "I don't think I've ever seen a boy as tickled as Wade was last night."

"When his mama gets back from Virginia the sleeping arrangements might suddenly change," Justin said, laughing.

A vehicle could be heard coming around the house and a white van with Alleghany Refrigeration painted on the side came into view. Justin slid his hand into his back pocket and gripped his Smith and Wesson Centennial Airweight .38 Special.

"They're on our side, Justin," DeMac said.

The van pulled into the carport and the roll-up door started closing.

"You guys even have a remote to open and shut my carport door?" Justin asked.

"Travis is with them," Chief said. "They all rode together to keep from having so many vehicles parked around here."

As soon as the door closed all the way, every door on the van opened up and people started piling out. There was Jimmy Hardy,

Travis, Agent Dan Loggins, Agent Robert Ritchie, Agent Roseanna Lankford, and three men that Justin had never seen before.

"Have you guys ever been to the circus and seen all those clowns when they come piling out of that little bitty car?" Justin asked. "That's what it looked like when the door came down."

"You're the only clown in this crowd," Jimmy Hardy said. "I do enjoy listening to Luther Van Dross though."

"Oh, Jimmy, you're not pissed off about that are you?"

"Like I said once before, I'd kick you in the ass, but if I did you would probably shoot me."

"Justin, let me introduce you to these men," Agent Loggins said. "This is Corey Wallace, Ed Reed, and Peter Ollinger."

"Nice to meet you, men," Justin said as he shook each man's hand.

"They will be in charge of the Special Response Teams when we move in to make our arrests," Dan Loggins said.

"Let's go inside and sit down," Justin said and he led the way as the ten men and one woman filed inside the house and gathered in the living room. Travis and Chief brought some chairs from the dining room to help accommodate the crowd and they all finally got seated and were ready to start the meeting. Jimmy Hardy stood and began to address the group.

"Let me begin by reminding everybody that everything that is said in this meeting is highly classified and will remain so for the rest of your lives, so unless you want to join these crooks in prison, do not repeat a word of what's said here today. Secondly, I want to emphasize how important this mission is to the security of the United States. Our number one priority is to take possession of Suitcase B so that it can't be used by a terrorist organization to bring a nuclear or biological device into this country. If we fail to accomplish this it could result in the deaths of tens of thousands of Americans, so we need to be at our best," Jimmy said and then paused to let it sink in.

"Gyurman Yahamen Tahare-Azar is flying out Saturday night along with a gangster named Ricky Stone to a secluded air-strip near Dayton, Ohio. As soon as they land we will arrest them and seize the suitcase, and from that point on the FBI will take charge of this operation and the CIA and Seal Team 4 will disappear. Under no circumstances can the CIA or the Department of the Navy be associated with the raid on Jack Billings's house or the arrest of the fugitives. This is a civilian operation that was conducted by the FBI and the FBI only. Is everybody perfectly clear on that?"

Everyone in the room said, "Yes, sir."

"Our number two priority is to arrest and interrogate the man carrying Suitcase B and find out the names and addresses of his contacts. That will no doubt eventually lead us to cell groups that are operating in this country, and we will either infiltrate these groups or we will destroy them. We are also especially interested in how the Terrorists are connected to organized crime since the arrangements for his stay were made through the mafia."

"And finally, our third priority is to make sure that no one is making a duplicate suitcase based on Suitcase B. The CIA doesn't think that anyone can build this suitcase except for the engineers in Canada that work for Specialty Products, but we need to make sure. Specialty Products has assured us that they will never build another one and they have destroyed the blueprints and withdrawn the patents that are associated with this product."

"The three priorities that I have outlined for you are critical to the security of this country and the future of mankind. Let's all pray that we are successful. Now I'm going to turn this meeting over to Special Agent Dan Loggins so he can tell you what the FBI is planning to bring to this party."

Jimmy took a seat and Agent Loggins stepped up to address the group.

"First of all I would like to inform Justin that our investigation of the shooting that he was involved in day before yesterday is complete, and there will be no charges filed by the FBI. A detailed report has been sent to the Ashe County District Attorney, the Ashe County Sheriff's Department, and the State Bureau of Investigation. Not only did we find no evidence of any wrong doing, we think you should be commended for stepping in and saving the lives of two law enforcement officers, and our report states that as such."

There was a small round of applause from everyone in the room and Agent Loggins waited for it to subside before continuing.

"As Jimmy explained to you earlier, the FBI will assume control of this operation as soon as we get the word that Suitcase B has been recovered and the two suspects are in custody. Our mission does not have national security concerns but it is very important nonetheless. We know through phone conversations that at least four fugitives are staying at the underground hotel and there are probably even more. One of those fugitives is Mike Savalous and he is on the FBI's top ten list and the Federal Marshall's top fifteen list. The other fugitives are Ricky Stone, who will be arrested along with Gyurman in Ohio, Sonny Milano, who is Jimmy Milano's son; and Quai Son Bien, who is Sonny's bodyguard.

"The biggest arrest though as far as the FBI is concerned will be made in Chicago at the home of Jimmy Milano," Agent Loggins continued. "We have been recording his phone conversations for almost three years thanks to the RICO laws, and he has never given us anything we could use until yesterday, so when we raid Jack Billing's house we will simultaneously raid Jimmy Milano's house in the suburbs of Chicago and arrest him also.

"The raid at both locations will begin at 10:45 a.m. on Sunday. Every Sunday at 10:45 the church bell at the New River Baptist Church is rung to signal its parishioners that it's time to gather for worship. That will be our signal to start. As Jimmy mentioned earlier, the CIA and Seal Team 4 will disappear, but not until we have completed our raid on Jack's house. They will remain in place and be our eyes and ears during this operation and will pack up and leave after we have secured the house and the hotel. They will not intervene unless it's necessary to save a life.

"Phase one of our plan is designed to seal off the house and the hotel and to shut down the landing strip. Corey Wallace will lead his team through the front gate. They will be traveling in an armored personnel carrier and will ram the front gate and knock it down. Two men will jump off the back of the APC and guard the front entrance while the rest of the team surrounds the house.

"At the same time that Corey's team enters the front gate, Ed Reed's team will arrive by helicopter and land on the airstrip. Their job will be to block the airstrip and surround the hangar. There is a good chance that somebody will attempt to fly out and escape once they realize that they are being raided, and it will be Corey's job to stop them.

"When the time comes to enter the hangar we can simply punch in the code that opens the door, thanks to the snipers that have been set up across the river. They were able to video an employee of Jacks when he punched in the code, and the CIA enhanced the video until they could tell exactly what the code is, but initially all we want to do is to secure the hangar and contain the suspects.

"Peter Ollinger's team will also arrive by helicopter at the same time as the other two teams. Two of his men will rappel out of the chopper onto the top of the mountain behind the house and take a position beside the air ducts and fresh air vents that come up from the hotel. The air ducts and the air vents are camouflaged and they are virtually invisible, but satellite images and pictures taken from a fighter jet confirm what we believe to be the ventilation system for the motel, and two agents will guard them to make sure that no one escapes through them. The rest of Peter's team will be dropped off near the garage area and will secure the garage, the muscle car building, the dojo, and the various equipment sheds until we decide to clear them.

"As soon as I receive word from all three teams that everything has been secured, I will try to make contact with the people inside by telephone. They will be ordered to come out one at a time, and if they do, we will take them into custody and isolate them.

"If we are unable to make contact through the telephone, then Corey, Ed, and Peter will use bull horns to order them outside. Our hope is that once they realize that they are surrounded, they will surrender to us, but I would be surprised to see any of the fugitives give up that easily since they all face long prison terms.

"Phase One will happen very quickly, probably in less than three minutes. Phase Two will be slow and methodical. Our objective in Phase Two is to clear all the structures and arrest everybody we find. We would obviously like to accomplish this without anyone getting hurt or killed, so we plan on going slow and being very careful. Like most of our operations we don't really know what to expect. We may come under fire and if we do we will respond accordingly, but we don't want this to become a shooting match if we can possibly avoid it. The last thing that the FBI needs is a Branch Davidian disaster or a Ruby Ridge.

"Special Agent Jim Wilson and his SWAT team are flying in today from Texas. They will be responsible for making entry into all the structures and clearing them. The plan that I submitted to FBI Headquarters included using our own teams to clear the structures, but when they saw the list of fugitives they vetoed my plan and sent for Jim Wilson. I personally think that we could have handled the job, but for the record, Jim's SWAT team is probably the best in the country. They will arrive by helicopter after all the structures are surrounded and secure. They will clear the garage first and then the muscle car building and then the Dojo and equipment sheds, and finally the house and hotel.

"Also traveling today to join our surprise party is a full contingent of K-9s. Our best bloodhounds, attack dogs, and drug and bomb sniffing dogs are on their way from Quantico and will arrive sometime after dark.

"If the SWAT team needs a dog to help search a room or wants to make sure there are no explosives, we want to have one on site for their use. And if by chance someone slips through our net we want to be able to put the bloodhounds on their track immediately.

"We want all the teams in place and ready to deploy by 2200 hours tomorrow night just in case something happens and we have to go in early.

"The two professional bodyguards from Security Concepts in California were arrested when we went to Jack's house to investigate the shooting. We arrested them for the sole purpose of removing them from the premises and they are presently staying in a hotel in Charlotte until Sunday evening when we will release them and let them fly back to California.

"Sheriff Bill Sisk will also be arrested on Sunday morning," Agent Loggins continued. "Agent Turner and Agent Lankford will get the honor of placing the cuffs on him. If he is at home, in a restaurant, at his office, or sitting on the front row of church, we will place him in custody. I hate a dirty cop and I'm glad that we have the opportunity to remove that worthless piece of trash!

"Well, that just about does it," Agent Loggins said. "Does anybody have any questions?" There was silence in the room.

"Does everybody know their assignments and what's expected from them?"

"Yes, sir!"

"If nobody has anything to discuss I'll turn this meeting back over to Agent Hardy." Dan said and then took his seat.

Jimmy stood to address the group again.

Ashley stirred the Seagram 7 and 7-Up and took a small sip before she carried it down the hall to Jack's office. At least he was waiting until ten o'clock to start drinking she thought as she knocked on his office door. He had been drinking constantly since Johnny had been killed and everybody had been staying as far away from him as they could.

"Come in!"

"Here's your drink, Jack," Ashley said as she walked in and set it on his desk. Jack's desk was covered in photographs and an empty shoe box was sitting on the floor beside him.

Jack didn't even look up so Ashley turned and left the room.

"When Ashley went back up the hallway she passed by Johnny Steele. "Is Jack in his office?"

"Yeah, good luck!" She said.

Johnny walked down the hall and knocked on Jack's door. "Come in!"

"You wanted to see me?" Johnny asked. "Come in and shut the door."

Johnny shut the door behind him and took a seat across from Jack's desk. "I need for you to round up some things for me," Jack said. "Here's a list."

Johnny took the paper and read it out loud. "A fanny pack, two pairs of handcuffs, a roll of duct tape, a nine millimeter Glock with two spare magazines, a cell phone, a condom, three pairs of disposable latex gloves, a butterfly knife, a pair of size ten Canoe shoes, and twenty feet of 3/8 window sash cord. When do you need it?"

"By tonight," Jack said as he took a big gulp of his drink.

"Okay, Jack, is that all?"

"One more thing. CJ was supposed to take the old white Chevy Blazer that they use on the farm and fill it up with gas and tint all the windows. Would you check and see if he's done that yet?"

"I saw him drive it up to the front of the house and leave it there about fifteen minutes ago," Johnny said.

"Okay, good," Jack said. "That's all I need." He reached down and picked up another stack of pictures.

Johnny started out the door and almost hit Danny Comer with it when he opened it.

"Excuse me," Danny said as he turned sideways to slip by Johnny's huge frame.

Jack didn't wait for Danny to ask him what he wanted, he just went ahead and told him. "Danny, I need to know if the FBI has Justin Hayes's phone line tapped."

"No, sir, I know they don't," Danny responded instantly.

"How can you be so sure?"

"When we put our tap on his line I took an ohms reading before we tapped it and after we tapped it, and the ohms reading is still the same this morning as it was when we tapped it on Monday."

"What is an ohms reading?"

"It's just a measurement of the phone line. If your phone line runs five miles before it gets to a switch, and my phone line runs seven miles before it gets to a switch, my line will measure more ohms than yours."

"Why do you need to know that?" Jack asked.

"Well, if I know how many ohms the line measures with our tap on it, I can tell by looking at the ohms reading if anything has changed. If someone removed our tap, or if somebody else tapped the line, the phone line would read a different amount of ohms. We put our tap on Justin's line on Monday, and the FBI didn't even get involved until Tuesday, and the ohms are still reading the same, so I'm sure that no one has tapped that line."

"Well, good, Danny. I'm glad that somebody around here knows what the hell there doing," Jack said. "That's all I needed to know."

"Thank you, sir," Danny said and he turned and left the room, shutting the door as he left.

Jack thumbed through the pictures on his desk until he came to one of Johnny and Billy sitting in a canoe in the middle of the river. Jack remembered that day. They got the canoe stuck on a rock shelf in the very center of the river and were rocking it up and down like a see-saw trying to free it from its perch. They were such happy boys when they were growing up and Jack loved to watch them laugh and play.

Jack couldn't remember any laughter in his house when he was a boy. The only thing he remembered was being hungry and cold and having to wear rags for clothes. He also remembered hiding under his bed when his father got drunk and started hitting everybody in the house.

Jack swore to himself that if he ever managed to escape his meager existence and his alcoholic father that he would always have food to eat and descent clothes to wear even if he had to work two jobs, and that's exactly what he did. When he turned thirteen he started working on a neighbor's dairy farm, getting up at 4:30 in the morning and walking two miles to start the morning milking. He would catch the school bus in front of the dairy and ride it to school, and then after school he would get off the bus at the dairy and go back to work, shoveling manure, mending fences, getting up hay, or whatever needed doing until it was time to start the evening milking. After dark Jack would walk to another neighbors and light the fire for that nights run of white lightning. He would tend to the fire until there was a glowing bed of coals for them to cook their "mash" over that night.

It wasn't long before Jack had enough money to buy Zeb and him each a new pair of shoes and they were able to eat a hot lunch in the school cafeteria. It also wasn't long before Jack's dad started searching the house for Jack's money so he could buy himself a bottle of whiskey with it. If he couldn't find Jack's stash of money, he would get furious and beat Jack until he would finally tell him where it was. There seemed to be no way out of the hell that they were enduring.

One night as Jack was getting ready to leave the liquor still and head back home, his boss sent him on an errand. He told him to take all the whisky in one particular crate and destroy it because it was poison and would kill you if you drank it. Jack poured the tainted whiskey into a stump hole, except for one quart that he took home and hid where he knew his father would find it. When Jack got up the following morning to head for the dairy, he found his father lying in the yard facedown in his own vomit, dead.

Jack learned two very important lessons at a very young age. First, if you want something, you have to go after it. And second, if someone stands in your way, run over them!

Jack stared at the picture of Johnny and Billy but no tears came to his eyes this morning. It was time to deal with the one that was standing in the way. It was time to run over Justin Hayes!

"As Agent Loggins mentioned earlier, we intercepted a phone call yesterday from Jack Billings to Jimmy Milano," Jimmy Hardy said to the crowd in Justin's living room. "This phone call was—"

"Excuse me, Jimmy. I hate to interrupt you but could we take a five-minute break?" Justin asked.

"Well, I guess so but we're almost through."

"I would appreciate it," Justin said and he winked at Jimmy.

"Okay, everybody, stretch your legs and get something to drink and we will resume in about ten minutes."

Everyone stood and some went toward the bathroom while others went toward the kitchen and Justin went straight toward Jimmy.

"What's wrong?" Jimmy asked as Justin approached him.

"It's Gabriel," Justin answered. "Something is wrong. He's warning me that I'm in danger."

"Are you sure?" Jimmy asked.

"I'm positive!" Justin said as he stepped over and looked out the window toward River Road.

"Well, don't stand in the window!" Jimmy said. "I'll call control at the tobacco barn and see if the snipers have seen anything." Jimmy reached for his phone but it rang before he touched it. Jimmy cut his eyes toward Justin and then answered it. "What's up?"

"Hart and Cat just called in and said that Jack and an Oriental man just got in a white Chevy Blazer and are traveling up River Road at a very slow speed. Jack is driving!"

"That's got to be Quai that's with him. Patch me through to the comm. network," Jimmy ordered.

"Ten-four, go ahead, you're on."

"All positions, white Blazer is carrying assassin and must be stopped if it tries to approach Rabbit Den. All snipers with a visual have a green light to incapacitate vehicle if it turns into the driveway. Do not let the vehicle approach the house! Over."

"Everyone get in here, Now!" Jimmy hollered and feet could be heard running through the house. Everyone was present in seconds.

"DeMac, you and Chief grab your gear. One of you take a position at the rear of the house and the other one come back in here and guard the front. Everybody else get your weapons ready and stay down."

Justin squatted down but continued to gaze at River Road. The white SUV finally came in sight and Justin could feel Gabriel pounding him with warnings. The vehicle couldn't have looked anymore suspicious or sinister as it crept along at about twenty-five miles an hour with its windows tinted black.

"Control, this is Crow's Nest. We are tracking vehicle but are unable to see inside because of the heavy window tint. Over."

"Crow's Nest, this is Boss Man. If you see a barrel sticking out a window then you have a green light. I repeat, all snipers, if vehicle approaches the house or anyone sees a weapon you are to engage," Jimmy said.

"Roger that, Boss Man, we got you covered."

Justin watched as the white Blazer crept by the front of the house. It appeared that it slowed down slightly to turn into the driveway, but it crept on by and continued down the road. You could almost here everyone in the room exhale as it went out of sight.

"Control, this is Boss Man, call Big Daddy and tell them we need satellite surveillance of this vehicle. If it stops and somebody gets out, we need to know immediately. Over."

"Roger that, Boss Man, calling now."

"What in the hell is going on Jimmy?" Justin asked. "Who is this assassin?"

"He's a professional, Justin," Jimmy said. "And he's damn good too!"

After looking over Justin's house, Quai was even more convinced that they needed to get him to leave home before they could kill him. A person could probably creep down to the house at night and kill the dogs with a silenced firearm, but since there were two of them it would be hard to kill them both before one of them barked and warned him of an intruder. A gunfight with this man was out of the question, so Quai thought that his plan to kidnap Carol and make him come to her rescue was probably the only way. He had seen the video from the Sheriff's Department that was taken when they interrogated Justin about the shooting, so he knew what Justin looked like. Now what he really wanted to know was what his girlfriend Carol looked like.

They wound their way through several twisting roads and made several turns until Quai was sure he couldn't find his way back. They finally came to a stop sign and could see the river again and Jack stopped the Blazer and just sat there.

"This is the north fork of the New River," Jack finally said. "Carol lives about two miles downstream so you can put the canoe in anywhere between here and her house."

Jack turned right and drove slowly down Cranberry Creek Road. When they came around the first curve in the road they could see two canoes that were beached on the opposite side of the river, and there were two young couples sitting on the bank passing a joint back and forth.

"Spring Break" Jack said as they passed by. "A lot of college kids come up here to canoe and kayak. The north fork of the New River is perfect for canoeing. It's wide and shallow and the worst rapids are only a class three, so it's real popular with college kids and Boy Scout troops and families that like to camp. It's also popular because the waters warmer than the other rivers and streams."

"Why is that?" Quai asked.

"The New River flows north instead of south. It's the only river in North America that flows from the south to the north. That's why the water is warmer."

"I don't want anybody to see me when I approach the house," Quai said.

"There aren't many people on the river this early in the year so you shouldn't have any trouble. If it was June or July it could be a problem because there will be a lot of people up and down this river."

They drove slowly down the winding road until they came to a place where the river and the road swung sharply to the right. Jack stopped the Blazer and turned to face Quai.

"This is probably the best place for you to enter the river. I can drop you off here and you can slide the canoe down this bank to the river. If anybody is on the river they won't be able to see you in this sharp turn and the road is wide enough for me to make a three point road turn and leave without having to drive by Carol's house. There's a set of rapids around this next bend that are probably only a class two, but you could capsize the canoe there and you wouldn't have to walk but maybe a half a mile before you got to her house." Jack started rolling again before he continued. "After we go around this next curve and then one more you will be able to see the house. It's a small white house on the right hand side and it's the only house for a mile in either direction."

True to Jack's word when they rounded the second curve Quai could see a small white house about a quarter of a mile away. It was nestled on the side of a hill surrounded by maple trees and there was an old barn and several sheds sitting behind it.

"And you're sure that she lives alone?" Quai asked.

"Yeah, I'm sure," Jack said. "She's an only child and her father passed away about ten years ago and her mother passed away last year."

"And now she is going to pass away," Quai said, smiling.

Jack felt a chill run down his back as he glanced over at Quai and saw him smiling. Jack had never had anyone killed except for the ones that had to be, at least in his way of thinking. He would never even think about killing Carol if there was any other way, but since it was the only way they could get to Justin, then so be it. But it did bother him that Quai was enjoying it so much. This guy is a real psycho Jack thought to himself.

As they neared the house they could see someone standing in the backyard. Jack slowed down to a crawl as Quai picked up the binoculars that were lying on the seat and peered through them. Carol was hanging sheets on the clothes line and the ten mile an hour breeze was fighting her. She was wearing blue jeans and a sweater as Quai studied her from her blowing brunette hair to her white sandals. She turned and watched the slow moving vehicle as it passed, but Quai kept staring at her through the binoculars. He knew that she couldn't see him through the dark tint on the windows and even if she could he didn't care. She was very attractive for an older woman and Quai found himself suddenly aroused. He wasn't surprised by his sudden arousal, he always got aroused when he looked at a woman that he knew he would eventually rape and kill. He just didn't know if it was the rape that aroused him, or the killing. It was probably both of them he thought as they finally rode out of sight.

"As Agent Dan Loggins mentioned to you earlier, we intercepted a phone call yesterday that finally gives the FBI the evidence they need to arrest Jimmy Milano," Jimmy Hardy said. "It was a call from Jack Billings to Jimmy to hire a hit man to kill Justin. The difference between this call and the calls that have been recorded over the last three years is that Jack called people by their real names. So the FBI has obtained a warrant to arrest Jimmy for aiding and abetting the hiring of someone for the purpose of committing first-degree murder. This is important because Jimmy would have probably fled as soon as he learned that we had raided Jack's house, and now he can be arrested before he has a chance to flee."

"The hit man that Jimmy recommended to Jack is named Quai Son Bien. Quai's parents immigrated to the United States from Korea before Quai was born so he is a naturalized citizen. His father was an accomplished pianist and his mother was an interpreter at the United Nations until their murders when Quai was eleven years old. After his parents were murdered in an apparent robbery, Quai moved to Chicago to live with his aunt. It is on the streets of Chicago where we believe that Quai started going wrong. He was arrested when he was in his early teens for several minor offences, but since then has virtually disappeared. The FBI believes that Quai started doing hits for several of the gangs in Chicago and eventually graduated up to work for the mob. He has a very high IQ and is extremely cautious. He likes to use a knife to dispatch his victims and he usually tortures them before he kills them. If there are any women in the house when Quai does a hit he will rape them and torture them before he finally kills them, and it doesn't matter how old they are either. The authorities in Chicago have DNA samples that link eleven of the murders together and they think that Quai is the murderer, but they can't get a DNA sample from him to compare it. They have followed him into bars and restaurants and when he is walking down the street, but he always wears gloves and never eats or drinks in public and he doesn't smoke or spit or anything that would give them the sample they need to put him away."

"The bad news is that Quai was already staying at Jack's hotel when Jimmy recommended him, so there was no travel time involved. The only good news is that Quai has always worked in an urban environment, so trying to hit someone in a rural setting has taken him out of his element. Regardless, he is very dangerous and we are very concerned for Justin's safety," Jimmy said and he looked at Justin to emphasize his concern.

"So with that having been said, Justin, we want you to stay inside your house until we raid Jack's and can arrest Quai along with everybody else that's in there. DeMac, we're going to leave you and Chief with Justin to guard him and we want one of you two to be awake at all times, understood?"

"Yes, sir!" both men said instantly.

"Justin, we don't want you to have any visitors if you can avoid it and we don't want you to get your mail anymore. We'll get it during the night and deliver it to your carport. Okay?"

"Whatever you say, Jimmy," Justin replied.

"They may try to place a bomb in your mailbox or even mail one to you that can be detonated with a remote control, so we don't want to take any chances. We also don't want you to go out on your front porch. We don't think that Quai has the skill to slip up on you without us knowing it, but let's not underestimate him."

"Travis, we have decided to put a team of snipers over at Jesse's house until this thing is over. There is a possibility that they may try to kidnap you to get to your dad, so we want to cover all the bases.

We have requested more help and they have agreed to it, so we have plenty of men to go around now. Eight more Seals were sent to us yesterday and four of them have been put in charge of guarding you and Jesse. The only thing I ask is that you let me know if you want to go see your dad so that we will be expecting you when you drive up."

"I will, and thank you for the protection," Travis said.

"The bottom line is that these people are very unpredictable and very dangerous, so everybody needs to be in a very heightened state of awareness until all the bad guys are locked up!" Jimmy said loudly. "Any questions or comments?"

The room was silent.

"Do you have anything else Agent Loggins?"

"No, I think we've pretty much covered it all," Dan Loggins said.

"This will be our first and last get together as a group, so I want to thank everybody ahead of time and wish everybody good luck. That's all I've got to say so let's go earn those government pensions. Justin, I want to speak to you and DeMac and Chief in private before I leave."

The group got up and wandered through the house toward the carport and Jimmy walked over to where Justin and DeMac and Chief were standing.

"Justin, I appreciate your skills with a handgun and a rifle, but I want you to promise me that you will take this threat seriously and stay inside this house," Jimmy said.

"I hear you loud and clear, Jimmy," Justin responded.

"I know that there's nothing wrong with your ears and you can hear me loud and clear, but I still want you to promise me that you won't leave this house."

"Oh, okay, Jimmy. I'll be a good boy and stay inside the house," Justin said.

"DeMac, if you or Chief see him go out onto the porch or try to walk down to the mailbox I want you to shoot him in the leg," Jimmy said.

"Yes, sir!" they both said.

"And if he says that his angel, or whatever it is, is warning him of danger I want you to take it seriously and I want to be notified," Jimmy said to DeMac.

"Yes, sir, we will go into condition red and notify you immediately," DeMac said.

"I'll see you on Sunday if not before," Jimmy said and then turned and headed for the carport.

The responsibility of gathering all the intelligence and keeping everybody safe and also coordinating all the agencies was taking a toll on Jimmy Hardy. You could see it in his face and by the way he walked. Justin felt kind of sorry for him and would be glad when this nightmare was finally over, for his sake and Jimmy's. Jimmy stepped into the carport and his cell phone rang again.

"Hello?" Jimmy said.

"This is Control, Boss Man. The snipers on Cranberry Creek Road that are guarding Carol Crissman have called and reported that the white Chevy Blazer rode through there slowly about five minutes ago."

"Hmm, that's kind of interesting, isn't it?" Jimmy said. "Tell them to send the video to the barn. I'll be there in about fifteen minutes."

"Roger that, Boss Man. Out."

Friday the Thirteenth

C hief was sitting in Justin's kitchen at a spot that allowed him to watch the front door as well as the back door when he heard the noise. It sounded like soft footsteps on the white oak hardwood floor, so he slowly raised his M-4 and flipped the selector switch to fire just as Justin stepped into the kitchen.

"Chieu-Hoi! Chieu-Hoi! I surrender!" Justin said as he made his way to the coffee pot.

Chief placed the rifle back on his lap and put the selector switch back in the 'safe' position. "Sorry about that," Chief said. "Just making sure."

"No problem, Chief. I need to quit wearing these moccasins and buy some tap shoes so that you'll know it's me walking around," Justin said with a grin.

"Don't shoot!" DeMac hollered before he stepped out of his bedroom and made his way to the kitchen. Justin handed DeMac a cup of coffee and then poured one for him before they joined Chief at the dining room table.

"I guess it was a quiet night?" DeMac asked.

"Totally, except for when they brought Justin's guns back. They said that there wasn't any mail."

"I got the mail yesterday before we had the meeting," Justin said. "Did they bring back all three guns?"

"Just a rifle and a snub-nose revolver," Chief said. "They're in the hall closet."

"Were there three guns?" DeMac asked.

"Yeah, I had a .45 automatic, but Sheriff Sisk took that off of me when I surrendered to him," Justin said.

"We'll bring that to Agent Loggins attention so you'll be sure to get it back after they arrest the good sheriff," DeMac said.

"Thank you," Justin said. "I don't want to lose that pistol. It's the one that you were firing the other day."

"You know, I thought that Ruger No. 1 rifles had a reputation for being inaccurate, but you made two incredible shots with yours," Chief said. "Actually three incredible shots when you count the five hundred-yard shot on the coyote."

"They do have a reputation for mediocre accuracy, but I rebuilt mine," Justin said. "It has a Douglas Match Barrel and a Kepplinger Single Set Trigger, and I bedded the forearm. It'll shoot three-inch groups at five hundred yards."

"Well, there is nothing mediocre about that," Chief said. "I keep forgetting that you're a gunsmith."

"What surprises me the most about you Justin is that you carry a J-framed revolver around with you instead of a .45," DeMac said. "You would think that after years of competition that you would be more comfortable with a .45."

"Of all the guns that a given man might own, the one that saves his life is the one that he has on him when he needs it," Justin said. "A typical forty-five will weigh around forty ounces, and they're too bulky to carry around all day, but a J-framed revolver weighs just seventeen ounces, and they fit into your pocket, so you tend to carry them with you wherever you go. That's why I carry a snub-nose revolver."

"Makes sense," DeMac said.

"If I suspect that there's going to be trouble and I have time to prepare for it, I will pick a forty-five every time, like I did the day that Jack and his goon came to see me. But if you're going to carry a pistol all day long, you can't beat a seventeen ounce revolver."

"Chief, now that I'm awake, you can go to bed and get some sleep whenever you get ready," DeMac said.

"Let's eat some breakfast first," Justin said as he stood up. "How about a ham, egg, and cheese omelet with Texas Pete hot sauce and a side order of hash brown potatoes and some biscuits with butter and sourwood honey."

"I think I can delay my beauty sleep long enough to eat an omelet," Chief said.

The clock radio that was sitting on the nightstand beside Jesse's bed switched from 6:29 to 6:30 and the bedroom was suddenly assaulted by a screeching alarm. Jesse reached over and cut the alarm off and swung her legs around to sit on the edge of the bed when Travis grabbed her and flipped her over backward. Jesse squealed and then started giggling as she finished her flip and landed on Travis's chest. Jesse spun around until she was lying on top of Travis and they kissed each other softly.

"Don't go," Travis pleaded.

·"I have to, Fridays are busy and my intern needs to get off early today," Jesse said.

"I love you, Jesse!"

"I love you too, Travis!"

Travis's arms were wrapped around Jesse and he started massaging her back slowly but forcefully as she kissed his neck and moaned. Travis couldn't believe how his life had changed in just seven days. It was one week ago that he had met this marvelous woman and now his entire life centered around her. He wanted to be with her every minute, and when they were apart, he couldn't think about anything but her. It was like his life had no real direction until he met her, and now he knew exactly where he wanted to be and what he wanted to do. It was a wonderful feeling.

Jesse was unable to speak. All she could manage to do was moan and kiss Travis's neck as his magical fingers worked their way down her back. This unexpected massage reminded Jesse of her grandmother Leah, and how she used to sit on the edge of the bed at night and rub her back as she told her bedtime stories. She told Jesse stories about Indian maidens who fell in love with brave warriors, and about Cinderella, who had to work so hard but eventually met a handsome Prince. Tears came to Jesse's eyes as she thought about her grandmother. She wished that she could have lived long enough to have been there when she graduated from college, and long enough to have met her handsome prince, who was driving her insane with his fingers as they finally reached her lower back. She needed to take a shower and to get ready to go to work, but right now she was paralyzed by pleasure. What a wonderful way to start your morning.

"Promise me something," Jesse moaned.

"What?"

"That you will do this every morning."

"Flip you over backward!"

"No, silly, massage my back."

"Every morning?"

"Yes, every morning."

"For how long?"

"For the rest of my life!"

"Jessica Longbow, are you proposing to me?"

"Well, no. Uh, are you going to massage my back every morning or not?"

"On one condition," Travis said.

"What's the condition?" Jesse asked.

"That you wear that red thong and those knee-high rubber boots when you feed the kittens."

"Every day?"

"At least once a week."

"I'll have to think about that."

"I think about it at least twenty times a day!" Travis said.

"I have never been so embarrassed."

"Believe me, honey, when you wear a thong, there is nothing to be embarrassed about!"

"I need to take a shower and go to work."

"I need a shower too."

"Well, come on and we can take a shower together," Jesse said. "It saves water."

"I'm a firm believer in water conservation!"

"The only thing firm about you is hanging between your legs, and we can take care of that when we take our shower," Jesse said.

"Race you to the bathroom!"

Bill Sisk sat at his desk reading an invitation. It was to the annual Sheriff's Association Banquet on Saturday, April 28 at the Embassy Suites Ballroom in Fayetteville, NC, but his concentration was broken when he heard loud voices coming from the front of the building. He immediately recognized one of the voices as belonging to his deputy Steve Lang. Steve was probably bringing in a drunk or a punk kid that was high as a kite, so Bill got up and walked down the hall toward the sound of the ruckus. When he reached the end of the hall he saw his deputy holding a double-barreled shotgun in one hand and dragging a prisoner with the other. The prisoner had his hands cuffed behind his back and his tee shirt was pulled up and over his head, completely covering his face.

"Jed, if you don't stop resisting, I'm going to pepper spray you!" Deputy Lang shouted. "Good morning, Sheriff."

"Good morning, Steve," Bill said. "What did shit for brains here do?"

"I didn't do a damn thing, Sheriff!" Jed shouted from underneath his shirt.

"He shot at Thad Bodenhiemer this morning when Thad drove by his house," Steve answered.

"If I would have shot at that son of a bitch, he would be dead!" Jed protested.

"He actually shot over his truck when he went by, but Thad had his granddaughter in the truck because she missed the school bus and he was taking her to school. She was scared to death," Steve said. "Then when I approached Jed to arrest him, he tried to spit on me!"

"Well, Jed, you're just about the dumbest son of a bitch in Ashe County," Bill said. "You have committed two felonies over a busted muffler."

"Two felonies!" Jed shouted. "How in the hell do you figure that, Sheriff?"

"Shooting at an occupied vehicle is one felony, and spitting at a police officer is another felony," Bill said. "You're probably going to do some time in prison over a damn busted muffler."

Jed started crying now that he realized how serious his offences were. "Sheriff, I just couldn't take it anymore. That son—"

"Shut up, Jed," Bill said. "Lock him up, Steve. Here, give me that shotgun and I'll lock it up in the property room."

Steve handed Bill the shotgun and led the weeping man down the hall and Bill turned and started down the steps that led to the basement. The property room was actually a vault that was constructed in the basement of the Sheriffs Department to secure guns and jewelry and confiscated drugs or anything else that was being held as evidence. Bill liked the feel of the shotgun and stopped at the bottom of the stairs to examine it. The barrel was tarnished but you could still read the inscription when you held it under the light.

"Parker Brothers" was all that Bill could make out, but that was all that he needed to know. A Parker double-barrel shotgun in 16-gauge was probably worth two or three thousand dollars, or maybe even more depending on its grade. Jed must have inherited this shotgun from his daddy or his granddaddy because he could never have afforded a gun worth this much money Bill thought.

Bill threw the shotgun up to his shoulder and swung it around like he was following the flight of a Bobwhite quail or a grouse that was exploding out of a laurel bush. The shotgun was perfectly balanced and came up smoothly and he was looking right down the barrels when the stock met his shoulder. It would be a crime to destroy such a magnificent shotgun. A shotgun like this needs to be in a private collection, Bill thought to himself. Kind of like my gun collection, he figured.

Bill unlocked the door to the vault and stepped inside. A gun rack was built against the far wall and Bill placed the shotgun in one of the empty slots. As he turned to leave he happened to notice a .45 automatic that was lying on a shelf beside the gun rack. It had a tag hanging from the trigger guard by a string, and on the tag someone had written "Justin Hayes No. 179." Bill remembered taking the pistol off of Justin when he arrested him, but he had forgotten it until now.

A plastic Ziploc bag was lying beside the pistol with a tag that had "No. 179" written on it and there were seven .45 ACP cartridges in the bag. Bill knew that the cartridges in the bag were the ones that came out of Justin's pistol the day that he was detained.

Bill picked the pistol up and racked the slide to make sure that it was unloaded and then took aim at the light bulb in the center of the room. CLICK! He smiled and then shoved the pistol under his belt and grabbed the bag of cartridges before he cut the lights off and exited the room. He would have to return this property back to its owner since there were no charges filed against him, and strangely enough, he was looking forward to it.

"You are still planning on going with me when I fly to Tampa to visit my daughter and her family, aren't you?" Teresa asked Justin. They had been talking on the phone for almost an hour.

"Can we join the mile high club?"

"Why, Justin Hayes, you dirty old man! I can't believe that you would ask me such a question," Teresa said. "Of course we can."

"Then count me in. When are we leaving?" Justin asked.

"We'll be leaving on Monday, May the seventh," Teresa answered. "Is that okay with you?"

"I'm sure that my calendar is clear. As a matter of fact, going with you to Florida is the only thing I have planned for 2006, and I'm looking forward to it. I need a vacation after all that's been going on around here lately."

"Are you absolutely positive that you're safe?" Teresa asked.

"Yes, ma'am. I have two bodyguards, two dogs, and four snipers that are guarding me right now."

"Would you tell me if you were in any danger?" Teresa asked.

"Absolutely not! But I'm perfectly safe. You have to believe me."

"Any idea when I can come back to Sparta?"

"A couple of days probably, either Sunday or Monday."

"I can't wait," Teresa sighed. "I love you, Justin."

"I can't wait either," Justin said. "I love you more."

"Well, I'm going to let you go, honey. I think I'll go to the office and check on my realtors. I might ride around this evening and look at some property since I don't have anything else to do."

"Well, you be careful. I love you," Justin said.

"I love you more," Teresa said. "Bye now."

"Bye."

Justin hung the phone up and then rubbed his ear. He wasn't used to talking on the phone that long and his ear was sore, but he would have talked to her all morning if she wanted too. When she called him earlier and he answered the phone, just hearing her voice made him happy. She was a very special lady and Justin knew it. If he could have placed an order for someone to spend his life with, it would have been Teresa. Actually, now that he thought about it, he did place an order for her when he asked God to send him someone.

Justin started to get up and go to the kitchen to get a glass of sweet tea when the phone rang again. The number on the caller ID was unfamiliar but he answered it anyway. "Hello?"

"Justin, is that you?"

"Who's asking?"

"It's Kathy, your ex-wife."

"Oh, Kathy, yes, this is me."

"I hope you don't hang up on me, but if you do I'll understand."

"No, I'm not going to hang up on you."

"Travis gave me your number and said he thought it would be okay if I called you."

"Sure, it's okay to call me. You can call me anytime you like."

"Thank you, Justin, I appreciate that," Kathy said and Justin could tell by her voice that she was about to cry. There was a moment of silence before either of them spoke and then they both tried to speak at the same time and then they both stopped talking to let the other one speak and another moment of silence followed.

"Travis tells me that you're having some health problems," Justin finally said.

"Yes, yes, I am. I'm not going to be around very much longer Justin, which is one of the reasons I wanted to call you. I called to apologize to you. I know that it's probably ridiculous for me to apologize to you after all these years, especially after what I did to you, but I wanted to anyway. I know I don't deserve it, but I hope you can find it in your heart to forgive me."

"I forgave you fifteen years ago Kathy. I was crushed when you left me, but I had a son to raise, and I didn't have the time or the energy to sit around and hate you, so I forgave you and moved on. Don't get me wrong, I hated you for a while. I even thought about hunting Paul down and giving him a good thrashing. But eventually I realized that all the hate was doing was ruining my life, and it was ruining Travis's life too."

"Well, what I did was the biggest mistake of my life," Kathy said. "My marriage to Paul was just for his convenience. He never really loved me, but he needed a wife and like a fool I ran away with him. It was exciting the first year, the fancy cars, the beautiful homes, the expensive clothes and jewelry, and the trips around the world, but eventually I caught him sleeping with other women, and when I confronted him about it he just laughed at me. He admitted that he slept with other women and thought that it was perfectly okay for him to sleep with whoever he pleased. From that moment on I wanted out of the marriage, but I had burned all my bridges and hurt so many people, you and Travis, and my mom and dad, and your mother and all our friends. I was trapped and he knew it."

"I'm sorry that it worked out like that, Kathy," Justin said. "I was serious when I called you and wished you the best."

"And I laughed at you," Kathy said. "I guess the joke was on me. You're a remarkable man Justin, and so is Travis. He is such a gentleman and he is so handsome. I've been calling him everyday, but I guess that you're aware of that."

"No, I didn't know that. I actually haven't seen much of him since he met Jesse."

"You can tell that they're madly in love with each other. I met her the second time that Travis came to see me and she seemed like a very sweet girl, and she is absolutely gorgeous!"

"She is a very sweet girl, and a talented veterinarian. He couldn't have found a better girl anywhere."

"Does her family live up there in Sparta?" Kathy asked.

"The only family that she has is a brother and he's in the military. She lives by herself on a farm and she owns and runs the only animal hospital in Sparta. From what Travis has told me, she has to work practically all the time to pay back her business loan and her college loan. She is a very hard worker and has a lot of character, and I really like her a lot. And like you said earlier, she is absolutely gorgeous."

"I like her a lot too," Kathy said. "I was scared to death to call you this morning Justin, but I'm glad now that I did."

"I'm glad you did too. It's good to talk to you after all these years."

"I'm so tired right now that I must go lie down Justin, but thank you for talking to me. Can I call you back sometime and talk some more?"

"Sure, you can, anytime you like."

"Talking to you has reminded me of how huge a mistake it was to leave you. I cherish the years that we spent together, Justin, and I'm so thankful that you raised our son to be a man that is just like you," Kathy said, crying. "Believe it or not, there is still a special place in my heart for you."

"We spent twenty years together, Kathy. There were some hard times and some bad times, but there were some good times too. You can call me anytime you like, and I'll be sure to remember you in my prayers."

"Thank you, Justin," Kathy cried, and then she hung up, too emotional to continue.

Billy pulled into the parking lot of the Sparta Fence Company and parked his truck. He was about to do something that he had never had to do before; ask for a job. The $2,000 that his dad had given him when he threw him out was slowly but surely dwindling away. Having to buy his own groceries and beer and fuel for his truck was eating away at his nest egg and he needed a job to keep from having to move back in with his dad.

Billy opened the front door of the business and walked up to the counter. Neil Simpson owned Sparta Fence Company and his wife Patty was sitting behind the counter when Billy walked in. Billy had known them all his life.

"Well, hey, Billy," Patty said. "Can I help you?"

"Yeah, I need to see Neil if I can."

"He's out back loading up some pipe. Just walk on through the warehouse and you'll see him back there somewhere."

"Okay, Patty," Billy said. "Thank you."

"You're welcome, honey."

Billy walked behind the counter and through the warehouse until he was standing on the loading dock at the back of the building. Neil was lowering a bundle of three inch galvanized pipe onto the bed of a truck with a fork-lift and he waved at Billy as soon as he saw him. As soon as the pipe was resting on the bed of the truck, Neil backed up and drove the fork-lift up the ramp and into the warehouse where he parked it.

"Hey Billy, what can I do for you?" Neil said as he climbed off the fork-lift.

"I need a job, Neil."

Neil stopped walking and stared at Billy. You could tell that what he just heard had startled him. "A job!"

"Yeah, I moved out of daddy's house and I'm living on my own, so I need a job to pay my bills," Billy explained. "Are you hiring?"

"Well, I just signed a contract with the Ashe County School Board to build ten thousand feet of fence around three elementary schools, so I could use a few more employees, at least for a few months."

"That would be great if you could find a place for me," Billy said.

"What does your daddy think about all this?"

"I don't know Neil, and I really don't care."

"It's hard work, Billy, digging holes, pouring concrete, stringing wire!"

"I know it's hard work, Neil, but I need a job and I don't know anywhere else to get one."

"There's no drinking, Billy. If you come in smelling of beer or I catch you drinking on the job you'll be fired immediately."

"I understand, Neil," Billy said. "I won't drink."

"Okay, Billy, I'll hire you on one condition. I'm going to call your dad, and if he okays it you can start to work Monday morning."

"He doesn't have anything to do with this, Neil!" Billy said. "This is between you and me!"

"Billy, I know your dad, and if I hired you and he didn't like it he would build a fence company across the street from me and undercut my prices until I went bankrupt. He could also make a few phone calls and get my contract cancelled with the school board since he's a county commissioner, so if he doesn't approve it then I won't hire you. I'm sorry, Billy, but that's just the way it is."

"Well, then, just forget it, Neil. I'll find a damn job somewhere else!" Billy said and then walked away. Billy stormed back through the warehouse and past the counter where Patty was doing paperwork.

"Did you find him, Billy?" Patty asked.

Billy walked out without answering her and jumped in his truck and left. Everybody in Ashe County was scared to death of Jack Billings he reckoned. He couldn't even get a damn job without his dad's approval. Billy slammed his fist into the dash as he pulled up to the highway. Instead of turning left on 117 and going home, he turned right and headed into town. Billy turned right at the first stoplight and drove past the Sparta Photo Center and then past Curry's Body Shop and turned in the gravel parking lot of the Rack-Um Billiards and Bar. It was kind of early, but he needed a beer. He needed several beers.

Since Justin couldn't go outside, he decided to spend his time in the kitchen. He had cooked a pot of cabbage with slices of Polish kielbasa sausage and course ground red pepper, and another pot of pinto beans flavored with a ham bone that he had saved since Christmas in the freezer. He was pouring cornbread mix into a muffin pan when he heard his dogs barking and he turned just as DeMac came rushing into the kitchen.

"Bill Sisk just pulled into your driveway," DeMac said. "He's coming up to the house."

"Well, let's see what the sheriff wants," Justin said.

DeMac was wearing a headset and you could tell that he was listening to someone talking.

"Jimmy says to try and avoid a confrontation with him, but to go ahead and see what he wants. If he tries to arrest you we will go ahead and take him down," DeMac said. "I'm going to wake Chief up and then slip around to the corner of the house. Chief will be hiding behind the front door in case he needs to back you up. Let your dogs keep him in his car until we get ready."

"Okay, DeMac, you guys go ahead and get ready."

Bill Sisk pulled up and parked in front of the house. Shogun and Scooter recognized the man who tried to come through the front door of the house two days ago, and they circled the car and barked and growled.

Chief came out of the bedroom wearing a headset and a pair of boxer shorts and was carrying his M-4. He took a position behind the door while DeMac slipped around to the front corner of the house. When DeMac got into position he told Chief he was ready and Chief nodded for Justin to go ahead. Justin opened the front door and then the glass storm door and stepped out onto the porch.

"Shogun! Scooter! Heel! Come on now, heel!"

Shogun was still growling when he ran up the steps and into the house and Scooter stopped on the porch and turned around to growl at the sheriff again.

"Get in the house, Scooter," Justin ordered. Scooter snorted to show his disapproval and finally jumped in the house and Justin closed the storm door.

Bill Sisk stepped out of his Ford Explorer carrying a clipboard full of papers and Justin's .45 automatic and a Ziploc bag with .45 ACP cartridges in it. He turned the clipboard up until it was flat and placed the pistol and shells on top of it.

"Mr. Hayes, I've come to return your pistol to you. I got a copy of the report from the FBI regarding the shooting the other day and you have been cleared of any wrongdoing. I also came to apologize to you. I think that you and I got off on the wrong foot the other day."

Justin wasn't sure where this was leading but there were several things that got his attention. For one, the sheriff was overly friendly which was a sure sign that something wasn't right. Secondly, he was wearing body armor under his shirt, and Bill Sisk was known for not wearing body armor even though his deputies were required to. And last but certainly not least, the .45 that was lying on top of the clipboard was cocked, and even a rookie officer knew better than to hand a pistol to somebody with it cocked, even if you knew it was unloaded.

Justin hooked his thumbs on each side of his blue jeans and pulled them up and then started tucking his shirttail in, but when his hands went behind his back he slipped his .38 out of his back pocket and tucked it under his belt with the grips tilted forward just in case he needed to draw it. "Excuse me just a minute sheriff, I think I'm getting a phone call," Justin said as he unclipped the cell phone and put it to his ear.

"Hello. Oh, hey there, Jimmy. I'm fine and how about yourself!" Justin said. Justin listened intently for several moments before continuing. "I know what you're thinking, Jimmy, but it's not going to be a problem. I can handle it by myself but I appreciate the offer. It's not going to work until somebody puts a pin in it, but I can do that later on by myself. Just tell your men not to worry about it and we'll settle up later." Justin pretended to be listening again. "Okay then, I'll talk to you later and thanks for calling."

Justin closed his phone and clipped it back on his side. "Sorry to keep you waiting, Sheriff, but that call was important."

"I need for you to sign this form Justin. It just says that your property was returned to you on this date and in good condition," Bill said.

"Eagle, this is Crow's Nest. That .45 that the sheriff is holding is cocked. Over."

"Crow's Nest, this is Eagle. Do not fire, Daddy Rabbit said he could handle it. Stand by for instructions. Over."

Justin walked down the porch steps and over to the Ford Explorer and placed both his hands on the right front fender.

"Is your son still here, Justin, or has he had to report back to the Navy?" Bill asked.

"No, he's not here," Justin said. "I'm all by myself."

"That's good, Justin," Bill said as he grabbed the .45 up and pointed it at Justin's chest. Bill jerked the trigger and the gun went click. Justin reached around and pulled out his Smith and Wesson .38 and pointed it straight at Bill's head.

"What the hell is—"

"They won't fire without a firing pin, Bill. I took the firing pin out before I walked down the mountain and surrendered to you," Justin said. "It only takes a few seconds to remove the firing pin from a .45, and you don't need any tools. Now unbuckle that Sam Brown rig and let it fall to the ground."

"Wait a minute, Justin. What are—"

"Bill, I'm trying to talk myself out of shooting you between the eyes, so if I were you, I would unbuckle that belt and do exactly what I was told."

Bill unbuckled his belt and let it fall to the ground.

"Now step over there where I can see you," Justin said. "Pull up your pant legs one at a time."

Bill pulled up one pant leg and then the other while Justin watched. When he pulled up the second one it revealed an ankle holster with what looked like a .32-caliber automatic in it.

"Unstrap that ankle holster and let it hit the ground," Justin ordered. "And don't touch the pistol when you do it."

Bill pulled the Velcro straps until they were free and let the rig hit the ground.

"Now take five steps backward and lie down and place your hands on the back of your head and intertwine your fingers," Justin said.

"What are you planning on doing, Hayes?"

Justin fired a round in between Bill's feet. Bill jumped backward and his face turned pale.

"If you speak again I'm going to shoot both your knees and then I'm going to sit on the porch and listen to you scream. Do you understand?"

Bill nodded yes and then took five steps backward and lay down with his fingers interlocked on the back of his head.

Justin picked up the ankle holster and the Sam Brown rig and carried them to the side of the Explorer. He opened the door and threw the guns and holsters over the back seat and all the way against the rear hatch. Justin then reached over to the shotgun that was mounted to the dash and shucked the shells out of it one at a time and threw them over the backseat as well. He then checked the glove box and found another small automatic and tossed it to the rear.

"Now get up," Justin said.

Bill stood up and stared straight ahead. He still looked pale and he was trembling.

Justin shoved his .38 back in his pocket and walked over until he was face to face with the· sheriff. "Now I'm going to get my .45 and go back inside my house and eat my lunch," Justin said. "And you're going to get into your Explorer and leave, understand?"

"Yeah, I understand," Bill said and it looked like he was getting his color back.

Justin picked his .45 up off the hood and grabbed the bag of shells and started up the front steps and Bill walked over to his Explorer and started to get in when Justin turned around and shouted, "Bill!"·

"What?"

"I let you live this time," Justin said, "but I won't the next time. If you come back on this property, I'll shoot you on sight!"

"But I'm the sheriff of this county!"

"If I ever catch you on this property, you'll be the dead sheriff of this county," Justin said as be opened the storm door. "Sic him, boys!"

Shogun and Scooter exploded through the doorway and jumped over the steps and down to the ground as Bill jumped in his vehicle and slammed the door.

Billy leaned on his cue stick and watched as Tony Fowler shot the nine ball into the side pocket. It was the third game that Tony had won and Pete Honeycutt had won the other two. Billy hadn't won a game yet. It was turning into a lousy day.

"Pay up boys!" Tony hollered as the ball fell into the leather pocket. Billy and Pete each through a five dollar bill onto the table and Tony scooped them up and shoved them in his pocket.

"What's wrong with you, Billy?" Tony said. "You usually shoot better than this!"

"I'm just having a shitty day, that's all," Billy grumbled.

"Somebody said you weren't living with your dad anymore," Pete said.

"I'm not, I moved out."

"Did it have anything to do with you driving that truck down the middle of the river?" Tony asked, smiling.

"Naw, I just needed to get away. I needed to get out on my own," Billy lied.

"I almost pissed in my pants when the old lady turned on the TV and I saw you and Johnny going down the river in that bad-ass truck," Pete said, laughing.

"It was funny as hell!" Tony said. "What possessed you to do something like that Billy?"

"I saw two guys fishing in the river and I thought that one of them was that sailor that I got in a fight with at the Hess station," Billy said. "I was gonna kick his ass, but it wasn't him."

"I'm surprised that you haven't kicked his ass yet!" Pete said.

"I haven't seen him. I can't find him," Billy said. "Dad said that he was up here to do some fishing, but I've rode up and down the north and south fork of the river and haven't seen him anywhere!"

"Oh, he's around all right, but you're not going to find him on the river," Tony said. "What do you mean by that?" Billy said as he took another sip of his beer.

"He's shacking up with the vet!" Tony said.

"The vet, You mean Jesse? Jesse Longbow?" Billy asked.

"Yeah, and I'm jealous as hell," Tony said. "Damn that's a fine looking woman!"

"Are you sure?" Billy asked.

"Hell yeah, Billy. Everybody in town knows it," Pete said. "My niece saw them in Jefferson at the Wal-Mart last Monday night and she said that they were holding hands and laughing and acting plumb silly!"

"So that's why I haven't been able to find him."

"Billy, there's people in town that say you can't beat him. That woman at the Hess station, Emma-Jean Boles, she said she saw the whole thing and that he beat you fair and square, and did it in a few seconds too!" Tony said. "Buddy Dixon and Jerry Morris said the same thing."

"Do you think you can take him, Billy?" Pete asked.

"What do you think, Pete?" Billy said, looking straight at him.

"I've seen you fight, Billy. Hell yeah, I think you can take him!"

"I can take him," Billy said. "He tricked me the first time, but the next time will be different. I'll show Emma-Jean and Buddy and Jerry and everybody else in this damn town who the best is! You'll see!"

"When you going to fight him, Billy?" Tony asked.

"Soon, Tony," Billy said as he drained the last swallow of beer from his bottle. "Real soon."

Jesse held the fishhook with a hemostat while Terry Shive, her intern, cut the barb off with a pair of wire cutters. Jesse carefully backed the hook out the same way that it went in until it was free and then tossed it onto the stainless steel surgical tray.

"There you go, Ginger, you're good as new," Jesse said to the whining yellow lab.

"I'm glad you came to work today," Terry said. "It's been crazy!"

"It usually is on Fridays," Jesse said. "When do you need to leave?"

"I need to leave by 3:30 if that's okay with you."

Jesse glanced at the clock. It was 2:30 now and she hadn't even eaten lunch yet. "Sure, it is. I need to run to the bank before you leave, so I'm going to run on now while I can and then pick up a sandwich on the way back. As soon as I get back you can run on."

"Thank you," Terry said. "I appreciate it."

Jesse pulled the surgical gloves off and threw them in the hazardous waste disposal and stepped over to the sink to wash her hands. "I'll be back in about fifteen minutes," she said as she finished drying her hands and grabbed her pocketbook. She walked out the back door and climbed in her Suburban and headed uptown. She turned in at the Wachovia Bank and jumped out with her pocketbook and went in. She still owed the bank over one hundred thousand dollars on her business loan and the payment was due on the fourteenth so it had to be paid today. Jesse walked up to the first teller and pulled out her checkbook and her payment book.

"Hey, Jesse, how are you?" the teller asked.

"Hey, Betty Sue. I'm fine. How's your cat doing?"

"She's getting better; she's starting to eat more."

"That's always a good sign," Jesse said. "I need to make a payment." Jesse slid her payment book across the counter and started writing her check.

"Tell me about this new man I been hearing about," Betty Sue said.

"Well, let's see, he's handsome, and smart, and sweet, and romantic, and funny, and I can't wait to get off of work so I can get back home and attack him!" Jesse said grinning.

"Eu-wheee, you go girl! You better keep your claws in him 'cause every woman in this town is talking about him. You can't hardly get an appointment to get your hair done since he came to town."

Jesse finished writing the check and slid it across the counter and waited for Betty Sue to give her a receipt, but Betty Sue was staring at the computer screen with a puzzled look on her face. She picked up Jesse's payment book and checked the loan number again. "Jesse, this loan is paid in full. There is a zero balance!"

"That's impossible, Betty Sue," Jesse said. "It must be a computer glitch or a mistake of some kind."

"I don't think so, honey. it shows that it was paid off at the main branch of Wachovia Bank in Greensboro, NC. Let me see if I can pull up a photocopy of the check. Yes, here it is. The check is signed by a Mrs. Kathy Maxwell. Do you know a Kathy Maxwell?"

"No, I don't know. Well, yes, I know Mrs. Maxwell, but are you sure, Betty Sue?"

"Yes, I'm positive, Jesse. I'm looking at a photocopy of the check. It was paid today at 1:09 at the main branch in Greensboro."

Jesse stood there speechless with her mouth open.

"I can't accept a payment on a loan that is paid in full," Betty Sue said. "You need to void that check Jesse. Jesse, are you all right? Jesse?"

Quai's teeth were chattering and his hands were so cold they ached. Jack had driven him to the drop-off point and helped him unload the canoe and then left. Quai had never been in a canoe, but figured if Boy Scouts and college students could do it, then he certainly could.

He figured wrong. He didn't go fifty feet before he managed to flip the canoe, and he had flipped it once more since then and the water was freezing. Jack had said that the water in the New River was warmer than the other rivers because it flowed from south to north, but if this water was warm then he would hate to see what a cold river felt like.

Quai thought about ditching the canoe and just walking the rest of the way, but this stretch of river was surrounded by the forest, and he wasn't about to walk through any forest. He wondered if there were bears watching him drift by, or maybe lions just waiting for him to come to shore. Maybe giant snakes were swimming under the canoe like in that movie he saw. This Rambo stuff was not for him.

Quai saw a large rock ahead and started paddling furiously to steer around it, but the canoe refused to turn and he slammed into it, spinning the canoe around backward. Why can't they put a steering wheel on these damn things, he thought to himself. He didn't know how he did it, but he managed to spin the canoe back around and he took a big breath and felt relieved until he looked ahead and saw the rapids. He was absolutely terrified. It looked like to him that he was going over Niagara Falls and he pissed on himself for the first time in years. As the canoe picked up speed and entered the rapids he screamed and dropped the paddle so he could grip the sides of the canoe. The canoe pitched back and forth and he held on like a six-year-old on a rollercoaster. In the center of the river were two huge rocks jutting up seven or eight feet into the air and he was heading straight through the center of them until the canoe bumped a small rock just under the surface and turned. The front of the canoe caught the rock on the right and the canoe spun around and flipped so fast that Quai didn't even have time to shut his eyes before he hit the water. He came up coughing and gagging and screamed for help. For someone who didn't want to be seen, he was making a hell of a racket. Quai finally grabbed onto a rock and got stopped. He felt for the bottom and then stood up and was amazed that the water was only two and a half feet deep, and then he sloshed to the shore where he collapsed.

Quai shivered as he lay on the rocky shore and tried to catch his breath. After several minutes he regained his composure and finally stood up. He looked upstream first and the canoe was nowhere in sight, so he looked downstream and the canoe was still nowhere in sight but something else was. The small white farmhouse that was surrounded by maple trees stood about a quarter of a mile away, and to Quai it was a beautiful sight.

Quai checked to make sure that his fanny pack was still attached to him and then spun it around and unzipped it. The contents were all enclosed in plastic Ziploc storage bags and he took the nine-millimeter Glock pistol out of its bag and shoved it under his belt and then pulled his shirttail out to conceal it. He would be warm soon, and Justin and Carol would be the ones that were cold.

Jesse locked the front door of the animal hospital and headed for the back. She was still in shock from her trip to the bank this evening. She had called Travis and told him that she couldn't accept such a gift and Travis said that when she got home they would call his mother and talk to her about it. Jesse grabbed her pocketbook and cut out the lights before stepping outside and locking the door. It had been an overly busy day and she couldn't wait to get back home and take a bath. Travis had already fed the horses and put fresh water in their buckets and he fed the chickens and the kittens so that Jesse could relax when she got home.

Jesse walked over to her suburban and got in and shut the door. As she cranked the engine she noticed an odor inside the cab and realized that the odor she smelled was beer.

Thinking that some jerk must have thrown a beer can into the back of her SUV, she turned around and was looking straight into the bloodshot eyes of Billy Billings. Jesse screamed and tried to open the door, but Billy was holding the door lock down with his left hand and stuck a pistol to her head with his right hand.

"What are you doing Billy?" Jesse screamed.

"I heard you had a new boyfriend Jesse. Is that true?"

"Billy, let me go! Get out of my truck!"

"You didn't answer my question! I heard you're shacking up with a sailor that I've been looking for."

"We broke up! He moved out yesterday. Now get out of my truck!" Jesse shouted.

"If he moved out yesterday, why did he leave his Jeep behind your house? I rode by there about an hour ago and saw it!"

"Billy, when Joshua gets back from Afghanistan he will hunt you down for this!"

"I'll worry about that when he gets back. Now drive!" Billy shouted and Jesse was engulfed in his beer breath.

"Billy, this is kidnapping!"

"Either you can drive me to your house, or me and you can stay here and party," Billy said in an evil voice. "I'm to the point where I really don't care. Johnny's dead, daddy threw me out of the house, I can't find a job, and everybody in town is talking about the sailor that kicked my ass, so I'm not worried about your brother Joshua or about being charged with kidnapping. Now either start driving, or start taking off your clothes!"

Quai turned and started up Carol's driveway. Everything about the place was neat and organized. The house was well cared for and there was nothing out of place. All the shrubbery was evenly spaced and even the two rocking chairs on the front porch were turned exactly the same. Quai was anxious to look in Carol's panty drawer. He would bet that all her panties were folded and stacked in neat rows. He would find out shortly.

Quai glanced around to make sure that no one was in sight and then walked up the steps and knocked on the front door.

"I'm coming!" a voice rang out and he could hear footsteps that were getting louder. There was a loud click as someone unlocked the door, and that was exactly what Quai wanted to hear. From this point on he was in charge of the outcome. The door swung open and there she stood in a bathrobe and bedroom slippers. He felt the excitement starting to build as he stood there wringing wet and shaking from the cold.

"Can I help you?" Carol asked.

"Yes, ma'am, I'm sorry to bother you but I turned my canoe over and it went downstream and left me stranded. Could I please use your phone to call my brother to come and get me?"

"Why, sure you can, bless your heart, you're all wet and cold," Carol said. "Come on in and I'll fix you some coffee and get you a towel to dry off with."

Carol turned and walked back through the house quickly and Quai stepped inside and shut the door behind him. He walked slowly through the living room and into the kitchen where Carol had gone. When he walked into the kitchen, Quai was shocked to see Carol sitting on the counter facing him with her legs crossed seductively and her bathrobe pulled open revealing her ample cleavage.

"Tell me something, Quai," Carol said. "Were you going to rape me before you killed Justin, or afterward?"

Quai's eyes were normally slanted, but were perfectly round now as he stared at this woman and wondered how she knew so much. He started to rush her but noticed two red dots on his chest, and tried to spin around just as the darts from the tasers entered his chest.

Jesse turned into her driveway and started up the hill and Billy pushed the barrel of the pistol against the back of her head to remind her not to try anything foolish.

"Why didn't you just drive up here and fight him like a man instead of kidnapping me?" Jesse asked Billy angrily.

"Because he would probably come out of the house with a shot-gun, that's why! Now shut up and do what I say!"

"Mayday! Mayday! Eagle this is Iceman. The Doc is pulling up and has white male in the backseat holding a pistol to her head. Do you copy?"

"Affirmative Iceman. What is your yardage?"

"Three-fifty to three seventy-five max. Chip shot Eagle!"

"Be ready to engage! Send me video."

"Video's rolling Eagle. Ready to engage. Over."

Maggie was going nuts so Travis stepped to the back door and saw Jesse when she drove by the house. His heart almost stopped when he saw Billy holding the pistol to her head and he ran toward them until Billy screamed for him to stop. Travis stood in the yard shaking with anger. If he hurts her I will kill him, he thought to himself.

"Now cut the engine off and throw the keys out the window," Billy ordered.

Jesse did as instructed. She would have never driven him here, even if it meant that she got raped, if she thought that he would hurt Travis. But she knew that a sniper was hidden on the side of the mountain somewhere, and she was hoping that he was good at his trade.

Billy pulled a set of handcuffs out of his back pocket and threw them on the seat beside of Jesse. "Snap one side on your wrist and then stick that arm through the steering wheel before you snap the other side on. Hurry!" Billy shouted as he stared at Travis through the window.

"Iceman, this is Eagle. We have backup rolling. Stand by."

"Roger that, Eagle."

"Lock that damn dog up or I'll shoot her!" Billy hollered to Travis.

Maggie was circling the suburban growling and Travis intercepted her and carried her over to Jesse's dog kennel and locked her inside. "Okay Billy, she's locked up! Now let Jesse go. This is between you and me!" Travis shouted.

Billy opened the back door and stepped out. He was holding the pistol down by his side and grinning at Travis as he turned to face him.

Jimmy was sitting on the edge of his seat in the tobacco barn as he watched the drama unfold. "Iceman, if Tango raises the pistol you are green light to shoot. Over!"

"Roger that Eagle. Taking up the slack."

"Are you okay, Jesse?" Travis hollered.

"I'm okay," Jesse responded.

"Let her go Billy. I'm warning you!"

"I can't do that sailor boy. I promised her that after I beat you to death that me and her would party some tonight," Billy said. "I'm looking forward to that almost as much as I am kicking your ass."

"You're not going to be able to kiss her with a broken jaw!"

"You'll never touch my jaw this time sailor boy," Billy said. "Fool me once, shame on you, fool me twice, shame on me. Now take your shirt off and empty your pockets. I want to make sure you're not armed."

Travis pulled his tee-shirt off and turned his pockets inside out. He unclipped his cell phone and stepped over to the clothes line and clipped it to one of the wires. He knew that Jimmy was listening to this and that a Seal sniper was watching it through a rifle scope. Travis took his key ring and threw it down in front of Billy.

"Take my Jeep and leave Billy and we'll forget this ever happened," Travis said. "You're drunk, and I don't want to kill you."

"You don't want to kill me!" Billy said and then started laughing. "I think you want me to leave because you're afraid to fight me!"

"You don't understand Billy. I've been to Japan and studied *Yo-ursu-cham-oron* under the great Master Gichin Funakoshi. Please just drive away! I don't want to kill you!" Travis pleaded.

"I've heard of Gichin Funakoshi, but I never heard of *Yo-ursu-cham-oron*," Billy said.

"*Yo-ursu-cham-oron* is Japanese for 'without moving a step,'" Travis explained. "I can channel my energy and strike you without ever moving, like a bullet coming out of the sky. It's just like you've been struck by a bullet. Please just drive away, there's been enough killing around here without you dying too!"

"Iceman, this is Eagle. Do you have a silencer?"

"Affirmative, Eagle, but it's not on the rifle."

"Screw it on, and hurry!"

"Sam Pasciuti didn't know what was going on but he just received an order, so he grabbed his drag bag and found the pocket that held the silencer. He unzipped the pocket and grabbed the silencer and quickly started screwing it on the Heckler and Koch PSG1 sniper rifle. "Silencer is on, Eagle!"

"Stand by for a shot, Iceman."

"You don't expect me to believe that bullshit, do you?" Billy said, grinning.

"I can prove it, Billy! I know you don't believe it and I didn't either until I went to Japan and saw it for myself," Travis said. "I can blow up that pistol you're holding by just pointing my fingers at it and channeling all my energy into it."

"I think you've been watching to many of those B-rated karate movies, that's what I think."

"If you lay the pistol on the ground beside your feet, I'll prove it to you. I'm twenty feet from you, and I'll destroy it without ever moving my feet!"

"I think you're just stalling for time because you're scared, sailor boy," Billy said grinning. "But I want to see this demonstration of *Yo-ursu-cham-oron*, so I'm going to lay the pistol on top of this log and let you channel your energy and destroy it." Billy walked toward the chicken house until he was standing beside a four foot section of a huge oak tree that had been turned up on its end so that it could be used for a table. It was where Jesse's grandmother Leah had chopped the heads off of hundreds of chickens and turkeys over the years. When Billy got beside the make-shift table he turned and stared at Travis. "Before I lay this pistol on top of this log, you need to know that if you try to rush me I'm going to pick it up and shoot you. So don't try any tricks, sailor boy."

"Iceman, this is Eagle. On my command, shoot the pistol. I repeat, when I say fire, shoot the pistol. Do you copy?"

"Roger that, Eagle, preparing for shot." Sam thought that he was going to have to shoot at a person, not a pistol. He took his laser ranger finder and pointed it at the log and pressed the button. The viewfinder read 357 yards. He then grabbed his ballistic log book and turned to the page with all his scope adjustments that he had recorded while firing the rifle with the silencer attached. The bullet trajectory was slightly different with the silencer attached, and trying to hit a pistol at 357 yards didn't leave him with any room for error. Sam dialed in his elevation and windage adjustments and turned his parallax adjustment until his sight picture was clear and crisp. He then settled into his shooting position and started searching for his natural point of aim, and gradually got into the bubble. Nothing existed except for what he could see through the rifle scope. The crosshairs were resting on the silver colored pistol with just a slight tremble every time his heart beat. "Ready to fire, Eagle."

"I've heard of some weird shit before, but this has got to be the weirdest!" Billy shouted. "Okay sailor boy, there's the pistol. Let's see you destroy it without moving your feet. But you can't put off this ass-whipping any longer. After this demonstration of *Yo-ursu-cham-oron* or whatever the hell you said it was, it's just you and me. I've been waiting a week, and I'm not going to wait any longer!"

"Okay, Billy, I'm going to raise my hands over my head, and when I lower them and point at the pistol, it will explode."

"Right. Sure it will." Billy laughed.

Travis shut his eyes and took a deep breath. He slowly raised both his arms until they were pointing straight up and they were clasped together like he was praying. He stood motionless for a long moment in deep concentration, and then opened his eyes widely and stared at the pistol. Suddenly Travis screamed, "Keeeyieee!" and jerked his arms down and pointed at the pistol with both his index fingers.

"Fire!" Eagle said.

Sam took the last six ounces of pressure left on the trigger of the PSG1 and the German-built sniper rifle fired.

Billy was laughing as he watched the sailor standing there screaming and pointing his fingers at the pistol—that is, until the pistol exploded and flew into about five pieces. Billy jumped backward with a jump that would have impressed Bruce Lee, and then stared at the log in disbelief.

Travis stood there trying to keep a straight face, but the look on Billy's face of shock, fear amazement, disbelief, and at least ten other emotions was just too much. He started to laugh and then held it in for just a brief moment, and then he heard Jesse giggling and he lost it. Travis busted out laughing and unknowingly started a chain reaction. The FBI agents and the Navy Seals in the tobacco barn busted out laughing, and the CIA and military personnel watching from the Pentagon busted out laughing, and finally Iceman, who was watching the show through his Schmidt and Bender sniper scope, couldn't stand it anymore and he started laughing too.

"Nice shot, Iceman! Over," Jimmy said in between laughs.

"I hope I don't have to make another one. I'm laughing too hard now, Eagle!"

"Don't worry, Iceman. The cavalry is coming up the driveway! Over."

A black van came flying up Jesse's driveway and almost went airborne when it crested the hill. The side door was open and men wearing camouflage and carrying automatic weapons were jumping out even before it came to a stop. They surrounded Billy and ordered him to the ground, and then put zip ties around his wrists and ankles.

"What the hell is going on?" Billy demanded.

"FBI! You're under arrest for kidnapping and assault with a deadly weapon. You have the right to remain silent. Everything you do or say.

While they were reading Billy his rights, one of the men on the Special Response Team found the handcuff key in Billy's pocket and threw it to Travis, who ran to the Suburban and released Jesse. They stood beside the driver's door and held each other tight. They didn't know whether to laugh or cry, so they did both. After a moment, one of the FBI agents stepped over to them.

"I'm Agent Corey Wallace with the FBI's Special Response Team. Are both of you all right?"

"Yes, we're fine," Jesse said as she wiped a tear from her face. "Thank you so much for your help."

"You're welcome, ma'am. Is there anything else I can do for you before we leave with the prisoner?"

"Let me talk to him a minute before you take him away," Travis said, and he and Jesse walked over to the side of the van where Billy was sitting surrounded by four officers.

Billy looked up at Travis and snarled, "This ain't over, sailor boy!"

"Actually, Billy, it is over, at least for a few years, because you're going to be in prison."

"Don't count on it. My daddy will get me out of this, and when he does, I'll be back!"

"Your daddy is going to be in there with you, Billy. The good news is, you'll get three meals a day and a roof over your head and if you want to practice your fighting skills, I'm sure that some of those boys in the federal penitentiary will be glad to oblige you."

"Answer me one thing. How did you blow up that pistol?"

"The ancient art of *Yo-ursu-cham-oron*, Billy," Travis said. "Let me write that down for you." Travis got a pencil and a piece of paper from one of the men and scribbled something on it before showing it to Billy.

"In Japanese, it's *Yo-ursu-cham-oron*. But in English, it's 'You're such a moron.'"

Billy stared at the piece of paper and then tried to lunge at Travis, but the officers pushed him to the ground.

"Fool me once, shame on you. Fool me twice, shame on me," Travis said. "Okay, Agent Wallace, take this piece of shit away."

Billy was screaming obscenities as the officers threw him into the van and then piled in on top of him and drove away. Jesse ran over to the kennel and let Maggie out and rubbed her head before walking back over and hugging Travis.

"Let's go inside, sweetie," Jesse said as she kissed Travis. "I need a hot bath, a cold beer, and a massage."

"Sounds great, but I need to do one more thing before we go inside," Travis said.

"What's that?"

"This," Travis said and he turned and faced the mountain. Travis snapped to attention and saluted the mountain, and then put his arm around Jesse and walked toward the house.

Iceman smiled and returned the salute even though he knew they would never see him. "You're welcome!" he said out loud.

The Calm before the Storm

Johnny Steele turned onto Cranberry Creek Road and drove slowly along as he searched the river. There had been no word from Quai and Jack had been up all night pacing back and forth wondering why he hadn't heard from him. Jack now sat motionless in the passenger seat. He was very near total exhaustion and he looked like he had aged ten years.

"You don't think he would have just taken off do you?" Johnny asked.

"No, he was looking forward to it," Jack said drearily. "He was almost drooling when we rode through here day before yesterday."

"I guess it's possible that he flipped the canoe and hit his head on a rock or something," Johnny added.

"I guess it's possible," Jack said, "but you know as well as I do that as soon as it gets hot weather they'll be little kids and fat women and even old folks coming through here everyday on canoes, and the only time you ever here about anybody drowning is when there drunk like my brother was when he drowned."

Johnny cruised along slowly for several more minutes until they rounded a curve and could see Carol's house in the distance.

"Keep it slow, Johnny. I want to look real good when we ride by," Jack said. "For all I know that sick bastard could still be in there cutting them up in pieces."

Johnny kept the Hummer steady as they crept by Carol's house. There were no lights on in the house and there was no sign of life.

"Her car is gone," Jack said. "There's not a vehicle anywhere in sight."

"I believe he took off, Jack," Johnny said. "I think staying cooped up inside the motel was starting to get on his nerves, and when he finally got out and tasted freedom again, he killed Carol and then stole her car and hit the road."

"Drive into town and find a payphone. I'm going to call his cell phone again and see if he'll answer it," Jack ordered.

"Look, Jack!" Johnny said pointing toward the river. "There's the canoe!"

Jack looked in the direction of the river and saw the canoe. It was washed up against some rocks and was floating on its side.

"Well, we know he ditched the canoe," Jack said. "Who knows, maybe he killed Justin after all, he wasn't in the front yard this morning with his dogs like he normally is."

"You want me to load up the canoe?"

"No, to hell with that canoe. Get me to a payphone!"

"Yes, sir."

"I don't think I'd ever make it in prison," Justin said to Teresa. "I've been cooped up for just two days and I'm already going insane!"

"If I was cooped up with you it wouldn't be so bad, would it?" Teresa said in her sexiest voice.

"I could probably live in a cave with you, darling," Justin answered as a car horn blew in the background at Teresa's house.

"Oh, I got to go, sweetie. My girlfriends are here to pick me up to go eat breakfast. I love you and I can't wait to see you again!"

"I love you too."

"I'll call you later on today," Teresa said, and Justin heard the car horn blow again. "Okay, honey. Bye now."

"Bye, darling."

Justin hung up the phone and looked out the window at the New River as it flowed by in all its grandeur. Being confined to his house was slowly killing him he thought as he watched two tom turkeys step out from behind some mountain laurel bushes and head to the river for a drink. "Rejoicing in Hope, patient in tribulation," Justin said, quoting a verse of scripture from the book of Romans. Justin leaned back and picked his Bible up off the end table and flipped it open. He stuck his finger on the page to randomly select a verse to read.

It was 1 Kings, chapter 20, the 29th verse. "And they pitched one over against the other seven days. And so it was, that in the seventh day the battle was joined; and the children of Israel slew of the Syrians an hundred thousand footman in one day. But the rest fled to Aphek, into the city; and there a wall fell upon twenty and seven thousand of the men that were left."

Justin tried to visualize what that battle must have looked like on that day many, many years ago. The Bible said that the children of Israel numbered only seven thousand, and that was counting the children, but on the day of this battle they slaughtered over a hundred thousand Syrian soldiers and then twenty-seven thousand of the survivors were killed when a wall fell on them. As hard as he tried, Justin couldn't imagine a battlefield with over a hundred thousand dead soldiers lying on it.

DeMac walked into the living room and stepped over to look out one of the picture windows. "Reading your Bible?" he asked.

"Yeah, I was just reading about the Israeli army," Justin said. "I sure am glad that when I was in the army we were fighting the Vietnamese instead of the Israelites!"

"They have an awesome army to be as small a country as they are," DeMac said.

"If you think their army is awesome now, you should read about it back before Christ!" Justin said.

"While I'm thinking about it, Jimmy called a little while ago and said he was going to stop by this morning and fill us in on what's going on," DeMac said. "He also said that Wade Shavers was planning on coming over here later on today, and he wants you to call him and make up some excuse to keep him at home."

"How does he know that?"

"He heard Wade telling one of his buddies about it over the phone."

"They have his phone tapped too?"

"It's the CIA, Justin," DeMac said, "They have everybody's phone tapped."

Justin picked up the phone book and flipped through it until he found the Shaver's phone number and then he dialed it.

"Shaver's Farm, Wade speaking."

"Wade, this is Justin. How you doing?"

"I'm doing good, Mr. Hayes."

"How are the dogs working out?"

"They're great, Mr. Hayes! They act like they already know what to do," Wade said excitedly.

"They do know what they're supposed to do," Justin said. "A friend of mine named Jimmy Hayworth runs a farm and a dog kennel in Oak Ridge, and that's where those dogs came from. Jimmy was training them when they were five months old to herd ducks."

"Ducks?" Wade asked.

"Yeah, that's how they start training pups to herd."

"The only thing that bothers me is sometimes they act like they want me to tell them what to do, and I don't know what to say to them."

"That's why I wanted to call you. Jimmy's coming up here the first of next month and he's going to house sit for me for a week while

I'm in Florida. He likes to trout fish and I told him you could show him where some good places are to fish, and in exchange, he's going to spend a couple of days with you and show you how to train your dogs. He's already trained your dogs to respond to a whistle."

"That will be so cool, Mr. Hayes. I really appreciate all you've done for me. Is there anything you need me to do for you?"

"Actually, there is, when Jimmy comes up here to fish, how about mowing my yard that week so that he won't have to do it."

"I sure will, Mr. Hayes. I'll mow it all summer if you want me to."

"No, that won't be necessary, Wade, just when I'm gone or if I get sick or something."

"Okay. Uh, Mr. Hayes, do you think I'm ready to start shooting farther than three hundred yards? I might get a shot at a coyote like you did that's over five hundred yards."

"Yes, you're ready as you'll ever be," Justin said, smiling. "Can I come over there today and try?" Wade asked.

"That's another reason I called you this morning Wade," Justin said. "I've managed somehow to catch a stomach virus and I'm squirting like a goose. Better not come over here for a day or two until I can get rid of this."

"Oh, okay. I' m sorry you're sick."

"It's no big deal, Wade. I just can't get too far away from the bathroom. I'll be better in a few days and I'll give you a call."

"Okay, Mr. Hayes. If you need anything just let me know."

"Okay, Wade, I'll holler if I need you. Bye now."

"Good-bye, Mr. Hayes."

Jack dialed the number for Quai's cell phone and listened as it rang. After six or seven rings it went to an automatic message center and Jack hung up. He was standing in an old phone booth that was located behind the Sparta Livestock Arena, totally hidden from any-one's view.

"Give me some more quarters," Jack said to Johnny.

Johnny handed Jack a handful of quarters and he fed them into the phone and dialed Carol's phone number. He listened intently as the phone rang and rang until it finally switched to Carol's voice mail. Jack hung the receiver up and bowed his head as he thought about what he should do next.

"I'm going to call Justin's house," Jack finally said. "I've got to know if he's dead or alive. He wasn't in his front yard this morning like he normally is. Maybe Quai killed the son of a bitch after all."

Jack fed more quarters into the thirty-year-old payphone and dialed Justin's number.

"Hello? Hello? Is anyone there?"

Jack hung the phone up. Justin was still alive and well. Dammit, no one could touch this man. Sheriff Sisk was scared to death of him. Tommy Sides disappeared in front of his house. Johnny Steele never even touched his pistol before he had him covered, he shot and killed two men and never spent one night in jail, and now the best assas-sin on the East Coast according to Jimmy Milano couldn't kill him! What the hell is going on, Jack wondered.

Jack jerked the receiver back off the cradle and started beating the payphone with it until it shattered and flew into several pieces. Johnny Steele stood there and didn't move and didn't speak.

"Let's go back to the house," Jack said. "I'm beginning to think that I'm going to have to kill the son of a bitch myself."

Shogun and Scooter both started barking as the white van with Alleghany Refrigeration painted on its side came up Justin's drive-way. Jimmy drove around back and parked at the carport. He gave the dogs a pat on the head before walking to the back door where

DeMac let him in. He looked exhausted. His eyes were red and he was walking slowly.

"Hey, DeMac. Hey, Justin. I just came by to fill you in on a couple of things."

"Stop. Stop right there!" Justin ordered.

"What do you mean stop?" Jimmy barked.

"I mean for you to stop!" Justin repeated. "Go into my bathroom and take a nice long shower and then come back in here and fill us in over a nice hot breakfast."

"I really don't have time."

"Bullshit! You're in charge of this operation and there are plenty of capable men that can run this thing for one hour while you shower and eat," Justin said. "You look like hell Jimmy!"

"I know I look rough, but—"

"What do you want for breakfast?" Justin asked.

"I really can't stay."

"French toast, hotcakes, eggs, sausage, ham, bacon, an omelet, oatmeal, liver pudding.

"I appreciate it, Justin, but—"

"If you don't take a shower and eat some breakfast, I'm going to walk down to Jack's house and beat on the front gate!"

"Knowing you, you probably would! Okay, okay. I'll go shower and talk to you over breakfast," Jimmy said as he started through the house. "Two eggs scrambled with ham and biscuits."

"Grits or hash brown potatoes?" Justin said smiling.

"Potatoes. You're a pain in the ass, Sergeant Hayes!"

"Thank you, sir," Justin said.

Travis and Jesse stood on the marble floor and held hands as they waited for someone to answer the door at the Maxwell residence. The door finally opened, but instead of the beautiful Latino maid, it was a butler that opened the door this time.

"May I help you?" the butler asked.

"I'm Mrs. Maxwell's son Travis, and this is my girlfriend Jessica. I would like to see my mother if it's possible."

"Please come in," the butler said as he held the door open and gestured with his other arm for them to step inside. "Mrs. Maxwell has told me all about you," the butler said. "My name is Walter. Mrs. Maxwell is feeling poorly this morning, so if you would be so kind as to wait here, I will go ask her if she can see you."

"Certainly," Travis responded.

The butler left rapidly and returned in a flash. "Mrs. Maxwell is thrilled that you have come and wants to see you immediately."

"Thank you, Walter," Travis said.

"Please follow me," Walter said and he led them down the hallway toward the master bedroom. Walter opened the bedroom door and gestured for them to enter. "Mrs. Maxwell is in the Sun Room. Can I get either of you something to drink?"

"No, thank you."

"Very well. Ring for me if you change your mind," Walter said and then he was gone.

Jesse and Travis walked through the magnificent bedroom toward the French doors that led into the Sun Room. Kathy was sitting there wearing a beautiful red silk robe. The robe was embroidered with a large gold dragon and a beautiful golden sunrise that was rising in between two Bonsai trees. Jesse and Travis both hugged Kathy before they took their seat. It broke Travis's heart when he looked at his mother. She was very pale and she trembled slightly as she sat there and tried to smile. It was obvious that she needed to be in bed, and Travis now wished that he had called her before they came.

"That's the most beautiful robe that I have ever seen," Jesse said to Kathy.

"Thank you. I bought it in Tokyo and I've always loved it."

"I guess we should have called before we came barging in," Travis said.

"Nonsense. You're family and you can come anytime you like. I'm so glad that you're here."

"Mrs. Maxwell," Jesse said.

"Kathy. Just call me Kathy, honey," she said smiling.

"Okay, Kathy. I was absolutely floored yesterday when I found out that you—"

"You're welcome, Jessica." Kathy interrupted her with a smile.

"But, Mrs. uh, Kathy, I can't possibly accept such a gift."

"Yes, you can and you will."

"But I'm just dating your son. I'm not even related to you and I've only met you once before today!"

"It doesn't matter," Kathy said. "It doesn't even matter if something happens and you two lovebirds break-up, although from what I've seen I don't think that will happen. There have been some dramatic changes in this house and in myself since you were here last. I'm sure you noticed that Maria is gone. I ran every woman in this house off and hired all men. If Paul wants to cheat on me in this house, then he'll have to become a homosexual to do it!" Kathy said and Travis and Jesse both couldn't help but to chuckle.

"I called Justin yesterday and spoke with him briefly, and after we talked I sat here and cried and cried as I thought about the twenty years that we spent together. Justin Hayes is probably the most remarkable man on this planet. He goes day to day with absolutely no thoughts about his own needs or desires. His number one priority in life has always been to help other people that were in need, and it used to drive me crazy. He used to say that the only real joy on this side of heaven was being able to help somebody, but I didn't care about anybody else. I only cared about myself. I wanted nicer things, a bigger house, a fancy car, expensive jewelry. I was greedy and selfish, and it has cost me dearly."

"Mama, you don't have to—"

"Let me finish, Travis, while I've got the strength," Kathy said. "Please!"

"Okay, Mama," Travis said as tears came to the corners of his eyes.

"Yesterday when I signed the check and had my attorney take it to the bank, I felt the best that I've felt in years. It was absolutely wonderful! Knowing that I helped somebody out was the most remarkable feeling that I have ever experienced. I have been sick for over three years, and none of my so-called friends or any of the wives of Paul's business associates have come to see me, not one!" Kathy said sternly. "But Jessica you came to see me, so I did some checking up on you. I found out how you have struggled all your life and I wanted to help you, not because you're dating my son, but because you are such a wonderful and sweet person and you have had such a hard life. So please Jessica, let me give you this gift. It means so much to me, more than you could ever imagine."

"Jesse was crying as she stared at Kathy. "I don't know what to say."

"Say thank you," Kathy said.

"Thank you," Jesse whimpered. "I don't deserve this."

"You're welcome, and you do deserve it," Kathy said and then she turned to face Travis. "Now as for you Travis, I abandoned you when you were ten years old and there is absolutely nothing that I can do now to make up for that."

"You don't have to do anything, Mama," Travis said.

"I know but I already have. I had my attorney set up a trust fund in your name for one hundred thousand dollars, but you can't collect it until I die. I don't think you're going to have to wait very long for that to happen."

"Mama, you don't have to do that!" Travis said. "I forgave you for leaving me, and I love you just like we were never apart!"

"I know you do, and do you know why?" Kathy said. "Because you're Justin Hayes son, that's why! You have no idea how good it felt to put one hundred thousand dollars of Paul Maxwell's money into an account for you."

"Mama, are you sure?"

"Travis," Kathy interrupted, "press that button beside you please."

Travis stopped talking and looked until he saw the button beside him that his mother was pointing at and he pushed it for her. Almost instantly a door could be heard shutting and Walter came across the bedroom and entered the Sun Room.

"You called me, Madam?"

"Yes, Walter. Would you bring us a bottle of champagne and three glasses please?"

"Certainly, Madam," Walter said and he turned and left quickly.

"I want to toast my new family," Kathy said. "My cancer is no longer in remission, and my poor old liver is just barely functioning, but my heart feels better than it has in years! I am finally at peace with myself, and it feels so wonderful."

"That's great, Mama," Travis said. "I'm glad you're finally at peace."

"I have had everything my heart desired, and yet I've been completely miserable for the last fifteen years, but now thanks to the two of you, I feel good again."

Jesse couldn't sit there any longer, so she got up and stepped around the coffee table and took Kathy in her arms and Travis soon joined them. Walter came in carrying a tray with three champagne glasses, and an ice bucket with a bottle of expensive champagne just barely visible above the shaved ice.

"Okay everyone, dry your eyes and get a glass," Kathy said. "I'm going to quit sitting around here crying and start smiling for a change."

Everyone grabbed a tissue and dried their eyes and took a glass from the tray that Walter was holding. Walter set the tray down and removed the bottle of champagne from the ice bucket and opened it expertly. He rested the bottle across the towel that was draped over his left forearm and poured all three glasses about half full.

Kathy held her glass up in front of her. I want everybody to propose a toast. I'll go first," she said as she straightened her back and stared at her glass. "To second chances and new beginnings!"

"To new beginnings!" Travis said and they all three touched their glasses and then drained them. Walter quickly filled their glasses again and then stepped back and stood like a statue.

It was Travis's turn. "To my father Justin Hayes, who told me to go see my mother, and to just follow my heart."

"To Justin Hayes," Kathy and Jesse said, and they all three touched their glasses again and then drained them.

"To my beloved grandmother Leah," Jesse said, "who never really had anything, but still taught me how to laugh and how to love."

"To Leah," Travis and Kathy said simultaneously, and they touched their glasses and drank.

"Let's go around again," Kathy said. "I'm having fun with my new family and I don't want to stop." Walter immediately stepped forward and filled their glasses again.

"To Jessica Longbow and Travis Hayes, the most beautiful couple that I've ever known," Kathy said. Jesse and Travis looked at each other the way that only two people madly in love with each other can, and they drained their glasses for the fourth time.

After their glasses were refilled again, Travis came to attention. "To this wonderful country that we live in, and to all the men and women who stand in harms way to protect it!"

"Hear, hear!" Walter suddenly blurted out, and Kathy, Travis, and Jesse all turned and stared at him.

"Oh, pardon me," Walter said, blushing. "I'm afraid I got carried away. I'm so sorry for the interruption. I beg your forgiveness."

"Walter, are you a veteran?" Travis asked with a puzzled look.

"Yes, sir, but that doesn't excuse my behavior. I am truly sorry for disrupting your gathering," Walter said with his head bowed.

"What branch?" Travis continued.

"Marine Corps, sir," Walter said without looking up. "Please continue with your party."

"Well, that would explain your outburst. Did you serve overseas?"

"Yes, sir, in Operation Iraqi Freedom from February 2003 until August of 2003 in the city of Fallujah, Al Anbar Province. Please ignore me, Mr. Hayes."

"Walter," Kathy said, "go get another glass and bring Ethan back with you."

"As you wish, Madam," Walter said with a red face and he practically ran from the room. He returned soon carrying another glass and another butler was following him.

"Ethan, take that champagne bottle away from Walter and pour his glass full," Kathy ordered. "Walter, you are officially off duty until I say otherwise."

"But, Madam—"

"It's your turn, Walter. Propose a toast!" Kathy said and she held her glass up in front of her.

"But, Madam, this is so inappropriate," Walter pleaded.

"I'll decide what's inappropriate around here!" Kathy blurted. "Now propose a toast before I pass out."

"Very well, Madam, if you insist," Walter finally conceded and he snapped to attention without spilling a drop of his champagne. "To the Corps, Semper Fidelis!"

"Hoo-ahh!" Travis grunted and they all touched their glasses and then drained them.

"Now, Walter and Ethan, help me to my bed," Kathy said. "I think I'm drunk."

Cecil walked into Jack's bedroom and stepped over to the window where Jack sat behind a spotting scope that was trained on Justin's house.

"Jack, I need to talk to you about a few things if you can spare a minute."

Jack swiveled around to face Cecil and Cecil was shocked at what he saw. "Jack, you look like death warmed over! You better start getting some rest or you're going to have a heart attack."

"I won't be able to rest until that son of a bitch is dead!" Jack said as he nodded his head toward Justin's house. "What is it you need to talk about?"

"For starters, Walt's body has been released to his wife and she had Jackson Funeral Home pick it up. The Wake is tomorrow night and the funeral is at 2:00 p.m. Monday. She called me this morning and hinted around that she didn't have the money to pay for the funeral."

"Call her back and tell her that I will pay for the funeral, but I want her to sign a waiver that states that we're not responsible for his death. I don't want her to come up three months from now and sue us after we paid to bury him."

"Okay, I'll draw up an agreement that protects us provided we pay for all his funeral expenses," Cecil said.

Jack pushed the intercom button. "Ashley, bring me a Seagram's 7 and a 7-Up."

"Yes, sir," Ashley's voice came back.

"I also got a call from the State Medical Examiner's Office and they have completed the autopsy on Johnny and are prepared to release his body. Johnny's mother, Amy, called me yesterday evening and she wants you to release the body to her. She said that she will pay for his funeral, but she wants to bury him in Mt. Airy and she doesn't want you to attend the funeral."

"That bitch!" Jack snarled as Ashley walked into the room with his drink. Ashley turned and left and Jack took a big swallow from the glass. "Go ahead and let her have the body," Jack said with tears starting down his face. "I don't think I could go to his funeral anyway."

"Very well. There's just one more thing. I tried to notify Billy about Walt and Johnny's funeral arrangements, but I couldn't get him to answer his phone, so I sent Lee to find him and he couldn't. He wasn't at home and nobody has seen him."

"Send Brooks Walker and Charles Moses. They can probably find him. And give them a couple hundred dollars to give to him when they do."

"Okay, Jack, I'll take care of it," Cecil said as he turned to leave.

"Cecil, have you ever heard of Alleghany Refrigeration?" Jack asked.

"I can't say that I have," Cecil said as he turned back around.

"I saw a white van drive up to Justin's a little while ago and that's what it said on the side of it."

"Want me to check it out?"

"Yeah, check it out and get back to me," Jack said as he looked back through the spotting scope.

"Okay, Jack, I'll find out where they're from."

"Thank you, Cecil. I'm going to take a nap, so just check back with me later on," Jack said as he drained the rest of his drink. Jack leaned back and shut his eyes and was asleep before Cecil left the room.

Jimmy finished off the eggs, ham, and hash brown potatoes that Justin had fixed for him and grabbed one more biscuit and started spreading butter and sourwood honey on it.

"You look much better," Justin said as he sipped his coffee.

"I feel much better. Thank you for your hospitality."

"You're welcome."

"Did you call Wade Shavers?" Jimmy asked.

"Yeah, I told him I had a stomach virus."

"Good," Jimmy said and then took a big bite of his biscuit. "This is the best honey I've ever eaten," Jimmy mumbled. "Where do you get it?"

"Good sourwood honey is just like moonshine, Jimmy, the best comes from the mountains of North Carolina, but you have to know somebody to get it."

"I see," Jimmy said as he swallowed the last bite. "Well, men, here's the latest. Quai Son Bien has been arrested. He pretended to capsize a canoe and then walked to Carol Crissman's house and she let him in so he could supposedly call somebody to come pick him up. We had two FBI agents waiting inside and when he came in they tased him."

"How did you know that he would show up there?" Justin asked.

"After they rode by here the other day, Jack and Quai drove over to Carol's house and rode by real slow and checked the place out. We figured that Quai was afraid to try and kill you at your house, so he decided to go to Carol's and overpower her, and then use her as bait to get you to come over there, then he would kill you and then rape and kill Carol.

"Where is Carol now?" Justin asked.

"She is being held in a safe house by the FBI until this thing is over."

"I'm glad you guys figured that out before she got hurt," Justin said.

"If we hadn't intercepted Quai, Carol would be more than just hurt," Jimmy said. "That sick bastard would have tortured and raped her, and then cut her up slowly until she died."

"I guess they thought that she was my girlfriend since they intercepted that call she made to me," Justin said.

"That call didn't leave much doubt that she was your girlfriend," DeMac said with a grin.

"Also," Jimmy continued, "Jack's son Billy has been arrested."

"Billy!" Justin shouted. "Besides driving that truck down the river I figured the only crime Billy was guilty of was being a drunk and a bully."

"That's true, Billy probably wouldn't have been charged with any crimes—that is, until yesterday. He kidnapped Jesse when she left work and made her drive him to her house so he could settle his score with Travis."

Justin tensed up and arched his eyebrows but before he could say anything Jimmy continued.

"Everybody's just fine, Justin. Jesse wasn't hurt and Travis wasn't hurt either. Billy was taken into custody by the FBI and charged with assault and kidnapping."

"What exactly happened?" Justin asked.

"Let me go get my laptop Justin," Jimmy said as he got up and headed outside to the van, "You have got to see this to believe it!" Jimmy came back with the laptop and Justin and DeMac watched the video three times before Jimmy closed the lid and refused to show it to them again.

"I think that's the funniest thing I've ever seen!" Justin said laughing. "Did you see how far Billy jumped when that pistol exploded?"

"That son of yours missed his calling," DeMac said. "He should have been a circus clown."

"There is no telling how many people have watched this video since we recorded it," Jimmy said.

"I've got to call him," Justin said.

"He's in Greensboro with Jesse and is going to stay there until tomorrow evening. They are staying at the Regency Hyatt in the honeymoon suite compliments of the United States government until after the raid."

"But why?" Justin asked.

"Logistics, Justin. We needed a place to put the armored personnel carrier, and a place for about thirty men to sleep until we launch the raid. We also needed a place for the canines and their handlers and Jesse's place was perfect. The tobacco barn was too small to accommodate everybody, so we put the APC in Jesse's barn and the men are sleeping in the loft, and the dogs are in Jesse's kennel, at least until tomorrow."

"So everything's still on schedule for tomorrow?" DeMac asked.

"Yeah, but we're ready to go now if something happens to warrant it. With Jack's man and his Kawasaki Mule missing, and now Quai and Billy missing, Jack may get suspicious and try to run. We may have to move in early. We're going to watch him real closely until this thing goes down."

"I got a call this morning but no one spoke and then they hung up," Justin said.

"I'll check it out when I get back to the barn," Jimmy said as he stood up and wiped his mouth. "Thank you again for a hot shower and a delicious breakfast."

"You're welcome, Jimmy," Justin said.

"Just because Quai has been captured that doesn't mean anything has changed. Stay in this house and let DeMac and Chief guard you, understand?"

"Yes, sir," Justin replied. "You were right about Jack, there's absolutely no telling what he might try next."

"Exactly, so be careful. If your guardian angel warns you about something, get down and let DeMac and Chief check it out."

"So you finally believe that I have a guardian angel?"

"I got to go," Jimmy said and he turned and walked away.

"We won't leave here until about midnight, so it will probably be around 1:45 a.m. when we land in Ohio," Donald said over the phone. "If we take back off by two we should be in Houston between seven and eight."

"Just call me before you take off in Ohio and I'll go ahead and leave then," Frank Crafton said. "It'll take me about four hours to drive from Corpus Christi to Houston, so I should be there when you land."

Someone knocked on Donald's door and it startled him. "I got to go. I'll call you from Dayton."

"Okay, brother. I'll see you in the morning."

Donald hung the phone up. "Come in," he said. Cecil Wood and Steve Helms walked in and shut the door behind them. Donald didn't know what they wanted to talk about, but from the look on their faces it had to be serious.

"Donald, Steve and I have been talking, and we think that something has got to be done to stop this vendetta that Jack has with Justin Hayes," Cecil said.

"He has lost his mind, Donald!" Steve blurted. "He is obsessed with killing him and he stays drunk from morning to night! Have you seen him today?"

"No, I haven't seen him since I walked out of that meeting day before yesterday," Donald said.

"He looks like death warmed over!" Steve said.

"He's going to have a heart attack or a stroke if we can't figure out a way to turn him around," Cecil said.

"I've been trying to get him to back off all week and he won't listen," Donald said. "Between the news coverage of the truck being driven down the river and the FBI investigating the shootout, the last thing Jack needs to do now is to kill Justin Hayes. But you guys know as well as I do that he won't stop until Justin Hayes is dead or he is one."

"We know how stubborn he is, but we have a plan," Cecil said. "If all three of us approach him this evening as a group and tell him we're leaving, maybe he'll stop and think this thing through. It's worth a shot, don't you think?"

"If he thinks that all three of us are packing up and leaving I think he'll back off, at least "for now," Steve said.

"I don't know if he will or not!" Donald said. "Where is he now?"

"He's passed out in his room," Cecil said. "He probably won't wake up till after dark."

"Have you said anything to Johnny, or Brett, or Danny, or Lee, or anybody else besides me?" Donald asked.

"No, we wanted to talk to you and see what you thought about it first," Steve said.

"I think it's a great idea. It's probably our only chance to turn Jack around before it's too late," Donald said. "But I think that everybody that knows about Roy's accident and about our plans for Justin should be involved too. Instead of just the three of us approaching Jack, why not get everybody to approach him?"

"Do you really think that that's necessary?" Cecil asked.

"Yes, I do. If everybody goes together, he really won't have any choice but to back off," Donald stressed.

"I don't know, Donald," Steve said. "That seems kind of over the top, if you know what I mean."

"You do realize that we're talking about Jack Billings here, don't you?" Donald said. "You both know how he is."

"Well, that much is true," Cecil mumbled. "He can be as stubborn as a mule."

"I don't want to approach him at all unless we are all together on this thing."

"You may be right," Steve wondered out loud.

"Why don't we have a meeting in one hour in the conference room and see what everybody thinks about it," Donald suggested.

Cecil and Steve both stood silently and pondered the suggestion. Donald could tell that they were unsure about involving everybody in on the plan.

"I guess it wouldn't hurt to get everybody together and see what they think," Steve finally said.

"Okay then," Cecil said. "It's 11:45 now. Let's get everybody to meet in the conference room at one p.m."

"That'll work," Donald said, "everybody will have time to eat lunch before the meeting."

"I'll go tell my people," Steve said as he turned to leave.

"I'll see you guys at one," Donald said.

"Okay, see you at one o'clock," Cecil said as he shut the door behind him. Donald picked up his phone and dialed it quickly.

"Hello!" Coy said when he answered his cell phone. "We leave at 1:05, just you and me. Understand?"

"Uh, a.m. or p.m.?" Coy asked.

"P.m., an hour and fifteen minutes from now."

"Gotcha!"

"Have that bird ready to fly at one."

"Hello?" Travis said when he answered his cell phone.

"Mr. Hayes, this is Special Agent Sam Smart from the Bureau of Alcohol, Tobacco, and Firearms. It has come to my attention that you have been practicing the ancient art of *Yoursu-cham-oron* without a Class Three Federal Firearms License."

"Oh, whew, you had me for just a minute there, Dad," Travis said.

"That's the funniest thing I've seen since you let those girls put beads in your hair when you were in high school," Justin said.

"Oh man, I forgot about that!" Travis said.

"I've got a picture of it."

"That's right, you did take a picture."

"Where in the world did you come up with *Yo-ursu-cham-oron?*" Justin asked.

"We were clowning around after karate class one night and someone came up with it," Travis said. "I don't remember who it was though."

"I heard you and your lady won a trip."

"We sure did! We've already checked into our room and it's unbelievable," Travis said. "We also made reservations for tonight at Sterling's. It's a very exclusive restaurant in downtown Greensboro."

"You must be feeling generous."

"That's the best part," Travis said. "Agent Loggins gave me a government credit card and told me not to be bashful with it!"

"That joint is probably formal wear only," Justin said. "Have you two lovebirds got anything to wear?"

"We're inside the Dreams Come True Boutique right now. Jesse is trying on evening gowns and I'm going to rent a tux. What about you dad? Are you all right?"

"Yeah, I got a little dose of cabin fever, but other than that I'm fine."

"Maybe by this time tomorrow this nightmare will be over," Travis said.

"It sounds like to me that the nightmare that you're having tonight is the kind of nightmare that I dream about, if that makes any sense," Justin said.

"You have a good point," Travis said laughing. "Hey, Dad, you're not going to believe what Mama did. She paid off Jesse's business loan and put a hundred thousand dollars in a trust fund for me whenever she dies."

"That's great! Shucks, that's better than great, that's fantastic!"

"She said that she was finally at peace with herself," Travis said somberly.

"She's a good woman," Justin said. "She just got off track and got in over her head. I'm glad she is finally at peace with herself."

"Me too."

"Well, you kids have a ball, and I'll talk to you sometime tomorrow."

"Okay, Dad," Travis said. "I love you, man!"

"Love you too, Hoss! Bye now."

"Bye."

Donald stared at his computer screen and waited nervously for the transaction to go through. Jack's overseas bank account had a balance of $9,658,233.27 in it. Donald was leaving $8,233.27 in Jack's account and transferring $9,650,000.00 into his personal account that was at the same bank. He had checked and double checked the account numbers and the secret numerical codes before he made his request, but the computer screen remained unchanged. The phone rang on his desk and startled him and he jumped before he answered it.

"Donald, everybody's in the conference room except for you and Coy and Jerry," Cecil Wood said.

"We'll be there in just a few minutes Cecil. We got tied up but we're on the way."

"Okay, see you in a few minutes."

Donald hung the phone up and went back to staring at his computer screen. "Come on, dammit!" he said out loud and just like the computer heard him, it made a dinging sound and displayed the transfer as complete. Donald quickly shut the computer down and started unplugging the hard drive. Donald didn't know if Jack could get Brett to retrieve his account number from his computer or not, but he knew he couldn't if the hard drive was gone. Donald slid the hard drive out from under his desk and placed it on a hand truck and started out the door, pushing the hand truck in front of him. He glanced at the wall clock as he exited the room. It was 1:02 p.m. As he entered the hall he could hear the chatter coming from the conference room at the end of the hall. This was the most critical part of the getaway, getting to the plane without someone seeing him and stopping him. He cleared the hall and was almost to the kitchen when he almost crashed into Ashley Yates.

She was carrying an ice bucket and was heading for the conference room. "Oh excuse me Donald."

"Excuse me, Ashley. We almost crashed, didn't we?"

"We sure did are you coming to the meeting?"

"Yes, I'll be there in just a minute."

"Speaking of crashing, did your computer crash?" Ashley asked, looking at the hard drive.

"It's been acting up lately," Donald explained. "Brett's getting me a new one."

"Okay, we'll see you in a few."

Donald picked up the pace as he went through the kitchen. He opened the door to the tunnel that led to the hangar and started jogging with the hand truck in front of him until he reached the end of the tunnel. Donald opened the door to the hangar and hurried inside. The King Air was facing the hangar doors with Coy sitting in the pilot's seat.

Jerry Simmons was standing about forty feet away from the plane with his hands on his hips. "What the hell is going on Donald? Aren't we supposed to be in the conference room for some sort of meeting?"

"We have a slight emergency, Jerry," Donald said. "Go on to the meeting and tell everybody that I'll be there in just a minute."

"Do you need some help with that?" Jerry asked.

"No, no, you go ahead. I can get this."

"Okay, but Coy is acting weird. He could have told me that there was an emergency," Jerry said obviously annoyed. He started walking back across the hangar as Donald reached the stairs that led up into the plane. Donald picked up the hard drive and practically ran up the steps. He threw the hard drive onto the nearest seat and then raised the steps and latched the door. Coy pushed the remote control to open the hangar doors and then started the planes twin engines as Donald jumped in the copilot's seat and fastened his safety belt. It seemed like to Donald that it was taking forever for the hangar doors to open. He looked back across the hangar and saw Jerry jogging back toward them with his hands over his ears and then he saw Johnny Steele step into the hangar and break into a run.

"We gotta go Coy!" Donald hollered.

The doors finally opened up enough for the King Air to slip through and Coy released the brake and steered the plane out onto the runway and opened up the throttle. The sudden acceleration forced Donald back into his seat as the plane sped down the runway and gracefully lifted off the ground.

As soon as Donald felt the plane clear the ground, a feeling of euphoria washed over him. He took a deep breath and slowly let it out. So far everything had worked perfectly.

"Well, Coy, you and I are officially millionaires," Donald said.

"Wee Doggies!" Coy squealed. "So you were able to transfer the money into your account before you left?"

"Nine million dollars' worth!" Donald shouted.

"Hot Dog! Is your brother going to pick us up when we get to Dallas?"

"He's going to be waiting for us, but not in Dallas," Donald answered. "We're going to land at a private airstrip near Houston. I have a map in my pocket with the coordinates."

"Why the change?" Coy asked.

"It's safer, not as many people." Donald said. "Is there anyway that Jack can track us?"

"Not unless I want him to."

"Good," Donald said. Donald had intentionally told Coy that they were going to Dallas instead of Houston just in case Coy slipped up and told somebody where they were headed. Donald was considering getting up and stepping back to the plane's wet bar to mix himself a drink when suddenly a voice came over the radio.

"Base to KSJ 135, come in, 135. Over," Jack Billing's voice came through the speaker. "Home base to KSJ 135, answer me, Donald. I know you can hear me!"

"Should we answer him?" Coy asked.

"No, turn it off or change frequencies or something. There's nothing he can say that I want to hear."

"I'll find you! By God I'll find both of you!" Jack was screaming when Coy switched the frequency on the radio.

"He'll kill us if he ever finds us," Coy said.

"He's not smart enough to find us, and now that he's broke, he can't afford to hire somebody that's smart enough to find us," Donald reassured Coy. "Besides, he'll probably be in prison in a matter of weeks, if not days."

"You're right, Donald," Coy said. "I think we're home free!"

Coy certainly didn't need to worry about Jack Billings, Donald thought to himself. As soon as Donald and his half brother got back to Corpus Christi, they were going to kill Coy anyway. Donald's half brother, Frank, was a licensed pilot and he already had a float plane waiting for them when they arrived. They would load Coy's body onto the plane, and drop him in the ocean on their way to Maine. The sharks would take care of the rest.

Plan B

The voice that came through the speaker in the tobacco barn left no doubt as to which sniper was reporting in. "Eagle, this is Redneck." The words oozed out in a slow Arkansas drawl. "The bird just flew the coop!"

"Roger that, Redneck," Jimmy Hardy answered. "How many on board?"

"At least two. Don't rightly know, but there was two fellers chasing them when they left the hangar."

"Eagle, that's affirmative. Two in the plane and two chasing them on foot," Joaquin "Mex" Murieta reported from his hide on top of the mountain beside Jack's house. Mex had a better angle from his location to see inside the plane.

"Roger that, Mex," Jimmy said as he flipped a switch on the control board. "Control, this is Eagle. The bird has flown and is occupied by two."

"Roger that, Eagle. Eye in the sky has a visual and will track the pigeon until it roosts. We still have no signal from the package."

Jimmy wasn't surprised. The tracking signal that was emitted from Suitcase B had disappeared from the screen over three weeks ago when it was carried inside the mountain, and it was still absent from the screen, which only meant that Suitcase B was still inside the mountain.

When Jimmy overheard Donald Crafton call his brother the second time and tell him that they were leaving in one hour, he didn't think that they would be taking the suitcase with them. There was only one man at Jack's hotel that knew about the special suitcase and that was Gyurman Yahamen Tahare-Azar. The big question was, "What will Jack do now?" and "What do we do now?" The CIA had intercepted the money transfer sent from Donald Crafton to the Imperial National Bank of Switzerland, and also the two phone calls to his brother in Corpus-Christi, Texas. As so often happens in covert operations, everything you spent hours and days planning suddenly changes, and everybody is left scrambling to figure out what Plan B is.

Jimmy and at least one of the senior CIA officials wanted to go ahead and launch the raid on Jack's house, but the FBI wanted to wait so they could take down Jimmy Milano at the same time. Finally the decision was made to just wait. Jack's property was isolated and it was surrounded by highly trained snipers. If anyone tried to leave, the snipers could stop them and then they wouldn't have any choice but to launch the raid, Jimmy Milano or no Jimmy Milano.

"Listen up, team, here's the game plan," Jimmy said into the mic. "If that hangar door opens up and that Cessna starts taxiing out onto the runway, you are to disable it. If anybody that we don't want to leave gets into a car or truck, you are to disable it also. If you do have to disable a car or truck, wait until it is on the bridge and then put a round through the engine block. That way it will block anyone else from leaving until we can get our troops there. Does everybody copy?"

"This is Hart, copy!"

"Redneck, copy!"

"Mex, copy!"

"Wizard, copy!"

"Doc, copy!"

"Okay, guys, make me proud," Jimmy said. "Kickoff could be at any second."

Jimmy swiveled around to face FBI Special Agent Dan Loggins. "How are your guys doing?"

"Everything's looking good. We have a Special Response Team en route to Houston's Gulf Port Airstrip and they should be there in plenty of time to welcome Donald Crafton. We also have two agents following Donald's half-brother Frank as he drives up to Houston from Corpus-Christi."

"I hope they don't get busted!" Jimmy responded. "Frank could send a text message to the plane and warn them not to land."

"They won't get busted," Dan said. "When Frank stopped to buy gas they put a GPS transponder on his car. They're following him from a mile back."

"Good," Jimmy said.

"I'm sorry we couldn't go ahead and launch the raid," Dan said, "But Jimmy Milano is sitting in a restaurant right now, and if we tried to take him down in the club somebody might get killed."

"It's no big deal," Jimmy said. "This is my first operation as the on-site coordinator and I'm just anxious to get it over with. We've only been here for three weeks but it seems like a year to me. I always thought that the guys sitting back at operations headquarters had it made, but I know different now. Trying to coordinate everybody without jeopardizing the mission or anybody's safety is enough to drive you insane!"

"It's a lot of pressure sometimes," Dan said.

"It's too much pressure for me," Jimmy said. "When you're crawling through the jungle or rappelling out of a helicopter the only thing you have to worry about is yourself and your team, but when you're in charge of the whole mission you have to worry about every-thing! I don't think I'm cut out for this shit."

"Seems to me that you're doing just fine," Dan replied. "You'll probably get used to it in time."

"I don't know, Dan." Jimmy sighed. "I just don't know."

The silence in the conference room was surreal. Everyone sat perfectly still, staring either straight ahead or down at the table in front of them. No one was eating or drinking or talking or making eye contact with anyone else in the room.

Jack fumbled with the paper wrapper that held the headache powder he so desperately needed. He finally managed to unfold it enough to pour it down his throat, and he chased the bitter medicine with a gulp from a nearby glass of water. The medicine may help relieve Jack's headache, but nothing could extinguish the anger that burned in his soul. A man that he trusted completely had betrayed him, and as much as he wanted to kill Justin Hayes, he now wanted to kill Donald Crafton more!

"Well, since all you people decided to have a meeting that I didn't know anything about, let's have a damn meeting!" Jack practically shouted. "Who wants to go first?"

There was silence in the room. There were thirteen people gathered around the huge marble table, but no one uttered a word.

"This is the strangest meeting I've ever been to!" Jack hollered like a school teacher scolding his students.

"Jack, we were having a meeting because we were concerned about you," Cecil finally said. "Since Johnny was killed you've been—"

"Angry!" Jack offered. "Hell yeah, I've been angry and you would be too if some son of a bitch murdered your nephew!"

"Not just angry, Jack, distraught, disconnected. We were all worried about you."

"Whose idea was it to have a meeting?"

"Donald. It was Donald's idea."

"He always was a clever son of a bitch," Jack said. "He gathered everybody into one room so that he could slip out the back door without anyone stopping him."

There was silence once again.

"Well, Donald Crafton isn't the only clever one around here!" Jack huffed. "Danny, did you do that errand that I asked you to do after our last meeting?"

"Yes, sir."

"Go get it."

"Yes, sir, right away," Danny said as he stood up to leave.

"Anthony, I need you to run the hotel until further notice. I don't want anyone to mention this little problem we have to any of our guests. Just tell the two guests that were supposed to leave tonight that there was a mechanical problem with the plane and that we had to fly it to a nearby airport to get it repaired. Tell them that it was for their safety."

"I'll handle it, sir," Anthony said.

"As for everybody else, do not worry about Billings Enterprises. This last week and what happened today is just a bump in the road. We have been in business for over twenty years and I intend to be in business for the next twenty years, so just do your jobs and let me worry about the rest. Okay?"

Several people around the table mumbled a "yes, sir."

"Now I want everyone to go back to work except for Cecil, Steve, and Johnny."

For the first time in fifteen minutes there was noise in the room as everyone scrambled to leave. The conference room had felt like a tomb to everyone that was gathered in it and everyone that filed through the door looked like they were escaping some sort of death chamber.

After the room emptied Jack turned to face Cecil. "Well, how much did he take?"

"$9,650,000," Cecil said.

"He left $ 8,233 in the account."

"Well, that was mighty nice of him, wasn't it?" Jack said as he rubbed his face with both his hands. "I remember when we set that overseas account up. You tried to convince me to give you the first five digits of the security code and to give Donald the last five digits so that both of you would have to be present to access the account. I wish I would have listened to you now."

"What are we going to do Jack?" Cecil asked.

"We're going to get it back! That's what we're going to do."

"But how?" Cecil asked.

"I got suspicious of Donald after our last meeting. He kept telling me that we needed to back off and we needed to sit back and watch and that there's something we don't know. I didn't like what he was saying or the tone of his voice, so I told Danny to put a recorder on Donald's private line. I hope we can find him from his phone conversations over the last two days. If we can't find him soon we'll just have to sell off some of my property and start over."

There was a soft knock on the door and then it opened and Danny Comer entered the room carrying a recorder. He took a seat beside of Jack and pushed the button that said Play.

"Hello?" Justin said when he answered his phone.

"Justin, this is Jimmy. Is everything okay over there?"

"Yeah, everything's fine, Jimmy. Is something wrong?"

"No, nothing's wrong. I was just checking."

"Everything's cool over here, Jimbo."

"We traced that phone call you got when they hung up on you. It was placed from a payphone in Sparta."

"So we don't know who placed the call then?"

"Yeah, we know who placed it. The phone was smashed to pieces but we still were able to lift fingerprints from it. It was Jack!"

"Hmmm, wonder why he called."

"He was checking to see if you were still alive, that's why! He can't find his assassin so he was checking to see if you were still breathing."

"Yeah, that makes sense. He was hoping that even though he couldn't find Quai that somehow he still managed to kill me."

"Exactly, and when he heard your voice he got so angry that he took it out on the phone."

"That stress will kill you!"

"Listen Justin, that payphone is at least thirty years old and it was built like a tank. It took a lot of force to smash it like he did, so I just-called to warn you. He knows you're still alive and he's very angry, so be very careful."

"Okay, Jimmy, we'll be on our toes. I'll tell DeMac and Chief."

"Okay, let me know about anything suspicious."

"We'll call you if we see anything strange."

"Do that. Bye."

"Bye."

"Don't say anything until I finish talking," Jimmy Milano's voice came over the phone in Jack's office. "I got your message, but I'm calling you from a restaurant instead of my office. This phone line should be secure, but I don't trust it as much as my private line, so be careful what you say. It would be better if we talked later if your problem can wait. If it can't wait, then go ahead."

"It can't wait," Jack said. "I don't know if you can help me or not, but if you can then time is of the essence."

"Okay, tell me what's going on."

"The man you normally talk to when you call to make arrangements has betrayed me. He cleaned out my bank account, and with the help of one of my pilots, he stole my plane. They are heading to a private airstrip near Houston, Texas. If you have any contacts near that area, I need for them to board my plane when it lands and force my pilot to turn around and fly my plane back to me. The job pays one million."

"One mill. Gees, the closest man I got is in New Orleans," Jimmy Milano said. "How much time do we have?"

"They left at one o'clock and it's a five-hour flight, so they should land in Houston around six."

"It's two o'clock where you are, right?"

"Yeah, it's two o'clock here," Jack answered. "We have four hours to get somebody there before they land."

"If my people can leave New Orleans by four o'clock in a private plane, they should be able to arrive before your guys get there, don't you think?"

"Yeah, yeah, I'm looking at a map, and it looks like an hour and a half flight from New Orleans to Houston so they should be there by five thirty and my guys won't land until six."

"I think I can help you," Jimmy said. "Let me make a phone call."

"Uh, if they can pull this off I'll pay them a million, but I need both my guys in good condition when they get here so that I can find out where they put my money, and it may take me a couple days to get my hands on it," Jack fumbled.

"Don't say anything to them about the money," Jimmy said. "You just pay me and I'll take care of them, okay?"

"Yeah, sure, I really appreciate it, and I won't forget it!"

"Is everything else okay down there?"

"Yeah, everything's good," Jack lied.

"Okay. I'll have my man call you in fifteen minutes."

"Thank you."

"I wouldn't care if the FBI needed to use my place once a month as long as they put me up in this hotel," Jesse said. Her head was just barely visible over the steaming water as she and Travis soaked in the honeymoon suite hot tub. Travis was sitting across from Jesse facing her and their legs were wrapped up together like they were afraid the other one would escape. A knock on the door startled them and they both sat straight up.

"Mr. Hayes, this is room service. We have a delivery for you, sir."

"Did you order something to be delivered here?" Travis asked Jesse as he stood up and pulled on his terrycloth robe.

"No, I didn't order anything," Jesse answered.

"Does it say who sent it?" Travis said loudly as he crossed the room toward the door.

"Yes, sir, a Mrs. Kathy Maxwell."

Travis opened the door and then realized he didn't have his wallet to tip the bellhop, so he jogged into the bedroom and returned carrying a five dollar bill. "Thank you," he said as he took the beautifully wrapped box and handed the five to the man.

"You're welcome, sir."

Travis closed and locked the door and then read the card that was trimmed in lace.

Jessica,
I'm sure this will look much prettier on you than on me.
Love you both,
Kathy Maxwell

Travis crossed the room and handed the package to Jesse before dropping his robe and returning to his place in the hot tub.

"What in the world has your mother done now?" Jesse asked as she read the card.

"There's no telling," Travis answered. "Open it."

Jesse unwrapped the box and took the lid off. Inside was the beautiful red silk robe that Kathy was wearing when they visited her earlier in the day.

"It's the robe that she bought in Tokyo! I can't believe it!" Jesse said, admiring the garment. "I told her how beautiful it was and she just gave it to me. Your mother is so sweet!"

"I can't believe it either," Travis said. "I didn't even have a mother until a few days ago. Of course I didn't have you either!"

"A lot has happened in just a week," Jesse said as she placed the robe and the box beside the hot tub.

Jesse and Travis stared at each other as they both sank back down in the hot water.

"Did you ever see the movie *Karate Kid*?" Travis asked. "I think everybody has seen *Karate Kid*," Jesse answered.

"Do you remember in the movie when Mr. Miagee sent Daniel LaRusso to find his girlfriend?" Travis asked. "Bonsai Danielson! Bonsai!" Travis hollered.

"Yes, I remember," Jesse said, laughing.

"Mr. Miagee told Danielson that he needed balance, not just in karate, but in his whole life," Travis said as he stared at the most beautiful blue eyes on earth. "I think I found my balance this week. I'm in love with you, Jesse!"

"I love you too," Jesse said and then she paused slightly before continuing. "Did you ever see the Disney movie *Cinderella*?"

"Well, I don't know. Uh, I might have seen it when I was just a little fellow," Travis kinda mumbled.

"We didn't have a TV when I was small, but my grandmother bought me the book for my fifth birthday," Jesse said as she stared at the ceiling. Travis could tell that she was traveling back into her childhood memories.

"I made her read me that book every night until I memorized every word. Every time I had to mop the floor or gather the eggs. or hang out the laundry. I just imagined that I was Cinderella," Jesse said, staring at the ceiling.

"I thought I had it bad because daddy made me clean up my room," Travis said. "You definitely came up hard, Jesse."

"Yes, I did, but tonight I get to put on a beautiful dress and a beautiful pair of high heeled shoes and get into a beautiful carriage and go to the Ball! The only difference is that my Prince will be with me when I arrive, and he will be going home with me when I leave!"

Jesse lowered her gaze until she was looking straight at Travis. "I'm in love with you too, Travis," she said with tears in her eyes.

Jack poured himself a bourbon and coke and sipped it as he walked back down the hall toward the conference room. He was feeling much better since he had talked to the two men in New Orleans. They had assured Jack that they would be waiting at the Gulf Port Airstrip when his plane arrived and that they could easily persuade Donald Crafton and Coy Beard to fly the plane back to North Carolina. As an added bonus, they both had flown into the Gulf Port Airstrip on several occasions and were very familiar with its layout. If everything went as planned they should be landing back at Jack's around midnight.

Jack walked into the conference room where Cecil, Johnny, and Lee continued to wait. "It's all arranged. The plane and our two wayward sons should be returning around midnight."

"Well, good!" Cecil said. "Maybe we can finally return things to normal around here!"

"Things aren't going to return to normal around here until Justin Hayes is dead," Johnny Steele grumbled.

"Well, at least we can operate the business if we get our plane and our money back!" Cecil argued. "We can do that with Justin Hayes alive!"

"It's my turn, Jack," Johnny said as Jack sat down at the head of the table.

"What are you talking about, Johnny?"

"We've tried to kill him three times and we failed three times. We sent Tommy to pour chemicals in the river and he disappeared. Then Justin was in the Ashe County jail for shooting Johnny and Chris, and Bill Sisk couldn't keep him there. You even hired a professional hit man and he disappeared. It's my turn to kill him!"

"What makes you so sure you can kill him?" Jack asked.

"Because the other times the plan was too complicated. There was too much that could go wrong," Johnny said. "My plan is simple. I call Bill Sisk and get him to pick me up and drive me over to the New River State Park. No one is allowed to drive on the access roads except for park rangers and law enforcement officers, so Bill can drive me around to the backside of the mountain that Justin lives on. From there I climb the mountain and come out directly behind Justin's house at the edge of the wood line. As soon as I make sure that no one is watching, I come straight down the hill until I'm standing behind his house, and I throw a Molotov cocktail through a window and set the house on fire. When he comes out, I kill him!"

"What if his dogs are outside and they see you when you run up?" Jack asked.

"Then I kill them before I throw the Molotov cocktail through the window. The dogs don't concern me. I've never seen a man or a dog that could live after being hit with a load of double-ought buckshot."

"It sounds too simple," Jack said.

"That's why it will work!" Johnny said. "Justin Hayes is not superman, he's just a man. He won't expect anyone to try and hit him at his house in the middle of the afternoon.

We'll catch him totally off guard!"

"It sounds like you've been thinking about this for some time."

"I've been thinking about it ever since he pointed that .45 at me." Johnny snarled, "What if he calls the fire department and they get there before he has to come out?"

"I thought about that too," Johnny said. "After Bill drops me off he can drive back around to River Road and set up a roadblock just before you get in sight of Justin's driveway. If the fire department or anybody comes down the road, he can stop them and tell them that there are reports of someone firing at vehicles. When I kill Justin, I'll throw him back inside and let his body burn up with the house. As soon as I get back to the top of the mountain I can call Bill's cell phone and tell him I'm through. By that time the house should be too far gone for the fire department to save. With his daddy dead and the house burned to the ground, I think his son will sell out and move."

"It sounds like your plan just might work Johnny," Cecil said, "But what about the investigation afterward? The fire department will investigate the cause of the fire, and they will know that an accelerant was used and the fire was arson. Then they will call the SBI and those guys will sort through every piece of evidence they can find. And even though Justin's body will be severely burned, an autopsy will reveal that he was killed by a shotgun blast and not a fire."

"Let them investigate!" Johnny said. "After I cross the mountain all I have to do is go straight down the other side until I come to Whiskey Creek. I can walk straight down the center of the creek until it empties into the New River, and then wait until dark. After dark I can cross the·river and walk up the other side until I come out right behind the hangar. If they put dogs on my scent they will probably loose it at Whiskey Creek, but if they don't they will definitely lose it at the river. And besides, I have an alibi! I was with you guys all day."

"I don't know, Johnny," Jack said.

"Come on, Jack! Let's get our money back and our plane back and kill that son of a bitch while were waiting. I've been waiting to settle up with him ever since he pointed that pistol at me, and I think the time is right. He killed Tommy and Johnny and now's the time to settle up! It won't be any easier to kill him a month from now, and when you wake up in the morning all your problems will be gone!"

The thought of waking up in the morning with his plane back in the hangar and Donald and Coy's bodies lying in the bottom of the mine was enticing, but if Justin Hayes was dead also, it would be a dream come true. Jack knew that he couldn't last much longer under the kind of stress he had been under the last week. He had lost ten pounds and he shook so bad in the morning when he first got up that he had to take a drink before he could sign his name. Maybe if Justin was dead he could finally buy that property and build Billy a house on the same spot. He wouldn't be living here, but at least he would be close.

"Let's do it!" Jack said.

"Who's there?" the voice demanded when Bill Sisk pushed the intercom button beside the cast iron gates at Jacks.

"It's the sheriff," Bill answered. "I tried my remote but it didn't work!"

"We changed the code. I'll open it for you."

The gate clicked and then started opening and Bill got back in his Explorer and drove in. He wondered if he was the reason they changed the code. He was hoping that since he was helping Johnny Steele to kill Justin that he could get back on Jack's good side, and the best part was that he didn't have to face Justin Hayes this time. Their last encounter was still fresh in his mind.

Bill made a circle and then backed up to the double carport that was built on the side of the house. As he was getting out, the roll-up door that was directly behind him started to rise and out stepped Johnny Steele wearing dress slacks and a white dress shirt.

"Open the rear hatch," Johnny said so Bill grabbed the handle and lifted the rear hatch. Johnny stepped back into the carport and then emerged carrying a black ballistic nylon bag that was three and a half feet long and one and a half feet wide and he tossed it into the back of the Explorer and shut the hatch. "Let's go," he said to Bill and he stepped around to the passenger side and climbed in.

"You're dressed awful nice to go hunting!"

"That's just in case somebody sees me on the way over," Johnny said, looking straight ahead. "People always look at a cop car when it passes."

"You're right about that," Bill said.

"Eagle, the High Sheriff just pulled up to the gates of hell," Hart reported.

"Give me video."

"You got it, Boss Man!"

Dan Loggins slid over beside Jimmy and stared at the monitor as it came to life. They watched as the Sheriff drove in and parked, and watched as the rear hatch raised and then shut. They couldn't see what they were doing at the back of the vehicle, but the Sheriff and Johnny Steele both walked around and got into the Explorer and headed back toward the front gate.

"Call the ball, Eagle," Hart's voice came over the speaker. "We are ready to engage."

"Red light, red light. Let them leave!"

"Roger that, Eagle, we are red light."

Jimmy and Dan watched as they drove through the gate and across the bridge and started up River Road.

"Crow's Nest, this is Eagle. Be advised, the sheriff is headed your way. If he turns into Daddy Rabbit's driveway, shut him down. You are Green Light to disable the vehicle. That goes for you too, Wizard."

"Roger that, Eagle," Duke responded. "I don't like Fords anyway."

"Wizard, send me video!"

"Roger that, Boss Man, you got it."

Jimmy and Dan watched as the blue Explorer came up River Road and drove past Justin's driveway and went out of sight around the curve.

"Wonder where those two are going?" Dan asked.

"I don't know," Jimmy answered, "But they sure are dressed nice, aren't they?"

"Maybe they're going to church," Dan said, trying to ease the tension in the room. "Maybe there's a revival somewhere nearby!"

"They better give their souls to Jesus," Jimmy said, "'cause after tomorrow their asses will be mine!"

"Amen, brother!" Dan chuckled. "Amen!"

Bill Sisk pulled his Ford Explorer beside trail marker 163 and cut off the ignition. They had wound their way through four miles of twisting and bumpy access roads that circled the New River State Park until they finally arrived here. At one point they came upon a tree that had fallen across the road and Bill thought that they would have to turn around, but Johnny got out and with the strength of a good mule, he dragged the tree out of the road.

"This is it," Bill said. "About three years ago a twelve-year-old boy wandered off and got lost and we put the dogs on him right here. The dogs went straight up the mountain and found him right behind Roy Hepler's place. Most of the time a kid will go downhill, but he went straight up like a mountain goat!"

Johnny didn't say anything, he just went straight to the back of the Explorer and opened the hatch and let the tailgate down. He dragged his black bag out onto the tailgate and unzipped it. Johnny quickly changed out of his dress clothes into a pair of black cargo pants and a black tee shirt and then put on a second chance bullet proof vest. He then pulled a fanny pack out of the bag and put his cell phone, a· disposable lighter, a flashlight, two expensive looking wine bottles full of gasoline, a couple of cotton rags, a bottle of water, a pair of small binoculars, and a box of 12-gauge double-ought buck-shot shells into the fanny pack and zipped it up before strapping it around his waist. Next he pulled out his .50 AE Desert Eagle pistol and stuck it in his vest, and finally he pulled out a FN Herstal tactical police shotgun with a collapsible stock. Johnny slung the shotgun over his shoulder and then put his dress clothes back in the bag before he zipped it back up and slung it over his other shoulder.

"How far to the top?"

"Maybe nine hundred feet," Bill answered. "It's not too far."

"Drive back around to River Road and wait for me to call you."

"Okay, Johnny."

Then he was gone, through the mountain laurel bushes and out of sight. Bill got back into his Explorer and did a three point road turn and started back. He glanced up the mountain one last time before he left. "Good luck Johnny!" he said. "You might need it!"

"I feel like I'm back in high school," Teresa said. "As soon as I get home, I run to the phone and call my boyfriend. I miss you so much!"

"I miss you too, sweetie," Justin said. "Maybe by this time tomorrow it will be over with."

"I sure hope so. Call me as soon as it is and I will meet you in the Jacuzzi!"

"Oh no, don't even mention that." Justin groaned. "I'm already going insane from being cooped up in this house without thinking about you in that Jacuzzi!"

"I think I'm going to run myself a hot bath and then call you back on my cell phone."

"You're killing me! You know that, don't you? You're absolutely killing me!"

"Why don't you get in your tub and we can talk to each other while we're soaking!"

"No, no. I couldn't stand it!"

"I could describe everything I'm doing while I'm sitting in the tub."

"You are such a little devil sometimes!"

"Are you excited?"

"If I tried to stand up and walk right now I would probably fall down!"

"Good. I'll call you after I get my bath run. Love you!"

"Love you too." Justin hung the phone up and grinned. That woman was something else. He managed to stand up and he hobbled to the kitchen to pour himself a glass of tea.

DeMac was sitting at the kitchen table reading the latest issue of the American Rifleman Magazine as Justin reached up to get himself a glass. Justin froze in mid-stride.

"What's the matter?" DeMac said looking up from his magazine.

"It's Gabriel! We're in danger, I can feel it!" Justin said.

DeMac jumped up and grabbed his M-4. "Chief! Chief! Condition Red!"

"I'm getting tired of fighting in my damn underwear!" Chief hollered as he ran out of the bedroom wearing his boxer shorts.

"Justin, get in the center of the house!" DeMac ordered. "Chief, you guard the front and I'll guard the back!" DeMac stepped over to the kitchen sink and scanned the tree line as he pulled out his cell phone.

"Eagle, this is Red Fox! Daddy Rabbit's getting some bad vibrations. We are Condition Red! I repeat, we are Condition Red!"

"Roger that, Red Fox. I'll notify Crow's Nest and Wizard."

Jimmy flipped a switch and grabbed the microphone. "Crow's Nest and Wizard, Rabbit Den is Condition Red. I repeat, Rabbit Den is Condition Red! Over."

"Roger that, Eagle, we got their back!"

Jimmy turned to face Dan Loggins. "Dan, how about putting one of your teams in a chopper and let them do a flyover."

"You're putting a lot of stock into a funny feeling, aren't you?"

"He hasn't been wrong yet!"

"Okay, I'll call them right now," Dan said as he swiveled back around.

"Listen up, everybody! Rabbit's Den is Condition Red! All eyes on the Rabbit's Den! Second string is doing a flyover!"

Bill Sisk checked the screen on his cell phone before answering. "Sheriff Sisk."

"I'm ready. Don't let anyone down the road until I call you back," Johnny said.

"Okay, Johnny. I'll block the road."

The line went dead.

"Hello?" Jack said when he answered the phone.

"Jack, I'm ready to go."

"Okay, be careful."

"I thought I would call you so you could watch."

"I'm going to watch, all right! You just be careful!"

"I'm going to show you how a pro does it! I'll call you back after I'm through."

"Okay. I'll have Michael cook you a steak and have it waiting for you when you get back."

"Sounds good. I'll see you about an hour after dark."

"See you then," Jack said and then hung up the phone. Jack spun his swivel rocker around so that it was facing the bay window. He adjusted the spotting scope so that it was pointed at the hill behind Justin's house.

"It's payback time, Hayes," Jack said. "Let me introduce you to my little friend!"

"Who was that calling Jack and what in the world does he want him to watch?" Dan Loggins asked Jimmy.

Jimmy didn't answer. He was deep in thought as he tried to make sense of the call that they just intercepted from Jack's phone line.

"I recognize that voice from somewhere," Jimmy finally said. "Where did I hear that voice?" Suddenly Jimmy's eyes grew wide and he grabbed his laptop and punched in a code. The screen lit up with the video of Jack Billings and Johnny Steele standing in front of Justin's front porch. Jimmy turned up the audio.

"You touch that pistol and I'll blow a hole right through those pretty white teeth!" Justin said and then he hollered, "Hush!" so the dogs would quit barking.

"If those dogs leave that porch I'll kill them!" Johnny replied to Justin. Jimmy backed the video up and then restarted it. "If those dogs leave that porch I'll kill them!" Johnny said again. Jimmy flipped a couple switches on the control board and listened. "I thought I would call you so you could watch."

"That's it. That's Johnny Steele's voice!" Jimmy shouted.

"But he left with the sheriff and he was wearing dress clothes!" Dan said.

"And it worked too, damn it!" Jimmy said as he grabbed the microphone. "Smitty, Duke, Wizard, Snake, DeMac, Chief, this is Eagle! We believe that Johnny Steele is in position somewhere to attack the Rabbit's Den. You are Green Light to shoot anyone approaching the Rabbit's Den! Find him and eliminate him! We have a chopper en route. Do not shoot at any helicopters."

Johnny Steele knelt down just inside the tree line and pulled out the two wine bottles and the cotton rags. He took the corks off the bottles and shoved a piece of cloth into the neck of each one. He took the disposable lighter and checked it to make sure it worked and then slid it into his front pants pocket. He then grabbed the binoculars and eased forward just enough to get a clear view of the back of Justin's house and machine shop. As long as Justin wasn't working in his shop he probably could make it down the hill without being seen. There were no lights on in the machine shop and all the doors appeared to be closed. There was no sign of Justin or the dogs either. He's probably sitting in his recliner taking a nap Johnny thought as he eased back and put the binoculars back in his bag. Johnny swung the shotgun around so that it was facing forward in its sling and picked up the two Molotov cocktails and stood up.

"I got him, Eagle," Smitty said. "He's standing straight behind the house, twelve o'clock from our position and he's holding two Molotov cocktails and a tactical shotgun!"

"I got him too!" Duke said, as he lay beside Smitty looking through the scope on his Barrett M82-A1 .50-caliber sniper rifle. "What's the yardage?"

"873 yards," Smitty said.

"Smitty, this is Eagle. Prepare your shot but wait until he commits. Wizard, can you see the tango?"

"Negative, Eagle, but if he steps out of the tree line I will be able to engage."

"Roger that, Wizard. Prepare your shot. Snake, slip out of your hide and circle around behind him and see if he is by himself. Duke, send me video from your location. DeMac, you need a man in the carport to engage the tango in case he makes it down the hill."

"Mayday! Mayday! Here he comes!" Smitty said as Johnny Steele started down the bill.

Jimmy Hardy and Dan Loggins and all the Navy Seals and Special Response Team members that were gathered at the tobacco barn crowded around the monitor as Johnny Steele made his run down the hill.

"Green light, green light, kill him!" Jimmy said into the microphone.

Smitty squeezed the rear sandbag that his rifle was resting on and watched as the crosshairs came down until they crossed Johnny's face and centered his chest. The rifle roared and the muzzle blast blew leaves and sticks and dirt into the air like a super charged leaf blower.

Wizard saw Johnny as soon as he stepped from the tree line and began tracking him as he traveled down the hill and from the right to the left. Wizard let his crosshairs catch up to the man's chest before he broke his shot. Grass and dirt filled the air around the sniper hide but Wizard stayed down on the rifle scope so he could make his next shot.

It wouldn't be necessary. Smitty's 671-grain match bullet arrived first and struck Johnny in the center of his chest and blew the biggest portion of his sternum and his heart and lungs and spine out through his back in a stream of gore almost three inches in diameter. Wizard's bullet arrived next, but since the body was falling forward and down, the bullet struck him in the side of the neck instead of in the chest and totally decapitated him, sending his head spinning into the air until it finally landed almost ten feet away from the body.

"Threat is neutralized, Eagle," Duke reported. "Continuing to search for targets. Over."

"Roger that, good job. Continue to search until Snake reports in."

Jimmy finally leaned back in his chair and wiped the sweat from his forehead. "I think you can call off your chopper, Dan."

Dan turned around and grabbed his microphone. "A Team, you can turn around. Threat has been neutralized."

"Roger that, Control, returning to base."

"Eagle, this is Snake. No sign of anyone behind the Rabbit's Den. Tango was acting solo. Over."

"Roger that, Snake, return to your hide. After dark we will remove the body. Good job, guys. Over."

Jack was somewhat skeptical about Johnny's plan to kill Justin, but the more he thought about it the more he liked it. He felt anxious as he sat in his bedroom looking through the spotting scope waiting for the action to begin. It was like being at a football game waiting for the opening kickoff. When Johnny finally broke away from the tree line and started down the hill, Jack felt like standing up and cheering. Jack watched as Johnny covered ten yards, then twenty yards, then thirty yards, what the—oh my God, no. Jack's last visual was an explosion of gore and Johnny's head arching away from his body.

Jack ran to the bathroom and threw up and then returned to the spotting scope to make sure what he saw was real. Johnny's headless body was lying on the hill with blood and bone and tissue strewn behind it for twenty feet up the hill. A helicopter in the distance flared and went back the way it was coming, and Jack ran back to the bathroom and threw up again.

"Control, this is A Team. Over."

"A Team, this is Control, go ahead," Dan said into his mic.

"We are returning to base, but thought you might want to know, the sheriff has a roadblock set up just around the curve from the Rabbit's Den. Over."

"Roger that, A Team," Dan said as he spun around to face Jimmy. "Did you hear that?"

"Yeah, does your chopper have a missile launcher on it?" Jimmy asked.

"No, but it has a .30-caliber machine gun mounted under its nose," Dan answered. "Tell your men to go back and strafe that son of a bitch!"

"You're kidding, aren't you?"

"Yeah, I'm kidding," Jimmy said. "I guess we better wait until tomorrow and arrest that piece of shit."

"I'm looking forward to it!" Dan said.

"I'm coming in there!" Travis hollered at the bathroom door.

"No, you're not!" Jesse shouted. "I'll be out in just a minute."

"Okay, I'll wait," Travis said as he paced back and forth across the floor. She insisted that he not see her until she was ready and Travis was as anxious as a new dad in the waiting room of the hospital. Finally he heard the door lock click and Jesse stepped out. Travis stopped in his tracks and gazed at her.

"Oh my God, Jesse. You are...you are absolutely gorgeous!"

And she was. Jesse had chosen a black off the shoulder evening gown that was jewel encrusted around the neck line and it dipped just low enough to reveal just a glimpse of cleavage. The gown was slightly gathered on her left hip and the scalloped hem line went down at a sharp angle toward her right ankle. There was a slit running up the right side that stopped halfway between her knee and hip showing off her beautiful legs, and the gown was just tight enough to high light her perfect figure. She topped it off with a dainty turquoise necklace and matching open toed high heel shoes. She was absolutely stunning.

"Do you like it?" She asked smiling.

"I'm...I'm speechless," Travis finally said. "You are the most beautiful woman that I have ever seen Jesse. My heart is about to jump out of my chest!"

"You're not just saying that are you?"

"Look. just look!" Travis said as he took her hand and led her over to the three-sided full-length mirror. "I'm searching for words to describe you," Travis said as he stood behind her as she looked at herself in the mirror. "Absolutely beautiful isn't enough. Maybe 'ravishing,' or 'utterly stunning.' No, that's not it. A 'vision of beauty.' I don't know how to describe the way you look tonight, but I don't think Cinderella was this beautiful."

"Thank you and you look so handsome in your tux" Jesse said as she turned around to face Travis.

"There's only one thing wrong with the way you look," Travis said. "Wrong! What's wrong?"

"I'll have to fight off every man that sees you."

"Well, you're pretty good at that too," Jesse said as she leaned over to kiss him.

"Finally!" Bill Sisk said out loud when his cell phone rang. No one had come down River Road but it had been a long time since he heard the gunfire. He looked at the sky over Justin's house to see if there was any smoke as he pushed the button to answer his cell phone. "Sheriff Sisk."

"It's over, Bill. Go back to town," Jack said.

"Did everything go all right? I don't see any smoke!"

"No, it didn't go all right, and you're not going to see any smoke."

"Is Johnny, uh—"

"What do you think, Bill?" Jack's voice exploded through the cell phone. "Hell, yes, he's dead, so get in your damn truck and go back to town!" Click.

The color drained from Bill's face and he just stood there for several seconds before he finally ran over to his Explorer and spun it around and headed back toward town.

Jack sat in his office sipping a Coca-Cola in hopes that it would settle his stomach. His head was spinning with questions. How in the hell did Justin Hayes manage to kill Johnny before he even traveled forty yards down the hill? He would have to be looking out a window with his rifle in his hands to shoot that fast. It doesn't make sense. No one is that lucky or that good. And what kind of rifle can blow a man's guts out his back and decapitate him at the same time? Something's not right. There have been too many strange things happening this week! That rifle didn't sound like any rifle that I've ever heard before. It sounded the same as when the road crew uses dynamite to blast through rock. What will Justin do with Johnny's body?

Will he call the Sheriff's Department or the SBI, or will he just bury it the same place he buried Tommy? Jack tried to sort through all the weekly events in his head, but it was too much information. He needed to write it all down. Jack grabbed a pen and a piece of paper and started making a list:

1. Tommy went to pour chemicals in the river and just vanished.
2. Justin sent pictures of Billy and Johnny driving the monster truck down the river to several television news stations, but never came forward to validate them.
3. Justin shot and killed Johnny and Chris, but was released by the FBI after just a few hours.
4. The FBI came the next morning to investigate Walt's murder and the shooting rampage of Chris and Johnny, and then arrested the two men from Security Concepts.
5. Quai was sent to overpower Carol Crissman and then use her as bait to lure Justin over to her house so he could kill him, and he has disappeared along with Carol.
6. Donald Crafton and Coy Beard stole my money and my plane and fled to Texas.
7. Johnny Steele storms Justin's house and is cut down immediately.

"It's too much," Jack said out loud, "Nobody is that lucky or that good dammit!"

Jack picked up his phone and dialed Cecil Wood. "Hey, Jack," Cecil answered.

"Did you check on that van I saw with Allegheny Refrigeration painted on the side?"

"Yes, but there has been so much going on I haven't had a chance to talk to you about it," Cecil answered. "There is no Allegheny

Refrigeration. I checked with the Better Business Bureau and the licensing department in Raleigh, and nobody's heard of them."

"What about Billy? Did Brooks Walker and Charles Moses find him?"

"No, they can't find him. The last place that Billy was seen was at the pool hall, and as much as I don't want to tell you this, the two guys that were shooting pool with him said he was talking about settling his score with Travis Hayes."

"Dammit, Cecil, I need to know things like that. He's my son!"

"I know, Jack. I'm sorry! It's just been so damn crazy around here I couldn't find the right time to tell you."

Jack hung the phone up and added this new information to his list.

8.   Allegheny Refrigeration is bogus.
9.   Billy's missing after going after Travis Hayes.

Jack looked over the list. There is no way in hell that one man could make this happen. It would take a team of men to pull this off. And if Allegheny Refrigeration is bogus, who is driving the van and why are they going to Justin's house? Something's not right. I must be missing something! Suddenly it dawned on Jack that he was saying the same things that Donald Crafton had been saying all week. Something's not right, we're missing something. Fear started seeping into Jack as he studied his notes. Justin did have a team working for him and it had to be the FBI. That's why he was released so quickly from jail! That's why Donald and Coy decided to run! That's why Tommy disappeared! That's who was in the helicopter that turned around and went back the way it came! That's why Johnny was cut down immediately! There were FBI sharpshooters protecting Justin's house, and they were probably watching this house also! With it all written down in front of him, it was as obvious as the nose on his face.

Jack felt sick on his stomach as he thought about what was sure to happen soon. The Feds would swoop down on them and arrest everyone except possibly the two maids and the two Mexicans that looked after the grounds. Everyone else would end up serving long prison terms. He probably would never live long enough to get back out of prison. It was over. He had built an empire, but it would collapse like a house of cards in a matter of days, if not hours.

Jack sat back in his chair and took a deep breath. Life was good until Justin Hayes moved into the neighborhood. The pool parties and the booze and the call girls, racing the muscle cars and going on trips to wherever you pleased, the five-star restaurants and the strip clubs, lap dances and massages and wearing expensive clothes, it was all gone!

Jack picked up his phone and started to dial Steve Helms, but after thinking about it for a moment, he laid the phone back in its cradle. He walked back down the hall to Steve's office and stepped inside.

"Oh, Jack," Steve said, looking up from some paperwork. "I heard about Johnny. I sure am sorry."

"Do Horatio and Antonio carry two-way radios?" Jack asked.

"Uh, yeah," Steve said, surprised by the question.

"How about calling them and telling them I'd like to see them before they leave today," Jack said.

"Sure, Jack. Uh, did they do something wrong?"

"No, no. They haven't done anything wrong," Jack assured Steve. "I just want them to translate something for me, that's all."

"Oh, okay then. I'll tell them to stop on their way out this evening."

"Thank you, Steve," Jack said and he turned and left.

"That's great, thanks for the call," Dan said and then closed his cell phone. "I just got word from Houston. They have arrested Donald's half brother Frank and the two gangsters from New Orleans, and have boarded Jack's airplane and arrested Donald Crafton and Coy Beard."

"So far so good!" Jimmy said.

"Not bad for second string," Dan said and cut his eyes over to Jimmy.

"Ah, hell, Dan, you know I didn't mean anything when I called your men second string."

"It doesn't bother me, but if those men on the Special Response Team hear you call them second string, their going to be pissed!"

"Well, we certainly don't need to get in a pissing contest," Jimmy said. "I apologize for calling your men second string, and it won't happen again."

"Fair enough, apology accepted."

"Thank you, Walter," Travis said as he and Jesse stepped out of the limousine in front of the Regency Hyatt Hotel. "I can't believe that mother sent a limo and a driver for us."

"It is my pleasure, sir," Walter said and bowed his head. "How was your meal?"

"It was unbelievable," Jesse spoke up. "I'm not even sure what some of the things I ate were, but it was all delicious."

"Sterling's has quite a reputation for exquisite food," Walter said.

"It was a perfect meal with a perfect lady," Travis said as he put his arm around Jesse. "Walter, I'm a little concerned about my mother though."

"Her health, sir?"

"No, she has the best doctors in the state," Travis said. "I'm worried about Paul Maxwell. Mama has spent a big chunk of his money and run off all his girlfriends. I'm afraid he might get angry enough to try and hurt her!"

"You needn't worry, sir." Walter answered. "I work for your mother, not Paul Maxwell. The reason your mother hired Ethan and I is because we are not just butlers, but bodyguards also. If Paul Maxwell acts inappropriately, I will toss him out on his duff. And if things become bad enough, I will call on my little friend." Walter opened his coat just enough for Travis to see the butt of a handgun.

"You cannot imagine how relieved I am to learn that."

"If something happens, I have been instructed to contact you immediately."

"Semper fi!" Travis said.

"Semper fi!" Walter answered.

Travis and Jesse nodded at the doorman when they entered the hotel and all heads turned and stared as they crossed the lobby and stepped onto the elevator.

"Honeymoon suite, please," Travis said to the operator.

"Congratulations," he replied. "You are quite an attractive couple."

"Thank you," Travis and Jesse said together. When they reached their floor Travis tipped the man and swiped his card to enter their room. As soon as Travis shut the door behind him he spun Jesse around and kissed her passionately. "You are so beautiful it's driving me insane!" He said as he searched for the zipper on the back of her gown.

"Easy, tiger, we have all night," Jesse said, smiling. "Besides, I have a special outfit to wear for you tonight."

"Don't tell me that I have to stand outside that bathroom and wait for you again!"

"Yes, you do!" Jesse said in between the kisses. "But it won't take me long to get ready."

"I won't be able to wait very long."

"I'll hurry, I promise."

"Please hurry!" Travis begged.

"Eagle, this is Hart," Harold Hartley reported from his hide. "The two Mexicans that do the yard maintenance have stopped their truck beside the house and gone inside."

"Give me video," Jimmy said.

"Okay, but I don't know how much you can see. It's getting dark out here fast."

Jimmy and Dan strained their eyes to make out the house and the truck. It had been eerily quiet at Jacks since the shooting of Johnny Steele. There had been no activity on the phone lines and no one was stirring around outside. The silence was driving Jimmy Hardy insane. He had never quit during a mission in his twenty-two years of service, and he wouldn't quit this one, but he had never wanted a mission to end as much as this one.

"Here they come," Hart said.

Jimmy and Dan could see two figures emerge from the side door and walk out to the truck and get in. The truck started up and headed toward the gate.

"Call the ball, Eagle," Hart said.

"Red light, red light, let them leave. They don't have anything to do with this mess and they don't live on the premises."

"Roger that, Eagle, we are red light."

The truck went through the gate and across the bridge and up River Road.

Travis took his tuxedo off and stripped down to his black briefs while Jesse was in the bathroom putting on her special outfit. He dimmed the lights and lit all the candles and then turned down the huge comforter on the king-sized heart shaped bed.

His imagination was only matched by his anticipation as he paced back and forth wondering what this special outfit was. Probably a "teddy" of some sort, either black or red, or possibly an edible outfit, like a cool-whip bikini! That would be so awesome he thought as he walked around the bedroom.

"I'm going crazy out here!" Travis shouted at the bathroom.

"I'm ready, but I want you to walk out on the balcony and wait until I call you before you come in the bedroom," Jesse hollered.

"Okay, I'm going," Travis shouted. He stepped over and drew the vertical blinds that covered the sliding glass door that led out onto the balcony. Travis slid the door open and stepped out onto the balcony. "Okay, I'm on the balcony!"

"Wait until I say so before you come into the bedroom!"

"Okay, but please hurry!"

Travis turned around and looked over the banister at the town of Greensboro at night. The world seemed so peaceful from sixteen floors up. He wondered how peaceful things were back at his dad's house and chastised himself for not calling earlier and checking.

"Okay, you can come in now!" Jesse's voice echoed through the door.

Travis walked back inside and shut the door and the blinds before trotting to the bedroom. When he entered the bedroom and saw Jesse he was totally awestruck. Jesse was standing beside the bed with her back toward Travis and she was bent over looking back through her legs at the expression on his face. She was wearing her red thong and knee-high rubber boots.

"Well, how's this outfit?" She said grinning. "Perfect! Absolutely positively perfect!"

Knock! Knock!

Before Anthony Tussey even opened the door that led into Jack's kitchen he could hear several people talking. That was unusual on Sunday mornings, especially before ten o'clock. He had set his alarm so he would wake up early since Jack had temporarily put him in charge of running the hotel. He hoped that if everything ran smoothly with him at the helm that maybe Jack would consider letting him run the hotel permanently. Even though he made twice as much money working for Jack as he would working for anyone else, the thought of being in charge and getting a substantial wage increase had him so excited that he could barely sleep last night.

Anthony opened the door and stepped into the kitchen and walked over to the coffeepot to pour a cup of coffee. Cecil, Steve, Lee, Jerry, and Ashley were seated around the island bar in the kitchen drinking coffee.

"Good morning, everyone," Anthony said. "I guess we got our plane back last night."

"No, we didn't!" Cecil said.

"Really?" Anthony said. "Has there been a change in the arrangements?"

"No one knows," Steve spoke up. "Lee waited in the hangar all night and Jerry waited in the control tower and the plane never showed up! We've tried to contact them on the radio, but so far there has been no response."

"Does Jack know?" Anthony asked.

"We don't know if he does or not," Cecil said. "He's not up yet."

"Maybe we should wake him," Anthony suggested.

"He has a do not disturb sign on his door," Ashley said. "I'm not going to wake him!"

"Me either!" Cecil and Steve said at the same time.

"Does he have a woman with him, Ashley?" Lee asked.

"I don't know if he does or not. If he does he slipped her in after I went to bed," Ashley said. "Normally that's the only reason he hangs the sign on his door though."

"I guess we're just going to have to wait until he gets up before we can find out what's going on," Cecil said.

The voice of Tracey Skeen suddenly came over the intercom in the kitchen. "Anthony?"

Anthony stepped over and pushed the talk button beside the speaker. "This is Anthony speaking."

"Anthony, Mr. Ignacio has been ringing his buzzer since seven o'clock this morning. He is very upset that he wasn't able to fly out last night and he wants to talk to Mr. Crafton about flying out today in the other plane. If he rings that damn buzzer one more time, I'm going to take a mop handle down there and knock that damn towel off his head!"

"Calm down Tracey," Anthony said. "If he buzzes again tell him that I will be there in five minutes."

"Yes, sir, I will," Tracey said. "I'm sorry but he got on my last nerve this morning."

"That's okay, just have a seat in the office and I'll bring you a cup of coffee. You can take a break while I go talk to him."

"Thank you."

"You're welcome." Anthony let go of the button and grabbed another coffee cup from the cabinet.

"I can go talk to him if you like," Cecil offered.

"No, that's okay, Cecil. I can handle it."

"We never fly anybody out during the day, and we never fly the Cessna at night, so he's just going to have to be patient!" Cecil said.

"Exactly what I intend to tell him," Anthony said as he turned to leave.

"I'll be right here if you need me," Lee said. "Since Johnny and Tommy are gone, I guess I'll have to handle any unruly guests."

"Thanks, Lee, but I'm sure I can calm Mr. Ignacio down," Anthony said. "I would like for someone to let me know when the plane will be back."

"We'll let you know as soon as we know," Cecil said.

"Thank you," Anthony said as he stepped through the door.

Scott Rhodes grabbed a bale of hay from Jesse's barn loft and handed it down to several waiting members of the Special Response Team. The smell of orchard grass brought back memories of his parent's farm in Ohio, and he wondered if his dad was doing the same thing that he was on this beautiful Sunday morning. Scott climbed down and carried the bale of hay through the barn and tossed it over the gate that led to the pasture. He opened the gate and picked the bale back up and carried it about forty yards away from the barn before he cut the twine that held it together. He tossed three equal portions of hay into three separate piles and then paused to look at Jesse's horses. They were standing about a hundred yards away, staring at Scott and wondering why thirty-five men spent the night in their barn.

"I don't blame you one bit!" Scott said to the horses. "I would stand way the hell over there too if this crowd moved into my house." Scott walked back to the barn and shut the gate behind him. He had to carry a scoopful of chicken feed over to the hen house and then he could finish getting himself ready for the raid.

"Hey, Scott," a voice echoed through the barn. "West Virginia wants to know if there are any sheep out there in the pasture!"

"Kiss my ass, Sonny!" another voice sounded.

"There's just one and she's mine!" Scott said bringing on a round of laughter from the men as they prepared for their morning operation. Scott carried a scoopful of chicken feed over to the hen house and returned to the barn just in time to hear the team leaders call everybody to attention. Corey Wallace stepped up onto a wheelbarrow to address the crowd since he was the senior man.

"Okay, guys, if I can have your attention for just a minute. I'm not going to rehash your assignments and your areas of responsibility. You all know what you're supposed to do. But I do need to tell you how we're going to leave this morning. At 10:30, approximately one hour from now, three Bell UH-lD Huey helicopters will land in the pasture behind this barn. As soon as they land, myself and my team will load into the Armored Personnel Carrier and leave. It will take us about fifteen minutes to arrive at our objective, so we should arrive at about 10:45. As we are leaving, you will be loading into the choppers. Ed Reed's team will load into the first helicopter and Peter Ollinger's team will load into the second helicopter. The third helicopter will already be manned by Jim Wilson's SWAT team from Texas. They should be nice and fresh this morning since they have been sleeping in the Federal Building in North Wilkesboro instead of a barn like we have."

A round of boos resonated from the crowd until Corey quieted them down. "Anyway, as we approach our objective, Special Agent Dan Loggins at Control Headquarters will coordinate the APC and all three helicopters and give us the go ahead to begin. Nothing happens until Control says go. Are there any questions?"

The group of warriors was silent as each man mentally rehearsed his assignment.

"Okay, here's what we know," Corey continued. "There are at least fifteen people and probably more on the premises that are to be arrested. At least four of them are fugitives from justice and probably won't surrender willingly since they are all looking at long prison terms." Corey paused briefly before he continued. "Here's what we don't know. We have no idea what kind of firepower they have or if any of them will be willing to use it against us. We don't think they have any explosives, like grenades or RPGs, but again let me emphasize that we don't know for sure what they have. Remember, there are three military sniper teams set up around the perimeter and if we need them we can call them. Any questions?"

Again there was silence.

"One last thing," Corey said as he lifted a poster up for the crowd to see. "The man you are looking at on this poster is one of the people that you will be arresting today. He is Egyptian and his name is Gyurman Yahamen Tahare-Azar but he goes by the alias Maschiek Abdullah Ignacio. Mr. Tahare-Azar is a known Al Qaida terrorist and is wanted by the CIA and the Department of Homeland Defense. He must be captured alive if at all possible. He will be carrying a suitcase and a laptop computer with him or either they will be close by when he is captured. Here is a picture of the suitcase," Corey said as he held up another poster.

"It is imperative that we recover the suitcase and the computer when we capture him. As soon as he is placed in custody, we will lead him out to the airstrip where a plane will land and pick him up along with the suitcase and the computer. After he flies away you will forget that you ever saw him. Does everybody understand me?"

The barn filled with the voices of over thirty men as they answered, "Yes, sir," in unison.

"If you shoot this man you better have a damn good reason. He is by far the most important objective of this operation and the suitcase is just as important as he is," Corey emphasized. "Are there any questions?"

"Should the suitcase be considered dangerous? Should we handle it like an explosive?" one of the men asked.

"No, the suitcase is harmless," Corey answered. "More than likely he will be arrested inside by the SWAT team, but if he manages to slip by them and runs outside you can pick the suitcase up without worrying about it exploding. Are there anymore questions?"

The barn was eerily quiet.

"Good luck," Corey said. "Now let's go catch some bad guys!"

"Ahhhhh!" Travis screamed as he jumped out of bed. "What's wrong, sweetheart?" Jesse shouted.

Travis stood beside the huge heart-shaped bed in the honeymoon suite of the Regency Hiatt Hotel naked as the day he was born with a look of complete bewilderment on his face.

"What's wrong, honey?" Jesse asked again. She was sitting up now, looking first at Travis and then at the bed.

Travis put his hands over his face and started laughing and laughed until he started coughing.

"What is so funny?" Jesse demanded.

"Oh my God, I can't breathe," Travis finally said in between the coughing and the laughing. Travis finally took a deep breathe and climbed back into bed.

"Do you do this often when you wake up in the morning?" Jesse asked.

"Only when there's a mirror hanging over the bed," Travis said as he pointed at the ceiling and started laughing some more. "When I woke up and opened my eyes there was a naked man over me and it totally freaked me out!"

Jesse laughed and then slid over against Travis and kissed him. "I saw the same naked man over me last night and it didn't freak me out."

"Last night was so amazing," Travis said.

"How about a massage this morning sailor?" Jesse said as she kissed him again.

"How much do you charge?"

"Not for you! A massage for me! You owe me one anyway since I wore the thong and the rubber boots."

"Okay, climb on the table."

Jesse slid over on top of Travis and buried her head in the pillow beside his head as he reached around her and started massaging her neck and shoulders. He stared at the mirror on the ceiling as he worked his hands down her back. She was gorgeous lying there on top of him, from her beautiful black hair down her slender body to her firm hips, and on down her shapely legs to the tips of her toes, and seeing her in the mirror lying on top of him was incredibly erotic.

"Hmmm, the massage table suddenly has a lump in it," Jesse moaned.

"Seeing you in that mirror is killing me," Travis said. "You are so beautiful and sexy, Jesse."

"Let me see," Jesse said as she flipped over on her back still lying on top of Travis. "Now massage this side while I watch."

Travis moved his hands up to her breasts as he kissed her ear. Jesse moaned as he began massaging her breasts with one hand while his other hand worked down her stomach until it was between her legs.

"You know what, darling?" Jesse panted.

"No, what?"

"We got to buy us a mirror."

"That was the best breakfast that I've ever had," Chief said rubbing his belly.

"If we had to stay here another week, Chief, we would be so fat we couldn't pass our PT test," DeMac said as he rubbed his belly also.

Justin just grinned at the two soldiers as they sat around the breakfast table trying to digest the mountain of food they just ate. "Well, I figured this would probably be our last meal together, so why not make it special."

Justin had taken three rib eye steaks out of the freezer last night and thawed them out so he could fix them for breakfast, along with scrambled eggs, silver dollar pancakes, hash brown potatoes, sliced cantaloupe, and hot biscuits.

"Well, it was definitely special!" DeMac said.

"Amen to that," Chief added.

"Now, as soon as I clean up these dishes, I'm going to get another cup of coffee and go sit on the front porch so I can watch the show this morning.' Justin said. "I've been cooped up in this house for three days and I'm about to go out of my mind!"

"Jimmy will go out of his mind if he finds out you're sitting on the front porch," DeMac said.

"I know, but I don't hardly see how I could be in much danger with the FBI assaulting Jack's place from every direction," Justin said.

"I don't either!" Chief said.

"Okay," DeMac said. "I'll agree to it, but I want you to sit in between me and Chief and I want you to wear a ballistic vest."

"That's fair enough," Justin said as he stood up from the table. "Now get out of here so I can clean up these dishes."

Marvin Wood stood in the vestibule of the New River Baptist Church and checked his pocket watch for the third time in two minutes. Marvin was a simple man, a little slow by most standards but as reliable as the sunrise and sunset. He couldn't teach a Sunday school class or lead the choir, but he could ring the bell every Sunday at 10:45 and he did so with vigor.

Marvin looked over the congregation to see who was present and who was missing. It appeared that everybody was here except for Justin Hayes and Carol Crissman. He had overheard somebody saying that they were sweet on each other and he wondered if they were together this morning. He had always liked the low cut dresses that Carol wore and the way her breasts came together in the center. As Marvin thought about that he suddenly turned red and felt ashamed of himself for thinking such thoughts in the house of God.

Marvin checked his watch again to help clear his mind. It was almost time to ring the bell. He stepped over to the side of the vestibule and took hold of the rope with one hand and held his watch with the other. When there was only ten seconds to go, Marvin put his watch up and counted out loud, "Nine, eight, seven, six, five, four, three, two, one." Ding, dong, ding, dong, ding, dong.

He had no way of knowing that he just signaled the beginning of a multistate and multimillion-dollar federal raid.

"FBI, open the door!"

"Federal marshal, open the door now!"

The two officers stepped aside so that the four man battering ram team could break down the door. "Hit it!" one of them said. The men lunged forward and shattered the three-inch thick solid oak door on the first strike, and then broke it down with the next one. The men that were swinging the ram fell inside and rolled out of the way so that the throng of FBI agents and Federal marshals could get by them.

Two men in suits came charging through the house but quickly went to the floor when they saw the muzzles of ten assault rifles pointed at them.

"Where's Jimmy?" the marshal shouted at the man on the floor. "I don't know!"

"You piece of shit, where's Jimmy? Somebody give me a taser!"

"He ain't got up yet, he's still in bed!" the man shouted.

The officers ran through the kitchen and started clearing rooms as they worked their way down the hall until they came to the last door. It was locked.

"FBI!" they shouted as one of them backed up and kicked the door in. A woman screamed and two miniature French Poodles barked as they entered the bedroom with their pistols leading the way. A pretty blond haired woman who looked to be in her twenties was sitting in the center of a king sized bed with the comforter pulled up tight around her neck.

"Let me see your hands!"

"I'm not dressed!" she cried.

"Let me see your hands! Do it now!"

The woman finally let go of the comforter and raised her hands as the comforter fell down, revealing two incredibly huge breasts.

"Where's Jimmy?"

"He's not here!"

"No, shit tits, we know that! Where did he go?"

"I don't know!"

The officers headed across the room. There were three doors in front of them. One led into a bathroom, one led into a walk-in closet, and the third led to a hallway that led to who knows where.

"He probably went down the hall, but let's clear these rooms first," the FBI agent said. They entered the bathroom first and cleared it before they eased their way into the closet. It was thirty feet long with clothes hanging on both sides. It was the perfect place to be ambushed and the two officers knew it. You can train in live fire shooting ranges and study every conceivable scenario, but there is just no way to safely clear a room full of clothes.

They eased along using one hand to shift the clothes so they could see behind them and the other hand to hold their Sigarms P220 .45-caliber pistols. They finally reached the end of the closet and started to turn around when the Marshal noticed that the shoe rack that was built against the end of the closet had a piano hinge running down the left side. He pulled on the shoe rack and it swung open effortlessly, revealing a small tunnel that was just big enough for a man to crawl through on his hands and knees. They shined their flashlights down the tunnel but it turned ninety degrees and prevented them from seeing very far.

"We need a K-9 in the master bedroom," the FBI agent said into his mic. "Roger that, we're on the way!"

The officers walked back to the bedroom to await the dog. "A couple of you guys check out that hallway and see where it leads! One of you find a robe for tits here and take her to the dining room."

An officer dressed in tactical gear entered the bedroom leading a large German Shepherd. The two French poodles started barking furiously and leapt off the bed but spun around and jumped back on the bed when the K-9 barked and then jumped at them.

"At the end of that closet," the marshal directed the dog handler.

The dog was leading as they entered the closet, and instantly started barking when he saw the opening to the tunnel. He knew exactly why he was brought here now.

"We're turning the dog loose!" the officer shouted into the opening. "Come out if you don't want to get bit!"

"Hold on! Just wait a damn minute, I'm coming out!" a voice echoed.

"Come out slowly with your hands in front of you!" the marshal shouted.

After about thirty seconds a pair of hands appeared at the opening and the two officers dragged Jimmy Milano out on the floor and cuffed him. They read him his rights and then stood him up.

"What is this about?" Jimmy snarled.

"We have a warrant for your arrest."

"What's the charge?"

"Aiding and abetting for the purpose of committing first-degree murder, aiding and abetting the harboring of fugitives, and tax evasion."

"I want to talk to my attorney! You don't have shit on me!"

"I think as soon as some of those good old boys in North Carolina get ready to cut a deal with us, we'll have a lot more on you than we do now," the FBI agent said and then grinned.

"I don't even know anybody in North Carolina!"

"Oh, by the way, we have a search warrant for your house too," the marshal said and then held it out so that Jimmy could see it.

"Would somebody please escort Mr. Milano out to the paddy wagon?"

Justin leaned over the railing that ran around his front porch and threw up. His stomach churned as he fought to regain his composure and what little bit of dignity he had left.

DeMac and Chief stood on either side of him wondering what they could do to help, but they had no idea what was happening to Justin.

Justin was excited as he watched the armored personnel carrier roll by his house on its way to meet up with Jack's wrought iron gate and he watched through binoculars as it crossed the bridge and knocked the gate down. What happened next caught him completely off guard. The three Huey helicopters came right down River Road, nose to tail and tree top high and passed by Justin's house in a blur. With no warning, Justin found himself back in Vietnam.

Justin knew that the main force would be jumping out of the choppers and sweeping the valley, and he along with a small blocking force were set up to intercept any Viet Cong that tried to slip out the back. Justin saw three men carrying AK-47s run across the dike that separated the two rice paddies and he quickly settled his crosshairs on the one bringing up the rear. The man's head snapped back and he crumbled to the ground as Justin worked the bolt on his rifle and shifted the cross hairs over to the next one. As he squeezed the trigger on his rifle he could hear machine guns and rockets going off, and smell the rotten stench of bodies burning as the Phantom Jets dropped their canisters of Napalm on the villages.

"Justin! Justin, are you all right?" DeMac shouted.

"Yeah, yeah, I'm all right now," Justin said as he wiped his mouth with the back of his hand. "I had a flashback. I was back in Nam. Oh, God, I could smell the burning bodies!"

"Let's go back inside!" DeMac said.

"No, I'm okay now," Justin said. "That's never happened before. I think it was the Hueys that brought it on. I didn't know they still used them."

"There's still quite a few of them around," Chief said.

"We lost 2,500 of them in Vietnam, and 2,200 pilots," Justin said as he sat back down in the rocking chair and picked his binoculars back up. He looked toward Jack's with a little hesitation, fearing that it could trigger another flashback. One of the helicopters went out of sight as it lowered itself on the other side of the mountain, while the other helicopter sat down beside of Jack's garage. Justin searched for the third helicopter and finally discovered that it had climbed to a higher altitude and was slowly circling.

"I wish Roy was sitting here with me this morning," Justin said as he watched the men surrounding the house. DeMac sat down to the left of Justin but Chief remained standing as he watched the action through his binoculars.

Justin suddenly felt a chill and wondered if he was coming down with a fever. Maybe that had something to do with him getting sick on his stomach, he thought. When Justin finally lowered his binoculars he caught a glimpse of movement in his peripheral vision and turned to his right. The empty rocking chair beside him was slowly rocking back and forth ever so slightly. Justin smiled. "Well, howdy, Roy."

"What did you say?" Chief said as he turned around.

"Nothing. Just talking to myself."

The buzzer that signaled that the gate was open suddenly went off and Ashley stepped into the living room to see who was coming in. She screamed when she saw the Armored Personnel Carrier sliding to a stop and armed men running in every direction. Cecil and Lee came running into the room.

"Oh shit!" Cecil hollered. "Go wake Jack!"

Ashley and Lee ran down the hall to Jack's bedroom and beat on the door.

"Jack! Wake up! It's an emergency! Wake up!" Ashley shouted. The thumping sound of a helicopter could be heard and it grew so loud it sounded like it was landing on the roof.

"Stand back!" Lee shouted, and he backed up and kicked Jack's door in. Ashley and Lee rushed in and saw Jack lying across his bed, naked as usual.

"Jack, wake up!" Ashley screamed. She started toward the bed but suddenly stopped. "That's not Jack."

Antonio Penta was lying sideways across Jack's bed with an empty bottle of tequila in his right hand and a smile across his face.

"More coffee, Sheriff?"

"Yeah, you can fill it up while you're here, darling," Bill said to the waitress. He was sitting in the back corner of the Allegheny Inn finishing off a stack of pancakes and an order of link sausage while he waited for his guest to arrive. Bill stuck his fork in the last piece of pancake and then stuck it in the last piece of sausage and swirled it around in the maple syrup before sticking it in his mouth. A man wearing a pair of faded blue jeans and a ragged sweatshirt entered the restaurant and came straight back to Bill's table and sat down.

"Well, hello, Eddie," Bill said. "Want some breakfast?"

"I'm not hungry, Sheriff," he said as he glanced around nervously.

"Breakfast is the most important meal, Eddie. You should eat something. I'll even pay for it."

The waitress walked back to their table carrying a menu and a cup of coffee. "Coffee, sir?"

"Yes, ma'am, thank you. This is all I want, I'm not eating."

"All right, holler if you change your mind, honey," she said as she left.

"What do you want, Sheriff?" Eddie Ledbetter asked as soon as the waitress was gone.

"I want to offer you a deal, Eddie."

"How do I know you're not setting me up?"

"'Cause the deal I'm offering you is just as illegal for me as it is for you. I would do more time than you would if we got caught!" Bill said.

"What do you want me to do?"

"I was looking over your background information yesterday and noticed that you were a demolition expert when you were in the Green Beret."

"That's true, so what?"

"Let's just say that I have a rock damning up the stream that feeds my pond and I need to blow it out of the way. Could you build me a bomb to do it?"

"I know how but I don't have a license to handle explosives," Eddie said.

"I'm not worried about a bullshit license, Eddie."

"I know, but I can't buy the stuff I need to build a bomb without a license."

"What if I provided you with whatever you needed, could you build it then?"

"Yeah, I could build it, but what's in it for me?"

"What if that bag of cocaine and that bottle of oxycodone that was found in your truck mysteriously disappeared from our evidence room?"

"I see where you going with this now," Eddie said.

"You're looking at some serious time, Eddie," Bill said.

"I know, I know! Okay, you have a deal, Sheriff, but just remember, if you double cross me I can always build another one when I get out of the joint!"

"I won't double cross you, Eddie. I need this bomb bad and I need it now so what do you need to build it."

"How big is the rock?"

"It's a little over six feet tall and weighs about 230 pounds," Bill said as he stared across the table at Eddie.

"Oh, that kind of rock," Eddie said as he took a napkin and wiped his forehead.

"I also need to set it off with some kind of remote. Can you do that?"

"Sure, no problem. All I need is a half a pound of plastic explosives, a blasting cap, and a cell phone. I have everything else I need in my shop."

Bill was looking straight at Eddie but suddenly shifted his gaze to the three people that just entered the restaurant. FBI agents Roseanna Lankford and Fred Turner, along with SBI agent Jerry Teddar casually crossed the room until they were standing directly across the table from Bill Sisk. Eddie got up and stepped over to the side.

"Good morning, officers, let me buy you some breakfast," Bill said and he started to reach behind his back like he was retrieving his wallet.

"Keep your hands on top of the table, Sheriff," Roseanna ordered.

"What's going on here?" Bill asked as he started to stand up.

Jerry Teddar pushed Bill back down. "You're under arrest, Sheriff, that's what's going on."

Roseanna stepped over beside Eddie Ledbetter and ripped the tape off his chest that was holding the recorder as Eddie held his sweatshirt up.

"I got a better deal than yours, Sheriff," Eddie said as he pulled the tape off that was holding the microphone.

"You people are out of your mind!" Bill said. "I was trying to find out where the missing explosives are that were stolen from the quarry." Bill started to reach behind himself again and this time Roseanna and Fred drew their guns.

"If you reach around your back one more time you're going to hear some explosives, Sheriff," Agent Turner said.

"You got to be kidding me! I wasn't going to go through with this deal! This is part of my investigation!"

"We're not arresting you for this, Sheriff," Roseanna said. "We're arresting you for the murder of Roy Hepler, along with aiding and abetting the harboring of fugitives and the attempted murder of Justin Hayes."

"When you called Eddie yesterday and told him you wanted to meet with him this morning, he immediately called me," Jerry Teddar said. "And I called FBI Agent Dan Loggins because I had a feeling that there was something strange going on after the shootout the other day. Turns out that they were going to arrest you this morning anyway, so this was the perfect way for Agent Lankford and Agent Turner to locate you this morning."

"Now stand up slowly and place your hands on top of your head," Roseanna ordered.

Bill placed his hands on the edge of the table and slowly started to stand and then suddenly flipped the table over onto the officers and reached for his gun. Roseanna stepped back but her heel caught in a crack in the linoleum and she tumbled over backward but not before firing one round that went an inch over Bill's head. Fred Turner fell sideways over an adjacent chair and never got a round off, but SBI Agent Jerry Teddar side-stepped the flying table and dishes and did what he had practiced at least a thousand times at the SBI indoor shooting range. He swept his coat out of the way as he grabbed his pistol and took a lower and wider stance as he presented his pistol and pumped five .40-caliber rounds into Bill Sisk's chest.

Bill staggered and then fell across the upside down table and all the broken dishes, and then let out a death moan.

"Jack's not here, Cecil!" Ashley shouted when she ran back into the kitchen.

"What do you mean he's not here?" Cecil shouted back.

"I think he left with Horatio last night. Antonio is passed out on Jack's bed."

Lee Hayworth ran through the kitchen and through the door that led to the hangar.

"Lee! Lee!" Cecil shouted, but Lee never broke his stride. The phone in the kitchen started ringing as Cecil tried to figure out what to do next. "Answer that, Ashley! It might be Jack!"

Ashley lifted the receiver and put it to her ear slowly. "Hello?"

"This is Special Agent Dan Loggins of the Federal Bureau of Investigation. It is imperative that you stay on the line with me and not hang up. I need to speak to Mr. Jack Billings."

"It's the FBI," Ashley said to Cecil. "They want to speak with Jack."

Cecil took the handset from Ashley. "Jack's not here! What do you want?"

"Who am I speaking with?" Dan asked.

"Is this your men outside the house?"

"Yes, the house and the hangar are totally surrounded. I have arrest warrants and search warrants and there is absolutely no way that anyone can escape. You have my word that no one will be hurt if they come out the front door with their hands up. If you surrender and do exactly what you are told, no one will be injured."

"Give me ten minutes to talk to my people," Cecil said.

"You have three minutes. I will call you back in exactly three minutes, and if you do not answer we will breach the doors and come in and arrest you. The end result is the same, but how it happens is entirely up to you!" Dan said as he hung up the phone.

When Jack came in sight of the house, at least seventy-five guineas began running in every direction and they squawked to the top of their lungs. The racket they made was incredibly loud but the noise that had Jack's attention the most was the barking of a large dog and it was getting louder. The flock of guineas parted down the center as a huge plott hound came down the dirt driveway barking and growling.

Jack was scared to death but he was in no shape to run or climb a tree. He had been walking cross country and up and down mountains for fourteen straight hours. His feet were blistered and bleeding, and his legs were cramping and stinging and he could barely stand, much less run from the growling black dog. Jack slid his right hand into his pants pocket and gripped the derringer that he had brought along with him. He kept a derringer and forty thousand dollars in a hidden wall safe in his bedroom just in case he ever had to run, and he had grabbed it before he left the house with Horatio.

The big hound slid to a stop about ten feet from Jack and stood there growling. "Who's out there!" someone shouted from the house.

"Buck, Buck Jones, it's Jack Billings! Call off your dog!"

"Buckshot, come here, boy! Buckshot, come on!"

The hound turned and started trotting toward the house, but he never stopped growling. Jack hobbled up the dirt driveway toward the shanty that Buck and his wife Vera called home. Buck was standing on the front porch in bib overhauls and holding a double barreled shotgun and Buckshot was now standing beside him.

"Jack Billings, well, I'll be damned, it is you!" Buck said. "What happened? Did you wreck your car and walk back here for help?"

"I need help, Buck, but I didn't wreck my car. The Feds are after me!"

"Revenuers?"

"No, the FBI," Jack said. "Mind if I come up on the porch and sit down? I've been walking all night and all morning."

"FBI, revenuers, federal marshals, you stir them up in a pot and you can't tell one from the other. You say they're chasing you? I ain't heard no dogs?"

"No, they're after me but they don't have dogs on me," Jack said. "I don't think they can follow me back to here."

"You'd be surprised where they can follow you!" Buck said. "Come on up and set down. Buckshot, you lay down and shut up."

"Thank you, Buck," Jack said and he slowly climbed the steps and sat down in a ladder back chair and started unlacing his boots. When Jack pulled his feet out of his boots there were bloodstains on his socks.

"Damn, Jack, you have been walking a spell!" Buck said. "Vera! Vera!"

An elderly woman wearing an apron pushed the screen door open just a few inches. She didn't speak, she just stood there with her cheek full of snuff and waited for instructions.

"Bring a pan of hot water and some Epsom salts," Buck ordered. She let the screen door shut and disappeared inside the house.

"Why they after you, Jack? You been growing marijuana would be my guess."

"No, Buck, not that," Jack said as he tried to pull off one of his socks. "I was hiding a couple guys from the law and they found out about it. They moved a secret agent into that house they built where Roy Hepler's old house used to stand, and he's been spying on me. He even shot and killed my nephew six days ago and they didn't even put him in jail!"

"I heard about a shooting the other day over your way," Buck said. "It's okay for those sons of bitches to kill people, Jack, it's only illegal if you and me do it!"

Vera pushed the screen door open and stepped out onto the porch carrying a large blue pan of hot water and she set it down in front of Jack. She reached in her apron and pulled out a box of Epsom salts and poured the contents into the water and then started to leave.

"Vera, bring Jack here a half a glass of apple brandy," Buck said as she was going back through the door. "Jack, you need to drink that brandy before you stick your feet in that water or you'll scream so loud the Feds will here you for sure."

"Thank you Buck, I really appreciate it."

Vera reappeared shortly and handed Jack a mason jar that was half full of crystal clear apple brandy and she handed one to Buck also, even though he didn't ask for it. Jack figured that Buck and Vera had been together for so long that they probably didn't have to talk to each other anymore to communicate. They were both over seventy years old and they got married when they were sixteen, so they had spent every night together for over fifty-five years except for the three and a half years that Buck spent in prison.

Jack put the glass of brandy to his lips and took a small sip. It was as smooth as ice water and he turned the glass up and drank about a third of it in one gulp.

"Better go kinda slow with that stuff, Jack," Buck said. "You'll be seeing demons if you don't!"

Jack immediately started feeling a warm glow that started in his stomach and rose up to his head. He knew that nobody in Ashe County made better moonshine than Buck Jones, and nobody hated the feds more than him either. Buck had come back from the Korean War in 1953 with several toes that were frost bitten, and he tried for awhile to work on his farm and ignore them, but the pain was too much to bear in the wintertime. When he finally approached the Veterans Administration a year later to try and get some help he was denied from receiving any benefits because he couldn't prove that it happened when he was serving in Korea. The VA claimed that it could have happened while he was working on his farm. To Buck it was the same thing as calling him a liar.

Vera was pregnant by this time so Buck just went back to work on his farm and suffered through the pain. Then the local and state politicians decided that, in order to preserve our precious natural resources, there needed to be a New River State Park, so with the help of a grant from the Federal Government they purchased the land for the park. A large portion of the land was the rich river bottoms that ran along the river, and the biggest majority of it was owned by Buck Jones. Buck was paid a paltry sum for his rich bottom land and was left with some rocky and hilly land that was impossible to farm.

By this time, Vera was pregnant with their third child. Since Buck didn't have any land he could farm he got a job at the Cisco Mine, the same property that Jack later bought to build his house on. He quickly worked his way to a foreman's position and things were starting to look up when the "government environmental people" decided that the Cisco Mine was hazardous to the New River and needed to be shut down. So Buck was unemployed again with three children and another one on the way. With no land, no job, and a wife and four children to raise, Buck did the only thing he could to survive and raise his family, he started making whiskey.

Buck worked as hard at making whiskey as he did at farming and mining and soon had a prosperous business. He raised a wife and five children and none of them ever went hungry or cold. On the day that Buck and Vera's youngest daughter, Suzy, was graduating from high school, Buck's oldest son was moving some supplies from one still to another when the revenuers jumped him. He had folded the windshield on the old Willis Jeep down on the hood and the sun's reflection was spotted by a passing plane and reported. Chuck Jones, Buck's oldest boy, was carrying a box of jars when the men jumped him and he threw them down and started running. When the jars shattered, one of the men thought it was gunfire and opened up on Chuck, killing him. They found Buck's still and all his supplies and sent him to prison for three and a half years. His hatred for the federal government grew every day that he sat in that jail cell and mourned the loss of his son, and it was that hatred that Jack was counting on to help him in his time of need.

Jack took another swallow of the brandy and then took a deep breath before placing his feet into the warm water. "Ughhh," Jack grunted through clinched teeth.

"You let them feet soak for awhile and I'll get Vera to bandage them up for you," Buck said.

"Buck, I can't tell you how much I appreciate this," Jack said through gritted teeth.

"We probably should move inside before they come flying in here with their guns and badges flashing," Buck said. "Them guineas will let us know when they get here."

"I don't think they'll be able to follow me here, Buck," Jack said. "I had a Mexican drop me off about a quarter of a mile above the New River Campground. I told him that I was going to wait until dark and then steal a canoe and go downstream into Virginia. After he drove off I waded at least a half a mile up river before I crossed over and started walking cross country toward your place."

"Well, if they do come, I got a root cellar out back I can put you in that they'll never find!"

"I got some money if you'll hide me out for a couple weeks, Buck."

"I'll hide you from those sons of bitches for free." Buck huffed. "What's your plan? You gonna lay low for a couple weeks and then make a run for it?"

"I'm not sure what I'm going to do," Jack said. "The only thing I'm sure of is I'm going to kill that son of a bitch that lives at Roy Hepler's place!"

Lee Hayworth ran through the tunnel and burst through the door into the hangar. His voice echoed in the large metal building as he screamed for Jerry. There was no one in the hangar so Lee grabbed his cell phone and dialed Jerry's number. He answered immediately.

"Hello?"

"Jerry, we got to get out of here! Where are you?"

"I'm lying on the floor in the control tower! What the hell's going on? There's a helicopter sitting on the airstrip and there are soldiers everywhere!"

"It's the FBI, Jerry! We got to get the hell out of here!"

"I can't go anywhere! They have the—"

Lee hung up. He just lost his only opportunity to escape, or maybe not. Maybe one of the guests knew how to fly a plane. Lee turned and ran down the hall that housed the guests. He ran past room number one because he figured the only thing that Wild Bill Hagee could operate was a Harley Davidson motorcycle. He paused when he ran by room number two but decided to keep going. Sonny Milano was a spoiled brat from Chicago that was too irresponsible to ever get a pilots license. Lee finally stopped at room number four and started beating on the door.

"Wait a damn minute!" Ricky Stone hollered from his bed.

Lee didn't have time to wait. "Can you fly a plane, Mr. Stone?" Lee shouted.

"Hell, no, I can't fly a plane! Why?"

Lee ran down to room number six and started to hit the door when it opened. Mike Savalous had heard the ruckus and was coming to see what was going on.

"Can you fly a plane, Mr. Savalous?" Lee asked impatiently.

"What kind of plane?"

"A Cessna, like the one in our hangar."

"Yeah, I can fly a small prop," Mike said. "I can't fly a jet."

"Then let's go," Lee said. "There are FBI agents surrounding the house!"

"Let me grab my glasses," Mike said as he turned and ran back in his room. He emerged from his room still wearing his pajamas but this time he had his glasses on. Ricky Stone, Bill Hagee, and Maschiek Ignacio had gathered in the hall by this time.

"What the hell is going on?" Wild Bill hollered as Lee and Mike headed for the hangar.

"We got to leave. The FBI is surrounding the house," Lee said.

"Well, I'm going too!" Ricky said.

"Hell yeah, me too!" Wild Bill shouted.

"I will go also," Maschiek said.

The crowd started down the hall in a trot toward the hangar. "There's only room for four people on that Cessna," Mike said. "Somebody's got to stay here and it can't be me because I'm the pilot!"

"One of you three needs to stay here," Lee said, looking back at Ricky, Bill, and Maschiek.

"Why don't you stay here, asshole?" Ricky said. "The guests are the ones that should get to leave."

"Why don't we leave this fucking Arab?" Bill said. "He ain't even American!"

Gyurman was bringing up the rear as the group entered the hangar in a fast trot. Once they cleared the door he ran past Bill Hagee and Ricky Stone and came up quickly beside Lee Hayworth and grabbed his handgun out of his holster. Gyurman shot Lee in the head while still running and then quickly spun around and shot Ricky and Bill. After the three men fell to the concrete he stepped over each one and shot them in the head once more and then turned to face Mike Savalous. "I must get my suitcase before we leave."

"We don't have time for luggage!" Mike shouted.

"Would you like to join your friends Mr. Savalous?"

"Okay, go get your suitcase and I'll warm up the plane."

"No, you go get my suitcase. It is beside my bed."

Mike took off back toward the hotel in a run.

"Shots fired! Shots fired!" The voice came over the speaker in the tobacco barn. "It sounds like they're coming from inside the hangar!"

Dan Loggins keyed the mic. "We don't have anybody in there do we?"

"Negative, Control. All our people are still outside!"

"Roger that. Continue to maintain the perimeter." Dan checked his watch and then dialed the number to Jack's house. Someone answered it on the first ring.

"You said that no one would be hurt!" Cecil shouted. "I can hear gunshots!"

"The shots you hear are coming from the hangar and we're not involved," Dan said. "None of my men have fired a shot!"

"Okay, okay, we're coming out."

"Come out the front door one at a time and follow the instructions that are given you. If you do, no one will be hurt. You have my word on that."

"We're coming out," Cecil said and then he hung up.

"Adam One, do you copy?"

"This is Adam One, Control," Corey Wallace answered.

"The occupants of the house have confirmed that they will be surrendering at the front door," Dan said.

"Roger, Control. We're ready for them."

"Control, this is SWAT. We have cleared the garage, the muscle car building, the equipment sheds, the dojo, and the control tower and have four in custody. Over."

"Roger that, SWAT. Take your prisoners to the front yard and assist Adam One with the rest of the prisoners. Over."

"Control, this is Bravo One. We can hear a plane running inside the hangar and the doors are starting to open!"

"Stop that plane if it tries to leave, Bravo One!" Dan said.

"Roger, Control!"

Jimmy Hardy took a seat at his control board and grabbed the mic. "Redneck, this is Eagle, prepare to disable the plane but wait for my green light."

"Ten-four, Eagle, waiting for your green light."

Every screen on the console was lit up as Jimmy and Dan coordinated the climax to this operation. There was video coming in from all the sniper hides as the FBI continued their assault. Jimmy and Dan turned their attention to the screen that showed the hangar doors as they slowly opened.

Gyurman crouched behind Mike Savalous and held the pistol to his head as they waited for the doors to open. Mike eased off the brake and let the plane ease forward slowly as the doors opened. When they neared the door Mike could see armed men on both sides of the door and the helicopter was blocking the airstrip.

"The runways blocked!" Mike shouted. "I can't get by that chopper!"

"Go around it," Gyurman said. "If you stop I will kill you!"

Mike let off the brake and headed for the grass on the side of the airstrip. A loud clanging sound filled the cabin as several members of the Special Response Team opened up on the engine compartment of the Cessna. Smoke poured out of the engine hood and the plane sputtered but it kept going through the grass and back up onto the runway.

"Green light! Green light! Shut it down, Redneck!" Jimmy hardy said into his mic.

Bill "Redneck" Stoughton took the last six ounces of pressure off the trigger of the Barrett .50-caliber sniper rifle and sent an armor-piercing round over four hundred yards through the engine of the small plane. A large piece of the engine and a portion of the hood flew off the plane and flames erupted across the nose of the aircraft.

Gyurman shot Mike Savalous through the back of his head and opened the door and jumped down onto the runway carrying the suitcase in his left hand and the pistol in his right. He started running down the runway and turned to fire a round at the agents before he noticed that his pistol was empty and the slide was locked back. He threw the pistol down and continued to run. Over twenty men eased their fingers off their triggers when they saw him throw down his pistol.

Dan and Jimmy watched on the monitor as a German Shepherd was released and started down the airstrip after Gyurman. He had a two hundred-yard head start but the K-9 quickly overcame him and took him down.

"Damn, that's beautiful!" Jimmy said.

"That was some amazing trigger discipline," Dan said. "It's a wonder that he didn't get shot!"

Jimmy and Dan shifted their attention to the front of Jack's house. There was a parade of people coming out the front door, and the officers were putting zip-ties on their wrists and seating them in the grass. The SWAT team had caught Jerry Simmons in the control tower and Brooks Walker, Steve Weavil, and Charles Moses in the equipment shed and seated them to one side. The rest were being seated in a circle in the yard. Cecil Wood, Ashley Yates, Steve Helms,

Danny Comer, C. J. Tysinger, Michael Bloom, Stephen Sanders, Anthony Tussey, Tracey Skeen and Jennifer Lopp were all sitting in the yard. Four members of the SWAT team came through the front door carrying Antonio Penta. They had wrapped him in a sheet and they dropped him on the ground in the center of the circle, still unconscious.

"Where's Brett?" Ashley whispered to Steve.

"No talking!" a man standing guard over them shouted.

Brett balanced on the metal framework of the fresh air vent over one hundred feet above the concrete floor and removed the last sheet metal screw that held the cover on. He grunted as he lifted the thirty-six-inch panel and set it to the side. He had no intention of going to prison with the rest of those fools.

He thought about the old saying his daddy used to say: "There's more than one way to skin a cat." Well, he had figured out another way to skin this cat. While the rest of those suckers were walking out the front door with their hands held up, he was looking for another way to escape, and this was it.

Brett twisted his body so he could slip into the ductwork. He could see daylight above him and the top of the duct was within easy reach. This is going to be easier than I thought, he was thinking, as he grabbed the top of the duct and hoisted himself up. Brett swung his body over the top and dropped about five feet to the ground. He smiled when he thought about his ingenuity but when he turned around he suddenly stopped smiling.

"FBI!" the two men with assault rifles shouted. "Get on the ground!"

"I'm just working on the ventilation system!" Brett hollered.

The man standing closest to Brett snickered at first and then started laughing and the other officer joined in and started laughing too.

"Thanks, man," The officer said. "That made my day. Now get on the ground!"

"Ghost Rider, this is Control. The runway is clear and you are cleared for landing. Over!"

"Roger, Control. Our ETA is one minute thirteen seconds."

Several members of the Special Response Team were standing beside the hangar waiting for the plane to pick up their prisoner. He was shackled and blindfolded like they had requested and the suitcase was handcuffed to an armed guard.

The black Bombardier 31-A Lear jet approached the runway with its nose up high and the back of the plane low, similar looking to the space shuttle when it's landing, and leveled off just before setting down. The whine of the engines was incredibly loud as it approached the hangar and spun around so that it was pointed back up the runway for its takeoff.

Gyurman Yahamen Tahare-Azar was led out to the plane as a set of steps slowly lowered to the ground. Two men inside the plane dragged Gyurman up the steps and disappeared into the plane as another man dressed in a suit stepped down to get Suitcase B.

"Where's the laptop computer that goes with the suitcase?" he asked.

"It's inside the suitcase, sir. I was told to look for it and that's where it is!"

"Thank you" was all he said as he stepped back into the plane. The stairs rose up and the door was latched, and the black unmarked jet screamed down the runway and disappeared into the sky.

Justin sat on his front porch all morning with DeMac and Chief sitting on either side of him watching the action at Jack's house. DeMac was wearing his headset but it wasn't patched through to the FBI's communication network so the only thing he heard was an occasional comment from one of the sniper hides. He did hear

Jimmy give Redneck the green light to disable the plane, and of course everyone within two or three miles heard the big fifty when it went off.

The armored personnel carrier finally drove back past Justin's and a virtual parade of black SUVs, vans, and Crown Victorias came by steadily hauling the prisoners to the Federal Building in North Wilkesboro.

"If it wasn't Sunday I believe I would just go trout fishing this evening," Justin said.

"You can't fish on Sunday in North Carolina?" Chief asked.

"It's not illegal to fish on Sunday," Justin said. "I just never felt right doing it."

"Justin, I need to get the okay from Jimmy before you start wandering around," DeMac said. "I know you've been penned up for a few days and want to get out, but it's still my responsibility to protect you until he says different."

"I think I'll call him," Justin said.

"There's no need to now," Chief said. "I think he just turned in."

The white van with High Country Tours painted on the side started up the driveway and Justin, DeMac, and Chief went around to the carport to greet them. The van pulled up and Jimmy Hardy and Dan Loggins got out.

"Well, gentlemen, is it finally over?" Justin asked.

"Yes and no," Dan said. "Let's go inside and talk."

"I don't like the sound of that!" Justin said as they headed for the kitchen table. As the men started to seat themselves, Justin grabbed five longnecks from the refrigerator. "I think we all have earned a cold beer!"

"Thank you," Dan and Jimmy both said.

Dan sat back and took a long swallow from his bottle and then stared across the table at Justin. "Well, do you want the good news or the bad news?"

"Give me the good news," Justin said.

"The good news is that the raid went off flawlessly," Dan said. "As a matter of fact, if the film from the sniper hides wasn't classified they could be used for training videos at the FBI academy. Jimmy Milano was arrested in Chicago without a shot being fired, and we arrested everybody at Jack's without firing a shot except for the shots that were fired to stop the plane from leaving. There wasn't even a single injury except for a couple nasty looking dog bites on our Egyptian friend."

"I guess you recovered the suitcase?" Justin asked.

"The suitcase and the laptop computer and Gyurman Yahamen Tahare-Azar are all three in Quantico, Virginia, as we speak," Jimmy said.

"What about Sheriff Sisk?"

"When they tried to arrest him he decided to shoot it out with them and SBI Agent Jerry Teddar shot and killed him," Dan said. "He was trying to bribe a man to build him a remote-controlled bomb when they approached him and I think you can guess what he was going to do with it."

"Okay, the raid went perfectly. You recovered the suitcase, captured the terrorist, killed the crooked sheriff, and rounded everybody up," Justin said. "So what's the bad news?"

"I didn't say we rounded everybody up," Dan said. "Jack wasn't there!"

"You mean he hasn't been arrested yet?" Justin said.

"Exactly," Dan said. "We can't find him. We think he left last night with one of the Mexicans that he hires to do the yard work and the landscaping. He probably figured out what was going on after Johnny Steele was killed and pretended to be one of the two Mexicans when they left at dark last night to go home. At least that's what we think happened."

"It's my fault," Jimmy said. "I should have stopped that truck last night when they left instead of assuming that it was the two Mexicans."

"That's no big deal, is it?" DeMac asked. "He'll probably be picked up in a few days."

"That's another problem," Dan explained. "There are a lot of people who live in these mountains that still have hard feelings toward the Federal Government left over from the days of Prohibition. They either had a grandfather or an uncle or a cousin that was killed by a federal agent or either they had some family member that went to prison for awhile. Jack knows everybody up here in these hills and more than likely knows someone that will help him hide. We have a team of investigators that are going to continue to look for him, but we know from experience that he may be hard to find."

"You're referring to Eric Rudolf," Justin said.

"Who is Eric Rudolf?" Chief asked. "The name sounds familiar."

"Eric Rudolf set off a series of bombs in several southern states killing two and injuring a hundred and fifty more and was declared a fugitive in May of 1998 and put on the FBI's most wanted list," Dan explained. "An extensive task force was sent to the mountains of North Carolina to track him down and I was part of that task force. We knew that he was in the area and we used dogs and helicopters and planes with thermal cameras and did extensive sweeps through those hills for months on end and could never find him. We also offered a huge reward for information but nobody ever came forward."

"I remember now," Chief said. "He was finally caught, wasn't he?"

"Yes, but it wasn't by us. A city policeman caught him going through a dumpster looking for food. It was in May of 2003, five years after we went after him. The point is we may not be able to find Jack for a long time."

"Well, I would like to propose a toast," Justin said. "To all the brave men of the FBI, SBI, CIA, and the Navy Seals, may God bless America!"

"Hear, hear!" everyone said as they clinked their bottles together over the kitchen table.

"Justin, I'm not sure you understand what we're telling you," Dan said. "Jimmy and I think that Jack may be free for a long time and we also think that he will try to kill you."

"And there won't be any snipers set up around your house to protect you," Jimmy said. "DeMac and Chief are the only ones that haven't already packed up and left, and they'll be leaving with me in the van."

"I understand perfectly," Justin said. "And I'm sure that Jack will probably try to kill me and when he does we'll settle this thing once and for all."

"I can always put you in the witness protection program until we catch him," Dan suggested.

"No way!" Justin instantly answered.

"Then I'll put two agents here to protect you as long as you need them."

"No, you won't either!" Justin said. "Listen to me. As long as there are people hanging around here protecting me, he won't try to kill me. If he has someone hiding him then time is on his side, and he will just wait until I'm unprotected. Jimmy, you and your men get out of here. And Dan, as soon as you get the crime scene processed, you and your men pack up and leave. Gabriel will let me know when Jack makes his move, and when he does I'll deal with him personally."

"Are you sure, Justin?" Dan said.

"I'm positive," Justin replied.

"I feel like I set you up and now I'm abandoning you," Jimmy said. "But I don't have a choice in the matter. The CIA has their suitcase and their terrorist and they have ordered me to leave immediately!"

"Then follow your orders, soldier," Justin said.

"I got thirty days' vacation coming to me," DeMac said. "I could stay and we could get in some fishing."

"You need to take that vacation time and get your ass back to Montana and rebuild that house," Justin said, staring into DeMac's eyes. "Where do you think I'm going to sleep when I come out there to hunt and fish with you?"

There was silence around the table as everybody seemed to be confused as to what they should do next. Jimmy finally broke the silence. "Justin, why don't you pack a bag and go to Quantico with us. My superiors want to talk to you about 'Gabriel' and this would be a good time to go."

"No way," Justin said. "I'm not talking to any government shrinks about Gabriel or anything else!"

"I told them that's what you would say," Jimmy said. "Will you at least sit down and write a brief description of your experiences, a couple pages maybe explaining what you think about it?"

"I'll send them my opinion if they promise to leave me alone."

"That's fair enough."

"Leave me an address."

It was silent again as everybody studied their empty beer bottle and wondered what to do next.

"Listen, guys," Justin finally said. "I understand your concerns, but you all know how this is going to play out. It has been my pleasure to have worked with you on this mission and I count it an honor, but there's only one thing left to do and that's to say our goodbyes. So Jimmy, you load Dan up in that van and drive him down to Jack's and then come back by here and pick up DeMac and Chief and let's get this over with."

After a brief pause Jimmy stood up and reached across the table to shake Justin's hand. "Care if I come back and visit you sometime?"

"You're welcome anytime," Justin said as he shook his hand. "All of you are welcome to come back anytime. And before I forget it, I got a quart jar of that sourwood honey you like so much over there on the counter. I told you that the only way you could get it was if you knew somebody."

"Thank you," Jimmy said and he turned and left. Dan shook Justin's hand and left without saying a word. DeMac and Chief packed their sea bags and shook Justin's hand and said their goodbyes and then stood outside waiting for Jimmy to pick them up.

Justin dialed Teresa's home phone number and after several rings her answering machine came on. "Sorry I wasn't available to take your call. Please call me on my cell phone or leave me a message. Thank you."

Justin dialed her cell phone and she answered it on the first ring. Hearing her voice brought a smile to his face.

"Hello?"

"Is this the dirty old man rescue society?" Justin said.

"Why, yes, it is. Do you know a dirty old man that needs rescuing?" Teresa said over the background noise of children playing and squealing.

"Yes, I do. He's mid fifties, six feet one and about two hundred and thirty pounds, sandy hair with a little gray mixed in. He's not real pretty, but he has a wonderful personality."

"I know exactly what he needs," Teresa said. "Where can I find this dirty old man?"

"You need to meet him in the parking lot of the Sparta Bed and Breakfast."

"How romantic, a secluded hideaway. I can be there in ten minutes."

"Ten minutes!" Justin practically shouted. "Did you buy an Apache helicopter?"

"No, I spent last night with Jerry and Mary Lou, and we're over at Buddy and Judy's right now. Cindy and Colby are playing on the floor with their new kittens. Buddy and Jerry were released from the hospital yesterday and asked me if I wanted to spend the night with them, so I followed them home. I was hoping you would call today. I love you!"

"I love you too, darling, but I can't be in Sparta in ten minutes. What about thirty minutes? I can't wait to see you!"

"I'll be there waiting for you when you pull up!"

"I'm on the way. Love you. Bye."

An Even Fifty

uck finally saw the mailbox he had been searching for and he hit the brakes hard and turned in the driveway. It had taken him three hours to drive from Sparta to Asheville and he was glad that he was finally here. His rusty 1991 Ford F150 truck was as worn out from the trip as Buck was as he steered it up the asphalt driveway toward a modest brick home.

Jack had provided the money for a new set of tires and a tune up, and also paid to get the old truck inspected and tags put back on it so that Buck could make this trip. As he drew closer to the house he could see that the driveway forked, with the right fork going to the brick house and the left fork going back to a cinder block building that was about two hundred feet behind the house. Buck took the left fork and drove up to the block building and parked. There were iron bars over the windows but the steel door was propped open and there were lights on inside. A sign hung beside the doorway: "The Powder Keg. Owner Steve Harrison, Certified Gunsmith."

This is the right place, Buck thought as he tried to get his stiff seventy-three-year-old body out of the truck. He finally managed to crawl out and shut the truck door, and then he paused to get his balance before walking up to the building and stepping inside. A woodstove sat against the wall to his right with an old couch and a couple rocking chairs surrounding it, and to his left was a counter that ran down about fifteen feet before turning ninety degrees and going all the way to the wall that the woodstove sat against. On the other side of the counter there was machinery of every description bolted to the concrete floor. Buck recognized a few of the machines, a pedestal grinder and a drill press, but for the most part he had no idea what the other machines were. A man who looked to be in his forties came walking through the shop and approached the counter.

"Can I help you?"

"Are you Steve Harrison?" Buck asked.

"That depends on if you're a customer or the IRS," the man said with a grin.

"My name is Buck Jones. Tim Hill told me to come see you."

"Tim Hill from Sparta?"

"Yes, sir, that would be him. He won the big rifle match this year in Hickory and he said you built his rifle."

"Yes, I did, a 6.5 × 284, I believe."

"I don't know about all that, but I need a rifle and it needs to be accurate and it needs to be powerful and Tim said to come talk to you."

"You must want a rifle for one thousand-yard matches."

"No, sir," Buck said. "It's for deer hunting."

"Deer hunting. Well, I normally build rifles for competition, but I can build you a deer rifle if that's what you want. What did you have in mind?"

"Well, that's part of the problem 'cause I don't have anything in mind. Let me just explain to you what I need and maybe you can help me out," Buck said. "I need a rifle that I can kill a big buck with at five hundred yards, and I need to drop him in his tracks before he jumps in the river."

"I see. Five hundred yards is a long way to shoot at a buck. Is there any way you can get closer?"

"No, sir, there ain't. Back in the spring of 1996 when the New River flooded and washed everything into Virginia, it changed its course and left me with just a narrow strip of land that borders the New River State Park. If I was a young man I could wade across the river and kill that buck, but I'm way too old for that now."

"This buck must be pretty big if you're going to get a custom rifle built just for him."

"He's the new state record if I can kill him!"

"Really?" Steve said. "How big is he?"

"He was a double drop-tine fourteen pointer this time last season," Buck said, holding his hands out about thirty inches apart. "He stays inside the state park where no one can hunt him, but when he gets to chasing does during the rut, they sometimes swim across the river to get away from him and he swims across right behind them. As soon as he steps up on the bank, I plan on killing him!"

"I understand what you need now," Steve said. "But there's one big problem, Mr. Jones. I'm booked up for over a year. Ever since Tim won that match with my rifle I've been taking orders right and left. I can't build you a rifle and have it ready by November."

"I can pay you big money if you move me to the top of the list."

"Everybody on that list is paying me big money, Mr. Jones."

"I see. Well, I guess I'm just out of luck then," Buck said dejectedly.

"Well, maybe not," Steve said." I can't build you a rifle before November, but I got a rifle here that was built just for killing deer at long range. It's a Beanfield Rifle."

"What's a Beanfield Rifle?" Buck asked.

"Have you ever heard of Kenny Jarrett?"

"I don't think so."

"Well, he's a gunsmith in South Carolina," Steve explained. "He had customers that wanted a rifle that they could kill a buck with if it was standing on the other side of those big soybean fields that they have down there. Jim Carmichael, the famous gun writer, wrote an article about Kenny Jarrett's rifles and he called them Beanfield Rifles and the name stuck."

"Why would you buy one of his rifles when you can build your own?"

"That's a good question," Steve said, grinning. "The truth is I had a customer who came on hard times and he gave me the rifle to settle his bill."

"Well, it sounds like it's just what I'm looking for," Buck said. "And I reckon it'll be cheaper than having you build a new one."

"Actually, Mr. Jones, I could build you a nice deer rifle for a lot less money than I can sell you this Beanfield Rifle."

"You mean a second hand rifle built by this Jarrett feller will cost me more money than a new rifle built by you?"

"I'm afraid so. Kenny Jarrett doesn't build any rifles for less than five thousand dollars and he's booked for over three years. I don't mean to judge you Mr. Jones, but from the way you're dressed and from the looks of your old truck out there, you don't look like a man who has lots of money."

"Well, Mr. Harrison, if I don't kill that buck this coming deer season then I don't think I'll have another chance. As you can see I am an old man, so go get this Beanfield Rifle and let's look at it."

"Are you sure you can afford it?"

Buck unzipped the front pocket on his bib overhauls and pulled out a roll of one hundred dollar bills that totaled over ten thousand dollars. "I can afford it, Mr. Harrison."

Justin studied the banister that ran down the staircase at the Sparta Bed and Breakfast as he descended the stairs. It was made of Chestnut and the craftsmanship was truly incredible. There weren't any CNC-controlled wood lathes back in 1908 when this building was erected, and you couldn't drive down to Home Depot and buy a bundle of spindles or a twenty-foot hand rail. It was built by a true craftsman with a draw knife and chisels and mauls and a carpenters plane. The reddish-blond wood of the hand-rail had been polished smooth by a million rough hands sliding down it, and probably the rear end of several mischievous boys taking a ride.

The Inn was originally built as a boarding house for the men who worked in the lumber yard, but the railway never made it to Sparta and the cost of shipping by truck eventually doomed the lumber business. Justin was glad it did, because he loved the huge timber that grew in these forests.

Justin nodded at several guests that were sitting in the lobby drinking coffee as he crossed the room and approached the counter. Phil and Robin Gulledge, the owners of the Inn, were busy behind the counter with various chores.

"Good morning, Mr. Hayes," Robin said. "Can I help you?"

"Yes, ma'am, I'd like to check out please," Justin answered with a smile.

"Alrighty, then, let's see here. It will be eighty-five dollars, please."

Justin handed her a one hundred dollar bill and the keys to the room and she leaned forward to hand him his change.

"Just keep the change, Mrs. Gulledge. I accidentally knocked the soap dish off the bathroom sink and it broke when it hit the floor. I think you can replace it with fifteen dollars."

"Well, okay then. Thank you for telling us."

"You're welcome," Justin said as he thought back to what he and Teresa were doing when they knocked the soap dish off.

"Uh, Mr. Hayes, can I speak with you a moment before you leave?" Phil asked.

"Certainly."

"Let's step out on the porch if you don't mind," Phil said and he led the way. Justin followed him and he held the front door open so that Justin could step onto the porch and then he stepped outside and shut the door behind him. "Mr. Hayes, I hesitate to say anything to you because I appreciate your business, but according to the register you have a local address."

"That's true," Justin said. "I own a home in Ashe County."

"Mr. Hayes, my wife and I are Christians and we hold ourselves to a higher standard than a lot of people. I'm not running a sleazy motel or a brothel here, so I'm afraid I'm going to have to ask you to not come back. I'm sorry, but that's the way I feel."

"I see, so you think that since I own a home locally that I'm secretly meeting a woman over here so that we can have sex without her husband or my wife finding out about it."

"You've been a guest here four or five times in the last three weeks. I can't think of any other reason except you're hiding your affair with her from someone!" Phil said sternly.

"Well, Phil, I can appreciate your concerns, and if you don't want Ms. Owens or me to come back then we'll go elsewhere. But just for the record, Ms. Owens is single and so am I. We meet here because it's too dangerous to go to my house."

"What's so dangerous about your house?" Phil huffed, and it was obvious that he didn't believe Justin.

"Jack Billings is hiding out somewhere in these mountains and he's going to try and kill me one of these days. I don't want Ms. Owens around when he does."

"Oh. I...of course. Justin Hayes, you're the man who killed Johnny Billings and Chris Reed!"

"Yeah, I'm afraid so, Phil."

"I didn't make the connection. You saved my nephew's life. Buddy Dixon is my nephew, my sister's boy! I'm so embarrassed. I apologize, Mr. Hayes, for questioning your character. You can stay here anytime you like. As a matter of fact, you can stay here for free!"

"That's okay, Phil," Justin said. "I hope they catch Jack pretty soon so that I can start living a normal life again. Have a nice day." Justin walked down the steps and out to the parking lot where Teresa was loading her suitcase into her Escalade.

Teresa shut the door and turned to face him. "I'm still perturbed at you."

"You're not perturbed, you're madder than hell!"

"Okay, you're right. I'm madder than hell! You said you would go with me to Florida!"

"I didn't know that a psychopath would be hiding in these hills trying to kill me when I promised you I would go."

"He may be hiding in these hills a year from now Justin! I don't like living like this, meeting each other secretly like we're hiding something!"

"That's what Phil thought."

"What?"

"Nothing, just forget it."

"My God, Justin, I own a home in this county and can't even spend a night in it!"

"It won't be much longer, honey. Jack is like a pressure cooker that is building up steam. He's getting madder and madder as every day passes. It's been three weeks since he went on the run, and he's just waiting for things to settle down before he makes his move. The Criminal Profilers at the FBI think he will make his move within the first twelve weeks."

"If the FBI would have caught him to begin with, we wouldn't be meeting here at the Sparta Bed and Breakfast!" Teresa snapped.

"Just be patient, honey. Go to Florida and enjoy your grandchildren. Maybe by the time you get back it will be over."

"What am I supposed to tell my daughter and son-in-law? That you're hunting a psychopath that is trying to kill you?"

Justin stood in front of Teresa suddenly not staring at her, but beyond her. His face was void of any expression, as blank as an empty page. A switch inside him had finally tripped. It wasn't exactly like a switch tripping, but more like someone had slowly but surely raised one side of a table until a single domino finally succumbed to the forces of nature and came crashing down. Nobody saw it coming, least of all him. Maybe it was because he had been waking every morning for the last three weeks wondering if today would be the day that Jack would try to kill him. Maybe it was because he had been riding an emotional rollercoaster that ranged from making love to a beautiful woman in front of a roaring fireplace to shooting two men to death that were firing machine guns at him. Maybe it went all the way back to Vietnam.

All Justin wanted this spring was to spend some time with his son and to do some trout fishing, but he had been plunged into a world of deceit. A world of hiding out in your own home, a world of wiretaps and murder, a world that was full of FBI agents, CIA agents, and Navy Seals, a world where your neighbor and the local sheriff were trying to kill you, a senseless and crazy world, like *Alice in Wonderland* with guns.

"Justin! Justin!" Teresa barked. "I said what do you want me to tell my daughter and son in-law!"

"Tell them that I'm trying to get an 'even fifty,' Teresa! Tell them that I'm an asshole! Tell them whatever the hell you want to!" Justin said and he turned and walked across the lot toward his truck.

"Justin, wait! Justin, I'm sorry! Please, Justin. I didn't mean to be so short with you." Justin climbed into his truck and drove down the street.

"He said they call it a Beanfield Rifle," Buck said as Jack studied the beautiful firearm that was lying across Buck's kitchen table. "A man in South Carolina builds them for people that want to kill a deer on the other side of those big soybean fields least that's what he said."

"I've never seen anything quite like it," Jack said. "I had some beautiful rifles, a couple Weatherbys and a couple of custom jobs, but nothing quite like this! What's all this other stuff?"

"That rifle comes with more damn paperwork than a new car," Buck said as he took another sip of his brandy. "That Jarrett feller shoots every rifle he builds about a hundred and fifty times before he sells it so he can break in the barrel and figure out what powder and bullet shoots the best, and then he loads up several boxes of shells for whoever buys the rifle. He also prints out a piece of paper that tells you how much the bullet drops and where you need to set your scope at to make those long shots. Then he sends the last three targets that he shoots and another piece of paper that tells you how fast the bullet is going and how much energy it has. least that's what that Harrison man said."

"It sounds like it's exactly what I need."

"As much money as you paid for it, I sure hope the hell it's what you need."

"It'll be worth every penny if I can kill that son of a bitch with it!"

"Here's the receipt and your change," Buck said as he reached in the front zipper pocket of his overhauls. Buck lay what was left of the roll of money along with several coins and the receipt on the table. Jack picked up the receipt and read it.

Beanfield Rifle Serial # W917321A
Gunsmith-Kenny Jarrett-- [Jarrett Rifles]
Caliber-- .300 Winchester Magnum
Action--Winchester Model 70
Stock--McMillan (custom order)
Sights- Leupold Mk3 - 6.5 x 20 x 50 Ballistic Mill Dot
Trigger- Jewell (24 ounce)
Finish--Gray Ghost
Price--$5,350.00

"It was kinda pricey, but I believe it's just what I need," Jack said. "Thank you, Buck, I appreciate you doing this for me. I appreciate everything you've done."

"Oh, I forgot something. Vera! Vera! Go get that plastic bag off the front seat of the truck!" Buck hollered. "That Harrison man said that I would need a laser range finder if I was going to try and shoot a buck that far, so I stopped at the gun store in North Wilkesboro on the way back and bought one. He said to take that range finder and figure out how far I was going to shoot and then practice at that distance."

"I think that makes good sense," Jack said. "I'll slip over there and fix me a place to shoot from and then use the range finder to see how far it is. Do you know somewhere we can go to practice?"

"We can go over to Piney Creek where those sons of bitches killed my son at!" Buck said. "It seems kinda fitting to practice there."

Jack noticed that tears had welled up in Buck's eyes and he understood completely. No one knows the pain of losing a child except for the people who have experienced it. The loss of his oldest son was like an open sore that had never healed, and Buck needed Justin killed as much as Jack did.

"We'll kill that son of a bitch, Buck," Jack said as he picked up the rifle and put it to his shoulder. "It's payback time for you and me!"

Justin was practically in a trance as he drove slowly down Highway 117 toward home. He felt numb all over, like the men you see at the veteran's hospital, sitting quietly in their wheelchairs or lying motionless in their beds. Men who were heroes. Men just like him who did what was asked of them and now couldn't live with the memories.

He had done nothing wrong! Not one damn thing! But he had killed one hundred and seventeen men. The military listed it at forty-seven, but he knew the real number. And now he had to kill one more!

Something was wrong inside him. Something was out of kilter. The flashback he suffered on his front porch when the Hueys flew by his house was a warning from his psyche that all the horrible things he had witnessed could return in the blink of an eye. The bodies jerking awkwardly at the sound of the shot, and then collapsing and lying there twitching from nerve impulses until the brain finally shut down and quit sending signals. The horrible stench of burning flesh that got in your clothes and stayed there for days. The little children who were trapped in a war that they didn't want or understand. The memories of what he had seen and done scared him much worse than being shot at.

He could conquer the demons around him, the evil neighbor, the crooked sheriff, even the drug-crazed assassins. But could he conquer the demons inside him? He was scared.

What's the magic number? How many men can you kill before you end up staring at a wall with a nurse constantly feeding you drugs to keep your body separated from your mind? A mind that was full of memories of young men dying in jungles and in rice patties, and in the middle of River Road! How do you fight this enemy?

Justin was only doing about thirty miles an hour when he rounded a curve and came in sight of Jesse's driveway, and as he drew closer he could see Jesse and Travis on horseback headed up the driveway toward Jesse's house. Travis saw his dad's truck and waved and motioned for him to turn in. Justin turned in and slowly followed them. Halfway up the driveway Jesse kicked the gray speckled Appaloosa she was riding in the haunches and both horses broke into a full run as they headed up the hill toward Jesse's house. It was an unexpected pleasure for Justin, watching the beautiful and powerful animals as they lunged forward, each trying to outdo the other. Jesse and Travis sped past the house and finally reigned in their horses in a cloud of dust as they approached the barn. Both were grinning when they dismounted.

"I won!" Jesse announced.

"You cheated!" Travis argued. "You didn't tell me we were going to race, you just took off!"

"I still won," Jesse said with her perfect smile. "Good morning, Justin."

"Good morning," Justin said as he walked up. "Those are two beautiful animals. You can tell that a veterinarian owns them."

"Hey, Pop," Travis said. "Has Teresa already left?"

"Yeah, she went home to pack for her trip."

"I hate you couldn't go with her," Travis said. "I know you were looking forward to it."

"Well, such is my life. I shouldn't have promised her that I would go with her, I guess," Justin said as he bent down to pet Maggie who had run up carrying a Frisbee in her mouth. Justin scratched her head and then took the Frisbee and sailed it across the yard, much to Maggie's delight. It never touched the ground. Maggie timed her leap perfectly and snatched the Frisbee out of the air and trotted back toward Justin proudly, hoping he would throw it again.

"Dogs are such amazing creatures," Justin said as he took the Frisbee and sailed it across the yard again. "They give themselves to you totally. The only thing they want is to serve you. They'll work all day for you, they'll protect you, they'll entertain you, and they'll love you. And it doesn't matter if you're a good person or not. All they want is a pat on the head."

"I don't guess I can change your mind about letting me move back in with you until this things over," Travis said. "I don't like you being over there by yourself."

"I'm not by myself," Justin said. "I got two dogs, remember?"

"You know what I mean. It wouldn't hurt for someone to be there with you. I don't want anything to happen to you Dad!"

"If Jack challenged you to a fist fight, what do you think his chances of beating you would be?" Justin asked Travis as he took the Frisbee from Maggie and threw it again.

"He wouldn't have a chance!" Travis said. "He's in his mid to late fifties, he's out of shape, and he's had no training. I would annihilate him!"

"Exactly," Justin said. "And that's exactly what's going to happen when he tries to shoot me. Shooting is what I do. It's what I'm trained to do, and when he comes after me, I'll annihilate him."

There was a short pause before Justin continued. "It would be like entering this beautiful Appaloosa in the Kentucky Derby. She's a beautiful animal, and she can outrun some horses, but she can't run with those thoroughbreds. Jack will no doubt try to kill me, but killing people is what I trained for. Killing people is what I do best!"

Justin took the Frisbee from Maggie once again and sailed it toward the house. "Well, I guess I better go. I've got some things to do before my date with destiny."

"Will you call me as soon as you know he's over there?"

"I'll call you when he's dead," Justin said as he climbed in his truck.

Travis and Jesse watched as Justin turned around and drove away. Jesse stepped over and put her arm around Travis's waist. "Something's wrong with him, Travis."

"I know." Travis sighed. "Something's very wrong!"

Monday Morning, May 7

Special Agent Dan Loggins switched the windshield wipers to the next highest speed as he turned onto River Road. It was a drizzly dreary Monday morning and the weather matched his mood perfectly. He, and every member of his team, had been working twelve and fourteen hour days trying to find Jack Billings and so far they had come up empty.

There was a $25,000 reward for information but so far there had been no response, nothing! These mountain people were good people but they were wary of strangers, and they didn't trust "government people."

Dan had called Justin twice yesterday but no one answered and Justin didn't return his calls, so he decided he better drop in and check on him. When he stopped by his office this morning there was a voice message from Travis on his answering machine. It said that he thought there was something wrong with his dad and he was worried about him. "Would you stop in and check on him?" Damn right I'll check on him! He wouldn't be walking around with a bulls-eye on his back if we had caught Jack in the first place. It was Jimmy Hardy's call to let the two men leave the night before the raid, but I was sitting right beside him and didn't say anything.

Dan pulled his cell phone out and dialed Justin's number. It rang six times before someone answered it. "Hello?"

"Justin, its Dan Loggins. I'm turning into your driveway. Open up the carport door and let me in."

"Okay," Justin said and then hung up.

Dan turned in and drove up the mountain and around to the back of the house. Justin was standing in the carport in his boxer shorts motioning for him to pull inside.

"Good morning," Dan said as he stepped out of his car. Justin just turned and walked back inside the house. You didn't have to be a detective to tell that he had just crawled out of bed. Dan followed Justin into the kitchen.

"Get a cup of coffee," Justin said as he poured himself one and stepped over to the kitchen table. Dan got a cup and joined him.

"You just get up?"

"Yeah, when you called."

"What ever happened to the man who got up every morning between 5:30 and 6:00?"

"I been busy the last few days, been staying up late."

"You're not having trouble sleeping are you?"

"Naw, I just been busy. By the way, I got all the stuff that I asked you for. I appreciate you doing that for me."

"No problem," Dan said. "Why aren't you answering your phone? You're worrying the hell out of a lot of people, Justin."

"Nobody's called me!" Justin countered.

"The hell they haven't!" Dan said. "I called you twice myself!"

"Well, let's just see!" Justin said and he hopped up and walked into the living room to look at his caller ID. There were two calls from Travis, three calls from Teresa, one call from Reverend McDowell, one call from Carol Crissman, and two calls from Dan Loggins.

"Okay, you're right," Justin said as he returned to the kitchen table. "I guess I was busy and didn't hear it."

"Be sure and check your voice mail everyday," Dan suggested. "If you don't, somebody's got to come over here and check on you."

Justin sipped his coffee and tried to recall the last two days. He had come home Saturday morning and he was angry. Angry that a man was stalking him! Angry that neither his son nor girlfriend could come visit him! Angry that he couldn't go to Florida with Teresa!

Angry that he couldn't go fishing! Angry that he had been thrust into his past! So angry that he went straight to his shooting range and shot a man silhouette target over a hundred times with one of his .45s before he finally calmed down. He then went to his living room and tried to sit down and relax, but he was too restless. He paced back and forth like a caged animal until the anger returned. He stared out the picture window at the river and the mountains beyond.

"Okay, Jack, you son of a bitch, how are you going to kill me? Where will you hide? Will you take the shot in the morning or in the afternoon, or maybe at dusk? What's the farthest shot you ever made? Will you try it if it's windy, or wait for a calm day? Cloudy or sunny? Do you know how the temperature affects your rifle and your ammo? Do you know how to read mirage? Do you understand bullet drop and wind drift? Do you know what natural respiratory pause is? How long can you lay motionless ignoring the cold or the heat, the sore muscles and the insect bites? Damn you, Jack Billings!"

Justin finally managed to calm himself down enough to start answering some of those questions. He worked through a multitude of possible scenarios in his mind of how a sniper would approach the problem, where he would hide, when he would shoot. And just when he thought he knew how it would transpire it dawned on him that Jack wasn't a sniper. He had no training. He couldn't possibly take the shot a trained sniper could. Justin realized that he had to start over. He had to forget his training and look at the scenario from Jack's perspective. He had to get into Jack's mind.

"Justin, are you all right?" Dan asked.

"Yeah, yeah, I'm all right," Justin said. "I'm just not awake yet, that's all."

"Justin, listen to me," Dan said like it was an order. "If and when Jack shows up over here, call me. I can have men here in twenty minutes. We can set up a perimeter and put a chopper in the air and we can flush him out!"

"He would kill at least one of your men and maybe more!" Justin said. "Jack's not going to prison Dan. He wouldn't make it in prison and he knows it. If he was hiding on the side of a mountain and your men went in after him, chances are good that he would kill at least one of them when they got close."

"We get paid to get shot at!"

"Tell that to the man's widow when you go to the funeral!"

"Okay, okay, just call me and I'll set my men up but keep them out of sight."

"When I call you, Dan, Jack will be dead!"

"Dammit, Justin," Dan shouted, but he stopped his tirade to answer his cell phone. "Dan Loggins," he said when he flipped his phone open.

"Dan, it's Roseanna."

"What's up?"

"I ran a search on the computer for any rifle that has been sold in the last three weeks within a one hundred mile radius of Sparta. Then I cross referenced that list with people that live in Ashe, Alleghany, and Wilkes County. There was nothing that really stood out so I extended the radius to a hundred and fifty miles. I've been sorting through them this morning and I have one that stinks like a can of sardines on a truck manifold."

"Tell me what you got!" Dan said.

"The rifle was sold in Asheville to a Mr. Buck Jones. He had to use his real name because of his driver's license, but he used a bogus address which as you know is a felony by itself. Anyway, I found him in the NCIC and he did three years in the federal penitentiary for bootlegging, and get this, his son was killed by federal marshals when they raided his still."

"What kind of rifle did he buy?"

"It's called a Beanfield Rifle. It's built by a company in South Carolina and it is specifically designed to kill deer at very long distances. It's a 300 Winchester Magnum with a twenty power scope. And wait till you hear this, he paid $5,350 for it. Oh, and by the way, Mr. Jones is seventy-three years old and lives solely on social security."

"Where does he live?"

"He lives at Route 9, Shatley Springs, about fifteen miles from Justin."

"Get everybody together and go ahead and get a search warrant. I'll be there in thirty minutes, and before I forget it, that's some damn fine police work, Agent Lankford!"

"Thank you, sir. I'll see you in thirty minutes."

"Dan put his cell phone back in his pocket and stood up. "I got to go, Justin."

"Got a hot tip?"

"Sounds real promising," Dan said. "Maybe you want have to kill Jack Billings after all!"

Jack shut his left eye and squinted with his right as he looked through the rifle scope at the fifty-five gallon drum that was 483 yards away. Buck had taken the rusty fifty-five gallon drum and spray painted a crude outline of a man in white paint, and then stood the drum up on the other side of a deep hollow, the same hollow he used to make illegal whiskey in, the same hollow his son died in. Then Buck took a fifty-pound bag of lime and spread it on the ground behind the drum so he could tell where the bullet hit in case Jack missed the target. It was a good thing he did because it took six shots before Jack ever hit the drum.

Jack had slipped over to the mountain across from-Justin's yesterday morning before daylight. Buck dropped him off at the low water bridge and sat there fishing until Jack returned. It took Jack all morning to crawl around and find the place he would shoot from. He first crawled down the mountain until he was about 325 yards from the house, but the banister that ran around Justin's front porch was in the way so he crawled back up the mountain until he had a shot that would clear it. It was 483 yards according to the range finder.

Jack studied the crosshairs as they bobbed up and down and left and right. It seemed so simple, just place the crosshairs on the target and pull the trigger. But he was learning that it was harder than it looked, much harder than shining a light in a deer's eyes and then shooting him from about a hundred yards away. Out of a total of eleven shots he had only hit the drum six times, and only three of those shots were on the target, one shot in the collarbone, one shot in the left shoulder, and the last shot which was in the left nipple, if the target would have had nipples.

He settled the crosshairs as much as he could and slowly pulled the trigger. The rifle slammed his already sore shoulder but he was rewarded by the clang that signaled he once again had hit the drum.

"Where'd you hit?" Buck asked before the echo of the rifle was even gone.

"Almost dead center," Jack said, smiling. "I think I'm getting the hang of this."

"You're getting better that's for sure," Buck said. "I think we better come back though and practice some more before you try."

"You're right, Buck," Jack said. "I'm not going to get but one shot and I got to make it count!"

"I speck we better git out of here for now before somebody comes to see what all the shooting is about. I'll go over there and cover up the drum with brush while you pack up your stuff."

"Okay, Buck," Jack said as he peered back through the scope. "That last shot would have killed him instantly!"

"I wouldn't care if you hit him a little to one side and the son of a bitch laid there and suffered awhile!" Buck said as he strained to get up.

"I wouldn't care either, Buck. Not one damn bit!"

Vera took a spoon and fished a small piece of fatback out of the pot and popped it in her mouth. Buck and Jack would be back soon and she had fixed a pot of pinto beans and a pot of cooked cabbage. She stepped over to the table and started to pick up the pan of cornbread when she heard the guineas squawking. Suddenly Buckshot started growling and jumped up and ran through the house, almost knocking the screen door off its hinges when he went through it.

Vera stepped into the den and looked through the screen door at the black Suburban that was sloshing up the driveway and there was a black van right on its bumper. She quickly stepped back into the kitchen and opened one of the cabinet doors and retrieved a brown grocery sack that was full of coal and she opened the door of the wood stove and threw it in. Vera shut the stove door and opened up the damper so that it could get plenty of air, and then set the pot of pintos and the pot of cabbage in the sink before picking up her Bible and walking back to the front porch. Vera called Buckshot back to the porch and snapped a chain on his collar, and then took a seat in one of the rockers and opened up her Bible.

There were men dressed in black and carrying black guns running to the back of the house as the man wearing a suit approached the front porch.

"FBI, ma'am. We have a warrant to search the house and the premises for a rifle. Are you Mrs. Jones?"

Vera sat rocking and reading her Bible. She never acknowledged his presence.

"If you don't answer my questions, ma'am, I can arrest you for obstructing justice!" Again, Vera sat in her rocker reading her Bible and ignored the officer.

"Where is your husband? Where is Buck Jones?"

Nothing.

"Search the house," Dan instructed several of his men. "Roseanna, watch her while we look around."

"That damn mule kicked every board off his barn stall!" Buck said. "Don't ever let a mule drink sour mash 'cause they get mean when they get drunk!"

Jack was laughing as Buck drove them home and told stories from his moonshining days. He hadn't laughed in a long time and it almost felt strange to him. They were almost back at Buck's house and he was glad because he was starving. He knew that Vera would have something fixed for dinner when they got there. Buck turned onto the dirt road that wound through the country and went by his driveway.

"I believe that when we go back to practice your shooting that you should just take one or two bullets with you," Buck said. "Instead of shooting ten rounds in ten minutes, spend ten minutes getting ready and then just shoot once."

"You're probably right, Buck," Jack said. "We'll try it and see what happens."

They rounded a curve and came in sight of Buck's driveway and Buck slammed on the brakes and threw Jack into the dashboard.

"What's wrong?" Jack hollered.

"Look," Buck said and he pointed in the direction of the house.

Jack searched the driveway and the woods but didn't see anything unusual. "I don't see anything, Buck."

"Look above the trees," Buck said in a strained voice.

Jack looked up over the trees and instantly saw the black smoke that was pouring out like it was coming from an industrial boiler. "Damn, is the house on fire?"

"No, there's police at the house. Probably Feds looking for you!" Buck said as he turned the steering wheel hard to the left and dumped the clutch. The old truck spun around in its tracks without ever getting close to either ditch. It was a move that any bootlegger could do in their sleep. Buck straightened the old truck up and raced back in the direction they had come.

"Where will we go now?" Jack shouted as he searched for something to hold on to.

"To the low water bridge to let you out! You got to take the shot tomorrow, Jack. If you don't you won't ever have another chance!"

"Can't we spend the night somewhere and leave out early tomorrow morning?"

"Every cop in four counties will be looking for this truck. You're just going to have to spend the night in the woods Jack! I'm sorry, but we don't have no choice. I'll give you my shirt and my coat to help keep you warm."

Jack knew that Buck was right. It was now or never, and never wasn't an option. Justin Hayes had to die! He had to die for Chuck Jones, Buck's oldest boy. He had to die for Johnny Billings, his nephew. He had to die for Tommy Sides and Johnny Steele and Bill Sisk. He had to die for taking away everything that he had ever worked for. Not taking the shot was not an option, taking the shot was a necessity. It is all I have left, the conclusion of my accomplishments, the final chapter of my life!

"Knowing that I'll be blowing a hole through his heart tomorrow will keep me warm tonight!" Jack said. "Don't you worry, Buck, I'll be just fine tonight. And tomorrow I'll slip over there and blow him to hell!"

Justin woke up and glanced over at the clock radio on his night stand. It was 4:17 a.m. He reached for his pistol and listened to see if his dogs were barking, but all he heard was silence. He rolled over on his back and stared at the ceiling. What triggered his body to wake up at this time of the morning? Did he have a nightmare? Did he need to use the bathroom? He could tell that he would never get back to sleep.

It was a wonder that he got to sleep at all with all the crap that was swirling around in his head. He had spent over an hour on the phone before he went to bed, calling people and apologizing for not returning their calls. He called Pastor McDowell and spoke with him briefly, and then he called Carol Crissman and chatted with her for about fifteen minutes. After hanging up with Carol he called Travis and assured him that he was all right and not to worry. And then he made the call that was most difficult for him—the call to Florida to talk to Teresa. They talked for half an hour, but the conversation seemed strained, like neither one of them knew where they stood with the other one. They finally told each other good night and Justin started to bed when the phone rang and the caller ID said it was Dan Loggins. Justin stared at the caller ID and hoped and prayed that he would hear the words, "We got him," but it wasn't to be. Dan said that they found where Jack was hiding and had arrested the woman, but she hadn't uttered a word since she had been in custody. A short time later a North Carolina State Trooper had spotted the truck her husband was driving and had chased the old coot for ten miles before finally executing the PIT maneuver on him and spinning him out. He too hadn't spoken a word since he was brought in.

Dan was apologetic as he went on to explain that they hadn't been able to find Jack or the rifle.

"What kind of rifle was it?" Justin had asked. "They call it a 'Beanfield Rifle.' Are you familiar with it?"

"Oh hell, yes, I'm familiar with it! Kenny Jarrett builds the finest long range bunting rifles in the world. If Jack misses the shot, he can't blame it on the rifle. A Kenny Jarrett rifle will easily shoot one-half minute of angle. A good rifleman can bust cantaloupes at five hundred yards with a Beanfield Rifle."

The purchase of such a precision rifle confirmed to Justin how Jack was planning on killing him. It didn't surprise him at all. With his house sitting so high on the mountain it was impossible to get a clear shot from either side. The shot would have to be taken from across the river so that the shooter could get enough elevation to clear the natural curve of the mountain. The only other option was to approach the house the same way Johnny Steele did, and Justin didn't think Jack had the physical ability or the stones for that.

Justin suddenly sat straight up in bed. He knew now why he was awake. Like a soft whisper in his ear or a gentle tingle in his spine, Gabriel had brought him awake. "You're in danger!" Lately Justin had wondered if Gabriel was still watching over him. His faith had definitely been weak. The load he had been carrying seemed to be too great, more than anyone could bear. But he was sure it was him. Jack was somewhere near, crawling closer and closer to try and kill him.

Justin climbed out of bed and stepped over to the double windows in his bedroom and stared through the blackness at the river and the mountains beyond. Yes, he was there. Thank you, Gabriel. Thank you God. Why did I ever doubt you?

Should he call Dan Loggins? This was the first time he had ever felt like he had a choice of whether he would kill somebody or not. He could call the FBI and they would handle it. He wouldn't have to kill anybody if he just picked up the phone and made the call. They would set up a perimeter around the mountain and then fly over it with a helicopter, shouting through a speaker for Jack to raise his hands and to walk down the mountain.

Then after two or three attempts they would send a Reactive Force or a Special Response Team up the mountain to flush him out. Jack would lie in his hiding place crying, knowing that he wouldn't get the chance to kill Justin, knowing that his life would soon be over. As the agents got closer and closer he would angrily pick the closest one out and place his crosshairs on his chest and blow his heart and lungs into Jell-O. Justin had seen it happen too many times in Vietnam. A platoon of soldiers would stomp through the jungle like a herd of elephants, and a lone gunman would hide and single one man out and blow his heart out when he got close enough.

Would I be responsible for that death? Not really. Would I feel guilty the rest of my life?

Probably. Come on, Jack, I've been waiting for you. Let's finally end this!

Jack was thinking that he had finally come full circle. He grew up hungry, wearing rags for clothes, and shivering from the cold. And now here he was again, hungry, wearing rags for clothes, and shivering from the cold!

He had curled up under a huge white pine tree and buried himself under a thick layer of pine needles to help keep him warm until the first hint of light would permit him to find his shooting blind. He didn't think the night would ever end, but eventually the black of the forest turned to a dark gray as the sun fought its way up toward the horizon, and Jack had to rush to get into his spot before it got too light. When he finally crawled into the brush pile where he planned on taking the shot he was sweating, and that proved to be a big mistake! In less than a minute he was shivering from the wetness of his body. His teeth chattered and his body shook and his anger grew with every passing second. Finally, as the sun grew higher and his body dried off, the shivering stopped. He was exhausted from the ordeal.

Now he faced another unexpected problem—trying to stay awake! As he slowly warmed up he started yawning and his eyelids fought him as he tried to bold them open. Maybe if he took a quick nap it would revive him? No, he would fall to sleep and miss his opportunity. Maybe Justin would come out on the front porch early like he used to, drinking coffee and watching his dogs run and play. Somehow he had to make himself stay awake!

Jack set the rifle on the bags that he brought on his earlier trip. Buck had taken an old pair of overhauls and cut the legs off at the knees and had Vera to sew up one end. Then he poured them full of dried peas and had her to sew up the other end. They were crude but effective. The rifle snuggled down in the pea bags and looked rock steady as he peered through the scope. There was a small limb blocking his view so he crawled forward about seven feet and snapped it so that he could see unobstructed. He reached into his coat and pulled out the box of shells and shoved three of the shells into the rifle's magazine before sliding the bolt forward and chambering a round. He was finally ready.

The morning dragged on, with seconds turning into minutes, and minutes turning into what seemed like hours. He was learning that the hardest part of being a sniper wasn't making the shot, but it was lying motionless and being patient. His back hurt and he had a pounding headache. He didn't know if the headache was caused by him being hungry or from the eye strain from staring through the scope, all he knew was that he had to keep watching through the scope. He felt like he could sleep for two days, but he knew that there wouldn't be any time for sleeping once he took the shot.

Jack wondered what he would do after he made the shot. Maybe he could dump the rifle in the river and then hike over to the New River Campground and steal a car. But where would he go? He had spent all his time planning the murder, but up until now hadn't given a thought to what he would do afterward.

Jack suddenly jerked his head and realized that he had nodded off. Dammit, how long have I been asleep? He looked through the scope and immediately realized that something was different. The curtains were open and there was a light on in the living room. He started shaking when he realized what he was seeing through the rifle scope.

Justin was sitting in a rocking chair in his living room facing the river and reading the newspaper. There was steam rising up from a cup of coffee that was sitting on the table beside him as he slowly rocked back and forth.

Jack took his thumb and flicked the safety off his rifle and lightly placed his finger on the trigger. The crosshairs looked like they were doing a dance, up and down and left and right. Jack took a couple quick breaths and tried to steady himself. It was better, but still too wobbly. He shut his eyes and forced himself to relax and breathe normally for several moments before opening his eyes again. Now he was steady! The crosshairs were centered on the newspaper as he pressed the trigger.

It sounded like a howitzer went off in the stillness of the spring morning and Jack scrambled to look through the scope and see what happened. He got just a glimpse of Justin and the rocking chair toppling over and he chambered another round and searched for movement in the house.

The whole world seemed to stop! The birds had quit singing and everything was stone still, including the living room of Justin's house. Then Jack saw it, the most beautiful sight he had ever seen. In the big picture window, perfectly dead center, was a bullet hole! There was absolutely no way that the bullet could pass through that hole without killing him. He was dead! Justin was finally dead! Bill Sisk couldn't do it, and Quai couldn't do it, and Johnny Steele couldn't do it, but by God Jack Billings did it!

Jack's eyes flooded with tears. He wished that Buck could have seen it. It would have done the old man some good. He wiped his eyes on his sleeve and looked back through the scope.

Justin sat on the floor of his living room gently pulling on the rope so that the rocking chair would continue to rock back and forth. He sat there for ten minutes before it finally happened. The 180-grain Nosler Partition bullet went "chink" as it came through the window and then immediately went "kaplop" as it buried into the thirty-inch square of ballistic gelatin. Justin immediately yanked the rope and toppled the mannequin and the rocking chair as the sound of the gunshot echoed across the mountain.

Justin had cut the chest out of the mannequin and had also cut the back out of the rocking chair so that the bullets flight wouldn't be altered in any way. The bullet passed through the picture window and through the newspaper but didn't touch anything else before it buried into the block of ballistic gelatin.

Justin had used ballistic gelatin in the past to test the performance of hunting bullets. It was the best way to tell what your ammunition would do because it closely simulated the density and viscosity of human and animal muscle tissue. Firing a bullet into ballistic gelatin gives you a rough idea of how far a bullet will penetrate into an animal, how well the bullet holds together and how much tissue damage will occur.

He had taken a thick cardboard box that was thirty inches square and wrapped it tightly with duct tape and lined it with plastic before he filled it with water and the proper amount of gelatin powder. After the gelatin set up he positioned the block about six feet behind the rocker so that any bullet that cleared the porch banister and went through the mannequin had to hit the block of gelatin somewhere.

Justin picked up the quarter inch steel rod that he had made and slid on his back across the hardwood floor until he was beside the block of gelatin. He reached up slowly and slid the rod down the hole the bullet had created as it plowed through the gelatin. The rod was fifteen inches long and he had welded a special fixture on the end of it to hold the laser that Dan Loggins had provided him with. As soon as he had the rod in place he slid back out of sight and stood up and walked through the kitchen and out through the carport, careful not to trip over the electric cord he had run out to his shop.

Justin walked back to his machine shop and stepped inside and climbed the ladder that went to the attic. Once in the attic he stepped over to the shooting platform that he had built and climbed up behind his rifle that was already sitting on a set of sandbags waiting for him. He had previously removed two of the slats that covered the gable end of his machine shop so that he had a seven inch slot to aim and shoot through.

"Let's just see where you are, Jack," Justin said as he reached over and grabbed the two electric cords and plugged them together. The powerful red laser that was attached to the end of the steel rod came alive and shot a red beam through the hole in the picture window and over the banister and straight across the valley into the side of the mountain across from Justin's house.

Justin looked through his firing slot to get a general idea of where the laser was before settling in behind his rifle. He knew that because of the bullets trajectory that the laser would be pointing several feet above where the shot was taken from. A 180-grain bullet fired from a 300 Winchester Magnum would fall approximately four feet before it reached a five hundred-yard target. If the rifle was zeroed to hit a five hundred-yard target the muzzle of the rifle would be pointed up, and the bullet would arc up several feet above the line of sight before it stated falling back down to hit the target. Because of that arc, the bullets path in the ballistic gelatin would be angling downward, and the laser would be shining higher on the mountain than the shooter. A ballistic engineer could easily figure out exactly how far the distance would be between the laser and the shooter, but Justin wasn't worried about it because he knew he could find him.

Justin placed his crosshairs on the spot where the laser was shining and started lowering them, looking for something that would give away Jack's hide. He saw it immediately. A limb had been snapped and it hung down at a ninety-degree angle. He might as well of hung a neon sign up that said, "Here I am!" Nothing in nature is at ninety-degree angles, you learn that the first week of sniper school.

Justin studied Jack's hiding place. He couldn't see Jack but he knew he was there. He was at least smart enough to stay back far enough so that he couldn't be seen but he made a critical mistake when he chose this spot. A mistake that would probably cost him his life. There was no possible way for him to escape from this spot without exposing himself. A trained sniper never shoots from a position until he's damn sure that there's an escape route. Jack was hiding in a blow-down. The wind had snapped a tree in two and when the top crashed down to the forest floor it had created a small clearing. There was no way to crawl out of there without exposing yourself.

Justin no longer needed the laser so he reached over and unplugged the two extension cords. His rifle was resting across a set of leather sand bags and the scope was pointed directly at Jack's hiding place. The rifle was a Remington 700 action with a #6 Shilen Select Match barrel chambered in 308 Winchester. You can call it a Model 21 or a Model 24 or a Model 40, or whatever you want to call it, but they're basically all the same thing, a Remington 700 action with a fat match grade barrel, bedded into a composite stock, and with a trigger that breaks like a glass rod. In the hands of a trained sniper it is the grim reaper, the merchant of death, and a first class ticket to the after-life. He had zeroed his rifle yesterday at five hundred yards. He shot four rounds into a two inch circle.

Justin took his range finder and checked the distance to the blow-down. It was 503 yards. Perfect! He wouldn't even have to adjust the scope, just aim and squeeze. "Checkmate Jack! I know where you are and you can't escape without me seeing you. Mess with the best and die like the rest!"

"Brrrrrrp, Brrrrrrp, Brrrrrrp!" Justin's cell phone vibrated against the plywood shooting platform. He reached down without ever taking his eye off the scope and retrieved the phone. He took his thumb and pushed the red button to disconnect the call and then laid the phone down beside him. "Brrrrrrp, Brrrrrrp, Brrrrrrp," the phone vibrated again.

Justin finally picked the phone up and reluctantly answered it. "What's up?"

"That's what I want to know," Dan Loggins said. "Have you been shooting?"

"No. Why?"

"Because my man said he heard a single rifle shot about ten minutes ago. Not a string of shots like somebody that was shooting targets, but a lone rifle shot!"

"What, man?"

"We have an agent down at Jack's guarding the place. We have chains and padlocks on all the doors, but we were afraid somebody would loot the place so we put an agent down there to guard it."

"You put an agent down there to watch me!"

"No, I swear to you, Justin, he's just guarding the place! Anyway, who's shooting?"

"I was just checking the zero on my rifle, that's all."

"You're a terrible liar, Justin. You already said that you haven't been shooting," Dan said. "What's going on? Did Jack take a shot at you?"

"Yeah, he took his shot. He's hiding in a blow-down straight across from my house," Justin said with a certain sense of relief.

"Justin, I normally wouldn't care how a citizen would want me to handle a situation like this, but I been thinking about what you said about Jack killing one of my men, so I'm asking you, how should we handle this?"

"Bring your chopper to the top of the mountain and let your team rappel down and line up along the ridge. Once they're in position get on the loudspeaker and order him to surrender. I don't think he will, but I guess you have to give him the option."

"You're right," Dan answered. "We have to announce ourselves and give him the chance to come peacefully."

"If he doesn't respond, I'll turn the laser back on so you will know where he is and then you can fire a tear gas canister into his hide to flush him out."

"Sounds good to me!" Dan said. "We'll be there in about twenty minutes. I'll call you back right before we arrive."

Justin set the cell phone down and stared through his scope.

Jack was totally confused. He knew for a fact that he had killed a man sitting in a rocking chair in Justin's living room, but just when he started to crawl out of his hide a red laser had shone through the picture window and into the mountain above him. At first he thought it was some sort of rifle sight and he rolled to his right as far as possible and was expecting to hear a rifle shot ring out across the valley. But when he dared to look again, the laser was gone. He didn't understand the laser but he knew he had to leave, so he rolled back over and started to crawl forward. As he neared the opening the forest floor directly in front of him suddenly erupted, showering his face with dirt and rocks and he scurried back and rolled to his right as the sound of the rifle echoed in the valley. Jack twisted his head around and searched for a way out of this death chamber! His heart sank as he searched left and right and behind him. There is no way to slip out of here! Who is shooting at me? An FBI sharpshooter! Justin's son! Who, dammit? Whoever it is has probably already called the Sheriff's Department or the FBI.

Jack slipped out of Buck's coat and took a stick and shoved it toward the opening. Dirt and rocks showered the entrance of the brush pile again as another bullet tore into the forest floor.

Justin slid the bolt back on his rifle and shoved two more shells into the magazine without ever removing his eye from the scope. What was next? Would Jack try to come out fast and take off running? If he does, should I kill him? If I don't kill him he might get away and then try to kill me again later! It has got to end today! Can I shoot him in the leg and just wound him? Probably not at this distance. The legs will be moving and even if I did he would probably bleed to death before they got him to the hospital.

Suddenly there was movement. This time it was a white rag that was tied to a stick and it was waving back and forth. After about thirty seconds a head appeared and then a body. Jack stood up in front of the brush pile, waving his white rag back and forth. He held his hands up and continued to wave the rag as he started picking his way down the mountain. He was a few ounces of pressure from eternity as Justin followed him in his rifle scope. As Jack walked slowly down

569

the mountain, he was nearing the point where Justin would no longer be able to see him for his house, so Justin scrambled down the ladder and ran through the house carrying his rifle until he burst through the front door and once again covered him with his crosshairs.

Jack finally reached the river and Justin wondered if he would dive in and try to ride the current to freedom, but he waded across with his hands still up and his flag waving. He crossed River Road and started up Justin's driveway.

Justin fought the urge to pull the trigger. A Bible verse came to his mind and he recited it softly, "Dearly beloved, avenge not yourselves, but rather give place unto wrath: for it is written, Vengeance is mine: I will repay, saith the Lord. Therefore if thine enemy hunger, feed him; if he thirst, give him drink: for in so doing thou shalt heap coals of fire on his head."

When Jack finally got within fifty feet, Justin stepped back into his house and quickly returned, carrying the large family Bible that always sat on the table in his living room. Justin leaned his rifle against the doorjamb and stepped over to the front steps and took a seat with the large Bible resting across his lap.

Jack finally stopped about twenty feet from the porch and he dropped the stick with the rag tied to it and bent over resting his hands on his knees. He was fighting for breath after walking up the steep driveway.

"I...I must say, Justin, you are full of surprises."

Justin sat on the steps staring at Jack but he remained silent.

"I...wasn't expecting you to...preach to me."

"I'm not a preacher, Jack. The Bible is sitting on my lap to remind me that I don't have the right to kill you."

Jack finally caught his breath and stood up straight and stared at Justin. "Where was your damn Bible when you murdered my nephew?"

"I didn't murder your nephew, Jack! I've killed 119 men, but I've never murdered anyone. There's a big difference in the way I killed Johnny and the way you killed Roy!"

"That old fool!" Jack shouted. "I hope he's burning in hell!"

"There is definitely a hell, Jack, but Roy's not there. He's sitting in that rocking chair behind me. You owned thousands of acres of land in three counties, but you murdered him for a lousy forty-three acres. This book that is sitting on my lap has a verse in it that you need to read sometime. It says, 'Be not deceived: God is not mocked: For that which a man soweth, that shall he also reap.'"

"Well, if Roy is sitting in that rocking chair like you say he is, he's got a front row seat to watch me kill you!" Jack hollered as he jammed his hand into his front pants pocket and grabbed his derringer, cocking it as it cleared his pocket.

Justin flipped open the huge Bible that was resting on his lap and pulled the Colt Gold Cup National Match .45 automatic out of the hollowed out pages and fired five 180-grain hollow points into Jack's chest. Jack's eyes were as big as saucers as he stumbled backward and fought to bring the derringer up. Each .45-caliber bullet that ripped through his chest knocked him back several inches until finally on the fifth round he dropped the derringer and fell straight back.

Justin lowered his pistol and stared at the dead man in front of him. There was no twitching or jerking and his eyes weren't fluttering. They were wide open and staring at the sky as blood finally filled his mouth and began to spill out and run down his cheek. A helicopter could be heard in the distance as his cell phone rang and snapped him out of his trance.

"Hello."

"We're almost there Justin! ETA is under a minute!"

"Take your time, Dan," Justin said. "He's dead."

Epilogue

Saturday, December 15, 2006

Justin stood in the fellowship hall of the New River Baptist Church eating a piece of cake and washing it down with some kind of green punch as the crowd began to filter in to get refreshments. There was nothing fancy or elaborate about this reception, or the ceremony that preceded it. No trumpets or flutes or candelabra. No soloist or caterer or photographer. Just two beautiful people pledging their love in front of their friends and family.

Jesse's brother, Joshua, escorted his sister down the isle. Her beautiful black hair was gathered in a bun and her face was literally glowing with joy. Joshua was dashing, wearing a black tuxedo with a red corsage in honor of his late grandmother, Leah. Justin and Travis, both wearing black tuxedos, stood beside each other and watched as the organist began playing the wedding march and the congregation stood and turned so they could see the bride come down the isle. Travis's mother Kathy was sitting in her wheelchair at the end of the first pew and Walter turned her so she could watch the procession. Jesse paused when she got beside of Kathy and bent over to kiss her before stepping up beside her soon-to-be husband. The bride and groom stared at one another and smiled as Pastor McDowell stepped forward to start the service.

Justin finished his cake and set his paper plate down and pulled the program out of his coat pocket. The ushers handed him the program as soon as he arrived at the church but he hadn't had an opportunity to look at it yet. The front cover was a picture trimmed in lace. It was a picture of a butterfly sitting on a rock in the middle of the river. The rock was protruding up through a section of rapids in the river, and the water surrounding the rock was spraying and splashing as it crashed around it. The colors were vibrant and beautiful and you could almost hear the water roar when you stared at it.

A round of applause suddenly erupted and Justin looked up from the program and watched as the crowd parted to welcome Mr. and Mrs. Travis Hayes. The newlyweds stepped to the front of the line and began welcoming their guests and thanking them for their presence. The crowd parted again as Walter entered the fellowship hall pushing Kathy in her wheelchair. Travis and Jesse immediately stepped across the room and hugged and kissed her and then had Walter bring her to the front of the line to sit beside them as they continued to greet their guests.

Teresa and her two nine-year-old granddaughters, Megan and Mindy, appeared in the entrance but instead of getting in line for refreshments they crossed the room and headed straight for Justin. The twin girls were dressed in matching red dresses with black patent leather shoes, and they broke into a run about halfway across the large room.

"Mr. Hayes! Mr. Hayes! It's snowing outside! It's snowing outside! Can we go sledding tonight? Will you take us sledding? Please! Please! Please!"

"Well, I don't know," Justin said as he leaned over and kissed Teresa when she walked up. "Did you make your bed this morning when you got up?"

"Yes, sir, we made it up before Nanna fixed breakfast. She made us!"

"Did you brush your teeth?"

"Yes, sir," both girls answered in unison and then smiled as if to offer proof.

"Well, okay then," Justin said. "If you're good the rest of the day and your Nanna says it's okay, I guess I'll take you sledding."

"Thank you, Mr. Hayes, thank you!" they squealed and then ran to look out the nearest window.

Justin watched the girls cross the room and then looked back at Teresa. "Well, when I saw Jesse walking down the aisle I didn't think I had ever seen a more beautiful woman, but now that you're here I'm not so sure."

"Thank you, sweetheart," Teresa said. "You're full of baloney, but thank you anyway. It was a beautiful wedding and I don't think I've ever seen a more beautiful bride and groom."

"Me either," Justin said. "Are the twins wearing you out?"

"They are so excited about this snow! They have never seen snow before and they are literally going crazy!"

"Bring them over to the house right before dark and I'll build a bonfire and let them sled down the front yard. I can pull them back up the driveway with the four-wheeler."

"That would be great. I'll bring some hot chocolate and some marshmallows to roast over the fire."

"Sounds like a plan to me."

"Maybe later on after I get them to bed you can come over and help me clean the snow off the Jacuzzi," Teresa said with a devilish grin.

"There's nothing I hate worse than a Jacuzzi that's covered with snow!"

"You're so full of shit, Justin Hayes," Teresa said and she kissed him and took off after her squealing granddaughters.

Justin grinned and then glanced back across the room and what he saw almost took his breath. Jesse was standing beside Travis and she was cradling a baby in her arms as Travis looked on.

The baby was named Justin Thomas Morris, born on July 9, 2006, to Deputy Jerry Morris and his wife, Mary Lou. He was named Thomas after his grandfather, Tom Morris, and he was named Justin after the man who saved his father's life during a shootout on River Road. Justin stared at the bride and groom as they passed the baby back and forth and made faces at it. It hadn't even dawned on him until now that he could soon be a grandpa.

Jerry Morris and Buddy Dixon stepped into the room, and like Teresa and the girls, they came straight for Justin. Buddy still had a noticeable limp from the bullet wound he suffered to his knee. Justin reached out and shook their hands when they walked up.

"Congratulations, Sheriff Dixon," Justin said. "I read in the paper where the citizens of Ashe County had a new sheriff."

"Technically I'm just the interim sheriff until the next election, but thank you anyway," Buddy said.

"And congratulations to you too, Jerry," Justin continued. "The paper said we had a new chief deputy."

"Thank you, Justin," Jerry said.

"I'm sure the citizens of Ashe County will vote you in office at the next general election."

"We'll see, Justin. The only problem is I can't pass the annual physical because I can't run with this bum knee." Buddy sighed.

"All the more reason you need to be the sheriff," Justin answered. "You need to co ordinate and manage the sheriff's department and let your deputies do the running."

"I might hire you to be my campaign manager when the election rolls around."

"I doubt that you'll even need a campaign manager by the time the election rolls back around. I don't think that anybody will run against you."

"I hope you're right."

"Before I forget, bring the kids over to the house about dark. I'm going to build a bonfire and let Teresa's granddaughters sled down the front yard."

"I'll tell Judy, we might just take you up on that."

Justin suddenly felt something poke him in the back and when he spun around he couldn't believe his eyes. "DeMac! Chief! Jimmy! I wasn't expecting you guys to come! It's good to see you. Can't you guys walk through the front door like everybody else or do you have to slip in the back way?"

"We would come in the front if we got here on time," DeMac said. "There's a truck jackknifed halfway up the mountain and we had to wait over an hour until they got it cleared."

"Well, I'm glad you guys could make it and I know that Travis and Jesse will be thrilled."

"Where's the champagne?" DeMac asked.

"If you popped the cork on a bottle of champagne in a Southern Baptist Church your Seal Team couldn't even save you. They would drag you outside and stone you to death," Justin said. "There is some pretty tasty punch up at the serving table though."

DeMac grinned before continuing, "I forgot I was in the Bible Belt of the South."

"Come by the house after you leave and I'll give you something that's better than any champagne that's ever been made."

"They didn't waste any time getting married, did they?" DeMac said.

"Well, they were going to wait until May but the doctors don't think that Travis's mother will live that long, so they decided to go ahead so that she could attend."

"I see," DeMac said. "Well, I think I'll get in line and congratulate the newlyweds."

"How's the house coming along?" Justin asked as DeMac started to step away.

"They have it framed up and closed in. They're working on the inside now. It'll be finished by trout season."

"Is that an invitation?"

"You bet it is. What's the biggest trout you caught this year?"

"Fourteen pounds seven ounces, but the big one got away," Justin said, grinning.

"When you come out to Montana I'll show you what a twenty pounder looks like!" DeMac said as he turned and walked toward the serving line.

"Chief, it's good to see you. Can you guys spend the night?"

"No, sir, we have to get back."

"You still can't call me Justin, can you?"

"No, sir, I guess not," Chief said. "How are Wade and his dogs doing?"

"They're doing great. The dogs ran a coyote out of the pasture last week and it made the mistake of stopping and looking back before it topped the hill. Wade killed him at four hundred yards. He called me and was so excited he couldn't even talk."

"Chief! Chief!" a voice called out across the noisy room. Justin and Chief turned and saw Wade Shaver practically running across the room toward them.

"I'll let him tell you about his dogs," Justin said.

"Okay, Justin. It was good to see you again," Chief said and then stepped toward Wade.

"Well, I'll be damned, you finally called me Justin instead of sir!"

Justin turned and faced Jimmy Hardy. "Jimmy, it's good to see you too. Are you still a spook?"

"Yeah, for right now I am," Jimmy said. "I've had some good job offers from private contractors but so far I'm still with Uncle Sam. The real question, Justin, is how are you doing? I mean really. I know you were having some trouble at first."

"I'm doing okay now. I was having some nightmares at first, waking up in the middle of the night soaking wet, and having flashbacks when I would hear a helicopter. That sort of thing."

"Did you go see a shrink?"

"No, I started trout fishing with the preacher. We would fish awhile and then sit down and talk while we were resting. I haven't had any nightmares or flashbacks for over two months."

"Well, good, Justin. I'm really glad to hear that. I felt bad about leaving you up here with a bull's-eye on your back. What about Teresa, are you two still seeing each other?"

"Oh yeah, we took it real slow for awhile, but lately we've been seeing each other a lot. I'm flying with her to Tampa, Florida, a week from now to spend Christmas with her at her daughter's house. She's around here somewhere with her two granddaughters."

"That's great, Justin," Jimmy said. "That makes me feel better."

"If I could have everyone's attention please!" Pastor McDowell's voice echoed in the packed fellowship hall. "If I could please have everyone's attention!" The room grew quiet as everyone stopped talking and faced Pastor McDowell. "Jesse, I mean Mrs. Jessica Hayes, is going to throw the bouquet now. Since it's snowing outside we have decided to do it right here, so if all the single women will gather up we'll see who will be the next one to get married."

"Justin, I hate to bring this up, especially at your son's wedding, but my superiors are still on my back about your 'guardian angel.' If you remember, you said you'll send them an explanation of some kind, and when they found out that I was coming up here to your son's wedding, they asked me to mention it to you."

"Jimmy, as the old saying goes, 'The check is in the mail.' I was going through some old paperwork the other day and found the address you gave me. I wrote out an explanation and mailed it day before yesterday."

"Well, good. Maybe they'll get off my back!"

Justin and Jimmy quit talking and turned so they could watch the throwing of the bouquet. Jesse slipped her heels off and Travis and DeMac helped her as she climbed up and stood in a chair with her back to the wild eyed crowd of single women. Carol Crissman was front and center and there were twenty or more women huddled up behind her with their shoes off and they were bent down so they could jump when the time came. The room became oddly quiet as the anticipation grew, and finally after a quick look over her shoulder, Jesse flung the bouquet. Twenty hands stabbed into the air, and the bouquet after being deflected a couple times, disappeared into the center of the melee. It resembled a goal line stand at the Super Bowl as women went flying together, knocking each other down as they fought for the prize. The squealing and screaming soon turned to laughter as the women helped each other up and hugged one another before finally wandering back to their families. When the crowd finally thinned there was applause as Teresa got up from the floor holding up the bouquet like a trophy. Everyone in the room clapped, and then as if on cue, they turned and stared at Justin.

Monday, December 17, 2006

Deputy Director William Reese arrived at his office at the Central Intelligence Agency fifteen minutes early like always. He stepped into his office and removed his knee length wool coat and hung it on the coat rack before sitting down behind his desk. His secretary, Sherry, appeared thirty seconds later carrying his coffee and his mail.

"Good morning, sir."

"Good morning, Sherry. Thank you."

"You're welcome, sir," she said as she left the room.

He flipped through his mail as he sipped his coffee until one particular envelope caught his eye. He had been waiting for this envelope for seven months. He hastily ripped it open.

To Whom It May Concern:

I, Justin Hayes, having verbally agreed to explain certain supernatural phenomenon that occurred during Operation Red Rover, submit the following.

Psalms 34:7–8

The angel of the Lord encampeth round about them that fear him, and delivereth them. Taste and see that the Lord is good: blessed is the man that trusteth in him.

This will be our first and last correspondence,

Sincerely,
Justin Hayes

About the Author

Bobby Hall is a retired lineman who lives in Denton, North Carolina. He enjoys hunting, fishing, gunsmithing, playing with his grandchildren, and good Southern cooking. He is a "simple man," who relies on his family, friends, and his Christian faith to see him through each day.